PRAISE!
Our Songs and Hymns

compiled by
JOHN W. PETERSON
NORMAN JOHNSON

edited by
NORMAN JOHNSON

SINGSPIRATION MUSIC
OF THE ZONDERVAN CORPORATION
GRAND RAPIDS, MICHIGAN 49506

PRINTED IN U.S.A.

87 88 89 / 26 27

CREDITS

Worship Resources:
CHARLES A. WICKMAN, Compiler

Editorial Assistance by

Karlene Fenn, Dave Hill, Maxine McMillan, Marian Poel, Doris Rikkers

Music Typography:
MUSICTYPE, Omaha, Arkansas

Don Ellingson

General Staff:

Editorial Assistance by

JIM LOUCKS, Phil Brower, Dave Culross, Lois Johnson, Don Wyrtzen

Secretarial Assistance by

LOIS JOHNSON, Bonnie Hess, Marti Thomas, Corinne VanderZon, Margaret Welmers

Technical Assistance by

Steve Dykstra, Don Holloway, John Idema, Art Jacobs, Wayne Leistra, Charles Van Horn, Florence Warfield

FOREWORD

Well over 300 times God's Word instructs His people to **praise Him!** Indeed, (if frequency has any relationship whatsoever to importance) praise, joyfulness, thanksgiving, song, rejoicing — even shouting — must be an attitude of life God considers highly significant, and in which His Church, both in our corporate worship and in our personal daily lives, is often deficient.

This volume, **PRAISE! Our Songs and Hymns,** is designed to foster the warmth, fervor, and all the other positive aspects associated with the spirit of praise. Whether used in private devotions at home, in a small study group, in a village chapel, or in a metropolitan "super-church," its purpose is above all to bring together many forms of musical expression in hope of deepening the two-way relationship between ourselves and our Maker.

As a rule, hymns mirror the times in which they were written — the moods, the tensions, the hopes, the life-styles of that day. Doctrinal controversy and definition (44, 49), civil strife and political struggle (13, 36, 74), early revivalism (19), scientific advances (18), personal faith versus ecclesiasticism (81, 61), a souvenir of the Billy Graham Crusades (16) — these are but some of the reflections detected in just the first few pages of this book. And in spite of their diverse origins, the amazing unity of focus makes them collectively one of the unfathomable wonders of God's purposive plan.

Hymnody, of course, has developed through the centuries because of a compelling need for believers to respond emotionally, artistically, and intellectually to the gracious and loving God they have come to know. Some can express themselves well through "God Is So Good," while others cannot. Some hearts glow with the singing of "A Mighty Fortress," but some do not . . .

In compiling this hymnal, we were totally of one mind in believing there are riches to be found and enjoyed at all levels of hymnody, and established as our goal the selection of representative material from all periods, all styles, all segments of the Church. We opted to look at the spiritual tone, the doctrinal integrity, the down-to-earth quality of a hymn as being more important than the classical purity of its melody or its rhythm, more essential than perfect meters and rhymes or heights of poetic beauty. Thus, side by side, might be found a historic hymn of worship and a heart-stirring southern gospel song — or a contemporary praise-chorus of a form that suggests spontaneity. For this we make no apology.

It has been a joyous and challenging task to bring this hymnal to reality. We are thankful to the many writers and publishers who have made their songs available. We are indebted to those colleagues who worked so untiringly through the months of production. We are grateful to God and His Church for the privilege of being participants in the heritage of sacred song and the opportunity to assist in its preservation for the generations to follow.

Finally, it is our prayer that God's people everywhere, both individually and collectively, will find their lives blessed and their worship enriched through the ministry and use of **PRAISE! Our Songs and Hymns.**

John W. Peterson and **Norman Johnson**

CONTENTS

Praise Song . . . .

Lord, Your creation is fantastic:

Let the oceans roar with praise,
Let the trees shout with joy,
Let the fields respond in gladness,
Let the mountains applaud in worship,
Let the stars sing in adoration.

Lord, You are supreme forever:

How wonderful are Your works,
How awesome is Your power,
How fair is Your justice,
How deep are Your thoughts,
How high are Your ways.

Lord, You are the source of music:

May I sing Your greatness,
May I celebrate Your glory,
May I proclaim Your majesty,
May I acknowledge Your sovereignty,
May I exalt Your deity.

Lord, how great You are!

— DON WYRTZEN

PART 1

THE UPWARD LOOK

OUR SONGS AND HYMNS OF WORSHIP AND ADORATION

". . . Let us offer
the sacrifice of praise to God continually,
that is, the fruit of our lips
giving thanks to His name."

Hebrews 13:15

1 — Everybody Sing Praise to the Lord!

JOHN W. PETERSON JOHN W. PETERSON

DESCANT for High Voices
Al - - - - - - le - lu - ia, Al - - - - - -
Ev-'ry-bod-y sing praise to the Lord, Ev-'ry-bod-y sing praise to
le - lu - ia, Al - - - - - le - lu - ia, For He is so
the Lord, Ev-'ry-bod-y sing praise to the Lord, For He is so
1 (opt. 2,3)
Final
broadly
won-der - ful! ful! For He is so won-der - ful!
won-der- ful! ful! For He is so won-der - ful!

Preferably, first time in key of C (without descant); second time in key of D♭ (by means of A♭7 at †), descant optional; third time in key of D (by means of A7 at †), with descant; fourth time in E♭ as written (by means of B♭7 at †), with descant. Build volume from *pp* to *ff* as the song progresses. Various antiphonal effects may be introduced.

WORSHIP

Sing Praise to God

JOHANN J. SCHÜTZ
Trans. by Frances E. Cox

Bohemian Brethren's *Kirchengesänge*

1. Sing praise to God who reigns a - bove, The God of all cre -
2. What God's al - might - y pow'r hath made His gra - cious mer - cy
3. The Lord is nev - er far a - way, But, thru all grief dis -
4. Thus all my toil - some way a - long I sing a - loud His

a - tion, The God of pow'r, the God of love, The God of our
keep - eth, By morn-ing glow or eve-ning shade His watch-ful eye
tress - ing, An ev - er - pres - ent help and stay, Our peace and joy
prais - es, That men may hear the grate-ful song My voice un - wea -

sal - va - tion. With heal - ing balm my soul He fills, And
ne'er sleep - eth. With - in the king - dom of His might, Lo!
and bless - ing. As with a moth - er's ten - der hand He
ried rais - es. Be joy - ful in the Lord, my heart! Both

ev - 'ry faith - less mur-mur stills: To God all praise and glo - ry!
all is just and all is right: To God all praise and glo - ry!
leads His own, His cho - sen band: To God all praise and glo - ry!
soul and bod - y bear your part: To God all praise and glo - ry!

Tune: MIT FREUDEN ZART—lower key at 118

3 — Praise to the Lord, the Almighty

JOACHIM NEANDER
Trans. by Catherine Winkworth
Stralsund Gesangbuch
Arr. in Crüger's Praxis Pietatas Melica
1. Praise to the Lord, the Al - might - y, the King of cre -
2. Praise to the Lord, who o'er all things so won - drous - ly
3. Praise to the Lord, who with mar - vel - ous wis - dom hath
4. Praise to the Lord! O let all that is in me a -
a - - tion! O my soul, praise Him, for He is thy
reign - eth, Shel - ters thee un - der His wings, yea, so
made thee, Decked thee with health, and with lov - ing hand
dore Him! All that hath life and breath, come now with
health and sal - va - tion! All ye who hear, Now to His
gen - tly sus - tain - eth! Hast thou not seen How thy de -
guid - ed and stayed thee! How oft in grief Hath not He
prais - es be - fore Him! Let the A - men Sound from His
tem - ple draw near; Join me in glad ad - o - ra - - tion!
sires e'er have been Grant-ed in what He or - dain - - eth?
brought thee re - lief, Spread-ing His wings for to shade thee!
peo - ple a - gain: Glad - ly for aye we a - dore Him!*

Tune: LOBE DEN HERREN
WORSHIP

The Lord Is King! — 4

NORMAN JOHNSON
Freely adapted from Josiah Conder

Attr. to Charles Dingley in *Revival Melodies*
Arr. by Norman Johnson

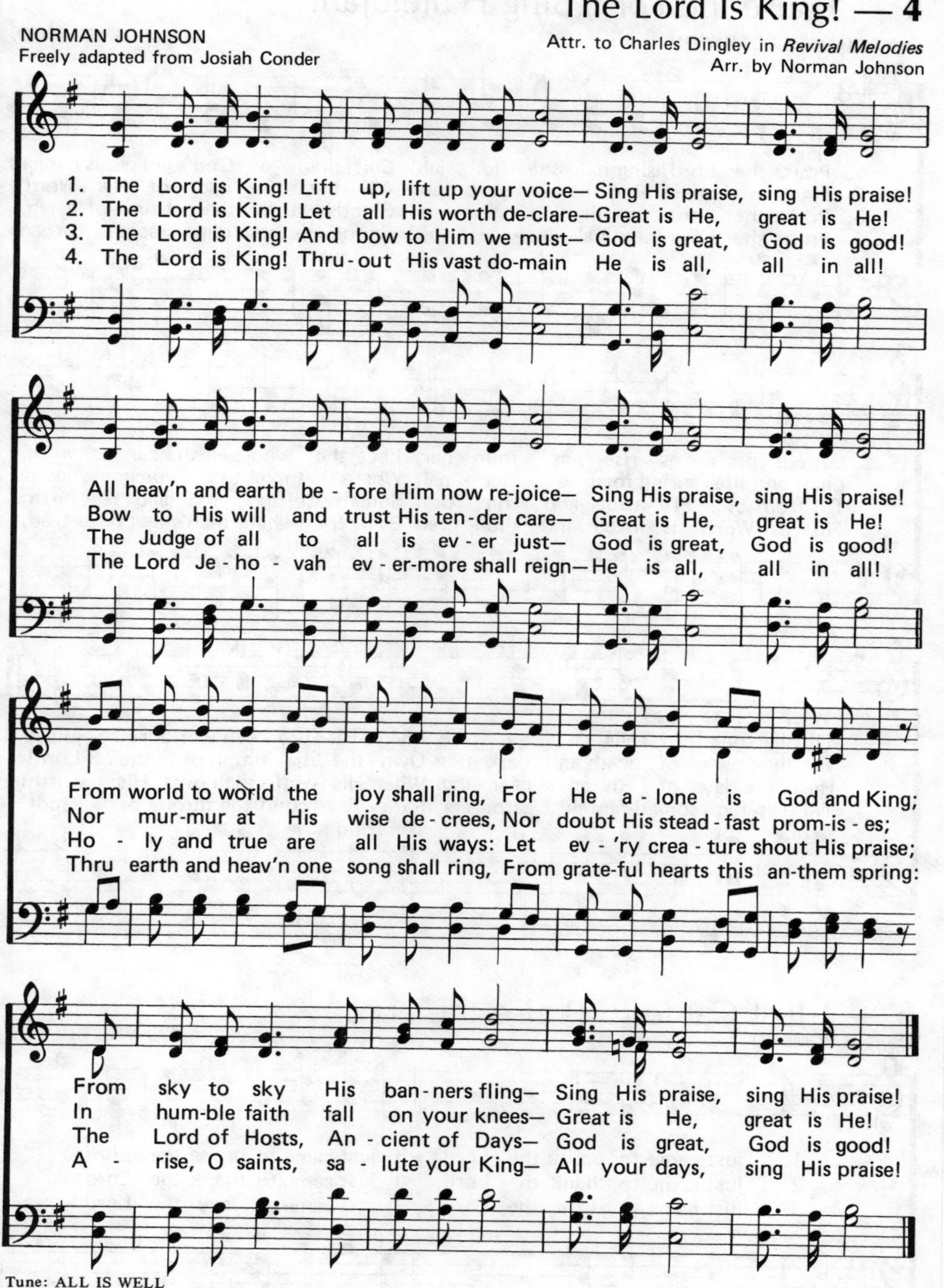
1. The Lord is King! Lift up, lift up your voice— Sing His praise, sing His praise!
2. The Lord is King! Let all His worth de-clare—Great is He, great is He!
3. The Lord is King! And bow to Him we must— God is great, God is good!
4. The Lord is King! Thru-out His vast do-main He is all, all in all!
All heav'n and earth be-fore Him now re-joice— Sing His praise, sing His praise!
Bow to His will and trust His ten-der care— Great is He, great is He!
The Judge of all to all is ev-er just— God is great, God is good!
The Lord Je-ho-vah ev-er-more shall reign—He is all, all in all!
From world to world the joy shall ring, For He a-lone is God and King;
Nor mur-mur at His wise de-crees, Nor doubt His stead-fast prom-is-es;
Ho-ly and true are all His ways: Let ev-'ry crea-ture shout His praise;
Thru earth and heav'n one song shall ring, From grate-ful hearts this an-them spring:
From sky to sky His ban-ners fling— Sing His praise, sing His praise!
In hum-ble faith fall on your knees— Great is He, great is He!
The Lord of Hosts, An-cient of Days— God is great, God is good!
A-rise, O saints, sa-lute your King— All your days, sing His praise!

Tune: ALL IS WELL

5 — Praise the Lord, Sing Hallelujah!

E. MARGARET CLARKSON NORMAN JOHNSON

1. Praise the Lord, sing hal - le - lu - jah! Chil - dren of God's gra-cious choice;
2. Man's im - pris - 'ning night is shat - tered At the im - pact of His Word;
3. Praise the Lord un - til His glo - ry Floods the far - thest realms of earth,
4. Praise the Lord, sing hal - le - lu - jah! Sound His sov-'reign grace a - broad,
Let His prais - es rise as thun - der, Let the whole earth hear His voice,
Light and life spring forth e - ter - nal Where that might - y voice is heard:
Till from ev - 'ry tribe and na - tion Souls rise up in glad re - birth:
Till His Word is loved and hon - ored Ev - 'ry - where man's feet have trod,
Till the song of His sal - va - tion Makes His bro - ken world re - joice!
Let the pow'rs of death and dark - ness Own the tri - umph of their Lord!
Haste the day of His ap - pear - ing, When His world shall own His worth!
Till His ran - somed fam-'ly gath - ers Safe - ly round the throne of God!*

Tune: VAN HORN (Alternate, REGENT SQUARE)

6 — I Just Came to Praise the Lord

WAYNE ROMERO WAYNE ROMERO

1. I just came to praise the Lord, I just came to praise the Lord;
2. I just came to thank the Lord, I just came to thank the Lord;
3. I just came to love the Lord, I just came to love the Lord;

I just came to praise His holy name, I just came to praise the Lord.
I just came to praise His holy name, I just came to thank the Lord.
I just came to praise His holy name, I just came to love the Lord.
We Praise Thee, O God, Our Redeemer — 7
JULIA C. CORY
Wade's Cantus Diversi
Arr. by Frank Anderson
1. We praise Thee, O God, our Re-deem-er, Cre-a-tor—In grate-ful de-vo-tion our trib-ute we bring; We lay it be-fore Thee, we kneel and a-dore Thee: We bless Thy ho-ly name, We bless Thy ho-ly name, We bless Thy ho-ly name, glad prais-es we sing.
2. We wor-ship Thee, God of our fa-thers, we bless Thee—Thru life's storm and tem-pest our guide hast Thou been; When per-ils o'er-take us, es-cape Thou wilt make us: And with Thy help, O Lord, And with Thy help, O Lord, And with Thy help, O Lord, our bat-tles we win.
3. With voic-es u-nit-ed our prais-es we of-fer—To Thee, great Je-ho-vah, glad an-thems we raise; Thy strong arm will guide us, our God is be-side us: To Thee our great Re-deem-er, To Thee our great Re-deem-er, To Thee our great Re-deem-er for-ev-er be praise!*
Tune: ADESTE FIDELES (different harmonization, higher key at 178)
Arr. © Singspiration 1979. All rights reserved.
WORSHIP

8 — To God Be the Glory
FANNY J. CROSBY
WILLIAM H. DOANE
1. To God be the glo - ry—great things He hath done! So loved He the
2. O per - fect re - demp-tion, the pur - chase of blood! To ev - 'ry be-
3. Great things He hath taught us, great things He hath done, And great our re-
world that He gave us His Son, Who yield - ed His life an a-
liev - er the prom-ise of God; The vil - est of - fen - der who
joic - ing thru Je - sus the Son; But pur - er and high - er and
tone-ment for sin And o-pened the Life-gate that all may go in.
tru - ly be lieves, That mo-ment from Je - sus a par - don re - ceives.
great - er will be Our won-der, our trans-port, when Je - sus we see.
CHORUS
Praise the Lord, Praise the Lord, Let the earth hear His voice! Praise the Lord,
Praise the Lord, Let the peo-ple re - joice! O come to the Fa - ther thru
WORSHIP

Je - sus the Son, And give Him the glo - ry—great things He hath done!
I Sing the Mighty Power of God — 9
ISAAC WATTS
Gesangbuch der Herzogl
1. I sing the might-y pow'r of God That made the moun-tains rise,
2. I sing the good-ness of the Lord That filled the earth with food;
3. There's not a plant or flow'r be - low But makes Thy glo - ries known;
That spread the flow-ing seas a - broad And built the loft - y skies.
He formed the crea-tures with His word And then pro-nounced them good.
And clouds a - rise and tem-pests blow By or - der from Thy throne;
I sing the wis - dom that or - dained The sun to rule the day;
Lord, how Thy won-ders are dis - played Wher - e'er I turn my eye:
While all that bor - rows life from Thee Is ev - er in Thy care,
The moon shines full at His com - mand, And all the stars o - bey.
If I sur - vey the ground I tread Or gaze up - on the sky!
And ev - 'ry - where that man can be, Thou, God, art pres - ent there.*
Tune: ELLACOMBE—lower key at 211
WORSHIP

10 — Sometimes "Alleluia"
CHUCK GIRARD
CHUCK GIRARD
Some-times "Al - le - lu - ia," Some-times "Praise the Lord!"
Fine
Some-times gen - tly sing - ing, Our hearts in one ac - cord. . .
1. O let us lift our voic - es, Look t'ward the sky and start to sing;
2. O let us know His pres - ence, Let sounds of prais-es fill the air;
D.C.
O let us now re - turn His love, Just let our voic - es ring!
O let us sing of Je - sus' love, To peo-ple ev - 'ry - where!
© Copyright 1974 by Dunamis Music. All rights reserved.
11 — Lord, We Praise You
OTIS SKILLINGS
OTIS SKILLINGS
1. Lord, we praise You, Lord, we praise You,
2. Lord, we thank You, Lord, we thank You,
3. Lord, we love You, Lord, we love You,
WORSHIP
© 1972 by Lillenas Publishing Co. All rights reserved.

Lord, we praise You, We praise You, Lord!
Lord, we thank You, We thank You, Lord!
Lord, we love You, We love You, Lord!

Where Two or Three Are Gathered — 12

JOHN W. PETERSON JOHN W. PETERSON

1. Where two or three are gath-ered, Gath-ered in Je - sus' name,
2. In Your name and for Your glo - ry We are met to - day;
In the midst He'll be— He prom-ised, Kin-dling a ho - ly flame.
Stir our hearts to praise and wor - ship, Teach us how to pray.
Come, come, Lord Je - sus, Come in love and pow'r;
Come, come, Lord Je - sus, Be our hal - lowed guest;
Qui - et - ly we wait be - fore You—Make this a sa - cred hour.
Breathe Your ho - ly breath up - on us— May ev - 'ry heart be blest.*

*Last four measures may be repeated softly as a Coda.

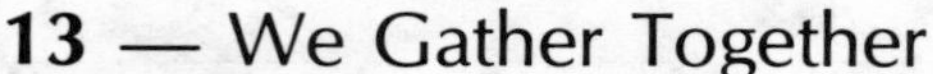

13 — We Gather Together

Netherlands folk song
Trans. by Theodore Baker

Netherlands melody
Nederlandtsch Gedenckclanck
Arr. by Edward Kremser

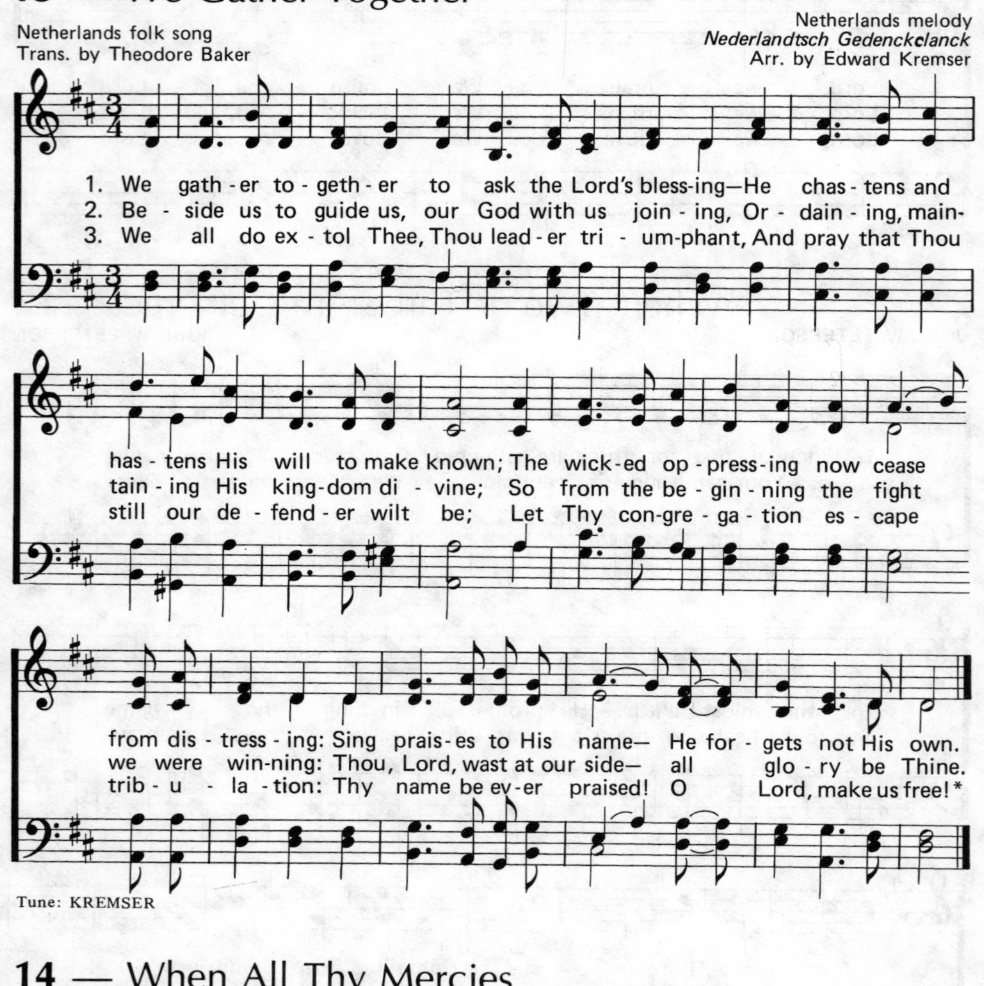
1. We gath-er to-geth-er to ask the Lord's bless-ing—He chas-tens and has-tens His will to make known; The wick-ed op-press-ing now cease from dis-tress-ing: Sing prais-es to His name— He for-gets not His own.
2. Be-side us to guide us, our God with us join-ing, Or-dain-ing, main-tain-ing His king-dom di-vine; So from the be-gin-ning the fight we were win-ning: Thou, Lord, wast at our side— all glo-ry be Thine.
3. We all do ex-tol Thee, Thou lead-er tri-um-phant, And pray that Thou still our de-fend-er wilt be; Let Thy con-gre-ga-tion es-cape trib-u-la-tion: Thy name be ev-er praised! O Lord, make us free! *

Tune: KREMSER

14 — When All Thy Mercies

JOSEPH ADDISON

Gardiner's *Sacred Melodies*

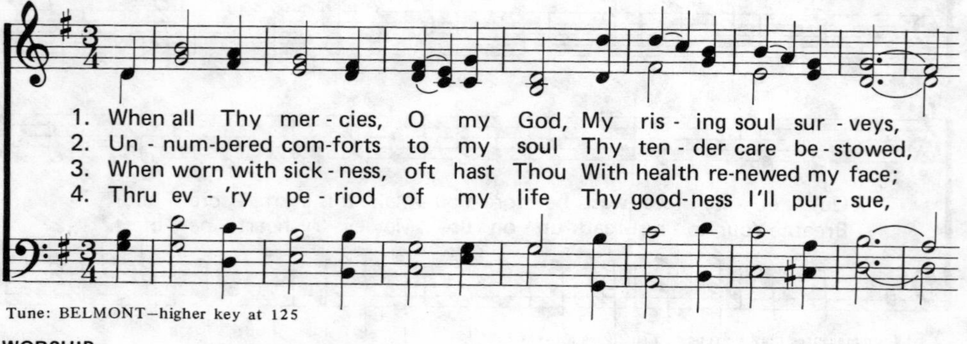
1. When all Thy mer-cies, O my God, My ris-ing soul sur-veys,
2. Un-num-bered com-forts to my soul Thy ten-der care be-stowed,
3. When worn with sick-ness, oft hast Thou With health re-newed my face;
4. Thru ev-'ry pe-riod of my life Thy good-ness I'll pur-sue,

Tune: BELMONT—higher key at 125

Trans-port - ed with the view, I'm lost In won - der, love and praise.
Be - fore my in - fant heart con-ceived From whom those com-forts flowed.
And, when in sins and sor - rows bowed, Re - vived my soul with grace.
And aft - er death, in dis - tant worlds, The glo - rious theme re - new.*
1. We bow and wor-ship Him, our Lord and King— For ev - er and ev - er His praise we'll sing; To Him all hon - or, love and thanks we bring— And to His at - tri-butes we cling.
2. We'll tell the world the glo - ry of His name— And tell how for sin - ners the Sav - ior came; We'll spread thru all the earth His won - drous fame— Un - chang-ing, al - ways He's the same!
3. Je - sus our Sav - ior lives for - ev - er - more— He rose from the grave to die no more; His mer - cy, grace and glo - ry we ex - plore— And, winged by faith, our spir - its soar.
4. He is de - serv - ing of all thanks and praise— With joy o - ver - flow - ing our hearts we raise; We'll sing and sing of Him for end - less days— This is our sac - ri - fice of praise.

Our Sacrifice of Praise — 15

Based on Hebrews 13:15
DON WYRTZEN

DON WYRTZEN

Tune: PARR

16 — How Great Thou Art!

STUART K. HINE | STUART K. HINE

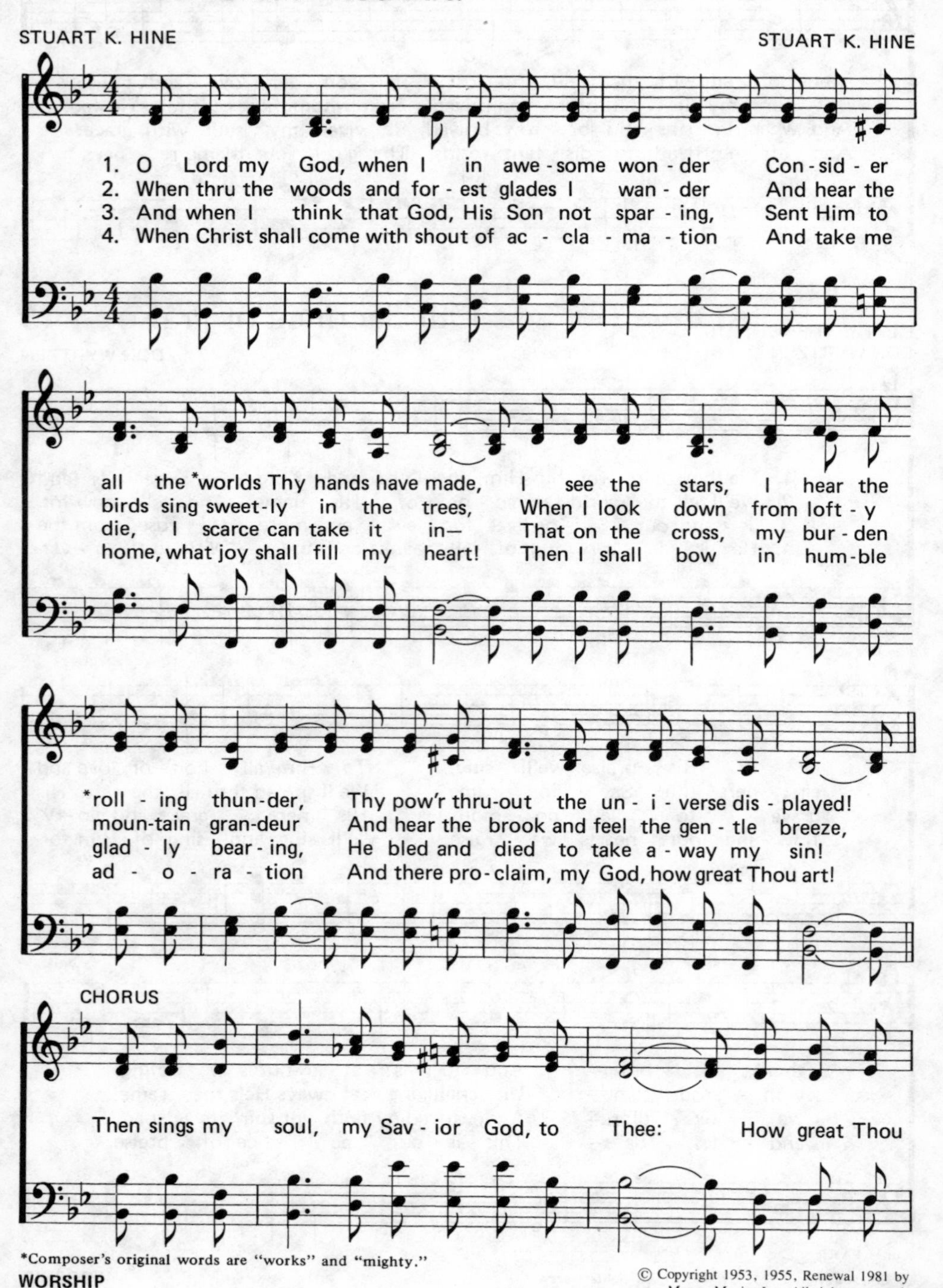

1. O Lord my God, when I in awe-some won-der Con-sid-er
2. When thru the woods and for-est glades I wan-der And hear the
3. And when I think that God, His Son not spar-ing, Sent Him to
4. When Christ shall come with shout of ac-cla-ma-tion And take me
all the *worlds Thy hands have made, I see the stars, I hear the
birds sing sweet-ly in the trees, When I look down from loft-y
die, I scarce can take it in— That on the cross, my bur-den
home, what joy shall fill my heart! Then I shall bow in hum-ble
*roll-ing thun-der, Thy pow'r thru-out the un-i-verse dis-played!
moun-tain gran-deur And hear the brook and feel the gen-tle breeze,
glad-ly bear-ing, He bled and died to take a-way my sin!
ad-o-ra-tion And there pro-claim, my God, how great Thou art!
CHORUS
Then sings my soul, my Sav-ior God, to Thee: How great Thou

*Composer's original words are "works" and "mighty."

WORSHIP

art, how great Thou art! Then sings my soul, my Sav - ior
God, to Thee: How great Thou art, how great Thou art!
Rejoice, Ye Pure in Heart — 17
EDWARD H. PLUMPTRE
ARTHUR H. MESSITER
1. Re - joice, ye pure in heart, Re - joice, give thanks and sing;
2. Bright youth and snow-crowned age, Strong men and maid - ens meek,
3. With voice as full and strong As o - cean's surg - ing praise,
4. Still lift your stand - ard high, Still march in firm ar - ray;
Your fes - tal ban - ner wave on high, The cross of Christ your King:
Raise high your free, ex - ult - ing song, God's wondrous prais - es speak:
Send forth the hymns our fa - thers loved, The psalms of an - cient days:
As war - riors thru the dark - ness toil Till dawns the gold - en day:
REFRAIN
Re - joice, re - joice, Re - joice, give thanks and sing!
Re - joice, re - joice,
Tune: MARION
WORSHIP

18 — God of Everlasting Glory
JOHN W. PETERSON
JOHN W. PETERSON
1. God of ev - er - last - ing glo - ry, Fill - ing earth and sky,
2. As we push man's fron-tiers for - ward In - to out - er space,
3. In the o - pen book of na - ture Faith re - mains un - moved—
4. Thru the course of hu - man his - t'ry Has Your pur - pose run,
Ev - 'ry - where Your won - ders o - pen To our search-ing eye:
Reach-ing for the stars and plan - ets, Still Your hand we trace;
Pat - terns of the Mas - ter-Build - er By each fact are proved;
And in sub - stance have we seen You In Your glo - rious Son:
In our tel - e - scop - ic prob - ing— Light years from our world,
In the lab - 'ra - to - ry's si - lence, Where Your se - crets hide,
So with rev - 'rent hearts we pon - der All the grand de - sign
He it was who came to save us And our hopes to raise—
In the at - om's theo - ried struc - ture Sci - ence has un - furled.
There the mar - vels of cre - a - tion Are for us sup - plied.
Of the u - ni - verse a - round us, Wrought by hands di - vine.
God of ev - er - last - ing glo - ry, Your great name we praise!*
Tune: BRETON ROAD
WORSHIP
© 1965, 1968, arr. 1979 by John W. Peterson Music Company. All rights reserved. Used by permission.

Brethren, We Have Met to Worship

GEORGE ATKINS
Attr. to William Moore
in *Columbian Harmony*
1. Breth-ren, we have met to wor-ship And a-dore the Lord our God;
2. Breth-ren, see poor sin-ners round you Slum-b'ring on the brink of woe;
3. Sis-ters, will you join and help us? Mo-ses' sis-ter aid-ed him;
4. Let us love our God su-preme-ly, Let us love each oth-er too;
Will you pray with all your pow-er While we try to preach the Word?
Death is com-ing, hell is mov-ing— Can you bear to let them go?
Will you help the trem-bling mour-ners Who are strugg-ling hard with sin?
Let us love and pray for sin-ners Till our God makes all things new.
All is vain un-less the Spir-it Of the Ho-ly One comes down;
See our fa-thers and our moth-ers And our chil-dren sink-ing down;
Tell them all a-bout the Sav-ior— Tell them that He will be found;
Then He'll call us home to heav-en, At His ta-ble we'll sit down;
Breth-ren, pray, and ho-ly man-na Will be show-ered all a-round.
Breth-ren, pray, and ho-ly man-na Will be show-ered all a-round.
Sis-ters, pray, and ho-ly man-na Will be show-ered all a-round.
Christ will gird Him-self and serve us With sweet man-na all a-round.

Tune: HOLY MANNA (Alternate, BEECHER)

20 — Revive Us Again

WILLIAM P. MACKAY

JOHN J. HUSBAND

1. We praise Thee, O God, for the Son of Thy love, For Je - sus who died and is now gone a - bove.
2. We praise Thee, O God, for Thy Spir - it of light, Who has shown us our Sav - ior and scat - tered our night.
3. All glo - ry and praise to the Lamb that was slain, Who has borne all our sins and has cleansed ev - 'ry stain.
4. Re - vive us a - gain— fill each heart with Thy love; May each soul be re - kin - dled with fire from a - bove.
CHORUS
Hal - le - lu - jah, Thine the glo - ry! Hal - le - lu - jah, a - men! Hal - le - lu - jah, Thine the glo - ry! Re - vive us a - gain.*

21 — The Lord Is in His Holy Temple

Habakkuk 2:20

Source unknown

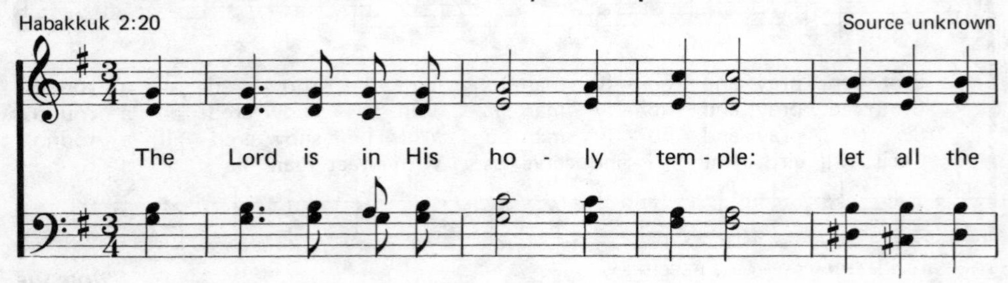

The Lord is in His ho - ly tem - ple: let all the

optional:
earth keep si - lence be - fore Him, A - men.
All Nature's Works His Praise Declare — 22
HENRY WARE, the younger
GOTTFRIED W. FINK
1. All na-ture's work His praise de - clare, To whom they all be - long;
2. To God the tribes of o - cean cry, And birds up - on the wing;
3. Great God, to You we con - se - crate Our voic - es and our skill;
There is a voice in ev - 'ry star, In ev - 'ry breeze a song.
To God the pow'rs that dwell on high Their tune - ful trib - ute bring.
We bid the peal - ing or - gan wait To speak a - lone Your will.
Sweet mu - sic fills the world a - broad With strains of love and pow'r;
Like them, let man the throne sur-round, With them loud cho - rus raise,
Lord, while the mu - sic round us floats, May earth - born pas - sions die;
The storm - y sea sings praise to God, The thun - der and the show'r.
While in - stru-ments of loft - ier sound As - sist His earth - ly praise.
O grant its rich and swell - ing notes May lift our souls on high! *

Tune: BETHLEHEM

23 — Thy Loving-Kindness Is Better Than Life

Based on Psalm 63:3-7
HUGH MITCHELL and JON DREVITS

HUGH MITCHELL
Arr. by Jon Drevits

1. Thy lov - ing - kind - ness is bet-ter than life, Thy lov - ing - kind - ness is bet-ter than life:
2. I lift my hands, Lord, un - to Thy name, I lift my hands, Lord, un - to Thy name:
3. Re - mem-b'ring Thee, Lord, I'm sat - is - fied, Re-mem-b'ring Thee, Lord, I'm sat - is - fied:
4. Safe in Thy shad - ow I will re - joice, Safe in Thy shad - ow I will re - joice:
My lips shall praise Thee, thus will I bless Thee— I will lift up my hands un-to Thy name.

24 — For Thine Is the Kingdom

Matthew 6:13b

NORMAN JOHNSON

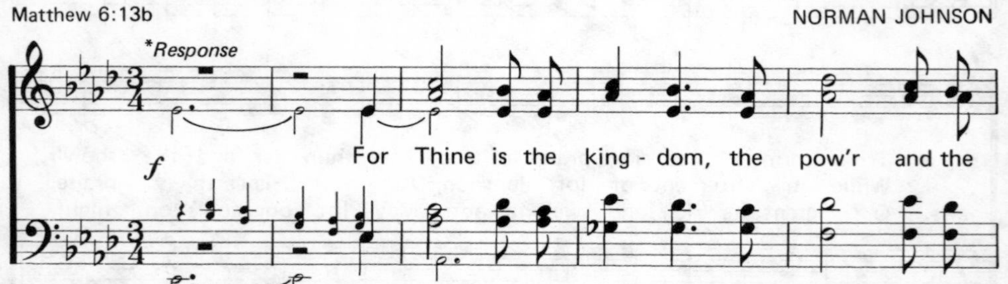
*Response
f
For Thine is the king - dom, the pow'r and the

*Choral or congregational response to the Invocation, Pastoral Prayer, Benediction—or may be used as a musical conclusion to the praying of "The Lord's Prayer."

glo - ry for - ev - er and ev - er! A - men.
Praise the Lord Who Reigns Above — 25
From Psalm 150
CHARLES WESLEY
JAMES NARES
in The Foundery Collection
1. Praise the Lord who reigns a - bove And keeps His courts be - low,
2. Cel - e - brate th'e - ter - nal God With harp and psal - ter - y,
3. Him in whom they move and live Let ev - 'ry crea - ture sing,
Praise the ho - ly God of love And all His great - ness show;
Tim - brels soft and cym - bals loud In His high praise a - gree;
Glo - ry to their Mak - er give And hom - age to their King;
Praise Him for His no - ble deeds, Praise Him for His match - less pow'r:
Praise Him, ev - 'ry tune - ful string, All the reach of heav'n - ly art:
Hal - lowed be His name be - neath, As in heav'n on earth a - dored:
Him from whom all good pro - ceeds Let earth and heav'n a - dore.
All the pow'rs of mu - sic bring, The mu - sic of the heart.
Praise the Lord in ev - 'ry breath, Let all things praise the Lord.*
Tune: AMSTERDAM
WORSHIP

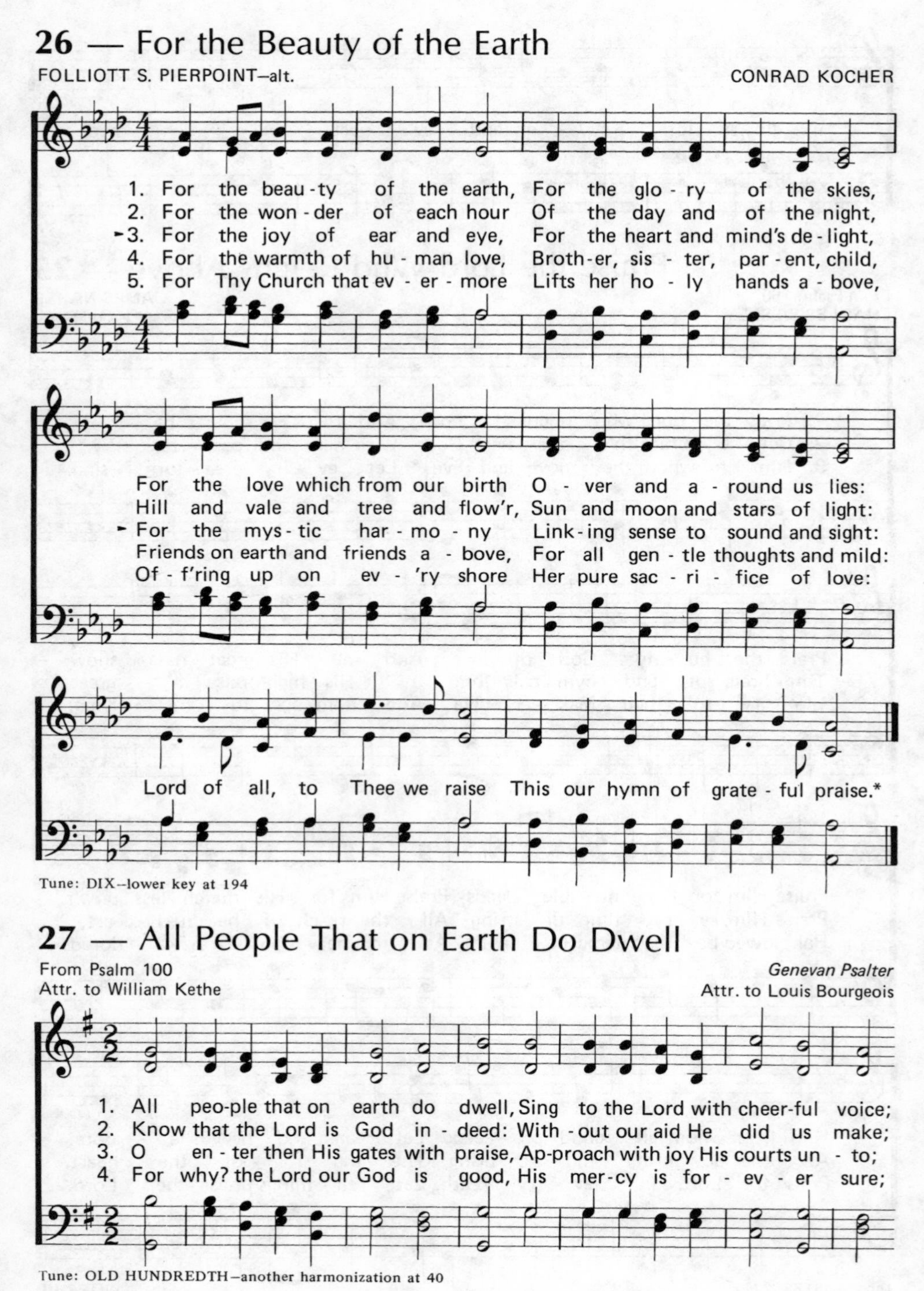
26 — For the Beauty of the Earth
FOLLIOTT S. PIERPOINT–alt.
CONRAD KOCHER
1. For the beau-ty of the earth, For the glo-ry of the skies,
2. For the won-der of each hour Of the day and of the night,
3. For the joy of ear and eye, For the heart and mind's de-light,
4. For the warmth of hu-man love, Broth-er, sis-ter, par-ent, child,
5. For Thy Church that ev-er-more Lifts her ho-ly hands a-bove,
For the love which from our birth O-ver and a-round us lies:
Hill and vale and tree and flow'r, Sun and moon and stars of light:
For the mys-tic har-mo-ny Link-ing sense to sound and sight:
Friends on earth and friends a-bove, For all gen-tle thoughts and mild:
Of-f'ring up on ev-'ry shore Her pure sac-ri-fice of love:
Lord of all, to Thee we raise This our hymn of grate-ful praise.*
Tune: DIX–lower key at 194
27 — All People That on Earth Do Dwell
From Psalm 100
Attr. to William Kethe
Genevan Psalter
Attr. to Louis Bourgeois
1. All peo-ple that on earth do dwell, Sing to the Lord with cheer-ful voice;
2. Know that the Lord is God in-deed: With-out our aid He did us make;
3. O en-ter then His gates with praise, Ap-proach with joy His courts un-to;
4. For why? the Lord our God is good, His mer-cy is for-ev-er sure;
Tune: OLD HUNDREDTH–another harmonization at 40

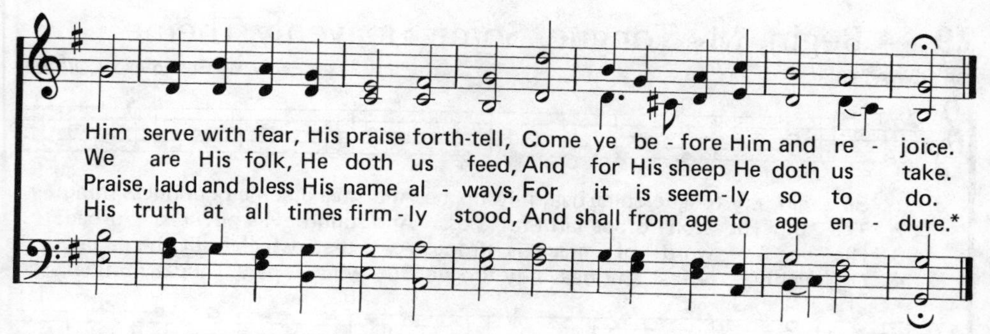
Him serve with fear, His praise forth-tell, Come ye be - fore Him and re - joice.
We are His folk, He doth us feed, And for His sheep He doth us take.
Praise, laud and bless His name al - ways, For it is seem-ly so to do.
His truth at all times firm-ly stood, And shall from age to age en - dure.*

O Worship the King — 28

ROBERT GRANT

Arr. from J. MICHAEL HAYDN

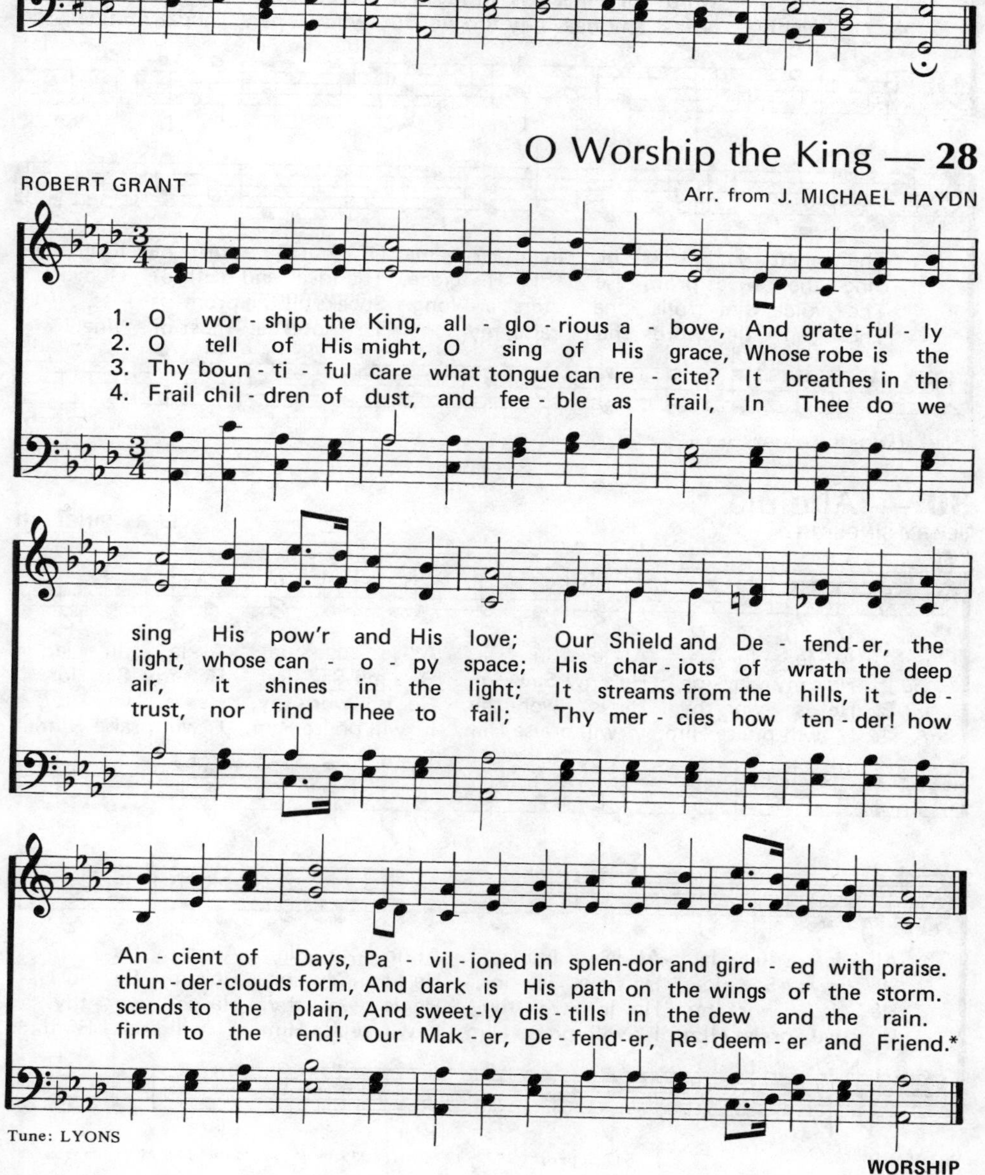
1. O wor - ship the King, all - glo - rious a - bove, And grate-ful-ly
2. O tell of His might, O sing of His grace, Whose robe is the
3. Thy boun - ti - ful care what tongue can re - cite? It breathes in the
4. Frail chil - dren of dust, and fee - ble as frail, In Thee do we
sing His pow'r and His love; Our Shield and De - fend-er, the
light, whose can - o - py space; His char - iots of wrath the deep
air, it shines in the light; It streams from the hills, it de -
trust, nor find Thee to fail; Thy mer - cies how ten - der! how
An - cient of Days, Pa - vil - ioned in splen-dor and gird - ed with praise.
thun - der-clouds form, And dark is His path on the wings of the storm.
scends to the plain, And sweet-ly dis - tills in the dew and the rain.
firm to the end! Our Mak - er, De - fend-er, Re - deem - er and Friend.*

Tune: LYONS

29 — Begin, My Tongue, Some Heavenly Theme
ISAAC WATTS
Henry W. Greatorex's Collection
1. Be - gin, my tongue, some heav'n-ly theme And speak some bound-less thing:
2. Tell of His won - drous faith-ful - ness And sound His pow'r a - broad;
3. His ver - y word of grace is strong As that which built the skies;
4. O might I hear Thy heav'n-ly tongue But whis - per, "Thou art mine!"
The might - y works or might-ier name Of our e - ter - nal King.
Sing the sweet prom - ise of His grace, The love and truth of God.
The voice that rolls the stars a - long Speaks all the prom - is - es.
Those gen - tle words shall raise my song To notes al - most di - vine.
Tune: MANOAH—lower key at 286
30 — Alleluia
JERRY SINCLAIR
JERRY SINCLAIR
p 1. Al - le - lu - ia, Al - le - lu - ia, Al - le - lu - ia, Al - le - lu - ia,
mp 2. He's my Sav - ior, He's my Sav - ior, He's my Sav - ior, He's my Sav - ior,
mf 3. He is wor - thy, He is wor - thy, He is wor - thy, He is wor - thy,
f 4. I will praise Him, I will praise Him, I will praise Him, I will praise Him,
Al - le - lu ia, Al - le - lu - ia, Al - le - lu - ia, Al - le - lu - ia!
He's my Sav - ior, He's my Sav - ior, He's my Sav - ior, He's my Sav - ior!
He is wor - thy, He is wor - thy, He is wor - thy, He is wor - thy!
I will praise Him, I will praise Him, I will praise Him, I will praise Him!

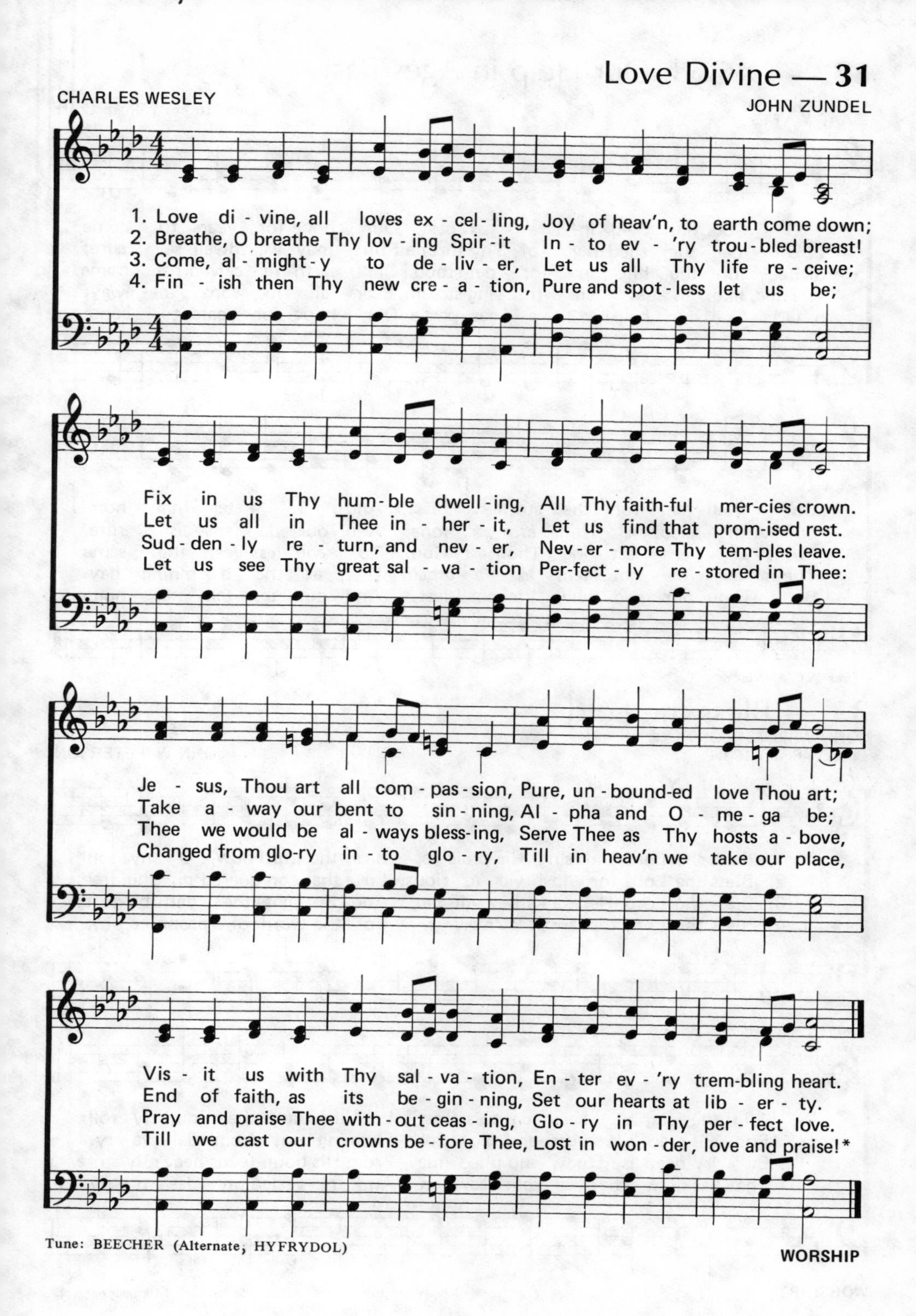
Love Divine — 31
CHARLES WESLEY
JOHN ZUNDEL
1. Love di - vine, all loves ex - cel - ling, Joy of heav'n, to earth come down;
2. Breathe, O breathe Thy lov - ing Spir - it In - to ev - 'ry trou - bled breast!
3. Come, al - might - y to de - liv - er, Let us all Thy life re - ceive;
4. Fin - ish then Thy new cre - a - tion, Pure and spot - less let us be;
Fix in us Thy hum - ble dwell - ing, All Thy faith - ful mer - cies crown.
Let us all in Thee in - her - it, Let us find that prom - ised rest.
Sud - den - ly re - turn, and nev - er, Nev - er - more Thy tem - ples leave.
Let us see Thy great sal - va - tion Per - fect - ly re - stored in Thee:
Je - sus, Thou art all com - pas - sion, Pure, un - bound - ed love Thou art;
Take a - way our bent to sin - ning, Al - pha and O - me - ga be;
Thee we would be al - ways bless - ing, Serve Thee as Thy hosts a - bove,
Changed from glo - ry in - to glo - ry, Till in heav'n we take our place,
Vis - it us with Thy sal - va - tion, En - ter ev - 'ry trem - bling heart.
End of faith, as its be - gin - ning, Set our hearts at lib - er - ty.
Pray and praise Thee with - out ceas - ing, Glo - ry in Thy per - fect love.
Till we cast our crowns be - fore Thee, Lost in won - der, love and praise!*

Tune: BEECHER (Alternate, HYFRYDOL)

32 — O God, Our Help in Ages Past

From Psalm 90
ISAAC WATTS
Attr. to William Croft
1. O God, our help in ages past, Our hope for years to come,
Our shelter from the stormy blast, And our eternal home!
2. Under the shadow of Thy throne Still may we dwell secure;
Sufficient is Thine arm alone, And our defense is sure.
3. Before the hills in order stood Or earth received her frame,
From everlasting Thou art God, To endless years the same.
4. Time, like an ever-rolling stream, Bears all its sons away;
They fly, forgotten, as a dream Dies at the op'ning day.
5. O God, our help in ages past, Our hope for years to come,
Be Thou our guide while life shall last, And our eternal home.*
Tune: ST. ANNE
33 — Bless the Lord
JOHN W. PETERSON
Chorus—Psalm 103:1
JOHN W. PETERSON
1. Bless the Lord and sing His praises, Bless the Lord now, O my soul;
Join the song all heaven raises, Let the anthem loudly roll!
2. Bless the Lord for love victorious, Love that conquered on the tree;
For His grace so great and glorious—Flowing out from Calvary.
3. Bless the Lord, He walks beside me, And He lights the path before;
Ev'ry need is now supplied me From His bounteous heav'nly store.
4. Bless the Lord for truth He's given— For the word of prophecy
That has drawn the veil from heaven And revealed my destiny.

CHORUS
Bless the Lord, O my soul! Bless the Lord, O my soul! Bless the Lord,
O my soul, And all that is with - in me bless His ho - ly name!
Bless His Holy Name — 34
Psalm 103:1
ANDRAÉ CROUCH
ANDRAÉ CROUCH
1. Bless the Lord, O my soul, and all that is with - in me, bless His
2. Bless the Lord, O my soul, and all that is with - in me, bless His
4. Bless the Lord, O my soul, and all that is with - in me, bless His
Fine
ho - ly name!
ho - ly name!
ho - ly name!
3. He has done great things, He has
D.C. al Fine
done great things, He has done great things—Bless His ho - ly name!
© Lexicon Music, Inc. 1973, arr. 1979. All rights reserved.
WORSHIP

35 — Come, Thou Fount

ROBERT ROBINSON—alt. JOHN WYETH

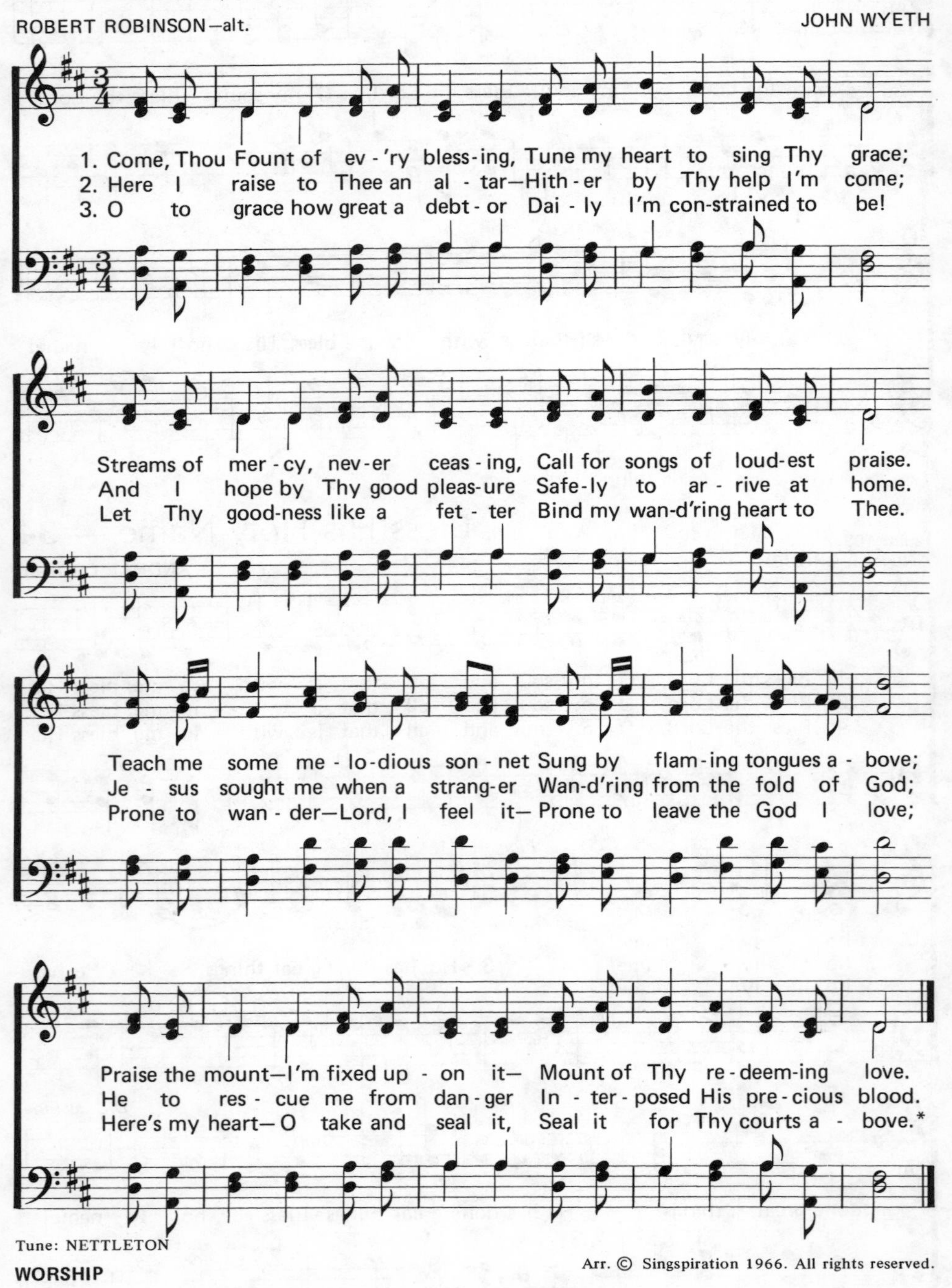
1. Come, Thou Fount of ev - 'ry bless-ing, Tune my heart to sing Thy grace;
2. Here I raise to Thee an al - tar—Hith - er by Thy help I'm come;
3. O to grace how great a debt - or Dai - ly I'm con-strained to be!
Streams of mer - cy, nev-er ceas - ing, Call for songs of loud-est praise.
And I hope by Thy good pleas-ure Safe-ly to ar - rive at home.
Let Thy good-ness like a fet - ter Bind my wan-d'ring heart to Thee.
Teach me some me - lo-dious son - net Sung by flam-ing tongues a - bove;
Je - sus sought me when a strang-er Wan-d'ring from the fold of God;
Prone to wan - der—Lord, I feel it— Prone to leave the God I love;
Praise the mount—I'm fixed up - on it— Mount of Thy re-deem-ing love.
He to res - cue me from dan-ger In - ter-posed His pre-cious blood.
Here's my heart— O take and seal it, Seal it for Thy courts a - bove.*

Tune: NETTLETON

WORSHIP

Now Thank We All Our God — 36

MARTIN RINKART
Trans. by Catherine Winkworth

JOHANN CRÜGER

1. Now thank we all our God With hearts and hands and voic - es,
2. O may this boun-teous God Thru all our life be near us,
3. All praise and thanks to God The Fa - ther now be giv - en,
Who won-drous things hath done, In whom His world re - joic - es;
With ev - er joy - ful hearts And bless - ed peace to cheer us;
The Son and Him who reigns With them in high - est heav - en—
Who from our moth-ers' arms Hath blessed us on our way
And keep us in His grace, And guide us when per - plexed,
The one e - ter - nal God Whom earth and heav'n a - dore—
With count - less gifts of love, And still is ours to - day.
And free us from all ills In this world and the next.
For thus it was, is now, And shall be ev - er - more.*

Tune: NUN DANKET

37 — All Creatures of Our God and King
FRANCIS of ASSISI
Trans. by William H. Draper
Geistliche Kirchengesäng
Arr. by Norman Johnson
1. All crea - tures of our God and King, Lift up your voice and
2. Thou rush - ing wind that art so strong, Ye clouds that sail in
3. Thou flow - ing wa - ter, pure and clear, Make mu - sic for thy
4. And all ye men of ten - der heart, For - giv - ing oth - ers,
5. Let all things their Cre - a - tor bless, And wor - ship Him in
with us sing, Al - le - lu - ia, Al - le - lu - ia! Thou
heav'n a - long, O praise Him! Al - le - lu - ia! Thou
Lord to hear, Al - le - lu - ia, Al - le - lu - ia! Thou
take your part, O sing ye! Al - le - lu - ia! Ye
hum - ble - ness, O praise Him! Al - le - lu - ia! Praise,
burn - ing sun with gold - en beam, Thou sil - ver moon with
ris - ing morn, in praise re - joice, Ye lights of eve - ning,
fire so mas - ter - ful and bright, That giv - est men both
who long pain and sor - row bear, Praise God and on Him
praise the Fa - ther, praise the Son, And praise the Spir - it,
soft - er gleam:
find a voice:
warmth and light, O praise Him, O praise Him! Al - le -
cast your care:
Three in One:

Tune: LASST UNS ERFREUEN—higher key at 38

lu - ia, Al - le - lu - ia! Al - le - lu - ia!*
Doxology — 38
THOMAS KEN
Geistliche Kirchengesänge
Arr. by Norman Johnson
Praise God, from whom all bless-ings flow, Praise Him, all crea-tures here be-
low: Al - le - lu - ia, Al - le - lu - ia! Praise Him a - bove, ye
heav'n-ly host, Praise Fa-ther, Son and Ho-ly Ghost: Al - le - lu - ia,
Al-le - lu - ia! Al-le - lu - ia, Al-le - lu - ia! Al-le - lu - ia!*
Tune: LASST UNS ERFREUEN—lower key at 37
Arr. © Singspiration 1968. All rights reserved.
WORSHIP: THE TRINITY

39 — Doxology

THOMAS KEN

Genevan Psalter
Attr. to Louis Bourgeois

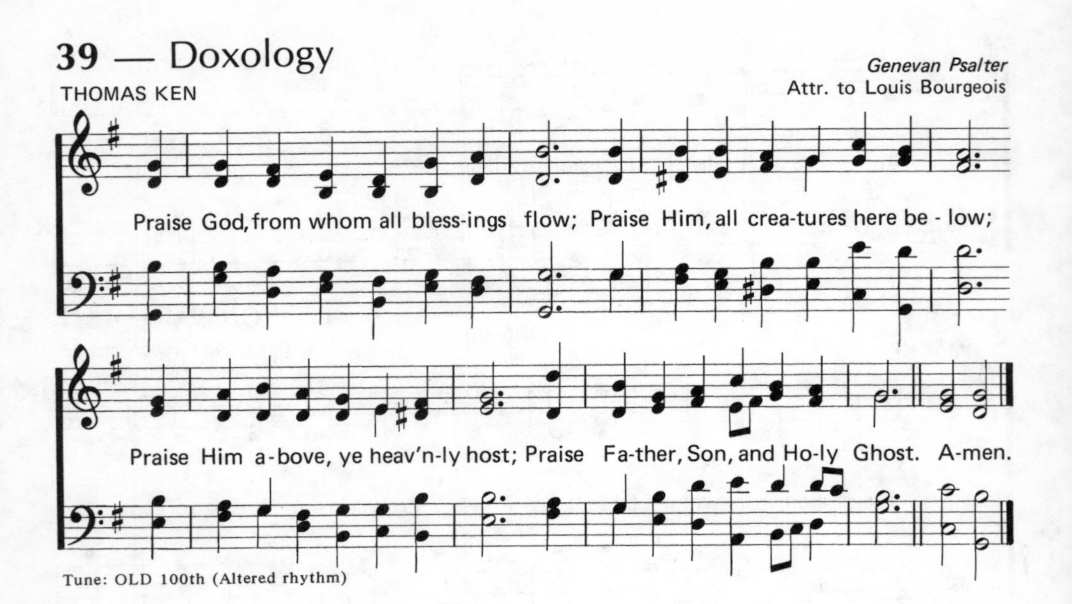

Praise God, from whom all bless-ings flow; Praise Him, all crea-tures here be - low;
Praise Him a-bove, ye heav'n-ly host; Praise Fa-ther, Son, and Ho-ly Ghost. A-men.

Tune: OLD 100th (Altered rhythm)

40 — Doxology

THOMAS KEN

Genevan Psalter
Attr. to Louis Bourgeois

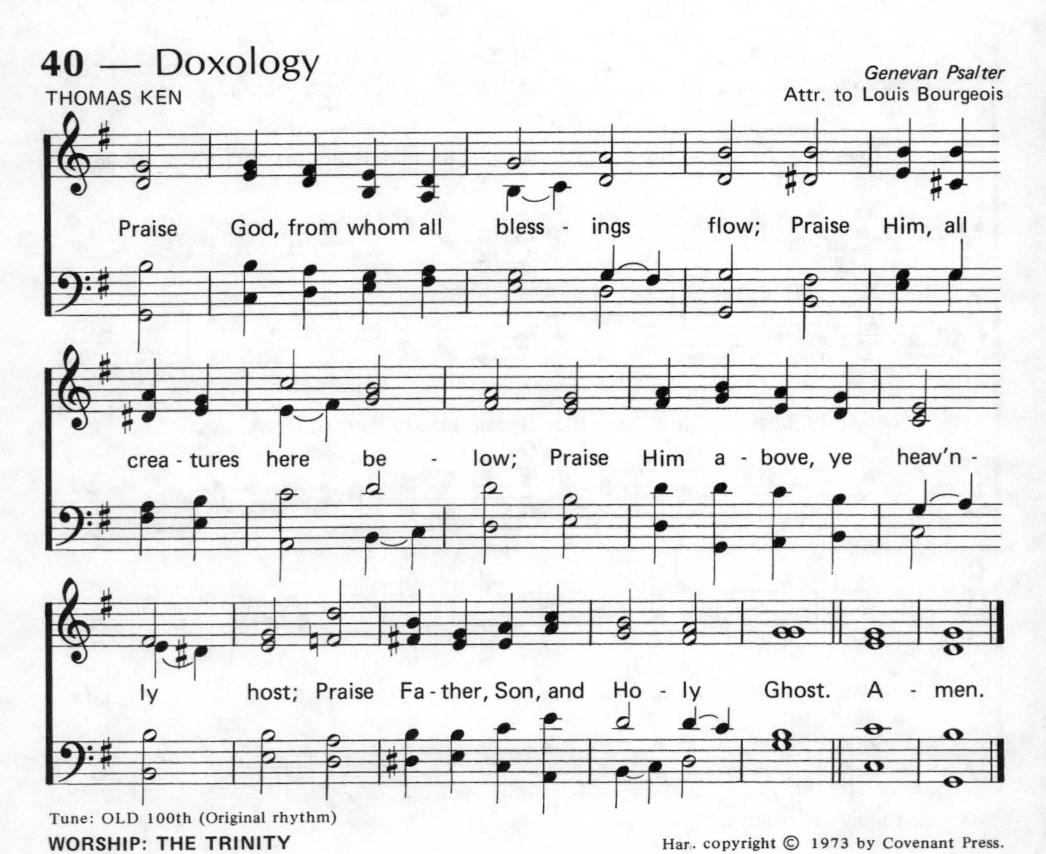

Praise God, from whom all bless - ings flow; Praise Him, all
crea - tures here be - low; Praise Him a - bove, ye heav'n -
ly host; Praise Fa - ther, Son, and Ho - ly Ghost. A - men.

Tune: OLD 100th (Original rhythm)

REGINALD HEBER

JOHN B. DYKES

1. Ho - ly, ho - ly, ho - ly, Lord God Al - might - y!
Ear - ly in the morn - ing our song shall rise to Thee;
Ho - ly, ho - ly, ho - ly! mer - ci - ful and might - y!
God in three per - sons, bless - ed Trin - i - ty!

2. Ho - ly, ho - ly, ho - ly! All the saints a - dore Thee,
Cast - ing down their gold - en crowns a - round the glass - y sea;
Cher - u - bim and ser - a - phim fall - ing down be - fore Thee,
Which wert and art and ev - er - more shalt be.

3. Ho - ly, ho - ly, ho - ly! Though the dark - ness hide Thee,
Though the eye of sin - ful man Thy glo - ry may not see;
On - ly Thou art ho - ly— there is none be - side Thee
Per - fect in pow'r, in love and pur - i - ty.

4. Ho - ly, ho - ly, ho - ly, Lord God Al - might - y!
All Thy works shall praise Thy name in earth and sky and sea;
Ho - ly, ho - ly, ho - ly! mer - ci - ful and might - y!
God in three per - sons, bless - ed Trin - i - ty!*

Tune: NICAEA

42 — Gloria Patri

Source unknown, 2nd century

CHARLES MEINEKE

Glo - ry be to the Fa - ther, and to the Son, and to the
Ho - ly Ghost: as it was in the be - gin - ning, is
now and ev - er shall be, world with-out end. A - men, A - men.

43 — Gloria Patri

Source unknown, 2nd century

HENRY W. GREATOREX

Glo - ry be to the Fa - ther, and to the Son, and to the
Ho - ly Ghost: as it was in the be - gin - ning, is now and

ev - er shall be, world with-out end. A - men, A - men.
8
TOBIAS CLAUSNITZER
Trans. by Catherine Winkworth
We Believe in One True God — 44
RICHARD REDHEAD
1. We be - lieve in one true God— Fa - ther, Son, and Ho - ly Ghost,
2. We be - lieve in Je - sus Christ, Son of God and Ma - ry's son,
3. We con - fess the Ho - ly Ghost, Who from both for - e'er pro-ceeds,
Ev - er - pre - sent help in need, Praised by all the heav'n - ly host,
Who de - scend-ed from His throne And for us sal - va - tion won,
Who up - holds and com-forts us In all tri - als, fears and needs.
By whose might-y pow'r a - lone All is made and wrought and done.
By whose cross and death are we Res-cued from sin's mis - er - y.
Blest and ho - ly Trin - i - ty, Praise for - ev - er be to Thee.*
Tune: REDHEAD—lower key at 216
Father, I Adore You — 45
TERRYE COELHO
TERRYE COELHO
I (Three-part round)
II
III
1. Fa - ther, I a - dore You, Lay my life be - fore You— How I love You!
2. Je - sus, I a - dore You, Lay my life be - fore You— How I love You!
3. Spir - it, I a - dore You, Lay my life be - fore You— How I love You!
© 1972 Maranatha! Music. All rights reserved.
WORSHIP: THE TRINITY

46 — Praise Ye the Triune God!

ELIZABETH R. CHARLES FRIEDRICH F. FLEMMING

1. Praise ye the Fa - ther for His lov - ing - kind - ness, Ten - der - ly
2. Praise ye the Sav - ior— great is His com - pas - sion, Gra - cious - ly
3. Praise ye the Spir - it, Com-fort - er of Is - rael, Sent of the
cares He for His err - ing chil - dren; Praise Him, ye an - gels,
cares He for His cho - sen peo - ple; Young men and maid - ens,
Fa - ther and the Son to bless us; Praise ye the Fa - ther,
praise Him in the heav - ens, Praise ye Je - ho - vah!
ye old men and chil - dren, Praise ye the Sav - ior!
Son, and Ho - ly Spir - it— Praise ye the Tri - une God!*

Tune: FLEMMING

47 — Glory Be to God on High

Traditional Traditional

1. Glo - ry be to God on high, Al - le - lu - ia!
2. Praise the Fa - ther, Spir - it, Son, Al - le - lu - ia!
3. Glo - ry be to God on high, Al - le - lu - ia!
4. Sing we prais - es un - to Thee, Al - le - lu - ia!
5. Glo - ry be to God on high, Al - le - lu - ia!

Tune: MICHAEL– higher key at 168

Glo - ry be to God on high, Al - le - lu - ia!
Praise the God - head, Three-in - One, Al - le - lu - ia!
Glo - ry be to God on high, Al - le - lu - ia!
For the truth that sets us free, Al - le - lu - ia!
Glo - ry be to God on high, Al - le - lu - ia!
Come, Thou Almighty King — 48
Source unknown
FELICE de GIARDINI
1. Come, Thou Al - might - y King, Help us Thy name to sing,
2. Come, Thou In - car - nate Word, Gird on Thy might - y sword,
3. Come, Ho - ly Com - fort - er, Thy sa - cred wit - ness bear
4. To Thee, great One in Three, E - ter - nal prais - es be,
Help us to praise: Fa - ther, all - glo - ri - ous, O'er all vic -
Our prayer at - tend: Come and Thy peo - ple bless, And give Thy
In this glad hour: Thou who al - might - y art, Now rule in
Hence ev - er - more: Thy sov - 'reign maj - es - ty May we in

to - ri - ous, Come and reign o - ver us, An - cient of Days.
word suc - cess— Spir - it of ho - li - ness, On us de - scend.
ev - 'ry heart— And ne'er from us de - part, Spir - it of pow'r.
glo - ry see, And to e - ter - ni - ty Love and a - dore.*

Tune: ITALIAN HYMN—lower key at 498

49 — Holy God, We Praise Thy Name

Te Deum
Attr. to Ignace Franz
Trans. by Clarence Walworth
Katholisches Gesangbuch
1. Ho - ly God, we praise Thy name— Lord of all, we bow be-fore Thee!
2. Hark, the loud ce - les - tial hymn An - gel choirs a - bove are rais - ing;
3. Lo, the ap - os - tol - ic train Joins Thy sa - cred name to hal - low;
4. Ho - ly Fa - ther, Ho - ly Son, Ho - ly Spir - it, Three we name Thee,
All on earth Thy scep - ter claim, All in heav'n a - bove a - dore Thee:
Cher - u - bim and ser - a - phim, In un - ceas - ing cho - rus prais-ing,
Proph-ets swell the glad re - frain, And the white-robed mar - tyrs fol - low;
While in es - sence on - ly One: Un - di - vid - ed God we claim Thee,
In - fi - nite Thy vast do - main, Ev - er - last - ing is Thy reign.
Fill the heav'ns with sweet ac - cord— Ho - ly, ho - ly, ho - ly Lord!
And, from morn to set of sun, Thru the Church the song goes on.
And a - dor - ing bend the knee, While we sing our praise to Thee.*
Tune: GROSSER GOTT
50 — Triune Blessing
II Corinthians 13:14
NORMAN JOHNSON
The grace of the Lord Je - sus Christ, and the love of God, and the com-

mun-ion of the Ho - ly Spir - it be with you all. A - men.
Suitable at beginning or close of worship.
Holy, Holy — 51
JIMMY OWENS
JIMMY OWENS
1. Ho - ly, ho - ly, ho - ly, ho - ly, Ho - ly, ho - ly,
2. Gra-cious Fa - ther, gra - cious Fa - ther, We're so blest to be Your
3. Pre-cious Je - sus, pre - cious Je - sus, We're so glad that You've re-
4. Ho - ly Spir - it, Ho - ly Spir - it, Come and fill our hearts a -
5. Ho - ly, ho - ly, ho - ly, ho - ly, Ho - ly, ho - ly,
6. Hal - le - lu - jah, hal - le - lu - jah, Hal - le - lu - jah,
Lord God Al - might - y; And we lift our hearts be-fore You as a
child - ren, gra - cious Fa - ther; And we lift our heads be-fore You as a
deemed us, pre - cious Je - sus; And we lift our hands be-fore You as a
new, Ho - ly Spir - it; And we lift our voice be-fore You as a
Lord God Al - might - y, And we lift our hearts be-fore You as a
hal - le - lu - jah; And we lift our hearts be-fore You as a
tok - en of our love, Ho - ly, ho - ly, ho - ly, ho - ly.
tok - en of our love, Gra-cious Fa - ther, gra - cious Fa - ther.
tok - en of our love, Pre-cious Je - sus, pre-cious Je - sus.
tok - en of our love, Ho - ly Spir - it, Ho - ly Spir - it.
tok - en of our love, Ho - ly, ho - ly, ho - ly, ho - ly.
tok - en of our love, Hal - le - lu - jah, hal - le - lu - jah.
© Lexicon Music, Inc. 1972, arr. 1979. All rights reserved.
WORSHIP: THE TRINITY

52 — Praise, My Soul, the King of Heaven

From Psalm 103
HENRY FRANCIS LYTE
JOHN GOSS
1. Praise, my soul, the King of heav - en, To His feet thy
2. Praise Him for His grace and fa - vor To our fa - thers
3. Fa - ther - like He tends and spares us, Well our fee - ble
4. An - gels in the height, a - dore Him, Ye be - hold Him
trib - ute bring; Ran - somed, healed, re - stored, for - giv - en,
in dis - tress; Praise Him, still the same as ev - er,
frame He knows; In His hands He gen - tly bears us,
face to face; Sun and moon, bow down be - fore Him,
Ev - er - more His prais - es sing: Al - le - lu - ia!
Slow to chide and swift to bless: Al - le - lu - ia!
Res - cues us from all our foes: Al - le - lu - ia!
Dwell - ers all in time and space: Al - le - lu - ia!
Al - le - lu - ia! Praise the Ev - er - last - ing King!
Al - le - lu - ia! Glo - rious in His faith - ful - ness!
Al - le - lu - ia! Wide - ly yet His mer - cy flows!
Al - le - lu - ia! Praise with us the God of grace! *
Tune: PRAISE MY SOUL

WORSHIP: THE FATHER

Joyful, Joyful, We Adore Thee

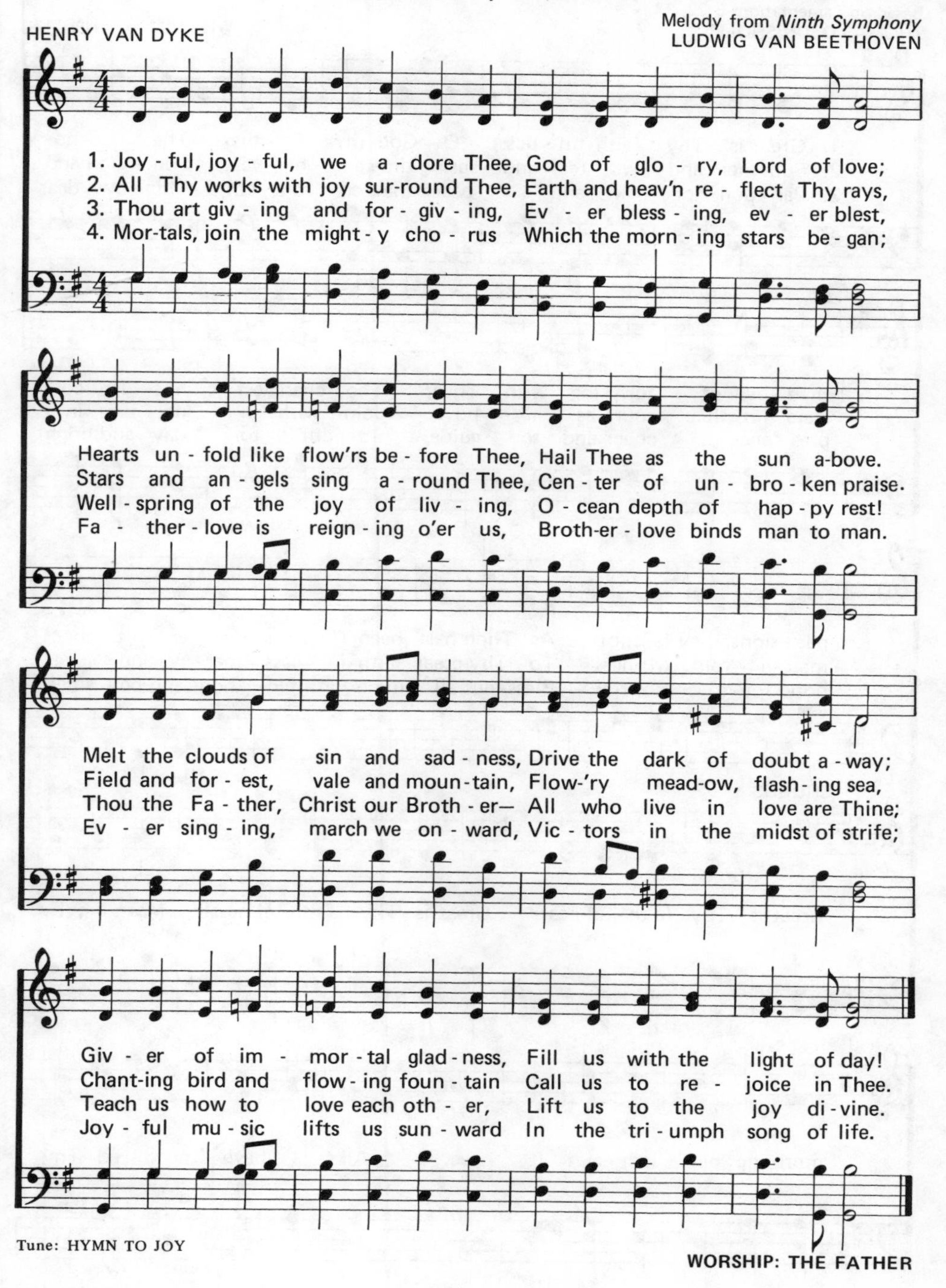
HENRY VAN DYKE
Melody from *Ninth Symphony*
LUDWIG VAN BEETHOVEN
1. Joy - ful, joy - ful, we a - dore Thee, God of glo - ry, Lord of love;
2. All Thy works with joy sur-round Thee, Earth and heav'n re - flect Thy rays,
3. Thou art giv - ing and for - giv - ing, Ev - er bless - ing, ev - er blest,
4. Mor-tals, join the might - y cho - rus Which the morn - ing stars be - gan;
Hearts un - fold like flow'rs be - fore Thee, Hail Thee as the sun a-bove.
Stars and an - gels sing a - round Thee, Cen - ter of un - bro - ken praise.
Well - spring of the joy of liv - ing, O - cean depth of hap - py rest!
Fa - ther - love is reign - ing o'er us, Broth-er - love binds man to man.
Melt the clouds of sin and sad - ness, Drive the dark of doubt a - way;
Field and for - est, vale and moun - tain, Flow-'ry mead-ow, flash - ing sea,
Thou the Fa - ther, Christ our Broth - er— All who live in love are Thine;
Ev - er sing - ing, march we on - ward, Vic - tors in the midst of strife;
Giv - er of im - mor - tal glad - ness, Fill us with the light of day!
Chant-ing bird and flow - ing foun - tain Call us to re - joice in Thee.
Teach us how to love each oth - er, Lift us to the joy di - vine.
Joy - ful mu - sic lifts us sun - ward In the tri - umph song of life.

Tune: HYMN TO JOY

54 — Great Is Thy Faithfulness
Based on Lamentations 3:22, 23
THOMAS O. CHISHOLM
WILLIAM M. RUNYAN
1. Great is Thy faith-ful-ness, O God my Fa-ther! There is no shad-ow of turn-ing with Thee; Thou chang-est not— Thy com-pas-sions, they fail not: As Thou hast been Thou for-ev-er wilt be.
2. Sum-mer and win-ter and spring-time and har-vest, Sun, moon and stars in their cours-es a-bove, Join with all na-ture in man-i-fold wit-ness To Thy great faith-ful-ness, mer-cy and love.
3. Par-don for sin and a peace that en-dur-eth, Thine own dear pres-ence to cheer and to guide, Strength for to-day and bright hope for to-mor-row— Bless-ings all mine, with ten thou-sand be-side!
CHORUS
Great is Thy faith-ful-ness! Great is Thy faith-ful-ness! Morn-ing by morn-ing new mer-cies I see; All I have need-ed Thy
WORSHIP: THE FATHER
Copyright 1923, renewal 1951 (ext.) by Hope Publishing Co.

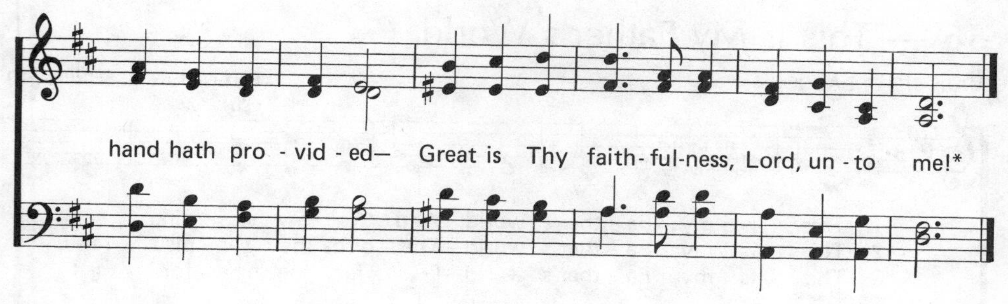
hand hath pro - vid - ed— Great is Thy faith-ful-ness, Lord, un - to me!*

Immortal, Invisible — 55

Based on I Timothy 1:17
WALTER CHALMERS SMITH

Welsh melody
Roberts' *Caniadau y Cyssegr*

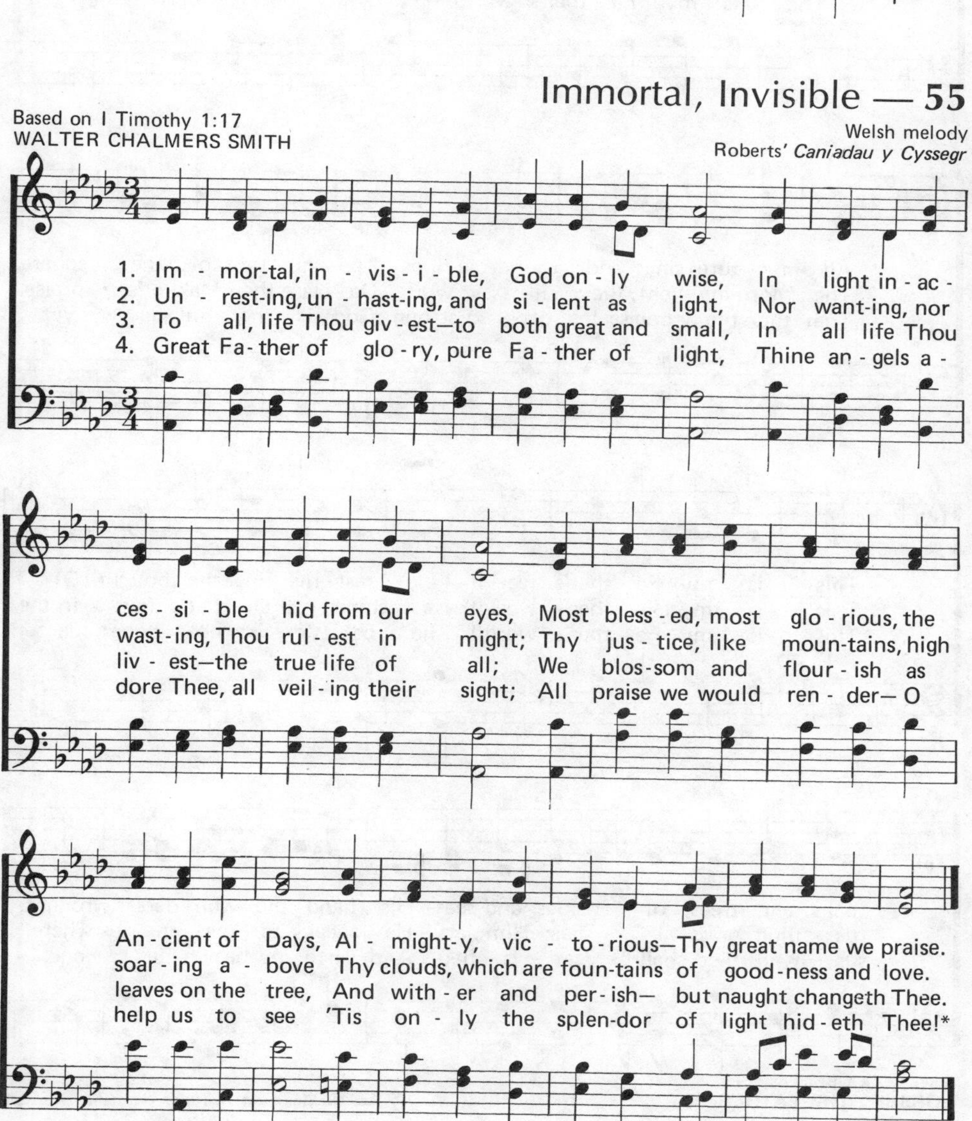
1. Im - mor-tal, in - vis - i - ble, God on - ly wise, In light in - ac -
2. Un - rest-ing, un - hast-ing, and si - lent as light, Nor want-ing, nor
3. To all, life Thou giv - est—to both great and small, In all life Thou
4. Great Fa - ther of glo - ry, pure Fa - ther of light, Thine an - gels a -
ces - si - ble hid from our eyes, Most bless - ed, most glo - rious, the
wast - ing, Thou rul - est in might; Thy jus - tice, like moun-tains, high
liv - est—the true life of all; We blos - som and flour - ish as
dore Thee, all veil - ing their sight; All praise we would ren - der— O
An - cient of Days, Al - might - y, vic - to - rious—Thy great name we praise.
soar - ing a - bove Thy clouds, which are foun-tains of good - ness and love.
leaves on the tree, And with - er and per - ish— but naught changeth Thee.
help us to see 'Tis on - ly the splen - dor of light hid - eth Thee!*

Tune: ST. DENIO—lower key at 415

56 — This Is My Father's World

MALTBIE D. BABCOCK
FRANKLIN L. SHEPPARD
1. This is my Fa - ther's world, And to my list - 'ning ears
2. This is my Fa - ther's world— The birds their car - ols raise;
3. This is my Fa - ther's world— O let me ne'er for - get
All na - ture sings, and round me rings The mu - sic of the spheres.
The morn-ing light, the lil - y white, De - clare their Mak - er's praise.
That tho the wrong seems oft so strong God is the Rul - er yet.
This is my Fa - ther's world! I rest me in the thought Of
This is my Fa - ther's world! He shines in all that's fair; In the
This is my Fa - ther's world! The bat - tle is not done; Je -
rocks and trees, of skies and seas— His hand the won - ders wrought.
rus - tling grass I hear Him pass— He speaks to me ev - 'ry - where.
sus who died shall be sat - is - fied, And earth and heav'n be one.

Tune: TERRA BEATA

WORSHIP: THE FATHER

Our Great Savior — 57

J. WILBUR CHAPMAN
ROWLAND H. PRICHARD
Arr. by Robert Harkness
1. Je - sus! what a Friend for sin - ners! Je - sus! Lov - er of my soul;
2. Je - sus! what a Strength in weak - ness! Let me hide my - self in Him;
3. Je - sus! what a Help in sor - row! While the bil - lows o'er me roll;
4. Je - sus! what a Guide and Keep - er! While the tem - pest still is high;
5. Je - sus! I do now a - dore Him, More than all in Him I find;
Friends may fail me, foes as - sail me, He, my Sav - ior, makes me whole.
Tempt - ed, tried, and some-times fail - ing, He, my Strength, my vic - t'ry wins.
E - ven when my heart is break - ing, He, my Com - fort, helps my soul.
Storms a - bout me, night o'er - takes me, He, my Pi - lot, hears my cry.
He has grant - ed me for - give - ness, I am His, and He is mine.
CHORUS
Hal - le - lu - jah! what a Sav - ior! Hal - le - lu - jah! what a Friend!
Sav - ing, help - ing, keep - ing, lov - ing, He is with me to the end.
Tune: HYFRYDOL—different harmonization at 172

58 — Fairest Lord Jesus
Münster Gesangbuch
4th vs. trans. by Joseph A. Seiss
Schlesische Volkslieder
Adapted by Richard S. Willis
1. Fair - est Lord Je - sus! Rul - er of all na - ture!
2. Fair are the mead - ows, Fair - er still the wood - lands,
3. Fair is the sun - shine, Fair - er still the moon - light,
4. Beau - ti - ful Sav - ior! Lord of the na - tions!
O Thou of God and man the Son! Thee will I cher - ish,
Robed in the bloom-ing garb of spring: Je - sus is fair - er,
And all the twink-ling star - ry host: Je - sus shines bright - er,
Son of God and Son of Man! Glo - ry and hon - or,
Thee will I hon - or, Thou my soul's glo - ry, joy and crown!
Je - sus is pur - er, Who makes the woe - ful heart to sing.
Je - sus shines pur - er Than all the an - gels heav'n can boast.
Praise, ad - o - ra - tion Now and for - ev - er - more be Thine!*
Tune: CRUSADERS' HYMN
59 — Praise the Savior
THOMAS KELLY
German melody
1. Praise the Sav - ior, ye who know Him! Who can tell how much we owe Him?
2. Je - sus is the name that charms us, He for con - flict fits and arms us;
3. Trust in Him, ye saints, for - ev - er— He is faith - ful, chang-ing nev - er;
4. Keep us, Lord, O keep us cleav - ing To Thy - self, and still be - liev - ing,
5. Then we shall be where we would be, Then we shall be what we should be;

Tune: ACCLAIM

WORSHIP: THE SON

Glad - ly let us ren - der to Him All we are and have.
Noth - ing moves and noth - ing harms us While we trust in Him.
Nei - ther force nor guile can sev - er Those He loves from Him.
Till the hour of our re - ceiv - ing Prom-ised joys with Thee.
Things that are not now, nor could be, Soon shall be our own.

May Jesus Christ Be Praised — 60

German hymn
Trans. by Edward Caswall

JOSEPH BARNBY

1. When morn-ing gilds the skies, My heart a - wak - ing cries:
2. Does sad - ness fill my mind? A sol - ace here I find:
3. In heav'n's e - ter - nal bliss The love - liest strain is this:
4. Be this, while life is mine, My can - ti - cle di - vine:
May Je - sus Christ be praised! A - like at work and prayer
May Je - sus Christ be praised! Or fades my earth - ly bliss?
May Je - sus Christ be praised! The pow'rs of dark - ness fear
May Je - sus Christ be praised! Be this th'e - ter - nal song
To Je - sus I re - pair: May Je - sus Christ be praised!
My com - fort still is this: May Je - sus Christ be praised!
When this sweet chant they hear: May Je - sus Christ be praised!
Thru all the a - ges long: May Je - sus Christ be praised!*

Tune: LAUDES DOMINI

61 — And Can It Be?
CHARLES WESLEY
THOMAS CAMPBELL
1. And can it be that I should gain An in - t'rest in
2. He left His Fa - ther's throne a - bove, So free, so in -
3. Long my im - pris - oned spir - it lay Fast bound in sin
4. No con - dem - na - tion now I dread: Je - sus, and all
the Sav - ior's blood? Died He for me, who caused His pain?
fi - nite His grace! Emp-tied Him - self of all but love,
and na - ture's night. Thine eye dif - fused a quick -'ning ray:
in Him, is mine! A - live in Him, my liv - ing Head,
For me, who Him to death pur - sued? A - maz - ing love!
And bled for Ad - am's help - less race! 'Tis mer - cy all,
I woke— the dun - geon flamed with light! My chains fell off,
And clothed in right - eous - ness di - vine, Bold I ap - proach
how can it be That Thou, my God shouldst
im - mense and free, For, O my God, it
my heart was free, I rose, went forth, and
th'e - ter - nal throne, And claim the crown, thru

Tune: SAGINA

WORSHIP: THE SON

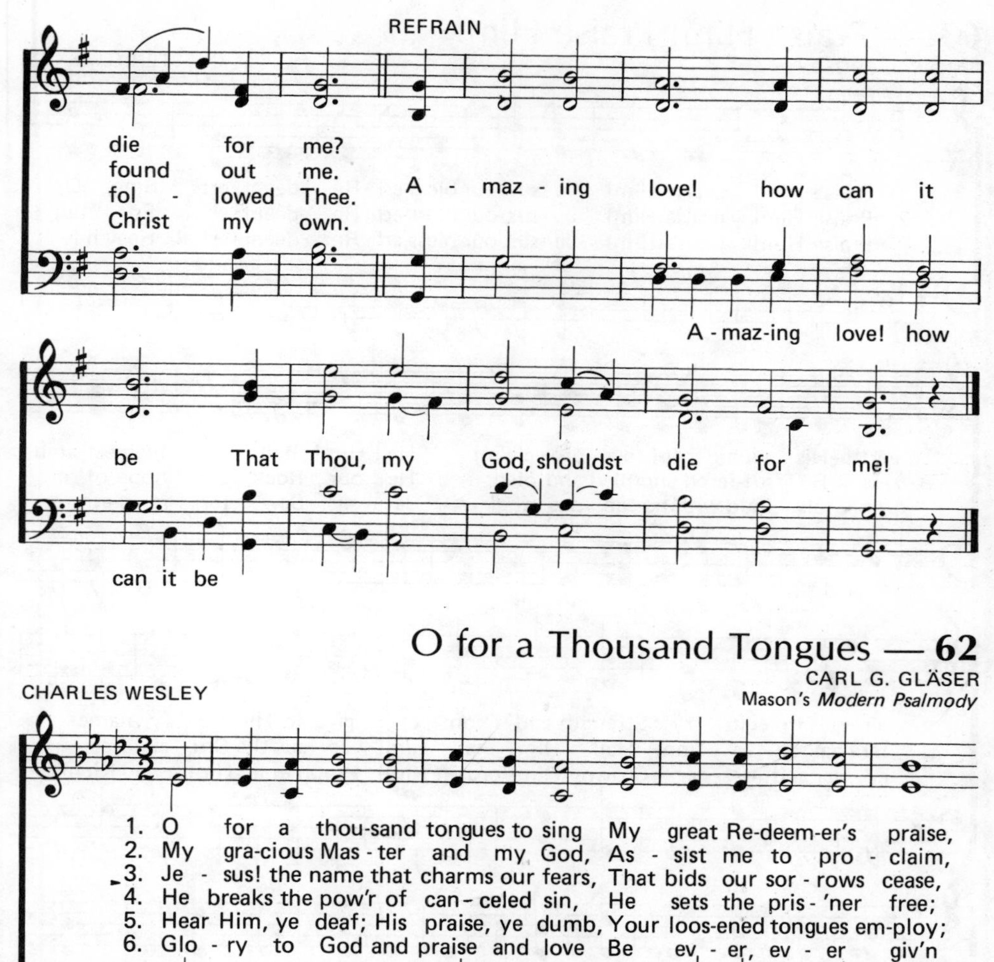
REFRAIN
die for me?
found out me.
fol - lowed Thee.
Christ my own.
A - maz - ing love! how can it be That Thou, my God, shouldst die for me!
A - maz-ing love! how can it be

O for a Thousand Tongues — 62

CHARLES WESLEY

CARL G. GLÄSER
Mason's *Modern Psalmody*

1. O for a thou-sand tongues to sing My great Re-deem-er's praise, The glo-ries of my God and King, The tri-umphs of His grace!
2. My gra-cious Mas - ter and my God, As - sist me to pro - claim, To spread thru all the earth a - broad The hon-ors of Thy name.
3. Je - sus! the name that charms our fears, That bids our sor - rows cease, 'Tis mu - sic in the sin - ner's ears, 'Tis life and health and peace.
4. He breaks the pow'r of can - celed sin, He sets the pris - 'ner free; His blood can make the foul - est clean— His blood a - vailed for me.
5. Hear Him, ye deaf; His praise, ye dumb, Your loos-ened tongues em-ploy; Ye blind, be - hold your Sav - ior come; And leap, ye lame, for joy.
6. Glo - ry to God and praise and love Be ev - er, ev - er giv'n By saints be - low and saints a - bove— The Church in earth and heav'n.*

Tune: AZMON

63 — Praise Him! Praise Him!
FANNY J. CROSBY
CHESTER G. ALLEN
1. Praise Him! praise Him! Je-sus, our bless-ed Re - deem-er! Sing, O
2. Praise Him! praise Him! Je-sus, our bless-ed Re - deem-er! For our
3. Praise Him! praise Him! Je-sus, our bless-ed Re - deem-er! Heav'n-ly
earth—His won-der-ful love pro-claim! Hail Him! hail Him! high-est arch-
sins He suf-fered and bled and died; He our Rock, our hope of e-
por - tals loud with ho-san - nas ring! Je - sus, Sav - ior, reign-eth for
an-gels in glo - ry, Strength and hon - or give to His ho - ly name!
ter - nal sal - va - tion, Hail Him! hail Him! Je-sus the Cru - ci - fied.
ev - er and ev - er, Crown Him! crown Him! Proph-et and Priest and King!
Like a shep - herd Je-sus will guard His chil - dren— In His arms He
Sound His prais - es— Je-sus who bore our sor - rows— Love un - bound-ed,
Christ is com - ing, o - ver the world vic-to-rious— Pow'r and glo - ry
REFRAIN
car - ries them all day long:
won-der-ful, deep and strong: Praise Him! praise Him! tell of His
un - to the Lord be - long:
WORSHIP: THE SON

ex-cel-lent great-ness! Praise Him! praise Him! ev-er in joy-ful song!
Come, Christians, Join to Sing — 64
CHRISTIAN HENRY BATEMAN
Source unknown
1. Come, Chris-tians, join to sing— Al-le-lu-ia! A-men!
2. Come, lift your hearts on high— Al-le-lu-ia! A-men!
3. Praise yet our Christ a-gain— Al-le-lu-ia! A-men!
Loud praise to Christ our King— Al-le-lu-ia! A-men!
Let prais-es fill the sky— Al-le-lu-ia! A-men!
Life shall not end the strain— Al-le-lu-ia! A-men!
Let all, with heart and voice, Be-fore His throne re-joice;
He is our guide and friend, To us He'll con-de-scend;
On heav-en's bliss-ful shore His good-ness we'll a-dore,
Praise is His gra-cious choice: Al-le-lu-ia! A-men!
His love shall nev-er end: Al-le-lu-ia! A-men!
Sing-ing for-ev-er-more, "Al-le-lu-ia! A-men!"
Tune: MADRID
Arr. © Singspiration 1968. All rights reserved.
WORSHIP: THE SON

65 — His Name Is Wonderful
AUDREY MIEIR
AUDREY MIEIR
His name is Won-der-ful, His name is Won-der-ful, His name is
He is the might-y King, Mas-ter of ev-'ry-thing, His name is
Won-der-ful, Je-sus, my Lord; Je-sus, my Lord.
He's the great Shep-herd, the Rock of all a-ges, Al-might-y
God is He; Bow down be-fore Him, Love and a-
dore Him, His name is Won-der-ful, Je-sus my Lord.
WORSHIP: THE SON
©Copyright 1959 by Manna Music, Inc. All rights reserved.

There's Something About That Name — 66
GLORIA GAITHER and
WILLIAM J. GAITHER
WILLIAM J. GAITHER
Je - sus, Je - sus, Je - sus; There's just some-thing a - bout that
name!
Mas-ter, Sav-ior, Je - sus, Like the fra-grance
aft-er the rain;
Je - sus, Je - sus, Je - sus, Let all
heav-en and earth pro - claim:
Kings and king-doms will
all pass a - way, But there's some-thing a - bout that name!
©Copyright 1970 by William J. Gaither. All rights reserved.
WORSHIP: THE SON

67 — O Come, Let Us Adore Him
Wade's Cantus Diversi
Traditional
1. O come, let us a - dore Him, O come, let us a - dore
2. We'll praise His name for - ev - er, We'll praise His name for - ev -
3. We'll give Him all the glo - ry, We'll give Him all the glo -
4. For He a - lone is wor - thy, For He a - lone is wor -
Him, O come, let us a - dore Him, Christ the Lord.
er, We'll praise His name for - ev - er, Christ the Lord.
ry, We'll give Him all the glo - ry, Christ the Lord.
thy, For He a - lone is wor - thy, Christ the Lord.
Tune: Refrain of ADESTE FIDELES
68 — Ye Servants of God
CHARLES WESLEY
Attr. to William Croft
1. Ye serv - ants of God, your Mas - ter pro - claim, And pub - lish a -
2. God rul - eth on high, al - might - y to save, And still He is
3. "Sal - va - tion to God, who sits on the throne!" Let all cry a -
4. Then let us a - dore, and give Him His right— All glo - ry and
broad His won - der - ful name; The name, all - vic - to - rious, of Je - sus
nigh, His pres - ence we have; The great con - gre - ga - tion His tri - umph
loud, and hon - or the Son; The prais - es of Je - sus the an - gels
pow'r, all wis - dom and might, All hon - or and bless - ing, with an - gels

Tune: HANOVER (Alternate, LYONS)

ex - tol: His king - dom is glo - rious, He rules o - ver all.
shall sing, As - crib - ing sal - va - tion to Je - sus, our King.
pro - claim, Fall down on their fac - es and wor - ship the Lamb.
a - bove, And thanks nev - er - ceas - ing, and in - fi - nite love.*
Jesus, We Just Want to Thank You — 69
GLORIA GAITHER and
WILLIAM J. GAITHER
WILLIAM J. GAITHER
1. Je - sus, we just want to thank You, Je - sus, we just want to thank You, Je - sus, we just want to thank You, Thank You for be - ing so good.
2. Je - sus, we just want to praise You, Je - sus, we just want to praise You, Je - sus, we just want to praise You, Praise You for be - ing so good.
3. Je - sus, we just want to tell You, Je - sus, we just want to tell You, Je - sus, we just want to tell You, We love You for be - ing so good.
4. Sav - ior, we just want to serve You, Sav - ior, we just want to serve You, Sav - ior, we just want to serve You, Serve You for be - ing so good.
5. Je - sus, we know You are com - ing, Je - sus, we know You are com - ing, Je - sus, we know You are com - ing, Take us to live in Your home.

Tune: THANK YOU

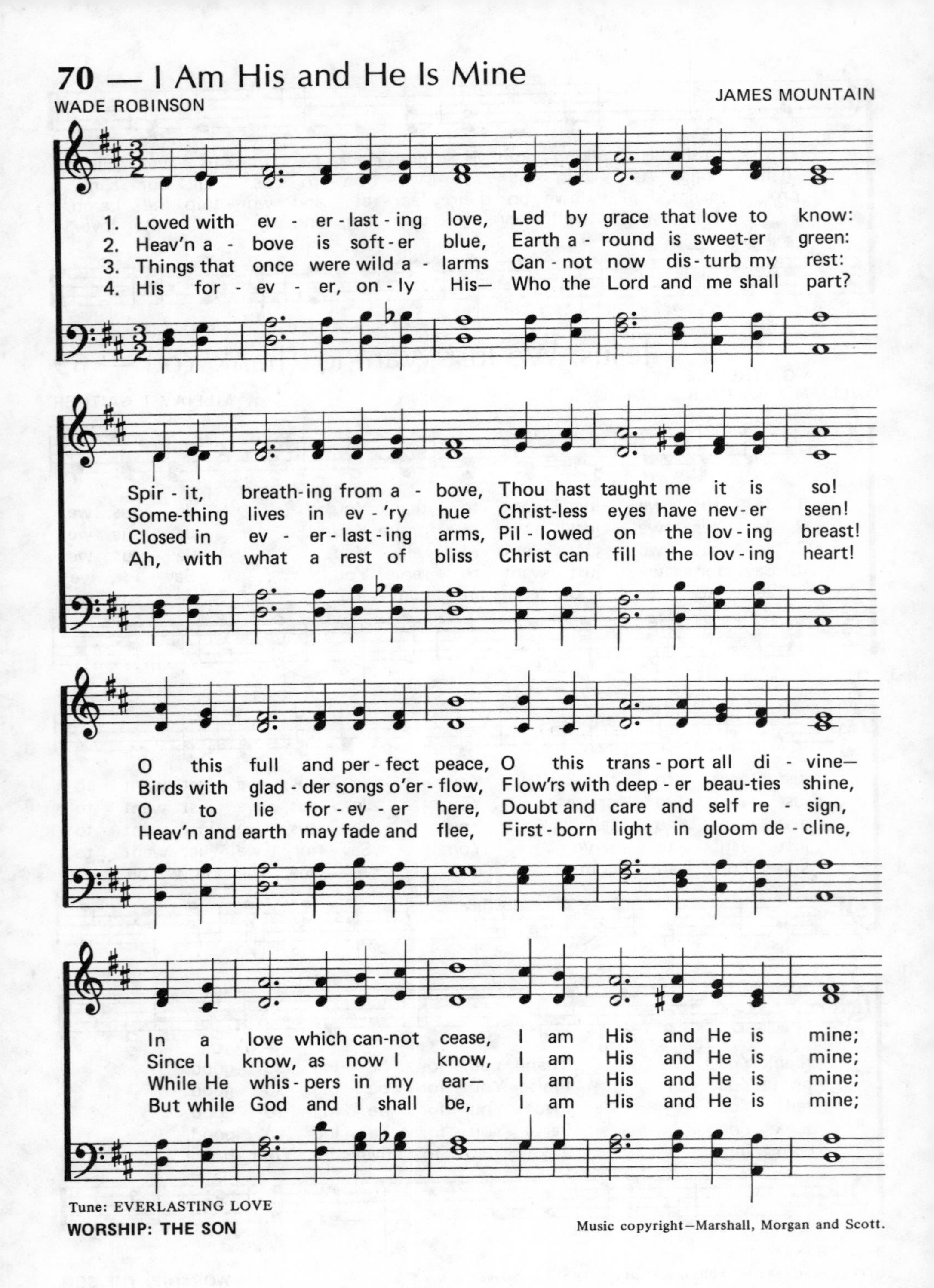
70 — I Am His and He Is Mine
WADE ROBINSON
JAMES MOUNTAIN
1. Loved with ev - er - last - ing love, Led by grace that love to know:
2. Heav'n a - bove is soft - er blue, Earth a - round is sweet-er green:
3. Things that once were wild a - larms Can - not now dis - turb my rest:
4. His for - ev - er, on - ly His— Who the Lord and me shall part?
Spir - it, breath-ing from a - bove, Thou hast taught me it is so!
Some-thing lives in ev - 'ry hue Christ-less eyes have nev-er seen!
Closed in ev - er - last - ing arms, Pil - lowed on the lov - ing breast!
Ah, with what a rest of bliss Christ can fill the lov - ing heart!
O this full and per - fect peace, O this trans - port all di - vine—
Birds with glad - der songs o'er - flow, Flow'rs with deep - er beau-ties shine,
O to lie for - ev - er here, Doubt and care and self re - sign,
Heav'n and earth may fade and flee, First - born light in gloom de - cline,
In a love which can-not cease, I am His and He is mine;
Since I know, as now I know, I am His and He is mine;
While He whis - pers in my ear— I am His and He is mine;
But while God and I shall be, I am His and He is mine;
Tune: EVERLASTING LOVE
WORSHIP: THE SON
Music copyright—Marshall, Morgan and Scott.

In a love which can-not cease, I am His and He is mine.
Since I know, as now I know, I am His and He is mine.
While He whis-pers in my ear— I am His and He is mine.
But while God and I shall be, I am His and He is mine.
Join All the Glorious Names — 71
ISAAC WATTS
JOHN DARWALL
1. Join all the glo-rious names Of wis-dom, love and pow'r That
2. Great Proph-et of my God, My tongue would bless Thy name; By
3. Je-sus, Thou great High Priest, Thou gav'st Thy blood and died; My
4. Di-vine, al-might-y Lord, My Con-q'ror and my King, Thy
5. Now let my soul a-rise And tread the tempt-er down; My
ev-er mor-tals knew, That an-gels ev-er bore: All are too
Thee the joy-ful news Of our sal-va-tion came: The joy-ful
guilt-y con-science seeks No sac-ri-fice be-side: Thy pow'r-ful
scep-ter and Thy sword, Thy reign-ing grace I sing: Thine is the
Cap-tain leads me forth To con-quest and a crown: A fee-ble
poor to speak His worth, Too poor to set my Sav-ior forth.
news of sins for-giv'n, Of hell sub-dued, and peace with heav'n.
blood didst once a-tone And now it pleads be-fore the throne.
pow'r— be-hold I sit In will-ing bonds be-neath Thy feet.
saint shall win the day, Tho death and hell ob-struct the way.*
Tune: DARWALL'S 148th—higher key at 245

72 — Thou Art Worthy

Based on Revelation 4:11, 5:9
1, (3) - PAULINE M. MILLS
2 - TOM SMAIL

PAULINE M. MILLS

1. Thou art wor - thy, Thou art wor - thy, Thou art wor-thy, O Lord,
To re-ceive glo-ry, glo - ry and hon - or, Glo - ry and hon - or and pow'r;
For Thou hast cre - at - ed, hast all things cre - at - ed, Thou hast cre - at - ed all things, And for Thy pleas-ure they are cre - at - ed: Thou art wor-thy, O Lord!

2. Thou art wor - thy, Thou art wor - thy, Thou art wor-thy, O Lamb,
To re-ceive bless-ing, glo - ry and hon - or And pow'r at the Fa - ther's right hand;
For Thou hast re - deemed us, hast ran - somed and cleaned us, By Thy blood set - ting us free, In white robes ar - rayed us, kings and priests made us: We are reign-ing in Thee!

3. Thou art wor - thy, Thou art wor - thy, Thou art wor-thy, O Lord,
To re-ceive glo-ry, glo - ry and hon - or, Glo - ry and hon - or and pow'r;
For Thou hast cre - at - ed, hast all things cre - at - ed, Thou hast cre - at - ed all things, And for Thy pleas-ure they are cre - at - ed: Thou art wor-thy, O Lord!

Worthy Is the Lamb — 73
Based on Revelation 5:12
DON WYRTZEN
Wor - thy is the Lamb that was slain, Wor - thy is the Lamb that was
slain, Wor-thy is the Lamb that was slain, to re - ceive:
Pow - er and rich - es and wis - dom and strength, Hon-or and glo - ry and
bless - ing! Wor - thy is the Lamb, Wor - thy is the Lamb, Wor-thy
is the Lamb that was slain, Wor - thy is the Lamb!
WORSHIP: THE SON

74 — Mine Eyes Have Seen the Glory

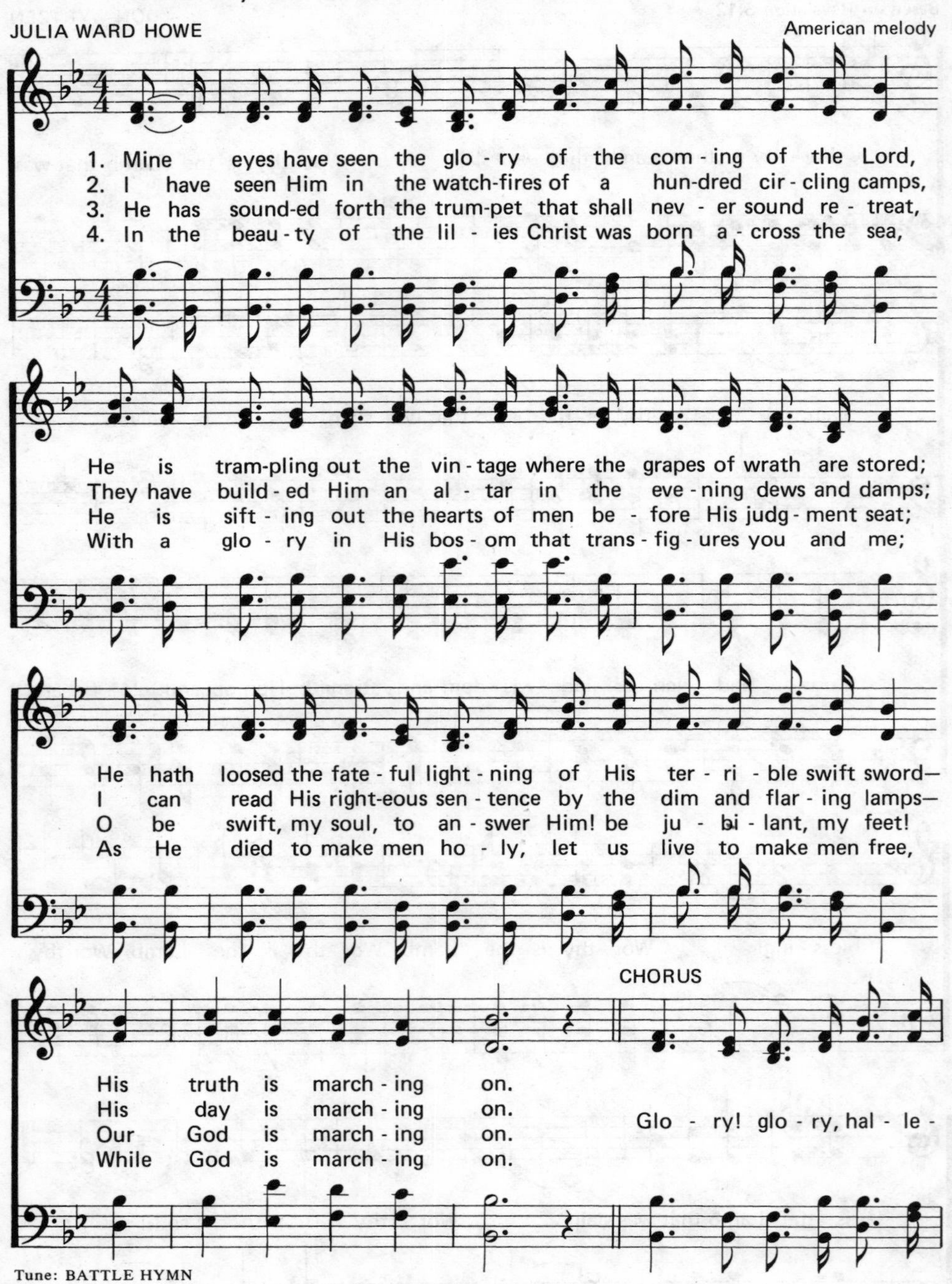
JULIA WARD HOWE
American melody
1. Mine eyes have seen the glo - ry of the com - ing of the Lord,
2. I have seen Him in the watch-fires of a hun-dred cir - cling camps,
3. He has sound-ed forth the trum-pet that shall nev - er sound re - treat,
4. In the beau - ty of the lil - ies Christ was born a - cross the sea,
He is tram-pling out the vin - tage where the grapes of wrath are stored;
They have build - ed Him an al - tar in the eve - ning dews and damps;
He is sift - ing out the hearts of men be - fore His judg - ment seat;
With a glo - ry in His bos - om that trans - fig - ures you and me;
He hath loosed the fate - ful light - ning of His ter - ri - ble swift sword—
I can read His right-eous sen - tence by the dim and flar - ing lamps—
O be swift, my soul, to an - swer Him! be ju - bi - lant, my feet!
As He died to make men ho - ly, let us live to make men free,
His truth is march - ing on.
His day is march - ing on.
Our God is march - ing on.
While God is march - ing on.
CHORUS
Glo - ry! glo - ry, hal - le -

Tune: BATTLE HYMN

WORSHIP: THE SON

lu - jah! Glo - ry! glo - ry, hal - le - lu - jah! Glo - ry!
glo - ry, hal - le - lu - jah! His truth is march - ing on.
All Glory to Jesus — 75
JOHN W. PETERSON
JOHN W. PETERSON
1. All glo - ry to Je - sus, be - got - ten of God, The great "I AM" is He; Cre - a - tor, sus - tain - er—but won - der of all, The Lamb of Cal - va - ry!
2. To think that the guard - ian of plan - ets in space, The Shep - herd of the stars, Is ten - der - ly lead - ing the church of His love, By hands with crim - son scars!
3. The King of all kings and the Lord of all lords, He reigns in glo - ry now; Some day He is com - ing earth's king - dom to claim, And ev - 'ry knee shall bow!
CODA
And ev - 'ry knee shall bow!

Tune: RIDGEMOOR

76 — Above Every Name
JOHN W. PETERSON
JOHN W. PETERSON
1. Names of kings and rul - ers we hon - or, Those whose portraits grace a pal - ace wall, Pre - cious name of "moth-er," Of a friend or lov - er, But the great - est name of them all:
2. He came down from heav - en to save us, O what pain and shame He suf-fered here; Mock - ing - ly they hailed Him, On a cross they nailed Him, That is why His name is so dear!
3. When in prayer I whis - per it soft - ly, At the throne of grace it is the key; An - gels love to hear it, Hell and de - mons fear it, Name of pow'r and vic - to - ry!
CHORUS (Based on Philippians 2:9-11)
A - bove ev - 'ry name is the name of Je - sus, A - bove ev - 'ry name is the name of Je - sus; A - bove ev - 'ry

WORSHIP: THE SON

name is the name of Je - sus, Ev-'ry knee shall bow, ev-'ry
tongue con - fess That He is Lord of all!
Jesus, Jesus, Jesus! — 77
Traditional
Traditional
Arr. by Eldon Burkwall
Je-sus, Je-sus, Je - sus:
Je-sus, Je-sus, Je - sus: Nev-er have I heard a
name that thrills my soul like Thine! Je-sus, Je-sus, Je -
Je-sus, Je-sus, Je -
sus:
sus: O what won-drous grace—that links that love - ly name with mine!

78 — How Sweet the Name of Jesus Sounds

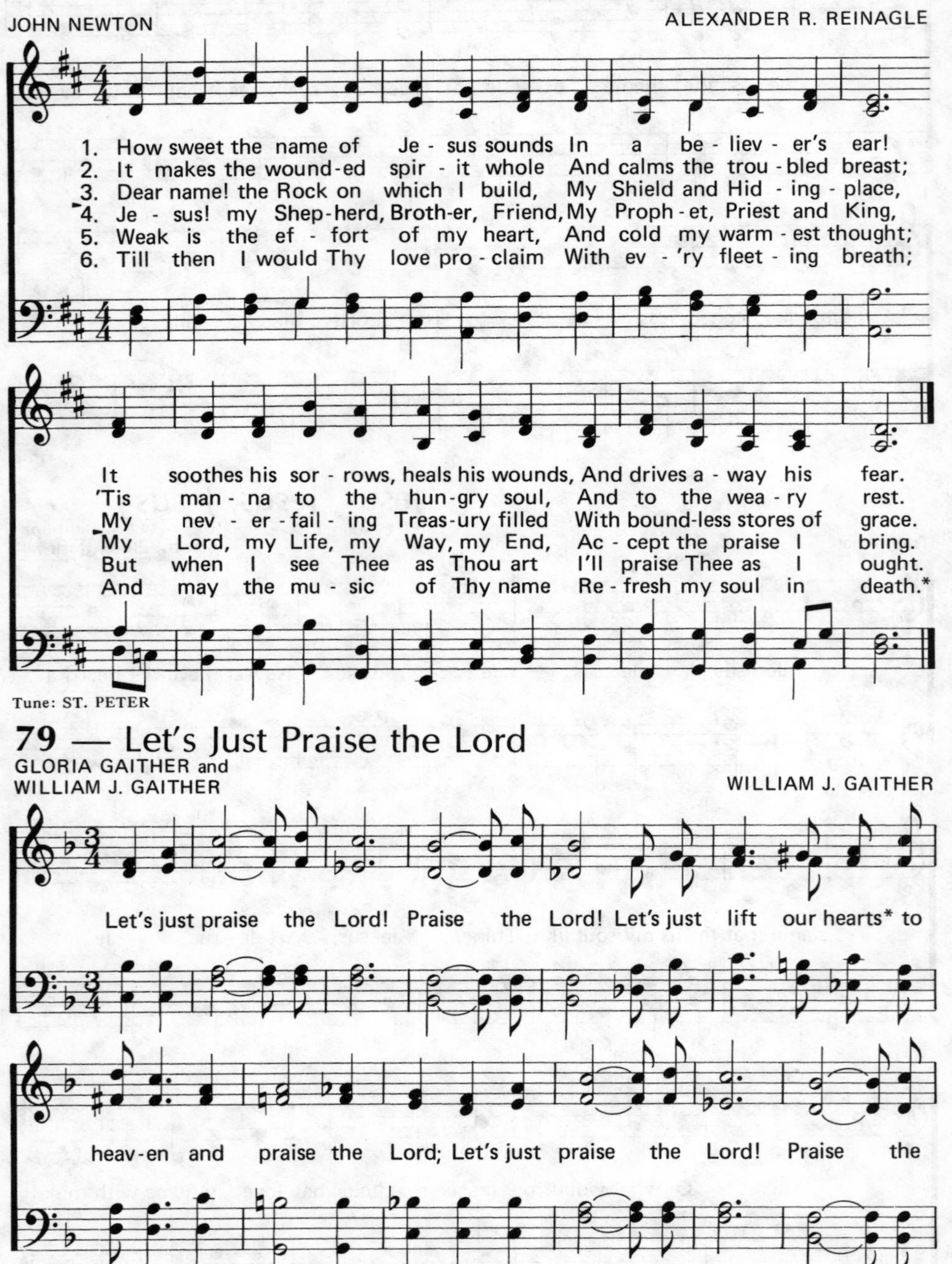
JOHN NEWTON
ALEXANDER R. REINAGLE
1. How sweet the name of Je - sus sounds In a be - liev - er's ear!
2. It makes the wound-ed spir - it whole And calms the trou - bled breast;
3. Dear name! the Rock on which I build, My Shield and Hid - ing - place,
4. Je - sus! my Shep-herd, Broth-er, Friend, My Proph - et, Priest and King,
5. Weak is the ef - fort of my heart, And cold my warm - est thought;
6. Till then I would Thy love pro - claim With ev - 'ry fleet - ing breath;
It soothes his sor - rows, heals his wounds, And drives a - way his fear.
'Tis man - na to the hun-gry soul, And to the wea - ry rest.
My nev - er - fail - ing Treas-ury filled With bound-less stores of grace.
My Lord, my Life, my Way, my End, Ac - cept the praise I bring.
But when I see Thee as Thou art I'll praise Thee as I ought.
And may the mu - sic of Thy name Re - fresh my soul in death.*
Tune: ST. PETER
79 — Let's Just Praise the Lord
GLORIA GAITHER and
WILLIAM J. GAITHER
WILLIAM J. GAITHER
Let's just praise the Lord! Praise the Lord! Let's just lift our hearts* to
heav-en and praise the Lord; Let's just praise the Lord! Praise the

*Alternatives: voices, hands.

Fine
Lord! Let's just lift our hearts* to heav-en and praise the Lord!
1. O we thank You for Your kind-ness, we thank You for Your love,
2. Just the pre-cious name of Je-sus is worth-y of our praise,
We have been in heav'n-ly plac-es, felt bless-ings from a-
Let us bow our knees be-fore Him, our hands to heav-en
bove; We've been shar-ing all the good things the fam-'ly can af-
raise; When He comes in clouds of glo-ry with Him we'll ev-er
D.C.
ford, Let's just turn our praise t'ward heav-en and praise the Lord.
reign, Let's just lift our hap-py voic-es and praise His name.

80 — Take the Name of Jesus with You
LYDIA BAXTER
WILLIAM H. DOANE
1. Take the name of Je - sus with you, Child of sor - row and of woe;
2. Take the name of Je - sus ev - er, As a shield from ev-'ry snare;
3. O the pre-cious name of Je - sus! How it thrills our souls with joy,
4. At the name of Je - sus bow - ing, Fall - ing pros-trate at His feet,
It will joy and com - fort give you— Take it, then, wher-e'er you go.
If temp - ta - tions round you gath - er, Breathe that ho - ly name in prayer.
When His lov - ing arms re - ceive us And His songs our tongues em-ploy!
King of kings in heav'n we'll crown Him When our jour - ney is com - plete.
CHORUS
Pre - cious name, O how sweet! Hope of earth and joy of heav'n;
Pre - cious name, O how sweet! Hope of earth and joy of heav'n.

S. TREVOR FRANCIS

THOMAS J. WILLIAMS

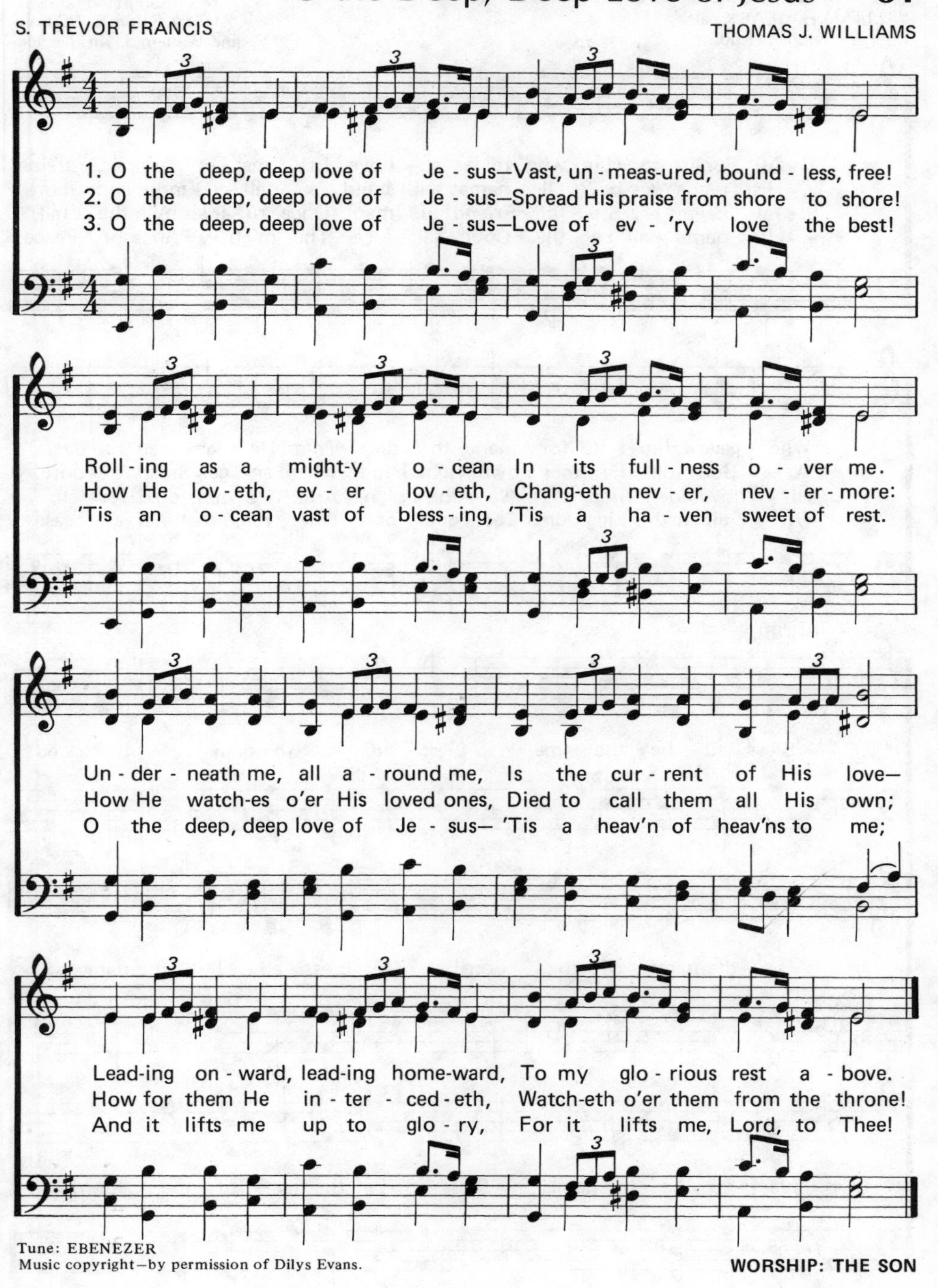
1. O the deep, deep love of Je - sus—Vast, un - meas-ured, bound - less, free!
2. O the deep, deep love of Je - sus—Spread His praise from shore to shore!
3. O the deep, deep love of Je - sus—Love of ev - 'ry love the best!
Roll - ing as a might-y o - cean In its full - ness o - ver me.
How He lov - eth, ev - er lov - eth, Chang-eth nev - er, nev - er - more:
'Tis an o - cean vast of bless - ing, 'Tis a ha - ven sweet of rest.
Un - der - neath me, all a - round me, Is the cur - rent of His love—
How He watch-es o'er His loved ones, Died to call them all His own;
O the deep, deep love of Je - sus— 'Tis a heav'n of heav'ns to me;
Lead-ing on - ward, lead-ing home-ward, To my glo - rious rest a - bove.
How for them He in - ter - ced - eth, Watch-eth o'er them from the throne!
And it lifts me up to glo - ry, For it lifts me, Lord, to Thee!

Tune: EBENEZER

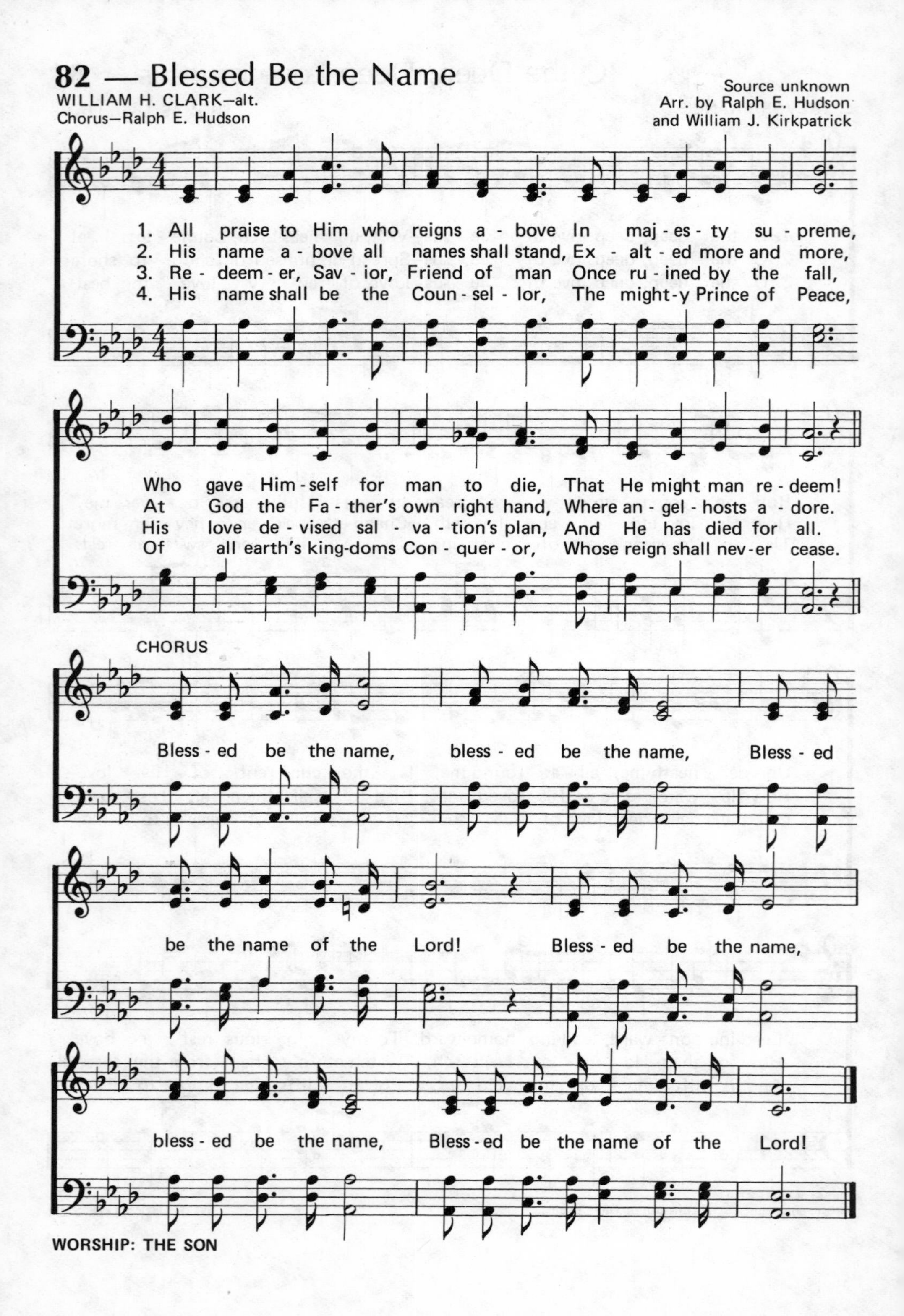

82 — Blessed Be the Name
WILLIAM H. CLARK—alt.
Chorus—Ralph E. Hudson
Source unknown
Arr. by Ralph E. Hudson
and William J. Kirkpatrick
1. All praise to Him who reigns a - bove In maj - es - ty su - preme,
2. His name a - bove all names shall stand, Ex - alt - ed more and more,
3. Re - deem - er, Sav - ior, Friend of man Once ru - ined by the fall,
4. His name shall be the Coun - sel - lor, The might - y Prince of Peace,
Who gave Him - self for man to die, That He might man re - deem!
At God the Fa - ther's own right hand, Where an - gel - hosts a - dore.
His love de - vised sal - va - tion's plan, And He has died for all.
Of all earth's king - doms Con - quer - or, Whose reign shall nev - er cease.
CHORUS
Bless - ed be the name, bless - ed be the name, Bless - ed
be the name of the Lord! Bless - ed be the name,
bless - ed be the name, Bless - ed be the name of the Lord!
WORSHIP: THE SON

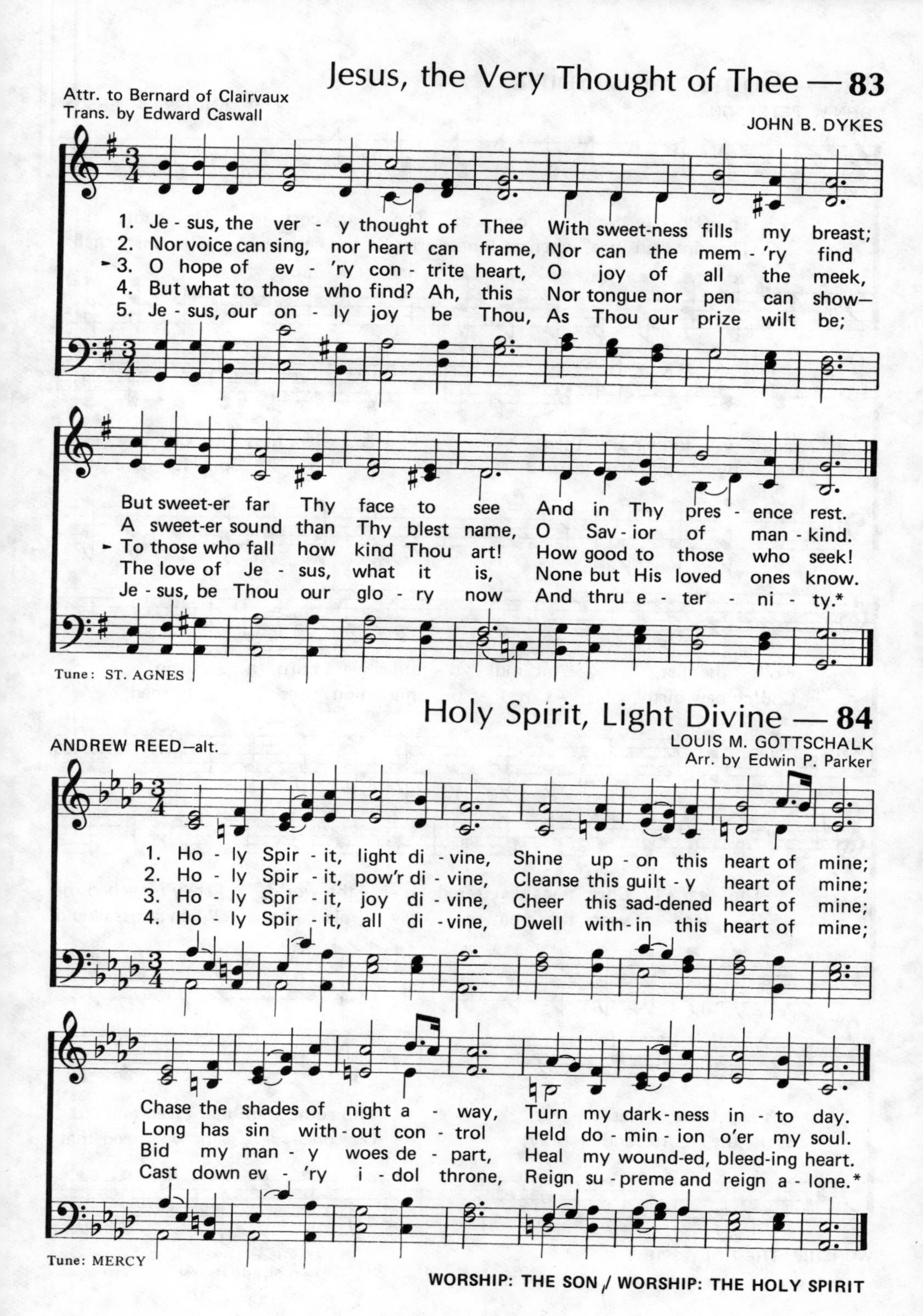
Jesus, the Very Thought of Thee — 83
Attr. to Bernard of Clairvaux
Trans. by Edward Caswall
JOHN B. DYKES
1. Je - sus, the ver - y thought of Thee With sweet-ness fills my breast;
2. Nor voice can sing, nor heart can frame, Nor can the mem - 'ry find
3. O hope of ev - 'ry con - trite heart, O joy of all the meek,
4. But what to those who find? Ah, this Nor tongue nor pen can show—
5. Je - sus, our on - ly joy be Thou, As Thou our prize wilt be;
But sweet-er far Thy face to see And in Thy pres - ence rest.
A sweet-er sound than Thy blest name, O Sav-ior of man - kind.
To those who fall how kind Thou art! How good to those who seek!
The love of Je - sus, what it is, None but His loved ones know.
Je - sus, be Thou our glo - ry now And thru e - ter - ni - ty.*
Tune: ST. AGNES
Holy Spirit, Light Divine — 84
ANDREW REED—alt.
LOUIS M. GOTTSCHALK
Arr. by Edwin P. Parker
1. Ho - ly Spir - it, light di - vine, Shine up - on this heart of mine;
2. Ho - ly Spir - it, pow'r di - vine, Cleanse this guilt - y heart of mine;
3. Ho - ly Spir - it, joy di - vine, Cheer this sad-dened heart of mine;
4. Ho - ly Spir - it, all di - vine, Dwell with-in this heart of mine;
Chase the shades of night a - way, Turn my dark-ness in - to day.
Long has sin with-out con - trol Held do - min - ion o'er my soul.
Bid my man - y woes de - part, Heal my wound-ed, bleed-ing heart.
Cast down ev - 'ry i - dol throne, Reign su - preme and reign a - lone.*
Tune: MERCY
WORSHIP: THE SON / WORSHIP: THE HOLY SPIRIT

85 — Come, Holy Spirit
JOHN W. PETERSON
JOHN W. PETERSON
1. The Ho - ly Spir - it came at Pen - te - cost, He came in mighty - y full - ness then; His wit - ness thru be - liev - ers won the lost, And mul - ti - tudes were born a - gain.
2. Then in an age when dark - ness gripped the earth, "The just shall live by faith" was learned; The Ho - ly Spir - it gave the Church new birth As ref - or - ma - tion fires burned.
The ear - ly Chris - tians scat - tered o'er the world, They preached the gos - pel fear - less - ly; Tho some were mar - tyred and to
In lat - er years the great re - viv - als came, When saints would seek the Lord and pray; O once a - gain we need that
WORSHIP: THE HOLY SPIRIT
© 1971, arr. 1979 by John W. Peterson Music Company. All rights reserved. Used by permission.

li - ons hurled, They marched a-long in vic - to - ry!
ho - ly flame To meet the chal - lenge of to - day!
CHORUS
Come, Ho - ly Spir - it, Dark is the hour; We need Your fill - ing,
Your love and Your might-y pow'r! Move now a - mong us, Stir us, we
pray; Come, Ho - ly Spir - it, Re-vive the Church to - day!
D.C.
CODA
Re - vive the Church to - day! Re - vive the Church to - day!

86 — Spirit of God, Descend upon My Heart
GEORGE CROLY
FREDERICK C. ATKINSON
1. Spir - it of God, de - scend up - on my heart: Wean it from
2. Hast Thou not bid us love Thee, God and King? All, all Thine
3. Teach me to feel that Thou art al - ways nigh; Teach me the
4. Teach me to love Thee as Thine an - gels love, One ho - ly
earth, through all its puls - es move. Stoop to my weak - ness, might-y
own— soul, heart and strength and mind. I see Thy cross—there teach my
strug - gles of the soul to bear— To check the ris - ing doubt, the
pas - sion fill - ing all my frame: The bap - tism of the heav'n-de-
as Thou art, And make me love Thee as I ought to love.
heart to cling; O let me seek Thee, and O let me find.
reb - el sigh; Teach me the pa - tience of un - an - swered prayer.
scend - ed Dove— My heart an al - tar and Thy love the flame.*
Tune: MORECAMBE—lower key at 157
87 — Breathe on Me, Breath of God
EDWIN HATCH
ROBERT JACKSON
1. Breathe on me, Breath of God, Fill me with life a - new,
2. Breathe on me, Breath of God, Un - til my heart is pure,
3. Breathe on me, Breath of God, Till I am whol - ly Thine,
4. Breathe on me, Breath of God, So shall I nev - er die,
Tune: TRENTHAM
WORSHIP: THE HOLY SPIRIT

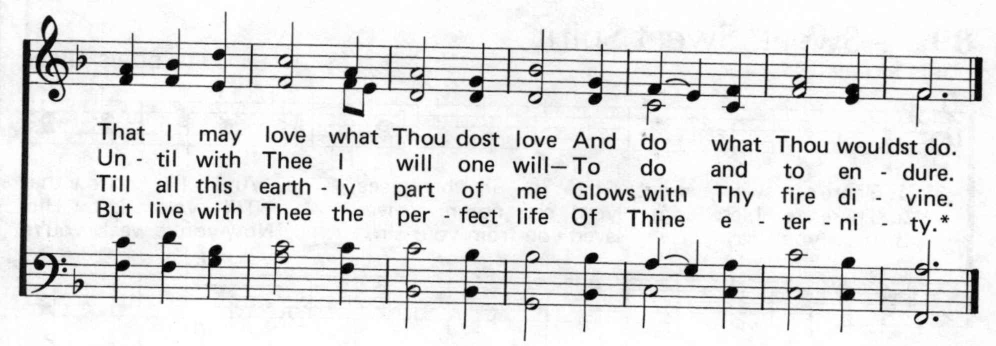
That I may love what Thou dost love And do what Thou wouldst do.
Un - til with Thee I will one will— To do and to en - dure.
Till all this earth - ly part of me Glows with Thy fire di - vine.
But live with Thee the per - fect life Of Thine e - ter - ni - ty.*

O Breath of Life — 88

BESSIE PORTER HEAD

NORMAN JOHNSON

1. O Breath of Life, come sweep-ing thru us, Re - vive Thy Church with life and pow'r; O Breath of Life, come cleanse, re - new us, And fit Thy Church to meet this hour.
2. O Wind of God, come bend us, break us, Till hum - bly we con - fess our need; Then in Thy ten - der - ness re - make us, Re - vive, re - store— for this we plead.
3. O Breath of Love, come breathe with - in us, Re - new - ing thought and will and heart; Come, Love of Christ, a - fresh to win us, Re - vive Thy Church in ev - 'ry part.
4. O Heart of Christ, once bro - ken for us, 'Tis there we find our strength and rest; Our bro - ken, con - trite hearts now sol - ace, And let Thy wait - ing Church be blest.
5. Re - vive us, Lord! Is zeal a - bat - ing While har - vest fields are vast and white? Re - vive us, Lord— the world is wait - ing! E - quip Thy Church to spread the light.*

Tune: CORONADO

89 — Sweet, Sweet Spirit
DORIS AKERS
DORIS AKERS
1. There's a sweet, sweet Spir - it in this place, And I know that
2. There are bless - ings you can - not re - ceive Till you know Him
3. If you say He saved you from your sin, Now you're weak, you're
it's the Spir - it of the Lord; There are sweet ex - pres-sions on each
in His full - ness and be - lieve; You're the one to prof - it when you
bound and can - not en - ter in, You can make it right if you will
face, And I know they feel the pres - ence of the Lord.
say, "I am going to walk with Je - sus all the way."
yield— You'll en - joy the Ho - ly Spir - it that we feel.
CHORUS
Sweet Ho - ly Spir - it, Sweet heav-en - ly Dove, Stay right here
with us, Fill - ing us with Your love. And for these
WORSHIP: THE HOLY SPIRIT
©Copyright 1962, arr. 1974 by Manna Music, Inc. All rights reserved.

bless - ings We lift our hearts in praise; With-out a doubt we'll know
that we have been re - vived, When we shall leave this place.

Spirit of the Living God — 90

DANIEL IVERSON

DANIEL IVERSON

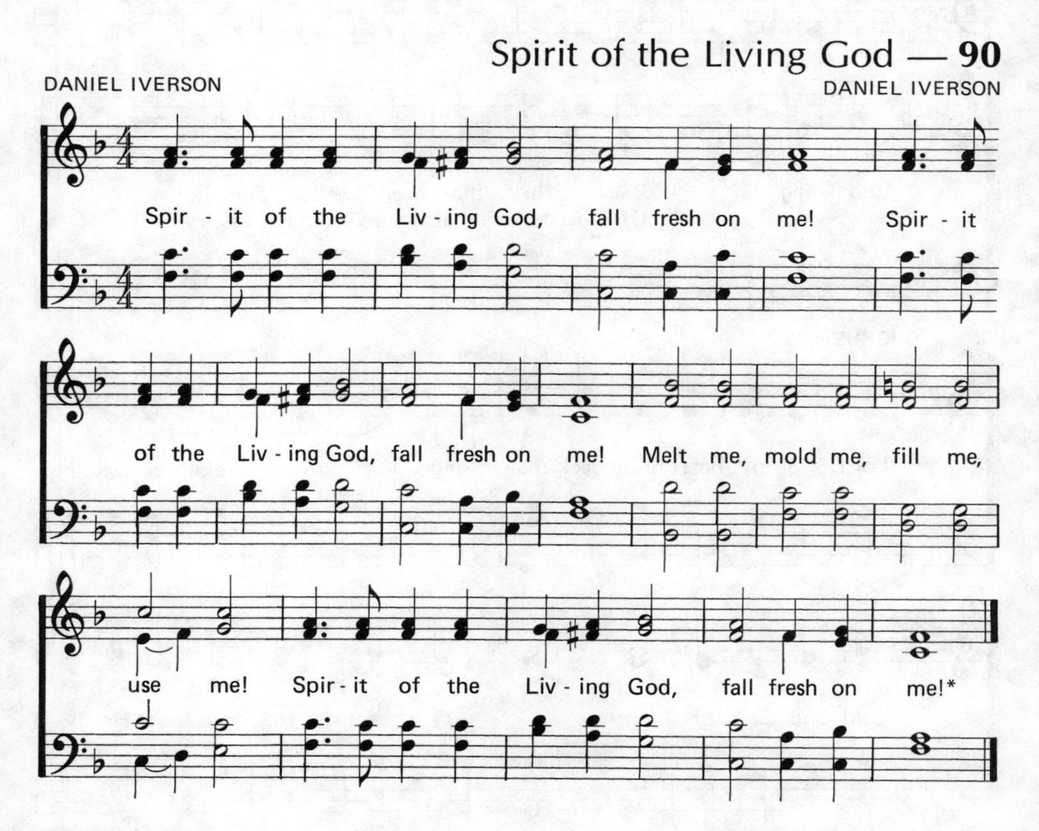
Spir - it of the Liv - ing God, fall fresh on me! Spir - it
of the Liv - ing God, fall fresh on me! Melt me, mold me, fill me,
use me! Spir - it of the Liv - ing God, fall fresh on me!*

91 — Bring Back the Springtime

KURT KAISER KURT KAISER

1. When in the spring the flow'rs are blooming bright and fair Aft - er the
2. Lord, make me like that stream that flows so cool and clear Down from the
gray of win - ter's gone, Once a - gain the lark be - gins its
mountains high a - bove; I will tell the world that won-drous
tun - ing Back in the mead-ows of my home.
sto - ry Of the streams that flowed from Cal-va - ry.
CHORUS
Lord, to my heart bring back the spring - time, Take a-way the
cold and dark of sin; O re-turn to me, sweet Ho - ly

WORSHIP: THE HOLY SPIRIT

Spir - it, May I warm and ten-der be a - gain.
Channels Only — 92
MARY E. MAXWELL
ADA ROSE GIBBS
1. How I praise Thee, pre-cious Sav-ior, That Thy love laid hold of me;
2. Emp-tied that Thou should-est fill me, A clean ves-sel in Thy hand,
3. Wit-ness-ing Thy pow'r to save me, Set-ting free from self and sin,
4. Je-sus, fill now with Thy Spir-it Hearts that full sur-ren-der know,
Thou hast saved and cleansed and filled me That I might Thy chan-nel be.
With no pow'r but as Thou giv-est Gra-cious-ly with each com-mand.
Thou who bought-est to pos-sess me, In Thy full-ness, Lord, come in.
That the streams of liv-ing wa-ter From our in-ner man may flow.
CHORUS
Chan-nels on-ly, bless-ed Mas-ter— But with all Thy won-drous pow'r
Flow-ing thru us, Thou canst use us Ev-'ry day and ev-'ry hour.

93 — The Comforter Has Come
FRANK BOTTOME
WILLIAM J. KIRKPATRICK
1. O spread the ti - dings 'round wher - ev - er man is found, Wher - ev - er hu - man hearts and hu - man woes a - bound; Let ev - 'ry Christian tongue pro - claim the joy - ful sound: The Com - fort - er has come!
2. Lo, the great King of kings, with heal - ing in His wings, To ev - 'ry cap - tive soul a full de - liv - 'rance brings; And thru the va - cant cells the song of tri - umph rings: The Com - fort - er has come!
3. O bound-less love di - vine! how shall this tongue of mine To won-d'ring mor-tals tell the match-less grace di - vine— That I, a child of hell, should in His im - age shine! The Com - fort - er has come!
CHORUS
The Com - fort - er has come, the Com - fort - er has come! The Ho - ly Ghost from heav'n—the Fa-ther's prom-ise giv'n; O spread the ti-dings
WORSHIP: THE HOLY SPIRIT

'round wher - ev - er man is found—The Com - fort - er has come!
Fill Me Now — 94
ELWOOD R. STOKES
JOHN R. SWENEY
1. Hov - er o'er me, Ho - ly Spir - it, Bathe my trem-bling heart and brow;
2. Thou canst fill me, gra - cious Spir - it, Tho I can - not tell Thee how;
3. I am weak-ness, full of weak - ness, At Thy sa - cred feet I bow;
4. Cleanse and com-fort, bless and save me, Bathe, O bathe my heart and brow;
Fill me with Thy hal-low'd pres - ence, Come, O come and fill me now.
But I need Thee, great - ly need Thee, Come, O come and fill me now.
Blest, di - vine, e - ter - nal Spir - it, Fill with pow'r, and fill me now.
Thou art com - fort - ing and sav - ing, Thou art sweet - ly fill - ing now.
CHORUS
Fill me now, fill me now, Je - sus, come and fill me now;
Fill me with Thy hal - low'd pres - ence—Come, O come and fill me now.
WORSHIP: THE HOLY SPIRIT

95 — Pentecostal Power

Based on Acts 2:1-4
CHARLES H. GABRIEL

CHARLES H. GABRIEL

1. Lord, as of old at Pen - te - cost Thou didst Thy pow'r dis - play,
2. For might - y works for Thee pre - pare And strength - en ev - 'ry heart;
3. All self con - sume, all sin de - stroy! With ear - nest zeal en - due
4. Speak, Lord! be - fore Thy throne we wait, Thy prom - ise we be - lieve,
With cleans - ing, pu - ri - fy - ing flame De - scend on us to - day.
Come, take pos - ses - sion of Thine own And nev - er - more de - part.
Each wait - ing heart to work for Thee— O Lord, our faith re - new!
And will not let Thee go un - til The bless - ing we re - ceive.
CHORUS
Lord, send the old - time pow - er, the Pen - te - cos - tal pow - er!
Thy flood - gates of bless - ing on us throw o - pen wide!
Lord, send the old - time pow - er, the Pen - te - cos - tal pow - er,

That sin-ners be con-vert-ed and Thy name glo-ri-fied!
Old-Time Power — 96
PAUL RADER
PAUL RADER
1. We are gath-ered for Thy bless-ing, We will wait up-on our God; We will trust in Him who loved us And who bought us with His blood.
2. We will glo-ry in Thy pow-er, We will sing of won-drous grace; In our midst, as Thou hast prom-ised, Come, O come and take Thy place.
3. Bring us low in prayer be-fore Thee And with faith our souls in-spire, Till we claim, by faith, the prom-ise Of the Ho-ly Ghost and fire.
CHORUS
Spir-it, now melt and move All of our hearts with love; Breathe on us from a-bove With old-time pow'r.
Copyright 1921, The Rodeheaver Co. ©Renewed 1949.
WORSHIP: THE HOLY SPIRIT

97 — Greater Is He That Is in Me

Based on I John 4:4; I Peter 5:8; Acts 2:2
LANNY WOLFE

LANNY WOLFE

Great-er is He that is in me, Great-er is He that is in me,
Great-er is He that is in me Than he that is in the world.
Fine
1. Sa - tan's like a roar - ing lion roam - ing to and fro,
2. On the day of Pen - te - cost, a rush - ing might - y wind
Seek - ing whom he may de - vour— the Bi - ble tells us so;
Blew in - to the up - per room, and bap - tized all of them
Man - y souls have been his prey— to fall in some weak hour: But
With a pow - er great - er than an - y earth - ly foe; And

WORSHIP: THE HOLY SPIRIT

D.C.
God has prom - ised us to - day His o - ver - com - ing pow'r.
I'm so glad I've got it too— I'll let the whole world know.
Where the Spirit of the Lord Is — 98
Based on II Corinthians 3:17
STEPHEN R. ADAMS
STEPHEN R. ADAMS
Where the Spir - it of the Lord is, there is peace; Where the
Spir - it of the Lord is, there is love; There is
com - fort in life's dark - est hour, There is light and life, there is
help and pow'r—In the Spir - it, in the Spir - it of the Lord.
© 1973 by Dimension Music. All rights reserved.
WORSHIP: THE HOLY SPIRIT

99 — Blessed Quietness

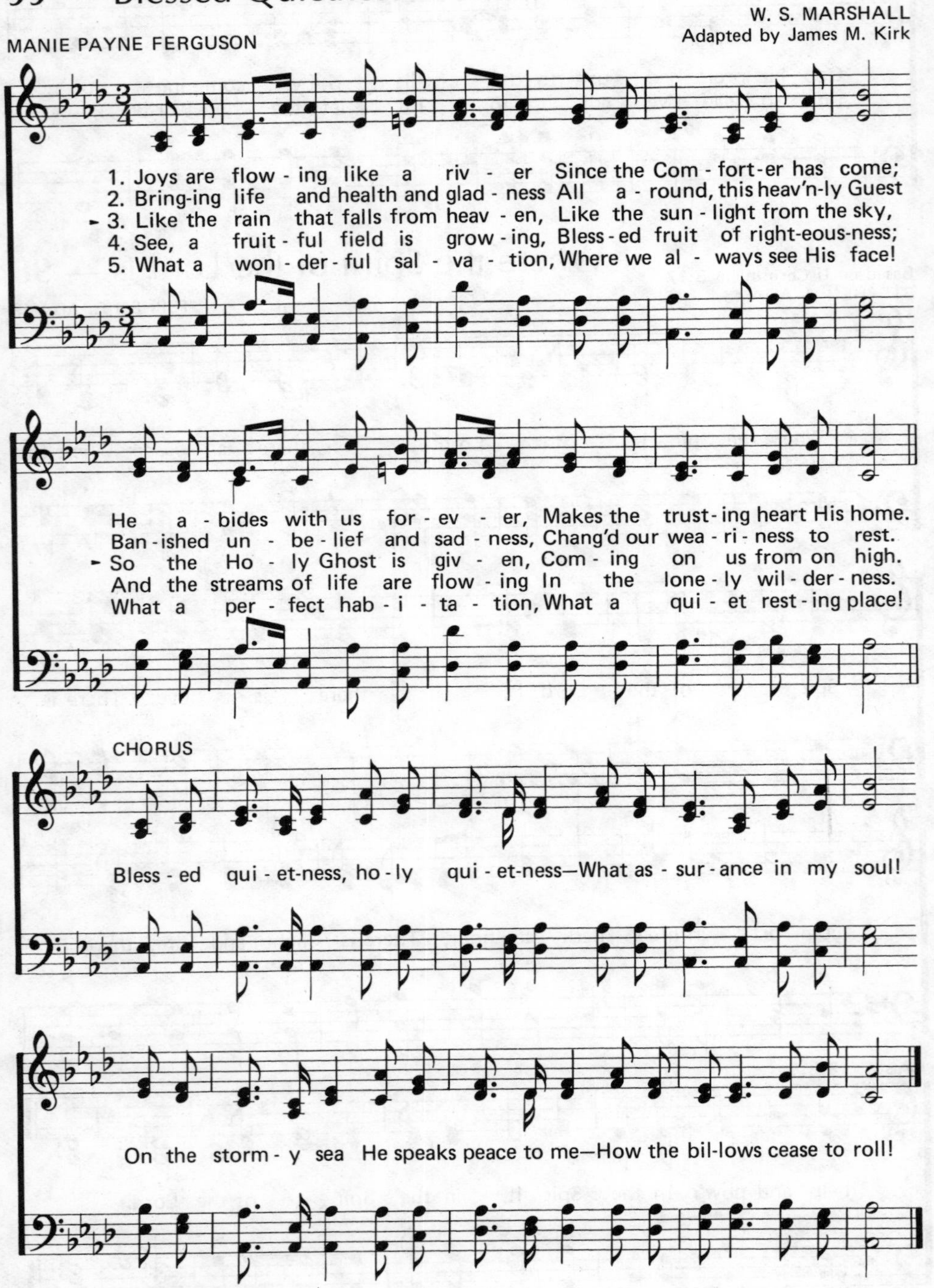
W. S. MARSHALL
Adapted by James M. Kirk
MANIE PAYNE FERGUSON
1. Joys are flow - ing like a riv - er Since the Com - fort-er has come;
2. Bring-ing life and health and glad - ness All a - round, this heav'n-ly Guest
3. Like the rain that falls from heav - en, Like the sun - light from the sky,
4. See, a fruit - ful field is grow - ing, Bless - ed fruit of right-eous-ness;
5. What a won - der - ful sal - va - tion, Where we al - ways see His face!
He a - bides with us for - ev - er, Makes the trust - ing heart His home.
Ban - ished un - be - lief and sad - ness, Chang'd our wea - ri - ness to rest.
So the Ho - ly Ghost is giv - en, Com - ing on us from on high.
And the streams of life are flow - ing In the lone - ly wil - der - ness.
What a per - fect hab - i - ta - tion, What a qui - et rest - ing place!
CHORUS
Bless - ed qui - et-ness, ho - ly qui - et-ness—What as - sur - ance in my soul!
On the storm - y sea He speaks peace to me—How the bil - lows cease to roll!

O Day of Rest and Gladness — 100

German melody
CHRISTOPHER WORDSWORTH
Arr. by Lowell Mason
1. O day of rest and glad-ness, O day of joy and light,
2. On thee, at the cre - a - tion, The light first had its birth;
3. To - day on wea - ry na - tions The heav'n-ly man - na falls;
4. New grac - es ev - er gain - ing From this our day of rest,
O balm of care and sad - ness, Most beau - ti - ful, most bright:
On thee, for our sal - va - tion, Christ rose from depths of earth;
To ho - ly con - vo - ca - tions The sil - ver trum - pet calls,
We reach the rest re - main - ing To spir - its of the blest;
On thee the high and low - ly, Thru ag - es joined in tune,
On thee our Lord vic - to - rious The Spir - it sent from heav'n;
Where gos - pel light is glow - ing With pure and ra - diant beams,
To Ho - ly Ghost be prais - es, To Fa - ther, and to Son:
Sing "Ho - ly, ho - ly, ho - ly" To the great God Tri - une.
And thus on thee, most glo - rious, A tri - ple light was giv'n.
And liv - ing wa - ter flow - ing With soul - re - fresh - ing streams.
The Church her voice up - rais - es To Thee, blest Three in One.*

Tune: MENDEBRAS

WORSHIP: SPECIAL TIMES (The Lord's Day)

101 — Amens
A - GENEVA
Louis Bourgeois
A - - - - men.
B - TWOFOLD
Dresden
A - men, A - - - men.
C - TWOFOLD
Norman Johnson
A - men, A - - - men.
© Singspiration 1979.
D - THREEFOLD
Denmark
A - men, A - men, A - - - men.
E - FOURFOLD
John Stainer
A - - men, A - - men, A - - - - men, A - - - men.
A - - men,
F - SEVENFOLD
John Stainer
A - men, A - - - - men,
A - men, A - men, A - - men, A - - - - men,
A - - men, A - - men,
A - - men,
A - - - - men, A - - - men, A - men.
A - - men,
WORSHIP: SPECIAL TIMES (Amens)

Go Out with Joy! — 102
NORMAN JOHNSON
NORMAN JOHNSON
CHORAL BENEDICTION
ff
Go out— go out with joy, to live in the pow'r of the Ris-en Christ!
Organ play lower clef only—no ped.
ped.
The Lord Bless You and Keep You — 103
Numbers 6:24-26
With trinitarian conclusion
NORMAN JOHNSON
The Lord bless you and keep you, The Lord make His face to shine up - on you
and be gra - cious un - to you; The Lord lift up His coun - te - nance up-
on you and give you peace, and give you peace. In the name of the
Fa-ther and of the Son and of the Ho-ly Spir - it. A - men.

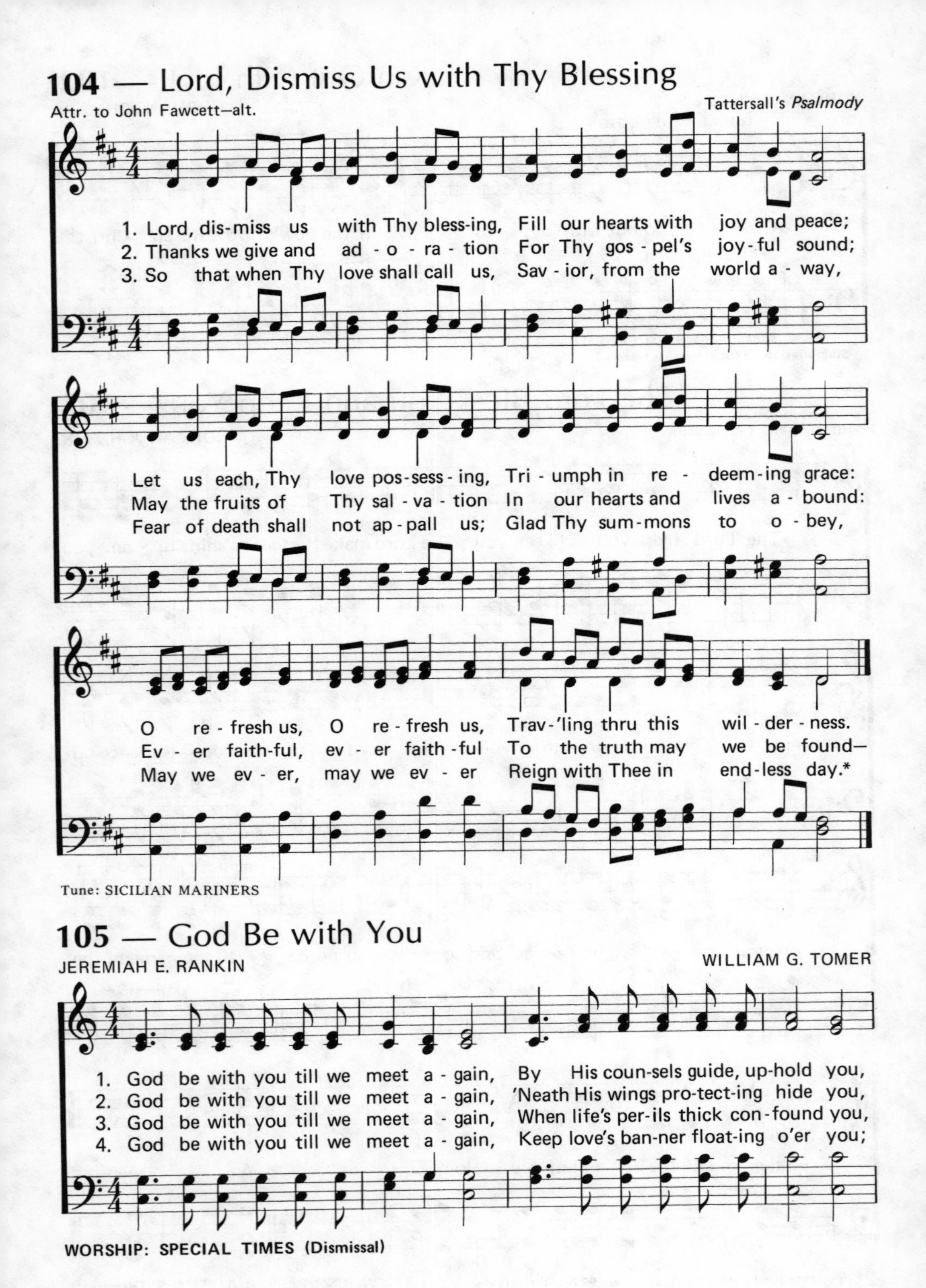
104 — Lord, Dismiss Us with Thy Blessing
Attr. to John Fawcett—alt.
Tattersall's Psalmody
1. Lord, dis-miss us with Thy bless-ing, Fill our hearts with joy and peace;
2. Thanks we give and ad - o - ra - tion For Thy gos - pel's joy-ful sound;
3. So that when Thy love shall call us, Sav - ior, from the world a - way,
Let us each, Thy love pos-sess-ing, Tri - umph in re - deem-ing grace:
May the fruits of Thy sal - va - tion In our hearts and lives a - bound:
Fear of death shall not ap - pall us; Glad Thy sum-mons to o - bey,
O re - fresh us, O re - fresh us, Trav-'ling thru this wil - der - ness.
Ev - er faith-ful, ev - er faith - ful To the truth may we be found—
May we ev - er, may we ev - er Reign with Thee in end-less day.*
Tune: SICILIAN MARINERS
105 — God Be with You
JEREMIAH E. RANKIN
WILLIAM G. TOMER
1. God be with you till we meet a - gain, By His coun-sels guide, up-hold you,
2. God be with you till we meet a - gain, 'Neath His wings pro-tect-ing hide you,
3. God be with you till we meet a - gain, When life's per-ils thick con-found you,
4. God be with you till we meet a - gain, Keep love's ban-ner float-ing o'er you;

With His sheep se - cure - ly fold you— God be with you till we meet a - gain.
Dai - ly man - na still pro - vide you— God be with you till we meet a - gain.
Put His arms un - fail - ing round you— God be with you till we meet a - gain.
Smite death's threat-'ning wave be - fore you— God be with you till we meet a - gain.

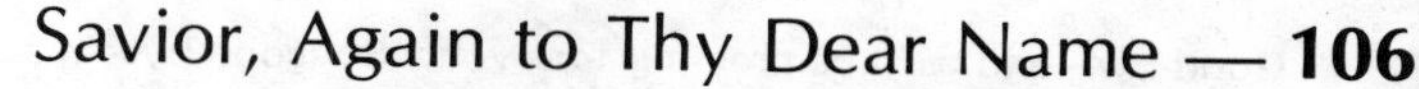

Savior, Again to Thy Dear Name — 106

JOHN ELLERTON

EDWARD J. HOPKINS

1. Sav - ior, a - gain to Thy dear name we raise With one ac - cord our part - ing hymn of praise; Once more we bless Thee ere our wor - ship cease, Then, low - ly kneel - ing, wait Thy word of peace.
2. Grant us Thy peace up - on our home-ward way: With Thee be - gan, with Thee shall end the day; Guard Thou the lips from sin, the hearts from shame, That in this house have called up - on Thy name.*
Tune: ELLERS

107 — Goodbye

WENDELL P. LOVELESS — WENDELL P. LOVELESS

Good-bye—our God is watching o'er you, Good-bye—His mer-cy go be-fore you;
Good-bye—and we'll be pray-ing for you, So good-bye—may God bless you.

108 — Now the Day Is Over

SABINE BARING-GOULD — JOSEPH BARNBY

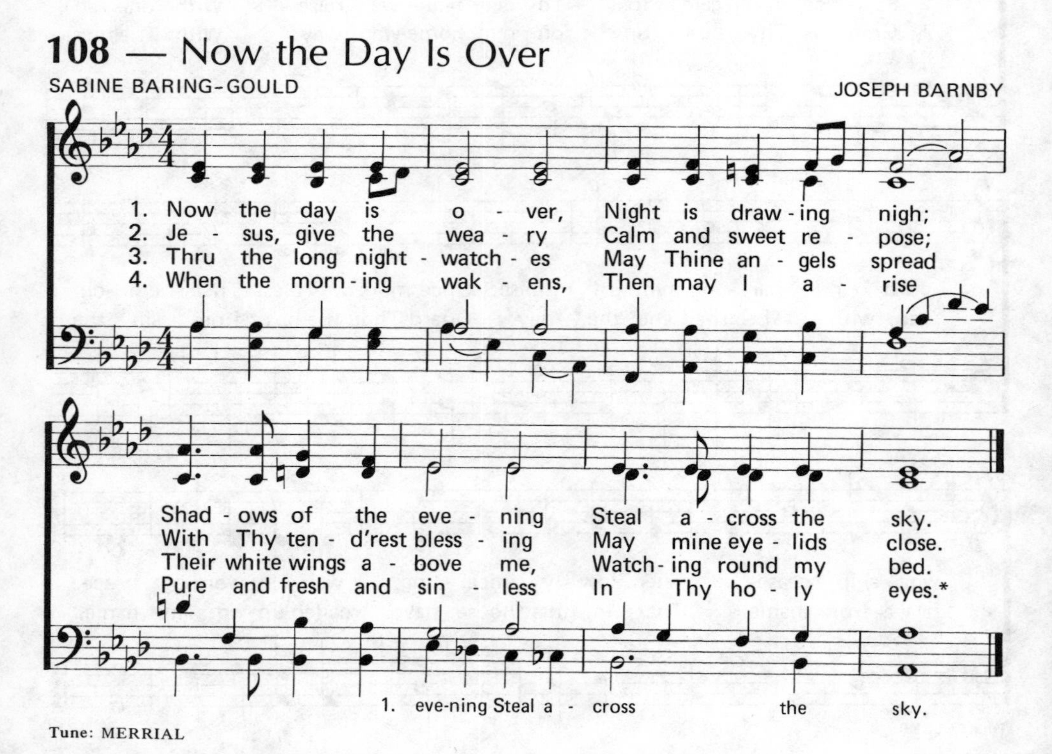
1. Now the day is o - ver, Night is draw - ing nigh;
2. Je - sus, give the wea - ry Calm and sweet re - pose;
3. Thru the long night - watch - es May Thine an - gels spread
4. When the morn - ing wak - ens, Then may I a - rise
Shad - ows of the eve - ning Steal a - cross the sky.
With Thy ten - d'rest bless - ing May mine eye - lids close.
Their white wings a - bove me, Watch - ing round my bed.
Pure and fresh and sin - less In Thy ho - ly eyes.*
1. eve-ning Steal a - cross the sky.

Tune: MERRIAL

WORSHIP: SPECIAL TIMES (Closing, Evening)

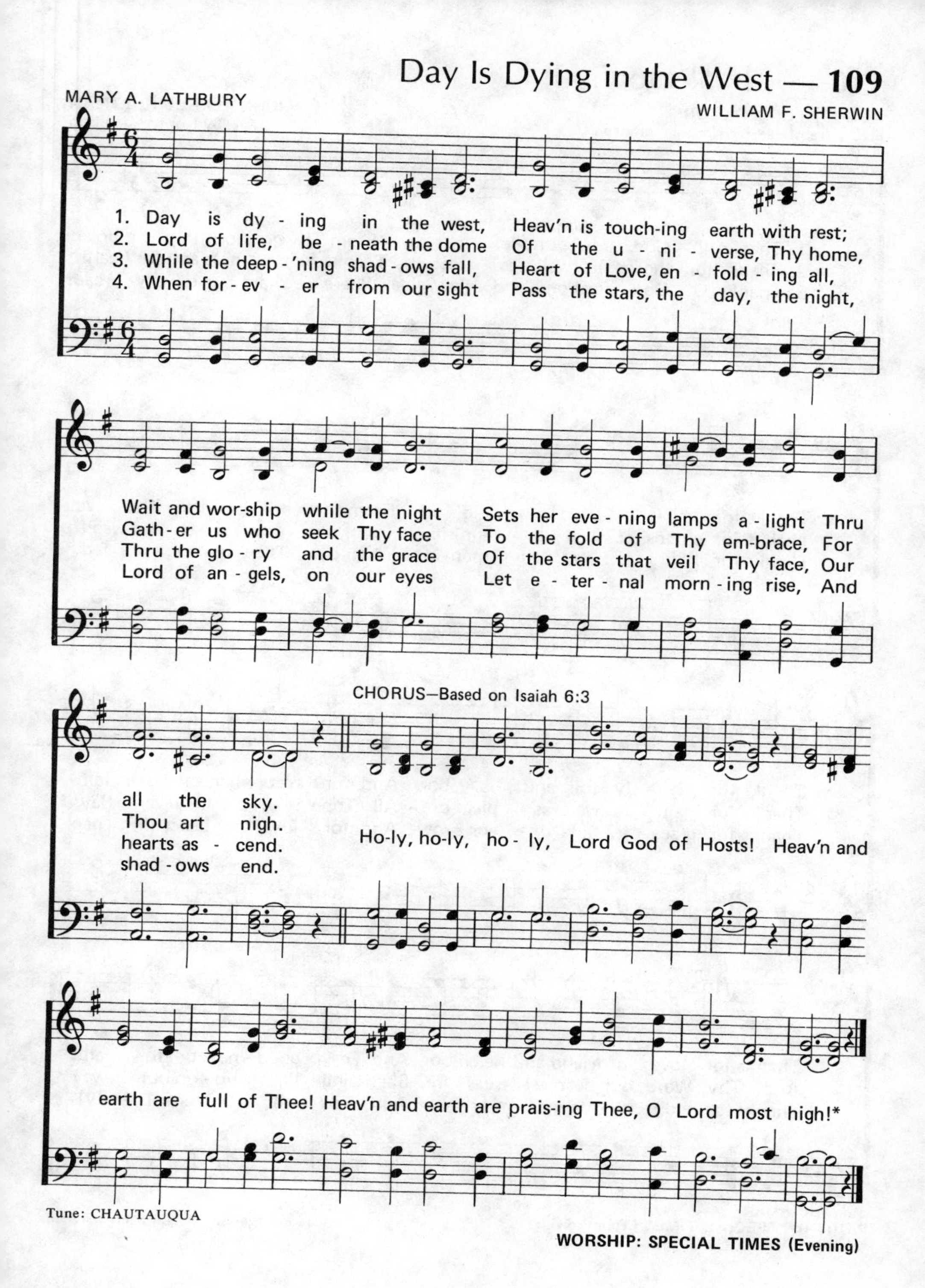
Day Is Dying in the West — 109
MARY A. LATHBURY
WILLIAM F. SHERWIN
1. Day is dy - ing in the west, Heav'n is touch-ing earth with rest; Wait and wor-ship while the night Sets her eve - ning lamps a - light Thru all the sky.
2. Lord of life, be - neath the dome Of the u - ni - verse, Thy home, Gath - er us who seek Thy face To the fold of Thy em-brace, For Thou art nigh.
3. While the deep - 'ning shad - ows fall, Heart of Love, en - fold - ing all, Thru the glo - ry and the grace Of the stars that veil Thy face, Our hearts as - cend.
4. When for - ev - er from our sight Pass the stars, the day, the night, Lord of an - gels, on our eyes Let e - ter - nal morn - ing rise, And shad - ows end.
CHORUS—Based on Isaiah 6:3
Ho-ly, ho-ly, ho - ly, Lord God of Hosts! Heav'n and earth are full of Thee! Heav'n and earth are prais-ing Thee, O Lord most high!*
Tune: CHAUTAUQUA

110 — Thanks to God!

AUGUST LUDVIG STORM
Freely translated by Norman Johnson

JOHN ALFRED HULTMAN
Arr. by Norman Johnson

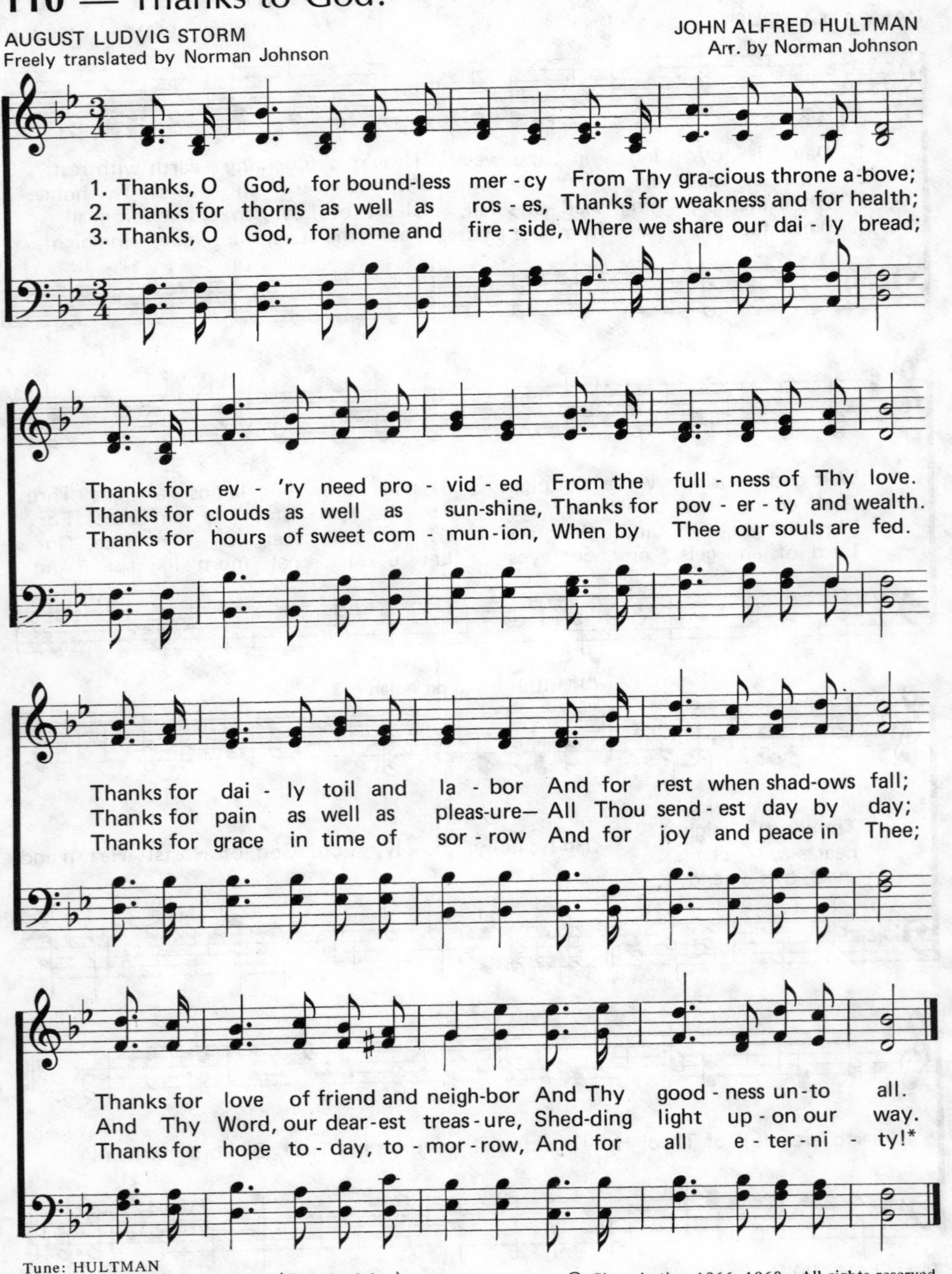
1. Thanks, O God, for bound-less mer-cy From Thy gra-cious throne a-bove;
2. Thanks for thorns as well as ros - es, Thanks for weakness and for health;
3. Thanks, O God, for home and fire - side, Where we share our dai - ly bread;
Thanks for ev - 'ry need pro - vid - ed From the full - ness of Thy love.
Thanks for clouds as well as sun-shine, Thanks for pov - er - ty and wealth.
Thanks for hours of sweet com - mun - ion, When by Thee our souls are fed.
Thanks for dai - ly toil and la - bor And for rest when shad-ows fall;
Thanks for pain as well as pleas-ure— All Thou send - est day by day;
Thanks for grace in time of sor - row And for joy and peace in Thee;
Thanks for love of friend and neigh-bor And Thy good - ness un-to all.
And Thy Word, our dear-est treas - ure, Shed-ding light up - on our way.
Thanks for hope to - day, to - mor - row, And for all e - ter-ni - ty!*

Tune: HULTMAN
WORSHIP: SPECIAL TIMES (Thanksgiving)

Come, Ye Thankful People — 111

HENRY ALFORD

GEORGE J. ELVEY

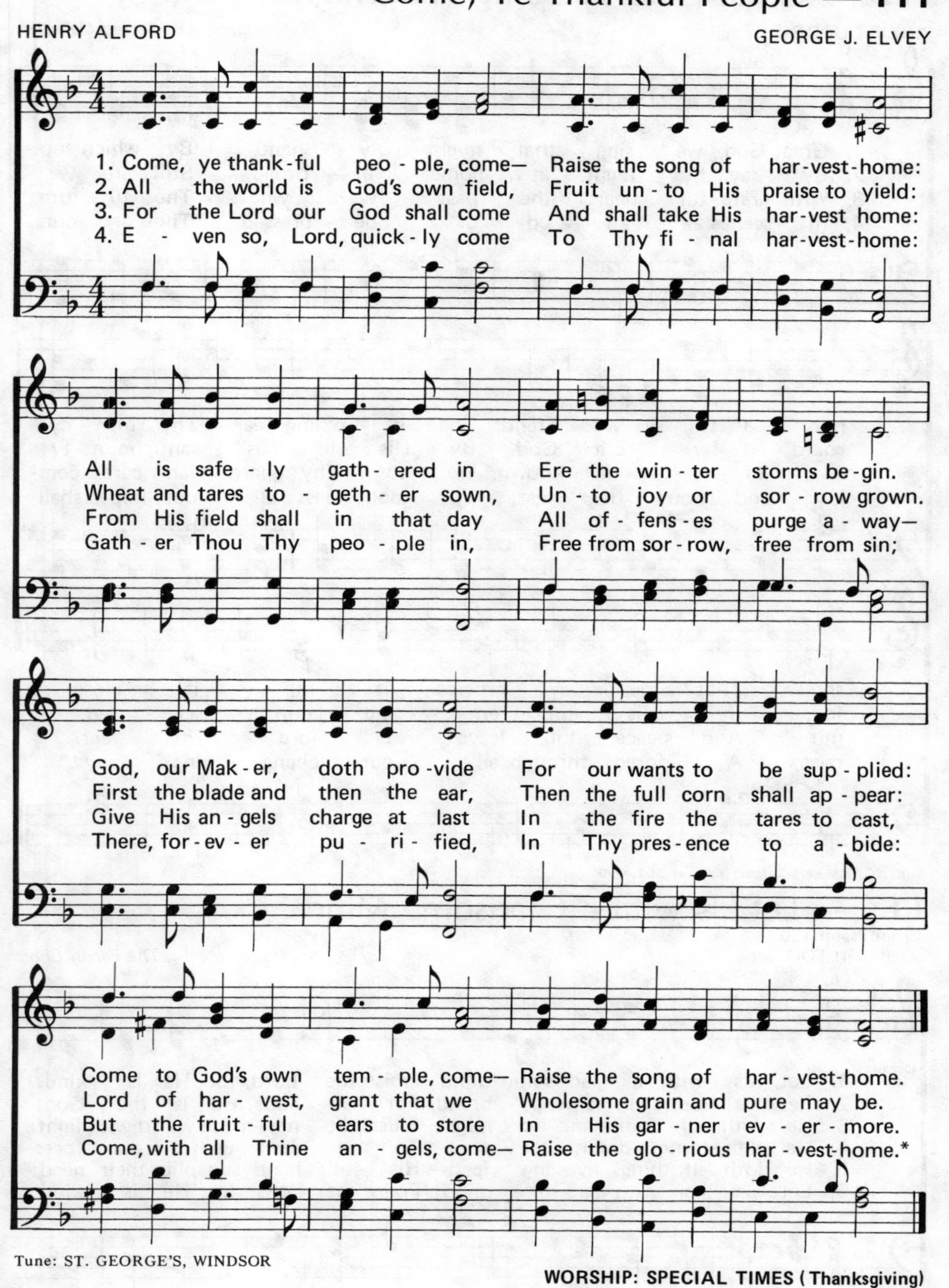
1. Come, ye thank - ful peo - ple, come— Raise the song of har - vest - home:
2. All the world is God's own field, Fruit un - to His praise to yield:
3. For the Lord our God shall come And shall take His har - vest home:
4. E - ven so, Lord, quick - ly come To Thy fi - nal har - vest - home:
All is safe - ly gath - ered in Ere the win - ter storms be - gin.
Wheat and tares to - geth - er sown, Un - to joy or sor - row grown.
From His field shall in that day All of - fens - es purge a - way—
Gath - er Thou Thy peo - ple in, Free from sor - row, free from sin;
God, our Mak - er, doth pro - vide For our wants to be sup - plied:
First the blade and then the ear, Then the full corn shall ap - pear:
Give His an - gels charge at last In the fire the tares to cast,
There, for - ev - er pu - ri - fied, In Thy pres - ence to a - bide:
Come to God's own tem - ple, come— Raise the song of har - vest - home.
Lord of har - vest, grant that we Wholesome grain and pure may be.
But the fruit - ful ears to store In His gar - ner ev - er - more.
Come, with all Thine an - gels, come— Raise the glo - rious har - vest - home.*

Tune: ST. GEORGE'S, WINDSOR

112 — Great God, We Sing That Mighty Hand

PHILIP DODDRIDGE—alt. Gardiner's *Sacred Melodies*

1. Great God, we sing that might - y hand By which sup -
2. By day, by night, at home, a - broad, Still are we
3. With grate - ful hearts the past we own: The fu - ture,
4. In scenes ex - alt - ed or de - pressed, Thou art our
port - ed still we stand; The o - p'ning year Thy mer - cy
guard - ed by our God, By His in - ces - sant boun - ty
all to us un - known, We to Thy guard - ian care com-
joy and Thou our rest; Thy good - ness all our hopes shall
shows, That mer - cy crowns it till it close.
fed, By His un - err - ing coun - sel led.
mit And, peace - ful, leave be - fore Thy feet.
raise, A - dored through all our chang - ing days.*

Tune: GERMANY—higher keys at 287, 490

113 — Let Us with a Gladsome Mind

From Psalm 136
JOHN MILTON—alt. *The Parish Choir*

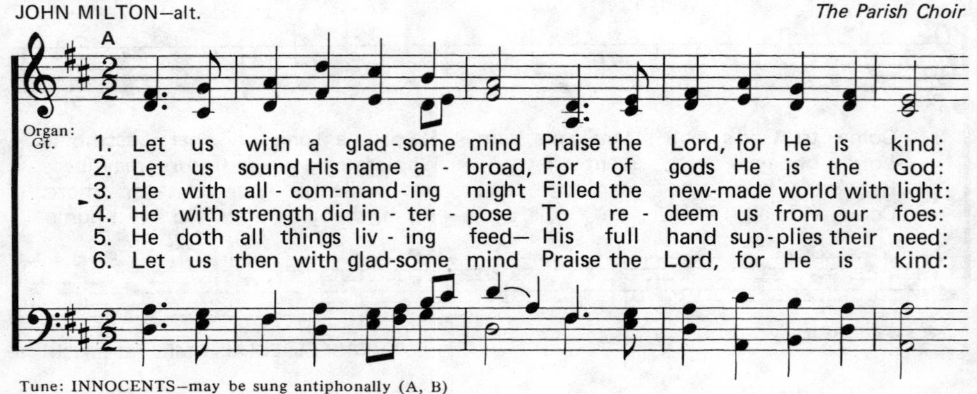

A
Organ:
Gt.
1. Let us with a glad - some mind Praise the Lord, for He is kind:
2. Let us sound His name a - broad, For of gods He is the God:
3. He with all - com - mand - ing might Filled the new-made world with light:
4. He with strength did in - ter - pose To re - deem us from our foes:
5. He doth all things liv - ing feed— His full hand sup - plies their need:
6. Let us then with glad - some mind Praise the Lord, for He is kind:

Tune: INNOCENTS—may be sung antiphonally (A, B)

B
Organ:
Sw.
For His mer-cies shall en - dure— Ev - er faith - ful, ev - er sure!*
Another Year Is Dawning — 114
FRANCES RIDLEY HAVERGAL
SAMUEL S. WESLEY
1. An - oth - er year is dawn - ing: Dear Fa - ther, let it be,
2. An - oth - er year of mer - cies, Of faith - ful - ness and grace;
3. An - oth - er year of serv - ice, Of wit - ness for Thy love;
In work-ing or, in wait - ing, An - oth - er year with Thee;
An - oth - er year of glad - ness In the shin - ing of Thy face;
An - oth - er year of train - ing For ho - lier work a - bove.
An - oth - er year of prog - ress, An - oth - er year of praise,
An - oth - er year of lean - ing Up - on Thy lov - ing breast;
An - oth - er year is dawn - ing: Dear Fa - ther, let it be,

An - oth - er year of prov - ing Thy pres - ence all the days;
An - oth - er year of trust - ing, Of qui - et, hap - py rest;
On earth or else in heav - en, An - oth - er year for Thee.*

Tune: AURELIA—higher key at 131

115 — The Church, O Lord, Is Thine
DAVID P. HANEY
JOHANN MARTIN SPIESS
1. The Church, O Lord, is Thine, Is Thine for - ev - er - more—
2. The Church, O Lord, is theirs, Whose toil this day hath brought—
3. The Church, O Lord, is ours, Is ours at high - est cost—
4. The Church, O Lord, is mine, And to its call I yield—
5. The Church, O Lord, is Thine, And we who bear Thy name,
(D.C.)
From age to age, from pole to pole, From shore to far - thest shore.
Their faith, their hope and fear - less love Our her - i - tage hath bought.
Thy cross, its shame and sac - ri - fice, And all the mar - tyred host.
To be as scat - tered, liv - ing seed In God's own har - vest field.
Un - til that day Thou dost ap - pear—Thy cho - sen Bride to claim.
CODA, after final stanza
Slower
The Church, O Lord, is Thine, Is Thine for - ev - er - more!*
Tune: SWABIA (Coda added by Editors for this hymn)
Words © Singspiration 1973. All rights reserved.
116 — We Bid You Welcome
JAMES MONTGOMERY
HEINRICH C. ZEUNER
1. We bid you wel - come in the name Of Je - sus, our ex - alt - ed Head:
2. Come as a shep - herd—guard and keep This fold from harm of earth and sin;
3. Come as a teach - er sent from God, Charged His whole counsel to de - clare;
Tune: MISSIONARY CHANT

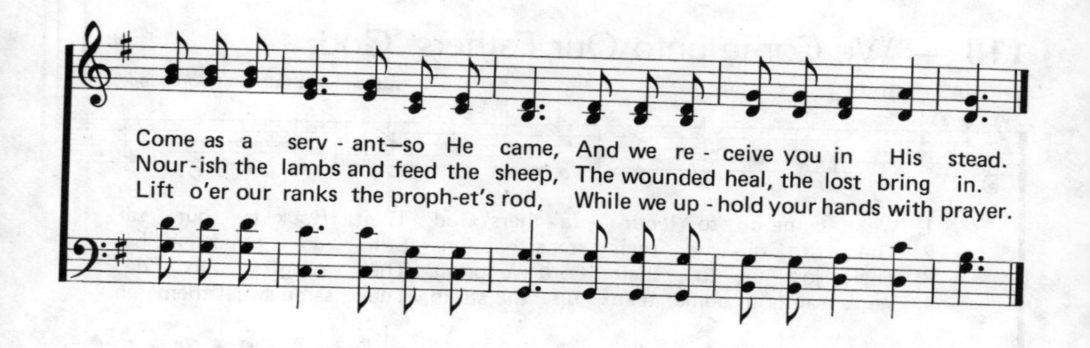
Come as a serv - ant—so He came, And we re - ceive you in His stead.
Nour-ish the lambs and feed the sheep, The wounded heal, the lost bring in.
Lift o'er our ranks the proph-et's rod, While we up - hold your hands with prayer.

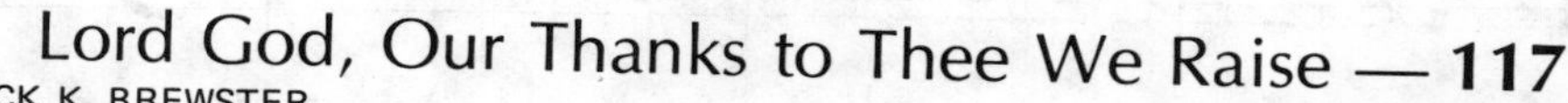

Lord God, Our Thanks to Thee We Raise — 117

FREDERICK K. BREWSTER

NORMAN JOHNSON

1. Lord, God, our thanks to Thee we raise For those who built this house of praise, Who long a - go to - geth - er stood To form a Chris - tian broth - er - hood.
2. Here have our chil - dren known Thy care And raised their tho'ts to Thee in prayer; Here have we shared the Wine, the Bread— Here have our liv - ing souls been fed.
3. Still thru the years be Thou our guide, Keep us from en - mi - ty and pride; Still help us choose the bet - ter part— A hum - ble and a thank - ful heart.
4. Be this our com - mon en - ter - prise: That truth be preach'd and prayer a - rise, That each may seek the oth - er's good And live and love as Je - sus would!
5. Cre - ate in us the word, the deed, That ours may be a liv - ing creed; And cause Thy grace in us to dwell— A - bide with us, Im - man - u - el!*

Tune: BREWSTER (Alternate: DUKE STREET)

WORSHIP: SPECIAL TIMES (Anniversary)

118 — We Come unto Our Fathers' God

THOMAS H. GILL

Bohemian Brethren's *Kirchengesänge*

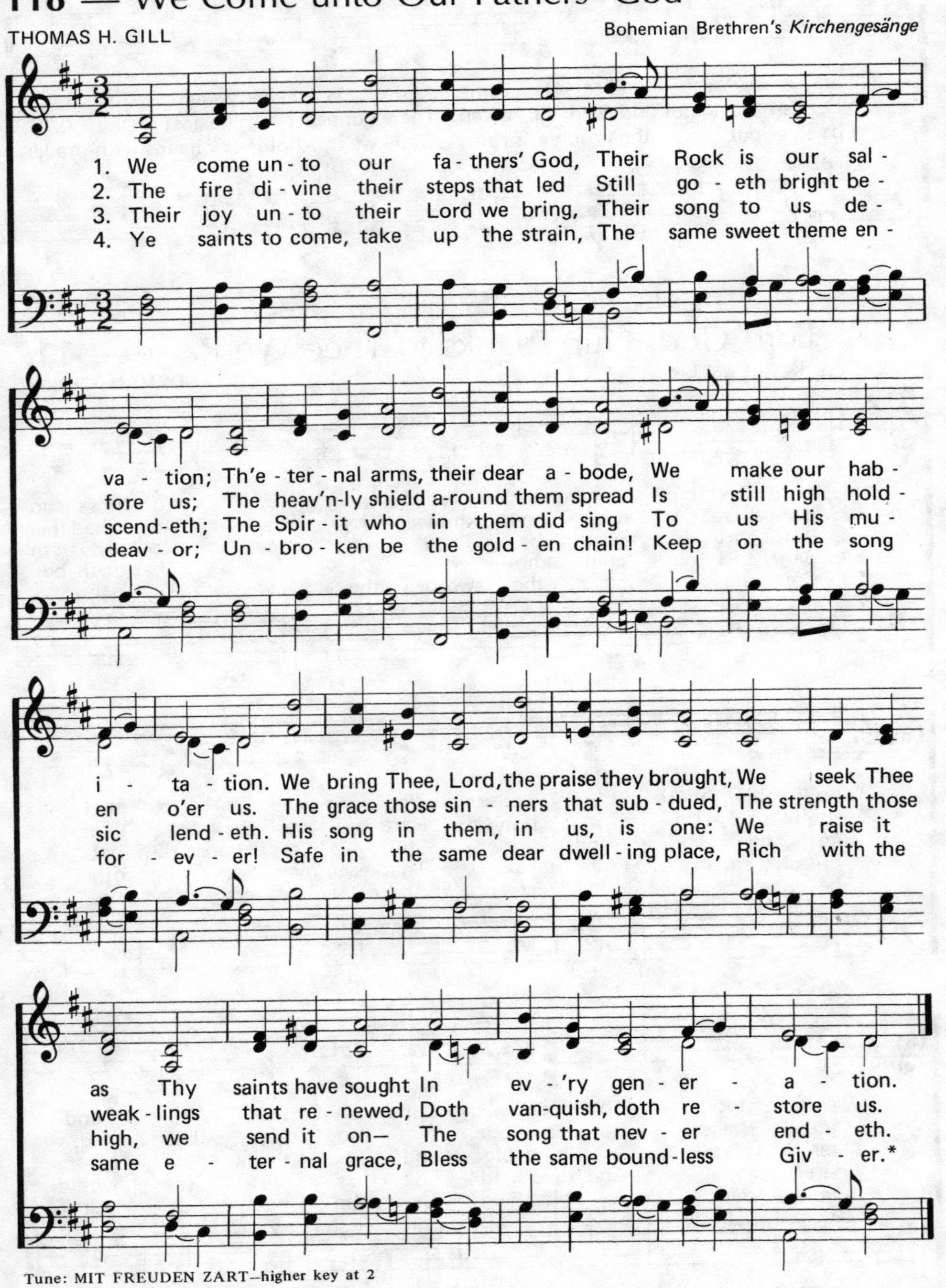
1. We come un - to our fa - thers' God, Their Rock is our sal -
2. The fire di - vine their steps that led Still go - eth bright be -
3. Their joy un - to their Lord we bring, Their song to us de -
4. Ye saints to come, take up the strain, The same sweet theme en -
va - tion; Th'e - ter - nal arms, their dear a - bode, We make our hab -
fore us; The heav'n-ly shield a-round them spread Is still high hold -
scend-eth; The Spir - it who in them did sing To us His mu -
deav - or; Un - bro - ken be the gold - en chain! Keep on the song
i - ta - tion. We bring Thee, Lord, the praise they brought, We seek Thee
en o'er us. The grace those sin - ners that sub - dued, The strength those
sic lend - eth. His song in them, in us, is one: We raise it
for - ev - er! Safe in the same dear dwell - ing place, Rich with the
as Thy saints have sought In ev - 'ry gen - er - a - tion.
weak - lings that re - newed, Doth van-quish, doth re - store us.
high, we send it on— The song that nev - er end - eth.
same e - ter - nal grace, Bless the same bound - less Giv - er.*

Tune: MIT FREUDEN ZART—higher key at 2

WORSHIP: SPECIAL TIMES (Memorial)

CLARA H. SCOTT   CLARA H. SCOTT

1. O - pen my eyes, that I may see Glimp-ses of truth Thou hast for me;
2. O - pen my ears, that I may hear Voic - es of truth Thou send-est clear;
3. O - pen my mouth, and let me bear Glad - ly the warm truth ev - 'ry-where;
Place in my hands the won-der-ful key That shall un-clasp and set me free.
And while the wave-notes fall on my ear, Ev - 'ry-thing false will dis - ap-pear.
O - pen my heart and let me pre-pare Love with Thy chil-dren thus to share.
Si - lent - ly now I wait for Thee, Read - y, my God, Thy will to see;
Si - lent - ly now I wait for Thee, Read - y, my God, Thy will to see;
Si - lent - ly now I wait for Thee, Read - y, my God, Thy will to see;
O - pen my eyes— il - lu - mine me, Spir - it di - vine!
O - pen my ears— il - lu - mine me, Spir - it di - vine!
O - pen my heart— il - lu - mine me, Spir - it di - vine!*

120 — Thy Word Have I Hid in My Heart

From Psalm 119
Adapted by Ernest O. Sellers

ERNEST O. SELLERS

1. Thy Word is a lamp to my feet, A light to my path al - way,
2. For - ev - er, O Lord, is Thy Word Es - tab-lished and fixed on high;
3. At morn-ing, at noon and at night I ev - er will give Thee praise;
4. Thru Him whom Thy Word hath fore-told, The Sav - ior and Morn-ing Star,
To guide and to save me from sin And show me the heav'n-ly way.
Thy faith-ful-ness un - to all men A - bid-eth for - ev - er nigh.
For Thou art my por-tion, O Lord, And shall be thru all my days!
Sal - va - tion and peace have been bro't To those who have strayed a - far.
CHORUS
Thy Word have I hid in my heart, (in my heart,) That I might not
sin a-gainst Thee; (a - gainst Thee;) That I might not sin, that
I might not sin, Thy Word have I hid in my heart.

THE WORD OF GOD

Standing on the Promises — 121

R. KELSO CARTER
NORMAN JOHNSON
In unison
1. Stand-ing on the prom-is-es of Christ my King, Through e-ter-nal a-ges let His prais-es ring! Glo-ry in the high-est I will shout and sing— Stand-ing on the prom-is-es of God, Stand-ing on the prom-is-es of God!
2. Stand-ing on the prom-is-es that can-not fail When the howl-ing storms of doubt and fear as-sail; By the liv-ing word of God I shall pre-vail— Stand-ing on the prom-is-es of God, Stand-ing on the prom-is-es of God!
3. Stand-ing on the prom-is-es of Christ the Lord, Bound to Him e-ter-nal-ly by love's strong cord, O-ver-com-ing dai-ly with the Spir-it's sword— Stand-ing on the prom-is-es of God, Stand-ing on the prom-is-es of God!
4. Stand-ing on the prom-is-es I can-not fall, Lis-t'ning ev-'ry mo-ment to the Spir-it's call, Rest-ing in my Sav-ior as my all in all— Stand-ing on the prom-is-es of God, Stand-ing on the prom-is-es of God!

Tune: TURLOCK

122 — Standing on the Promises
R. KELSO CARTER
R. KELSO CARTER
1. Stand-ing on the prom-is-es of Christ my King, Thru e-ter-nal a-ges let His prais-es ring! Glo-ry in the high-est I will shout and sing— Stand-ing on the prom-is-es of God.
2. Stand-ing on the prom-is-es that can-not fail When the howl-ing storms of doubt and fear as-sail; By the liv-ing word of God I shall pre-vail— Stand-ing on the prom-is-es of God.
3. Stand-ing on the prom-is-es of Christ the Lord, Bound to Him e-ter-nal-ly by love's strong cord, O-ver-com-ing dai-ly with the Spir-it's sword— Stand-ing on the prom-is-es of God.
4. Stand-ing on the prom-is-es I can-not fall, Lis-t'ning ev-'ry mo-ment to the Spir-it's call, Rest-ing in my Sav-ior as my all in all— Stand-ing on the prom-is-es of God.
CHORUS
Stand-ing, stand-ing, Stand-ing on the prom-is-es of God my Sav-ior;
THE WORD OF GOD

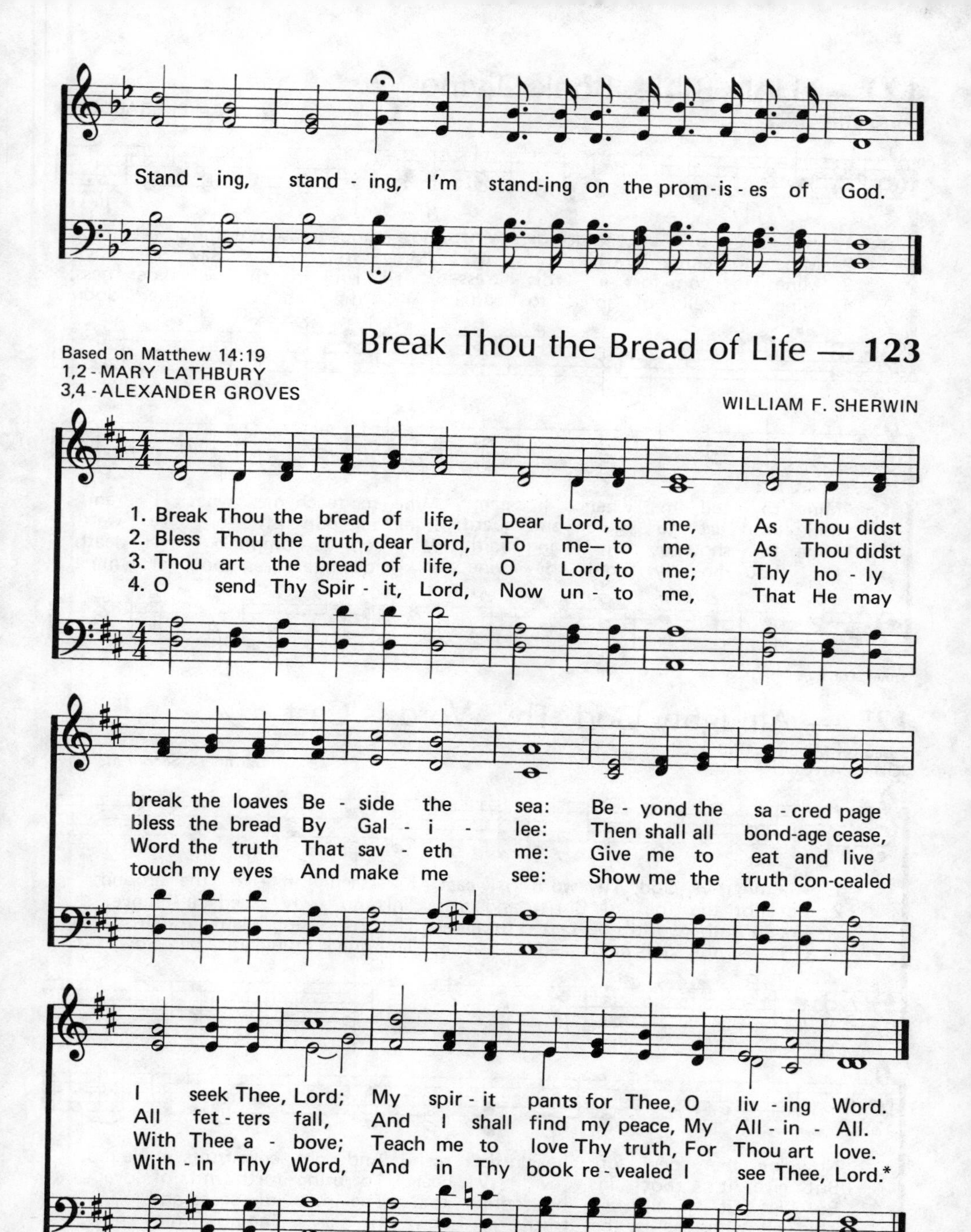
Stand - ing, stand - ing, I'm stand-ing on the prom - is - es of God.
Break Thou the Bread of Life — 123
Based on Matthew 14:19
1,2 - MARY LATHBURY
3,4 - ALEXANDER GROVES
WILLIAM F. SHERWIN
1. Break Thou the bread of life, Dear Lord, to me, As Thou didst break the loaves Be - side the sea: Be - yond the sa - cred page I seek Thee, Lord; My spir - it pants for Thee, O liv - ing Word.
2. Bless Thou the truth, dear Lord, To me— to me, As Thou didst bless the bread By Gal - i - lee: Then shall all bond-age cease, All fet - ters fall, And I shall find my peace, My All - in - All.
3. Thou art the bread of life, O Lord, to me; Thy ho - ly Word the truth That sav - eth me: Give me to eat and live With Thee a - bove; Teach me to love Thy truth, For Thou art love.
4. O send Thy Spir - it, Lord, Now un - to me, That He may touch my eyes And make me see: Show me the truth con-cealed With - in Thy Word, And in Thy book re - vealed I see Thee, Lord.*

Tune: BREAD OF LIFE

124 — Holy Bible, Book Divine

JOHN BURTON, Sr. WILLIAM B. BRADBURY

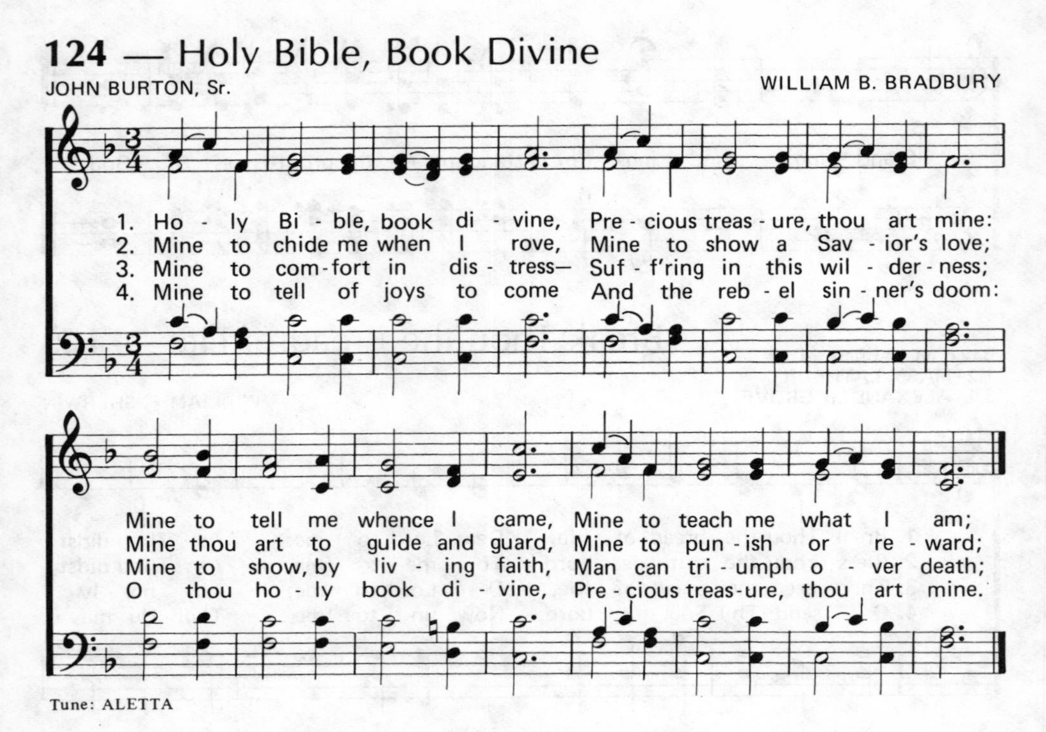
1. Ho - ly Bi - ble, book di - vine, Pre - cious treas - ure, thou art mine:
2. Mine to chide me when I rove, Mine to show a Sav - ior's love;
3. Mine to com - fort in dis - tress— Suf - f'ring in this wil - der - ness;
4. Mine to tell of joys to come And the reb - el sin - ner's doom:
Mine to tell me whence I came, Mine to teach me what I am;
Mine thou art to guide and guard, Mine to pun - ish or re - ward;
Mine to show, by liv - ing faith, Man can tri - umph o - ver death;
O thou ho - ly book di - vine, Pre - cious treas - ure, thou art mine.

Tune: ALETTA

125 — Almighty God, Thy Word Is Cast

Based on Matthew 13:3-9

JOHN CAWOOD Gardiner's *Sacred Melodies*

1. Al - might - y God, Thy word is cast Like seed in - to the ground;
2. Let not the foe of Christ and man This ho - ly seed re - move,
3. Let not the world's de - ceit - ful cares The ris - ing plant de - stroy,
4. Oft as the pre - cious seed is sown, Thy quick - 'ning grace be - stow,
Now let the dew of heav'n de - scend And right - eous fruits a - bound.
But give it root in ev - 'ry heart, To bring forth fruits of love.
But let it yield a hun - dred - fold The fruits of peace and joy.
That all whose souls the truth re - ceive Its sav - ing pow'r may know.*

Tune: BELMONT—higher key at 14

How Wonderful That Book Divine — 126

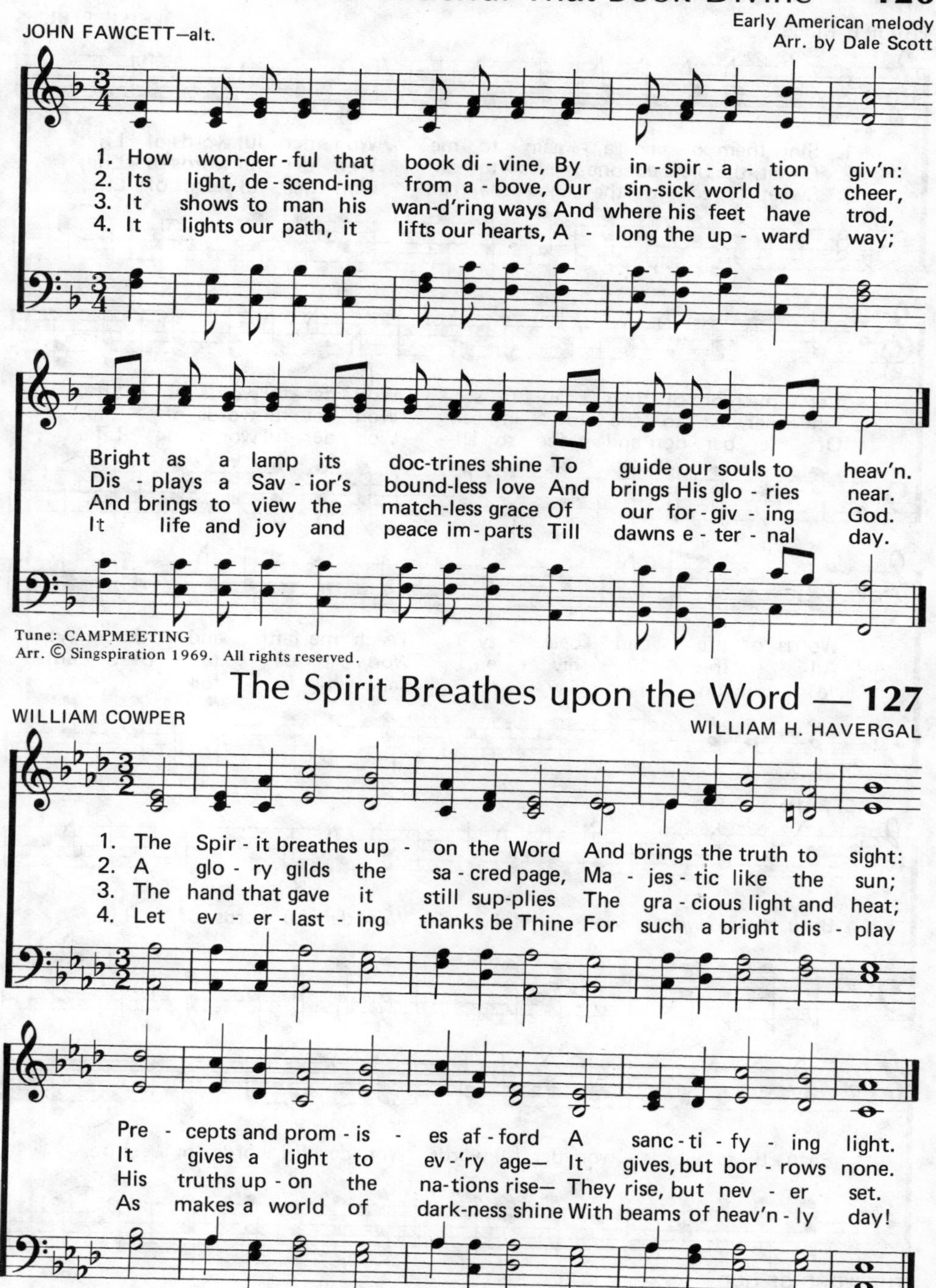

Early American melody
Arr. by Dale Scott
JOHN FAWCETT—alt.
1. How won-der-ful that book di-vine, By in-spir-a-tion giv'n:
2. Its light, de-scend-ing from a-bove, Our sin-sick world to cheer,
3. It shows to man his wan-d'ring ways And where his feet have trod,
4. It lights our path, it lifts our hearts, A-long the up-ward way;
Bright as a lamp its doc-trines shine To guide our souls to heav'n.
Dis-plays a Sav-ior's bound-less love And brings His glo-ries near.
And brings to view the match-less grace Of our for-giv-ing God.
It life and joy and peace im-parts Till dawns e-ter-nal day.
Tune: CAMPMEETING
Arr. © Singspiration 1969. All rights reserved.
The Spirit Breathes upon the Word — 127
WILLIAM COWPER
WILLIAM H. HAVERGAL
1. The Spir-it breathes up-on the Word And brings the truth to sight:
2. A glo-ry gilds the sa-cred page, Ma-jes-tic like the sun;
3. The hand that gave it still sup-plies The gra-cious light and heat;
4. Let ev-er-last-ing thanks be Thine For such a bright dis-play
Pre-cepts and prom-is-es af-ford A sanc-ti-fy-ing light.
It gives a light to ev-'ry age— It gives, but bor-rows none.
His truths up-on the na-tions rise— They rise, but nev-er set.
As makes a world of dark-ness shine With beams of heav'n-ly day!

Tune: EVAN (Alternate, ORTONVILLE, adapted)

128 — Wonderful Words of Life

PHILIP P. BLISS

PHILIP P. BLISS

1. Sing them o - ver a - gain to me— Won - der - ful words of Life;
2. Christ, the bless-ed one, gives to all Won - der - ful words of Life;
3. Sweet - ly ech - o the gos - pel call— Won - der - ful words of Life;

Let me more of their beau - ty see— Won - der - ful words of Life.
Sin - ner, list to the lov - ing call— Won - der - ful words of Life.
Of - fer par - don and peace to all— Won - der - ful words of Life.

Words of life and beau - ty, Teach me faith and du - ty:
All so free - ly giv - en, Woo - ing us to heav - en:
Je - sus, on - ly Sav - ior, Sanc - ti - fy for - ev - er:

REFRAIN

Beau - ti - ful words, won - der - ful words, Won - der - ful words of Life;

Beau - ti - ful words, won - der - ful words, Won - der - ful words of Life.

Glorious Things of Thee Are Spoken — 129
Based on Psalm 87:3
JOHN NEWTON
FRANZ JOSEPH HAYDN
1. Glo - rious things of thee are spo - ken, Zi - on, cit - y of our God;
2. See, the streams of liv - ing wa - ters, Spring-ing from e - ter - nal love,
3. Round each hab - i - ta - tion hov-'ring, See the cloud and fire ap - pear
He whose word can - not be bro - ken Formed thee for His own a - bode:
Well sup - ply thy sons and daugh - ters And all fear of want re - move:
For a glo - ry and a cov - 'ring, Show - ing that the Lord is near!
On the Rock of A - ges found-ed, What can shake thy sure re-pose?
Who can faint while such a riv - er Ev - er flows their thirst to as-suage?
Glo-rious things of thee are spo - ken, Zi - on, cit - y of our God;
With sal - va - tion's walls sur-round-ed, Thou mayst smile at all Thy foes.
Grace which, like the Lord, the giv - er, Nev - er fails from age to age.
He whose word can - not be bro - ken Formed thee for His own a - bode.

Tune: AUSTRIAN HYMN

130 — Christ Is Made the Sure Foundation

Based on Ephesians 2:19-22
Latin hymn, 7th century
Trans. by John M. Neale—alt.
HENRY T. SMART
1. Christ is made the sure foun - da - tion, Christ the head
2. To this tem - ple, where we call Thee, Come, O Lord
3. Here vouch - safe to all Thy serv - ants What they ask
4. Laud and hon - or to the Fa - ther, Laud and hon -
and cor - ner - stone, Chos - en of the Lord and pre - cious,
of hosts, to - day; With Thy wont - ed lov - ing-kind - ness
of Thee to gain, What they gain from Thee for - ev - er
or to the Son, Laud and hon - or to the Spir - it,
Bind - ing all the Church in one: Ho - ly Zi - on's
Hear Thy peo - ple as they pray, And Thy full - est
With the bless - ed to re - tain, And here - aft - er
Ev - er three and ev - er one: One in might and
help for - ev - er And her con - fi - dence a - lone.
ben - e - dic - tion Shed with - in its walls al - way.
in Thy glo - ry Ev - er - more with Thee to reign.
one in glo - ry, While un - end - ing a - ges run.*

Tune: REGENT SQUARE

SAMUEL J. STONE SAMUEL S. WESLEY

1. The Church-'s one foun - da - tion Is Je - sus Christ her Lord;
2. E - lect from ev - 'ry na - tion, Yet one o'er all the earth,
3. 'Mid toil and trib - u - la - tion And tu - mult of her war,
4. Yet she on earth hath un - ion With God the Three in One,
She is His new cre - a - tion By wa - ter and the Word:
Her char - ter of sal - va - tion One Lord, one faith, one birth;
She waits the con - sum - ma - tion Of peace for - ev - er - more;
And mys - tic sweet com - mun - ion With those whose rest is won:
From heav'n He came and sought her To be His ho - ly bride;
One ho - ly name she bless - es, Par - takes one ho - ly food,
Till with the vi - sion glo - rious Her long - ing eyes are blest,
O hap - py ones and ho - ly! Lord, give us grace that we,
With His own blood He bought her, And for her life He died.
And to one hope she press - es, With ev - 'ry grace en - dued.
And the great Church vic - to - rious Shall be the Church at rest.
Like them, the meek and low - ly, On high may dwell with Thee.

Tune: AURELIA—lower key at 114

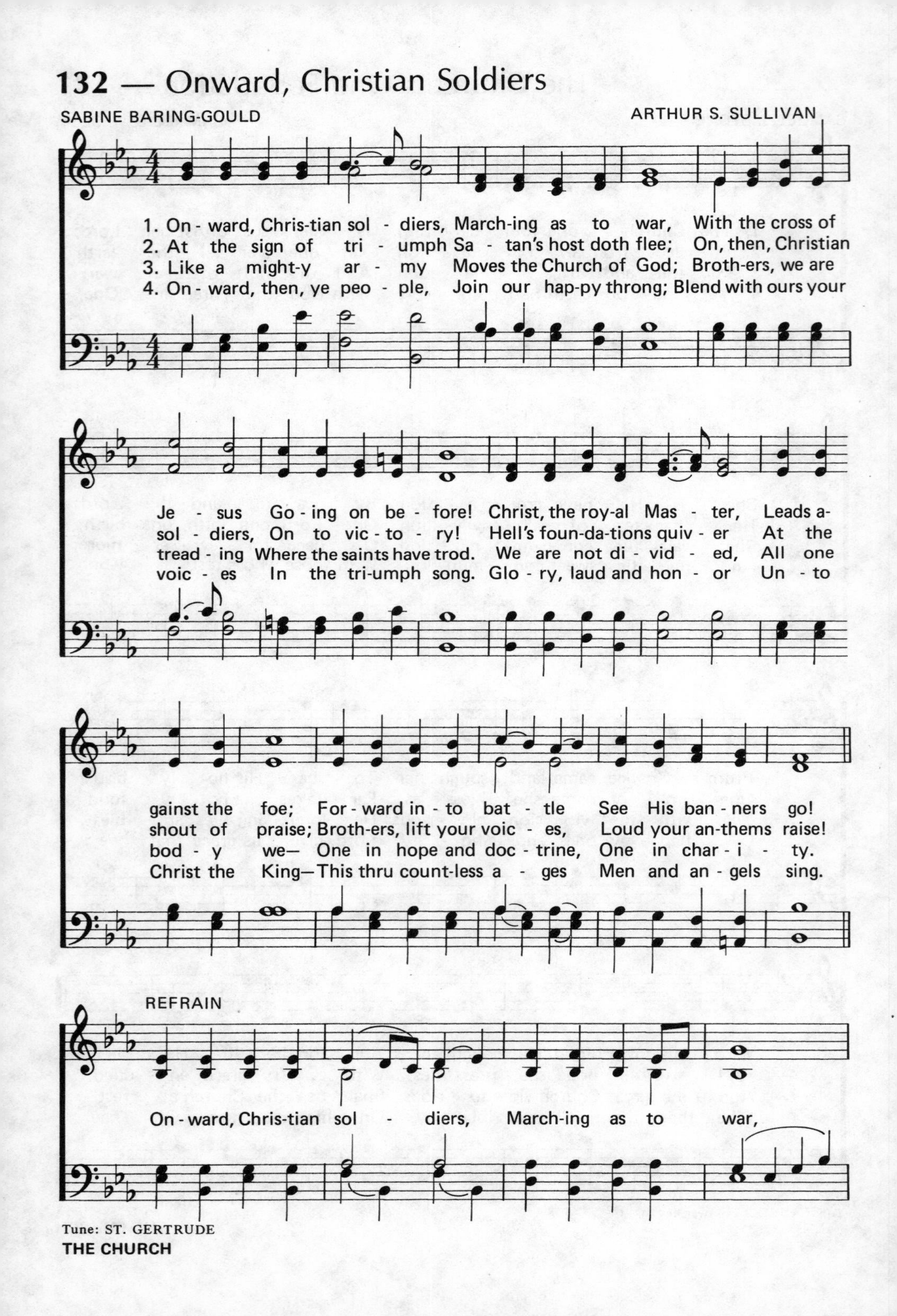
132 — Onward, Christian Soldiers
SABINE BARING-GOULD
ARTHUR S. SULLIVAN
1. On - ward, Chris-tian sol - diers, March-ing as to war, With the cross of
2. At the sign of tri - umph Sa - tan's host doth flee; On, then, Christian
3. Like a might-y ar - my Moves the Church of God; Broth-ers, we are
4. On - ward, then, ye peo - ple, Join our hap-py throng; Blend with ours your
Je - sus Go - ing on be - fore! Christ, the roy-al Mas - ter, Leads a-
sol - diers, On to vic - to - ry! Hell's foun-da-tions quiv - er At the
tread - ing Where the saints have trod. We are not di - vid - ed, All one
voic - es In the tri-umph song. Glo - ry, laud and hon - or Un - to
gainst the foe; For - ward in - to bat - tle See His ban - ners go!
shout of praise; Broth-ers, lift your voic - es, Loud your an-thems raise!
bod - y we— One in hope and doc - trine, One in char - i - ty.
Christ the King—This thru count-less a - ges Men and an - gels sing.
REFRAIN
On - ward, Chris-tian sol - diers, March-ing as to war,
Tune: ST. GERTRUDE
THE CHURCH

With the cross of Je - sus Go - ing on be - fore!
8
Faith of Our Fathers — 133
FREDERICK W. FABER
HENRI F. HEMY
Adapted by James G. Walton
1. Faith of our fa - thers, liv - ing still In spite of dun - geon, fire and sword— O how our hearts beat high with joy When-e'er we hear that glo - rious word!
2. Our fa - thers, chained in pris - ons dark, Were still in heart and con - science free; How sweet would be their chil - dren's fate If they, like them, could die for thee!
3. Faith of our fa - thers, we will love Both friend and foe in all our strife; And preach thee too, as love knows how, By kind - ly words and vir - tuous life.
Faith of our fa - thers, ho - ly faith, We will be true to thee till death!*
Tune: ST. CATHERINE
THE CHURCH

134 — I Love Thy Kingdom, Lord!
TIMOTHY DWIGHT
AARON WILLIAMS
1. I love Thy king - dom, Lord! The house of Thine a - bode—
2. I love Thy Church, O God! Her walls be - fore Thee stand,
3. For her my tears shall fall, For her my prayers as - cend,
4. Be - yond my high - est joy I prize her heav'n - ly ways—
5. Sure as Thy truth shall last, To Zi - on shall be giv'n
The Church our blest Re - deem - er saved With His own pre - cious blood.
Dear as the ap - ple of Thine eye And grav - en on Thy hand.
To her my cares and toils be giv'n Till toils and cares shall end.
Her sweet com - mun - ion, sol - emn vows, Her hymns of love and praise.
The bright - est glo - ries earth can yield, And bright - er bliss of heav'n.*
Tune: ST. THOMAS
135 — Blest Be the Tie That Binds
JOHN FAWCETT
HANS G. NAEGELI
1. Blest be the tie that binds Our hearts in Chris - tian love! The
2. Be - fore our Fa - ther's throne We pour our ar - dent prayers; Our
3. We share our mu - tual woes, Our mu - tual bur - dens bear; And
4. When we a - sun - der part It gives us in - ward pain; But
fel - low - ship of kin - dred minds Is like to that a - bove.
fears, our hopes, our aims are one, Our com - forts and our cares.
oft - en for each oth - er flows The sym - pa - thiz - ing tear.
we shall still be joined in heart, And hope to meet a - gain.
Tune: DENNIS

ANNE ORTLUND ANNE ORTLUND

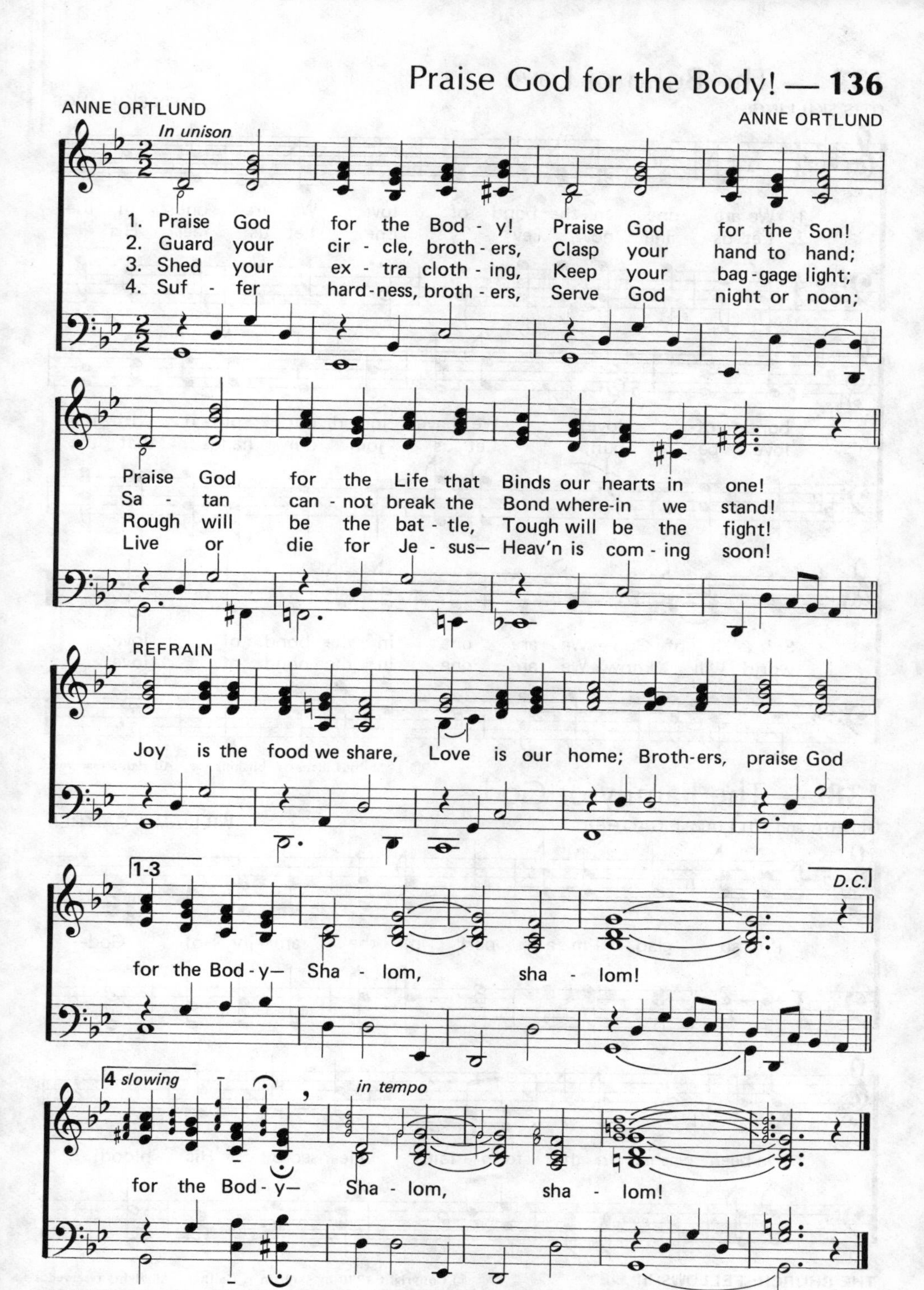
In unison
1. Praise God for the Bod - y! Praise God for the Son!
2. Guard your cir - cle, broth - ers, Clasp your hand to hand;
3. Shed your ex - tra cloth - ing, Keep your bag - gage light;
4. Suf - fer hard - ness, broth - ers, Serve God night or noon;
Praise God for the Life that Binds our hearts in one!
Sa - tan can - not break the Bond where - in we stand!
Rough will be the bat - tle, Tough will be the fight!
Live or die for Je - sus— Heav'n is com - ing soon!
REFRAIN
Joy is the food we share, Love is our home; Broth - ers, praise God
1-3
for the Bod - y— Sha - lom, sha - lom!
D.C.
4 slowing
in tempo
for the Bod - y— Sha - lom, sha - lom!

BODY—the fellowship of believers, the Church. SHALOM—a Hebrew greeting, "Peace!"
For Choir use, women sing SSA, men sing melody in unison.

137 — The Bond of Love
OTIS SKILLINGS
OTIS SKILLINGS
1. We are one in the bond of love, We are one in the bond of love; We have joined our spir - it with the Spir - it of God— We are one in the bond of love.
2. Let us sing now, ev - 'ry - one, Let us feel His love be - gun; Let us join our hands that the world will know We are one in the bond of love.
© 1971 by Lillenas Publishing Co. All rights reserved.
138 — The Family of God
GLORIA and WILLIAM J. GAITHER
WILLIAM J. GAITHER
I'm so glad I'm a part of the fam - ily of God— I've been washed in the foun - tain, cleansed by His blood!
THE CHURCH: FELLOWSHIP
© Copyright 1970 by William J. Gaither. All rights reserved.

Joint heirs with Je-sus as we trav-el this sod—
For I'm part of the fam-ily, the fam-ily of God.
Christian Love — 139
LOUIS PAUL LEHMAN
LOUIS PAUL LEHMAN
1. Chris-tian love, Chris-tian love! In the Spir-it we are one:
2. Chris-tian love, Chris-tian love! Grace and faith have made it plain:
3. Chris-tian love, Chris-tian love! How the an-gels stand a-mazed:
We par-take of great sal-va-tion, By His cross we're blood re-
Jus-ti-fied as God now sees us, We re-joice and live in
Join these Chris-tians by the hand, Shout and sing to glo-ry-
la-tion— Chris-tian love, Chris-tian love, Chris-tian love!
Je-sus— Chris-tian love, Chris-tian love, Chris-tian love!
land— Chris-tian love, Chris-tian love, Chris-tian love!

140 — There's a Quiet Understanding
TEDD SMITH
TEDD SMITH
1. There's a qui - et un - der-stand - ing When we're gath-ered in the Spir- it, It's a prom-ise that He gives us— When we gath-er in His name; There's a love we feel in Je - sus, There's a man-na that He feeds us, It's a prom-ise that He gives us
2. And we know when we're to-geth - er, Shar - ing love and un-der-stand- ing, That our broth-ers and our sis - ters Feel the one-ness that He brings; Thank You, thank You, thank You, Je - sus, For the way You love and feed us, For the man-y ways You lead us—
1
When we gath - er in His name.
2
Thank You, thank You, Lord.
THE CHURCH: FELLOWSHIP
Copyright © 1973 and arr. © 1977 by Hope Publishing Co. All rights reserved.

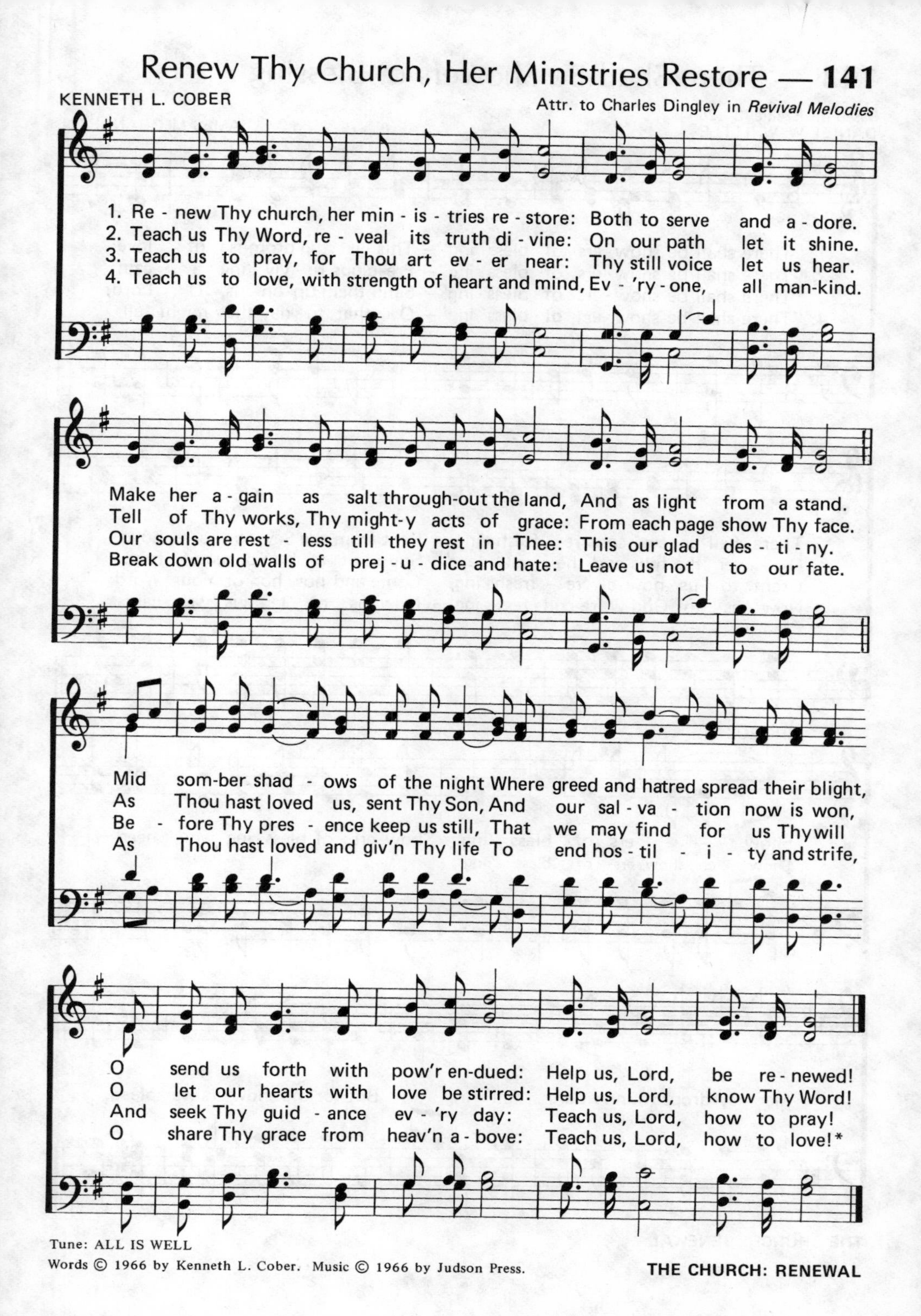
Renew Thy Church, Her Ministries Restore — 141
KENNETH L. COBER
Attr. to Charles Dingley in Revival Melodies
1. Re - new Thy church, her min - is - tries re - store: Both to serve and a - dore.
2. Teach us Thy Word, re - veal its truth di - vine: On our path let it shine.
3. Teach us to pray, for Thou art ev - er near: Thy still voice let us hear.
4. Teach us to love, with strength of heart and mind, Ev - 'ry - one, all man-kind.
Make her a - gain as salt through-out the land, And as light from a stand.
Tell of Thy works, Thy might-y acts of grace: From each page show Thy face.
Our souls are rest - less till they rest in Thee: This our glad des - ti - ny.
Break down old walls of prej - u - dice and hate: Leave us not to our fate.
Mid som-ber shad - ows of the night Where greed and hatred spread their blight,
As Thou hast loved us, sent Thy Son, And our sal - va - tion now is won,
Be - fore Thy pres - ence keep us still, That we may find for us Thy will
As Thou hast loved and giv'n Thy life To end hos - til - i - ty and strife,
O send us forth with pow'r en-dued: Help us, Lord, be re - newed!
O let our hearts with love be stirred: Help us, Lord, know Thy Word!
And seek Thy guid - ance ev - 'ry day: Teach us, Lord, how to pray!
O share Thy grace from heav'n a - bove: Teach us, Lord, how to love!*

Tune: ALL IS WELL

THE CHURCH: RENEWAL

142 — There Shall Be Showers of Blessing

Based on Ezekiel 34:26
DANIEL W. WHITTLE
JAMES McGRANAHAN
1. "There shall be show - ers of bless - ing"— This is the prom - ise of love;
2. "There shall be show - ers of bless - ing"— Precious re - viv - ing a - gain;
3. "There shall be show - ers of bless - ing"— Send them up - on us, O Lord;
4. "There shall be show - ers of bless - ing"— O that to - day they might fall,
There shall be sea - sons re - fresh - ing, Sent from the Sav - ior a - bove.
O - ver the hills and the val - leys, Sound of a - bun - dance of rain.
Grant to us now a re - fresh - ing, Come and now hon - or Your Word.
Now as to God we're con - fess - ing, Now as on Je - sus we call!
CHORUS
Show - ers of bless - ing, Show - ers of bless - ing we need;
Show - ers, show - ers of bless - ing,
Mer - cy - drops round us are fall - ing, But for the show - ers we plead.

JOHN ELLERTON
ARTHUR H. MANN
Arr. by Frank Anderson
1. Shine Thou up - on us, Lord, True light of men to - day,
2. Breathe Thou up - on us, Lord, Thy Spir - it's liv - ing flame,
3. Speak Thou for us, O Lord, In all we say of Thee:
4. Live Thou with-in us, Lord— Thy mind and will be ours:
And through the writ - ten Word Thy ver - y self dis - play,
That so with one ac - cord Our lips may tell Thy name;
Ac - cord - ing to Thy Word Let all our teach - ing be,
Be Thou be-loved, a - dored And served with all our pow'rs,
That so, from hearts which burn With gaz - ing on Thy face,
Give Thou the hear - ing ear, Fix Thou the wan-d'ring thought,
That so Thy lambs may know Their own true Shep-herd's voice,
That so our lives may teach Thy chil - dren what Thou art,
Thy lit - tle ones may learn The won - ders of Thy grace.
That those we teach may hear The great things Thou hast wrought.
Wher - e'er He leads them go, And in His love re - joice.
And plead, by more than speech, For Thee with ev - 'ry heart.*

Tune: ANGEL'S STORY

144 — O Grant Us Light

LAURENCE TUTTIETT

GEORGE J. ELVEY

1. O grant us light, that we may know The wis - dom Thou a - lone canst give, That truth may guide wher - e'er we go, And vir - tue bless wher - e'er we live.
2. O grant us light, that we may see Where er - ror lurks in hu - man lore, And turn our doubt - ing minds to Thee, And love Thy sim - ple Word the more.
3. O grant us light, that we may learn How dead is life from Thee a - part, How sure is joy for all who turn To Thee an un - di - vid - ed heart.*

Tune: ST. CRISPIN

145 — A Student's Prayer

JOHN W. PETERSON

Leavitt's *Christian Lyre*
Possibly from W. A. Mozart

1. God, the all - wise, and Cre - a - tor Of the hu - man in - tel-lect,
2. O how vast the shores of learn - ing— There are still un - chart - ed seas,
3. May the things we learn, so mea - ger, Nev - er lift our hearts in pride

Tune: ELLESDIE—higher key at 447

Guide our search for truth and knowl-edge, All our thoughts and ways di-rect.
And they call to bold ad-ven-ture Those who turn from sloth and ease.
Till in fool-ish self-re-li-ance We would wan-der from Your side.
Help us build the tow'rs of learn-ing That would make us wise, as-tute,
But we need Your hand to guide us In the stud-ies we pur-sue,
Let them on-ly bind us clos-er, Lord, to You, in whom we find
On the rock of Ho-ly Scrip-ture: Truth re-vealed and ab-so-lute.
And the pres-ence of Your Spir-it To il-lu-mine all we do.
Ver-y foun-tain-head of wis-dom, Light and life of all man-kind.*

My Lord, I Do Not Ask to Stand — 146

NORMAN E. RICHARDSON
FLORENCE I. JUDSON-BRADLEY

1. My Lord, I do not ask to stand
   As king or prince of high degree;
   I only pray that hand in hand
   A child and I may come to Thee.

2. To teach a tender voice to pray,
   Two childish eyes Thy face to see,
   Two feet to guide in Thy straight way—
   This fervently I ask of Thee.

3. O grant Thy patience to impart
   Thy holy law, Thy words of truth;
   Give, Lord, Thy grace, that my whole heart
   May overflow with love for youth.

4. As step by step we tread the way,
   Trusting and confident and free,
   A child and I shall day by day
   Find sweet companionship with Thee.*

Tune: ST. CRISPIN (at 144) or MARYTON (at 508)

147 — A Christian Home

BARBARA B. HART

JEAN SIBELIUS
Arr. for *Praise!*

1. O give us homes built firm up-on the Sav-ior, Where Christ is head and
2. O give us homes with god-ly fa-thers, moth-ers, Who al-ways place their
3. O give us homes where Christ is Lord and Mas-ter, The Bi-ble read, the
4. O Lord, our God, our homes are Thine for-ev-er! We trust to Thee their

coun-sel-lor and guide; Where ev-'ry child is taught His love and fa-vor
hope and trust in Him; Whose ten-der pa-tience tur-moil nev-er both-ers,
pre-cious hymns still sung; Where pray'r comes first in peace or in dis-as-ter,
prob-lems, toil and care; Their bonds of love no en-e-my can sev-er

And gives his heart to Christ, the cru-ci-fied: How sweet to know that
Whose calm and cour-age trou-ble can-not dim; A home where each finds
And praise is nat-ural speech to ev-'ry tongue; Where mountains move be-
If Thou art al-ways Lord and Mas-ter there: Be Thou the cen-ter

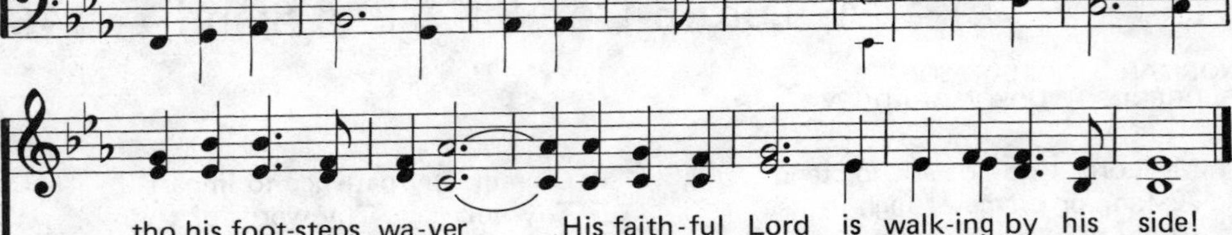

tho his foot-steps wa-ver His faith-ful Lord is walk-ing by his side!
joy in serv-ing oth-ers, And love still shines tho days be dark and grim.
fore a faith that's vast-er, And Christ suf-fi-cient is for old and young.
of our least en-deav-or— Be Thou our guest, our hearts and homes to share.*

Tune: FINLANDIA—higher key at 334

Happy the Home When God Is There — 148
HENRY WARE, the younger
JOHN B. DYKES
1. Hap-py the home when God is there And love fills ev - 'ry breast,
When one their wish and one their prayer And one their heav'n-ly rest.
2. Hap-py the home where Je - sus' name Is sweet to ev - 'ry ear,
Where chil-dren ear - ly lisp His fame And par - ents hold Him dear.
3. Hap-py the home where prayer is heard And praise is wont to rise,
Where par-ents love the sa - cred Word And all its wis - dom prize.
4. Lord, let us in our homes a - gree This bless - ed peace to gain;
U - nite our hearts in love to Thee, And love to all will reign.*
Tune: BEATITUDO–lower key at 316
Our Thanks, O God, for Parents — 149
LOIS S. JOHNSON
LOIS S. JOHNSON
1. Our thanks, O God, for par - ents Who fol - low in Thy way,
And who, with glad and trust - ing hearts, Ex - alt Thee ev - 'ry day.
2. Our thanks, O God, for par - ents Who show, by word and deed,
Com - mit - ment to Thy will and plan, And Thy com-mand-ments heed.
3. Our thanks, O God, for par - ents Who meet Thee oft in prayer,
And who, for all life's toil and care, Find strength and wis - dom there.
4. How bless - ed are the chil - dren Who in their par - ents see
The ten - der Fa - ther - love of God, And find their way to Thee.*

Tune: SOLIE

The word "mothers" or "fathers" may be substituted for other occasions.

150 — Lord of Life and King of Glory

CHRISTIAN BURKE

Swedish folk melody
Sionstoner
Arr. by Frank Anderson

1. Lord of life and King of glo - ry, Who didst deign a child to be,
2. Grant to us pure hearts, and pa-tient, That in all we do or say
3. When our grow-ing sons and daugh-ters Look on life with ea - ger eyes,
4. May we keep our ho - ly call - ing Stain-less in its fair re - nown,
Cra - dled on a moth-er's bo - som, Throned up - on a moth-er's knee:
Lit - tle ones our deeds may cop - y And be nev - er led a - stray,
Grant us then a deep - er in - sight And new pow'rs of sac - ri - fice:
That, when all the work is o - ver And we lay the bur - den down,
For the chil - dren Thou hast giv - en We must an - swer un - to Thee.
Lit - tle feet our steps may fol - low In a safe and nar - row way.
Hope to trust them, faith to guide them, Love that noth - ing good de - nies.
Then the chil - dren Thou hast giv - en Still may be our joy and crown.*

Tune: TILLFLYKT

151 — Faith of Our Mothers

A. B. PATTEN

1. Faith of our mothers, living still
   In cradle song and bedtime prayer,
   In nursery lore and fireside love,
   Thy presence still pervades the air:
   Faith of our mothers, living faith,
   We will be true to thee till death!

2. Faith of our mothers, loving faith,
   Fount of our childhood's trust and grace,
   O may thy consecration prove
   Source of a finer, nobler race:
   Faith of our mothers, loving faith,
   We will be true to thee till death!

Tune: ST. CATHERINE—music at 133

3. Faith of our mothers, guiding faith,
For youthful longing, youthful doubt,
How blurred our vision, blind our way,
Thy providential care without:
Faith of our mothers, guiding faith,
We will be true to thee till death!

4. Faith of our mothers, Christian faith,
In truth beyond our stumbling creeds,
Still serve the home and save the Church
And breathe thy spirit thru our deeds:
Faith of our mothers, Christian faith,
We will be true to thee till death!*

Thou Gracious God, Whose Mercy Lends — 152

OLIVER WENDELL HOLMES

ROBERT SCHUMANN

1. Thou gra - cious God, whose mer - cy lends The light of home, the smile of friends: Our gath - ered flock Thine arms en - fold, As in the peace - ful days of old.
2. Wilt Thou not hear us while we raise, In sweet ac - cord of sol - emn praise, The voic - es that have min - gled long In joy - ous flow of mirth and song?
3. For all the bless - ings life has brought, For all its sor - r'wing hours have taught, For all we mourn, for all we keep, The hands we clasp, the loved that sleep;
4. The noon - tide sun - shine of the past, These brief, bright mo - ments fad - ing fast; The stars that gild our dark-'ning years, The twi - light ray from ho - lier spheres:
5. We thank Thee, Fa - ther— let Thy grace Our lov - ing cir - cle still em - brace, Thy mer - cy shed its heav'n-ly store, Thy peace be with us ev - er - more.*

Tune: CANONBURY—higher key at 510

153 — In Jordan's Stream

Based on Matthew 3:13-17

JOHN W. PETERSON JOHN W. PETERSON

1. In Jor - dan's stream the Sav - ior stood Ful - fill - ing right - eous - ness;
2. To - day we gath - er in Thy name, And 'tis a sa - cred hour;
3. Our wit - ness to the world a - round Of Thy re - deem - ing grace;
4. Nor would we cease to fol - low Thee, Con - tent with this a - lone;
And like a dove the Spir - it came His heart and life to bless.
Bless these who fol - low in Thy steps, De - scend in love and pow'r.
A wit - ness of our love for Thee, Our hope to see Thy face.
On thru the gar - den, Cal - va - ry, Thy lot shall be our own.*

Tune: BRIDGEWATER (Alternate, SERENITY)

154 — We Bless the Name of Christ, the Lord

SAMUEL F. COFFMAN

THOMAS HASTINGS
Arr. by John W. Peterson

1. We bless the name of Christ the Lord, We bless Him for His ho - ly Word,
2. We fol - low Him with pure de - light To sanc - ti - fy His sa - cred rite;
3. Bap - tized in God—the Fa - ther, Son, And Ho - ly Spir - it—Three in One,
4. By grace we "Ab - ba, Fa - ther" cry, By grace the Com - fort - er comes nigh;
Who loved to do His Fa - ther's will And all His right - eous - ness ful - fill.
And thus our faith with wa - ter seal To prove o - be - dience that we feel.
With con - science free we rest in God, In love and peace, thru Je - sus' blood.
And for Thy grace our love shall be For - ev - er, on - ly, Lord, for Thee.*

Tune: RETREAT

See Israel's Gentle Shepherd Stand — 155

Based on Mark 10:14
PHILIP DODDRIDGE

WILLIAM V. WALLACE

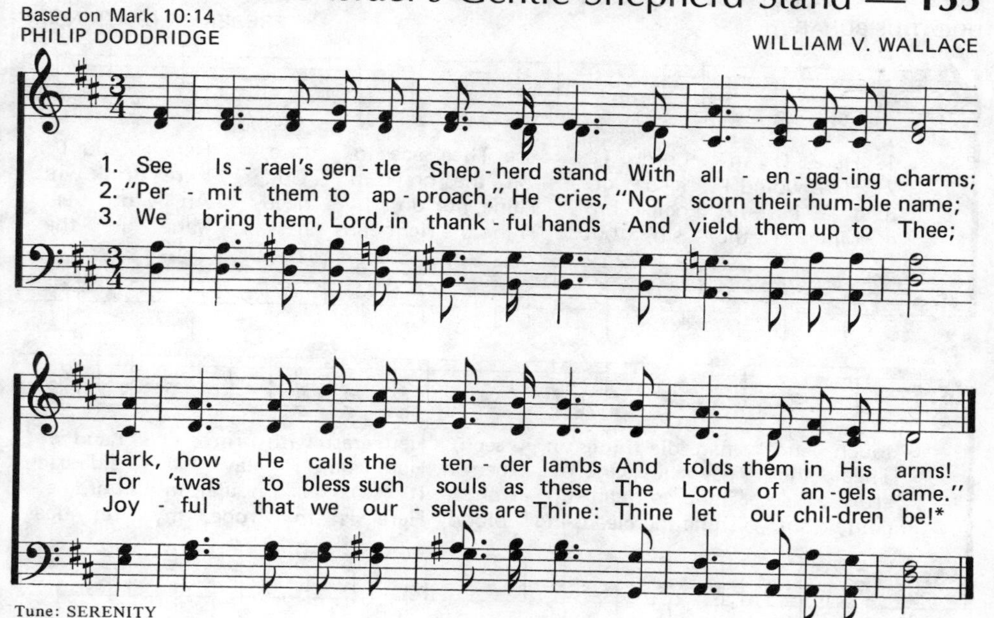
1. See Is - rael's gen - tle Shep - herd stand With all - en - gag - ing charms;
2. "Per - mit them to ap - proach," He cries, "Nor scorn their hum - ble name;
3. We bring them, Lord, in thank - ful hands And yield them up to Thee;
Hark, how He calls the ten - der lambs And folds them in His arms!
For 'twas to bless such souls as these The Lord of an - gels came."
Joy - ful that we our - selves are Thine: Thine let our chil - dren be!*

Tune: SERENITY

This Child We Dedicate to Thee — 156

From the German
Trans. by Samuel Gilman–alt.

HENRY K. OLIVER

1. This child we ded - i - cate to Thee, O God of grace and pu - ri - ty!
2. O may Thy Spir - it gen - tly draw Its will - ing soul to keep Thy law;
In Thy great love its life pro - long, Shield it, we pray, from sin and wrong.
May vir - tue, pi - e - ty and truth Dawn e - ven with its dawn - ing youth.*

Tune: FEDERAL STREET (Alternate, RETREAT)

157 — Here, O My Lord, I See Thee Face to Face
HORATIUS BONAR
FREDERICK C. ATKINSON
1. Here, O my Lord, I see Thee face to face, Here would I
2. Here would I feed up - on the bread of God, Here drink with
3. I have no help but Thine, nor do I need An - oth - er
4. Mine is the sin, but Thine the right-eous - ness, Mine is the
touch and han - dle things un - seen, Here grasp with firm - er hand e -
Thee the roy - al wine of heav'n, Here would I lay a - side each
arm save Thine to lean up - on; It is e - nough, my Lord, e -
guilt, but Thine the cleans-ing blood; Here is my robe, my ref - uge
ter - nal grace, And all my wea - ri - ness up - on Thee lean.
earth - ly load, Here taste a - fresh the calm of sin for - giv'n.
nough in - deed— My strength is in Thy might, Thy might a - lone.
and my peace, Thy blood, Thy right - eous - ness, O Lord, my God.*
Tune: MORECAMBE—higher key at 86
158 — According to Thy Gracious Word
JAMES MONTGOMERY
THOMAS A. ARNE
1. Ac - cord-ing to Thy gra - cious word, In meek hu-mil - i - ty,
2. Thy bod - y, bro - ken for my sake, My bread from heav'n shall be;
3. Geth - sem - a - ne can I for - get? Or there Thy con - flict see,
4. When to the cross I turn mine eyes And rest on Cal - va - ry,
5. Re - mem-ber Thee and all Thy pains And all Thy love to me;
6. And when these fail - ing lips grow dumb And mind and mem-'ry flee,
Tune: ARLINGTON—higher key at 499

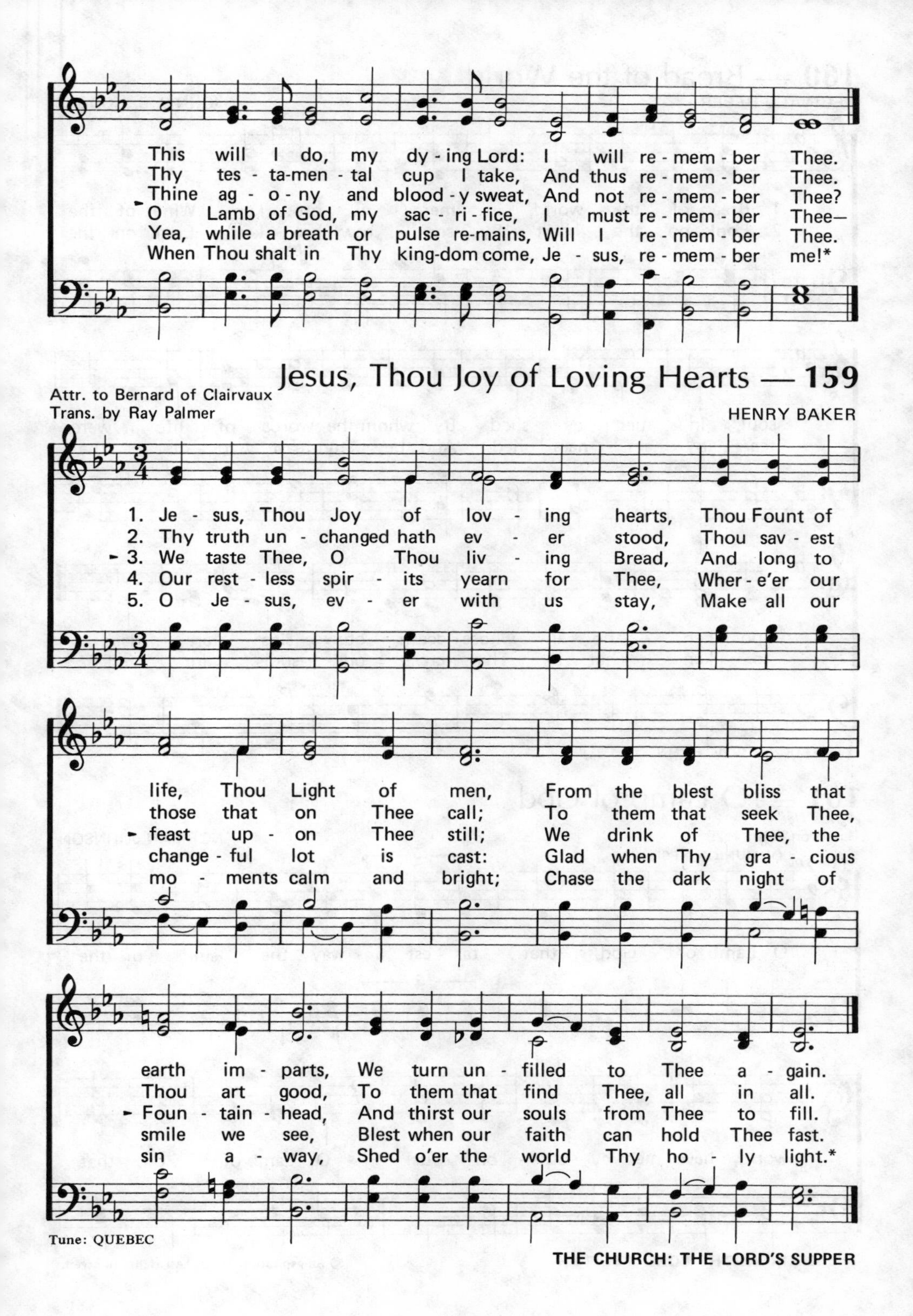
This will I do, my dy-ing Lord: I will re-mem-ber Thee.
Thy tes-ta-men-tal cup I take, And thus re-mem-ber Thee.
Thine ag-o-ny and blood-y sweat, And not re-mem-ber Thee?
O Lamb of God, my sac-ri-fice, I must re-mem-ber Thee—
Yea, while a breath or pulse re-mains, Will I re-mem-ber Thee.
When Thou shalt in Thy king-dom come, Je-sus, re-mem-ber me!*
Jesus, Thou Joy of Loving Hearts — 159
Attr. to Bernard of Clairvaux
Trans. by Ray Palmer
HENRY BAKER
1. Je-sus, Thou Joy of lov-ing hearts, Thou Fount of life, Thou Light of men, From the blest bliss that earth im-parts, We turn un-filled to Thee a-gain.
2. Thy truth un-changed hath ev-er stood, Thou sav-est those that on Thee call; To them that seek Thee, Thou art good, To them that find Thee, all in all.
3. We taste Thee, O Thou liv-ing Bread, And long to feast up-on Thee still; We drink of Thee, the Foun-tain-head, And thirst our souls from Thee to fill.
4. Our rest-less spir-its yearn for Thee, Wher-e'er our change-ful lot is cast: Glad when Thy gra-cious smile we see, Blest when our faith can hold Thee fast.
5. O Je-sus, ev-er with us stay, Make all our mo-ments calm and bright; Chase the dark night of sin a-way, Shed o'er the world Thy ho-ly light.*
Tune: QUEBEC
THE CHURCH: THE LORD'S SUPPER

160 — Bread of the World
REGINALD HEBER
JOHN S. B. HODGES
1. Bread of the world, in mer - cy bro - ken, Wine of the soul, in mer - cy shed, By whom the words of life were spo - ken, And in whose death our sins are dead:
2. Look on the heart by sor - row bro - ken, Look on the tears by sin - ners shed, And be Thy feast to us the to - ken That by Thy grace our souls are fed. *
Tune: EUCHARISTIC HYMN
161 — O Lamb of God
Agnus Dei
Based on John 1:29
NORMAN JOHNSON
COMMUNION RESPONSE
p
3
O Lamb of God, that tak - est a - way the sin of the world, have mer - cy up - on us! O Lamb of God, that
THE CHURCH: THE LORD'S SUPPER
© Singspiration 1970. All rights reserved.

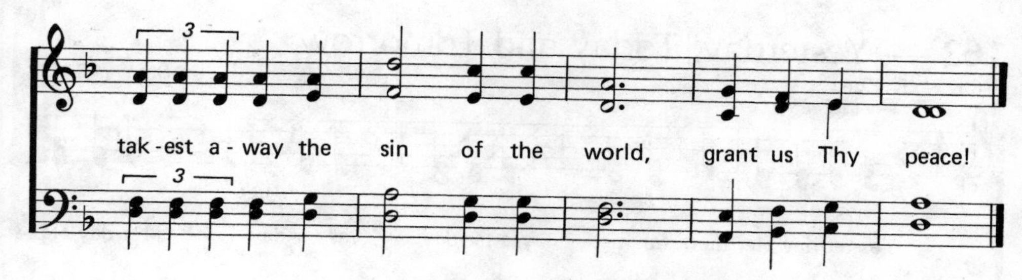
3
tak-est a-way the sin of the world, grant us Thy peace!
3

Let Us Break Bread Together — 162

Traditional

Traditional Spiritual
Arr. by Larry Leader

1. Let us break bread to-geth-er on our knees, (on our knees;)
2. Let us drink the cup† to-geth-er on our knees, (on our knees;)
3. Let us praise God to-geth-er on our knees, (on our knees;)
Let us break bread to-geth-er on our knees, (on our knees;)
Let us drink the cup† to-geth-er on our knees, (on our knees;)
Let us praise God to-geth-er on our knees, (on our knees;)
When I fall on my knees, With my face to the ris-ing
sun, O Lord, have mer-cy on me. (on me.)

†Optionally "wine."

163 — Yesterday, Today and Tomorrow
JACK WYRTZEN
DON WYRTZEN
Two-part
Yes-ter-day He died for me, yes-ter-day, yes-ter-day, Yes-ter-day He
died for me, yes-ter-day, Yes-ter-day He died for me, died for me— This is
his-to - ry. To-day He lives for me, to-day, to-day,
To-day He lives for me, to-day, To-day He lives for me, lives for
me— This is vic-to - ry. Tomorrow He comes for me, He comes,
3
CHRIST: HIS MISSION
© Singspiration 1966, arr. 1979. All rights reserved.

3
He comes, To-mor-row He comes for me, He comes, To-mor-row He
comes for me, comes for me— This is mys-ter - y. O friend, do
f
you know Him? know Him? know Him? O friend, do you know Him? know
Him? O friend, do you know Him? do you know Him? Je-sus Christ the Lord,
Je - sus Christ the Lord, Je - sus Christ the Lord!

164 — For God So Loved the World

1 - ELDON BURKWALL (based on John 1:11,12)
2 - FRANCES TOWNSEND (based on John 3:16)
3 - Source unknown

ALFRED B. SMITH

1. He came un - to His own—His own re-ceived Him not, But all who
2. For God so loved the world He gave His on - ly Son To die on
3. If God so loved the world Then we should love it too, And strive to

will be - lieve The pow - er will re - ceive To be the sons of God
Cal-v'ry's tree, From sin to set me free; Some day He's com-ing back—
live for Him, Lost sin - ners seek to win, So they'll be read - y when

By trust - ing in His name: I'm so glad that Je - sus came!
What glo - ry that will be: Won - der - ful His love to me!
He comes to earth a - gain: Joy - ful will that meet-ing be!

165 — Hallelujah, What a Savior!

PHILIP P. BLISS

PHILIP P. BLISS

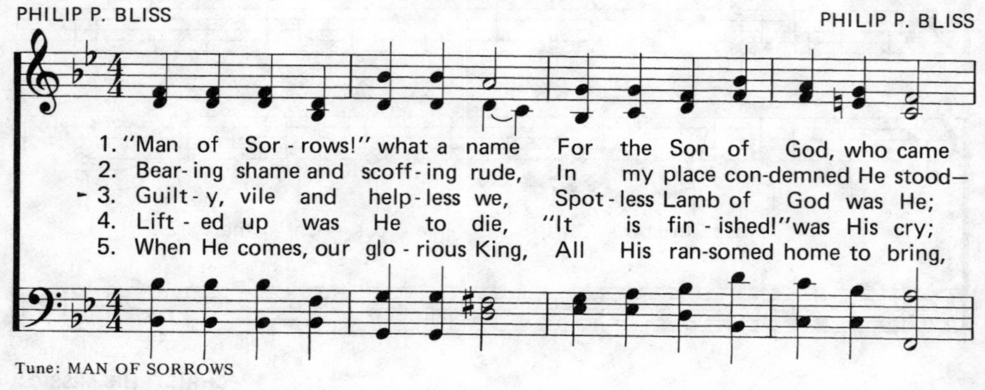
1. "Man of Sor - rows!" what a name For the Son of God, who came
2. Bear - ing shame and scoff - ing rude, In my place con-demned He stood—
3. Guilt - y, vile and help - less we, Spot - less Lamb of God was He;
4. Lift - ed up was He to die, "It is fin - ished!" was His cry;
5. When He comes, our glo - rious King, All His ran-somed home to bring,

Tune: MAN OF SORROWS

Ru - ined sin - ners to re - claim! Hal - le - lu - jah, what a Sav - ior!
Sealed my par - don with His blood: Hal - le - lu - jah, what a Sav - ior!
Full a - tone-ment! can it be? Hal - le - lu - jah, what a Sav - ior!
Now in heav'n ex - alt - ed high: Hal - le - lu - jah, what a Sav - ior!
Then a - new this song we'll sing: Hal - le - lu - jah, what a Sav - ior!
Wounded for Me — 166
1 - W. G. OVENS
2-5 - GLADYS WESTCOTT ROBERTS
W. G. OVENS
1. Wound-ed for me, wound-ed for me, There on the cross
2. Dy - ing for me, dy - ing for me, There on the cross
3. Ris - en for me, ris - en for me, Up from the grave
4. Liv - ing for me, liv - ing for me, Up in the skies
5. Com - ing for me, com - ing for me, One day to earth
He was wound-ed for me; Gone my trans - gres - sions, and
He was dy - ing for me; Now in His death my re -
He has ris - en for me; Now ev - er - more from death's
He is liv - ing for me; Dai - ly He's plead - ing and
He is com - ing for me; Then with what joy His dear
now I am free, All be-cause Je - sus was wound-ed for me.
demp-tion I see, All be-cause Je - sus was dy - ing for me.
sting I am free, All be-cause Je - sus has ris - en for me.
pray - ing for me, All be-cause Je - sus is liv - ing for me.
face I shall see, O how I praise Him—He's com-ing for me!
CHRIST: HIS MISSION

167 — One Day!

J. WILBUR CHAPMAN | CHARLES H. MARSH

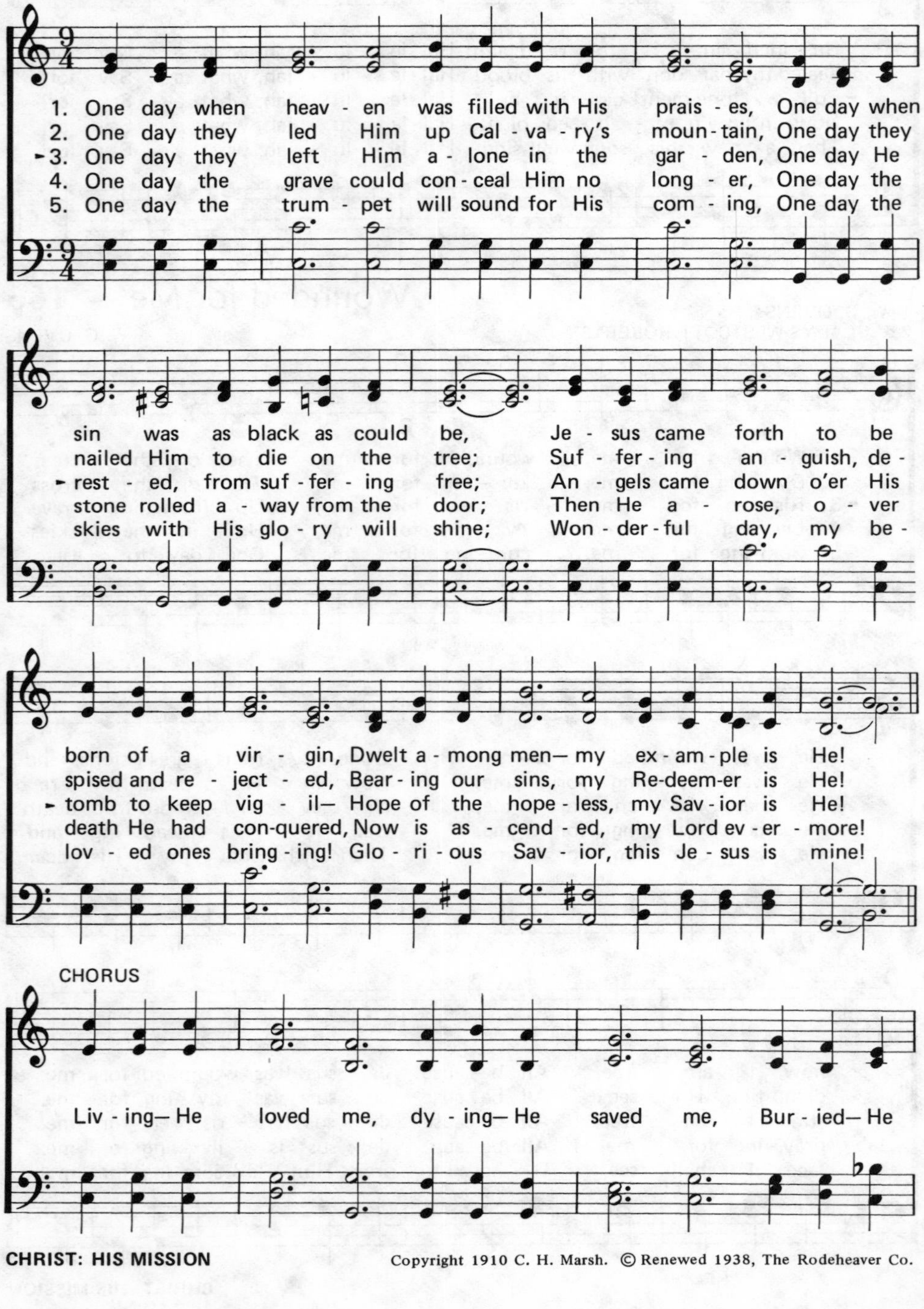

1. One day when heav - en was filled with His prais - es, One day when
2. One day they led Him up Cal - va - ry's moun - tain, One day they
3. One day they left Him a - lone in the gar - den, One day He
4. One day the grave could con - ceal Him no long - er, One day the
5. One day the trum - pet will sound for His com - ing, One day the

sin was as black as could be, Je - sus came forth to be
nailed Him to die on the tree; Suf - fer - ing an - guish, de -
rest - ed, from suf - fer - ing free; An - gels came down o'er His
stone rolled a - way from the door; Then He a - rose, o - ver
skies with His glo - ry will shine; Won - der - ful day, my be -

born of a vir - gin, Dwelt a - mong men— my ex - am - ple is He!
spised and re - ject - ed, Bear - ing our sins, my Re - deem - er is He!
tomb to keep vig - il— Hope of the hope - less, my Sav - ior is He!
death He had con - quered, Now is as - cend - ed, my Lord ev - er - more!
lov - ed ones bring - ing! Glo - ri - ous Sav - ior, this Je - sus is mine!

CHORUS

Liv - ing— He loved me, dy - ing— He saved me, Bur - ied— He

car - ried my sins far a - way; Ris - ing— He jus - ti - fied
free - ly, for - ev - er: One day He's com - ing— O glo - ri - ous day!
Traditional
Stanzas 2ab, 3b by E. B.
Traditional
Arr. by Eldon Burkwall
Refr.: Come and praise the Lord our King, Hal - le - lu - jah! Come and
1. Christ was born in Beth - le - hem, Hal - le - lu - jah! Son of
up an earth - ly child, Hal - le - lu - jah! Of the
2. As a man He toiled and taught, Hal - le - lu - jah! And in
Fa - ther's will de - fined, Hal - le - lu - jah! Grace and
for stanzas
for refrain
praise the Lord our King, Hal - le - lu - jah!
God and Son of Man, Hal - le - lu - jah! He grew
world but un - de - filed, Hal - le - lu - jah! Come and
love our souls He sought, Hal - le - lu - jah! He His
truth in Him com - bined, Hal - le - lu - jah! Come and

Come and Praise — 168

3. Jesus died at Calvary, . . .
Rose again triumphantly, . . .
Thru the gift of His own blood, . . .
Reconciling us to God, . . .
Refrain

4. He will cleanse us from our sin, . . .
If we come by faith to Him, . . .
Then we'll live with Him some day, . . .
And forever with Him stay, . . .
Refrain

Tune: MICHAEL—lower key at 47

169 — Thou Didst Leave Thy Throne

EMILY E. S. ELLIOTT | TIMOTHY R. MATTHEWS

1. Thou didst leave Thy throne and Thy king - ly crown When Thou
2. Heav-en's arch - es rang when the an - gels sang, Pro -
3. The fox - es found rest, and the birds their nest In the
4. Thou cam - est, O Lord, with the liv - ing word That should
5. When the heav'ns shall ring and the an - gels sing At Thy

cam - est to earth for me; But in Beth - le - hem's home was there
claim - ing Thy roy - al de - gree; But of low - ly birth didst Thou
shade of the for - est tree; But Thy couch was the sod, O Thou
set Thy peo - ple free; But with mock - ing scorn and with
com - ing to vic - to - ry, Let Thy voice call me home, say - ing,

found no room For Thy ho - ly na - tiv - i - ty. O
come to earth, And in great hu - mil - i - ty. O
Son of God, In the des - erts of Gal - i - lee. O
crown of thorn They bore Thee to Cal - va - ry. O
"Yet there is room—There is room at My side for thee." My

come to my heart, Lord Je - sus—There is room in my heart for Thee!
come to my heart, Lord Je - sus—There is room in my heart for Thee!
come to my heart, Lord Je - sus—There is room in my heart for Thee!
come to my heart, Lord Je - sus—There is room in my heart for Thee!
heart shall re-joice, Lord Je - sus, When Thou com - est and call - est for me!

Tune: MARGARET

CHRIST: HIS MISSION

Joy to the World! — 170

From Psalm 98
ISAAC WATTS
Adapted from GEORGE F. HANDEL
Arr. by Lowell Mason
1. Joy to the world! the Lord is come! Let earth re - ceive her King; Let ev - 'ry heart pre - pare Him room, And heav'n and na - ture sing, And heav'n and na - ture sing, And heav'n, and heav'n and na - ture sing.
2. Joy to the earth! the Sav - ior reigns! Let men their songs em - ploy; While fields and floods, rocks, hills and plains Re - peat the sound-ing joy, Re - peat the sound - ing joy, Re - peat, re - peat the sound - ing joy.
3. No more let sins and sor - rows grow, Nor thorns in - fest the ground; He comes to make His bless - ings flow Far as the curse is found, Far as the curse is found, Far as, far as the curse is found.
4. He rules the world with truth and grace, And makes the na - tions prove The glo - ries of His right - eous - ness And won - ders of His love, And won - ders of His love, And won - ders, won - ders of His love.
1. And heav'n and na - ture sing, And heav'n and na - ture sing,

Tune: ANTIOCH

171 — O Come, O Come, Emmanuel

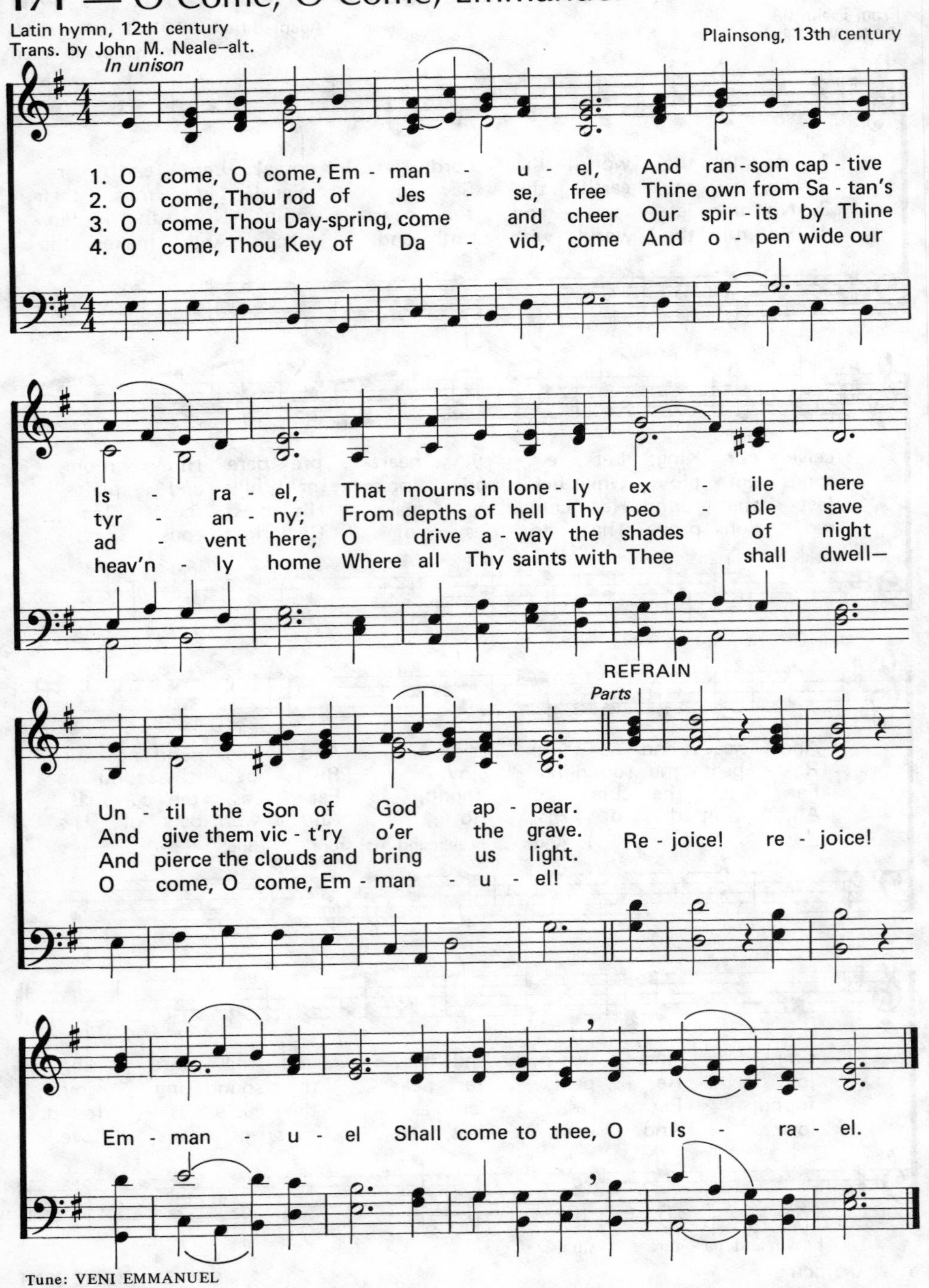

Latin hymn, 12th century
Trans. by John M. Neale–alt.
Plainsong, 13th century
In unison
1. O come, O come, Em - man - u - el, And ran - som cap - tive Is - ra - el, That mourns in lone - ly ex - ile here Un - til the Son of God ap - pear.
2. O come, Thou rod of Jes - se, free Thine own from Sa - tan's tyr - an - ny; From depths of hell Thy peo - ple save And give them vic - t'ry o'er the grave.
3. O come, Thou Day-spring, come and cheer Our spir - its by Thine ad - vent here; O drive a - way the shades of night And pierce the clouds and bring us light.
4. O come, Thou Key of Da - vid, come And o - pen wide our heav'n - ly home Where all Thy saints with Thee shall dwell— O come, O come, Em - man - u - el!
REFRAIN
Parts
Re - joice! re - joice! Em - man - u - el Shall come to thee, O Is - ra - el.

Tune: VENI EMMANUEL

CHRIST: HIS ADVENT

Come, Thou Long-Expected Jesus — 172
CHARLES WESLEY
ROWLAND H. PRICHARD
1. Come, Thou long - ex - pect - ed Je - sus, Born to set Thy
2. Born Thy peo - ple to de - liv - er, Born a child and
peo - ple free; From our fears and sins re - lease us, Let
yet a King, Born to reign in us for - ev - er– Now
us find our rest in Thee. Is - rael's Strength and Con - so -
Thy gra - cious King - dom bring. By Thine own e - ter - nal
la - tion, Hope of all the earth Thou art: Dear De - sire of
Spir - it Rule in all our hearts a - lone; By Thine all suf -
ev - 'ry na - tion, Joy of ev - 'ry long - ing heart.
fi - cient mer - it Raise us to Thy glo - rious throne.*

Tune: HYFRYDOL–another harmonization at 57 (Alternate, STUTTGART, doubled)

173 — O Thou Joyful, O Thou Wonderful

1 - JOHANNES D. FALK
2,3 - Source unknown
Trans. by Henry Katterjohn

Tattersall's *Psalmody*

1. O thou joy - ful, O thou won-der-ful Grace - re - veal - ing Christ - mas - tide! Je - sus came to win us From all sin with- in us: Glo - ri - fy the ho - ly Child!
2. O thou joy - ful, O thou won-der-ful Love - re - veal - ing Christ - mas - tide! Loud ho - san - nas sing - ing And all prais - es bring - ing: May thy love with us a - bide!
3. O thou joy - ful, O thou won-der-ful Peace - re - veal - ing Christ - mas - tide! Dark-ness dis - ap - pear - eth, God's own light now near - eth: Peace and joy to all be - tide!

Tune: O SANCTISSIMA

174 — Lift Up Your Heads

Based on Psalm 24:7-10
GEORG WEISSEL
Trans. by Catherine Winkworth

JEAN BAPTISTE CALKIN

1. Lift up your heads, ye might - y gates: Be - hold the
2. O blest the land, the cit - y blest, Where Christ the
3. Fling wide the por - tals of your heart: Make it a
4. Re - deem - er, come! I o - pen wide My heart to
5. So come, my Sov - 'reign, en - ter in! Let new and

Tune: WALTHAM—higher key at 196 (Alternate, DUKE STREET)

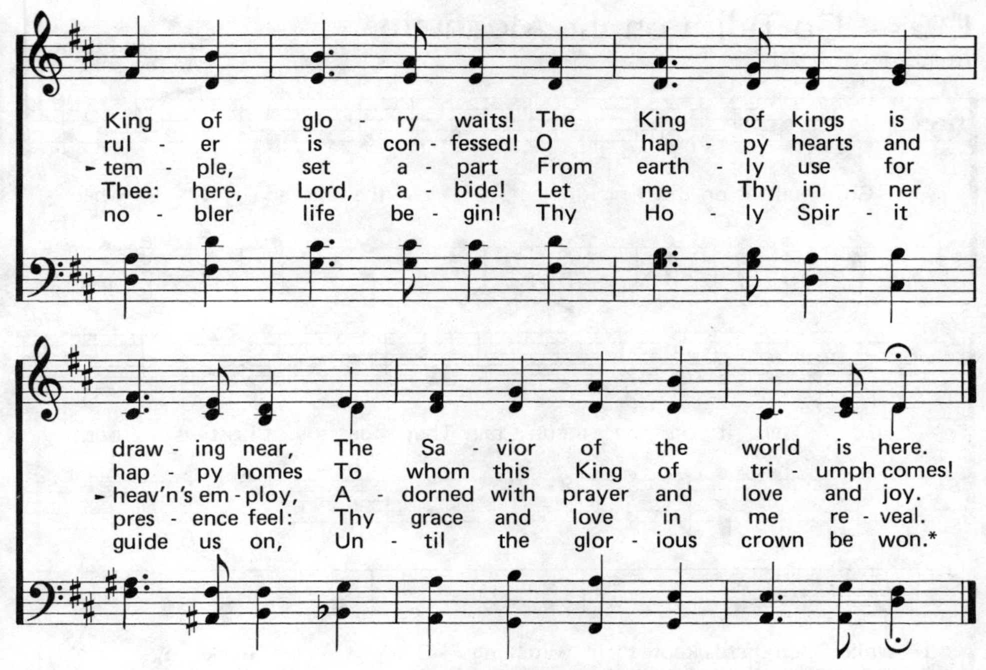
King of glo - ry waits! The King of kings is
rul - er is con - fessed! O hap - py hearts and
temple, set a - part From earth - ly use for
Thee: here, Lord, a - bide! Let me Thy in - ner
no - bler life be - gin! Thy Ho - ly Spir - it
draw - ing near, The Sa - vior of the world is here.
hap - py homes To whom this King of tri - umph comes!
heav'n's em - ploy, A - dorned with prayer and love and joy.
pres - ence feel: Thy grace and love in me re - veal.
guide us on, Un - til the glor - ious crown be won.*

Hark! the Glad Sound! — 175

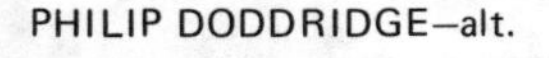
PHILIP DODDRIDGE—alt.

THOMAS HAWEIS
Arr. by Jon Drevits

CALL TO WORSHIP
Briskly (in 2)
Advent: Hark! the glad sound! the Sav - ior comes—The Sav - ior prom - ised long:
Christmas: Joy - ful ho - san - nas, Prince of Peace, Thy wel - come now pro - claim,
Let ev - 'ry heart pre - pare a throne And ev - 'ry voice a song!
While heav'n's e - ter - nal arch - es ring With Thy be - lov - ed name!

Tune: RICHMOND (variant)

176 — Go Tell It on the Mountain
Traditional
Traditional Spiritual
Arr. by Jon Drevits
Go tell it on the moun - tain, O - ver the hills and ev - 'ry-where—
Go tell it on the moun - tain That Je - sus Christ is born!
Fine
1. While shep - herds kept their watch-ing O'er si - lent flocks by night,
2. The shep - herds feared and trem - bled When lo! a - bove the earth
3. Down in a low - ly man - ger The hum-ble Christ was born,
Be - hold, thru - out the heav - ens There shone a ho - ly light.
Rang out the an - gel cho - rus That hailed our Sav - ior's birth.
And God sent us sal - va - tion That bless - ed Christ-mas morn.
D.C.
Music © Singspiration 1966. All rights reserved.
177 — Let All Mortal Flesh Keep Silence
Liturgy of St. James
Trans. by Gerard Moultrie
French melody, 17th century
Arr. by Eldon Burkwall
p
CHRISTMAS RESPONSE—in unison
Let all mor-tal flesh keep si - lence, And with fear and trem-bling stand;
Pon-der noth-ing earth-ly mind-ed— For with bless-ing in His hand

Tune: PICARDY

CHRIST: HIS BIRTH

Christ our God to earth de - scend - eth, Our full hom-age to de - mand.
O Come, All Ye Faithful — 178
Latin hymn, 18th century
Trans. by Frederick Oakeley
Wade's Cantus Diversi
1. O come, all ye faith - ful, joy - ful and tri - um - phant; Come ye, O come ye to Beth - le - hem; Come and be - hold Him, born the King of an - gels:
2. Sing, choirs of an - gels, sing in ex - ul - ta - tion; Sing, all ye bright hosts of heav'n a - bove; Glo - ry to God, all glo - ry in the high - est:
3. Yea, Lord, we greet Thee, born this hap-py morn - ing; Je - sus, to Thee be all glo - ry giv'n; Word of the Fa - ther, now in flesh ap - pear - ing:
REFRAIN
O come, let us a - dore Him, O come, let us a - dore Him, O come, let us a - dore Him, Christ, the Lord.
Tune: ADESTE FIDELES
CHRIST: HIS BIRTH

179 — Angels We Have Heard on High
French melody
Arr. by John W. Peterson
French carol
1. An - gels we have heard on high, Sweet - ly sing - ing o'er the plains,
2. Shep-herds, why this ju - bi - lee? Why your joy - ous strains pro - long?
3. Come to Beth - le - hem and see Him whose birth the an - gels sing;
4. See Him in a man - ger laid— Je - sus, Lord of heav'n and earth;
And the moun-tains, in re - ply, Ech - o - ing their joy - ous strains.
What the glad - some ti - dings be Which in - spire your heav'n - ly song?
Come a - dore, on bend - ed knee, Christ the Lord, the new - born King.
Ma - ry, Jo - seph, lend your aid, With us sing our Sav - ior's birth.
CHORUS
Glo - - - - - - - - - - - ri - a
in ex - cel - sis De - o! Glo - - - - -
- - - - - - ri - a in ex - cel - sis De - o!

Tune: GLORIA

CHRIST: HIS BIRTH

What Child Is This? — 180

WILLIAM C. DIX

English melody

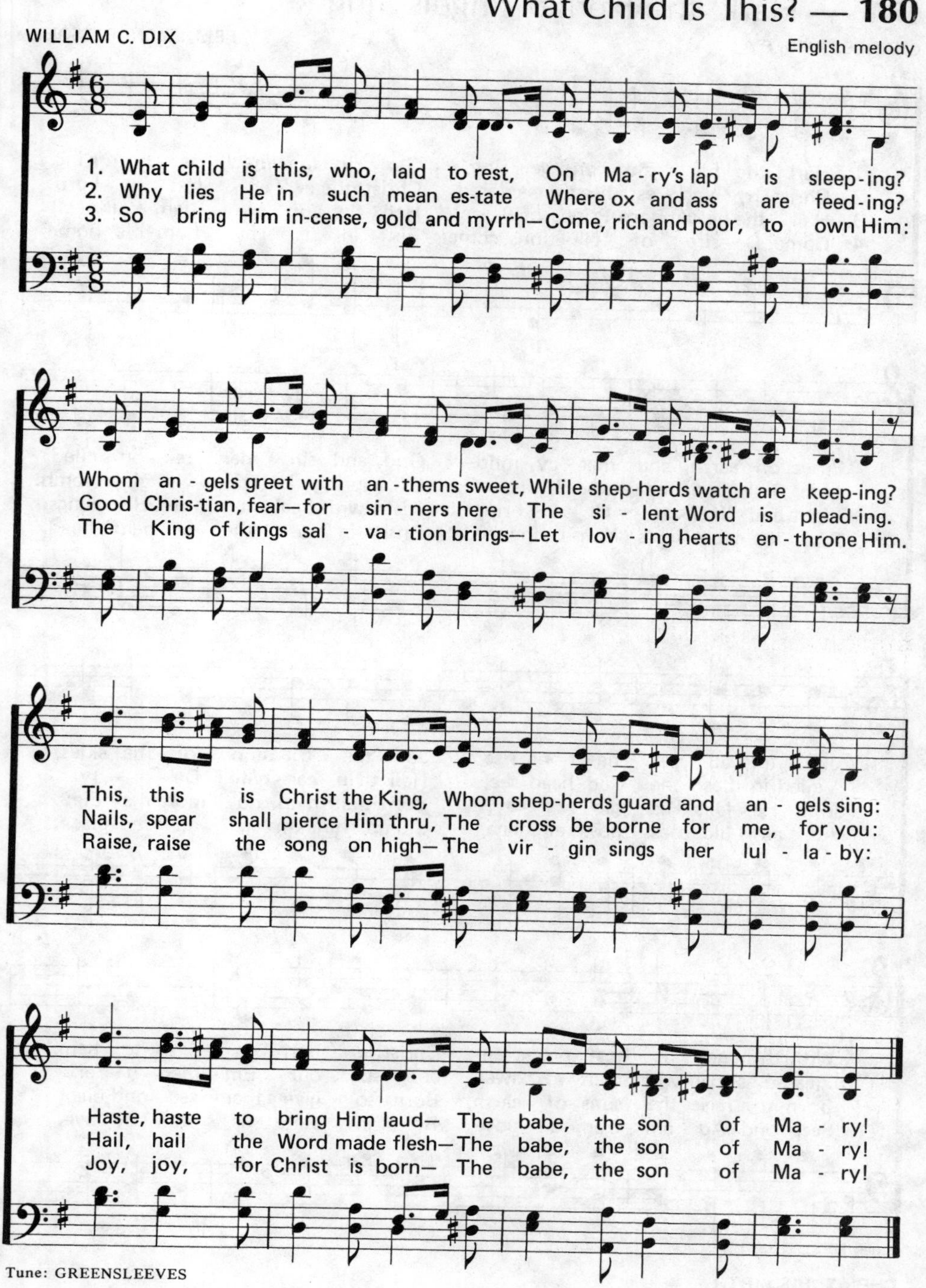
1. What child is this, who, laid to rest, On Ma-ry's lap is sleep-ing?
2. Why lies He in such mean es-tate Where ox and ass are feed-ing?
3. So bring Him in-cense, gold and myrrh—Come, rich and poor, to own Him:
Whom an-gels greet with an-thems sweet, While shep-herds watch are keep-ing?
Good Chris-tian, fear—for sin-ners here The si-lent Word is plead-ing.
The King of kings sal-va-tion brings—Let lov-ing hearts en-throne Him.
This, this is Christ the King, Whom shep-herds guard and an-gels sing:
Nails, spear shall pierce Him thru, The cross be borne for me, for you:
Raise, raise the song on high—The vir-gin sings her lul-la-by:
Haste, haste to bring Him laud—The babe, the son of Ma-ry!
Hail, hail the Word made flesh—The babe, the son of Ma-ry!
Joy, joy, for Christ is born—The babe, the son of Ma-ry!

Tune: GREENSLEEVES

181 — Hark! the Herald Angels Sing
CHARLES WESLEY
FELIX MENDELSSOHN
1. Hark! the her - ald an - gels sing, "Glo - ry to the new-born King;
2. Christ, by high - est heav'n a - dored, Christ, the ev - er - last - ing Lord:
3. Hail the heav'n-born Prince of Peace! Hail the Sun of Right-eous-ness!
4. Come, De - sire of Na - tions, come! Fix in us Thy hum - ble home;
Peace on earth, and mer - cy mild— God and sin - ners rec - on - ciled!"
Late in time be - hold Him come, Off - spring of a vir - gin's womb.
Light and life to all He brings, Ris'n with heal - ing in His wings.
Rise, the wom - an's con - q'ring seed, Bruise in us the ser - pent's head.
Joy - ful, all ye na - tions, rise, Join the tri - umph of the skies;
Veiled in flesh the God - head see, Hail th'in - car - nate De - i - ty!
Mild He lays His glo - ry by, Born that man no more may die;
Ad - am's like - ness now ef - face, Stamp Thine im - age in its place:
With th'an-gel - ic hosts pro - claim, "Christ is born in Beth - le - hem."
Pleased as man with men to dwell, Je - sus, our Em - man - u - el.
Born to raise the sons of earth, Born to give them sec - ond birth.
Sec - ond Ad - am from a - bove, Re - in - state us in Thy love.

Tune: MENDELSSOHN

CHRIST: HIS BIRTH

Hark! the her - ald an - gels sing, "Glo - ry - to the new-born King!"

Angels, from the Realms of Glory — 182

JAMES MONTGOMERY

HENRY SMART

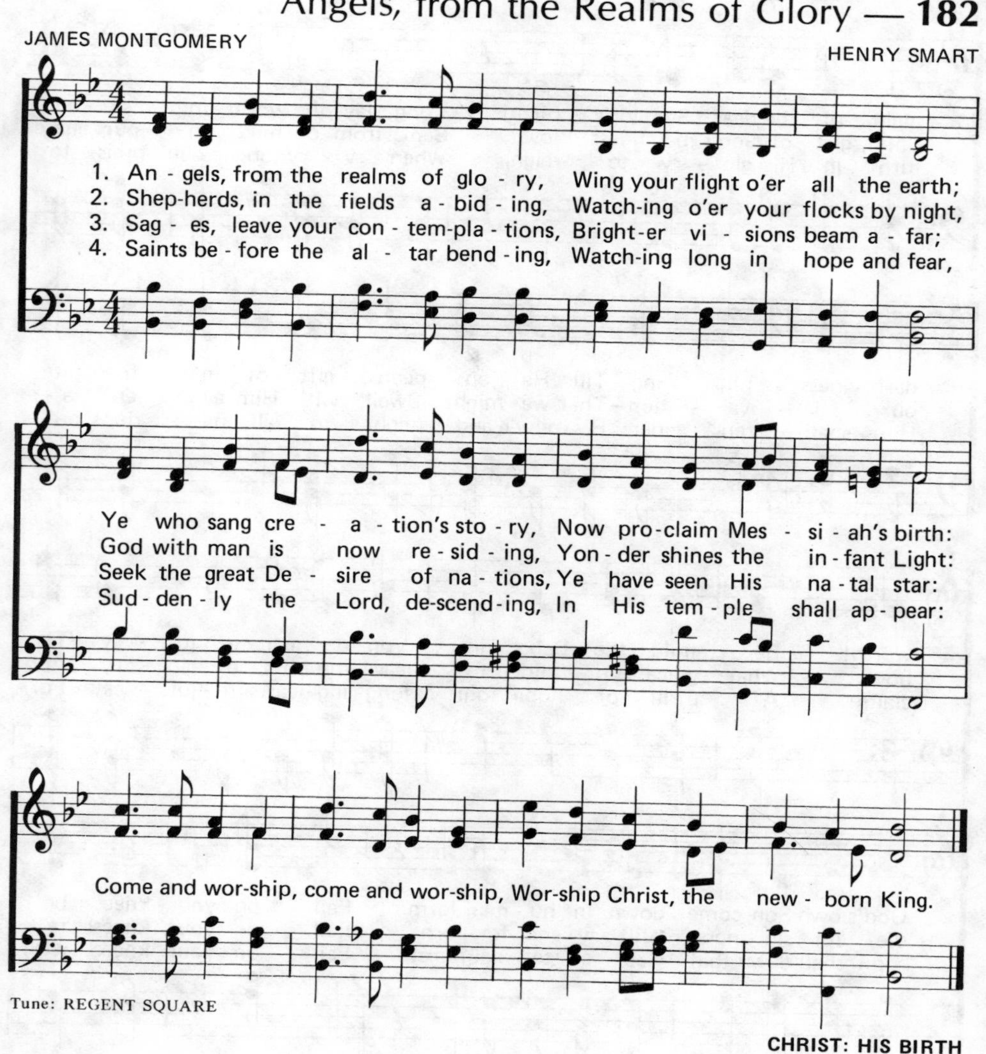
1. An - gels, from the realms of glo - ry, Wing your flight o'er all the earth;
2. Shep-herds, in the fields a - bid - ing, Watch-ing o'er your flocks by night,
3. Sag - es, leave your con - tem-pla - tions, Bright-er vi - sions beam a - far;
4. Saints be - fore the al - tar bend - ing, Watch-ing long in hope and fear,
Ye who sang cre - a - tion's sto - ry, Now pro-claim Mes - si - ah's birth:
God with man is now re - sid - ing, Yon - der shines the in - fant Light:
Seek the great De - sire of na - tions, Ye have seen His na - tal star:
Sud - den - ly the Lord, de-scend - ing, In His tem - ple shall ap - pear:
Come and wor-ship, come and wor-ship, Wor-ship Christ, the new - born King.

Tune: REGENT SQUARE

183 — O Holy Night!
JOHN S. DWIGHT
Revised by Avis B. Christiansen
ADOLPHE ADAM
Arr. by Eldon Burkwall
1. O ho - ly night! the stars are bright - ly shin - ing— It is the
2. With hum-ble hearts we bow in ad - o - ra - tion Be - fore this
3. O day of joy, when in e - ter - nal splen - dor He shall re -
night of the dear Sav - ior's birth! Long lay the world in sin and
Child, gift of God's match-less love, Sent from on high to pur - chase
turn in His glo - ry to reign, When ev - 'ry tongue due praise to
dark - ness pin - ing— Till He ap - peared, gift of in - fi - nite
our sal - va - tion—That we might dwell with Him ev - er a -
Him shall ren - der, His pow'r and might to all na - tions pro -
worth! Be - hold the Babe in yon - der man - ger low - ly— 'Tis
bove. What grace un - told— to leave the bliss of glo - ry And
claim! A thrill of hope our long - ing hearts re - joic - es, For
God's own Son come down in hu - man form: Fall on your knees be -
die for sin - ners guilt - y and for - lorn: Fall on your knees! re -
soon shall dawn that glad e - ter - nal morn: Fall on your knees! with
CHRIST: HIS BIRTH
© Singspiration 1975, 1979. All rights reserved.

fore the Lord most ho - ly!
peat the won-drous sto - ry! O night di - vine— O night
joy lift up your voic - es!
when Christ was born! O night di - vine— O night, O night di - vine!
JOSEPH MOHR
Trans. by John F. Young
Silent Night! Holy Night! — 184
FRANZ GRÜBER
1. Si - lent night! ho - ly night! All is calm, all is bright
2. Si - lent night! ho - ly night! Shep-herds quake at the sight;
3. Si - lent night! ho - ly night! Son of God, love's pure light
Round yon vir - gin moth-er and Child, Ho - ly In-fant, so ten-der and mild—
Glo-ries stream from heav-en a-far, Heav'n-ly hosts sing al-le-lu-ia!
Ra-diant beams from Thy ho-ly face With the dawn of re-deem - ing grace—
Sleep in heav-en-ly peace, Sleep in heav-en-ly peace.
Christ the Sav-ior is born! Christ the Sav-ior is born!
Je - sus, Lord, at Thy birth, Je - sus, Lord, at Thy birth.
Tune: STILLE NACHT
CHRIST: HIS BIRTH

185 — When Lights Are Lit on Christmas Eve
*NORMAN JOHNSON
PEDER KNUDSEN
1. When lights are lit on Christ-mas Eve And chil - dren laugh and sing,
2. When can - dles glow on Christ-mas Eve And snow falls glis - t'ning white,
3. When car - ols ring on Christ-mas Eve And bells in stee - ples chime,
4. When gifts are brought on Christ-mas Eve And laid a - round the tree,
I seem to hear a Ba - by's cry And an - gels ech - o - ing.
I seem to see the Christ-mas star That filled the world with light.
I seem to feel the won-drous joy Of that first Christ - mas - time.
I seem to know the pres - ence of God's gift of love to me.
Tune: CHRISTMAS EVE
*Freely derived from the Norwegian of Marie Wexelsen.
© Singspiration 1968. All rights reserved.
186 — Away in a Manger
1, 2 - Source unknown
3 - JOHN THOMAS McFARLAND
JAMES R. MURRAY
Arr. by Frank Anderson
1. A - way in a man-ger, no crib for a bed, The lit - tle Lord
2. The cat - tle are low - ing, the Ba - by a - wakes, But lit - tle Lord
3. Be near me, Lord Je - sus! I ask Thee to stay Close by me for -
Je - sus laid down His sweet head; The stars in the sky looked
Je - sus, no cry - ing He makes; I love Thee, Lord Je - sus! look
ev - er, and love me, I pray; Bless all the dear chil - dren in

Tune: AWAY IN A MANGER

CHRIST: HIS BIRTH

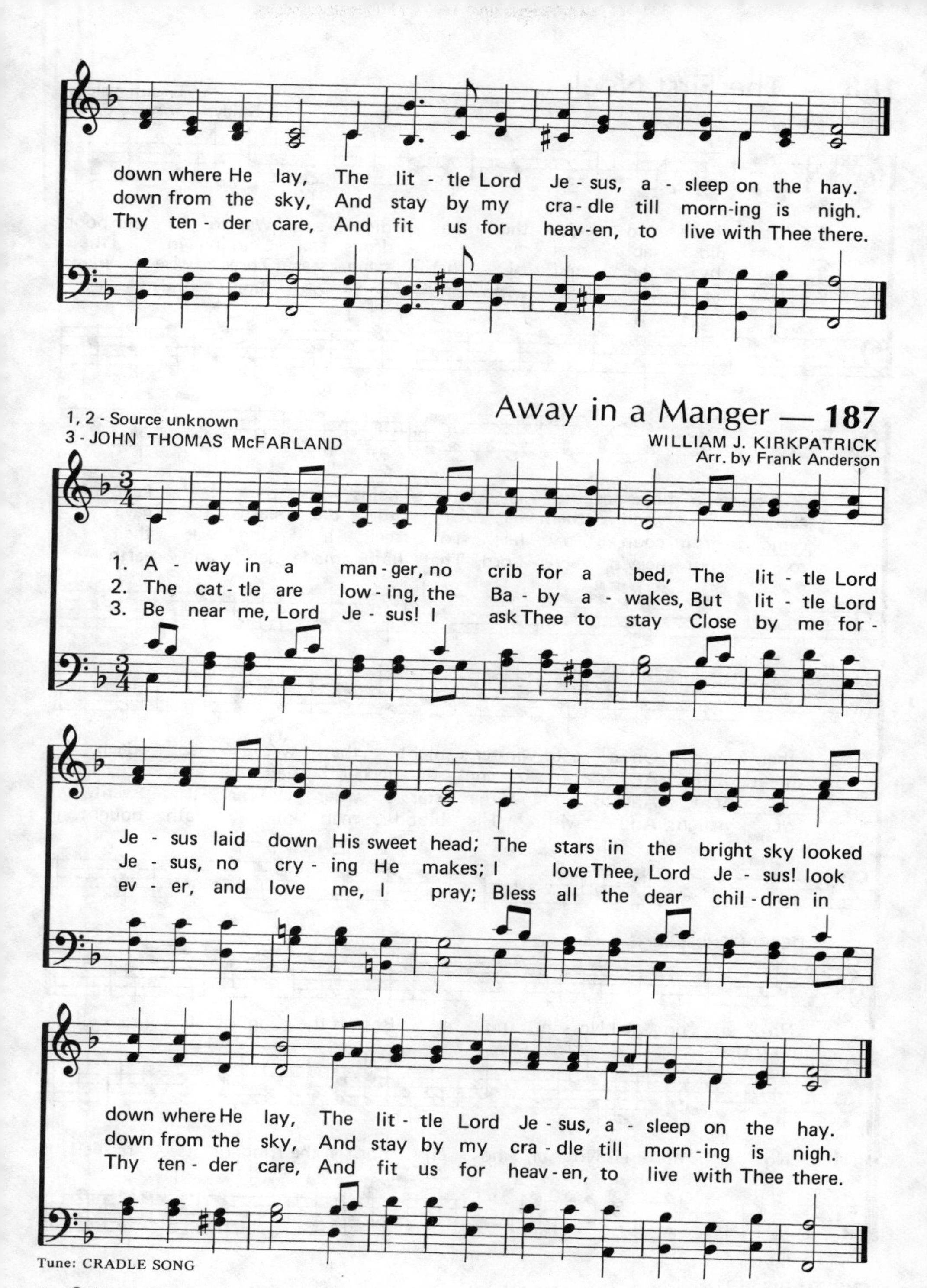
down where He lay, The lit - tle Lord Je - sus, a - sleep on the hay.
down from the sky, And stay by my cra - dle till morn-ing is nigh.
Thy ten - der care, And fit us for heav-en, to live with Thee there.
Away in a Manger — 187
1, 2 - Source unknown
3 - JOHN THOMAS McFARLAND
WILLIAM J. KIRKPATRICK
Arr. by Frank Anderson
1. A - way in a man - ger, no crib for a bed, The lit - tle Lord
2. The cat - tle are low - ing, the Ba - by a - wakes, But lit - tle Lord
3. Be near me, Lord Je - sus! I ask Thee to stay Close by me for -
Je - sus laid down His sweet head; The stars in the bright sky looked
Je - sus, no cry - ing He makes; I love Thee, Lord Je - sus! look
ev - er, and love me, I pray; Bless all the dear chil - dren in
down where He lay, The lit - tle Lord Je - sus, a - sleep on the hay.
down from the sky, And stay by my cra - dle till morn - ing is nigh.
Thy ten - der care, And fit us for heav - en, to live with Thee there.
Tune: CRADLE SONG

188 — The First Noel
English melody
Sandys' Christmas Carols
English carol
1. The first no - el the an - gel did say Was to cer - tain poor shep-herds in fields as they lay— In fields where they lay keep-ing their sheep, On a cold win-ter's night that was so deep.
2. Then did ap - pear a won - drous star Shin-ing in the east, be - yond them far; Un - to the earth it gave great light, And so it con - tin - ued both day and night.
3. And by the light of that same star, Three wise men came from coun - try far; To seek a king was their in - tent, And to fol - low the star wher - ev - er it went.
6. Now let us all with one ac - cord Sing prais - es to our heav'n - ly Lord, That hath made heav'n and earth of naught, And with His blood man - kind hath bought.
DESCANT (Optional for 1,4,6)
No - el, no - el! No - el, no - el! Born is the King of Is - ra - el!
REFRAIN
No - el, no - el! No - el, no - el! Born is the King of Is - ra - el!

Optional stanzas:

4. This star drew nigh to the northwest,
O'er Bethlehem it took its rest;
And there it did both stop and stay
Right over the place where Jesus lay.

Noel, noel! Noel, noel!
Born is the King of Israel!

5. Then entered in those wise men three,
Full rev'rently upon their knee,
And offered there, in His presence,
Their gold and myrrh and frankincense.

Noel, noel! Noel, noel!
Born is the King of Israel!

While Shepherds Watched Their Flocks — 189

NAHUM TATE

Arr. from GEORGE F. HANDEL
in Weyman's *Melodia Sacra*

1. While shep - herds watched their flocks by night, All seat - ed on the ground, The an - gel of the Lord came down And glo - ry shone a - round, And glo - ry shone a - round.
2. "Fear not!" said he, for might - y dread Had seized their trou - bled mind; "Glad ti - dings of great joy I bring To you and all man - kind, To you and all man - kind.
3. "To you in Da - vid's town this day Is born, of Da - vid's line, The Sav - ior who is Christ the Lord, And this shall be the sign— And this shall be the sign:
4. "The heav'n - ly Babe you there shall find To hu - man view dis - played, All mean - ly wrapt in swath - ing - bands And in a man - ger laid, And in a man - ger laid."
5. "All glo - ry be to God on high, And to the earth be peace: Good will hence - forth from heav'n to men Be - gin and nev - er cease! Be - gin and nev - er cease!"

Tune: CHRISTMAS

CHRIST: HIS BIRTH

190 — Ring the Bells

HARRY BOLLBACK

HARRY BOLLBACK
Ring the bells, ring the bells, Let the whole world know Christ was born in
Beth - le - hem Man - y years a - go: Born to die that man might live,
Came to earth new life to give, Born of Ma - ry, born so low,
Man - y years a - go. God the Fa - ther gave His Son, Gave His own be -
lov - ed One To this wick - ed, sin - ful earth, To bring man - kind His

love, new birth: Ring the bells, ring the bells, Let the whole world know
Christ the Sav - ior lives to - day As He did so long a - go!
While by Our Sheep — 191
German carol
Trans. by Theodore Baker—alt.
17th century carol
Trier Gesangbuch
1. While by our sheep we watched at night, Glad tid-ings bro't an an - gel bright:
2. There shall be born, so he did say, In Beth - le - hem a Child to - day:
3. There shall the Child lie in a stall, This Child who shall re - deem us all:
4. This gift of God we'll cher - ish well— Je - sus, our Lord Em - man - u - el:
How great our joy! (Great our joy!) Joy, joy, joy! (Joy, joy, joy!)
Praise we the Lord in heav'n on high! (Praise we the Lord in heav'n on high!)
f
p (echo)
CHRIST: HIS BIRTH

192 — O Little Town of Bethlehem

PHILLIPS BROOKS

LEWIS H. REDNER

1. O lit - tle town of Beth - le - hem, How still we see thee lie!
2. For Christ is born of Ma - ry— And gath - ered all a - bove,
3. How si - lent - ly, how si - lent - ly The won - drous gift is giv'n!
4. O ho - ly Child of Beth - le - hem, De - scend to us, we pray;
A - bove thy deep and dream - less sleep The si - lent stars go by.
While mor - tals sleep, the an - gels keep Their watch of won - d'ring love.
So God im - parts to hu - man hearts The bless - ings of His heav'n.
Cast out our sin and en - ter in— Be born in us to - day.
Yet in thy dark streets shin - eth The ev - er - last - ing Light—
O morn - ing stars, to - geth - er Pro - claim the ho - ly birth,
No ear may hear His com - ing, But, in this world of sin,
We hear the Christ - mas an - gels The great glad ti - dings tell;
The hopes and fears of all the years Are met in thee to - night.
And prais - es sing to God the King, And peace to men on earth.
Where meek souls will re - ceive Him still The dear Christ en - ters in.
O come to us, a - bide with us, Our Lord Em - man - u - el!

Tune: ST. LOUIS

CHRIST: HIS BIRTH

It Came upon the Midnight Clear — 193

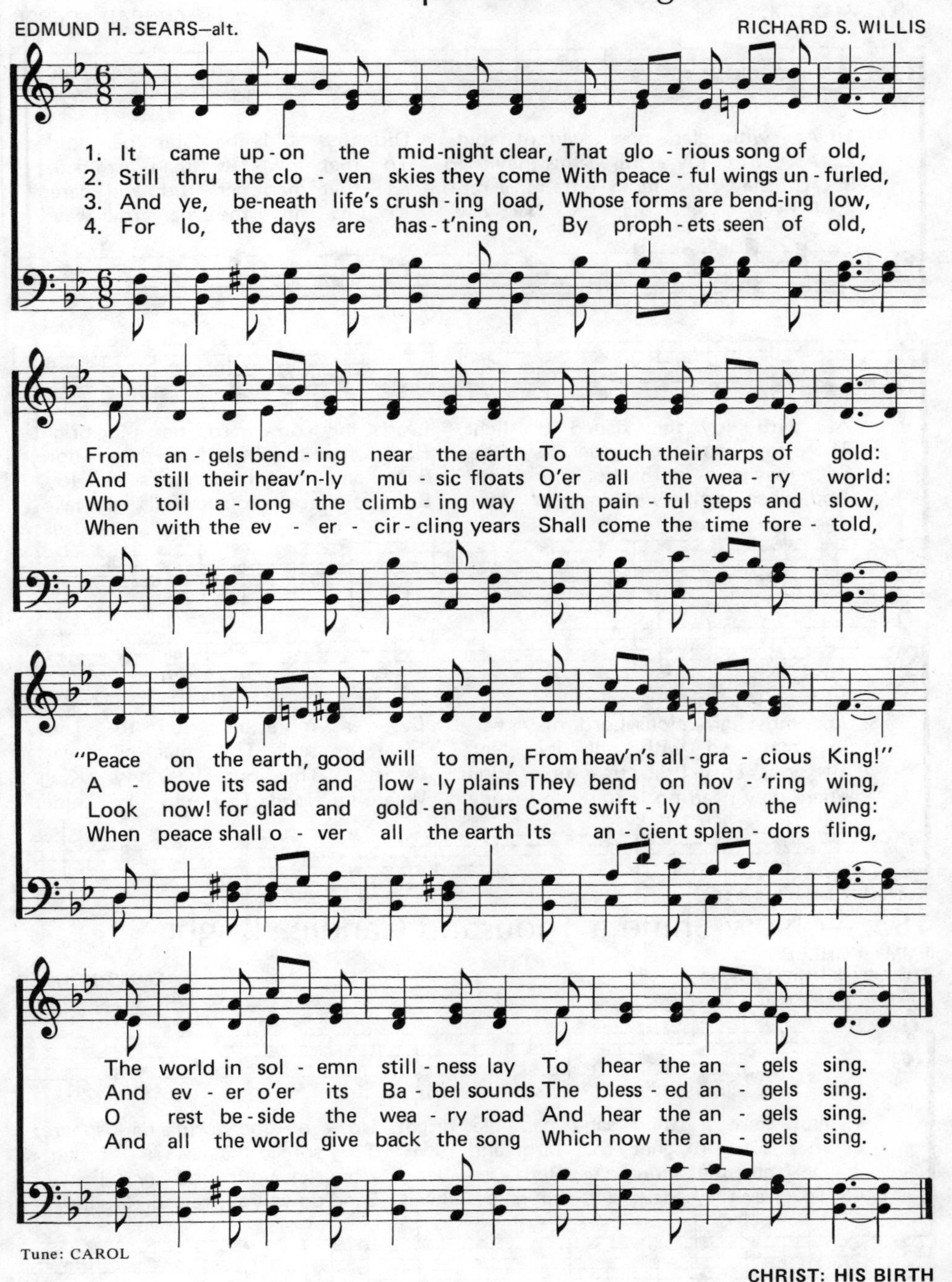
EDMUND H. SEARS—alt.
RICHARD S. WILLIS
1. It came up-on the mid-night clear, That glo - rious song of old,
2. Still thru the clo - ven skies they come With peace - ful wings un - furled,
3. And ye, be-neath life's crush - ing load, Whose forms are bend-ing low,
4. For lo, the days are has - t'ning on, By proph - ets seen of old,
From an - gels bend - ing near the earth To touch their harps of gold:
And still their heav'n-ly mu - sic floats O'er all the wea - ry world:
Who toil a - long the climb - ing way With pain - ful steps and slow,
When with the ev - er - cir - cling years Shall come the time fore - told,
"Peace on the earth, good will to men, From heav'n's all - gra - cious King!"
A - bove its sad and low - ly plains They bend on hov - 'ring wing,
Look now! for glad and gold - en hours Come swift - ly on the wing:
When peace shall o - ver all the earth Its an - cient splen - dors fling,
The world in sol - emn still - ness lay To hear the an - gels sing.
And ev - er o'er its Ba - bel sounds The bless - ed an - gels sing.
O rest be - side the wea - ry road And hear the an - gels sing.
And all the world give back the song Which now the an - gels sing.
Tune: CAROL

194 — As with Gladness Men of Old
WILLIAM C. DIX
CONRAD KOCHER
1. As with glad-ness men of old Did the guid-ing star be-hold—
2. As with joy-ful steps they sped To that low-ly man-ger-bed,
3. As they of-fered gifts most rare At that man-ger rude and bare,
4. Ho-ly Je-sus, ev-'ry day Keep us in the nar-row way;
As with joy they hailed its light, Lead-ing on-ward, beam-ing bright—
There to bend the knee be-fore Him whom heav'n and earth a-dore,
So may we with ho-ly joy, Pure and free from sin's al-loy,
And, when earth-ly things are past, Bring our ran-somed souls at last
So, most gra-cious Lord, may we Ev-er-more be led to Thee.
So may we with will-ing feet Ev-er seek Thy mer-cy seat.
All our cost-liest treas-ures bring, Christ, to Thee, our heav'n-ly King.
Where they need no star to guide, Where no clouds Thy glo-ry hide.*
Tune: DIX—higher key at 26
195 — Now Shine a Thousand Candles Bright
EMMY KÖHLER
Trans. by J. Irving Erickson
and Karl A. Olsson
EMMY KÖHLER
Arr. by Jon Drevits
1. Now shine a thou-sand can-dles bright Up-on the world's dark sphere;
2. In sub-urb, ghet-to, farm and town They spread the news a-broad
3. O star that shone o'er Beth-le-hem, Now let your kind-ly light
4. To ev-'ry dark and an-guished heart Send down your ray di-vine,
Tune: CHRISTMAS CANDLES
CHRIST: HIS BIRTH
Words copyright © 1973 by Covenant Press. Music arr. © Singspiration 1979. All rights reserved.

The deep blue sky is set a - light As myr - iad flames ap - pear.
That Je - sus Christ is born to - night, Our Sav - ior and our God.
With tran-quil hope and glo - ry shine In ev - 'ry home to - night.
And may the light of God's own love Like Christ-mas can - dles shine.
I Heard the Bells on Christmas Day — 196
HENRY W. LONGFELLOW
J. BAPTISTE CALKIN
1. I heard the bells on Christ - mas day Their old
2. I thought how, as the day had come, The bel -
3. And in de - spair I bowed my head: "There is
4. Yet pealed the bells more loud and deep: "God is
5. Then ring - ing, sing - ing on its way, The world
fa - mil - iar car - ols play, And wild and sweet the
fries of all Chris - ten - dom Had rolled a - long th'un -
no peace on earth," I said, "For hate is strong, and
not dead, nor doth He sleep; The wrong shall fail, the
re - volved from night to day— A voice, a chime, a
words re - peat Of peace on earth, good - will to men.
bro - ken song Of peace on earth, good - will to men.
mocks the song Of peace on earth, good - will to men."
right pre - vail, With peace on earth, good - will to men."
chant sub - lime Of peace on earth, good - will to men!
Tune: WALTHAM—lower key at 174
CHRIST: HIS BIRTH

197 — We Three Kings

JOHN H. HOPKINS, Jr. JOHN H. HOPKINS, Jr.

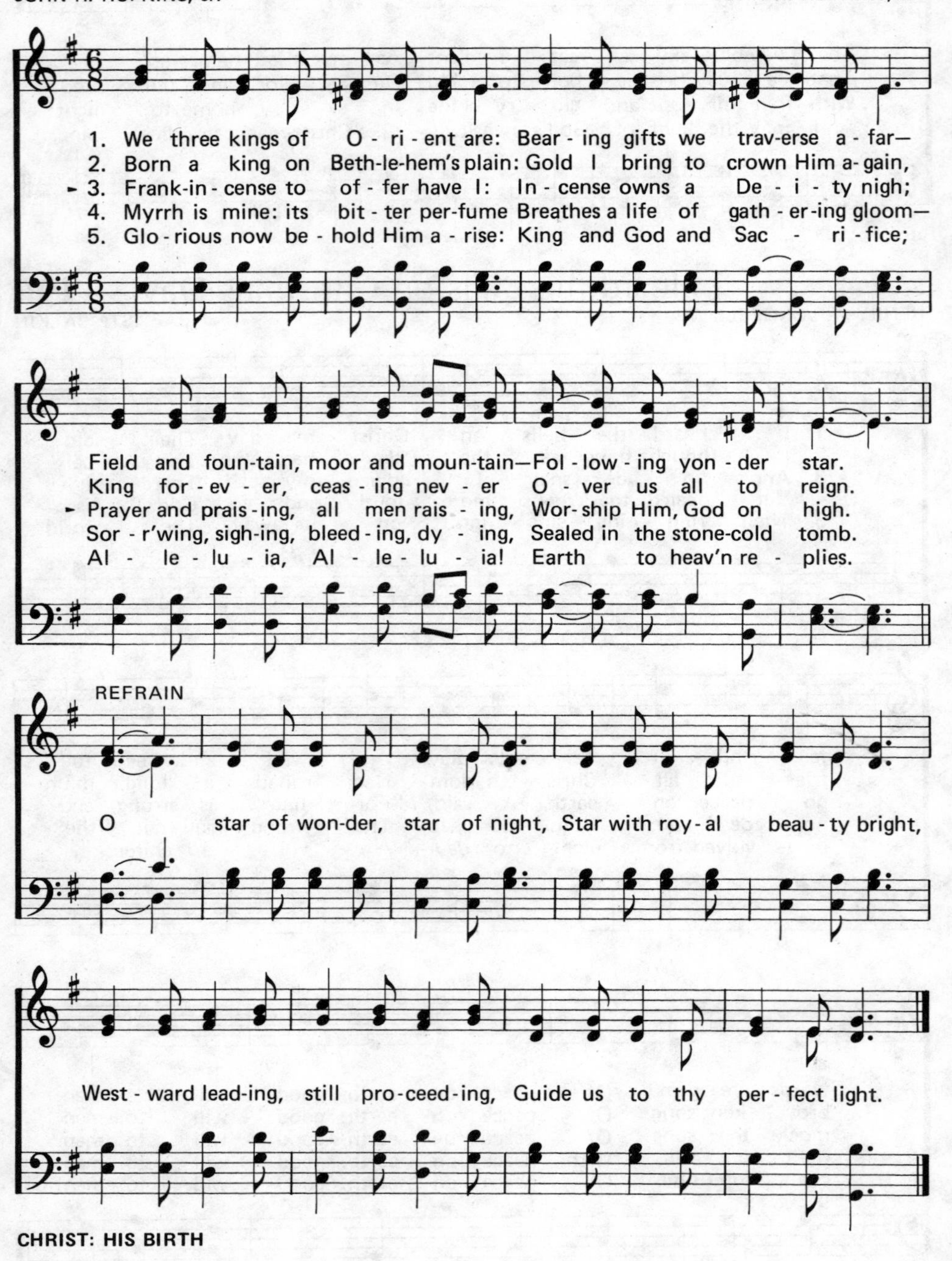

1. We three kings of Orient are: Bearing gifts we traverse afar—
2. Born a king on Bethlehem's plain: Gold I bring to crown Him again,
3. Frankincense to offer have I: Incense owns a Deity nigh;
4. Myrrh is mine: its bitter perfume Breathes a life of gathering gloom—
5. Glorious now behold Him arise: King and God and Sacrifice;
Field and fountain, moor and mountain—Following yonder star.
King forever, ceasing never Over us all to reign.
Prayer and praising, all men raising, Worship Him, God on high.
Sorr'wing, sighing, bleeding, dying, Sealed in the stone-cold tomb.
Alleluia, Alleluia! Earth to heav'n replies.
REFRAIN
O star of wonder, star of night, Star with royal beauty bright,
Westward leading, still proceeding, Guide us to thy perfect light.

CHRIST: HIS BIRTH

Good Christian Men, Rejoice — 198
Latin carol, 14th century
Trans. by John M. Neale
German melody, 14th century
Har. by John Stainer
1. Good Chris-tian men, re - joice With heart and soul and voice;
2. Good Chris-tian men, re - joice With heart and soul and voice;
3. Good Chris-tian men, re - joice With heart and soul and voice;
Give ye heed to what we say: News! news! Je - sus Christ is born to - day!
Now ye hear of end - less bliss: Joy! joy! Je - sus Christ was born for this!
Now ye need not fear the grave: Peace! peace! Je - sus Christ was born to save!
Ox and ass be - fore Him bow, And He is in the man - ger now:
He has o - pened heav-en's door, And man is bless - ed ev - er - more:
Calls you one and calls you all To gain His ev - er - last - ing hall:
Christ is born to - day! Christ is born to - day!
Christ was born for this! Christ was born for this!
Christ was born to save! Christ was born to save!
Tune: IN DULCI JUBILO

199 — Love Was When
JOHN E. WALVOORD
DON WYRTZEN
1. Love was when God be - came a man Locked in time and space with-out rank or place;
Love was God born of Jew - ish kin, Just a car - pen - ter with some fish - er-men.
2. Love was when God be - came a man Down where I could see love that reached to me;
Love was God dy - ing for my sin— And so trapped was I my whole world caved in.
1
2
Love was when Je - sus walked in his - to - ry— Lov - ing - ly He brought a new life that's free;
Love was when Je - sus rose to walk with me— Lov - ing - ly He brought a new life that's free;
Love was God nailed to bleed and die To reach and love one such as I.
Love was God— on - ly He would try To reach and love one such as I.
CHRIST: HIS EARTHLY MINISTRY
© Singspiration 1970, arr. 1974. All rights reserved.

The Healer — 200
LOIS IRWIN
Chorus—Isaiah 53:5
LOIS IRWIN
1. On the cross cru - ci - fied, in great sor - row He died— The giv - er of life was He; Yet my Lord was de - spised and re - ject - ed of men, This Je - sus of Cal - va - ry.
2. Came the lep - er to Christ, say - ing "Sure - ly I know That Thou, Lord, canst make me whole!" When his great faith was seen, Je - sus said, "Yes, I will," And touched him and made him clean.
3. He has healed my sick soul, made me ev - 'ry whit whole, And He'll do the same for you; He's the same yes - ter - day and to - day and for aye, This heal - er of men to - day.
CHORUS
He was wound-ed for our trans - gres-sions, He was bruised for our in - iq - ui - ties; Sure-ly He bore our sor-rows, And by His stripes we are healed.
Copyright Zondervan Fiesta 1955, Renewal 1983, arr. 1975. All rights reserved.
CHRIST: HIS EARTHLY MINISTRY

201 — Down from His Glory

EDUARDO di CAPUA
Arr. by Norman Johnson

WILLIAM E. BOOTH-CLIBBORN

1. Down from His glo - ry— ev - er - liv - ing sto - ry—
2. What con - de - scen - sion, bring-ing us re - demp - tion,
3. With - out re - luc - tance— flesh and blood His sub - stance—

My God and Sav - ior came, and Je - sus was His name;
That in the dead of night, not one faint hope in sight,
He took the form of man, re - vealed the hid - den plan;

Born in a man - ger— to His own a stran - ger,
God—gra - cious, ten - der— laid a - side His splen - dor,
O glo - rious mys - t'ry— sac - ri - fice of Cal - v'ry!

A man of sor - rows, tears and ag - o - ny!
Stoop - ing to woo, to win, to save my soul!
And now I know He is the great "I AM"!

CHORUS

O how I love Him! how I a - dore Him! My breath, my

sun - shine, my all in all! The great Cre - a - tor be -
came my Sav - ior, And all God's full - ness dwell-eth in Him!
Lonesome Valley — 202
Traditional
St. 3-FRANK ANDERSON
Traditional Spiritual
Arr. by Frank Anderson
1. Je - sus walked this lone - some val - ley, He had to
2. Je - sus went to stand His tri - al, He had to
3. Now in ev - 'ry lone - some val - ley, The trials and
walk it by Him - self; O no - bod - y else could
stand it by Him - self; O no - bod - y else could
sor - rows we must face, O Je - sus Him-self will
walk it for Him— He had to walk it by Him - self.
stand it for Him— He had to stand it by Him - self.
be there with us— To fill the shad - ows with His grace.
3

203 — Tell Me the Story of Jesus

FANNY J. CROSBY | JOHN R. SWENEY

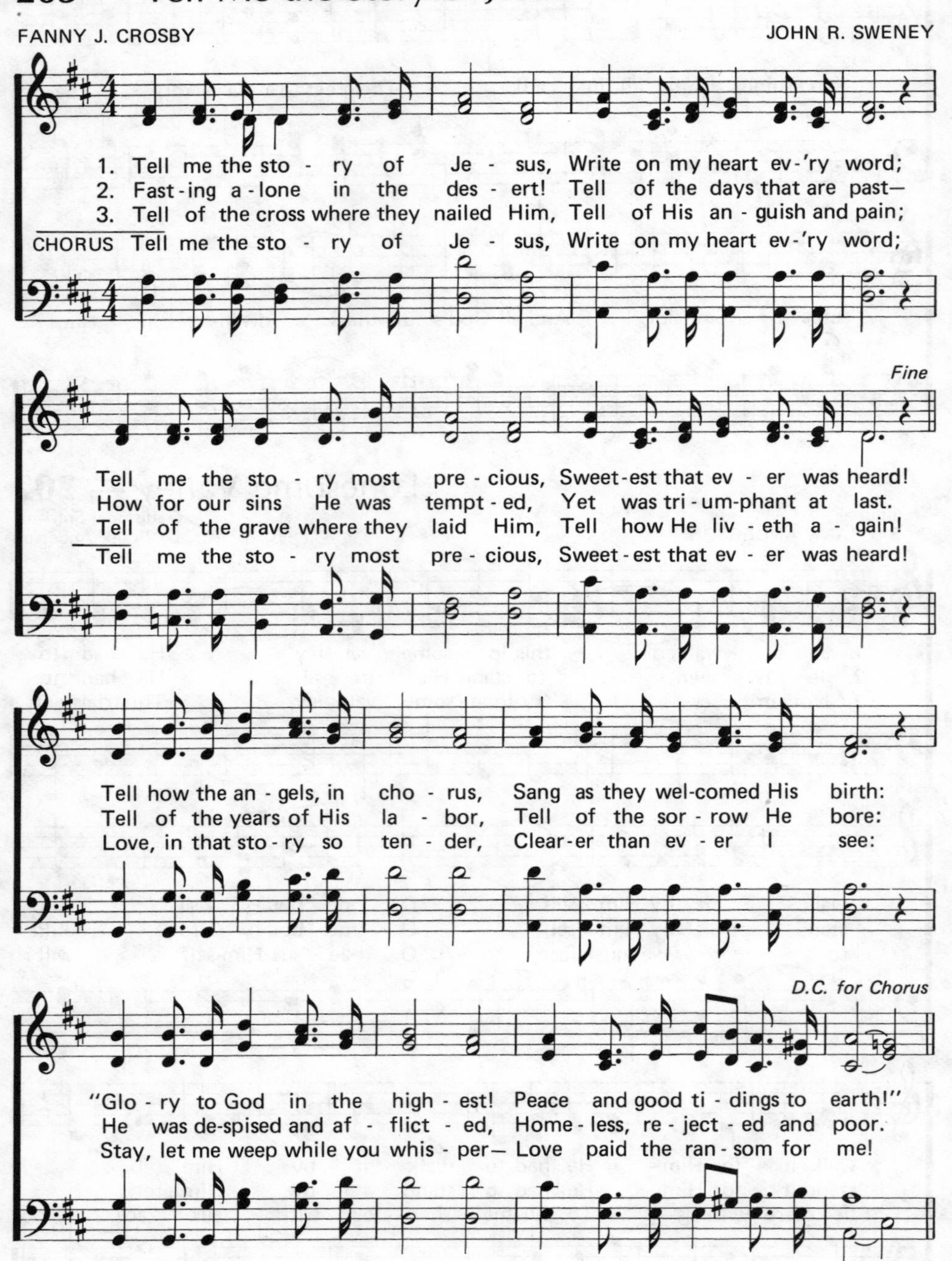
1. Tell me the sto - ry of Je - sus, Write on my heart ev-'ry word;
2. Fast-ing a-lone in the des - ert! Tell of the days that are past—
3. Tell of the cross where they nailed Him, Tell of His an - guish and pain;
CHORUS Tell me the sto - ry of Je - sus, Write on my heart ev-'ry word;
Fine
Tell me the sto - ry most pre - cious, Sweet-est that ev - er was heard!
How for our sins He was tempt - ed, Yet was tri - um-phant at last.
Tell of the grave where they laid Him, Tell how He liv - eth a - gain!
Tell me the sto - ry most pre - cious, Sweet-est that ev - er was heard!
Tell how the an - gels, in cho - rus, Sang as they wel-comed His birth:
Tell of the years of His la - bor, Tell of the sor - row He bore:
Love, in that sto - ry so ten - der, Clear-er than ev - er I see:
D.C. for Chorus
"Glo - ry to God in the high - est! Peace and good ti - dings to earth!"
He was de-spised and af - flict - ed, Home-less, re - ject - ed and poor.
Stay, let me weep while you whis - per— Love paid the ran - som for me!

CHRIST: HIS EARTHLY MINISTRY

That Beautiful Name — 204

JEAN PERRY

MABEL JOHNSTON CAMP

1. I know of a name, a beau - ti - ful name, That an - gels bro't
2. The one of that name my Sav - ior be - came, My Sav - ior of
3. I love that blest name, that won - der - ful name, Made high - er than

down to earth; They whis-pered it low, one night long a - go,
Cal - va - ry; My sins nailed Him there, my bur - dens He bare—
all in heav'n; 'Twas whis-pered, I know, in my heart long a - go—

To a maid-en of low - ly birth.
He suf-fered all this for me.
To Je - sus my life I've giv'n.

REFRAIN

That beau - ti - ful name, that beau - ti - ful name From sin has pow'r to free us! That beau-ti-ful name, that won-der-ful name, That match-less name is Je - sus!

205 —Behold the Lamb of God
John 1:29b
NORMAN JOHNSON
Be-hold, be-hold the Lamb of God who takes a - way the sin of the world.
Be - hold,
© Singspiration 1970, arr. 1979. All rights reserved.
206 —O Love How Deep, How Broad, How High
Latin hymn, 15th century
Trans. by Benjamin Webb—alt.
Williams' Supplement to Psalmody
Adapted by Edward Miller
1. O love how deep, how broad, how high! Be - yond man's
2. For us bap - tized, for us He bore His des - ert
3. For us He prayed, for us He taught, For us His
4. For us to wick - ed men be - trayed, Both scourged and
5. For us He rose from death a - gain, For us He
6. To Him whose bound - less love has won Sal - va - tion
gift to proph - e - sy— That God, the Son of God,
fast, and hun - gered sore; For us temp - ta - tions sharp
dai - ly works He wrought—By words and signs and ac -
mocked—with thorns ar - rayed, He bore the shame - ful cross
went on high to reign; For us He sent His Spir -
for us through His Son, To God the Fa - ther glo -
should take Our mor - tal form for mor - tals' sake.
He knew, For us the temp - ter o - ver - threw.
tions, thus Still seek - ing not Him - self, but us.
and death— For us gave up His fi - nal breath.
it here To guide, to strength - en and to cheer.
ry be, Both now and through e - ter - ni - ty.
Tune: ROCKINGHAM OLD
CHRIST: HIS EARTHLY MINISTRY

Traditional
Adapted for *Praise!*

Traditional Spiritual
Arr. for *Praise!*

Sing Refrain twice before first stanza.
1 + Final
A - men, a - men! A - men, a - men, a - men!
SOLO or Section of Congregation
1. See Him in the man - ger, Just a lit - tle ba - by—
2. See Him in the tem - ple, Talk - ing to the el - ders—
3. See Him at the sea - side, Preaching 'bout the King-dom—
men! A - men, a -
Hear the an - gels sing - ing!
Mar - vel at His wis - dom!
Mir - a - cles and won - ders!
After final stanza
D.C.
Sing it o - ver!
men! A - men, a - men, a - men!

4. See Him in the garden,
Bowed in deepest sorrow—
Praying to His Father!

5. See Him there on Calv'ry,
Dying for our sins—
Loving and forgiving!

6. See Him Easter morning,
Risen from the dead—
He will live forever!

7. Now He is our Savior,
And His name is Jesus—
Glory, hallelujah!

208 — All Glory, Laud and Honor
THEODULPH of ORLEANS
Trans. by John M. Neale
MELCHIOR TESCHNER
1. All glo - ry, laud and hon - or To Thee, Re - deem - er, King,
2. The com - pa - ny of an - gels Are prais - ing Thee on high,
3. To Thee, be - fore Thy pas - sion, They sang their hymns of praise;
To whom the lips of chil - dren Made sweet ho - san - nas ring:
And mor - tal men and all things Cre - at - ed make re - ply:
To Thee, now high ex - alt - ed, Our mel - o - dy we raise:
Thou art the King of Is - rael, Thou Da - vid's roy - al Son,
The peo - ple of the He - brews With palms be - fore Thee went;
Thou didst ac - cept their prais - es— Ac - cept the praise we bring,
CHORAL DESCANT (optional)
3. Who in all good de - light - est, Thou good and gra - cious King!*
Who in the Lord's name com - est, The King and bless - ed One!
Our praise and prayer and an - thems Be - fore Thee we pre - sent.
Who in all good de - light - est, Thou good and gra - cious King!*
Tune: ST. THEODULPH
CHRIST: HIS TRIUMPHAL ENTRY

O Zion, Acclaim Your Redeemer — 209

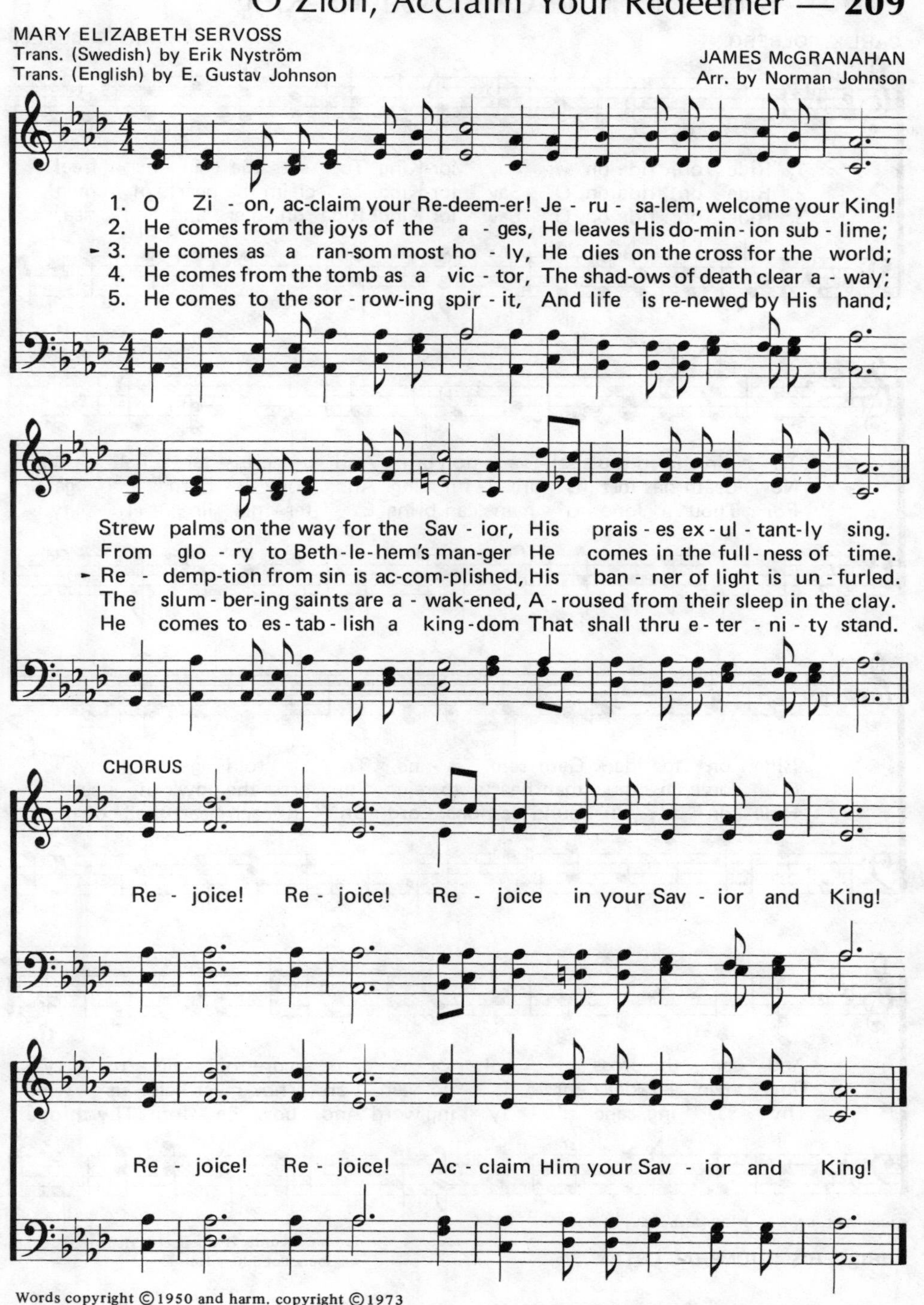
MARY ELIZABETH SERVOSS
Trans. (Swedish) by Erik Nyström
Trans. (English) by E. Gustav Johnson
JAMES McGRANAHAN
Arr. by Norman Johnson
1. O Zi - on, ac-claim your Re-deem-er! Je - ru - sa-lem, welcome your King!
2. He comes from the joys of the a - ges, He leaves His do-min - ion sub - lime;
3. He comes as a ran-som most ho - ly, He dies on the cross for the world;
4. He comes from the tomb as a vic - tor, The shad-ows of death clear a - way;
5. He comes to the sor - row-ing spir - it, And life is re-newed by His hand;
Strew palms on the way for the Sav - ior, His prais - es ex - ul - tant-ly sing.
From glo - ry to Beth-le-hem's man-ger He comes in the full-ness of time.
Re - demp-tion from sin is ac-com-plished, His ban - ner of light is un - furled.
The slum - ber-ing saints are a - wak-ened, A - roused from their sleep in the clay.
He comes to es-tab-lish a king-dom That shall thru e - ter - ni - ty stand.
CHORUS
Re - joice! Re - joice! Re - joice in your Sav - ior and King!
Re - joice! Re - joice! Ac - claim Him your Sav - ior and King!

CHRIST: HIS TRIUMPHAL ENTRY

210 — Ride On, Ride On, O Savior-King

CARL K. SOLBERG HENRY S. CUTLER

1. Ride on, ride on, O Sav - ior-King, To set the sin - ner free!
2. Ride on, ride on, O Sav - ior-King, To claim the hearts of men!
3. Ride on, ride on, O Sav - ior-King! Ride on o'er land and sea,
To sin-cursed souls sal - va - tion bring And peace e - ter - nal - ly!
Now death has lost its dread - ful sting And hope is born a - gain.
For Thou a - lone to man can bring E - ter - nal lib - er - ty.
Ride on to dark Geth - sem - a - ne, To un - told ag - o - ny,
O come, in hu - man hearts to reign—Sup - press the pow'r of sin!
Ride on to sin - bound na - tions, Lord, Un - til each heart shall own
And on the cross of Cal - va - ry Pro - cure our vic - to - ry!
Our own en - deav - or is in vain—Lord, Thou must help us win!
Thy sav - ing, sanc - ti - fy - ing word And bow be - fore Thy throne!*

Tune: ALL SAINTS NEW—higher key at 455

CHRIST: HIS TRIUMPHAL ENTRY

JENNETTE THRELFALL

Gesangbuch der Herzogl

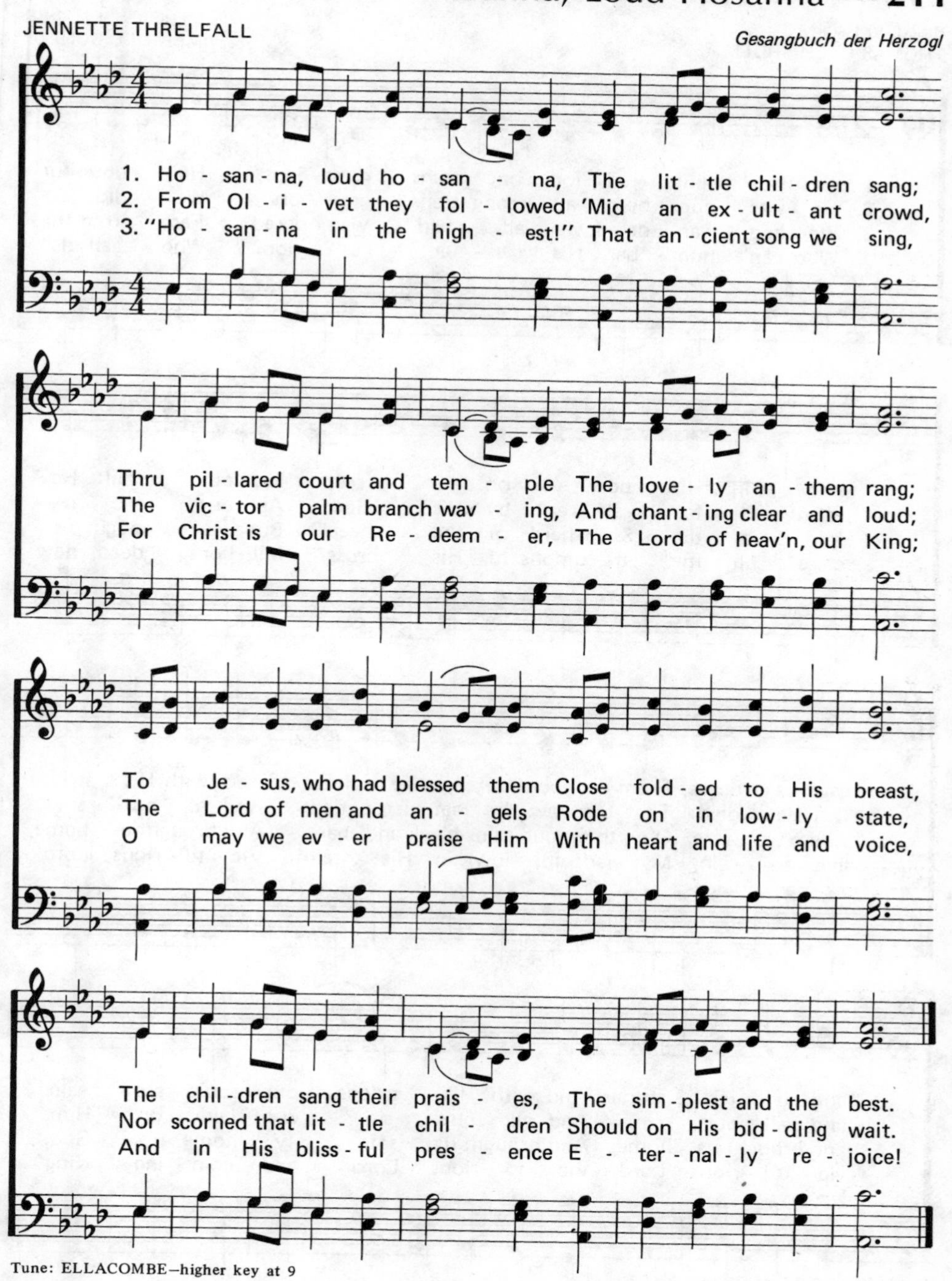
1. Ho - san - na, loud ho - san - na, The lit - tle chil - dren sang;
2. From Ol - i - vet they fol - lowed 'Mid an ex - ult - ant crowd,
3. "Ho - san - na in the high - est!" That an - cient song we sing,
Thru pil - lared court and tem - ple The love - ly an - them rang;
The vic - tor palm branch wav - ing, And chant - ing clear and loud;
For Christ is our Re - deem - er, The Lord of heav'n, our King;
To Je - sus, who had blessed them Close fold - ed to His breast,
The Lord of men and an - gels Rode on in low - ly state,
O may we ev - er praise Him With heart and life and voice,
The chil - dren sang their prais - es, The sim - plest and the best.
Nor scorned that lit - tle chil - dren Should on His bid - ding wait.
And in His bliss - ful pres - ence E - ter - nal - ly re - joice!

Tune: ELLACOMBE—higher key at 9

212 — He Was Wounded for Our Transgressions

Based on Isaiah 53
THOMAS O. CHISHOLM

MERRILL DUNLOP

1. He was wound - ed for our trans - gress - ions, He bore our
2. He was num - bered a - mong trans - gress - ors, We did es -
3. We had wan - dered, we all had wan - dered Far from the
4. Who can num - ber His gen - er - a - tion? Who shall de -
sins in His bod - y on the tree; For our guilt He
teem Him for - sak - en by His God; As our sac - ri -
fold of the Shep - herd of the sheep; But He sought us
clare all the tri - umphs of His cross? Mil - lions, dead, now
gave us peace, From our bon - dage gave re - lease, And with His stripes,
fice He died That the law be sat - is - fied, And all our sin,
where we were, On the moun - tains bleak and bare, And brought us home,
live a - gain, Myr - iads fol - low in His train! Vic - to - rious Lord,
and with His stripes, And with His stripes our souls are healed.
and all our sin, And all our sin was laid on Him.
and brought us home, And brought us safe - ly home to God.
vic - to - rious Lord, Vic - to - rious Lord and com - ing King!

CHRIST: HIS PASSION

O Sacred Head, Now Wounded — 213

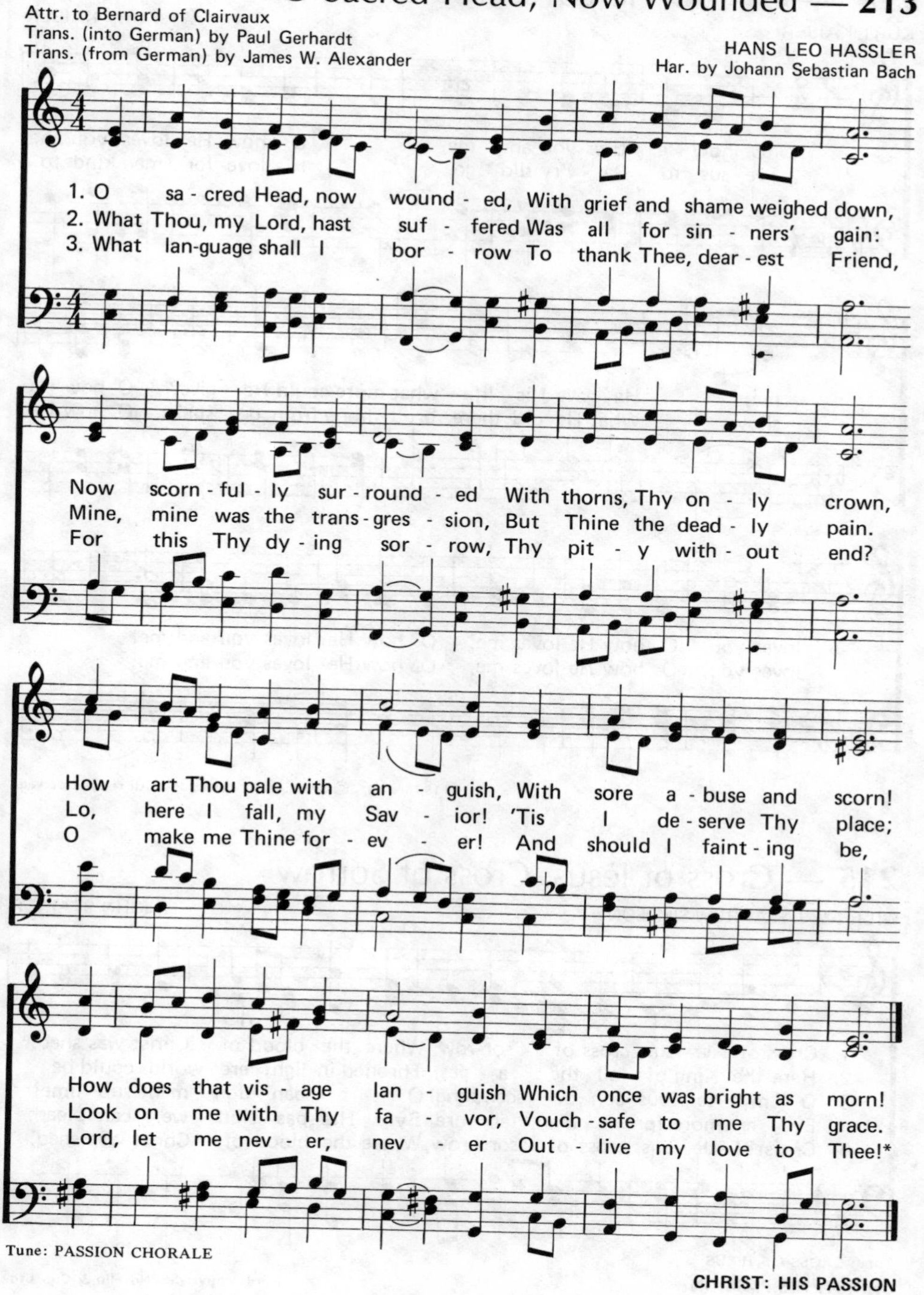
Attr. to Bernard of Clairvaux
Trans. (into German) by Paul Gerhardt
Trans. (from German) by James W. Alexander
HANS LEO HASSLER
Har. by Johann Sebastian Bach
1. O sa - cred Head, now wound - ed, With grief and shame weighed down,
2. What Thou, my Lord, hast suf - fered Was all for sin - ners' gain:
3. What lan-guage shall I bor - row To thank Thee, dear - est Friend,
Now scorn - ful - ly sur - round - ed With thorns, Thy on - ly crown,
Mine, mine was the trans - gres - sion, But Thine the dead - ly pain.
For this Thy dy - ing sor - row, Thy pit - y with - out end?
How art Thou pale with an - guish, With sore a - buse and scorn!
Lo, here I fall, my Sav - ior! 'Tis I de - serve Thy place;
O make me Thine for - ev - er! And should I faint - ing be,
How does that vis - age lan - guish Which once was bright as morn!
Look on me with Thy fa - vor, Vouch - safe to me Thy grace.
Lord, let me nev - er, nev - er Out - live my love to Thee!*

Tune: PASSION CHORALE

214 — O How He Loves You and Me!

KURT KAISER KURT KAISER

1. O how He loves you and me, O how He loves you and me; He gave His life— what more could He give? O how He loves you, O how He loves me, O how He loves you and me!
2. Je-sus to Cal-v'ry did go, His love for man-kind to show; What He did there bro't hope from de-spair: O how He loves you, O how He loves me, O how He loves you and me!

215 — Cross of Jesus, Cross of Sorrow

WILLIAM J. SPARROW-SIMPSON JOHN STAINER

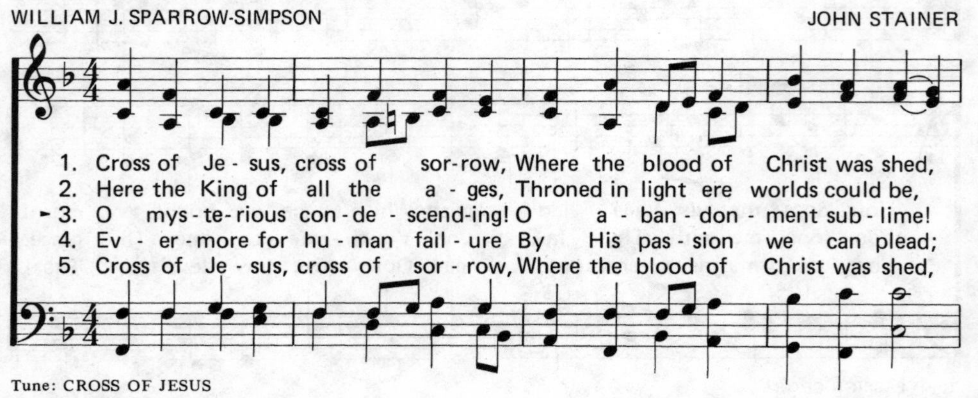
1. Cross of Je-sus, cross of sor-row, Where the blood of Christ was shed,
2. Here the King of all the a-ges, Throned in light ere worlds could be,
3. O mys-te-rious con-de-scend-ing! O a-ban-don-ment sub-lime!
4. Ev-er-more for hu-man fail-ure By His pas-sion we can plead;
5. Cross of Je-sus, cross of sor-row, Where the blood of Christ was shed,

Tune: CROSS OF JESUS

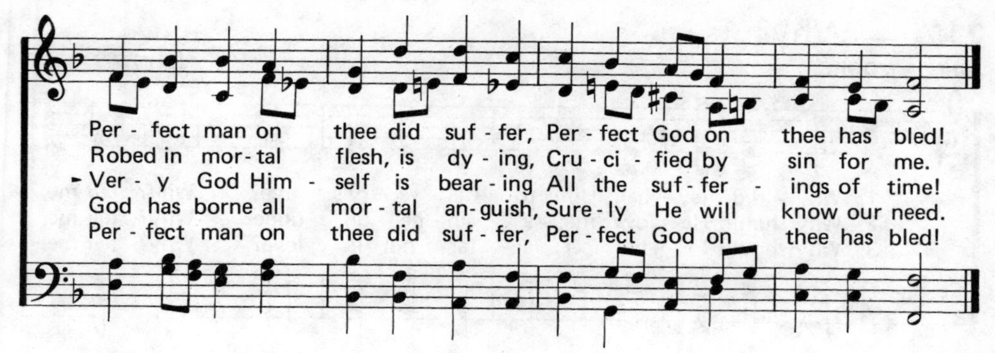

Per - fect man on thee did suf - fer, Per - fect God on thee has bled!
Robed in mor - tal flesh, is dy - ing, Cru - ci - fied by sin for me.
Ver - y God Him - self is bear - ing All the suf - fer - ings of time!
God has borne all mor - tal an - guish, Sure - ly He will know our need.
Per - fect man on thee did suf - fer, Per - fect God on thee has bled!

Go to Dark Gethsemane — 216

JAMES MONTGOMERY

RICHARD REDHEAD

1. Go to dark Geth - sem - a - ne, You that feel the temp - ter's pow'r;
2. Fol - low to the judg - ment hall, View the Lord of life ar - raigned;
3. Cal - v'ry's mourn - ful moun - tain climb; There, a - dor - ing at His feet,
Your Re - deem - er's con - flict see, Watch with Him one bit - ter hour:
O the worm - wood and the gall! O the pangs His soul sus - tained!
Mark the mir - a - cle of time, God's own sac - ri - fice com - plete:
Turn not from His griefs a - way— Learn of Je - sus Christ to pray.
Shun not suf - f'ring, shame or loss— Learn of Him to bear the cross.
"It is fin - ished!" hear Him cry— Learn of Je - sus Christ to die.

Tune: REDHEAD No. 76--higher key at 44

217 — Why?

JOHN M. MOORE JOHN M. MOORE

1. Why did they nail Him to Cal - va - ry's tree? Why? tell me,
2. Why should He love me, a sin - ner un - done? Why? tell me,
3. Why should I lin - ger a - far from His love? Why? tell me,
why was He there? Je - sus the Help - er, the Heal - er, the
why should He care? I do not mer - it the love He has
why should I fear? Some-how I know I should ven-ture and
Friend— Why? tell me, why was He there?
shown— Why? tell me, why should He care?
prove— Why? tell me, why should I fear?
CHORUS
All my in - iq - ui - ties
on Him were laid— He nailed them all to the tree; Je - sus the
debt of my sin ful - ly paid— He paid the ran - som for me.

CHRIST: HIS PASSION

Blessed Redeemer — 218

AVIS B. CHRISTIANSEN

HARRY DIXON LOES

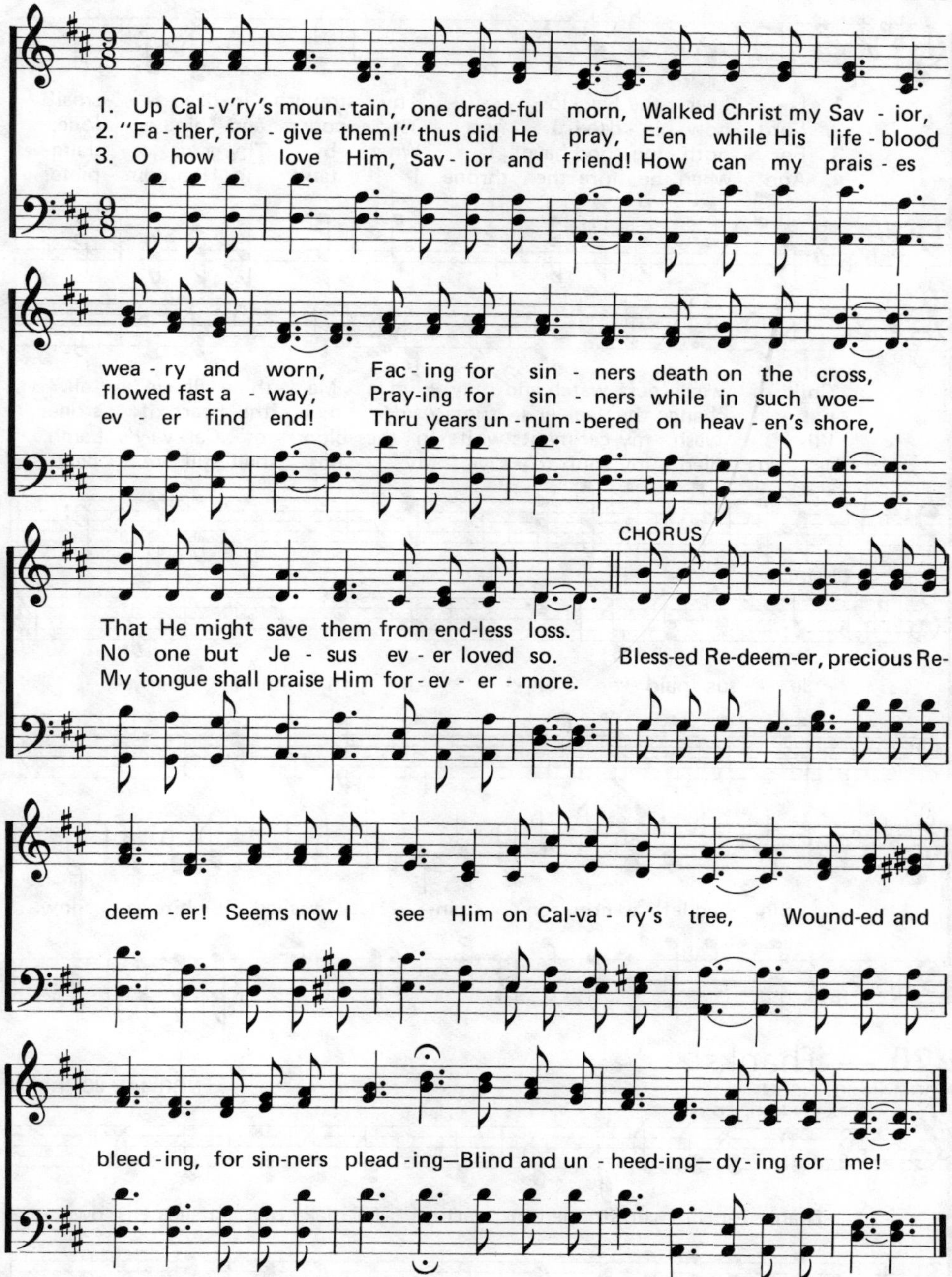

1. Up Cal - v'ry's moun - tain, one dread-ful morn, Walked Christ my Sav - ior, wea - ry and worn, Fac - ing for sin - ners death on the cross, That He might save them from end-less loss.
2. "Fa - ther, for - give them!" thus did He pray, E'en while His life - blood flowed fast a - way, Pray-ing for sin - ners while in such woe— No one but Je - sus ev - er loved so.
3. O how I love Him, Sav - ior and friend! How can my prais - es ev - er find end! Thru years un - num - bered on heav - en's shore, My tongue shall praise Him for - ev - er - more.

CHORUS

Bless-ed Re-deem-er, precious Re- deem - er! Seems now I see Him on Cal-va - ry's tree, Wound-ed and bleed - ing, for sin-ners plead - ing—Blind and un - heed-ing— dy - ing for me!

219 — Jesus Paid It All
ELVINA M. HALL
JOHN T. GRAPE
1. I hear the Sav - ior say, "Thy strength in-deed is small!
2. Lord, now in - deed I find Thy pow'r, and Thine a - lone,
3. For noth - ing good have I Where - by Thy grace to claim—
4. And when be - fore the throne I stand in Him com - plete,
Child of weak - ness, watch and pray, Find in Me thine all in all."
Can change the lep - er's spots And melt the heart of stone.
I'll wash my gar-ments white In the blood of Cal - v'ry's Lamb.
"Je - sus died my soul to save," My lips shall still re - peat.
CHORUS
Je - sus paid it all, All to Him I owe;
Sin had left a crim-son stain— He washed it white as snow.
220 — Thanks
NORMAN JOHNSON
NORMAN JOHNSON
PRAYER RESPONSE
Thanks for Him who stooped to earth To make our needs His own;
CHRIST: HIS PASSION
© Singspiration 1970. All rights reserved.

Thanks for ac - cess thru His blood Un - to our Fa - ther's throne.*
Lead Me to Calvary — 221
JENNIE EVELYN HUSSEY
WILLIAM J. KIRKPATRICK
1. King of my life I crown Thee now— Thine shall the glo - ry be;
2. Show me the tomb where Thou wast laid, Ten - der - ly mourned and wept;
3. Let me like Ma - ry, thru the gloom, Come with a gift to Thee;
4. May I be will - ing, Lord, to bear Dai - ly my cross for Thee;
Lest I for - get Thy thorn-crowned brow, Lead me to Cal - va - ry.
An - gels in robes of light ar - rayed Guard - ed Thee whilst Thou slept.
Show to me now the emp - ty tomb— Lead me to Cal - va - ry.
E - ven Thy cup of grief to share— Thou hast borne all for me.
CHORUS
Lest I for - get Geth - sem - a - ne, Lest I for - get Thine ag - o - ny,
Lest I for - get Thy love for me, Lead me to Cal - va - ry.*

222 — There Is a Green Hill Far Away
CECIL F. ALEXANDER
GEORGE C. STEBBINS
1. There is a green hill far a - way, Out - side a cit - y wall,
2. We may not know, we can - not tell, What pains He had to bear;
3. He died that we might be for-giv'n, He died to make us good,
4. There was no oth - er good e-nough To pay the price of sin;
Where the dear Lord was cru - ci - fied, Who died to save us all.
But we be - lieve it was for us He hung and suf - fered there.
That we might go at last to heav'n, Saved by His pre - cious blood.
He on - ly could un - lock the gate Of heav'n and let us in.
CHORUS
O dear - ly, dear - ly has He loved! And we must love Him too,
And trust in His re - deem - ing blood, And try His works to do.

Tune: GREEN HILL

CHRIST: HIS PASSION

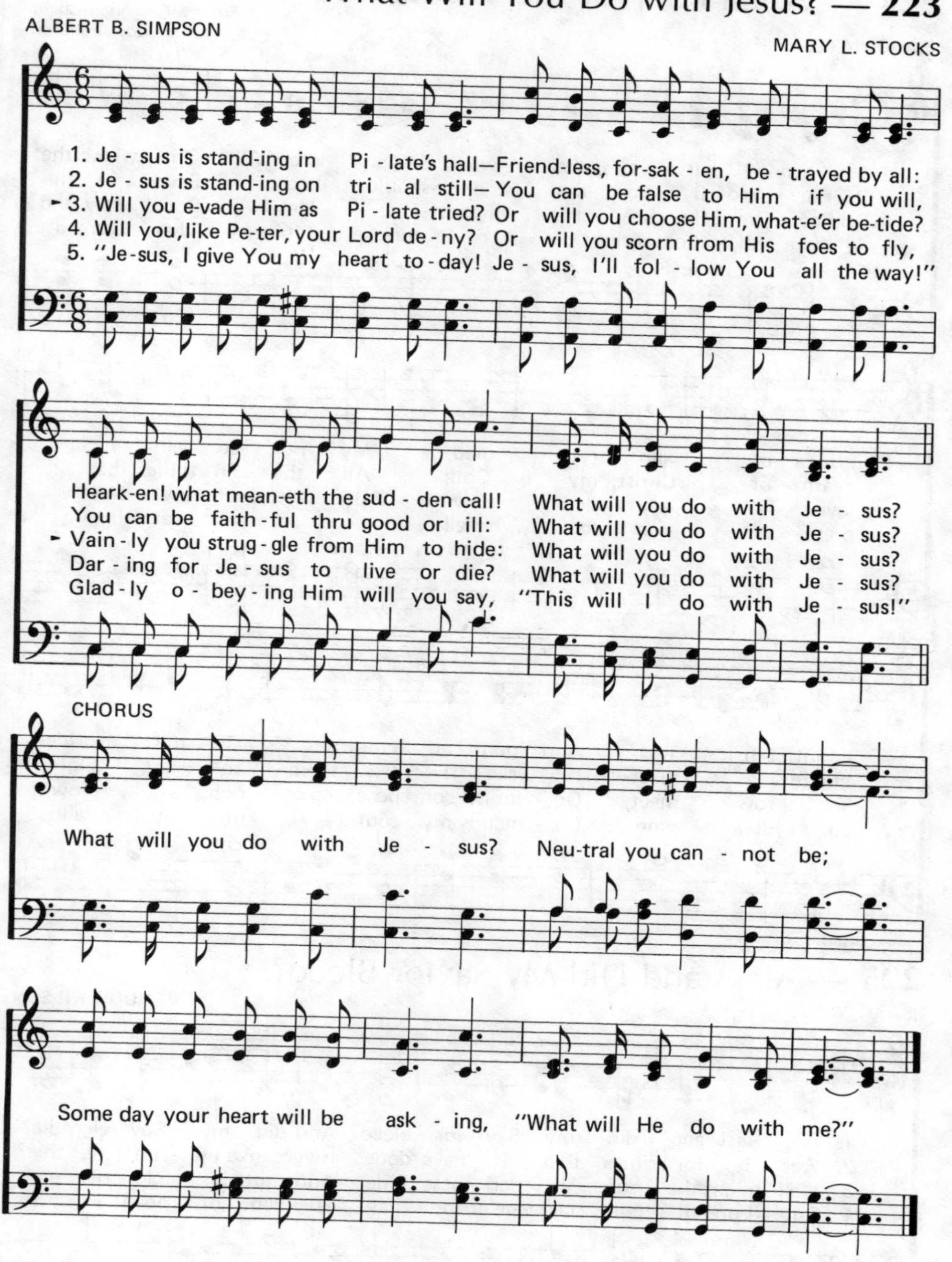
ALBERT B. SIMPSON
MARY L. STOCKS
1. Je - sus is stand-ing in Pi - late's hall—Friend-less, for-sak - en, be - trayed by all:
2. Je - sus is stand-ing on tri - al still— You can be false to Him if you will,
3. Will you e-vade Him as Pi - late tried? Or will you choose Him, what-e'er be-tide?
4. Will you, like Pe-ter, your Lord de - ny? Or will you scorn from His foes to fly,
5. "Je-sus, I give You my heart to-day! Je - sus, I'll fol - low You all the way!"
Heark-en! what mean-eth the sud - den call! What will you do with Je - sus?
You can be faith-ful thru good or ill: What will you do with Je - sus?
Vain-ly you strug-gle from Him to hide: What will you do with Je - sus?
Dar - ing for Je - sus to live or die? What will you do with Je - sus?
Glad-ly o - bey-ing Him will you say, "This will I do with Je - sus!"
CHORUS
What will you do with Je - sus? Neu-tral you can - not be;
Some day your heart will be ask - ing, "What will He do with me?"

224 — When I Survey the Wondrous Cross

ISAAC WATTS

From a Gregorian Chant
Arr. by Lowell Mason

1. When I sur - vey the won - drous cross On which the
2. For - bid it, Lord, that I should boast, Save in the
3. See, from His head, His hands, His feet, Sor - row and
4. Were the whole realm of na - ture mine, That were a

Prince of glo - ry died, My rich - est gain I
death of Christ, my God; All the vain things that
love flow min - gled down; Did e'er such love and
pres - ent far too small: Love so a - maz - ing,

count but loss, And pour con - tempt on all my pride.
charm me most— I sac - ri - fice them to His blood.
sor - row meet, Or thorns com - pose so rich a crown?
so di - vine, De - mands my soul, my life, my all.

Tune: HAMBURG

225 — Alas! and Did My Savior Bleed?

ISAAC WATTS

HUGH WILSON

1. A - las! and did my Sav - ior bleed? And did my Sov-'reign die?
2. Was it for crimes that I have done He groaned up - on the tree?
3. Well might the sun in dark - ness hide And shut his glo - ries in,
4. But drops of grief can ne'er re - pay The debt of love I owe;

Tune: MARTYRDOM

Would He de - vote that sa - cred head For such a worm as I?
A - maz - ing pit - y! grace un-known! And love be - yond de - gree!
When Christ, the might - y Mak - er, died For man the crea - ture's sin.
Here, Lord, I give my-self a - way—'Tis all that I can do.

'Tis Midnight—and on Olive's Brow — 226

Based on Luke 22:39-48
WILLIAM B. TAPPAN

WILLIAM B. BRADBURY

1. 'Tis mid-night—and on Ol - ive's brow The star is
2. 'Tis mid-night—and from all re - moved The Sav - ior
3. 'Tis mid-night—and for oth - ers' guilt The Man of
4. 'Tis mid-night—and from heav - en's plains Is borne the
dimmed that late - ly shone; 'Tis mid - night— in the
wres - tles lone with fears; E'en that dis - ci - ple
Sor - rows weeps in blood; Yet He that hath in
song that an - gels know; Un - heard by mor - tals
gar - den now The suf - f'ring Sav - ior prays a - lone.
whom He loved Heeds not His Mas - ter's grief and tears.
an - guish knelt Is not for - sak - en by His God.
are the strains That sweet - ly soothe the Sav - ior's woe.

Tune: OLIVE'S BROW

227 — At the Cross

ISAAC WATTS
Chorus—Ralph E. Hudson

RALPH E. HUDSON

1. A - las! and did my Sav - ior bleed? And did my Sov - 'reign die?
2. Was it for crimes that I have done He groaned up - on the tree?
3. Well might the sun in dark - ness hide And shut his glo - ries in,
4. But drops of grief can ne'er re - pay The debt of love I owe:
Would He de - vote that sa - cred head For such a worm as I?
A - maz - ing pit - y! grace un-known! And love be - yond de - gree!
When Christ, the might - y Mak - er, died For man the crea-ture's sin.
Here, Lord, I give my - self a - way—'Tis all that I can do!
CHORUS
At the cross, at the cross where I first saw the light And the
bur - den of my heart rolled a - way— It was there by faith
I re - ceived my sight, And now I am hap - py all the day!

CHRIST: HIS PASSION

Were You There? — 228
Traditional
Traditional Spiritual
1. Were you there when they cru - ci - fied my Lord? Were you there when they cru - ci - fied my Lord?
2. Were you there when they nailed Him to the tree? Were you there when they nailed Him to the tree? O!
3. Were you there when they laid Him in the tomb? Were you there when they laid Him in the tomb?
†opt. Were you there when He rose up from the dead? Were you there when He rose up from the dead?
†May be omitted, especially for Holy Week services.
Some-times it caus - es me to trem-ble, trem-ble, trem-ble!
Were you there when they cru - ci - fied my Lord?
Were you there when they nailed Him to the tree?
Were you there when they laid Him in the tomb?
Were you there when He rose up from the dead?

229 — Rise Again
DALLAS HOLM
DALLAS HOLM
1. Go a - head— drive the nails in My hands, Laugh at Me where I stand;
Go a - head and say it is - n't Me— The day will come when you will see!
REFRAIN
(1) 'Cause I'll rise a - gain— There's no pow'r on earth can tie Me down!
(2) 'Cause I'll rise a - gain— There's no pow'r on earth can tie Me down!
(3) 'Cause I'll come a - gain— There's no pow'r on earth can keep Me back!
1,2 (to sts. 2 & 3)
3
Fine
Yes, I'll rise a - gain— Death can't keep Me in the ground!
Yes, I'll rise a - gain— Death can't keep Me in the ground!
Yes, I'll come a - gain— Come to take My peo-ple back!
2. Go a - head and mock My name—My love for you is still the same;
3. Go a - head and say I'm dead and gone—But you will see that you were wrong;
CHRIST: HIS RESURRECTION
© 1977 by Dimension Music. All rights reserved.

D.S.
Go a - head and bur - y Me— But ver - y soon I will be free!
Go a - head and try to hide the Son— But all will see that I'm the one!
The Day of Resurrection — 230
JOHN of DAMASCUS
Trans. by John M. Neale
HENRY SMART
1. The day of res - ur - rec - tion! Earth, tell it out a - broad—
2. Our hearts be pure from e - vil, That we may see a - right
3. Now let the heav'ns be joy - ful, Let earth her song be - gin,
The Pass - o - ver of glad - ness, The Pass - o - ver of God!
The Lord in rays e - ter - nal Of res - ur - rec - tion light;
The world re - sound in tri - umph And all that is there - in;
From death to life e - ter - nal, From this world to the sky,
And, lis - t'ning to His ac - cents, May hear, so calm and plain,
Let all things seen and un - seen Their notes of glad - ness blend,
Our Christ has bro't us o - ver With hymns of vic - to - ry!
His own "All hail!" and, hear - ing, May raise the vic - tor - strain.
For Christ the Lord has ris - en, Our Joy that has no end!*

Tune: LANCASHIRE—higher key at 460

231 — Christ the Lord Is Risen Today

CHARLES WESLEY

Lyra Davidica

1. Christ the Lord is ris'n to - day, Al - le - lu - ia!
2. Lives a - gain our glo - rious King, Al - le - lu - ia!
3. Love's re - deem - ing work is done, Al - le - lu - ia!
4. Soar we now where Christ has led, Al - le - lu - ia!
Sons of men and an - gels say: Al - le - lu - ia!
Where, O death, is now thy sting? Al - le - lu - ia!
Fought the fight, the bat - tle won, Al - le - lu - ia!
Fol - l'wing our ex - alt - ed Head, Al - le - lu - ia!
Raise your joys and tri - umphs high, Al - le - lu - ia!
Dy - ing once He all doth save, Al - le - lu - ia!
Death in vain for - bids Him rise, Al - le - lu - ia!
Made like Him, like Him we rise, Al - le - lu - ia!
Sing, ye heav'ns, and earth re - ply: Al - le - lu - ia!
Where thy vic - to - ry, O grave? Al - le - lu - ia!
Christ has o - pened Par - a - dise, Al - le - lu - ia!
Ours the cross, the grave, the skies, Al - le - lu - ia!

Tune: EASTER HYMN

CHRIST: HIS RESURRECTION

ROBERT LOWRY
ROBERT LOWRY
1. Low in the grave He lay— Je - sus, my Sav - ior! Wait - ing the com-ing day— Je - sus, my Lord!
2. Vain - ly they watch His bed— Je - sus, my Sav - ior! Vain - ly they seal the dead— Je - sus, my Lord!
3. Death can-not keep his prey— Je - sus, my Sav - ior! He tore the bars a - way— Je - sus, my Lord!
CHORUS Faster
Up from the grave He a - rose, With a might-y tri-umph o'er His foes; He a - rose a Vic - tor from the dark do - main, And He lives for - ev - er with His saints to reign: He a - rose! He a - rose! Hal - le - lu - jah! Christ a - rose!
He a-rose,
He a-rose!
He a-rose!
He a-rose!

233 — He's Living Today!
JOHN W. PETERSON
JOHN W. PETERSON
1. The Sav - ior died a world to save, They sealed his bod - y in a grave; But He could not be bound In the tomb's cold ground, And soon He would be found a - live a - gain! A - live a - gain!
(2. It seemed to) them that all was loss, Their dreams were dashed by a Ro - man cross; They did not un - der - stand The pow'r in His hand— That He would rise and stand a - live a - gain! A - live a - gain!
(3. How sweet the) prom - ise He did give: "Be - cause I live, you too shall live." We share His vic - to - ry! We'll rise a - gain as He, To live with Him in heav'n e - ter - nal - ly! E - ter - nal - ly!
CHORUS
He's liv - ing to - day! He's liv - ing to - day! Let ev - 'ry - one know, Wher - ev - er you go! That's why the church bells are
CHRIST: HIS RESURRECTION
© John W. Peterson Music Company 1974, arr. 1979. All rights reserved.

ring-ing and the choirs are sing-ing In such a won-der-ful way—O
hear what they say:
1,2
He's liv-ing to-day!
2. It seemed to
3. How sweet the
3
He's liv-ing to-day!
He's liv-ing to-day!
He Is Lord — 234
Traditional
Based on Philippians 2:11
Traditional
Arr. by Dale Scott
He is Lord, He is Lord! He is ris-en from the dead and He is Lord!
Ev-'ry knee shall bow, ev-'ry tongue con-fess That Je-sus Christ is Lord.

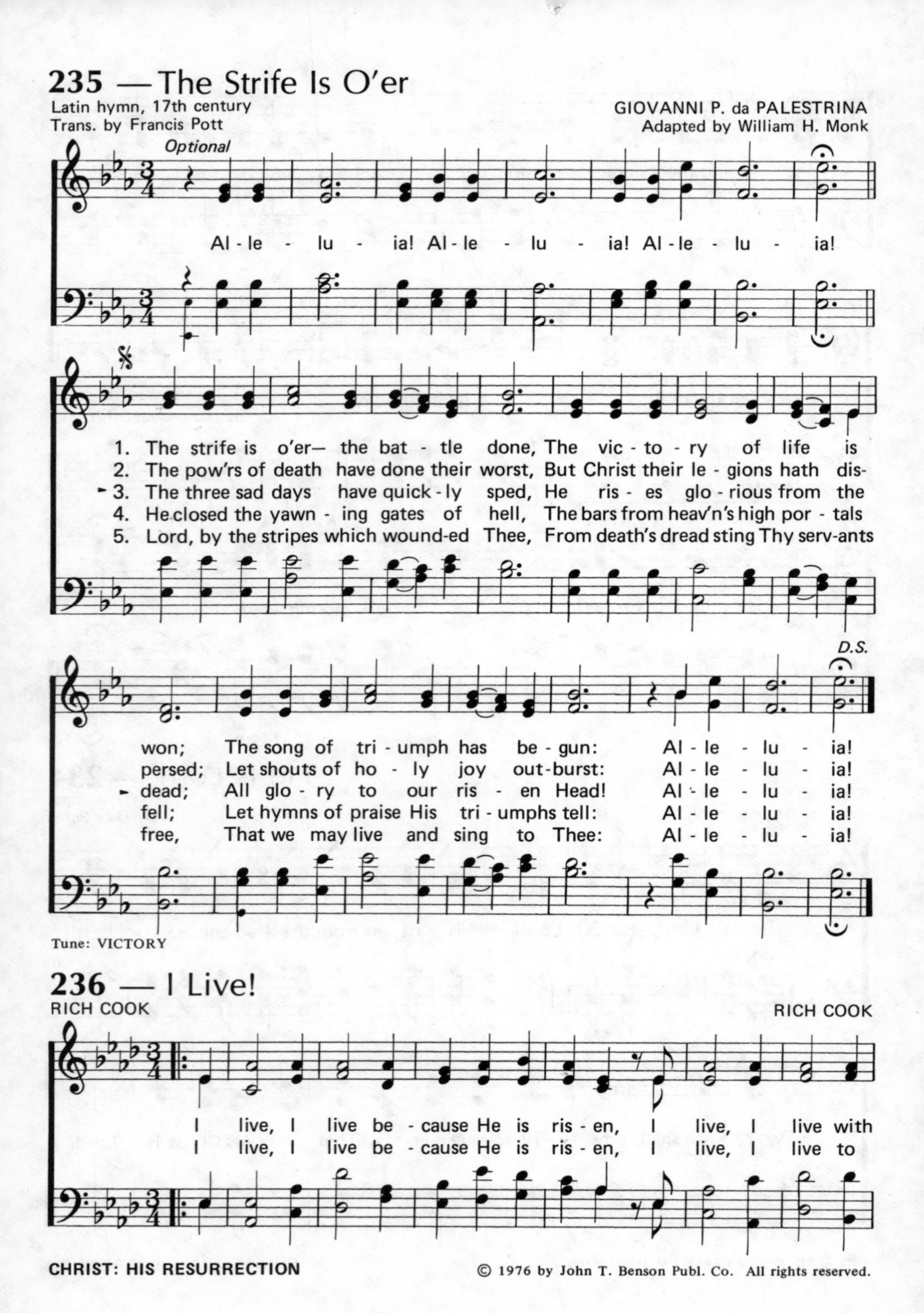
235 — The Strife Is O'er
Latin hymn, 17th century
Trans. by Francis Pott
GIOVANNI P. da PALESTRINA
Adapted by William H. Monk
Optional
Al - le - lu - ia! Al - le - lu - ia! Al - le - lu - ia!
1. The strife is o'er— the bat - tle done, The vic - to - ry of life is won; The song of tri - umph has be - gun: Al - le - lu - ia!
2. The pow'rs of death have done their worst, But Christ their le - gions hath dis - persed; Let shouts of ho - ly joy out - burst: Al - le - lu - ia!
3. The three sad days have quick - ly sped, He ris - es glo - rious from the dead; All glo - ry to our ris - en Head! Al - le - lu - ia!
4. He closed the yawn - ing gates of hell, The bars from heav'n's high por - tals fell; Let hymns of praise His tri - umphs tell: Al - le - lu - ia!
5. Lord, by the stripes which wound - ed Thee, From death's dread sting Thy serv - ants free, That we may live and sing to Thee: Al - le - lu - ia!
D.S.
Tune: VICTORY
236 — I Live!
RICH COOK
RICH COOK
I live, I live be - cause He is ris - en, I live, I live with
I live, I live be - cause He is ris - en, I live, I live to
CHRIST: HIS RESURRECTION
© 1976 by John T. Benson Publ. Co. All rights reserved.

pow'r o - ver sin;
wor - ship Him. Thank You, Je - sus! Thank You, Je - sus! Be -
cause You're a - live, be-cause You're a - live, Be-cause You're a-live, I live!
Jesus Lives! — 237
JOHN W. PETERSON
JOHN W. PETERSON
1. Je - sus lives! Je - sus lives! Je - sus lives who was cru - ci - fied;
2. Je - sus lives! Je - sus lives! He has con-quered the an - cient foe;
3. Je - sus lives! Je - sus lives! Lives a - gain, nev - er-more to die!
(D.C.)
La - bor done, vic - t'ry won, Je - sus lives! the grave is de - nied!
Spread the word, glo - rious word: Je - sus lives! the whole world must know.
Sav - ior-King— praise we sing, Je - sus lives! and so, too, shall I!
CODA (optional)
Je - sus lives! Je - sus lives! Je - sus lives! and so, too, shall I!

238 — Because He Lives

GLORIA GAITHER and
WILLIAM J. GAITHER

WILLIAM J. GAITHER

1. God sent His Son— they called Him Je - sus, He came to love, heal and for - give; He lived and died to buy my par - don, An emp - ty grave is there to prove my Sav - ior lives.
2. How sweet to hold a new - born ba - by And feel the pride and joy he gives; But great - er still the calm as - sur - ance: This child can face un - cer - tain days because Christ lives.
3. And then one day I'll cross the riv - er, I'll fight life's fi - nal war with pain; And then, as death gives way to vic - tory, I'll see the lights of glo - ry— and I'll know He lives.

CHORUS

Be - cause He lives I can face to - mor - row, Be - cause He lives all fear is gone; Be - cause I know He holds the

fu - ture And life is worth the liv - ing— just be-cause He lives.
Come, Ye Faithful, Raise the Strain — 239
JOHN of DAMASCUS
Trans. by John M. Neale
ROBERT WILLIAMS
Har. by John Roberts
1. Come, ye faith - ful, raise the strain Of tri-um - phant glad - ness:
2. 'Tis the spring of souls to - day: Christ hath burst His pris - on,
3. "Al - le - lu - ia!" now we cry To our King im - mor - tal,
God hath brought His peo - ple forth In - to joy from sad - ness;
From the frost and gloom of death Light and life have ris - en;
Who, tri - um - phant, burst the bars Of the tomb's dark por - tal;
Now re - joice, Je - ru - sa - lem, And with true af - fec - tion
All the win - ter of our sins, Long and dark, is fly - ing
"Al - le - lu - ia!" with the Son, God the Fa - ther prais - ing,
Wel - come with un - ceas - ing praise Je - sus' res - ur - rec - tion.
From His light, to whom we give Thanks and praise un - dy - ing.
"Al - le - lu - ia!" yet a - gain To the Spir - it rais - ing.*
Tune: LLANFAIR
CHRIST: HIS RESURRECTION

240 — All Hail the Power

EDWARD PERRONET
Alt. by John Rippon

OLIVER HOLDEN

1. All hail the pow'r of Je - sus' name! Let an - gels pros - trate fall;
2. Ye cho - sen seed of Is - rael's race, Ye ran-somed from the fall,
3. Let ev - 'ry kin - dred, ev - 'ry tribe, On this ter - res - trial ball,
4. O that with yon - der sa - cred throng We at His feet may fall!

Bring forth the roy - al di - a - dem, And crown Him Lord of all;
Hail Him who saves you by His grace, And crown Him Lord of all;
To Him all maj - es - ty as - cribe, And crown Him Lord of all;
We'll join the ev - er - last - ing song, And crown Him Lord of all;

Bring forth the roy - al di - a - dem, And crown Him Lord of all!
Hail Him who saves you by His grace, And crown Him Lord of all!
To Him all maj - es - ty as - cribe, And crown Him Lord of all!
We'll join the ev - er - last - ing song, And crown Him Lord of all!*

Tune: CORONATION

241 — All Hail the Power

EDWARD PERRONET
Alt. by John Rippon

WILLIAM SHRUBSOLE

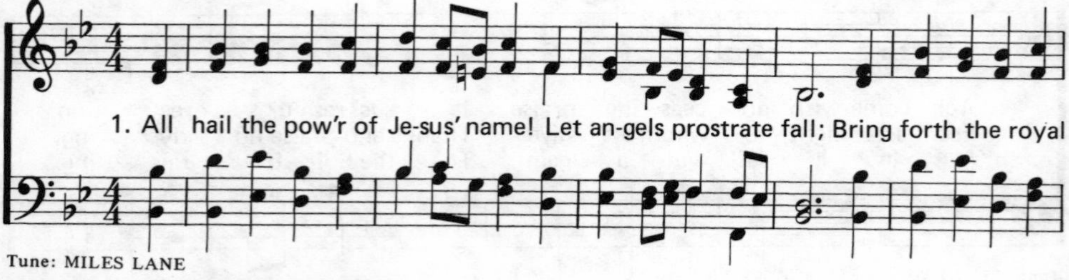

1. All hail the pow'r of Je-sus' name! Let an-gels prostrate fall; Bring forth the royal

Tune: MILES LANE

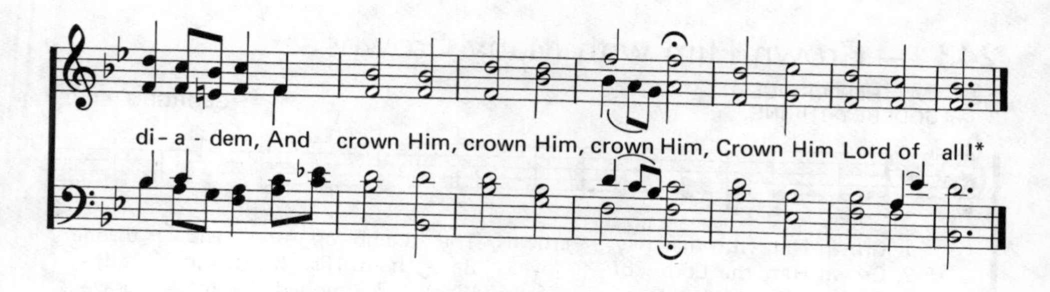
di - a - dem, And crown Him, crown Him, crown Him, Crown Him Lord of all!*

Majestic Sweetness Sits Enthroned — 242

SAMUEL STENNETT

THOMAS HASTINGS

1. Ma - jes - tic sweet - ness sits en-throned Up - on the
2. No mor - tal can with Him com - pare A - mong the
3. He saw me plunged in deep dis - tress And flew to
4. To Him I owe my life and breath And all the
5. Since from His boun - ty I re - ceive Such proofs of
Sav - ior's brow; His head with ra - diant glo - ries crowned, His
sons of men; Fair - er is He than all the fair Who
my re - lief; For me He bore the shame - ful cross And
joys I have; He makes me tri - umph o - ver death And
love di - vine, Had I a thou - sand hearts to give, Lord,
lips with grace o'er - flow, His lips with grace o'er - flow.
fill the heav'n - ly train, Who fill the heav'n - ly train.
car - ried all my grief, And car - ried all my grief.
saves me from the grave, And saves me from the grave.
they should all be Thine, Lord, they should all be Thine.*

Tune: ORTONVILLE—lower key at 326

243 — Crown Him with Many Crowns

1,2,4 - MATTHEW BRIDGES
3 - GODFREY THRING

GEORGE J. ELVEY

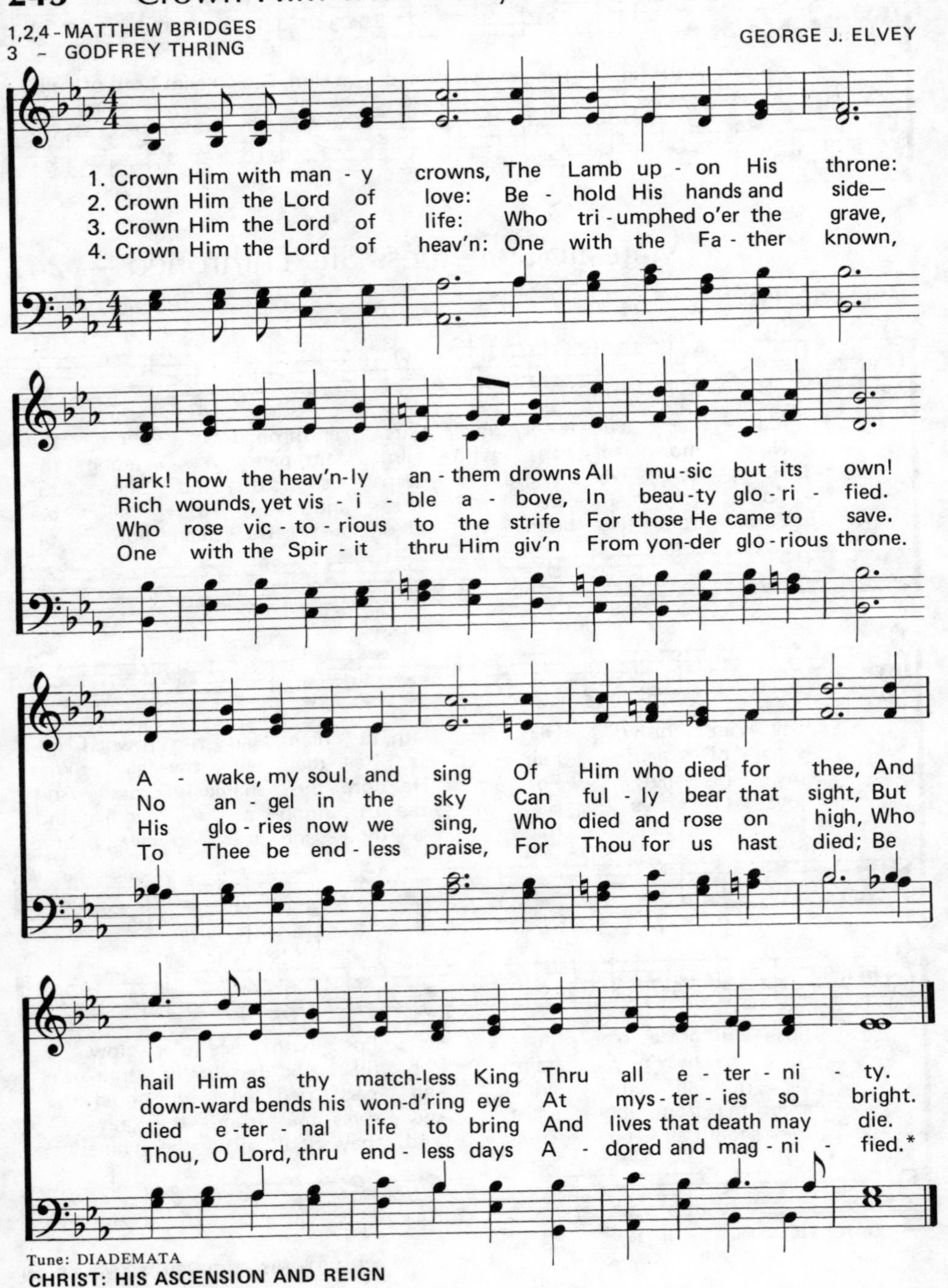
1. Crown Him with man - y crowns, The Lamb up - on His throne: Hark! how the heav'n-ly an - them drowns All mu-sic but its own! A - wake, my soul, and sing Of Him who died for thee, And hail Him as thy match-less King Thru all e - ter - ni - ty.
2. Crown Him the Lord of love: Be - hold His hands and side— Rich wounds, yet vis - i - ble a - bove, In beau-ty glo - ri - fied. No an - gel in the sky Can ful - ly bear that sight, But down-ward bends his won-d'ring eye At mys - ter - ies so bright.
3. Crown Him the Lord of life: Who tri - umphed o'er the grave, Who rose vic - to - rious to the strife For those He came to save. His glo - ries now we sing, Who died and rose on high, Who died e - ter - nal life to bring And lives that death may die.
4. Crown Him the Lord of heav'n: One with the Fa - ther known, One with the Spir - it thru Him giv'n From yon-der glo - rious throne. To Thee be end - less praise, For Thou for us hast died; Be Thou, O Lord, thru end - less days A - dored and mag - ni - fied.*

Tune: DIADEMATA

CHRIST: HIS ASCENSION AND REIGN

At the Name of Jesus — 244

Based on Philippians 2:5-11
CAROLINE M. NOEL
FRANCES R. HAVERGAL
1. At the name of Je - sus Ev - 'ry knee shall bow, Ev-'ry tongue con-
2. At His voice cre - a - tion Sprang at once to sight, All the an - gel
3. Hum-bled for a sea - son To re - ceive a name From the lips of
4. Bore it up tri - um - phant, With its hu - man light, Thru all ranks of
5. In your hearts en - throne Him: There let Him sub - due All that is not
6. Broth-ers, this Lord Je - sus Shall re - turn a - gain, With His Fa-ther's
fess Him King of glo - ry now; 'Tis the Fa-ther's pleas - ure We should
fac - es, All the hosts of light, Thrones and dom - i - na - tions, Stars up -
sin - ners Un - to whom He came: Faith-ful - ly He bore it Spot-less
crea - tures To the cen - tral height, To the throne of God - head, To the
ho - ly, All that is not true; Crown Him as your cap - tain In temp-
glo - ry, O'er the earth to reign; For all wreaths of em - pire Meet up-
call Him Lord, Who from the be - gin - ning Was the might - y Word.
on their way, All the heav'n-ly or - ders In their great ar - ray.
to the last, Brought it back vic-to - rious When from death He passed—
Fa - ther's breast— Filled it with the glo - ry Of that per - fect rest.
ta - tion's hour, Let His will en - fold you In its light and pow'r.
on His brow, And our hearts con-fess Him King of glo - ry now.

Tune: HERMAS, abridged (Alternate, WYE VALLEY, as at 492)

245 — Rejoice—the Lord Is King!
CHARLES WESLEY
JOHN DARWALL
1. Re - joice—the Lord is King! Your Lord and King a - dore!
2. Je - sus the Sav - ior reigns, The God of truth and love;
3. His king - dom can - not fail— He rules o'er earth and heav'n;
4. Re - joice in glo - rious hope! Our Lord the judge shall come
Re - joice, give thanks, and sing And tri - umph ev - er - more:
When He had purged our stains He took His seat a - bove:
The keys of death and hell Are to our Je - sus giv'n:
And take His serv - ants up To their e - ter - nal home:
Lift up your heart, lift up your voice! Rejoice, again, I say, re - joice!*
Tune: DARWALL'S 148th—lower key at 71
246 — Jesus Shall Reign
Based on Psalm 72
ISAAC WATTS
JOHN HATTON
1. Je - sus shall reign wher - e'er the sun Does his suc - ces - sive jour - neys run,
2. To Him shall end - less prayer be made, And praises throng to crown His head;
3. Peo - ple and realms of ev - 'ry tongue Dwell on His love with sweetest song,
4. Let ev - 'ry crea - ture rise and bring Hon - ors pe - cu - liar to our King,

Tune: DUKE STREET

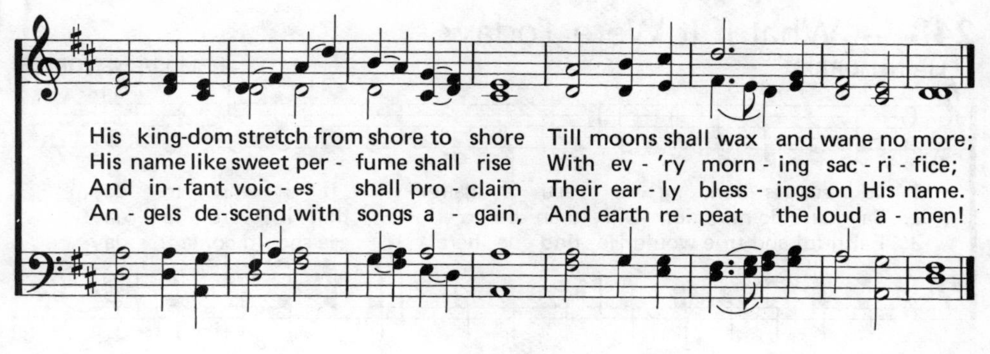
His king-dom stretch from shore to shore Till moons shall wax and wane no more;
His name like sweet per - fume shall rise With ev - 'ry morn - ing sac - ri - fice;
And in - fant voic - es shall pro - claim Their ear - ly bless - ings on His name.
An - gels de-scend with songs a - gain, And earth re - peat the loud a - men!

Look, Ye Saints! the Sight Is Glorious — 247

THOMAS KELLY

WILLIAM H. MONK

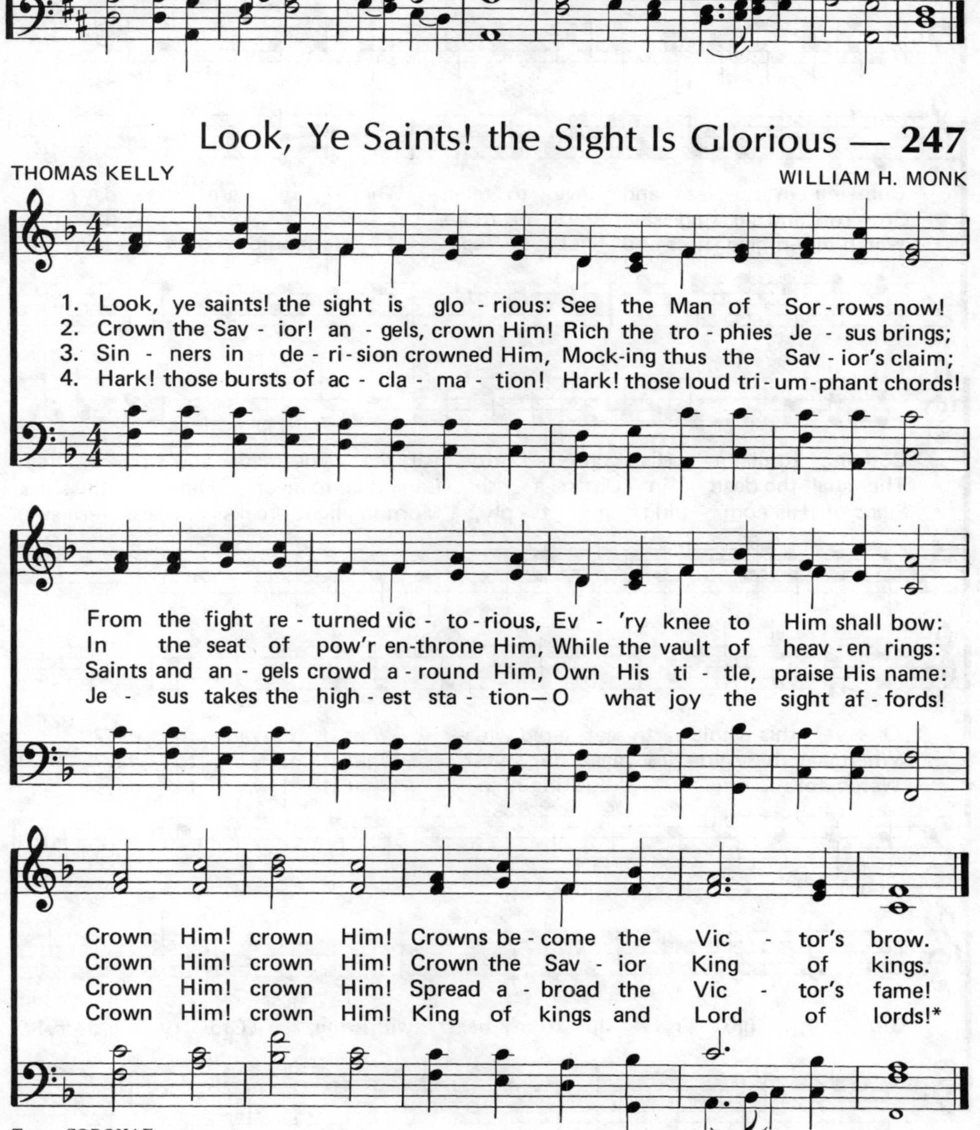
1. Look, ye saints! the sight is glo - rious: See the Man of Sor - rows now!
2. Crown the Sav - ior! an - gels, crown Him! Rich the tro - phies Je - sus brings;
3. Sin - ners in de - ri - sion crowned Him, Mock-ing thus the Sav - ior's claim;
4. Hark! those bursts of ac - cla - ma - tion! Hark! those loud tri - um - phant chords!
From the fight re - turned vic - to - rious, Ev - 'ry knee to Him shall bow:
In the seat of pow'r en-throne Him, While the vault of heav - en rings:
Saints and an - gels crowd a - round Him, Own His ti - tle, praise His name:
Je - sus takes the high - est sta - tion— O what joy the sight af - fords!
Crown Him! crown Him! Crowns be - come the Vic - tor's brow.
Crown Him! crown Him! Crown the Sav - ior King of kings.
Crown Him! crown Him! Spread a - broad the Vic - tor's fame!
Crown Him! crown Him! King of kings and Lord of lords!*

Tune: CORONAE

248 — What If It Were Today?
LELIA N. MORRIS
LELIA N. MORRIS
1. Je - sus is com - ing to earth a - gain— What if it were to - day?
2. Sa - tan's do-min - ion will then be o'er— O that it were to - day!
3. Faith-ful and true would He find us here If He should come to - day?
Com-ing in pow-er and love to reign— What if it were to - day?
Sor - row and sigh-ing shall be no more— O that it were to - day!
Watch-ing in glad - ness and not in fear, If He should come to - day?
Com-ing to claim His cho - sen Bride, All the re-deemed and pu - ri - fied,
Then shall the dead in Christ a - rise, Caught up to meet Him in the skies;
Signs of His com - ing mul - ti - ply, Morn-ing light breaks in east - ern sky;
rit.
a tempo
O - ver this whole earth scat - tered wide— What if it were to - day?
When shall these glo - ries meet our eyes? What if it were to - day?
Watch, for the time is draw - ing nigh— What if it were to - day?
CHORUS
Glo - ry, glo - ry! Joy to my heart 'twill bring, Glo - ry, glo - ry!
CHRIST: HIS RETURN
Copyright 1912, renewal 1940 (ext.), and arr. ©1979 by Hope Publishing Co.

When we shall crown Him King; Glo - ry, glo - ry! Haste to pre -
pare the way— Glo - ry, glo - ry! Je - sus will come some day!
Based on Revelation 7:9-15
ALMEDA J. PEARCE
When He Shall Come — 249
ALMEDA J. PEARCE
1. When He shall come, re - splen - dent in His glo - ry, To take His own from out this vale of night, O may I know the joy at His ap - pear - ing— On - ly at morn to walk with Him in white!
2. When I shall stand with - in the court of heav - en Where white-robed pil - grims pass be - fore my sight— Earth's mar-tyred saints and blood-washed o-ver - com - ers— These then are they who walk with Him in white!
3. When He shall call, from earth's re - mot - est cor - ners, All who have stood tri - um - phant in His might, O to be wor - thy then to stand be - side them, And in that morn to walk with Him in white!
Tune: PEARCE

250 — Jesus Is Coming Again
JOHN W. PETERSON
JOHN W. PETERSON
1. Mar - vel - ous mes-sage we bring, Glo - ri - ous car - ol we sing,
2. For - est and flow-er ex - claim, Moun-tain and mead-ow the same,
3. Stand-ing be-fore Him at last, Tri - al and trou-ble all past,
Won - der - ful word of the King: Je - sus is com - ing a - gain! (a - gain!)
All earth and heav-en pro - claim: Je - sus is com - ing a - gain! (a - gain!)
Crowns at His feet we will cast: Je - sus is com - ing a - gain! (a - gain!)
CHORUS
In unison
Com - ing a - gain, Com - ing a - gain;
May - be morn - ing, may - be noon, May - be eve-ning and may - be soon!
Com - ing a - gain, Com - ing a - gain;
CHRIST: HIS RETURN
© 1957 by John W. Peterson Music Company.
All rights reserved. Used by permission.

Parts
O what a won-der-ful day it will be— Je-sus is com-ing a - gain!
Lo! He Comes, with Clouds Descending — 251
CHARLES WESLEY—alt.
JOHN GOSS
1. Lo! He comes with clouds de - scend - ing, Once for our sal - va - tion slain; Thou - sand thou - sand saints at - tend - ing Swell the tri - umph of His train: Al - le - lu - ia! al - le - lu - ia! God ap - pears on earth to reign.
2. Ev - 'ry eye shall now be - hold Him, Robed in dread - ful maj - es - ty; Those who set at naught and sold Him, Pierced and nailed Him to the tree, Deep - ly wail - ing, deep - ly wail - ing, Shall the true Mes - si - ah see.
3. Yea, a - men! let all a - dore Thee, High on Thine e - ter - nal throne; Sav - ior, take the pow'r and glo - ry, Claim the king - dom for Thine own: Al - le - lu - ia! al - le - lu - ia! Thou shalt reign and Thou a - lone.*
Tune: PRAISE MY SOUL
CHRIST: HIS RETURN

252 — Christ Returneth!

H. L. TURNER

JAMES McGRANAHAN

1. It may be at morn, when the day is a - wak - ing, When sun - light thru dark-ness and shad-ow is break-ing, That Je - sus will come in the full - ness of glo - ry To re - ceive from the world His own.
2. It may be at mid - day, it may be at twi - light, It may be, per - chance, that the black-ness of mid - night Will burst in - to light in the blaze of His glo - ry When Je - sus re - ceives His own.
3. O joy! O de - light! should we go with - out dy - ing, No sick - ness, no sad - ness, no dread and no cry - ing— Caught up thru the clouds with our Lord in - to glo - ry When Je - sus re - ceives His own.

CHORUS

O Lord Je - sus, how long, how long Ere we shout the glad song—Christ re - turn-eth! Hal - le - lu - jah! Hal - le - lu - jah, A - men! Hal - le - lu - jah, A - men!

Chariot of Clouds — 253

JOHN W. PETERSON

JOHN W. PETERSON

1. Some day we'll leave this world of sin With all its dark de - spair,
2. Then faith at last will turn to sight As heav - en looms be - fore,
3. O glo - rious day! when in clear view Will stand the Lord we love,

And, like E - li - jah, rise to meet Our Sav - ior in the air.
And in that land of love and light We'll live for - ev - er - more.
And we can wor - ship at His feet Be - yond the stars a - bove.

CHORUS

We'll be caught up in a char - i - ot of clouds! We'll be caught up in a char - i - ot of clouds! Like E - li - jah of old, to the man - sions of gold, We'll be caught up in a char - i - ot of clouds.

254 — With the Sound of Trumpets

JOHN W. PETERSON | JOHN W. PETERSON

1. With the sound of trum-pets an-nounc-ing from the sky: "Je - sus is com-ing from heav-en on high!" See, now the pearl-y gates are o-pen, Christ is pass-ing, pass - ing thru them; All the u-ni - verse is watch-ing as the King, our Sav-ior - King de-scends to take His throne! With the sound of trum-pets! Tri-um-phant

2. With the sound of trum-pets in re-gal maj-es - ty: Je - sus is com-ing— tri - um-phant is He! And in His glo-rious train are mil-lions, Saints and an-gels— heav - en's ar-mies, O how awe-some is the great and grand dis - play of pow'r in - vin - ci - ble of Christ the Lord! By His ver - y bright-ness His en - e -

CHRIST: HIS RETURN

is the song! Je - sus is com - ing to right ev - 'ry wrong:
mies are slain! And all earth's king-doms are now His do - main:
1
D.C.
2
Cli - max of his - t'ry, a - wait-ed so long!
Je - sus is com - ing, is com-ing to reign!
He Is Coming Again — 255
MABEL JOHNSTON CAMP
MABEL JOHNSTON CAMP
He is com - ing a - gain, He is com - ing a - gain, The ver - y same
Je - sus re - ject - ed of men; He is com - ing a - gain, He is
com - ing a - gain, With pow'r and great glo - ry He is com-ing a - gain!

256 — I'll Fly Away
ALBERT E. BRUMLEY
ALBERT E. BRUMLEY
1. Some glad morn-ing when this life is o'er, I'll fly a - way; fly a-way;
2. When the shad-ows of this life have gone, fly a-way,
3. Just a few more wea-ry days and then,
To a home on God's ce-les-tial shore,
Like a bird from pris-on bars has flown,
To a land where joys shall nev-er end,
I'll fly a-way. fly a-way, fly a-way.
CHORUS
I'll fly a - way, O glo-ry, fly a-way, I'll fly a - way; fly a-way,
in the morn-ing; When I die,
hal-le-lu-jah, by and by, I'll fly a-way. fly a-way, fly a-way.
Copyright Albert E. Brumley & Sons 1932, renewal © 1960. All rights reserved.
CHRIST: HIS RETURN

Will Jesus Find Us Watching? — 257
FANNY J. CROSBY
WILLIAM H. DOANE
1. When Je - sus comes to re - ward His serv - ants, Wheth - er it be
2. If at the dawn of the ear - ly morn - ing He shall call us
3. Have we been true to the trust He left us? Do we seek to
4. Bless - ed are those whom the Lord finds watch - ing, In His glo - ry
noon or night, Faith - ful to Him will He find us watch - ing,
one by one, When to the Lord we re - store our ta - lents,
do our best? If in our hearts there is naught con - demns us,
they shall share; If He shall come at the dawn or mid - night,
With our lamps all trimmed and bright?
Will He an - swer us, "Well done"?
We shall have a glo - rious rest.
Will He find us watch - ing there?
CHORUS
O can we say we are read - y,
broth - er? Read - y for the soul's bright home? Say, will He find
you and me still watch - ing, Wait - ing, wait - ing when the Lord shall come?
CHRIST: HIS RETURN

258 — Jesus Is Coming!

JOHN W. PETERSON JOHN W. PETERSON

1. Some-day when this age has run the course that God in - tend-ed,
2. O it is a bless-ed hope to those who know the Sav - ior,
3. Man - y peo - ple doubt that Je - sus real - ly is re - turn-ing,
4. If you know Him not, then let there be no hes - i - ta - tion,
An - cient Bi - ble proph - e - cy will sure - ly be ful - filled;
Bless - ed in the man - y joys that it will ush - er in;
"Where's the prom - ise of His com - ing?" mock - ing - ly they cry;
Trust Him as your Lord and Sav - ior now with - out de - lay;
As the Sav - ior left the earth that day when He as - cend-ed,
Pu - ri - fy - ing hope that has the pow'r to change be - hav - ior,
Aft - er He has come and judg-ment fires a - round are burn-ing,
By His grace and mer - cy you can be a new cre - a - tion,
So He'll come a - gain— the Fa - ther has willed.
Keep - ing from the world's de - file - ment and sin.
They will know the truth that now they de - ny.
And be read - y then to meet Him that day.

CHRIST: HIS RETURN

CHORUS
Je - sus is com - ing, Though we know not when;
Yes, He is com - ing, Je - sus is com-ing a - gain.
Lift Up the Trumpet — 259
JESSIE E. STROUT
Alt. by Eldon Burkwall
GEORGE E. LEE
Arr. by Eldon Burkwall
1. Lift up the trumpet and loud let it ring: Je - sus is com-ing a - gain!
2. Na - tions are an - gry—by this do we know: Je - sus is com-ing a - gain!
3. Fierce fires and earthquakes confirm to the throng: Je - sus is com-ing a - gain!
4. Shout from the hilltops the joy - ful re - frain: Je - sus is com-ing a - gain!
Take heart, ye pil-grims, re-joice now and sing: Je - sus is com-ing a - gain!
Knowl-edge in-creas-es, men run to and fro: Je - sus is com-ing a - gain!
Tem-pests and whirlwinds the an-them pro-long: Je - sus is com-ing a - gain!
Com - ing in glo - ry— the Lamb that was slain: Je - sus is com-ing a - gain!
Com-ing a-gain, com - ing a-gain, Je - sus is com - ing a - gain!

260 — Is It the Crowning Day?

HENRY OSTROM CHARLES H. MARSH

1. Je - sus may come to - day— Glad day! glad day! And I would
2. I may go home to - day— Glad day! glad day! Seems like I
3. Faith-ful I'll be to - day— Glad day! glad day! And I will
see my Friend; Dan - gers and trou - bles would end If
hear their song: Hail to the ra - di - ant throng If
free - ly tell Why I should love Him so well, For
CHORUS
Je - sus should come to - day.
I should go home to - day. Glad day! glad day! Is it the crown-ing
He is my all to - day.
day? I'll live for to - day, nor anx - ious be, Je - sus, my Lord, I
soon shall see; Glad day! glad day! Is it the crown-ing day?

PART 2

THE INWARD LOOK

OUR SONGS AND HYMNS OF EXPERIENCE AND FELLOWSHIP

"Let the word of Christ
dwell in you richly in all wisdom,
teaching and admonishing one another
in psalms and hymns and spiritual songs,
singing with grace in your hearts
to the Lord."

Colossians 3:16

261 — Ye Must Be Born Again

Based on John 3:3
WILLIAM T. SLEEPER
GEORGE C. STEBBINS

1. A rul - er once came to Je - sus by night To ask Him the
2. Ye chil-dren of men, at - tend to the word So sol-emn - ly
3. O ye who would en-ter that glo - ri - ous rest And sing with the
way of sal - va - tion and light; The Mas - ter made an - swer in
ut - tered by Je - sus the Lord; And let not this mes - sage to
ran-somed the song of the blest, The life ev - er - last - ing if
words true and plain, "Ye must be born a - gain."
you be in vain, "Ye must be born a - gain."
ye would ob - tain, "Ye must be born a - gain."
CHORUS
"Ye must be
born a - gain, Ye must be born a - gain; I ver - i - ly,
ver - i - ly say un - to thee, Ye must be born a - gain."

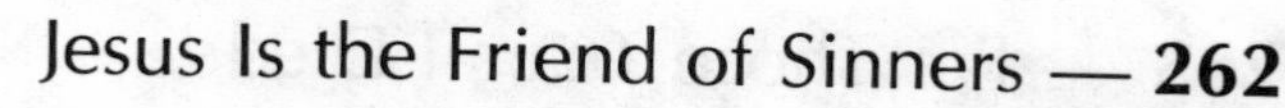
Jesus Is the Friend of Sinners — 262

JOHN W. PETERSON
JOHN W. PETERSON
1. Je - sus is the friend of sin - ners, Friend of sin - ners, friend of sin - ners; Je - sus is the friend of sin - ners— He can set you free.
2. If you trust Him, He will save you, He will save you, He will save you; If you trust Him, He will save you— Give you life a - new.
3. He will walk a - long be - side you, Walk be - side you, walk be - side you; He will walk a - long be - side you— Guide you day by day.
1,2
3
3
4. He will lead you on to glo - ry, On to glo - ry, on to glo - ry; He will lead you on to glo - ry— Home for - ev - er - more!

263 — For Those Tears I Died
MARSHA STEVENS
MARSHA STEVENS
1. You said You'd come and share all my sor-rows, You said You'd be there for all my to-mor-rows; I came so close to send-ing You a-way, But just like You prom-ised You came there to stay— I just had to pray!
2. Your good-ness so great I can't un-der-stand, And, dear Lord, I know that all this was planned; I know You're here now and al-ways will be, Your love loosed my chains and in You I'm free— But Je-sus, why me?
3. Je-sus, I give You my heart and my soul! I know that with-out God I'd nev-er be whole; Sav-ior, You o-pened all the right doors, And I thank You and praise You from earth's humble shores— Take me, I'm Yours!
REFRAIN
And Je-sus said, "Come to the wa-ter, stand by My side, I know you are thirst-y— you
SALVATION

won't be de - nied; I felt ev - 'ry tear - drop when in dark - ness you
cried, And I strove to re - mind you that for those tears I died."

Not What These Hands Have Done — 264

HORATIUS BONAR
NORMAN JOHNSON
1. Not what these hands have done Can save this guilt - y soul;
2. Not what I feel or do Can give me peace with God;
3. Thy work a - lone, O Christ, Can ease this weight of sin;
4. Thy love to me, O God— Not my poor love to Thee—
5. Thy grace a - lone, O God, To me can par - don speak;
6. I bless the Christ of God, I rest on love di - vine;
Not what this toil - ing flesh has borne Can make my spir - it whole.
Not all my prayers and sighs and tears Can bear my aw - ful load.
Thy blood a - lone, O Lamb of God, Can give me peace with - in.
Can rid me of this dark un - rest And set my spir - it free.
Thy pow'r a - lone, O Son of God, Can this sore bond - age break.
And with un - fal - t'ring lip and heart I call this Sav - ior mine!*

Tune: AURORA

265 — There Is a Fountain
WILLIAM COWPER
American melody
1. There is a foun - tain filled with blood Drawn from Im-man-uel's veins,
2. The dy - ing thief re - joiced to see That foun-tain in his day,
3. Dear dy - ing Lamb, Thy pre-cious blood Shall nev - er lose its pow'r,
4. E'er since by faith I saw the stream Thy flow-ing wounds sup - ply,
5. When this poor lisp-ing, stam-m'ring tongue Lies si - lent in the grave,
And sin - ners plunged be-neath that flood Lose all their guilt - y stains:
And there may I, though vile as he, Wash all my sins a - way:
Till all the ran - somed Church of God Be saved to sin no more:
Re - deem - ing love has been my theme And shall be till I die:
Then in a no - bler, sweet - er song I'll sing Thy pow'r to save:
Lose all their guilt - y stains, Lose all their guilt - y stains;
Wash all my sins a - way, Wash all my sins a - way;
Be saved to sin no more, Be saved to sin no more;
And shall be till I die, And shall be till I die;
I'll sing Thy pow'r to save, I'll sing Thy pow'r to save;
And sin - ners plunged be - neath that flood Lose all their guilt - y stains.
And there may I, though vile as he, Wash all my sins a - way.
Till all the ran - somed Church of God Be saved to sin no more.
Re - deem - ing love has been my theme And shall be till I die.
Then in a no - bler, sweet - er song I'll sing Thy pow'r to save.
Tune: CLEANSING FOUNTAIN

SALVATION

My Hope Is in the Lord — 266
NORMAN J. CLAYTON
NORMAN J. CLAYTON
1. My hope is in the Lord Who gave Him - self for me,
2. No mer - it of my own His an - ger to sup - press:
3. And now for me He stands Be - fore the Fa - ther's throne:
4. His grace has planned it all— 'Tis mine but to be - lieve,
And paid the price of all my sin at Cal - va - ry.
My on - ly hope is found in Je - sus' right - eous - ness.
He shows His wound-ed hands and names me as His own.
And rec - og - nize His work of love, and Christ re - ceive.
REFRAIN
For me He died, For me He lives;
For me He died, He died, For me, for me He lives, He lives;
And ev - er - last - ing life and light He free - ly gives.
Copyright 1945 Norman J. Clayton. © Renewed 1973 Norman Clayton Publishing Co.
SALVATION

267 — Burdens Are Lifted at Calvary
JOHN M. MOORE
JOHN M. MOORE
1. Days are filled with sor-row and care, Hearts are lone-ly and drear;
2. Cast your care on Je - sus to - day, Leave your wor-ry and fear;
3. Trou-bled soul, the Sav-ior can see Ev - 'ry heart-ache and tear;
Bur - dens are lift - ed at Cal - va - ry— Je - sus is ver - y near.
Bur - dens are lift - ed at Cal - va - ry— Je - sus is ver - y near.
Bur - dens are lift - ed at Cal - va - ry— Je - sus is ver - y near.
REFRAIN
Bur-dens are lift - ed at Cal - va - ry, Cal - va - ry, Cal - va - ry;
Bur - dens are lift - ed at Cal - va - ry— Je - sus is ver - y near.
Copyright Singspiration 1952, renewal 1980. All rights reserved.
268 — Thank You, Lord
SETH SYKES
SETH and BESSIE SYKES
Thank you, Lord, for sav - ing my soul, Thank you, Lord, for mak-ing me whole;
SALVATION
Copyright Singspiration 1940, renewal 1968. All rights reserved.

Thank you, Lord, for giv - ing to me Thy great sal - va - tion so rich and free.
Nothing But the Blood — 269
ROBERT LOWRY
ROBERT LOWRY
1. What can wash a - way my sin? Noth-ing but the blood of Je - sus;
2. For my par - don this I see— Noth-ing but the blood of Je - sus;
3. Noth - ing can for sin a - tone— Noth-ing but the blood of Je - sus;
4. This is all my hope and peace— Noth-ing but the blood of Je - sus;
What can make me whole a - gain? Noth-ing but the blood of Je - sus.
For my cleans-ing this my plea— Noth-ing but the blood of Je - sus.
Naught of good that I have done— Noth-ing but the blood of Je - sus.
This is all my right - eous - ness— Noth-ing but the blood of Je - sus.
REFRAIN
O! pre - cious is the flow That makes me white as snow;
No oth - er fount I know, Noth-ing but the blood of Je - sus.
SALVATION

270 — O Let Your Soul Now Be Filled with Gladness
PETER JÖNSSON ASCHAN
Trans. by Karl A. Olsson
Swedish folk melody
Arr. by A. Royce Eckhardt
1. O let your soul now be filled with glad - ness, Your heart re-deemed re -
2. If you seem emp - ty of an - y feel - ing, Re - joice—you are His
3. It is a good ev - 'ry good tran - scend - ing That Christ has died for
joice in - deed! O may the thought ban - ish all your sad - ness That
ran - somed bride! If those you cher - ish seem not to love you And
you and me! It is a glad - ness that has no end - ing There-
in His blood you have been freed, That God's un - fail - ing love is yours,
dark as - sails from ev - 'ry side, Still yours the prom-ise, come what may,
in God's won - drous love to see! Praise be to You, O spot - less Lamb,
That you the on - ly Son were giv - en, That by His
In loss and tri - umph, in laugh - ter, cry - ing, In want and
Who thru the des - ert my soul are lead - ing To that fair
death He has o-pened heav - en, That you are ran-somed as you are.
rich - es, in liv - ing, dy - ing, That you are pur-chased as you are.
cit - y of joy ex - ceed - ing, For which You bought me as I am.
Tune: RANSOMED SOUL
SALVATION
Copyright © 1972 by Covenant Press.

Fill My Cup, Lord — 271

RICHARD BLANCHARD
RICHARD BLANCHARD
1. Like the woman at the well I was seek-ing For things that could not sat-is-fy; And then I heard my Sav-ior speak-ing: "Draw from My well that nev-er shall run dry."
2. There are mil-lions in this world who are crav-ing The pleas-ures earth-ly things af-ford; But none can match the won-drous treas-ure That I find in Je-sus Christ my Lord.
3. So, my broth-er, if the things this world gave you Leave hun-gers that won't pass a-way, My bless-ed Lord will come and save you, If you kneel to Him and hum-bly pray:
CHORUS
Fill my cup, Lord— I lift it up, Lord! Come and quench this thirst-ing of my soul; Bread of heav-en, feed me till I want no more—Fill my cup, fill it up and make me whole!
SALVATION

272 — All in the Name of Jesus
STEPHEN R. ADAMS
STEPHEN R. ADAMS
1. Truth and beau-ty and hap - pi - ness— It's all in the name of
2. Care and com-fort and heal-ing and grace— It's all in the name of
Je - sus, Health and heav - en and peace and rest— It's
Je - sus, Wel-come and par - don, a hid - ing place— It's
all in the name of Je-sus; Joy and glad-ness, for - give - ness
all in the name of Je-sus; Warmth and sunshine and friend-ship
too, Life ev - er - last - ing and free: All that I've
true, Ful - fill - ment and bless-ing un - told: Hope for to -
longed for and all I need— It's all in the name of Je - sus.
mor - row and help for to - day— It's all in the name of Je - sus.
SALVATION
© 1975 by Dimension Music. All rights reserved.

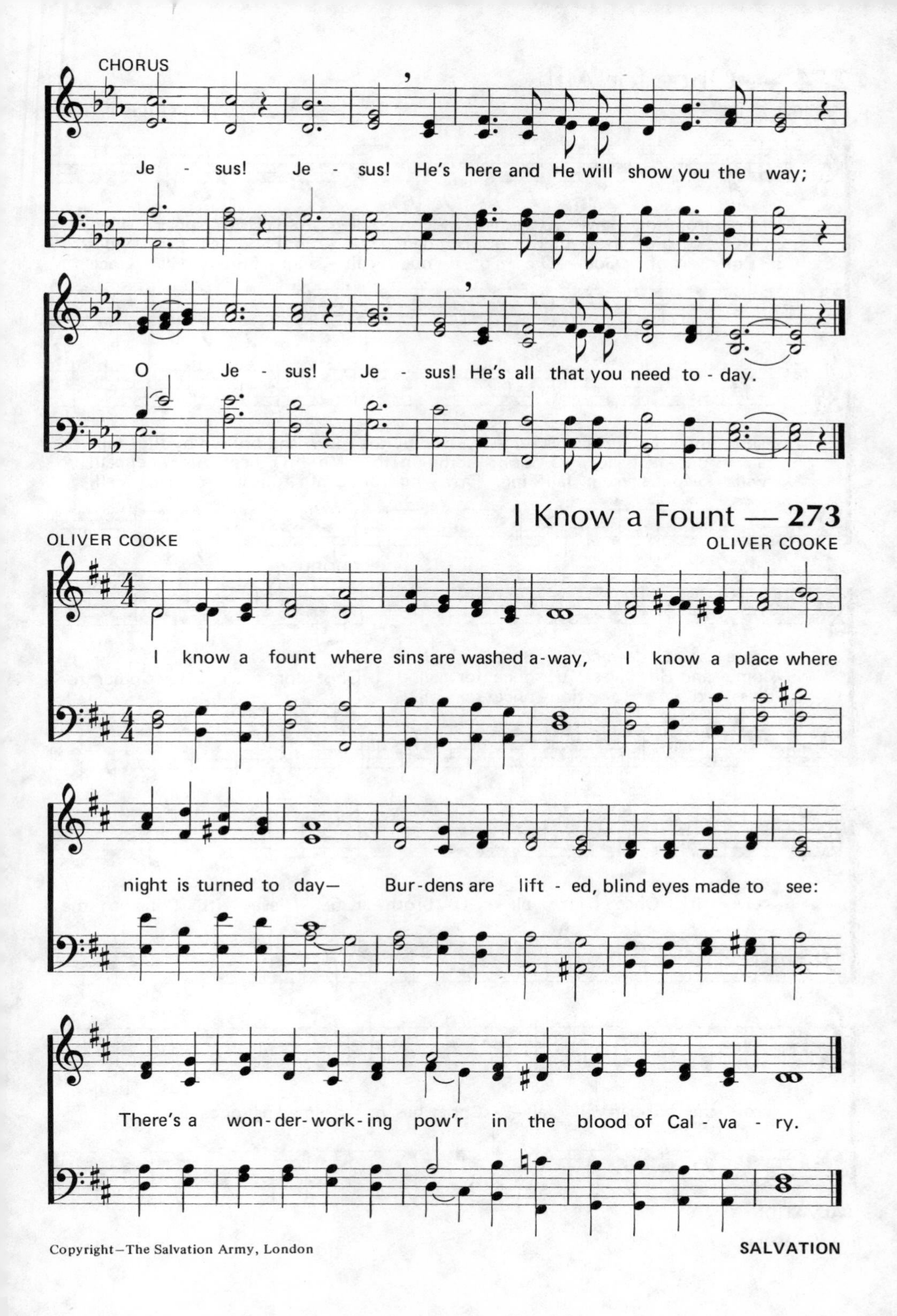
CHORUS
Je - sus! Je - sus! He's here and He will show you the way;
O Je - sus! Je - sus! He's all that you need to - day.
I Know a Fount — 273
OLIVER COOKE
OLIVER COOKE
I know a fount where sins are washed a-way, I know a place where
night is turned to day— Bur-dens are lift - ed, blind eyes made to see:
There's a won-der-work-ing pow'r in the blood of Cal - va - ry.
Copyright—The Salvation Army, London
SALVATION

274 — Once for All!

PHILIP P. BLISS PHILIP P. BLISS

1. Free from the law— O hap-py con - di - tion! Je - sus has bled, and there is re - mis - sion; Cursed by the law and bruised by the fall, Grace has re - deemed us once for all.
2. Now we are free—there's no con-dem - na - tion! Je - sus pro - vides a per - fect sal - va - tion; "Come un-to Me—" O hear His sweet call! Come—and He saves us once for all.
3. Chil-dren of God— O glo - ri - ous call - ing! Sure-ly His grace will keep us from fall - ing; Pass - ing from death to life at His call, Bless - ed sal - va - tion—once for all.
CHORUS
Once for all— O sin-ner, re - ceive it! Once for all— O broth - er, be - lieve it! Cling to the cross, the bur-den will fall— Christ has re - deemed us once for all!

O Happy Day! — 275
PHILIP DODDRIDGE
EDWARD F. RIMBAULT
1. O hap - py day that fixed my choice On Thee, my Sav - ior and my God!
2. O hap - py bond that seals my vows To Him who mer - its all my love!
3. 'Tis done, the great trans - ac - tion's done— I am my Lord's and He is mine;
4. Now rest, my long - di - vid - ed heart, Fixed on this bliss - ful cen - ter, rest;
Well may this glow - ing heart re - joice And tell its rap - tures all a - broad.
Let cheer - ful an - thems fill His house, While to that sa - cred shrine I move.
He drew me, and I fol - lowed on, Charmed to con - fess the voice di - vine.
Nor ev - er from my Lord de - part, With Him of ev - 'ry good pos - sessed.
CHORUS
Hap - py day, hap - py day, When Je - sus washed my sins a - way!
He taught me how to watch and pray And live re - joic - ing ev - 'ry day;
Hap - py day, hap - py day, When Je - sus washed my sins a - way!

SALVATION

276 — The Blood Will Never Lose Its Power
ANDRAÉ CROUCH
ANDRAÉ CROUCH
1. The blood that Je - sus shed for me,
2. It soothes my doubts and calms my fears,
Way back on Cal - va - ry— The blood that gives me strength from
And it dries all my tears; The blood that gives me strength from
day to day— It will nev - er lose its pow'r.
day to day— It will nev - er lose its pow'r.
REFRAIN
It reach-es to the high - est moun - tain, It flows to the
low - est val - ley; The blood that gives me strength from
© Copyright 1966, arr. 1979 by Manna Music, Inc. All rights reserved.
SALVATION

day to day— It will nev - er lose its pow'r.
My Faith Has Found a Resting Place — 277
LIDIE H. EDMUNDS
Norwegian melody
1. My faith has found a rest - ing place—Not in de - vice nor creed:
2. E - nough for me that Je - sus saves—This ends my fear and doubt;
3. My heart is lean - ing on the Word—The writ - ten Word of God:
4. My great Phy - si - cian heals the sick— The lost He came to save;
I trust the Ev - er - liv - ing One— His wounds for me shall plead.
A sin - ful soul I come to Him— He'll nev - er cast me out.
Sal - va - tion by my Sav - ior's name—Sal - va - tion thru His blood.
For me His pre - cious blood He shed—For me His life He gave.
REFRAIN
I need no oth - er ar - gu - ment, I need no oth - er plea; It
is e - nough that Je - sus died, And that He died for me.
Tune: NO OTHER PLEA
SALVATION

278 — Calvary Covers It All
ETHEL ROBINSON TAYLOR
ETHEL ROBINSON TAYLOR
1. Far dear - er than all that the world can im - part Was the mes - sage that came to my heart, How that Je - sus a - lone for my sin did a - tone— And Cal - va - ry cov - ers it all.
2. The stripes that He bore and the thorns that He wore Told His mer - cy and love ev - er - more; And my heart bowed in shame as I called on His name— And Cal - va - ry cov - ers it all.
3. How match - less the grace, when I looked in the face Of this Je - sus, my cru - ci - fied Lord; My re - demp - tion com - plete I then found at His feet— And Cal - va - ry cov - ers it all.
4. How bless - ed the thought that my soul, by Him bought, Shall be His in the glo - ry on high, Where with glad - ness and song I'll be one of the throng— And Cal - va - ry cov - ers it all.
CHORUS
Cal - va - ry cov - ers it all, My past with its sin and stain; My guilt and de - spair Je - sus took on Him there, And Cal - va - ry cov - ers it all.
SALVATION
Copyright 1934, Mrs. Walter G. Taylor.
©Renewed 1962, The Rodeheaver Co. All rights reserved.

My Sins Are Blotted Out, I Know! — 279
Based on Acts 3:19
MERRILL DUNLOP
MERRILL DUNLOP
1. What a won-drous mes-sage in God's Word! My sins are blot - ted out, I know! If I trust in His re - deem-ing blood, My sins are blot-ted out, I know!
2. Once my heart was black, but now what joy, My sins are blot - ted out, I know! I have peace that noth - ing can de - stroy, My sins are blot-ted out, I know!
3. I shall stand some day be - fore my King, My sins are blot - ted out, I know! With the ran - somed host I then shall sing: "My sins are blot-ted out, I know!"
CHORUS
My sins are blot-ted out, I know! I know! My sins are blot - ted out, I know! I know! They are bur - ied in the depths of the deep-est sea: My sins are blot-ted out, I know! I know!

280 — There's a Wideness in God's Mercy
FREDERICK W. FABER
LIZZIE S. TOURJÉE
1. There's a wide-ness in God's mer-cy Like the wide-ness of the sea;
2. There is wel-come for the sin-ner And more grac-es for the good;
3. For the love of God is broad-er Than the meas-ure of man's mind,
4. If our love were but more sim-ple, We should take Him at His word,
There's a kind-ness in His jus-tice Which is more than lib-er-ty.
There is mer-cy with the Sav-ior, There is heal-ing in His blood.
And the heart of the E-ter-nal Is most won-der-ful-ly kind.
And our lives would be all sun-shine In the sweet-ness of our Lord.
Tune: WELLESLEY
Arr. © Singspiration 1968. All rights reserved.
281 — I Am Not Skilled to Understand
DORA GREENWELL
WILLIAM J. KIRKPATRICK
1. I am not skilled to understand What God has will'd, what God has plan'd;
2. I take Him at His word in-deed—"Christ died for sin-ners," this I read—
3. That He should leave His place on high And come for sin-ful man to die,
4. And O that He ful-filled may see The trav-ail of His soul in me,
5. Yes, liv-ing, dy-ing, let me bring My strength, my sol-ace from this spring:
I on-ly know at His right hand Is One who is my Sav-ior!
For in my heart I find a need Of Him to be my Sav-ior!
You count it strange? so once did I, Be-fore I knew my Sav-ior!
And with His work con-tent-ed be, As I with my dear Sav-ior!
That He who lives to be my King Once died to be my Sav-ior!
Tune: GREENWELL
SALVATION

Tell Me the Old, Old Story — 282
A. CATHERINE HANKEY
WILLIAM H. DOANE
1. Tell me the old, old sto - ry Of un - seen things a - bove, Of Je - sus
2. Tell me the sto - ry slow - ly, That I may take it in— That won-der-
3. Tell me the same old sto - ry When you have cause to fear That this world's
and His glo - ry, Of Je - sus and His love. Tell me the sto-ry
ful re - demp - tion, God's rem-e - dy for sin. Tell me the sto-ry
emp - ty glo - ry Is cost-ing me too dear. Tell me the sto-ry
sim - ply, As to a lit - tle child, For I am weak and wea - ry,
oft - en, For I for-get so soon; The ear-ly dew of morn - ing
al - ways, If you would real - ly be, In an - y time of trou - ble,
CHORUS
And help-less and de - filed.
Has passed a - way at noon. Tell me the old, old sto - ry, Tell me the
A com-fort - er to me.
old, old sto - ry, Tell me the old, old sto - ry Of Je - sus and His love.
SALVATION

283 — There Is Power in the Blood
LEWIS E. JONES
LEWIS E. JONES
1. Would you be free from the bur - den of sin? There's pow'r in the blood,
2. Would you be free from your pas - sion and pride? There's pow'r in the blood,
3. Would you be whit - er, much whit - er than snow? There's pow'r in the blood,
4. Would you do serv - ice for Je - sus your King? There's pow'r in the blood,
pow'r in the blood; Would you o'er e - vil a vic - to - ry win? There's
pow'r in the blood; Come for a cleans-ing to Cal - va - ry's tide— There's
pow'r in the blood; Sin - stains are lost in its life - giv - ing flow—There's
pow'r in the blood; Would you live dai - ly His prais - es to sing? There's
CHORUS
won - der - ful pow'r in the blood. There is pow'r, pow'r, won-der-work-ing
pow'r In the blood of the Lamb; There is pow'r, pow'r,
In the blood
won-der-work-ing pow'r In the pre - cious blood of the Lamb.
SALVATION

Turn Your Eyes upon Jesus — 284
HELEN H. LEMMEL
HELEN H. LEMMEL
1. O soul, are you wea-ry and trou - bled? No light in the dark-ness you see? There's light for a look at the Sav - ior, And life more a - bun-dant and free!
2. Thru death in-to life ev-er-last - ing He passed, and we fol - low Him there; O-ver us sin no more has do-min - ion—For more than con-q'rors we are!
3. His word shall not fail you—He prom - ised; Be - lieve Him, and all will be well: Then go to a world that is dy - ing, His per-fect sal-va-tion to tell!
CHORUS
Turn your eyes up-on Je - sus, Look full in His won-der-ful face, won-der-ful face, And the things of earth will grow strange-ly dim In the light of His glo-ry and grace.
Copyright Singspiration 1922, renewal 1950. All rights reserved.
SALVATION

285 — If I Gained the World

Based on Luke 9:25

ANNA ÖLANDER (composite translation)

Swedish melody

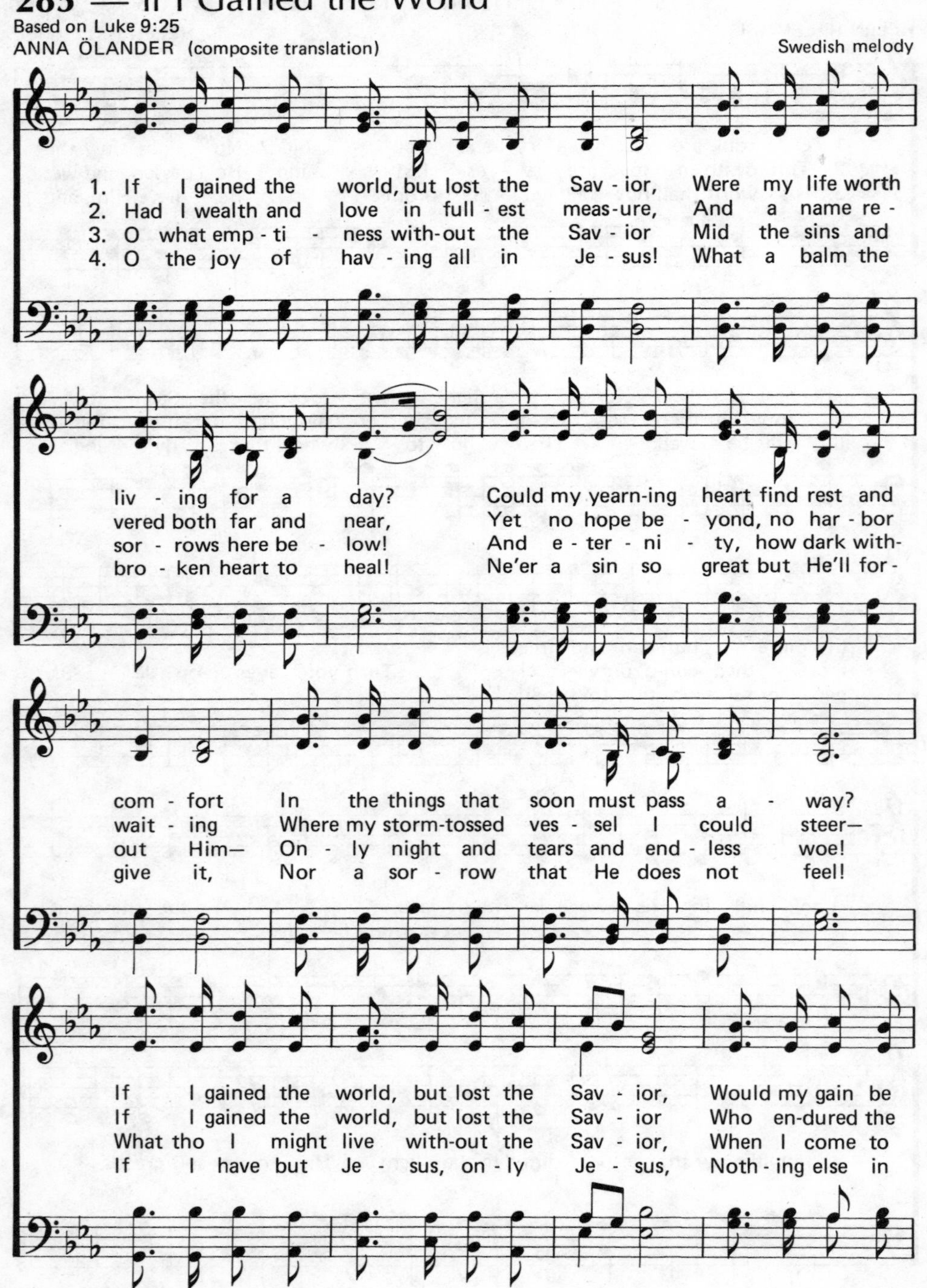
1. If I gained the world, but lost the Sav - ior, Were my life worth
2. Had I wealth and love in full - est meas-ure, And a name re -
3. O what emp - ti - ness with-out the Sav - ior Mid the sins and
4. O the joy of hav - ing all in Je - sus! What a balm the
liv - ing for a day? Could my yearn-ing heart find rest and
vered both far and near, Yet no hope be - yond, no har - bor
sor - rows here be - low! And e - ter - ni - ty, how dark with-
bro - ken heart to heal! Ne'er a sin so great but He'll for-
com - fort In the things that soon must pass a - way?
wait - ing Where my storm-tossed ves - sel I could steer—
out Him— On - ly night and tears and end - less woe!
give it, Nor a sor - row that He does not feel!
If I gained the world, but lost the Sav - ior, Would my gain be
If I gained the world, but lost the Sav - ior Who en-dured the
What tho I might live with-out the Sav - ior, When I come to
If I have but Je - sus, on - ly Je - sus, Noth - ing else in

Tune: TRUE RICHES

SALVATION

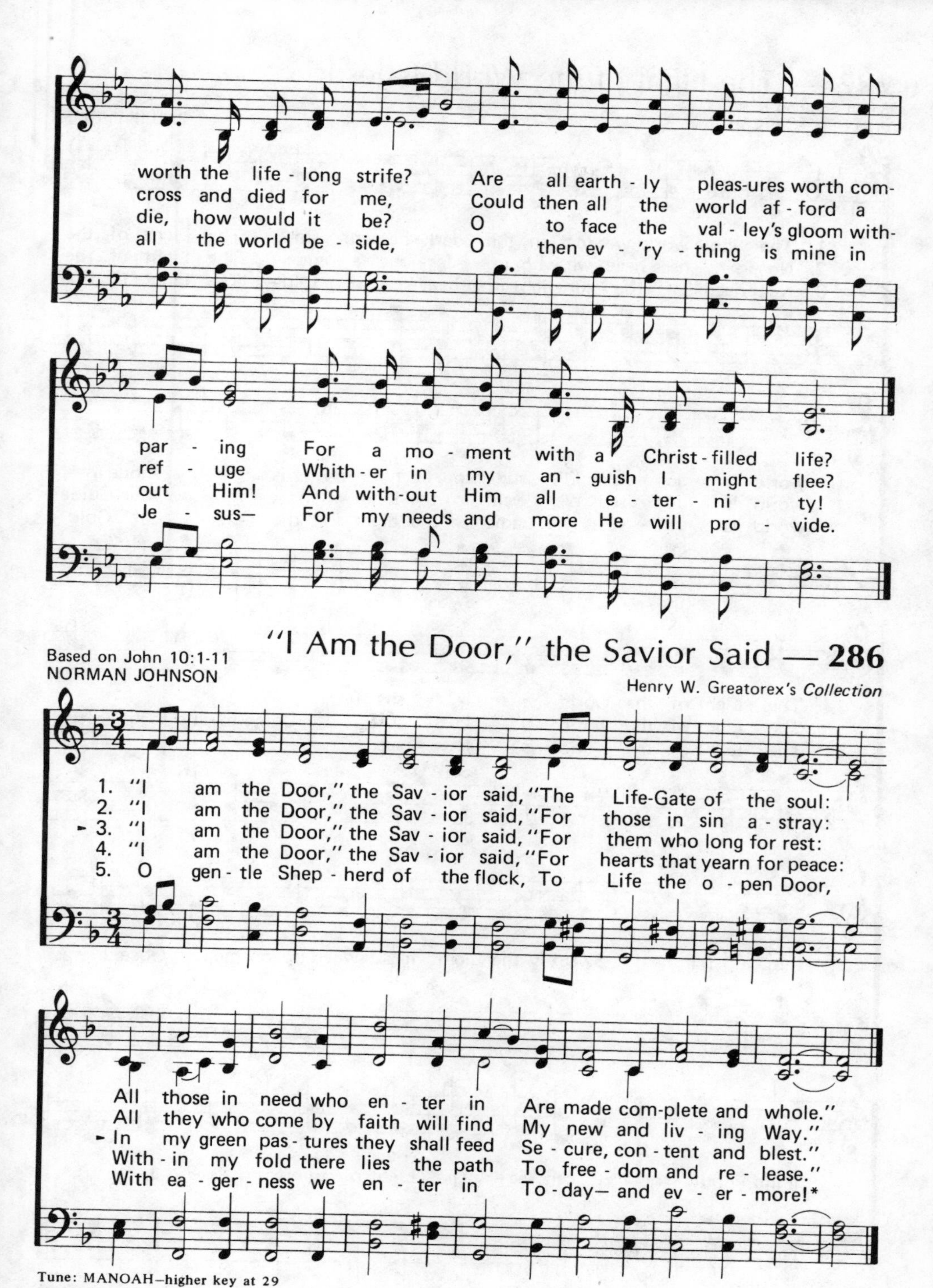
worth the life-long strife? Are all earth-ly pleas-ures worth com-
cross and died for me, Could then all the world af-ford a
die, how would it be? O to face the val-ley's gloom with-
all the world be-side, O then ev-'ry-thing is mine in
par-ing For a mo-ment with a Christ-filled life?
ref-uge Whith-er in my an-guish I might flee?
out Him! And with-out Him all e-ter-ni-ty!
Je-sus— For my needs and more He will pro-vide.
"I Am the Door," the Savior Said — 286
Based on John 10:1-11
NORMAN JOHNSON
Henry W. Greatorex's Collection
1. "I am the Door," the Sav-ior said, "The Life-Gate of the soul:
2. "I am the Door," the Sav-ior said, "For those in sin a-stray:
3. "I am the Door," the Sav-ior said, "For them who long for rest:
4. "I am the Door," the Sav-ior said, "For hearts that yearn for peace:
5. O gen-tle Shep-herd of the flock, To Life the o-pen Door,
All those in need who en-ter in Are made com-plete and whole."
All they who come by faith will find My new and liv-ing Way."
In my green pas-tures they shall feed Se-cure, con-tent and blest."
With-in my fold there lies the path To free-dom and re-lease."
With ea-ger-ness we en-ter in To-day— and ev-er-more!*

Tune: MANOAH–higher key at 29

287 — The Light of the World Is Jesus

Based on John 8:12
PHILIP P. BLISS

PHILIP P. BLISS

1. The whole world was lost in the dark - ness of sin— The Light of the
2. No dark - ness have we who in Je - sus a - bide— The Light of the
3. No need of the sun - light in heav - en, we're told— The Light of that

world is Je - sus; Like sun - shine at noon - day His glo - ry shone in—
world is Je - sus; We walk in the Light when we fol - low our Guide—
world is Je - sus; The Lamb is the Light in the Cit - y of Gold—

The Light of the world is Je - sus.
The Light of the world is Je - sus.
The Light of the world is Je - sus.

REFRAIN

Come to the Light, 'tis shin - ing for thee! Sweet - ly the Light has dawned up - on me; Once I was

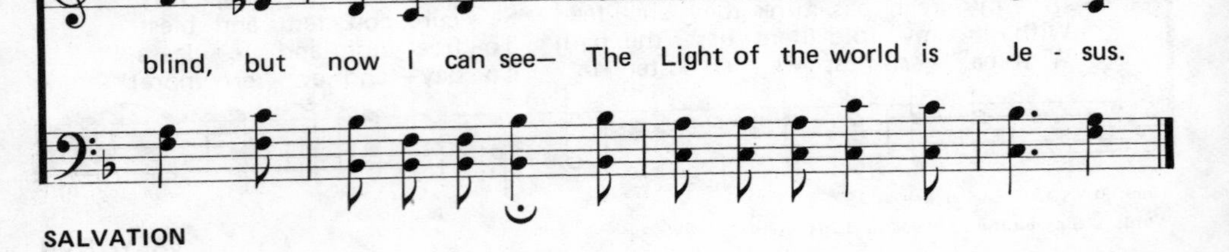
blind, but now I can see— The Light of the world is Je - sus.

SALVATION

I Know Whom I Have Believed — 288

Based on II Timothy 1:12
DANIEL W. WHITTLE
JAMES McGRANAHAN
1. I know not why God's won-drous grace To me He has made known,
2. I know not how this sav - ing faith To me He did im - part,
3. I know not how the Spir - it moves, Con - vinc - ing men of sin,
4. I know not what of good or ill May be re-served for me,
5. I know not when my Lord may come— At night or noon-day fair,
Nor why, un-wor-thy, Christ in love Re - deemed me for His own.
Nor how be-liev - ing in His Word Wrought peace with-in my heart.
Re - veal - ing Je - sus thru the Word, Cre - at - ing faith in Him.
Of wea - ry ways or gold - en days Be - fore His face I see.
Nor if I'll walk the vale with Him Or meet Him in the air.
CHORUS
But "I know whom I have be - liev - ed, And am per - suad - ed that He is
a - ble To keep that which I've com-mit-ted Un-to Him a-gainst that day."
SALVATION

289 — Jesus, Thy Blood and Righteousness

NICOLAUS L. von ZINZENDORF
Trans. by John Wesley

Gardiner's *Sacred Melodies*

1. Je - sus, Thy blood and right - eous - ness My beau - ty are, my glo - rious dress; 'Midst flam - ing worlds, in these ar - rayed, With joy shall I lift up my head.
2. Bold shall I stand in Thy great day, For who aught to my charge shall lay? Ful - ly ab - solved through these I am, From sin and fear, from guilt and shame.
3. Lord, I be - lieve Thy pre - cious blood, Which at the mer - cy seat of God For - ev - er doth for sin - ners plead, For me, e'en for my soul was shed.
4. Lord, I be - lieve were sin - ners more Than sands up - on the o - cean shore, Thou hast for all a ran - som paid, For all a full a - tone - ment made.*
Tune: GERMANY—lower key at 112, higher key at 490
290 — The Love of God
FREDERICK M. LEHMAN
FREDERICK M. LEHMAN
1. The love of God is great-er far Than tongue or pen can ev - er
2. When years of time shall pass a - way And earth-ly thrones and kingdoms
3. Could we with ink the o - cean fill And were the skies of parch-ment

tell, It goes be - yond the high-est star And reach-es to the low-est
fall, When men, who here re-fuse to pray, On rocks and hills and mountains
made, Were ev-'ry stalk on earth a quill And ev-'ry man a scribe by
hell; The guilt-y pair, bowed down with care, God gave His Son to
call, God's love so sure shall still en - dure, All mea-sure - less and
trade, To write the love of God a - bove Would drain the o - cean
win: His err-ing child He rec-on-ciled And par-doned from his sin.
strong: Re-deem-ing grace to Ad-am's race— The saints' and an - gels' song.
dry, Nor could the scroll con-tain the whole Tho stretched from sky to sky.
CHORUS
O love of God, how rich and pure! How mea-sure-less and strong!
It shall for ev - er-more en - dure— The saints' and an - gels' song.
SALVATION

291 — Wonderful Grace of Jesus
HALDOR LILLENAS
HALDOR LILLENAS
1. Won - der - ful grace of Je - sus, Great - er than all my sin;
2. Won - der - ful grace of Je - sus, Reach - ing to all the lost,
3. Won - der - ful grace of Je - sus, Reach - ing the most de - filed,
How shall my tongue de - scribe it, Where shall its praise be - gin?
By it I have been par - doned, Saved to the ut - ter - most;
By its trans-form - ing pow - er Mak - ing him God's dear child,
Tak - ing a - way my bur - den, Set - ting my spir - it free,
Chains have been torn a - sun - der, Giv - ing me lib - er - ty,
Pur - chas - ing peace and heav - en For all e - ter - ni - ty—
For the won - der - ful grace of Je - sus reach - es me.
For the won - der - ful grace of Je - sus reach - es me.
And the won - der - ful grace of Je - sus reach - es me.
CHORUS
the match-less grace of Je - sus,
Won - der - ful the match-less grace of Je - sus, Deep - er
Men
GRACE
Copyright 1918, renewal 1946 (ext.) by Hope Publishing Co.

the roll - ing sea;
Won - der - ful grace,
all - suf - fi - cient for
me, for e - ven me;
than the might-y roll - ing sea;
High - er than the
moun-tain, spark-ling like a foun - tain,
All - suf - fi - cient grace for e - ven
me;
Broad - er than the scope of my trans -
gres - sions,
trans -
gres - sions, sing it!
Great - er far than all my sin and shame;
my sin and shame;
O mag - ni - fy the pre - cious name of Je - sus, Praise His name!
GRACE

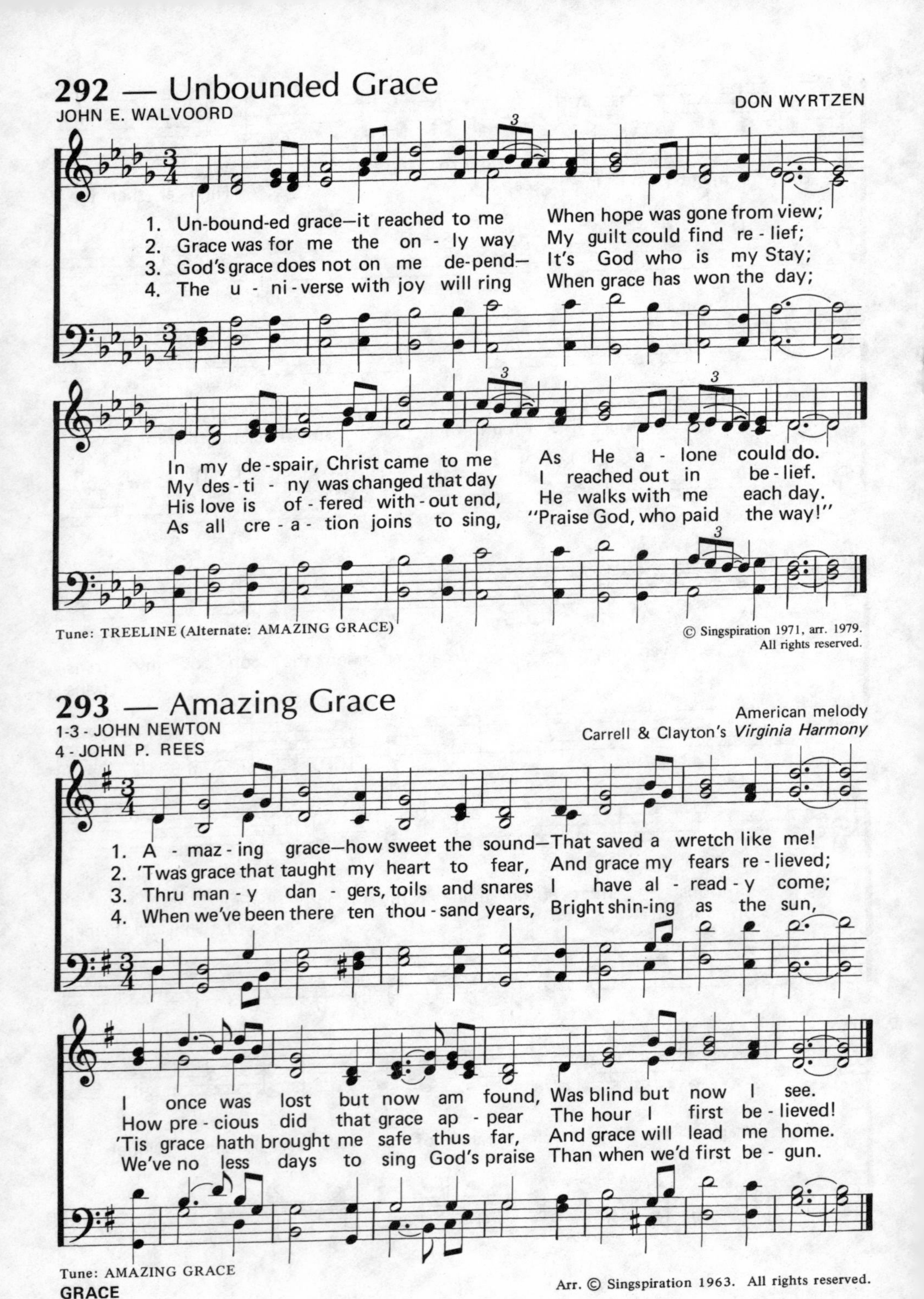
292 — Unbounded Grace
JOHN E. WALVOORD
DON WYRTZEN
1. Un-bound-ed grace—it reached to me When hope was gone from view;
2. Grace was for me the on - ly way My guilt could find re - lief;
3. God's grace does not on me de-pend— It's God who is my Stay;
4. The u - ni - verse with joy will ring When grace has won the day;
In my de-spair, Christ came to me As He a - lone could do.
My des - ti - ny was changed that day I reached out in be - lief.
His love is of - fered with - out end, He walks with me each day.
As all cre - a - tion joins to sing, "Praise God, who paid the way!"
Tune: TREELINE (Alternate: AMAZING GRACE)
© Singspiration 1971, arr. 1979.
All rights reserved.
293 — Amazing Grace
1-3 - JOHN NEWTON
4 - JOHN P. REES
American melody
Carrell & Clayton's Virginia Harmony
1. A - maz - ing grace—how sweet the sound—That saved a wretch like me!
2. 'Twas grace that taught my heart to fear, And grace my fears re - lieved;
3. Thru man - y dan - gers, toils and snares I have al - read - y come;
4. When we've been there ten thou - sand years, Bright shin-ing as the sun,
I once was lost but now am found, Was blind but now I see.
How pre - cious did that grace ap - pear The hour I first be - lieved!
'Tis grace hath brought me safe thus far, And grace will lead me home.
We've no less days to sing God's praise Than when we'd first be - gun.
Tune: AMAZING GRACE
GRACE
Arr. © Singspiration 1963. All rights reserved.

Great God of Wonders — 294
SAMUEL DAVIES
JOHN NEWTON
1. Great God of won - ders! all Thy ways Are match-less, God - like
2. In won-der lost, with trem-bling joy, We take the par - don
3. O may this strange, this match-less grace, This God - like mir - a -
and di - vine; But the fair glo - ries of Thy grace More God-like
of our God: Par - don for crimes of deep - est dye, A par - don
cle of love, Fill the whole earth with grate - ful praise, And all th'an-
and un - ri - valed shine, More God - like and un - ri - valed shine.
bought with Je - sus' blood, A par - don bought with Je - sus' blood.
gel - ic choirs a - bove, And all th'an - gel - ic choirs a - bove.
REFRAIN
Who is a par-d'ning God like Thee? Or who has grace so
rich and free? Or who has grace so rich and free? free?
1
2
GRACE

295 — Only a Sinner

JAMES M. GRAY DANIEL B. TOWNER

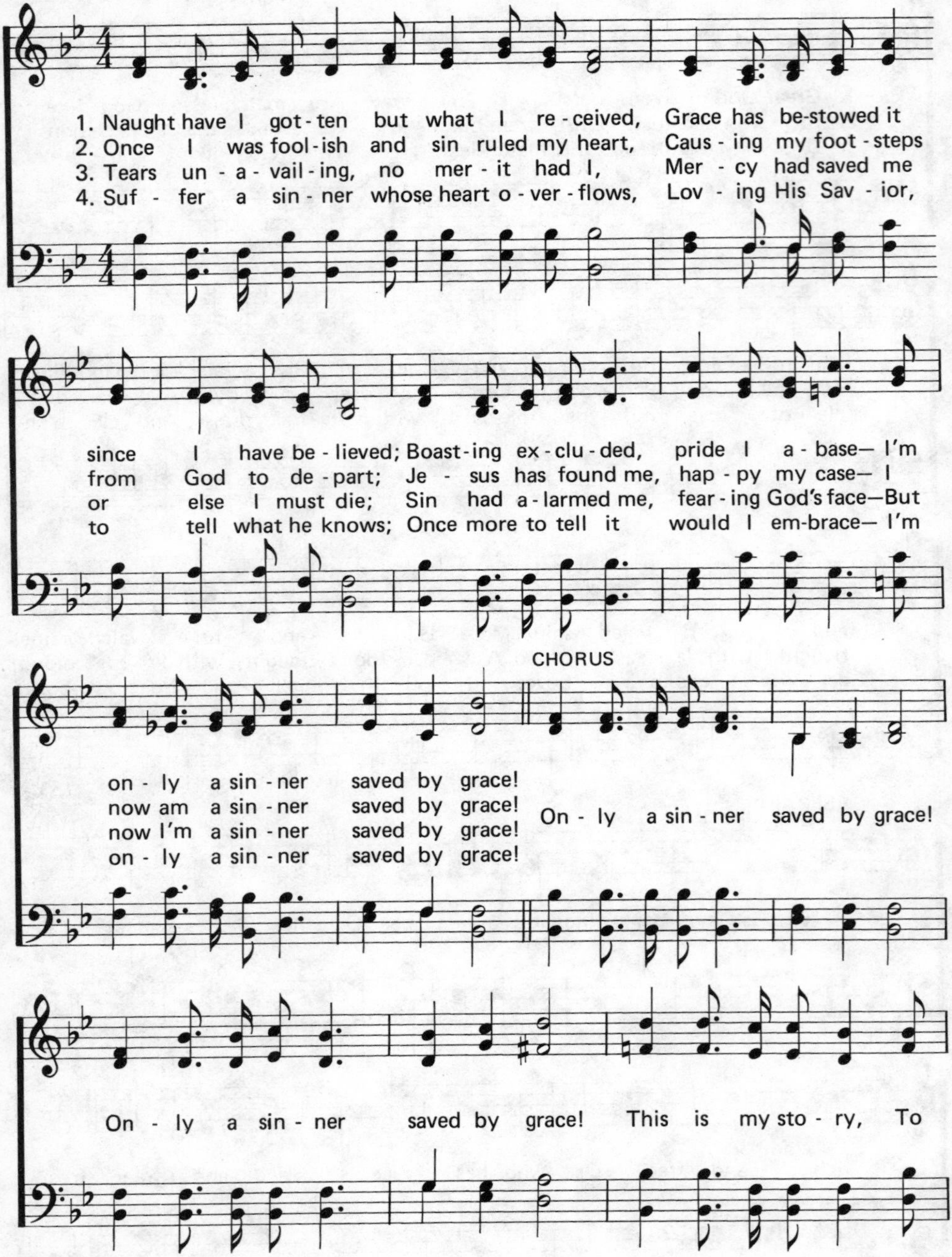

1. Naught have I got - ten but what I re - ceived, Grace has be-stowed it
2. Once I was fool - ish and sin ruled my heart, Caus - ing my foot - steps
3. Tears un - a - vail - ing, no mer - it had I, Mer - cy had saved me
4. Suf - fer a sin - ner whose heart o - ver - flows, Lov - ing His Sav - ior,

since I have be - lieved; Boast - ing ex - clu - ded, pride I a - base— I'm
from God to de - part; Je - sus has found me, hap - py my case— I
or else I must die; Sin had a - larmed me, fear - ing God's face—But
to tell what he knows; Once more to tell it would I em-brace— I'm

on - ly a sin - ner saved by grace!
now am a sin - ner saved by grace!
now I'm a sin - ner saved by grace!
on - ly a sin - ner saved by grace!

CHORUS

On - ly a sin - ner saved by grace!

On - ly a sin - ner saved by grace! This is my sto - ry, To

God be the glo - ry— I'm on - ly a sin - ner saved by grace!
Grace! 'Tis a Charming Sound — 296
1, 3 - PHILIP DODDRIDGE
2, 4 - AUGUSTUS M. TOPLADY
IRA D. SANKEY
1. Grace! 'tis a charm-ing sound, Har - mo - nious to the ear; Heav'n
2. 'Twas grace that wrote my name In life's e - ter - nal book;'Twas
3. Grace taught my wan-d'ring feet To tread the heav'n-ly road; And
4. O let Thy grace in - spire My soul with strength di - vine; May
with the ech - o shall re - sound, And all the earth shall hear.
grace that gave me to the Lamb, Who all my sor - rows took.
new sup-plies each hour I meet, While press - ing on to God.
all my pow'rs to Thee as - pire, And all my days be Thine.
CHORUS
Saved by grace a - lone! This is all my plea:
Je - sus died for all man - kind, And Je - sus died for me.
GRACE

297 — Grace Greater Than Our Sin

JULIA H. JOHNSTON

DANIEL B. TOWNER

1. Mar - vel - ous grace of our lov - ing Lord, Grace that ex - ceeds our
2. Sin and de - spair, like the sea - waves cold, Threat - en the soul with
3. Dark is the stain that we can - not hide— What can a - vail to
4. Mar - vel - ous, in - fi - nite, match - less grace, Free - ly be - stowed on
sin and our guilt! Yon - der on Cal - va - ry's mount out - poured—
in - fi - nite loss; Grace that is great - er— yes, grace un - told—
wash it a - way? Look! there is flow - ing a crim - son tide—
all who be - lieve! You that are long - ing to see His face,
There where the blood of the Lamb was spilt.
Points to the ref - uge, the might - y cross.
Whit - er than snow you may be to - day.
Will you this mo - ment His grace re - ceive?
CHORUS
Grace, grace,
Mar - vel - ous grace,
God's grace,
in - fi - nite grace,
Grace that will par - don and cleanse with - in;
Grace,
Mar - vel - ous

GRACE

grace, God's grace, Grace that is great-er than all our sin!
grace, in - fi - nite grace,
Only Trust Him — 298
JOHN H. STOCKTON
JOHN H. STOCKTON
1. Come, ev - 'ry soul by sin op-pressed—There's mer-cy with the Lord,
2. For Je - sus shed His pre-cious blood, Rich bless-ings to be - stow;
3. Yes, Je - sus is the Truth, the Way, That leads you in - to rest:
And He will sure-ly give you rest By trust-ing in His word.
Plunge now in - to the crim-son flood That wash-es white as snow.
Be - lieve in Him with - out de - lay And you are ful - ly blest.
CHORUS
On - ly trust Him, on - ly trust Him, On - ly trust Him now;
He will save you, He will save you, He will save you now.
INVITATION

299 — Room at the Cross for You

IRA F. STANPHILL — IRA F. STANPHILL

1. The cross up - on which Je - sus died Is a shel - ter in which we can hide; And its grace so free is suf - fi - cient for me, And deep is its foun - tain—as wide as the sea.
2. Tho mil - lions have found Him a friend And have turned from the sins they have sinned, The Sav - ior still waits to o - pen the gates And wel - come a sin - ner be - fore it's too late.
3. The hand of my Sav - ior is strong, And the love of my Sav - ior is long; Through sun - shine or rain, through loss or in gain, The blood flows from Cal - v'ry to cleanse ev - 'ry stain.
CHORUS
There's room at the cross for you, There's room at the cross for you; Tho mil-lions have come, There's still room for one—Yes, there's room at the cross for you.

INVITATION

The Savior Is Waiting — 300

RALPH CARMICHAEL
RALPH CARMICHAEL
1. The Sav - ior is wait - ing to en - ter your heart— Why don't you let Him come in? There's noth - ing in this world to keep you a - part— What is your an - swer to Him?
2. If you'll take one step toward the Sav - ior, my friend, You'll find His arms o - pen wide; Re - ceive Him and all of your dark - ness will end, With - in your heart He'll a - bide.
REFRAIN
Time aft - er time He has wait - ed be - fore, And now He is wait - ing a - gain To see if you're will - ing to o - pen the door— O how He wants to come in!

INVITATION

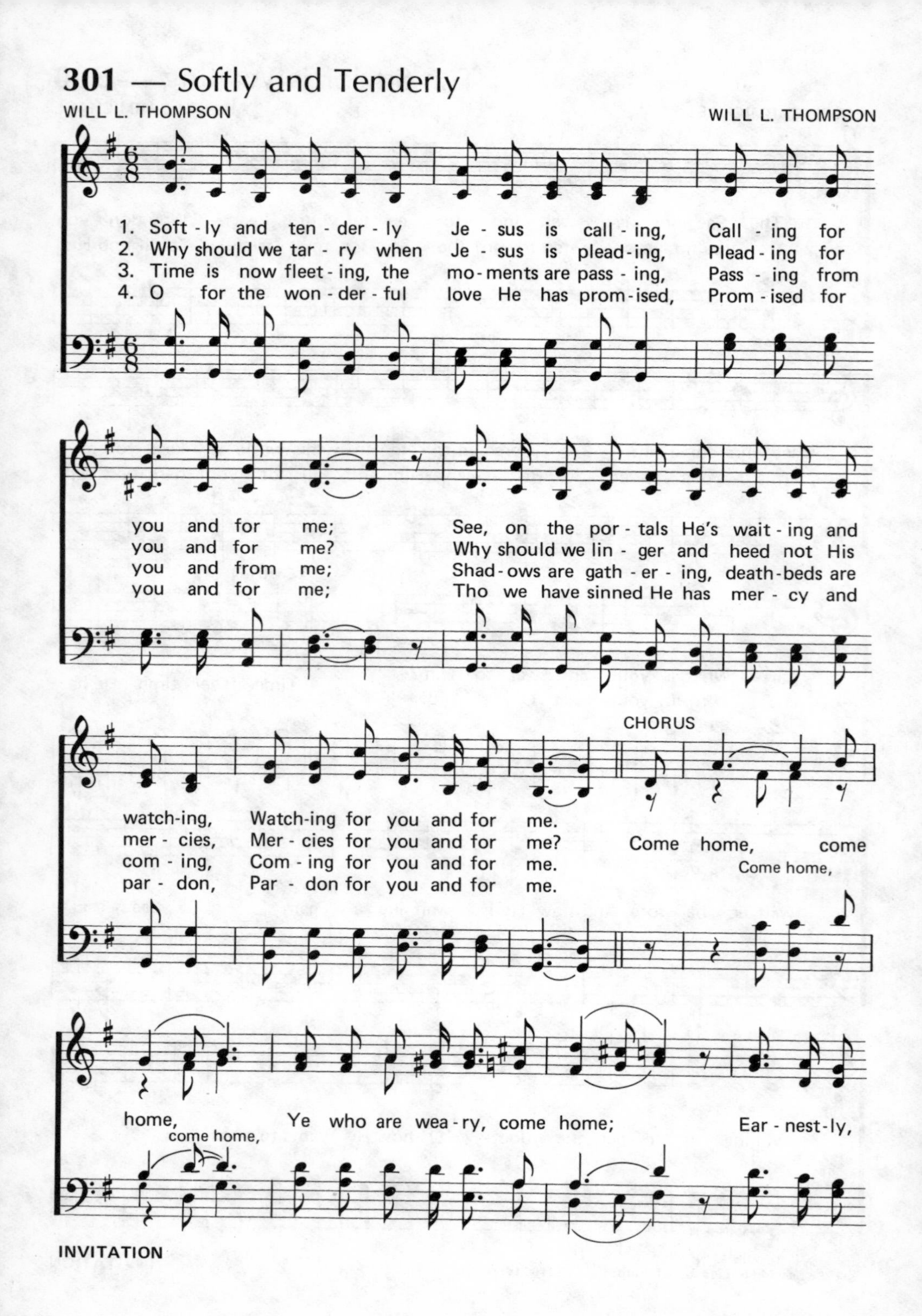
301 — Softly and Tenderly
WILL L. THOMPSON
WILL L. THOMPSON
1. Soft - ly and ten - der - ly Je - sus is call - ing, Call - ing for
2. Why should we tar - ry when Je - sus is plead - ing, Plead - ing for
3. Time is now fleet - ing, the mo - ments are pass - ing, Pass - ing from
4. O for the won - der - ful love He has prom - ised, Prom - ised for
you and for me; See, on the por - tals He's wait - ing and
you and for me? Why should we lin - ger and heed not His
you and from me; Shad - ows are gath - er - ing, death - beds are
you and for me; Tho we have sinned He has mer - cy and
CHORUS
watch - ing, Watch - ing for you and for me.
mer - cies, Mer - cies for you and for me? Come home, come
com - ing, Com - ing for you and for me. Come home,
par - don, Par - don for you and for me.
home, Ye who are wea - ry, come home; Ear - nest - ly,
come home,
INVITATION

ten-der-ly, Je-sus is call-ing— Call-ing, "O sin-ner, come home!"
Have You Any Room for Jesus? — 302
Based on Revelation 3:20
Source unknown
C. C. WILLIAMS
1. Have you an-y room for Je-sus, He who bore your load of sin?
2. Room for pleas-ure, room for busi-ness— But, for Christ the Cru-ci-fied,
3. Have you an-y room for Je-sus, As in grace He calls a-gain?
4. Room and time now give to Je-sus, Soon will pass God's day of grace;
As He knocks and asks ad-mis-sion, Sin-ner, will you let Him in?
Not a place that He can en-ter In the heart for which He died?
O to-day is time ac-cept-ed, Lat-er you may call in vain.
Soon your heart left cold and si-lent, And your Sav-ior's plead-ing cease.
REFRAIN
Room for Je-sus, King of glo-ry! Has-ten now, His word o-bey;
Swing the heart's door wide-ly o-pen, Bid Him en-ter while you may.
Tune: ANY ROOM
INVITATION

303 — Come with Your Heartache
OSWALD J. SMITH
REDD HARPER
1. Come with your heart-ache, your sor - row and care, Come to the Sav - ior to - day; Je - sus will com - fort— O why then de - spair? He will not turn you a - way.
2. Come with your heart-ache— the Sav - ior will hear, Come and un - bur - den your soul; Je - sus has prom - ised to dry ev - 'ry tear—Hearts, bro-ken hearts, He makes whole.
3. Come with your heart-ache— the world can - not heal! Why should you suf - fer a - lone? On - ly the Sav - ior your heart - ache can feel— Je - sus still cares for His own.
CHORUS
Come with your heart-ache, O come to Him now— He will not turn you a - way; Je - sus is wait-ing your bur-dens to share— Come with your heart-ache to-day.
INVITATION
Copyright Zondervan Herman Corp. 1955. Renewal 1983, arr. 1974. All rights reserved.

For You I Am Praying — 304
S. O'MALLEY CLUFF
IRA D. SANKEY
1. I have a Sav - ior—He's plead - ing in glo - ry, A dear, lov - ing Sav - ior, tho earth-friends be few; And now He is watch - ing in ten - der - ness o'er me—But O that my Sav - ior were your Sav - ior too.
2. I have a Fa - ther—to me He has giv - en A hope for e - ter - ni - ty, bless - ed and true; And soon He will call me to meet Him in heav - en—But O that He'd let me bring you with me too!
3. When Christ has found you, tell oth - ers the sto - ry, That my lov - ing Sav - ior is your Sav - ior too; Then pray that your Sav - ior will bring them to glo - ry, And prayer will be an - swered—'twas an - swered for you!
CHORUS
For you I am pray - ing, For you I am pray - ing, For you I am pray - ing, I'm pray - ing for you.

INVITATION

305 — Almost Persuaded

Based on Acts 26:28
PHILIP P. BLISS

PHILIP P. BLISS

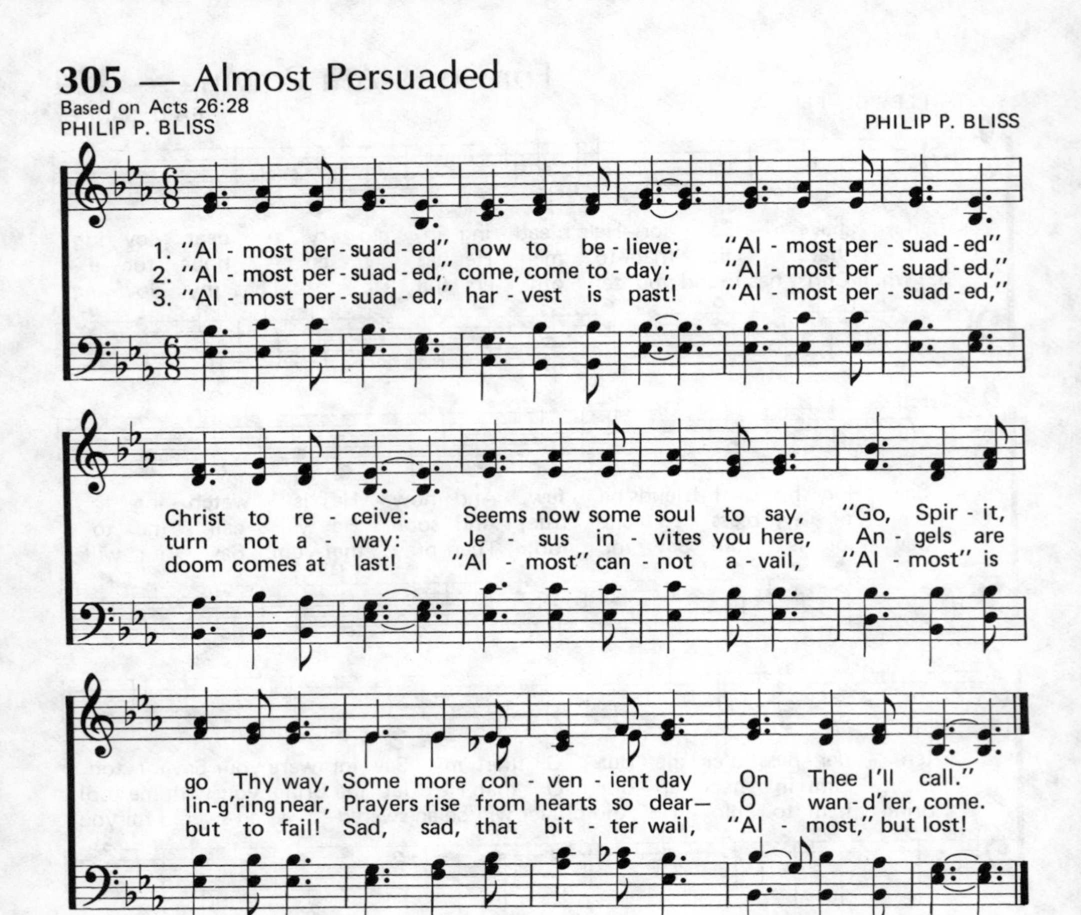
1. "Al - most per - suad - ed" now to be - lieve; "Al - most per - suad - ed" Christ to re - ceive: Seems now some soul to say, "Go, Spir - it, go Thy way, Some more con - ven - ient day On Thee I'll call."
2. "Al - most per - suad - ed," come, come to - day; "Al - most per - suad - ed," turn not a - way: Je - sus in - vites you here, An - gels are lin-g'ring near, Prayers rise from hearts so dear— O wan - d'rer, come.
3. "Al - most per - suad - ed," har - vest is past! "Al - most per - suad - ed," doom comes at last! "Al - most" can - not a - vail, "Al - most" is but to fail! Sad, sad, that bit - ter wail, "Al - most," but lost!

306 — Just As I Am

CHARLOTTE ELLIOTT

WILLIAM B. BRADBURY

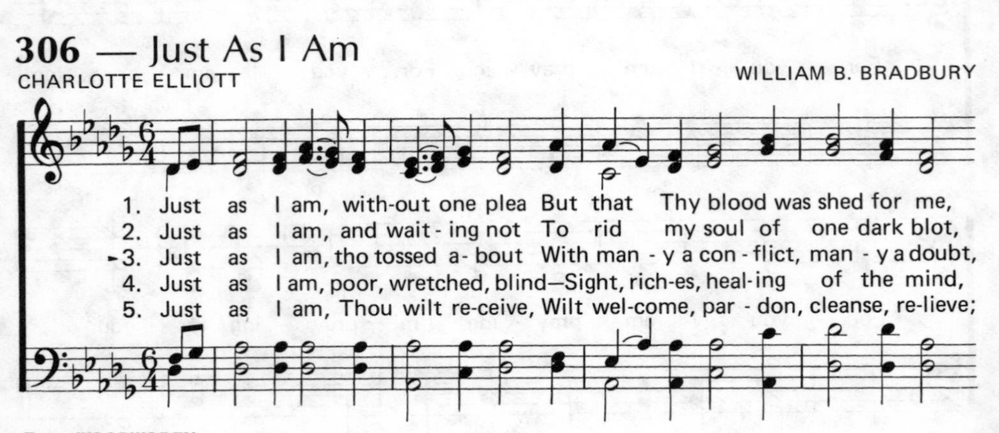
1. Just as I am, with-out one plea But that Thy blood was shed for me,
2. Just as I am, and wait - ing not To rid my soul of one dark blot,
3. Just as I am, tho tossed a- bout With man - y a con - flict, man - y a doubt,
4. Just as I am, poor, wretched, blind—Sight, rich-es, heal-ing of the mind,
5. Just as I am, Thou wilt re-ceive, Wilt wel-come, par - don, cleanse, re-lieve;

Tune: WOODWORTH

INVITATION

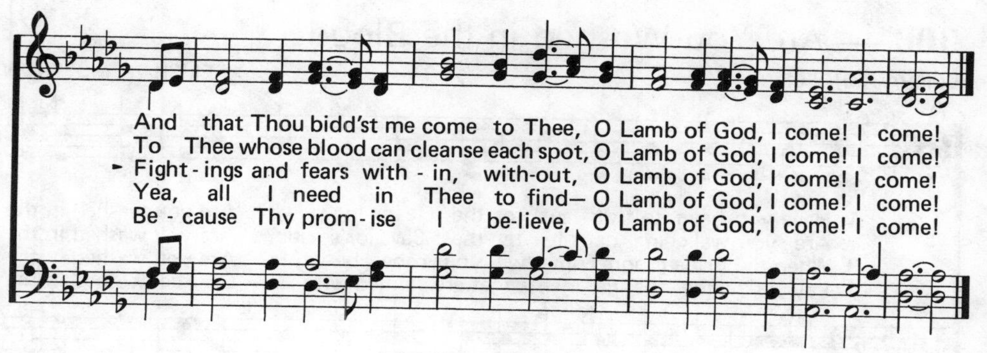
And that Thou bidd'st me come to Thee, O Lamb of God, I come! I come!
To Thee whose blood can cleanse each spot, O Lamb of God, I come! I come!
Fight-ings and fears with-in, with-out, O Lamb of God, I come! I come!
Yea, all I need in Thee to find— O Lamb of God, I come! I come!
Be-cause Thy prom-ise I be-lieve, O Lamb of God, I come! I come!

God's Final Call — 307

JOHN W. PETERSON

JOHN W. PETERSON

1. Some day you'll hear God's fi-nal call to you To take His of-fer of sal-va-tion true— This could be it, my friend, if you but knew: God's fi-nal call, God's fi-nal call.
2. How can you live an-oth-er day in sin, Think-ing some day with Christ you will be-gin? O will you hear, a-bove the world's loud din, God's fi-nal call, God's fi-nal call?
3. If you re-ject God's fi-nal call of grace, You'll have no chance your foot-steps to re-trace— All hope will then be gone, and doom you'll face: O hear His call! O hear His call!

INVITATION

308 — Are You Washed in the Blood?

ELISHA A. HOFFMAN ELISHA A. HOFFMAN

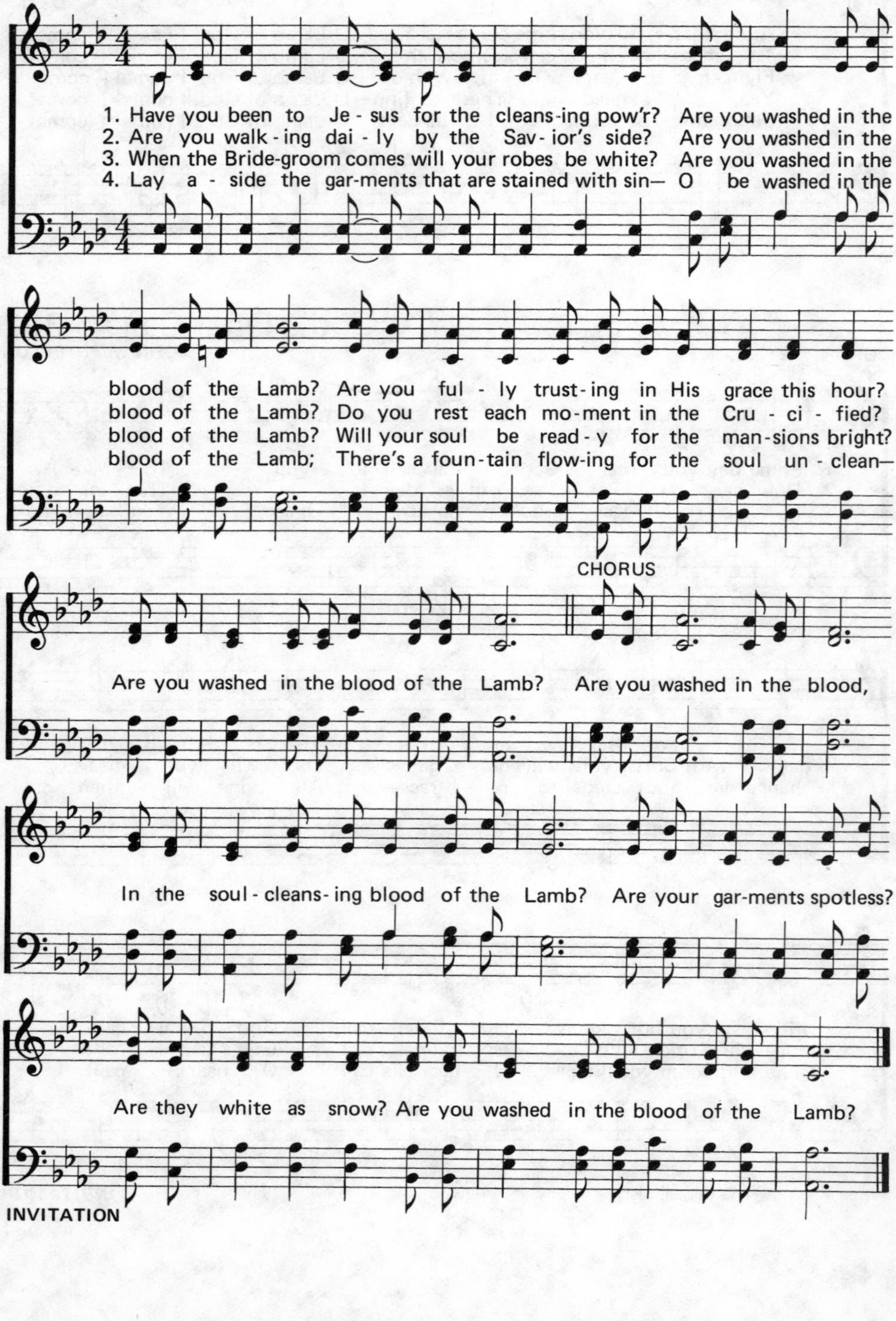

1. Have you been to Je - sus for the cleans-ing pow'r? Are you washed in the
2. Are you walk - ing dai - ly by the Sav - ior's side? Are you washed in the
3. When the Bride-groom comes will your robes be white? Are you washed in the
4. Lay a - side the gar-ments that are stained with sin— O be washed in the

blood of the Lamb? Are you ful - ly trust - ing in His grace this hour?
blood of the Lamb? Do you rest each mo - ment in the Cru - ci - fied?
blood of the Lamb? Will your soul be read - y for the man - sions bright?
blood of the Lamb; There's a foun - tain flow - ing for the soul un - clean—

Are you washed in the blood of the Lamb?

CHORUS

Are you washed in the blood,

In the soul - cleans - ing blood of the Lamb? Are your gar - ments spotless?

Are they white as snow? Are you washed in the blood of the Lamb?

INVITATION

Rise and Be Healed — 309
MILTON BOURGEOIS
MILTON BOURGEOIS
1. Has fear and doubt come a-gainst your mind? Has your faith been sore-ly tried? Lift up your eyes— here com-eth your help! It is Je-sus— for you He has died!
2. If by faith you reach out to Him, He will meet your ev-'ry need; He will re-spond to the cry of your heart, He will touch you and set you free!
CHORUS
Rise and be healed in the name of Je-sus— Let faith a-rise in your soul! Rise and be healed in the name of Je-sus— He will make you ev-'ry whit whole!
© 1972 by Crown Royal Music Co. All rights reserved.
INVITATION

310 — Pass Me Not
FANNY J. CROSBY
WILLIAM H. DOANE
1. Pass me not, O gen-tle Sav-ior— Hear my hum-ble cry!
2. Let me at a throne of mer-cy Find a sweet re-lief;
3. Trust-ing on-ly in Thy mer-it, Would I seek Thy face;
4. Thou the spring of all my com-fort, More than life to me!
While on oth-ers Thou art call-ing, Do not pass me by.
Kneel-ing there in deep con-tri-tion— Help my un-be-lief.
Heal my wound-ed, bro-ken spir-it, Save me by Thy grace.
Whom have I on earth be-side Thee? Whom in heav'n but Thee?
CHORUS
Sav-ior, Sav-ior, Hear my hum-ble cry!
While on oth-ers Thou art call-ing, Do not pass me by.
311 — Into My Heart
HARRY D. CLARKE
HARRY D. CLARKE
In-to my heart, in-to my heart, Come in-to my heart, Lord Je-sus;
REPENTANCE AND FORGIVENESS
Copyright 1924, renewal 1952, and arr. © 1979
by Hope Publishing Co. All rights reserved.

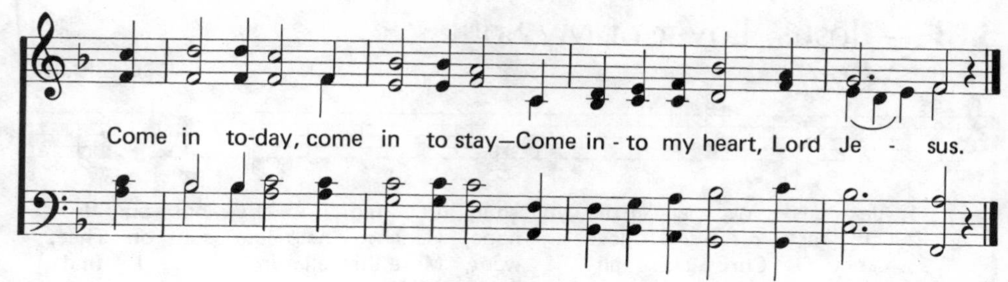
Come in to-day, come in to stay—Come in-to my heart, Lord Je - sus.

Lord, I'm Coming Home — 312

WILLIAM J. KIRKPATRICK

WILLIAM J. KIRKPATRICK

1. I've wan-dered far a - way from God— Now I'm com-ing home;
2. I've wast - ed man - y pre - cious years— Now I'm com-ing home;
3. I've tired of sin and stray - ing, Lord— Now I'm com-ing home;
4. My soul is sick, my heart is sore— Now I'm com-ing home;
The paths of sin too long I've trod— Lord, I'm com-ing home.
I now re - pent with bit - ter tears— Lord, I'm com-ing home.
I'll trust Thy love, be - lieve Thy word— Lord, I'm com-ing home.
My strength re - new, my hope re - store— Lord, I'm com-ing home.
CHORUS
Com-ing home, com-ing home, Nev - er - more to roam;
O - pen now Thine arms of love— Lord, I'm com-ing home.

313 — Jesus, Lover of My Soul

CHARLES WESLEY

JOSEPH PARRY

1. Je - sus, lov - er of my soul, Let me to Thy bos - om fly,
2. Oth - er ref - uge have I none, Hangs my help - less soul on Thee;
3. Thou, O Christ, art all I want, More than all in Thee I find;
4. Plen-teous grace with Thee is found, Grace to cov - er all my sin;

While the near - er wa - ters roll, While the tem - pest still is high.
Leave, ah, leave me not a - lone, Still sup - port and com - fort me.
Raise the fall - en, cheer the faint, Heal the sick and lead the blind.
Let the heal - ing streams a-bound, Make and keep me pure with - in.

Hide me, O my Sav - ior, hide, Till the storm of life is past;
All my trust on Thee is stayed, All my help from Thee I bring;
Just and ho - ly is Thy name— I am all un - righ - teous - ness;
Thou of life the foun - tain art, Free - ly let me take of Thee;

Safe in - to the ha - ven guide, O re - ceive my soul at last!
Cov - er my de - fense - less head With the shad - ow of Thy wing.
False and full of sin I am, Thou art full of truth and grace.
Spring Thou up with - in my heart, Rise to all e - ter - ni - ty.*

Tune: ABERYSTWYTH (Alternate, MARTYN)

REPENTANCE AND FORGIVENESS

Jesus, I Come — 314

WILLIAM T. SLEEPER

GEORGE C. STEBBINS

1. Out of my bond-age, sor - row and night, Je - sus, I come, Je - sus, I come;
2. Out of my shame-ful fail - ure and loss, Je - sus, I come, Je - sus, I come;
3. Out of un - rest and ar - ro - gant pride, Je - sus, I come, Je - sus, I come;
4. Out of the fear and dread of the tomb, Je - sus, I come, Je - sus, I come;

In - to Thy free-dom, glad - ness and light, Je - sus, I come to Thee.
In - to the glo - rious gain of Thy cross, Je - sus, I come to Thee.
In - to Thy bless-ed will to a - bide, Je - sus, I come to Thee.
In - to the joy and light of Thy home, Je - sus, I come to Thee.

Out of my sick - ness in - to Thy health, Out of my want and in - to Thy
Out of earth's sor - rows in - to Thy balm, Out of life's storms and in - to Thy
Out of my - self to dwell in Thy love, Out of de - spair in - to raptures a-
Out of the depths of ru - in un - told, In - to the peace of Thy shel-ter-ing

wealth, Out of my sin and in - to Thy-self, Je - sus, I come to Thee.
calm, Out of dis - tress to ju - bi-lant psalm, Je - sus, I come to Thee.
bove, Up - ward for aye on wings like a dove, Je - sus, I come to Thee.
fold, Ev - er Thy glo - rious face to be - hold, Je - sus, I come to Thee.

315 — Rock of Ages
AUGUSTUS M. TOPLADY
THOMAS HASTINGS
1. Rock of A - ges, cleft for me, Let me hide my-self in Thee;
2. Could my tears for - ev - er flow, Could my zeal no re - spite know,
3. When I draw my fi - nal breath, When my eyes shall close in death,
Let the wa - ter and the blood, From Thy wound - ed side which flowed,
This for sin could not a - tone— Thou must save, and Thou a - lone:
When I rise to worlds un-known And be - hold Thee on Thy throne,
Be of sin the dou-ble cure: Save from wrath and make me pure.
In my hand no price I bring, Sim - ply to Thy cross I cling.
Rock of A - ges, cleft for me, Let me hide my-self in Thee.*
Tune: TOPLADY (Alternate; REDHEAD)
316 — O for a Closer Walk with God
WILLIAM COWPER
JOHN B. DYKES
1. O for a clos - er walk with God, A calm and heav'n-ly frame,
2. Where is the bless - ed - ness I knew When first I saw the Lord?
3. Re-turn, O ho - ly Dove, re - turn, Sweet mes-sen - ger of rest;
4. The dear-est i - dol I have known, What-e'er that i - dol be,
5. So shall my walk be close with God, Calm and se - rene my frame;
Tune: BEATITUDO–higher key at 148

A light to shine up - on the road That leads me to the Lamb.
Where is the soul - re - fresh - ing view Of Je - sus and His Word?
I hate the sins that made Thee mourn And drove Thee from my breast.
Help me to tear it from Thy throne And wor - ship on - ly Thee.
So pur - er light shall mark the road That leads me to the Lamb.*
Cleanse Me — 317
Based on Psalm 139:23
J. EDWIN ORR
Maori melody
1. Search me, O God, and know my heart to - day; Try me, O Sav - ior, know my thoughts, I pray. See if there be some wick - ed way in me; Cleanse me from ev - 'ry sin and set me free.
2. I praise Thee, Lord, for cleans-ing me from sin; Ful - fill Thy Word and make me pure with-in. Fill me with fire where once I burned with shame; Grant my de - sire to mag - ni - fy Thy name.
3. Lord, take my life and make it whol - ly Thine; Fill my poor heart with Thy great love di - vine. Take all my will, my pas - sion, self and pride; I now sur - ren - der, Lord—in me a - bide.
4. O Ho - ly Ghost, re - viv - al comes from Thee; Send a re - viv - al— start the work in me. Thy Word de - clares Thou wilt sup - ply our need; For bless - ings now, O Lord, I hum - bly plead.*

Tune: MAORI

318 — Whiter Than Snow

Based on Psalm 51
JAMES NICHOLSON
WILLIAM G. FISCHER
1. Lord Je - sus, I long to be per - fect - ly whole; I
2. Lord Je - sus, for this I most hum - bly en - treat; I
3. Lord Je - sus, be - fore You I pa - tient - ly wait; Come
want You for - ev - er to live in my soul; Break down ev - 'ry
wait, bless - ed Lord, at Your cru - ci - fied feet; By faith, for my
now and with - in me a new heart cre - ate; To those who have
i - dol, cast out ev - 'ry foe— Now wash me and I shall be
cleans - ing I see Your blood flow— Now wash me and I shall be
sought You, You nev - er said "No"— Now wash me and I shall be
whit - er than snow.
REFRAIN
Whit - er than snow, yes, whit - er than
snow— Now wash me and I shall be whit - er than snow.

Blessed Assurance — 319
FANNY J. CROSBY
PHOEBE P. KNAPP
1. Bless - ed as - sur - ance, Je - sus is mine! O what a fore - taste of
2. Per - fect sub - mis - sion, per - fect de - light! Vi - sions of rap - ture now
3. Per - fect sub - mis - sion—all is at rest, I in my Sav - ior am
glo - ry di - vine! Heir of sal - va - tion, pur - chase of God,
burst on my sight; An - gels de - scend - ing bring from a - bove
hap - py and blest; Watch - ing and wait - ing, look - ing a - bove,
Born of His Spir - it, washed in His blood.
Ech - oes of mer - cy, whis - pers of love.
Filled with His good - ness, lost in His love.
CHORUS
This is my sto - ry,
this is my song, Prais - ing my Sav - ior all the day long; This is my
sto - ry, this is my song, Prais - ing my Sav - ior all the day long.

320 — Trust and Obey
JOHN H. SAMMIS
DANIEL B. TOWNER
1. When we walk with the Lord In the light of His Word, What a glo - ry He
2. Not a shad - ow can rise, Not a cloud in the skies, But His smile quick - ly
3. Not a bur - den we bear, Not a sor - row we share, But our toil He does
4. But we nev - er can prove The de - lights of His love Un - til all on the
5. Then in fel - low - ship sweet We will sit at His feet, Or we'll walk by His
sheds on our way! While we do His good will He a - bides with us still,
drives it a - way; Not a doubt nor a fear, Not a sigh nor a tear,
rich - ly re - pay; Not a grief nor a loss, Not a frown nor a cross,
al - tar we lay, For the fa - vor He shows And the joy He be - stows
side in the way; What He says we will do, Where He sends we will go—
And with all who will trust and o - bey.
Can a - bide while we trust and o - bey.
But is blest if we trust and o - bey.
Are for them who will trust and o - bey.
Nev - er fear, on - ly trust and o - bey.
CHORUS
Trust and o - bey— For there's
no oth - er way To be hap - py in Je - sus But to trust and o - bey.

It Is Well with My Soul — 321

HORATIO G. SPAFFORD

PHILIP P. BLISS

1. When peace, like a riv - er, at - tend - eth my way, When sor - rows like
2. Tho Sa - tan should buf-fet, tho tri - als should come, Let this blest as -
3. My sin— O the bliss of this glo - ri - ous tho't— My sin, not in
4. And, Lord, haste the day when my faith shall be sight, The clouds be rolled

sea - bil - lows roll— What - ev - er my lot, Thou hast taught me to say,
sur - ance con - trol, That Christ hath re - gard - ed my help - less es - tate
part, but the whole, Is nailed to the cross, and I bear it no more:
back as a scroll: The trump shall re - sound and the Lord shall de - scend,

It is well, it is well with my soul.
And hath shed His own blood for my soul.
Praise the Lord, praise the Lord, O my soul!
"E - ven so"— it is well with my soul.

CHORUS

It is well (It is well)
with my soul, (with my soul,) It is well, it is well with my soul.

322 — I Just Keep Trusting My Lord

JOHN W. PETERSON | JOHN W. PETERSON

1. I just keep trust - ing my Lord as I walk a - long,
2. I just keep trust - ing my Lord on the nar - row way,
I just keep trust-ing my Lord and He gives a song;
I just keep trust-ing my Lord as He leads each day;
(D.S.) Tho the storm-clouds dark-en the sky o'er the heav'n-ly trail,
(D.S.) Tho the road is wea-ry at times and I'm sad and blue,
Fine
I just keep trust-ing my Lord— He will nev - er fail!
I just keep trust-ing my Lord— He will see me through!
He's a faith - ful friend, such a faith - ful friend,
He's a faith - ful guide, such a faith - ful guide,

D.S.
I can count on Him to the ver - y end;
He is al - ways there walk - ing by my side;
Trusting Jesus — 323
EDGAR PAGE STITES
IRA D. SANKEY
1. Sim - ply trust - ing ev - 'ry day, Trust - ing thru a storm - y way;
2. Bright - ly does His Spir - it shine In - to this poor heart of mine;
3. Sing - ing if my way is clear, Pray - ing if the path be drear;
E - ven when my faith is small, Trust - ing Je - sus— that is all.
While He leads I can - not fall, Trust - ing Je - sus— that is all.
If in dan - ger, for Him call, Trust - ing Je - sus— that is all.
CHORUS
Trust - ing as the mo - ments fly, Trust - ing as the days go by;
Trust - ing Him what - e'er be - fall, Trust - ing Je - sus— that is all.
ASSURANCE AND TRUST

324 — 'Tis So Sweet to Trust in Jesus

LOUISA M. R. STEAD | WILLIAM J. KIRKPATRICK

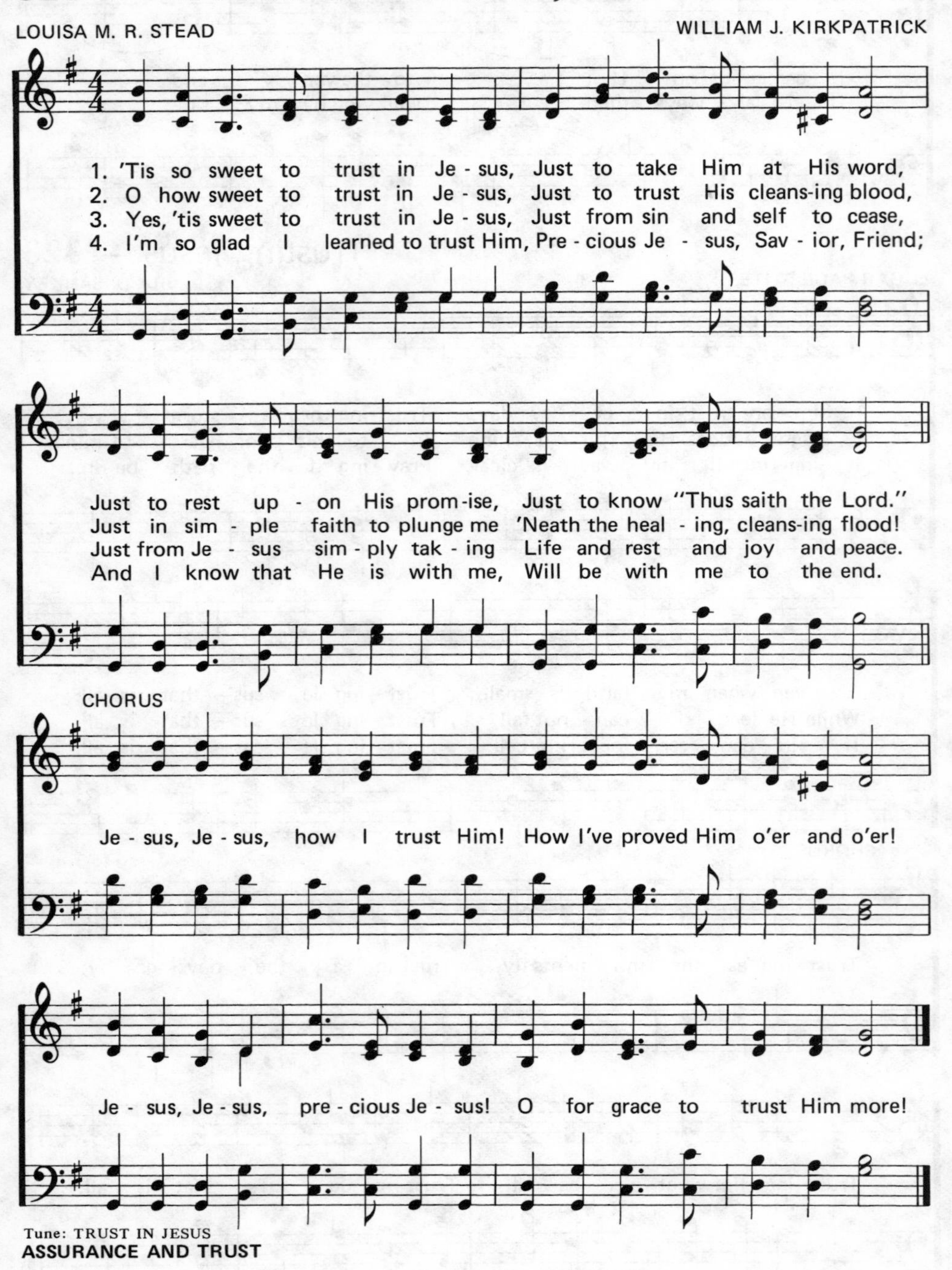
1. 'Tis so sweet to trust in Je - sus, Just to take Him at His word,
2. O how sweet to trust in Je - sus, Just to trust His cleans-ing blood,
3. Yes, 'tis sweet to trust in Je - sus, Just from sin and self to cease,
4. I'm so glad I learned to trust Him, Pre - cious Je - sus, Sav - ior, Friend;
Just to rest up - on His prom-ise, Just to know "Thus saith the Lord."
Just in sim - ple faith to plunge me 'Neath the heal - ing, cleans-ing flood!
Just from Je - sus sim - ply tak - ing Life and rest and joy and peace.
And I know that He is with me, Will be with me to the end.
CHORUS
Je - sus, Je - sus, how I trust Him! How I've proved Him o'er and o'er!
Je - sus, Je - sus, pre - cious Je - sus! O for grace to trust Him more!

Tune: TRUST IN JESUS

ASSURANCE AND TRUST

Jesus, I Am Resting — 325

JEAN SOPHIA PIGOTT
JAMES MOUNTAIN
1. Je - sus, I am rest - ing, rest - ing In the joy of what Thou art;
2. Sim-ply trust-ing Thee, Lord Je - sus, I be-hold Thee as Thou art,
3. Ev - er lift Thy face up - on me As I work and wait for Thee;
CODA Je - sus, I am rest - ing, rest - ing In the joy of what Thou art;
I am find - ing out the great - ness Of Thy lov - ing heart.
And Thy love, so pure, so change-less, Sat - is - fies my heart—
Rest - ing 'neath Thy smile, Lord Je - sus, Earth's dark shad-ows flee.
I am find - ing out the great - ness Of Thy lov - ing heart.*
Fine
Thou hast bid me gaze up - on Thee, And Thy beau - ty fills my soul,
Sat - is - fies its deep - est long-ings, Meets, sup-plies its ev - 'ry need,
Bright-ness of my Fa - ther's glo - ry, Sun - shine of my Fa-ther's face,
For by Thy trans - form - ing pow - er Thou hast made me whole.
Com - pass - eth me round with bless - ings: Thine is love in - deed!
Keep me ev - er trust - ing, rest - ing, Fill me with Thy grace.†

Tune: TRANQUILLITY

†D.C. for Coda

326 — All Things Work Out for Good

Based on Romans 8:28
JOHN W. PETERSON
THOMAS HASTINGS
1. All things work out for good, we know— Such is God's
2. This is the faith that keeps me still, No mat - ter
3. So now the fu - ture holds no fear, God guards the
4. Some day the path He chose for me Will all be
great de - sign; He or - ders all our steps be - low For
what the test, And lets me glo - ry in His will— For
work be - gun; And mor - tals are im - mor - tal here Un -
un - der - stood; In heav - en's clear - er light I'll see All
pur - pos - es di - vine, For pur - pos - es di - vine.
well I know 'tis best, For well I know 'tis best.
til their work is done, Un - til their work is done.
things worked out for good, All things worked out for good.
Tune: ORTONVILLE—higher key at 242
Words © Singspiration 1961. All rights reserved.
327 — Children of the Heavenly Father
LINA SANDELL
Trans by. Ernst W. Olson
Swedish folk melody
1. Chil-dren of the heav'n-ly Fa-ther Safe-ly in His bos-om gath - er;
2. God His own doth tend and nour - ish, In His ho - ly courts they flour-ish;
3. Nei - ther life nor death shall ev - er From the Lord His chil-dren sev - er;
4. Though He giv - eth or He tak - eth, God His chil-dren ne'er for - sak - eth;
Tune: TRYGGARE KAN INGEN VARA

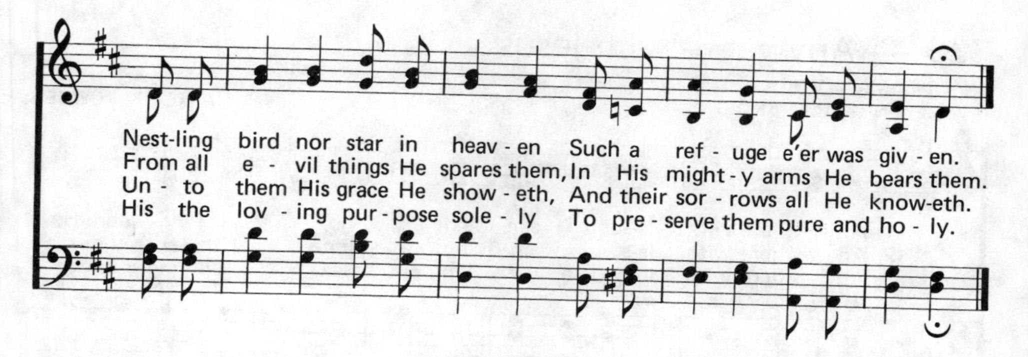
Nest-ling bird nor star in heav-en Such a ref-uge e'er was giv-en.
From all e-vil things He spares them, In His might-y arms He bears them.
Un-to them His grace He show-eth, And their sor-rows all He know-eth.
His the lov-ing pur-pose sole-ly To pre-serve them pure and ho-ly.

He's Got the Whole World in His Hands — 328

Traditional

Traditional Spiritual
Arr. by Frank Anderson

Let ♫ = ♩³♪
1. He's got the whole wide world in His hands, He's got the big round world in His hands, He's got the whole wide world in His hands—He's got the whole world in His hands.
2. He's got the wind and the rain in His hands, He's got the sun and the moon in His hands, He's got the wind and the rain in His hands—He's got the whole world in His hands.
3. He's got the ti-ny lit-tle ba-by in His hands, He's got the help-less lit-tle ba-by in His hands, He's got the ti-ny lit-tle ba-by in His hands—He's got the whole world in His hands.
4. He's got you and me, broth-er, in His hands, He's got you and me, sis-ter, in His hands, He's got you and me, broth-er, in His hands—He's got the whole world in His hands.
5. He's got ev-'ry-bod-y in His hands, He's got ev-'ry-bod-y in His hands, He's got ev-'ry-bod-y in His hands—He's got the whole world in His hands.

329 — Anywhere with Jesus

1,2 - JESSIE B. POUNDS
3 - HELEN G. ALEXANDER

DANIEL B. TOWNER

1. An-y-where with Je-sus I can safe-ly go, An-y-where He leads me in this world be-low; An-y-where with-out Him dear-est joys would fade, An-y-where with Je-sus I am not a-fraid.
2. An-y-where with Je-sus I am not a-lone, Oth-er friends may fail me—He is still my own; Tho His hand may lead me o-ver drear-y ways, An-y-where with Je-sus is a house of praise.
3. An-y-where with Je-sus o-ver land and sea, Tell-ing souls in dark-ness of sal-va-tion free; Read-y as He sum-mons me to go or stay, An-y-where with Je-sus when He points the way.
REFRAIN
An-y-where! an-y-where! Fear I can-not know;
An-y-where with Je-sus I can safe-ly go.

Moment by Moment — 330

DANIEL W. WHITTLE
MAY WHITTLE MOODY
1. Dy - ing with Je - sus by death reck-oned mine, Liv - ing with Je - sus a new life di - vine, Look-ing to Je - sus till glo - ry doth shine— Mo-ment by mo-ment, O Lord, I am Thine.
2. Nev - er a tri - al that He is not there, Nev - er a bur-den that He doth not bear; Nev - er a sor - row that He doth not share— Mo-ment by mo-ment, I'm un - der His care.
3. Nev - er a weak-ness that He doth not feel, Nev - er a sick-ness that He can - not heal; Mo - ment by mo-ment, in woe or in weal, Je - sus, my Sav-ior, a - bides with me still.
CHORUS
Mo-ment by mo-ment I'm kept in His love, Mo-ment by mo-ment I've life from a - bove; Look-ing to Je - sus till glo - ry doth shine, Mo-ment by mo-ment, O Lord, I am Thine.

Tune: WHITTLE

331 — Until Then

STUART HAMBLEN
STUART HAMBLEN
1. My heart can sing when I pause to re-mem-ber A heart-ache here is but a step-ping stone A-long a trail that's wind-ing al-ways up-ward— This trou-bled world is not my fi-nal home.
2. The things of earth will dim and lose their val-ue If we re-call they're bor-rowed for a-while; And things of earth that cause the heart to trem-ble, Re-mem-bered there, will on-ly bring a smile.
3. This wea-ry world with all its toil and strug-gle May take its toll of mis-er-y and strife; The soul of man is like a wait-ing fal-con— When it's re-leased, it's des-tined for the skies.
REFRAIN
But un-til then my heart will go on sing-ing, Un-til then with joy I'll car-ry on— Un-til the day my

eyes be-hold the cit - y, Un-til the day God calls me home.
All Will Be Well — 332
MARY PETERS
Welsh melody
1. Through the love of God, our Sav - ior, All will be well;
2. Though we pass through trib - u - la - tion, All will be well;
3. We ex-pect a bright to - mor - row— All will be well;
Free and change-less is His fa - vor— All, all is well.
Ours is such a full sal - va - tion— All, all is well.
Faith can sing through days of sor - row, All, all is well.
Pre - cious is the blood that healed us, Per - fect is the grace that sealed us,
Hap - py when in God con - fid - ing, Fruit-ful if in Christ a - bid - ing,
On our Fa - ther's love re - ly - ing, Je - sus ev - 'ry need sup - ply - ing,
Strong the hand stretched out to shield us— All must be well.
Ho - ly through the Spir - it guid - ing— All must be well.
Or in liv - ing or in dy - ing— All must be well.
Tune: AR HYD Y NOS
ASSURANCE AND TRUST

333 — A Mighty Fortress

MARTIN LUTHER
Trans. by Frederick H. Hedge
MARTIN LUTHER
1. A might-y for - tress is our God, A bul-wark nev-er fail - ing; Our
2. Did we in our own strength con-fide Our striv-ing would be los - ing, Were
3. And tho this world, with dev - ils filled, Should threaten to un - do us, We
4. That word a - bove all earth-ly pow'rs—No thanks to them—a - bid - eth; The
help - er He a - mid the flood Of mor - tal ills pre - vail - ing. For
not the right Man on our side, The Man of God's own choos - ing. Dost
will not fear, for God hath willed His truth to tri - umph thru us. The
Spir - it and the gifts are ours Thru Him who with us sid - eth. Let
still our an - cient foe Doth seek to work us woe— His craft and pow'r are
ask who that may be? Christ Je - sus, it is He— Lord Sab - a - oth His
prince of dark - ness grim, We trem-ble not for him— His rage we can en -
goods and kin - dred go, This mor-tal life al - so— The bod - y they may
great, And, armed with cru - el hate, On earth is not his e - qual.
name, From age to age the same, And He must win the bat - tle.
dure, For lo! his doom is sure: One lit - tle word shall fell him.
kill, God's truth a - bid-eth still: His king-dom is for - ev - er.*

Tune: EIN' FESTE BURG

ASSURANCE AND TRUST

Be Still, My Soul — 334
KATHARINA von SCHLEGEL
Trans. by Jane L. Borthwick
JEAN SIBELIUS
Arr. for Praise!
1. Be still, my soul— the Lord is on thy side! Bear pa-tient-ly the
2. Be still, my soul— thy God doth un-der-take To guide the fu-ture
3. Be still, my soul— the hour is has-t'ning on When we shall be for-
cross of grief or pain; Leave to thy God to or-der and pro-vide—
as He has the past; Thy hope, thy con-fi-dence let noth-ing shake—
ev-er with the Lord, When dis-ap-point-ment, grief, and fear are gone,
In ev-'ry change He faith-ful will re-main. Be still, my soul— thy
All now mys-te-rious shall be bright at last. Be still, my soul— the
Sor-row for-got, love's pur-est joys re-stored. Be still, my soul—when
best, thy heav'n-ly friend Thru thorn-y ways leads to a joy-ful end.
waves and winds still know His voice who ruled them while He dwelt be-low.
change and tears are past, All safe and bless-ed we shall meet at last.

Tune: FINLANDIA—lower key at 147
Music by permission of Breitkopf & Härtel.

335 — He Hideth My Soul

FANNY J. CROSBY | WILLIAM J. KIRKPATRICK

1. A won - der - ful Sav - ior is Je - sus my Lord, A won - der - ful
2. A won - der - ful Sav - ior is Je - sus my Lord— He tak - eth my
3. With num - ber - less bless - ings each mo - ment He crowns, And, filled with His
4. When clothed in His brightness trans - port - ed I rise To meet Him in

Sav - ior to me; He hid - eth my soul in the cleft of the
bur - den a - way; He hold - eth me up and I shall not be
full - ness di - vine, I sing in my rap - ture, "O glo - ry to
clouds of the sky, His per - fect sal - va - tion, His won - der - ful

CHORUS

rock, Where riv - ers of pleas - ure I see.
moved, He giv - eth me strength as my day.
God For such a Re - deem - er as mine!"
love, I'll shout with the mil - lions on high.

He hid - eth my soul

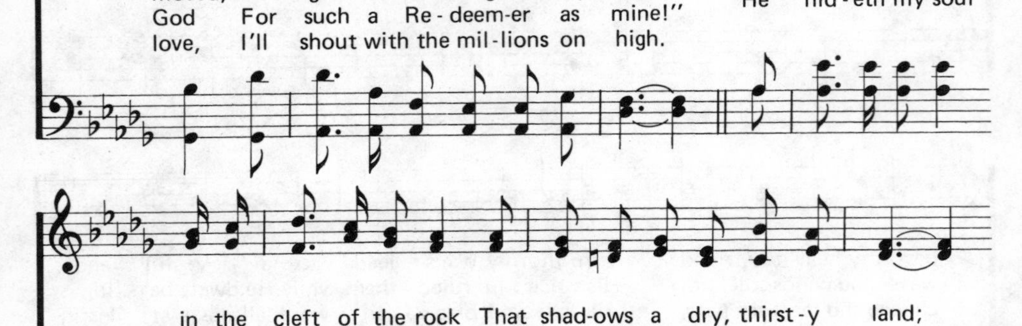
in the cleft of the rock That shad - ows a dry, thirst - y land;

ASSURANCE AND TRUST

He hid-eth my life in the depths of His love, And cov-ers me
there with His hand, And cov-ers me there with His hand.
Yesterday, Today, Forever — 336
Based on Hebrews 13:8
ALBERT B. SIMPSON
JAMES H. BURKE
1
Yes-ter-day, to-day, for-ev-er, Je-sus is the same;
All may change but Je-sus nev-er—
2
Glo-ry to His name! Glo-ry to His name! Glo-ry to His
name! All may change but Je-sus nev-er— Glo-ry to His name!

337 — Nothing Is Impossible
EUGENE L. CLARK
EUGENE L. CLARK
Noth-ing is im - pos - si - ble when you put your trust in God;
Noth-ing is im - pos - si - ble when you're trust - ing in His Word.
Heark-en to the voice of God to thee: "Is there an - y -
thing too hard for Me?" Then put your trust in God a - lone and
rest up-on His Word— For ev - 'ry-thing, O ev - 'ry - thing,
Copyright © 1966 and arr. copyright © 1975 by the Good News Broadcasting Ass'n., Inc. All rights reserved.
ASSURANCE AND TRUST

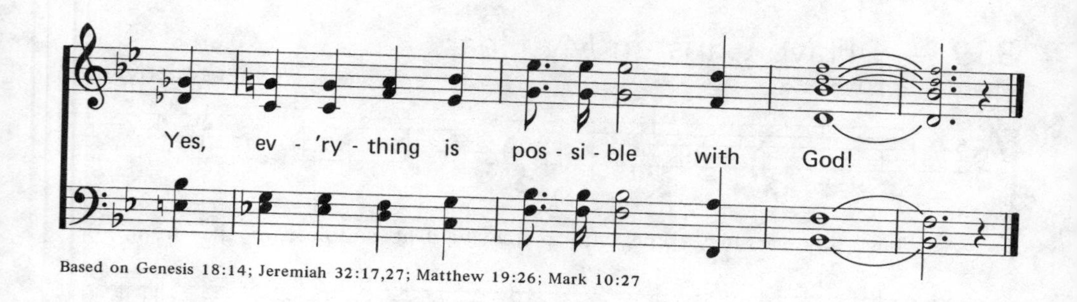
Yes, ev - 'ry - thing is pos - si - ble with God!
Based on Genesis 18:14; Jeremiah 32:17,27; Matthew 19:26; Mark 10:27

How Firm a Foundation — 338

"K"—in Rippon's *Selection of Hymns*

American melody
Caldwell's *Union Harmony*

1. How firm a foun - da - tion, ye saints of the Lord, Is laid for your
2. "Fear not, I am with thee—O be not dis-mayed, For I am thy
3. "When thru the deep wa - ters I call thee to go, The riv - ers of
4. "When thru fi - ery tri - als thy path-way shall lie, My grace, all-suf-
5. "The soul that on Je - sus hath leaned for re - pose, I will not, I
faith in His ex - cel - lent Word! What more can He say than to
God, I will still give thee aid; I'll strength-en thee, help thee, and
woe shall not thee o - ver - flow; For I will be with thee thy
fi - cient, shall be thy sup - ply; The flame shall not hurt thee—I
will not de - sert to his foes; That soul, tho all hell should en-
you He hath said— To you, who for ref - uge to Je - sus have fled?
cause thee to stand, Up - held by my gra-cious, om - nip - o - tent hand.
trou - bles to bless, And sanc - ti - fy to thee thy deep-est dis - tress.
on - ly de - sign Thy dross to con-sume and thy gold to re - fine.
deav - or to shake, I'll nev - er—no, nev - er—no, nev - er for - sake!"
Tune: FOUNDATION

339 — I Have Christ in My Heart
WENDELL P. LOVELESS
WENDELL P. LOVELESS
What tho wars may come, with march-ing feet and beat of the drum, For
I have Christ in my heart! What tho na-tions rage as we ap-proach the
end of the age, For I have Christ in my heart! God is still on the
throne—Al-might-y God is He, And He cares for His own thru all e-
ter-ni-ty; So let come what may—what-ev-er it is, I on-ly
ASSURANCE AND TRUST
Copyright 1940, renewal 1968, and arr. © 1975 by Hope Publishing Co.

say That I have Christ in my heart, I have Christ in my heart!
8va
The Solid Rock — 340
EDWARD MOTE
WILLIAM B. BRADBURY
1. My hope is built on noth-ing less Than Je-sus' blood and right-eous-ness;
2. When dark-ness veils His love-ly face, I rest on His un-chang-ing grace;
3. His oath, His cov-e-nant, His blood Sup-port me in the whelm-ing flood;
4. When He shall come with trumpet sound, O may I then in Him be found,
I dare not trust the sweet-est frame, But whol-ly lean on Je-sus' name.
In ev-'ry high and storm-y gale My an-chor holds with-in the veil.
When all a-round my soul gives way, He then is all my hope and stay.
Dressed in His right-eous-ness a-lone, Fault-less to stand be-fore the throne.
REFRAIN
On Christ, the sol-id Rock, I stand— All oth-er ground is
sink-ing sand, All oth-er ground is sink-ing sand.
Tune: SOLID ROCK
ASSURANCE AND TRUST

341 — I Know Who Holds Tomorrow
IRA F. STANPHILL
IRA F. STANPHILL
1. I don't know a - bout to - mor - row, I just live
2. Ev - 'ry step is get - ting bright - er As the gold -
3. I don't know a - bout to - mor - row, It may bring
from day to day; I don't bor - row from its sun - shine,
en stairs I climb; Ev - 'ry bur - den's get - ting light - er,
me pov - er - ty; But the one who feeds the spar - row
For its skies may turn to gray. I don't wor - ry o'er the
Ev - 'ry cloud is sil - ver - lined. There the sun is al - ways
Is the one who stands by me. And the path that be my
fu - ture, For I know what Je - sus said; And to - day
shin - ing, There no tear will dim the eye, At the end -
por - tion May be through the flame or flood; But His pres -
I'll walk be - side Him, For He knows what is a - head.
- ing of the rain - bow Where the moun - tains touch the sky.
- ence goes be - fore me And I'm cov - ered with His blood.
ASSURANCE AND TRUST
Copyright Singspiration 1950, renewal 1978. All rights reserved.

REFRAIN
Man - y things a - bout to - mor - row I don't
seem to un - der - stand; But I know who
holds to - mor - row, And I know who holds my hand.
God Moves in a Mysterious Way — 342
WILLIAM COWPER
Scottish Psalter
1. God moves in a mys - te - rious way His won - ders to per - form;
2. You fear - ful saints, fresh cour - age take: The clouds you so much dread
3. Judge not the Lord by fee - ble sense, But trust Him for His grace;
4. His pur - pos - es will rip - en fast, Un - fold - ing ev - 'ry hour;
5. Blind un - be - lief is sure to err And scan His work in vain;
He plants His foot - steps in the sea And rides up - on the storm.
Are big with mer - cy, and shall break In bless - ings on your head.
Be - hind a frown - ing prov - i - dence Faith sees a smil - ing face.
The bud may have a bit - ter taste, But sweet will be the flow'r.
God is His own in - ter - pret - er, And He will make it plain.
Tune: DUNDEE
ASSURANCE AND TRUST

343 — Like a River Glorious

FRANCES R. HAVERGAL

JAMES MOUNTAIN

1. Like a riv - er glo - rious Is God's per - fect peace, O - ver all vic - to - rious In its bright in - crease; Per - fect, yet it flow - eth Full - er ev - 'ry day, Per - fect, yet it grow - eth Deep - er all the way.
2. Hid - den in the hol - low Of His bless - ed hand, Nev - er foe can fol - low, Nev - er trai - tor stand; Not a surge of wor - ry, Not a shade of care, Not a blast of hur - ry Touch the spir - it there.
3. Ev - 'ry joy or tri - al Fall - eth from a - bove, Traced up - on our di - al By the Sun of Love; We may trust Him ful - ly All for us to do— They who trust Him whol - ly Find Him whol - ly true.

REFRAIN

Stayed up - on Je - ho - vah, Hearts are ful - ly blest— Find - ing, as He prom - ised, Per - fect peace and rest.

Tune: WYE VALLEY

PEACE AND COMFORT

All Your Anxiety — 344
EDWARD HENRY JOY
EDWARD HENRY JOY
1. Is there a heart o'er-bound by sor-row? Is there a life weighed
2. No oth-er friend so keen to help you, No oth-er friend so
3. Come then at once— de - lay no long-er! Heed His en - treat - y
down by care? Come to the cross—each bur - den bear-ing,
quick to hear; No oth-er place to leave your bur-den,
kind and sweet; You need not fear a dis - ap - point-ment—
All your anx - i - e - ty— leave it there.
No oth - er one to hear your prayer.
You shall find peace at the mer - cy seat.
CHORUS
All your anx - i - e - ty,
all your care,
Bring to the mer-cy seat—leave it there;
Nev-er a bur-den He can-not bear,
Nev-er a friend like Je - sus!

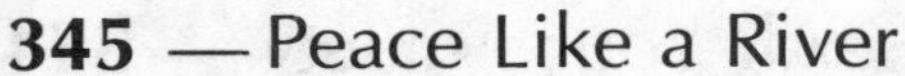

345 — Peace Like a River

Traditional

Traditional
Arr. by Dale Scott

1. I've got peace like a riv-er, I've got peace like a riv - er, I've got peace like a riv-er in my soul; I've got peace like a riv-er, I've got peace like a riv-er, I've got peace like a riv-er in my soul.
2. I've got love like a riv-er, I've got love like a riv - er, I've got love like a riv-er in my soul; I've got love like a riv-er, I've got love like a riv-er, I've got love like a riv-er in my soul.
3. I've got joy like a riv-er, I've got joy like a riv - er, I've got joy like a riv-er in my soul; I've got joy like a riv-er, I've got joy like a riv-er, I've got joy like a riv-er in my soul.

346 — Jesus Never Fails

ARTHUR A. LUTHER

ARTHUR A. LUTHER

1. Earth-ly friends may prove un-true, Doubts and fears as - sail; One still loves and
2. Tho the sky be dark and drear, Fierce and strong the gale, Just re - mem-ber
3. In life's dark and bit - ter hour Love will still pre - vail; Trust His ev - er-

CHORUS
cares for you, One who will not fail.
He is near And He will not fail. Je-sus nev-er fails, Je-sus
last-ing pow'r—Je - sus will not fail.
nev-er fails; Heav'n and earth may pass a - way, But Je - sus nev-er fails.
O Lord! — 347
Traditional
Traditional
1. Some-one's lone - ly, Lord—give him friends, Some-one's lone - ly, Lord—give him
2. Some-one's fight-ing, Lord—give him peace, Some-one's fight-ing, Lord—give him
3. Some-one's hat - ing, Lord—give him love, Some-one's hat - ing, Lord—give him
4. Some-one's doubting, Lord—give him faith, Some-one's doubting, Lord—give him
5. We are liv - ing, Lord—help us care, We are liv - ing, Lord—help us
friends, Some-one's lone - ly, Lord—give him friends... O Lord, give him friends.
peace, Some-one's fight-ing, Lord—give him peace... O Lord, give him peace.
love, Some-one's hat - ing, Lord—give him love... O Lord, give him love.
faith, Some-one's doubting, Lord—give him faith... O Lord, give him faith.
care, We are liv - ing, Lord—help us care... O Lord, help us care.
Tune: KUM BA YAH

348 — Does Jesus Care?
FRANK E. GRAEFF
J. LINCOLN HALL
1. Does Je - sus care when my heart is pained Too deep - ly for
2. Does Je - sus care when my way is dark With a name - less
3. Does Je - sus care when I've tried and failed To re - sist some temp-
4. Does Je - sus care when I've said good-bye To the dear - est on
mirth and song— As the bur - dens press, and the cares dis - tress,
dread and fear? As the day - light fades in - to deep night shades,
ta - tion strong? When for my deep grief I find no re - lief,
earth to me, And my sad heart aches till it near - ly breaks—
CHORUS
And the way grows wea - ry and long?
Does He care e - nough to be near?
Tho my tears flow all the night long?
Is it aught to Him? does He see?
O yes, He cares— I
know He cares! His heart is touched with my grief; When the

days are wea-ry, the long nights drear-y, I know my Sav-ior cares.
There Is a Balm in Gilead — 349
Based on Jeremiah 8:22
Traditional
Traditional Spiritual
Arr. by Jon Drevits—alt.
Slowly
There is a balm in Gil-e-ad To make the wound-ed whole;
Fine
There is a balm in Gil-e-ad To heal the sin-sick soul.
1. Some-times I feel dis-cour-aged And think my work's in vain,
2. If you can-not preach like Pe-ter, If you can-not pray like Paul,
D.C.
But then the Ho-ly Spir-it Re-vives my soul a-gain.
You can tell the love of Je-sus And say He died for all.
Arr. © Singspiration 1979, alt. 1981. All rights reserved.
PEACE AND COMFORT

350 — Wonderful Peace
W. G. COOPER
Arr. by Larry Leader
W. D. CORNELL—alt.
1. Far a - way in the depths of my spir - it to - night Rolls a mel - o - dy sweet - er than psalm; In ce - les - tial-like strains it un - ceas - ing - ly falls O'er my soul like an in - fi - nite calm.
2. What a treas - ure I have in this won - der - ful peace Bur - ied deep in the heart of my soul, So se - cure that no pow - er can mine it a - way While the years of e - ter - ni - ty roll.
3. I am rest - ing to - night in this won - der - ful peace, Rest-ing sweet - ly in Je - sus' con - trol, And I'm kept from all dan - ger by night and by day—Now His glo - ry is flood - ing my soul.
4. And I know when I rise to that cit - y of peace Where the Au - thor of peace I shall see, That one of the an - thems the ran-somed will sing In that heav - en - ly king - dom shall be:
5. O soul, are you here with - out com - fort and rest, Walk-ing down the rough path-way of time? Make Je - sus your friend ere the shad-ows grow dark—O ac - cept this sweet peace so sub - lime!
CHORUS
Peace! peace! won - der - ful peace, Com-ing down from the Fa-ther a - bove, Sweep o - ver my

spir - it for - ev - er, I pray, In fath - om - less bil-lows of love.
No One Understands Like Jesus — 351
JOHN W. PETERSON
JOHN W. PETERSON
1. No one un-der-stands like Je - sus, He's a friend be-yond com - pare;
2. No one un-der-stands like Je - sus, Ev - 'ry woe He sees and feels;
3. No one un-der-stands like Je - sus When the foes of life as - sail;
4. No one un-der-stands like Je - sus When you fal-ter on the way;
Meet Him at the throne of mer - cy, He is wait-ing for you there.
Ten - der - ly He whis-pers com - fort, And the bro-ken heart He heals.
You should nev-er be dis - cour - aged, Je - sus cares and will not fail.
Tho you fail Him, sad - ly fail Him, He will par - don you to - day.
REFRAIN
No one un - der-stands like Je - sus When the days are dark and grim;
No one is so near, so dear as Je - sus— Cast your ev - 'ry care on Him.

352 — Come, Ye Disconsolate
1, 2 - THOMAS MOORE—alt.
3 - THOMAS HASTINGS
SAMUEL WEBBE
1. Come, ye dis - con - so-late, wher - e'er ye lan - guish— Come to the mer - cy-seat, fer - vent - ly kneel; Here bring your wound - ed hearts, here tell your an - guish: Earth has no sor-row that heav'n can-not heal.
2. Joy of the des - o - late, light of the stray - ing, Hope of the pen - i - tent, fade - less and pure! Here speaks the Com - fort - er, ten - der - ly say - ing, "Earth has no sor-row that heav'n can-not cure."
3. Here see the Bread of Life, see wa - ters flow - ing Forth from the throne of God, pure from a - bove; Come to the feast of love— come ev - er know - ing Earth has no sor-row but heav'n can re - move.
Tune: CONSOLATOR
353 — Peace, Perfect Peace
EDWARD H. BICKERSTETH
GEORGE T. CALDBECK
1. Peace, per - fect peace— in this dark world of sin?
2. Peace, per - fect peace— by throng-ing du - ties pressed?
3. Peace, per - fect peace— with sor - rows surg - ing round?
4. Peace, per - fect peace— with loved ones far a - way?
5. Peace, per - fect peace— our fu - ture all un - known?

Tune: PAX TECUM

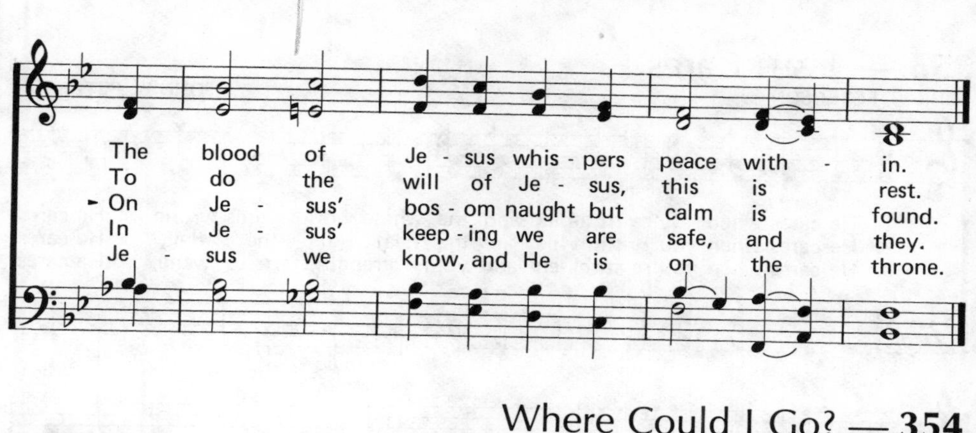
The blood of Je - sus whis - pers peace with - in.
To do the will of Je - sus, this is rest.
On Je - sus' bos - om naught but calm is found.
In Je - sus' keep - ing we are safe, and they.
Je - sus we know, and He is on the throne.

Where Could I Go? — 354

JAMES B. COATS

JAMES B. COATS

1. Liv - ing be - low in this old sin - ful world, Hard - ly a com - fort can af - ford; Striv - ing a - lone to face temp - ta - tions sore, Where could I go but to the Lord?
2. Neigh - bors are kind, I love them ev - 'ry one, We get a - long in sweet ac - cord; But when my soul needs man - na from a - bove, Where could I go but to the Lord?
3. Life here is grand with friends I love so dear, Com - fort I get from God's own Word; Yet when I face the chill - ing hand of death, Where could I go but to the Lord?
Chorus Where could I go, O where could I go, Seek - ing a ref - uge for my soul? Need - ing a friend to help me in the end, Where could I go but to the Lord?
D.C. for Chorus

355 — Jesus Cares
JOHN W. PETERSON
JOHN W. PETERSON
1. He cares when you're trou-bled and the whole world seems wrong, He cares
2. He cares when you stum-ble in the heat of the day, He cares
3. He cares when you're strick-en and your strength starts to wane, He cares
when the tri - als try to si - lence your song; He cares when you're
when you're bur-dened and too wea - ry to pray; He cares when you
when you trem - ble with fe - ver and pain; He cares when you've
lone - ly, tho you laugh with the throng— Je - sus cares.
fail Him, when your feet go a - stray— Je - sus cares.
strug-gled but the work seems in vain— Je - sus cares.
CHORUS
Yes, Je - sus cares, He cares when your heart aches;
Take Him your man - y bur-dens: Je - sus cares.
PEACE AND COMFORT
© John W. Peterson Music Company 1972, arr. 1974. All rights reserved.

In the Cross of Christ I Glory — 356
JOHN BOWRING
ITHAMAR CONKEY
1. In the cross of Christ I glo-ry, Tow'r-ing o'er the wrecks of time;
2. When the woes of life o'er-take me, Hopes de-ceive and fears an-noy,
3. When the sun of bliss is beam-ing Light and love up-on my way,
4. Bane and bless-ing, pain and pleas-ure, By the cross are sanc-ti-fied;
All the light of sa-cred sto-ry Gath-ers round its head sub-lime.
Nev-er shall the cross for-sake me: Lo! it glows with peace and joy.
From the cross the ra-diance stream-ing Adds more lus-ter to the day.
Peace is there that knows no meas-ure, Joys that thru all time a-bide.
Tune: RATHBUN
O the Love, the Love of Jesus! — 357
JOHN W. PETERSON
JOHN W. PETERSON
1. O the love, the love of Je-sus, O the love, the love of Je-sus,
2. O the grace, the grace of Je-sus, O the grace, the grace of Je-sus,
3. O the life, the life of Je-sus, O the life, the life of Je-sus,
4. O the pow'r, the pow'r of Je-sus, O the pow'r, the pow'r of Je-sus,
5. O the hope there is in Je-sus, O the hope there is in Je-sus,
O the love, the love of Je-sus—There is no great-er love than this!
O the grace, the grace of Je-sus—It is great-er than all my sin!
O the life, the life of Je-sus—By His Spir-it it flows thru me!
O the pow'r, the pow'r of Je-sus—There is noth-ing He can-not do!
O the hope there is in Je-sus—He is com-ing a-gain some day!
© John W. Peterson Music Company 1978, arr. 1979. All rights reserved.
PEACE AND COMFORT

358 — God Will Take Care of You
CIVILLA D. MARTIN
W. STILLMAN MARTIN
1. Be not dis-mayed what - e'er be - tide, God will take care of you;
2. Thru days of toil when heart doth fail, God will take care of you;
3. All you may need He will pro-vide, God will take care of you;
4. No mat-ter what may be the test, God will take care of you;
Be - neath His wings of love a - bide, God will take care of you.
When dan-gers fierce your path as - sail, God will take care of you.
Noth-ing you ask will be de - nied, God will take care of you.
Lean, wea-ry one, up - on His breast, God will take care of you.
CHORUS
God will take care of you, Thru ev - 'ry day, o'er all the way;
He will take care of you, God will take care of you.
take care of you.

Guide Me, O Thou Great Jehovah — 359

WILLIAM WILLIAMS
Trans. by Peter Williams

JOHN HUGHES

1. Guide me, O Thou great Je - ho - vah, Pil - grim thru this bar - ren land;
2. O - pen now the crys - tal foun - tain Whence the healing stream doth flow;
3. When I tread the verge of Jor - dan, Bid my anx-ious fears sub-side;
I am weak, but Thou art might - y— Hold me with Thy pow'r-ful hand:
Let the fire and cloud - y pil - lar Lead me all my jour - ney thru:
Bear me thru the swell - ing cur - rent, Land me safe on Ca - naan's side:
Bread of heav - en, Bread of heav - en, Feed me till I want no
Strong De - liv - 'rer, strong De - liv - 'rer, Be Thou still my strength and
Songs of prais - es, songs of prais - es I will ev - er give to
more, (want no more,) Feed me till I want no more.
shield, (strength and shield,) Be Thou still my strength and shield.
Thee, (give to Thee,) I will ev - er give to Thee.*

Tune: CWM RHONDDA

360 — He Giveth More Grace
ANNIE JOHNSON FLINT
HUBERT MITCHELL
1. He giv - eth more grace when the bur-den grows great-er, He send - eth more strength when the la - bors in - crease; To add - ed af - flic - tion He add - eth His mer - cy, To mul - ti - plied tri - als His mul - ti - plied peace.
2. When we have ex - haust - ed our store of en - dur-ance, When our strength has failed ere the day is half done, When we reach the end of our hoard-ed re - sourc-es, Our Fa - ther's full giv - ing is on - ly be - gun.
CHORUS
His love has no lim - it, His grace has no meas - ure, His pow'r has no boun - da - ry known un - to men; For out of His in - fi - nite

rich - es in Je - sus He giv - eth and giv - eth and giv - eth a - gain!
Each Step of the Way — 361
REDD HARPER
REDD HARPER
1. I'm fol-low-ing Je - sus one step at a time,
2. The path-way is nar - row, but He leads me on,
I live for the mo - ment in His love di - vine;
I walk in His shad - ow, my fears are all gone;
Why think of to - mor - row? just live for to - day,
My spir - it grows strong - er each mo - ment, each day,
I'm fol-low-ing Je - sus each step of the way.
For Je - sus is lead - ing each step of the way.

362 — Jesus Is Walking with Me

JOHN W. PETERSON JOHN W. PETERSON

1. I've been thru the val - ley, I've been thru the fire, I've walked thru deep
2. I've known dis - ap - point - ment, I've suf - fered some loss, I've felt on my
3. I've laughed on the moun - tain, I've sa - vored suc - cess, Re - joiced in my

wa - ter, I've bowed in the mire; I've fought in the bat - tle with
shoul - der the weight of a cross; I've wept in the dark - ness and
bless - ings— in more than in less; I've tast - ed the good life while

cour - age all gone, But this is the rea - son I al - ways go on:
wished for the light, But some - how His pres - ence gave songs in the night.
prais - ing His name, But sun - shine or shad - ow it's al - ways the same.

CHORUS

Je - sus is with me— my shep - herd and guide, All that I

need He is there to pro - vide; That makes the dif - f'rence—this

GUIDANCE AND CARE

friend by my side, Je - sus is walk - ing with me.
Leaning on the Everlasting Arms — 363
ELISHA A. HOFFMAN
ANTHONY J. SHOWALTER
1. What a fel - low-ship, what a joy di - vine, Lean - ing on the ev - er - last - ing arms; What a bless - ed - ness, what a peace is mine,
2. O how sweet to walk in this pil - grim way, Lean - ing on the ev - er - last - ing arms; O how bright the path grows from day to day,
3. What have I to dread, what have I to fear, Lean - ing on the ev - er - last - ing arms? I have bless - ed peace with my Lord so near,
Lean - ing on the ev - er - last-ing arms.
CHORUS
Lean - ing, lean - ing, Safe and se - cure from all a - larms; Lean - ing, lean - ing, Lean-ing on the ev - er - last - ing arms.
GUIDANCE AND CARE

364 — He Leadeth Me
JOSEPH H. GILMORE
WILLIAM B. BRADBURY
1. He lead - eth me! O bless - ed thought! O words with heav'n - ly com - fort fraught! What - e'er I do, wher - e'er I be, Still 'tis God's hand that lead - eth me.
2. Some - times 'mid scenes of deep - est gloom, Some - times where E - den's bow - ers bloom, By wa - ters still, o'er trou - bled sea, Still 'tis His hand that lead - eth me!
3. Lord, I would clasp Thy hand in mine, Nor ev - er mur - mur nor re - pine; Con - tent, what - ev - er lot I see, Since 'tis my God that lead - eth me!
4. And when my task on earth is done, When by Thy grace the vic - t'ry's won, E'en death's cold wave I will not flee, Since God thru Jor - dan lead - eth me.
CHORUS
He lead - eth me, He lead - eth me, By His own hand He lead - eth me; His faith - ful fol - l'wer I would be, For by His hand He lead - eth me.
GUIDANCE AND CARE

Hymns for the Young
Attr. to Dorothy A. Thrupp

WILLIAM B. BRADBURY

1. Sav - ior, like a shep-herd lead us, Much we need Thy ten-der care;
2. We are Thine—do Thou be-friend us, Be the guard-ian of our way;
3. Thou hast prom-ised to re - ceive us, Poor and sin - ful tho we be;
4. Ear - ly let us seek Thy fa - vor, Ear - ly let us do Thy will;
In Thy pleas-ant pas-tures feed us, For our use Thy folds pre - pare:
Keep Thy flock, from sin de - fend us, Seek us when we go a - stray:
Thou hast mer - cy to re - lieve us, Grace to cleanse and pow'r to free:
Bless - ed Lord and on - ly Sav - ior, With Thy love our bos-oms fill:
Bless - ed Je - sus, bless-ed Je - sus, Thou hast bought us, Thine we are;
Bless - ed Je - sus, bless-ed Je - sus, Hear, O hear us when we pray;
Bless - ed Je - sus, bless-ed Je - sus, Ear - ly let us turn to Thee;
Bless - ed Je - sus, bless-ed Je - sus, Thou hast loved us, love us still;
Bless - ed Je - sus, bless - ed Je - sus, Thou hast bought us, Thine we are.
Bless - ed Je - sus, bless - ed Je - sus, Hear, O hear us when we pray.
Bless - ed Je - sus, bless - ed Je - sus, Ear - ly let us turn to Thee.
Bless - ed Je - sus, bless - ed Je - sus, Thou hast loved us, love us still.*

Tune: BRADBURY

366 — The Lord's My Shepherd

Psalm 23
From the *Scottish Psalter*

JESSIE SEYMOUR IRVINE

1. The Lord's my Shep - herd—I'll not want; He makes me down to lie
2. My soul He doth re - store a - gain, And me to walk doth make
3. Yea, tho I walk thru death's dark vale, Yet will I fear no ill,
4. My ta - ble Thou hast fur - nish - ed In pres - ence of my foes;
5. Good-ness and mer - cy all my life Shall sure - ly fol - low me,
In pas - tures green— He lead - eth me The qui - et wa - ters by.
With-in the paths of right - eous - ness, E'en for His own name's sake.
For Thou art with me, and Thy rod And staff me com - fort still.
My head Thou dost with oil a - noint, And my cup o - ver - flows.
And in God's house for - ev - er - more My dwell - ing place shall be.*

Tune: CRIMOND

367 — If You Will Only Let God Guide You

GEORG NEUMARK
Trans. by Catherine Winkworth—alt.

Swedish folk melody
Arr. by Larry Leader

1. If you will on - ly let God guide you, And hope in
2. On - ly be still and wait His lei - sure In cheer-ful
3. Sing, pray, and keep His ways un - swerv - ing— So do your
Him through all your ways, What-ev - er comes, He'll stand be - side
hope, with heart con - tent To take what - e'er the Fa - ther's pleas-
part to prove Him true; Trust in His word, no self re - serv -

Tune: CELEBRATION

you And bear you through the e - vil days; Who trusts in
ure And all - dis - cern - ing love have sent; Nor doubt your
ing— Let Him ful - fill His work in you; God nev - er
God's un-chang-ing love Builds on the Rock that will not move.
in - most wants are known To Him who chose you for His own.
yet for - sook at need The soul that trust - ed Him in - deed.

The King of Love My Shepherd Is — 368

From Psalm 23
HENRY W. BAKER

JOHN B. DYKES

1. The King of love my Shep - herd is, Whose good-ness fail - eth nev - er;
2. Where streams of liv - ing wa - ter flow My ran-somed soul He lead - eth,
3. Per - verse and fool - ish oft I strayed, But yet in love He sought me,
4. In death's dark vale I fear no ill With Thee, dear Lord, be - side me;
5. And so thru all the length of days Thy good - ness fail - eth nev - er:
I noth - ing lack if I am His And He is mine for - ev - er.
And where the ver - dant pas - tures grow With food ce - les - tial feed - eth.
And on His shoul - der gen - tly laid, And home re - joic - ing bro't me.
Thy rod and staff my com - fort still, Thy cross be - fore to guide me.
Good Shep-herd, may I sing Thy praise With - in Thy house for - ev - er.*

Tune: DOMINUS REGIT ME

369 — Surely Goodness and Mercy

Based on Psalm 23
JOHN W. PETERSON
and ALFRED B. SMITH
JOHN W. PETERSON
and ALFRED B. SMITH
1. A pil - grim was I, and a - wan-d'ring— In the cold night of
2. He re - stor - eth my soul when I'm wea - ry, He giv - eth me
3. When I walk thru the dark lone-some val - ley, My Sav - ior will
sin I did roam When Je - sus the kind Shepherd found me—
strength day by day; He leads me be - side the still wa - ters,
walk with me there; And safe - ly His great hand will lead me
CHORUS
And now I am on my way home.
He guards me each step of the way.
To the man - sions He's gone to pre - pare.
Sure - ly good - ness
and mer - cy shall fol - low me All the days, all the
days of my life; Sure - ly good - ness and mer - cy shall

GUIDANCE AND CARE

(opt. D.C.)
fol - low me All the days, all the days of my life.
May be omitted until final chorus
And I shall dwell in the house of the Lord for - ev - er, And I shall
feast at the ta - ble spread for me; Sure - ly good - ness
and mer - cy shall fol - low me All the days, all the days of
my life, All the days, all the days of my life.

370 — Day by Day

LINA SANDELL BERG
Trans. by Andrew L. Skoog

OSCAR AHNFELT

1. Day by day and with each pass-ing mo - ment, Strength I find to
2. Ev - 'ry day the Lord Him-self is near me With a spe - cial
3. Help me then in ev - 'ry trib-u - la - tion So to trust Your
meet my tri-als here; Trust-ing in my Fa-ther's wise be - stow-ment,
mer-cy for each hour; All my cares He fain would bear, and cheer me,
prom-is-es, O Lord, That I lose not faith's sweet con-so - la - tion
I've no cause for wor-ry or for fear. He whose heart is kind be -
He whose name is Coun-sel-lor and Pow'r. The pro - tec - tion of His
Of-fered me with-in Your ho-ly Word. Help me, Lord, when toil and
yond all meas-ure Gives un - to each day what He deems best— Lov-ing-
child and treas-ure Is a charge that on Him-self He laid; "As your
trou-ble meet-ing, E'er to take, as from a fa-ther's hand, One by
ly, its part of pain and pleas-ure, Min-gling toil with peace and rest.
days, your strength shall be in meas-ure," This the pledge to me He made.
one, the days, the moments fleet-ing, Till I reach the prom-ised land.

Tune: BLOTT EN DAG

GUIDANCE AND CARE

God Is So Good — 371

Traditional

Traditional

1. God is so good, God is so good, God is so good— He's so good to me.
2. He cares for me, He cares for me, He cares for me— He's so good to me.
3. He's all I need, He's all I need, He's all I need— He's so good to me.
*4. God is so good, God is so good, God is so good— He's so good to me.

*Prior to the final stanza the worship leader may call for additional impromptu stanzas suited to the occasion, such as "He answers prayer..."—"I'll do His will..."—"I love Him so..."

The Branch of Healing — 372

Based on Exodus 15:22-26
ALBERT B. SIMPSON—alt.

THOMAS HASTINGS
Arr. by John W. Peterson

1. There is a heal - ing branch that grows Where ev - 'ry "bit - ter wa - ter" flows; This is our health - re - new - ing tree: "I am the Lord that heal - eth thee."
2. There is an old ap - point - ed way For those who heark - en and o - bey; A - bove the gate these words we see: "I am the Lord that heal - eth thee."
3. There is a prom - ise that has stood Since Is - rael crossed the part - ed flood; It stands to - day for you and me: "I am the Lord that heal - eth thee."
4. There is a great Phy - si - cian still Whose hand has all its an - cient skill; At His com-mand dis - ease must flee: "I am the Lord that heal - eth thee."

Tune: RETREAT

373 — In Pleasant Places
JOHN W. PETERSON
JOHN W. PETERSON
1. Sweet it is to fol - low the Sav - ior, Sweet to have Him close by my side; Care - ful - ly the path - way He choos - es, He is such a won - der - ful guide.
2. E - ven when the storm clouds are threat-'ning, There's no need to wor - ry or fear; Je - sus will be there to pro - tect me, When I call for help He will hear.
3. Now my life in - deed is worth liv - ing, Christ has made the dif - f'rence for me; There's a joy, a glo - ry, a won - der, Ev - 'ry day His good - ness I see.
4. Some day He will take me to heav - en, Safe - ly I'll be led by His hand; Pleas - ant are the plac - es a - wait - ing There with - in that beau - ti - ful land.
CHORUS
In pleas - ant plac - es Je - sus leads me, Like a shep - herd

GUIDANCE AND CARE

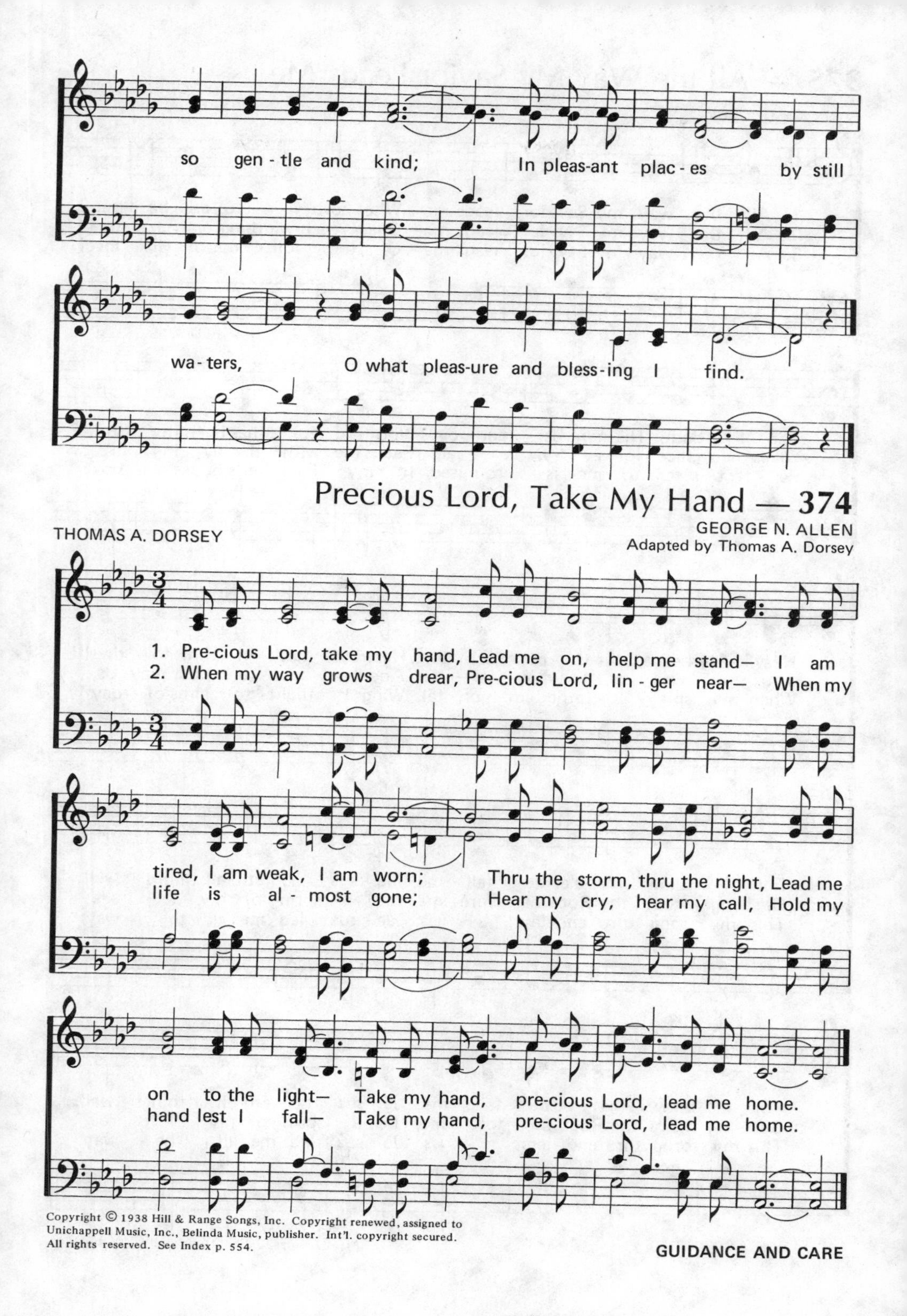
so gen-tle and kind; In pleas-ant plac-es by still
wa-ters, O what pleas-ure and bless-ing I find.
Precious Lord, Take My Hand — 374
THOMAS A. DORSEY
GEORGE N. ALLEN
Adapted by Thomas A. Dorsey
1. Pre-cious Lord, take my hand, Lead me on, help me stand— I am
2. When my way grows drear, Pre-cious Lord, lin-ger near— When my
tired, I am weak, I am worn; Thru the storm, thru the night, Lead me
life is al-most gone; Hear my cry, hear my call, Hold my
on to the light— Take my hand, pre-cious Lord, lead me home.
hand lest I fall— Take my hand, pre-cious Lord, lead me home.
Copyright © 1938 Hill & Range Songs, Inc. Copyright renewed, assigned to Unichappell Music, Inc., Belinda Music, publisher. Int'l. copyright secured. All rights reserved. See Index p. 554.
GUIDANCE AND CARE

375 — All the Way My Savior Leads Me
FANNY J. CROSBY
ROBERT LOWRY
Arr. by Larry Leader
1. All the way my Sav - ior leads me— What have I to ask be - side?
2. All the way my Sav - ior leads me— Cheers each wind-ing path I tread,
3. All the way my Sav - ior leads me— O the full - ness of His love!
Can I doubt His ten - der mer - cy, Who thru life has been my Guide?
Gives me grace for ev - 'ry tri - al, Feeds me with the liv - ing bread.
Per - fect rest to me is prom-ised In my Fa - ther's house a - bove.
Heav'n - ly peace, di - vin - est com - fort, Here by faith in Him to dwell!
Tho my wea - ry steps may fal - ter And my soul a - thirst may be,
When my spir - it, clothed im - mor - tal, Wings its flight to realms of day,
For I know, what-e'er be - fall me, Je - sus do - eth all things well;
Gush-ing from the Rock be - fore me, Lo! a spring of joy I see;
This my song thru end - less a - ges: Je - sus led me all the way;
For I know, what-e'er be - fall me, Je - sus do - eth all things well.
Gush-ing from the Rock be - fore me, Lo! a spring of joy I see.
This my song thru end - less a - ges: Je - sus led me all the way.
GUIDANCE AND CARE

1,4 - WILLIAM WHITING—alt.
2,3 - ROBERT NELSON SPENCER

JOHN B. DYKES

1. Al - might - y Fa - ther, strong to save, Whose arm hath bound the
2. O Christ, the Lord of hill and plain, O'er which our traf - fic
3. O Spir - it, whom the Fa - ther sent To spread a - broad the
4. O Trin - i - ty of love and pow'r, Our breth - ren shield in

rest - less wave, Who bidd'st the might - y o - cean deep
runs a - main By moun - tain pass or val - ley low:
fir - ma - ment: O Wind of heav - en, by Thy might
dan - ger's hour; From rock and tem - pest, fire and foe,

Its own ap - point - ed lim - its keep: O hear us when we
Wher - ev - er, Lord, Thy breth-ren go, Pro - tect them by Thy
Save all who dare the ea - gle's flight, And keep them by Thy
Pro - tect them where - so - e'er they go: Thus ev - er - more shall

cry to Thee For those in per - il on the sea.
guard - ing hand From ev - 'ry per - il on the land.
watch - ful care From ev - 'ry per - il in the air.
rise to Thee Glad praise from air and land and sea.*

Tune: MELITA

377 — Jesus, Savior, Pilot Me
EDWARD HOPPER
JOHN E. GOULD
1. Je - sus, Sav - ior, pi - lot me O - ver life's tem-pes-tuous sea:
2. As a moth-er stills her child, Thou canst hush the o - cean wild;
3. When at last I near the shore, And the fear - ful break-ers roar
Un - known waves be-fore me roll, Hid - ing rocks and treach-'rous shoal;
Bois - t'rous waves o - bey Thy will When Thou say'st to them, "Be still!"
'Twixt me and the peace-ful rest— Then, while lean - ing on Thy breast,
Chart and com-pass come from Thee— Je - sus, Sav - ior, pi - lot me!
Won-drous Sov-'reign of the sea, Je - sus, Sav - ior, pi - lot me!
May I hear Thee say to me, "Fear not— I will pi - lot thee!"*
Tune: PILOT
378 — Be Thou My Vision
Irish hymn, c. 8th century
Trans. by Mary E. Byrne
Versified by Eleanor H. Hull
Irish melody
Arr. by Norman Johnson
1. Be Thou my Vi - sion, O Lord of my heart— Naught be all
2. Be Thou my wis - dom, be Thou my true word— I ev - er
3. Be Thou my shield and my sword for the fight, Be Thou my
4. Rich - es I heed not nor man's emp - ty praise— Thou mine in -
5. High King of heav - en, when vic - t'ry is won, May I reach
Tune: SLANE

GUIDANCE AND CARE / ASPIRATION

else to me save that Thou art; Thou my best thought by day or by night— Wak-ing or sleep-ing, Thy pres-ence my light.
with Thee and Thou with me, Lord; Thou my great Fa-ther and I Thy true son— Thou in me dwell-ing, and I with Thee one.
dig-ni-ty, be Thou my might; Thou my soul's shel-ter and Thou my high tow'r, Raise Thou me heav'nward, O pow'r of my pow'r.
her-i-tance now and al-ways; Thou and Thou on-ly be first in my heart— High King of heav-en, my treas-ure Thou art.
heav-en's joys, O bright heav'n's Sun! Heart of my own heart, what-ev-er be-fall, Still be my Vi-sion, O Rul-er of all.*
Sun of My Soul — 379
JOHN KEBLE
Katholisches Gesangbuch
1. Sun of my soul, Thou Sav-ior dear, It is not night if Thou be near; O may no earth-born cloud a-rise To hide Thee from Thy serv-ant's eyes!
2. When the soft dews of kind-ly sleep My wea-ry eye-lids gen-tly steep, Be my last thought, how sweet to rest For-ev-er on my Sav-ior's breast!
3. A-bide with me from morn till eve, For with-out Thee I can-not live; A-bide with me when night is nigh, For with-out Thee I dare not die.
4. Be near to bless me when I wake, Ere thru the world my way I take; A-bide with me till in Thy love I lose my-self in heav'n a-bove.*
Tune: HURSLEY

380 — Higher Ground

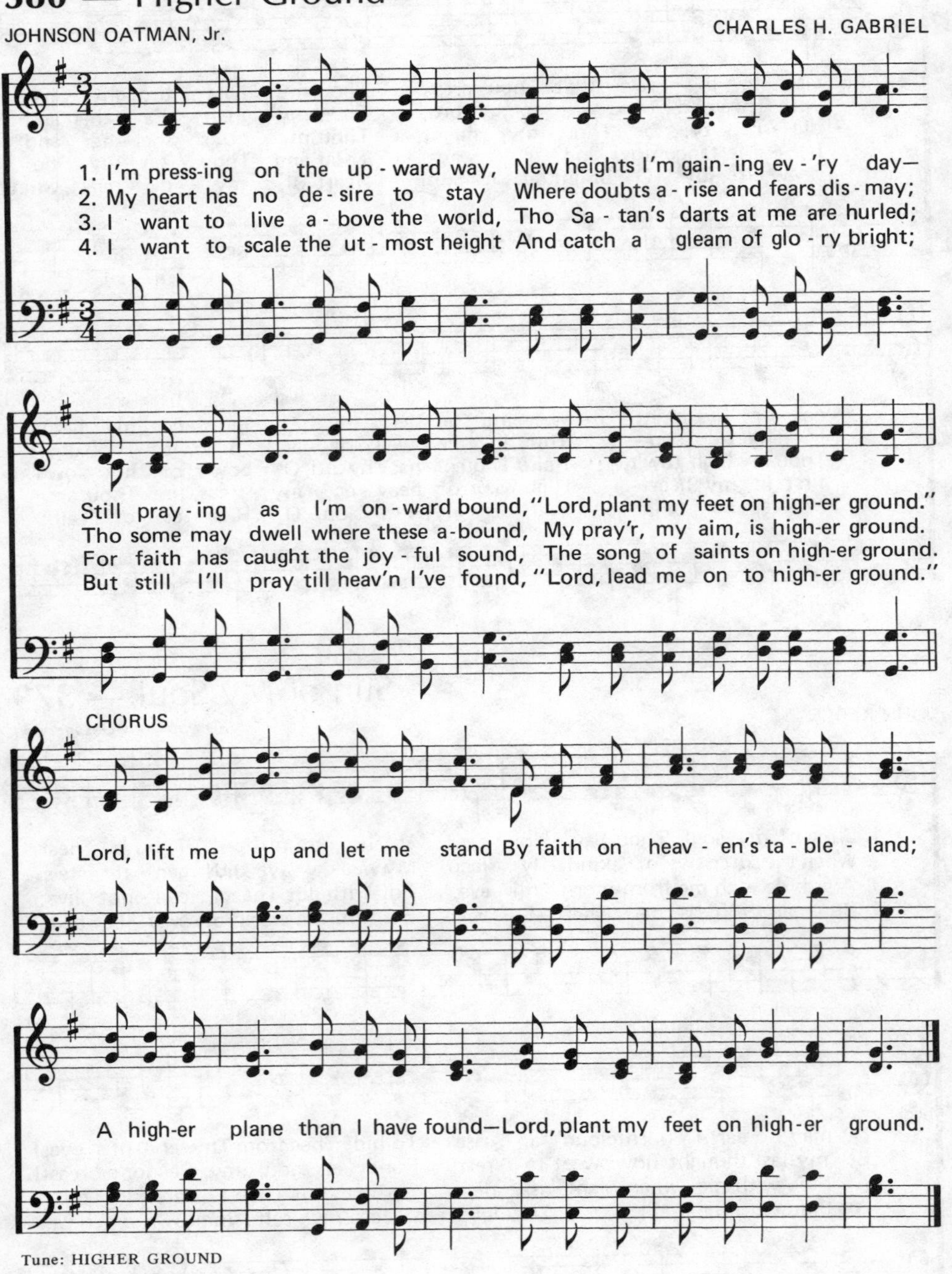
JOHNSON OATMAN, Jr.
CHARLES H. GABRIEL
1. I'm press-ing on the up-ward way, New heights I'm gain-ing ev-'ry day—
2. My heart has no de-sire to stay Where doubts a-rise and fears dis-may;
3. I want to live a-bove the world, Tho Sa-tan's darts at me are hurled;
4. I want to scale the ut-most height And catch a gleam of glo-ry bright;
Still pray-ing as I'm on-ward bound, "Lord, plant my feet on high-er ground."
Tho some may dwell where these a-bound, My pray'r, my aim, is high-er ground.
For faith has caught the joy-ful sound, The song of saints on high-er ground.
But still I'll pray till heav'n I've found, "Lord, lead me on to high-er ground."
CHORUS
Lord, lift me up and let me stand By faith on heav-en's ta-ble-land;
A high-er plane than I have found—Lord, plant my feet on high-er ground.

Tune: HIGHER GROUND

ASPIRATION

Traditional
Traditional Spiritual
1. Lord, I want to be a Christ-ian in-a my heart, in-a my heart, Lord, I want to be a Chris-tian in-a my heart;
2. Lord, I want to be more lov-ing in-a my heart, in-a my heart, Lord, I want to be more lov-ing in-a my heart;
3. Lord, I want to be more ho-ly in-a my heart, in-a my heart, Lord, I want to be more ho-ly in-a my heart;
4. Lord, I want to be like Je-sus in-a my heart, in-a my heart, Lord, I want to be like Je-sus in-a my heart;
heart,
In-a my heart, In-a my heart,
In-a my heart, In-a my heart,
Lord, I want to be a Chris-tian in-a my heart.
Lord, I want to be more lov-ing in-a my heart.
Lord, I want to be more ho-ly in-a my heart.
Lord, I want to be like Je-sus in-a my heart.

ASPIRATION

382 — I Need Thee Every Hour

ANNIE S. HAWKS
Chorus—Robert Lowry
ROBERT LOWRY
1. I need Thee ev-'ry hour, Most gra - cious Lord; No ten - der voice like Thine Can peace af - ford.
2. I need Thee ev-'ry hour, Stay Thou near by; Temp-ta-tions lose their pow'r When Thou art nigh.
3. I need Thee ev-'ry hour, In joy or pain; Come quick-ly and a - bide, Or life is vain.
4. I need Thee ev-'ry hour, Most Ho - ly One; O make me Thine in- deed, Thou bless - ed Son!
CHORUS
I need Thee, O I need Thee, Ev - 'ry hour I need Thee! O bless me now, my Sav-ior— I come to Thee!
383 — Let the Beauty of Jesus Be Seen in Me
ALBERT W. T. ORSBORN
TOM JONES
Let the beau-ty of Je-sus be seen in me— All His won-der-ful pas-sion and pu - ri - ty! O Thou Spir-it di - vine, All my

ASPIRATION

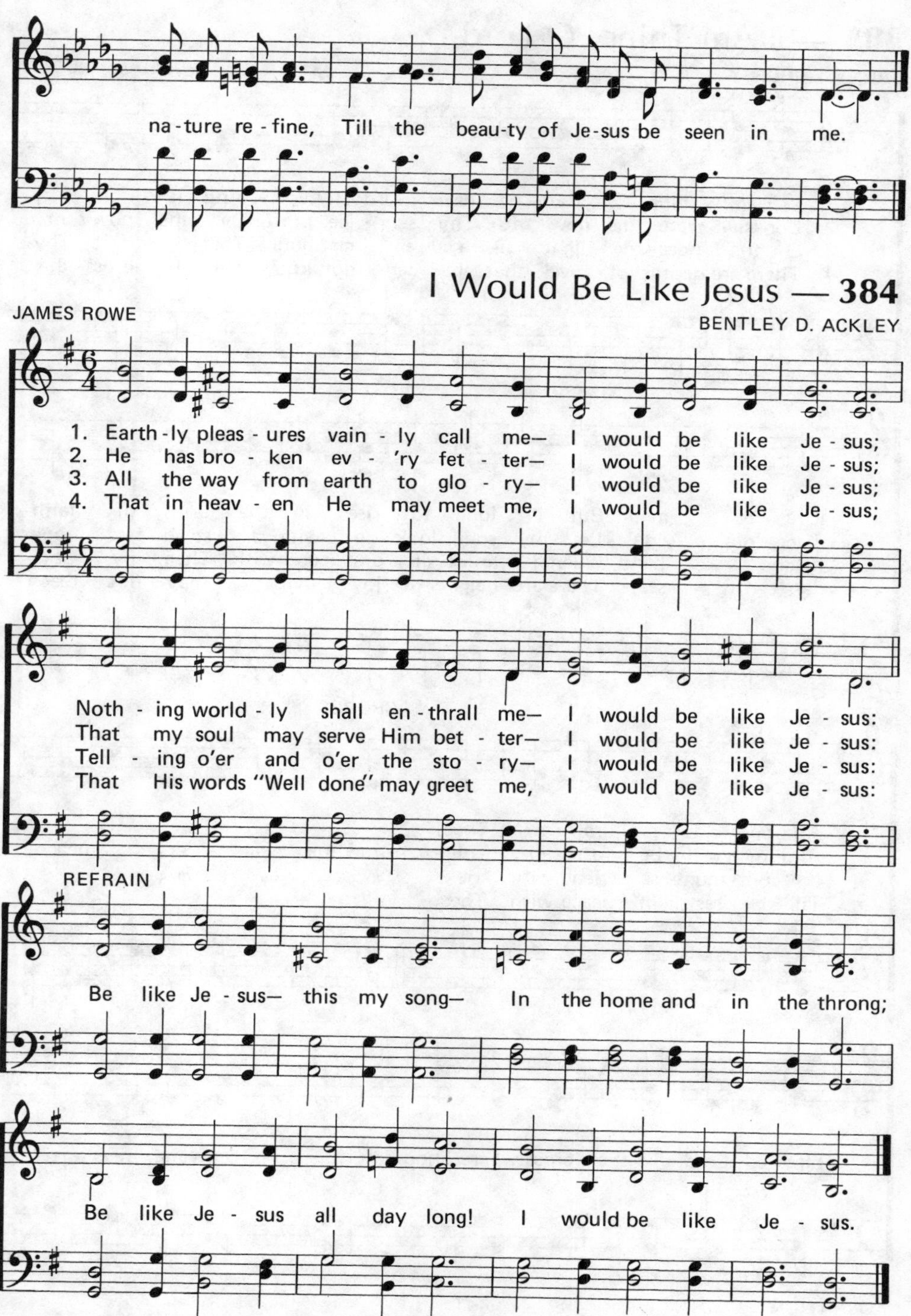
na-ture re-fine, Till the beau-ty of Je-sus be seen in me.
I Would Be Like Jesus — 384
JAMES ROWE
BENTLEY D. ACKLEY
1. Earth-ly pleas-ures vain-ly call me— I would be like Je-sus;
2. He has bro-ken ev-'ry fet-ter— I would be like Je-sus;
3. All the way from earth to glo-ry— I would be like Je-sus;
4. That in heav-en He may meet me, I would be like Je-sus;
Noth-ing world-ly shall en-thrall me— I would be like Je-sus:
That my soul may serve Him bet-ter— I would be like Je-sus:
Tell-ing o'er and o'er the sto-ry— I would be like Je-sus:
That His words "Well done" may greet me, I would be like Je-sus:
REFRAIN
Be like Je-sus— this my song— In the home and in the throng;
Be like Je-sus all day long! I would be like Je-sus.

ASPIRATION

385 — I Am Thine, O Lord
FANNY J. CROSBY
WILLIAM H. DOANE
1. I am Thine, O Lord— I have heard Thy voice, And it told Thy
2. Con-se - crate me now to Thy serv - ice, Lord, By the pow'r of
3. O the pure de- light of a sin - gle hour That be - fore Thy
4. There are depths of love that I can - not know Till I cross the
love to me; But I long to rise in the arms of faith
grace di - vine; Let my soul look up with a stead - fast hope
throne I spend, When I kneel in pray'r and with Thee, my God,
nar - row sea; There are heights of joy that I may not reach
CHORUS
And be clos - er drawn to Thee.
And my will be lost in Thine. Draw me near - er, near-er,
I com - mune as friend with friend.
near - er, near - er,
Till I rest in peace with Thee.
bless-ed Lord, To the cross where Thou hast died; Draw me near - er,
ASPIRATION

near - er, near - er, bless - ed Lord, To Thy pre - cious, bleed - ing side.

My Jesus, I Love Thee — 386

WILLIAM R. FEATHERSTON

ADONIRAM J. GORDON

1. My Je - sus, I love Thee, I know Thou art mine— For Thee all the fol - lies of sin I re - sign; My gra - cious Re - deem - er, my Sav - ior art Thou: If ev - er I loved Thee, my Je - sus, 'tis now.
2. I love Thee be - cause Thou hast first lov - ed me And pur-chased my par - don on Cal - va - ry's tree; I love Thee for wear - ing the thorns on Thy brow: If ev - er I loved Thee, my Je - sus, 'tis now.
3. I'll love Thee in life, I will love Thee in death, And praise Thee as long as Thou lend - est me breath; And say when the death - dew lies cold on my brow, "If ev - er I loved Thee, my Je - sus, 'tis now."
4. In man-sions of glo - ry and end - less de - light, I'll ev - er a - dore Thee in heav - en so bright; I'll sing with the glit - ter - ing crown on my brow, "If ev - er I loved Thee, my Je - sus, 'tis now."*

Tune: GORDON

ASPIRATION

387 — Near to Thy Heart
Based on John 13:23
JOHN W. PETERSON
JOHN W. PETERSON
1. Near to Thy heart, O Christ di - vine, Lean-ing like John on Thy breast—
2. Near to Thy heart O may I be, Hear-ing Thy sweet words of love,
3. Near to Thy heart where all is peace, Lost in the light of Thy face,
Till with Thy glo - ry I will shine, Near to Thy heart I'd rest.
Learn-ing Thy pre-cious will for me, Seek-ing those things a - bove.
There will my faith and trust in - crease, There will I grow in grace.*
Tune: SUSQUEHANNA
© John W. Peterson Music Company 1956. All rights reserved.
388 — May the Mind of Christ My Savior
KATE B. WILKINSON
A. CYRIL BARHAM-GOULD
1. May the mind of Christ my Sav - ior Live in me from day to day,
2. May the Word of God dwell rich - ly In my heart from hour to hour,
3. May the peace of God my Fa - ther Rule my life in ev - 'ry - thing,
4. May the love of Je - sus fill me As the wa - ters fill the sea;
5. May I run the race be - fore me, Strong and brave to face the foe,
6. May His beau - ty rest up - on me As I seek the lost to win,
By His love and pow'r con - trol - ling All I do and say.
So that all may see I tri - umph On - ly thru His pow'r.
That I may be calm to com - fort Sick and sor - row - ing.
Him ex - alt - ing, self a - bas - ing— This is vic - to - ry.
Look - ing on - ly un - to Je - sus As I on - ward go.
And may they for - get the chan - nel, See - ing on - ly Him.*

Tune: ST. LEONARDS

ASPIRATION

Make Me a Blessing — 389

IRA B. WILSON　　　　GEORGE S. SCHULER

1. Out in the high-ways and by-ways of life, Man - y are wea-ry and sad:
2. Tell the sweet sto-ry of Christ and His love, Tell of His pow'r to for - give:
3. Give as 'twas giv-en to you in your need, Love as the Mas-ter loved you;

Car - ry the sun-shine where darkness is rife, Mak-ing the sor-row-ing glad.
Oth - ers will trust Him if on - ly you prove True, ev-'ry mo-ment you live.
Be to the help-less a help - er in - deed, Un - to your mis-sion be true.

CHORUS

Make me a bless - ing, make me a bless - ing! Out of my life
Out, out of my

may Je - sus shine; Make me a bless - ing, O Sav - ior, I
life

pray, Make me a bless - ing to some - one to - day.
pray Thee, my Sav - ior,

ASPIRATION

390 — Christ Be Beside Me

Adapted by James Quinn
from *St. Patrick's Breastplate*

Traditional Gaelic melody
Arr. by Norman Johnson

In unison
1. Christ be be - side me, Christ be be - fore me, Christ be be - hind me— King of my heart; Christ be with - in me, Christ be be - low me, Christ be a - bove me— nev - er to part.
2. Christ on my right hand, Christ on my left hand, Christ all a - round me— shield in the strife; Christ in my sleep - ing, Christ in my sit - ting, Christ in my ris - ing— Light of my life.
3. Christ be in all hearts think - ing a - bout me, Christ be on all tongues tell - ing of me; Christ be the vi - sion in eyes that see me, In ears that hear me Christ ev - er be.
4. Christ be be - side me, Christ be be - fore me, Christ be be - hind me— King of my heart; Christ be with - in me, Christ be be - low me, Christ be a - bove me— nev - er to part.

Tune: BUNESSAN

391 — My Desire

LILLIAN PLANKENHORN

LILLIAN PLANKENHORN

My de - sire— to be like Je - sus, My de - sire— to be like Him! His

ASPIRATION

Spir - it fill me, His love o'er-whelm me: In deed and word to be like Him!
More About Jesus — 392
ELIZA E. HEWITT
JOHN R. SWENEY
1. More a - bout Je - sus would I know, More of His grace to oth - ers show,
2. More a - bout Je - sus let me learn, More of His ho - ly will dis - cern;
3. More a - bout Je - sus— in His Word Hold-ing com-mun-ion with my Lord,
4. More a - bout Je - sus on His throne, Rich - es in glo - ry all His own,
More of His sav - ing full - ness see, More of His love who died for me.
Spir - it of God, my teach - er be, Show-ing the things of Christ to me.
Hear - ing His voice in ev - 'ry line, Mak - ing each faith - ful say - ing mine.
More of His king - dom's sure in-crease, More of His com - ing—Prince of Peace.
REFRAIN
More, more a - bout Je - sus, More, more a - bout Je - sus;
More of His sav - ing full - ness see, More of His love who died for me!
ASPIRATION

393 — My Faith Looks Up to Thee

RAY PALMER
LOWELL MASON
1. My faith looks up to Thee, Thou Lamb of Cal-va-ry, Sav-ior di-vine; Now hear me when I pray, Take all my sin a-way, O let me from this day Be whol-ly Thine!
2. May Thy rich grace im-part Strength to my faint-ing heart, My zeal in-spire; As Thou hast died for me, O may my love to Thee Pure, warm and change-less be— A liv-ing fire!
3. While life's dark maze I tread And griefs a-round me spread, Be Thou my guide; Bid dark-ness turn to day, Wipe sor-row's tears a-way, Nor let me ev-er stray From Thee a-side.
4. When ends life's tran-sient dream, When death's cold sul-len stream Shall o'er me roll, Blest Sav-ior, then, in love, Fear and dis-trust re-move— O bear me safe a-bove, A ran-somed soul.*
Tune: OLIVET

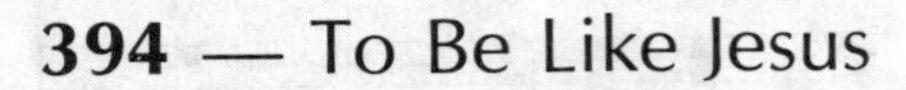

394 — To Be Like Jesus

Traditional

Traditional
Arr. by Frank Anderson

To be like Je-sus, to be like Je-sus! All I ask— to be like Him!

ASPIRATION

All thru life's jour-ney from earth to glo-ry, All I ask— to be like Him.
Close to Thee — 395
FANNY J. CROSBY
SILAS J. VAIL
1. Thou my ev - er - last - ing por - tion, More than friend or life to me;
2. Not for ease or world - ly pleas - ure, Nor for fame my pray'r shall be;
3. Lead me thru the vale of shad - ows, Bear me o'er life's fit - ful sea;
All a - long my pil - grim jour - ney, Sav - ior, let me walk with Thee.
Glad - ly will I toil and suf - fer, On - ly let me walk with Thee.
Then the gate of life e - ter - nal May I en - ter, Lord, with Thee.
Close to Thee, close to Thee, Close to Thee, close to Thee;
Close to Thee, close to Thee, Close to Thee, close to Thee;
Close to Thee, close to Thee, Close to Thee, close to Thee;
All a - long my pil - grim jour - ney, Sav - ior, let me walk with Thee.
Glad - ly will I toil and suf - fer, On - ly let me walk with Thee.
Then the gate of life e - ter - nal May I en - ter, Lord, with Thee.
ASPIRATION

396 — Nothing Between

CHARLES A. TINDLEY
CHARLES A. TINDLEY
1. Noth-ing be - tween my soul and the Sav - ior, Naught of this world's de - lu - sive dream: I have re - nounced all sin - ful pleas-ure— Je - sus is mine, there's noth-ing be - tween.
2. Noth-ing be - tween, like world - ly pleas-ure: Hab - its of life, tho harm-less they seem, Must not my heart from Him ev - er sev - er— He is my all, there's noth-ing be - tween.
3. Noth-ing be - tween, not e - ven hard tri - als, Tho the whole world a - gainst me con - vene; Watch-ing with prayer and much self-de - ni - al— Tri-umph at last, with noth-ing be - tween!
CHORUS
Noth - ing be - tween my soul and the Sav-ior, So that His bless - ed face may be seen; Noth-ing pre - vent-ing the least of His fa - vor: Keep the way clear—let noth-ing be-tween.

ASPIRATION

O to Be Like Thee! — 397
THOMAS O. CHISHOLM
WILLIAM J. KIRKPATRICK
1. O to be like Thee! bless-ed Re - deem - er, This is my con - stant long - ing and prayer; Glad - ly I'll for - feit all of earth's treas - ures, Je - sus, Thy per - fect like - ness to wear.
2. O to be like Thee! full of com - pas - sion, Lov - ing, for - giv - ing, ten - der and kind; Help - ing the help - less, cheer - ing the faint - ing, Seek - ing the wan-d'ring sin - ner to find.
3. O to be like Thee! while I am plead - ing, Pour out Thy Spir - it, fill with Thy love; Make me a tem - ple meet for Thy dwell - ing, Fit me for life and heav - en a - bove.
CHORUS
O to be like Thee! O to be like Thee, Bless-ed Re - deem - er, pure as Thou art! Come in Thy sweet - ness, come in Thy full - ness—Stamp Thine own im - age deep on my heart.

ASPIRATION

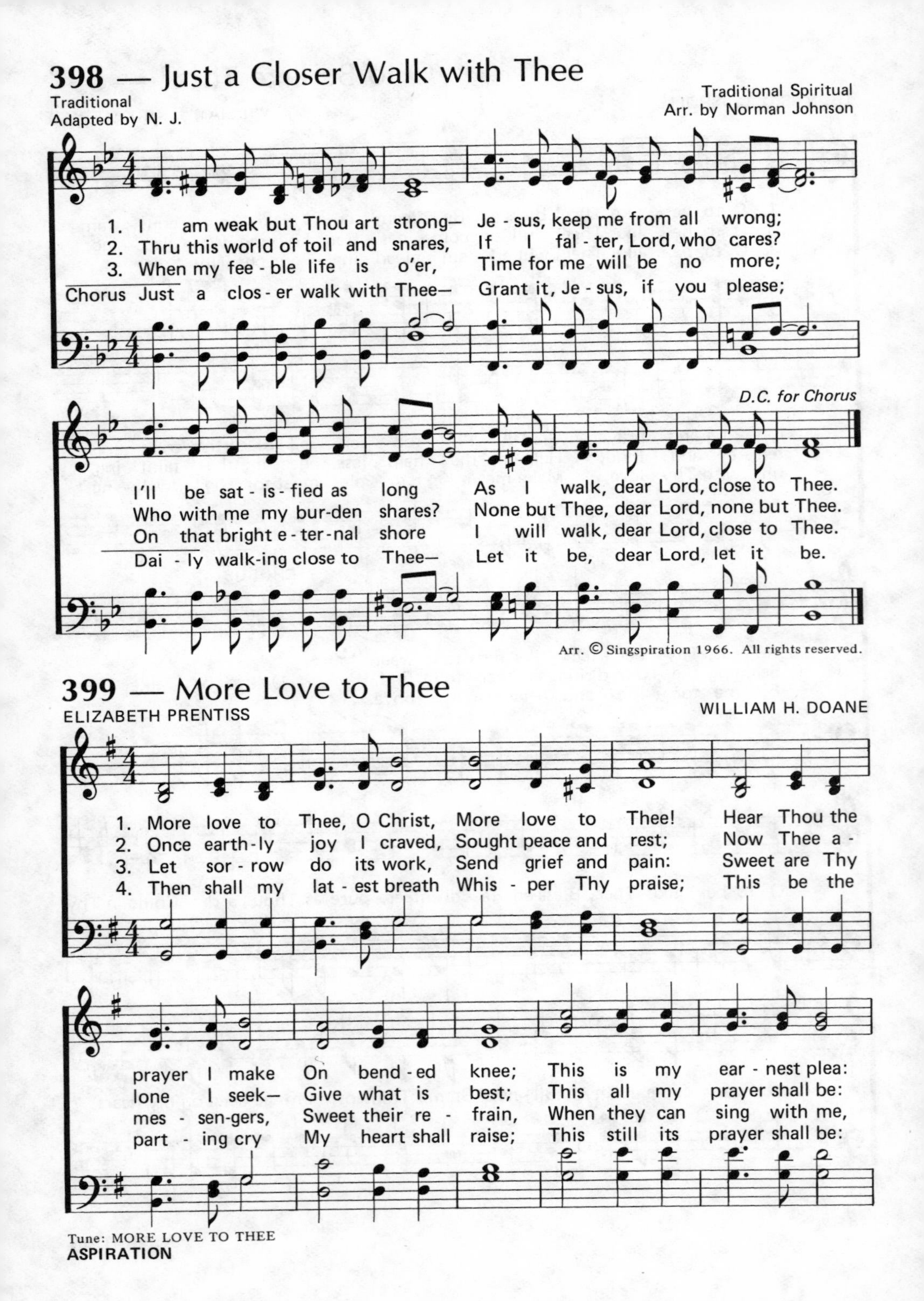
398 — Just a Closer Walk with Thee
Traditional
Adapted by N. J.
Traditional Spiritual
Arr. by Norman Johnson
1. I am weak but Thou art strong— Je - sus, keep me from all wrong;
2. Thru this world of toil and snares, If I fal - ter, Lord, who cares?
3. When my fee - ble life is o'er, Time for me will be no more;
Chorus Just a clos - er walk with Thee— Grant it, Je - sus, if you please;
D.C. for Chorus
I'll be sat - is - fied as long As I walk, dear Lord, close to Thee.
Who with me my bur-den shares? None but Thee, dear Lord, none but Thee.
On that bright e - ter - nal shore I will walk, dear Lord, close to Thee.
Dai - ly walk-ing close to Thee— Let it be, dear Lord, let it be.
Arr. © Singspiration 1966. All rights reserved.
399 — More Love to Thee
ELIZABETH PRENTISS
WILLIAM H. DOANE
1. More love to Thee, O Christ, More love to Thee! Hear Thou the
2. Once earth - ly joy I craved, Sought peace and rest; Now Thee a -
3. Let sor - row do its work, Send grief and pain: Sweet are Thy
4. Then shall my lat - est breath Whis - per Thy praise; This be the
prayer I make On bend - ed knee; This is my ear - nest plea:
lone I seek— Give what is best; This all my prayer shall be:
mes - sen-gers, Sweet their re - frain, When they can sing with me,
part - ing cry My heart shall raise; This still its prayer shall be:
Tune: MORE LOVE TO THEE
ASPIRATION

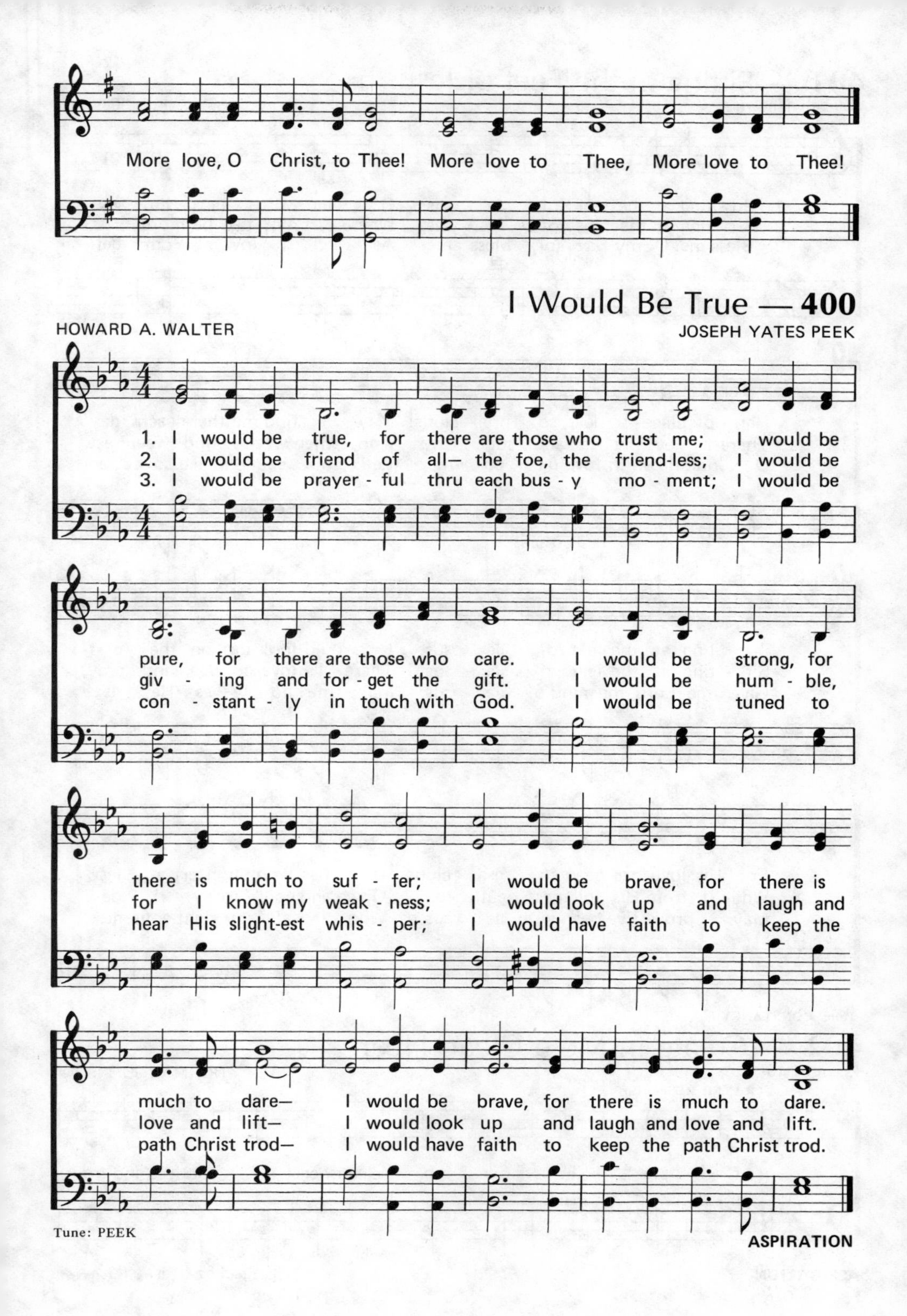
More love, O Christ, to Thee! More love to Thee, More love to Thee!
I Would Be True — 400
HOWARD A. WALTER
JOSEPH YATES PEEK
1. I would be true, for there are those who trust me; I would be pure, for there are those who care. I would be strong, for there is much to suffer; I would be brave, for there is much to dare— I would be brave, for there is much to dare.
2. I would be friend of all— the foe, the friend-less; I would be giv - ing and for - get the gift. I would be hum - ble, for I know my weak - ness; I would look up and laugh and love and lift— I would look up and laugh and love and lift.
3. I would be prayer - ful thru each bus - y mo - ment; I would be con - stant - ly in touch with God. I would be tuned to hear His slight-est whis - per; I would have faith to keep the path Christ trod— I would have faith to keep the path Christ trod.
Tune: PEEK
ASPIRATION

401 — Sitting at the Feet of Jesus
Source unknown
Source unknown
1. Sit - ting at the feet of Je - sus, O what words I hear Him say!
2. Sit - ting at the feet of Je - sus, Where can mor - tal be more blest?
3. Bless me, O my Sav - ior, bless me, As I sit low at Your feet!
Hap - py place—so near, so pre - cious! May it find me there each day!
There I lay my sins and sor - rows, And, when wea-ry, find sweet rest.
O look down in love up - on me, Let me see Your face so sweet!
Sit - ting at the feet of Je - sus, I would look up - on the past,
Sit - ting at the feet of Je - sus, There I love to weep and pray,
Give me, Lord, the mind of Je - sus, Make me ho - ly as He is;
For His love has been so gra - cious— It has won my heart at last.
While I from His full-ness gath - er Grace and com-fort ev - 'ry day.
May I prove I've been with Je - sus, Who is all my right-eous-ness.*
Tune: CONSTANCY
402 — Create in Me a Clean Heart
Psalm 51:10
NORMAN JOHNSON
PRAYER RESPONSE
Cre - ate in me a clean heart, O God, and re -
ASPIRATION

optional
new a right spir - it with - in me. A - men.
Near the Cross — 403
FANNY J. CROSBY
WILLIAM H. DOANE
1. Je - sus, keep me near the cross— There a pre - cious foun - tain,
2. Near the cross, a trem - bling soul, Love and mer - cy found me;
3. Near the cross! O Lamb of God, Bring its scenes be - fore me;
4. Near the cross I'll watch and wait, Hop - ing, trust - ing ev - er,
Free to all, a heal - ing stream, Flows from Cal - v'ry's moun - tain.
There the Bright and Morn - ing Star Sheds its beams a - round me.
Help me walk from day to day With its shad - ows o'er me.
Till I reach the gold - en strand Just be - yond the riv - er.
CHORUS
In the cross, in the cross Be my glo - ry ev - er,
Till my rap - tured soul shall find Rest, be - yond the riv - er.*
ASPIRATION

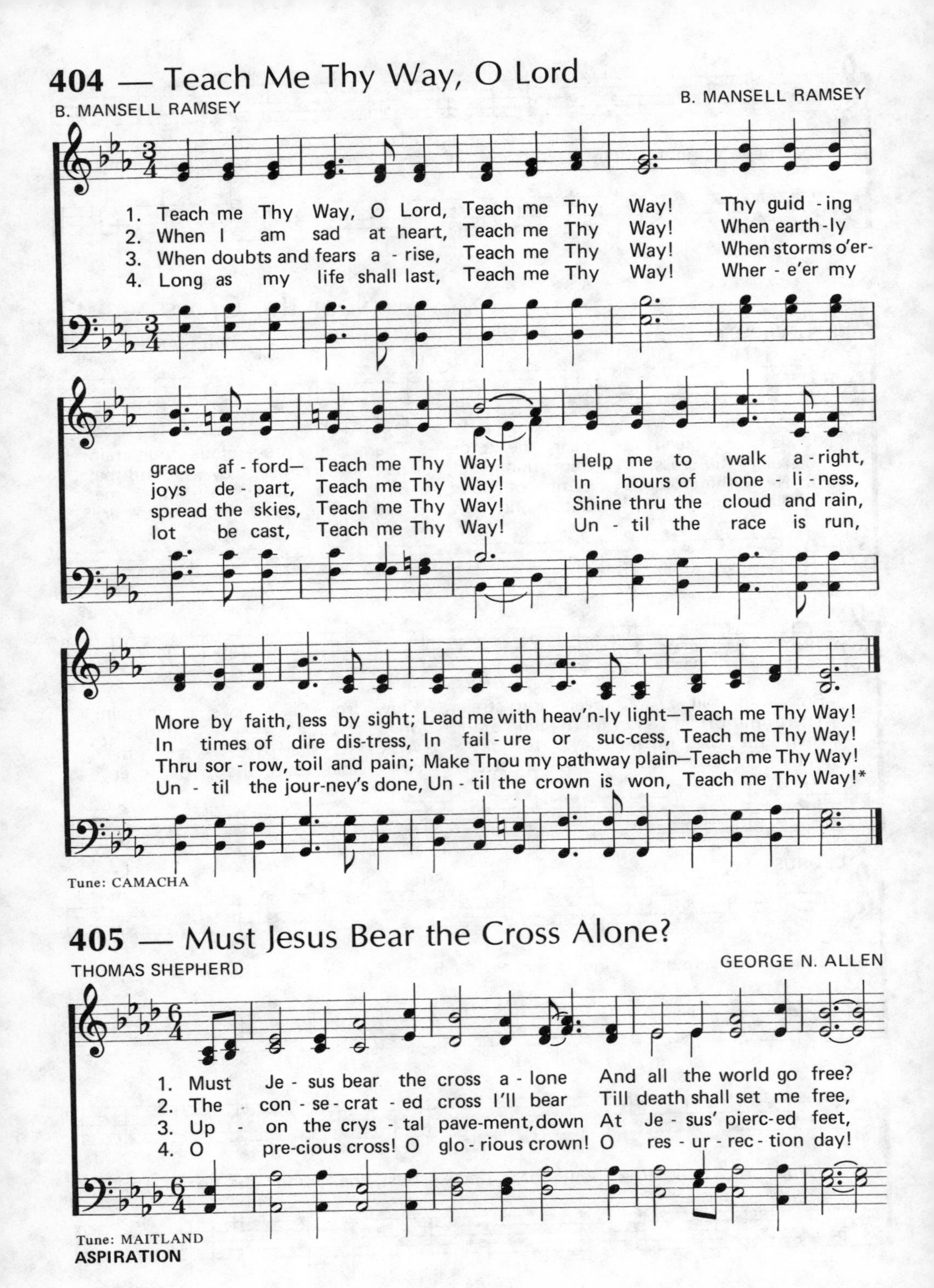
404 — Teach Me Thy Way, O Lord
B. MANSELL RAMSEY
B. MANSELL RAMSEY
1. Teach me Thy Way, O Lord, Teach me Thy Way! Thy guid - ing
2. When I am sad at heart, Teach me Thy Way! When earth - ly
3. When doubts and fears a - rise, Teach me Thy Way! When storms o'er-
4. Long as my life shall last, Teach me Thy Way! Wher - e'er my
grace af - ford— Teach me Thy Way! Help me to walk a - right,
joys de - part, Teach me Thy Way! In hours of lone - li - ness,
spread the skies, Teach me Thy Way! Shine thru the cloud and rain,
lot be cast, Teach me Thy Way! Un - til the race is run,
More by faith, less by sight; Lead me with heav'n-ly light—Teach me Thy Way!
In times of dire dis-tress, In fail - ure or suc-cess, Teach me Thy Way!
Thru sor - row, toil and pain; Make Thou my pathway plain—Teach me Thy Way!
Un - til the jour-ney's done, Un - til the crown is won, Teach me Thy Way!*
Tune: CAMACHA
405 — Must Jesus Bear the Cross Alone?
THOMAS SHEPHERD
GEORGE N. ALLEN
1. Must Je - sus bear the cross a - lone And all the world go free?
2. The con - se - crat - ed cross I'll bear Till death shall set me free,
3. Up - on the crys - tal pave-ment, down At Je - sus' pierc-ed feet,
4. O pre-cious cross! O glo - rious crown! O res - ur - rec - tion day!
Tune: MAITLAND
ASPIRATION

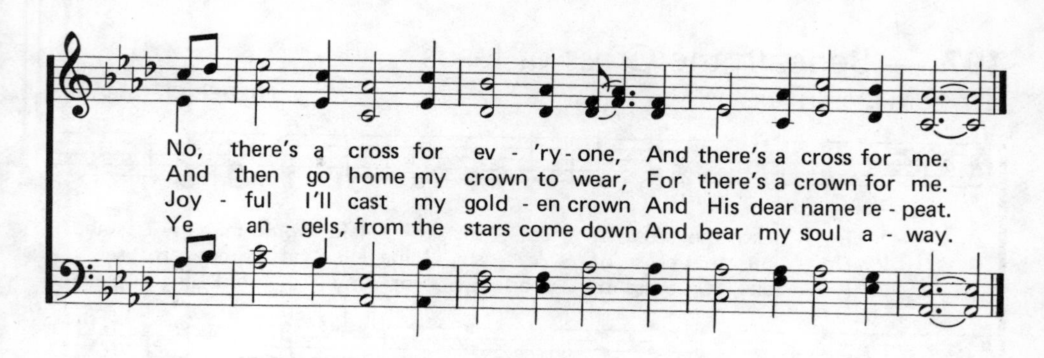

No, there's a cross for ev - 'ry - one, And there's a cross for me.
And then go home my crown to wear, For there's a crown for me.
Joy - ful I'll cast my gold - en crown And His dear name re - peat.
Ye an - gels, from the stars come down And bear my soul a - way.

Dear Lord and Father of Mankind — 406

JOHN G. WHITTIER

FREDERICK C. MAKER

1. Dear Lord and Fa - ther of man-kind, For - give our fe - v'rish ways! Re - clothe us in our right - ful mind; In pur - er lives Thy serv - ice find, In deep - er rev - 'rence, praise.
2. In sim - ple trust like theirs who heard, Be - side the Syr - ian sea, The gra - cious call - ing of the Lord, Let us, like them, with - out a word Rise up and fol - low Thee.
3. O sab - bath rest by Gal - i - lee! O calm of hills a - bove, Where Je - sus knelt to share with Thee The si - lence of e - ter - ni - ty, In - ter - pret - ed by love—
4. Drop Thy still dews of qui - et - ness Till all our striv - ings cease; Take from our souls the strain and stress, And let our or - dered lives con - fess The beau - ty of Thy peace.
5. Breathe thru the heats of our de - sire Thy cool - ness and Thy balm; Let sense be dumb, let flesh re - tire; Speak thru the earth - quake, wind and fire, O still small voice of calm!*

Tune: REST

ASPIRATION

407 — Beneath the Cross of Jesus

ELIZABETH C. CLEPHANE | FREDERICK C. MAKER

1. Be - neath the cross of Je - sus I fain would take my stand,
2. Up - on that cross of Je - sus Mine eye at times can see
3. I take, O cross, thy shad - ow For my a - bid - ing - place—
The shad - ow of a might - y Rock With - in a wea - ry land;
The ver - y dy - ing form of one Who suf fered there for me;
I ask no oth - er sun - shine than The sun - shine of His face;
A home with-in the wil - der - ness, A rest up - on the way
And from my smit-ten heart with tears Two won-ders I con - fess—
Con - tent to let the world go by, To know no gain nor loss,
From the burn-ing of the noon-day heat And the bur-den of the day.
The won-ders of His glo - rious love And my own worth-less-ness.
My sin - ful self my on - ly shame, My glo - ry all the cross.

Tune: ST. CHRISTOPHER

ASPIRATION

ELISHA A. HOFFMAN

ELISHA A. HOFFMAN

1. I must tell Je - sus all of my tri - als, I can - not bear these bur - dens a - lone; In my dis - tress He kind - ly will help me, He ev - er loves and cares for His own.
2. I must tell Je - sus all of my trou - bles, He is a kind, com - pas - sion - ate friend; If I but ask Him, He will de - liv - er, Make of my trou - bles quick - ly an end.
3. O how the world to e - vil al - lures me! O how my heart is tempt - ed to sin! I must tell Je - sus, and He will help me O - ver the world the vic - t'ry to win.
CHORUS
I must tell Je - sus! I must tell Je - sus! I can - not bear my bur - dens a - lone; I must tell Je - sus! I must tell Je - sus! Je - sus can help me, Je - sus a - lone.

PRAYER

409 — Teach Me to Pray
ALBERT S. REITZ
ALBERT S. REITZ
1. Teach me to pray, Lord, teach me to pray— This is my heart-cry day unto day; I long to know Thy will and Thy way— Teach me to pray, Lord, teach me to pray.
2. Power in prayer, Lord, power in prayer— Here 'mid earth's sin and sorrow and care; Men lost and dying, souls in despair— O give me power, power in prayer!
3. My weakened will, Lord, Thou canst renew— My sinful nature Thou canst subdue; Fill me just now with power anew— Power to pray and power to do!
4. Teach me to pray, Lord, teach me to pray— Thou art my pattern day unto day; Thou art my surety now and for aye— Teach me to pray, Lord, teach me to pray.
CHORUS
Living in Thee, Lord, and Thou in me— Constant abiding, this is my plea; Grant me Thy

PRAYER

pow - er, bound-less and free— Pow-er with men and pow-er with Thee.
Near to the Heart of God — 410
CLELAND B. McAFEE
CLELAND B. McAFEE
1. There is a place of qui - et rest, Near to the heart of God,
2. There is a place of com-fort sweet, Near to the heart of God,
3. There is a place of full re-lease, Near to the heart of God,
A place where sin can - not mo - lest, Near to the heart of God.
A place where we our Sav - ior meet, Near to the heart of God.
A place where all is joy and peace, Near to the heart of God.
CHORUS
O Je - sus, blest Re - deem - er, Sent from the heart of God,
Hold us who wait be - fore Thee Near to the heart of God.
Tune: McAFEE
PRAYER

411 — Spend a Little Time with Jesus in Prayer

JOHN W. PETERSON — JOHN W. PETERSON

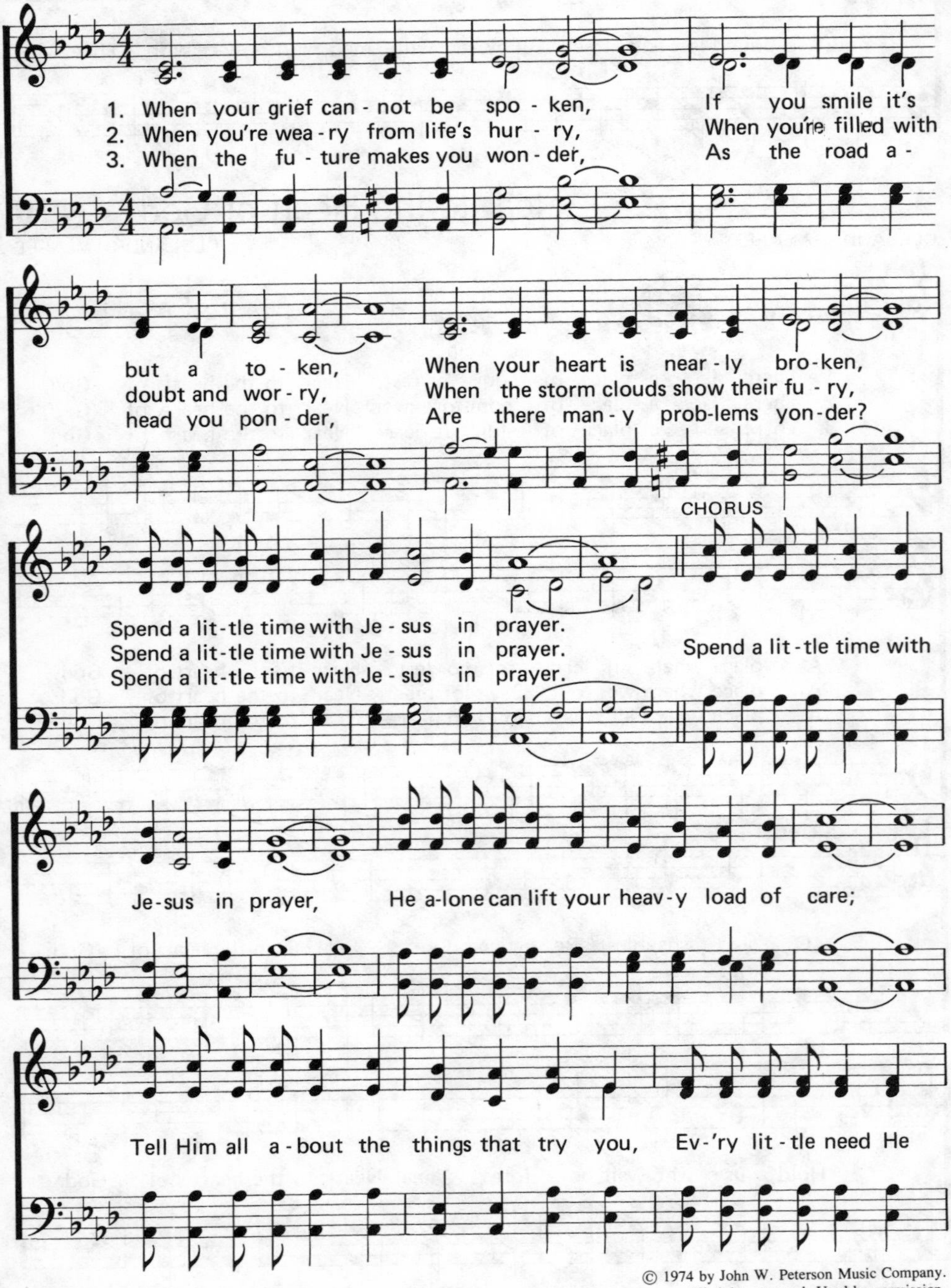

1. When your grief can - not be spo - ken, If you smile it's but a to - ken, When your heart is near - ly bro - ken, Spend a lit - tle time with Je - sus in prayer.
2. When you're wea - ry from life's hur - ry, When you're filled with doubt and wor - ry, When the storm clouds show their fu - ry, Spend a lit - tle time with Je - sus in prayer.
3. When the fu - ture makes you won - der, As the road a - head you pon - der, Are there man - y prob - lems yon - der? Spend a lit - tle time with Je - sus in prayer.

CHORUS

Spend a lit - tle time with Je - sus in prayer, He a - lone can lift your heav - y load of care; Tell Him all a - bout the things that try you, Ev - 'ry lit - tle need He

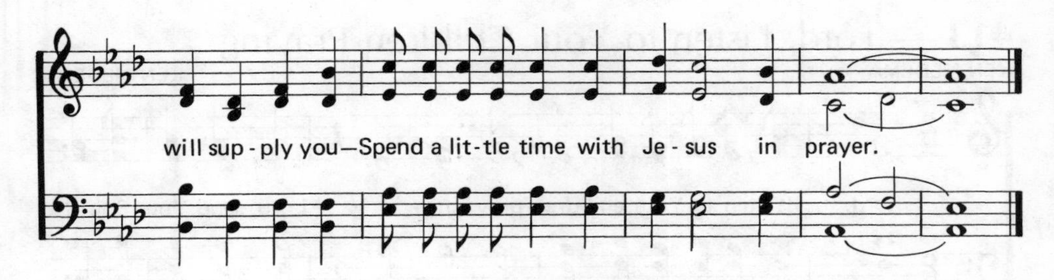
will sup - ply you—Spend a lit - tle time with Je - sus in prayer.

What a Friend We Have in Jesus — 412

JOSEPH SCRIVEN

CHARLES C. CONVERSE

1. What a Friend we have in Je - sus, All our sins and griefs to bear!
2. Have we tri - als and temp - ta - tions? Is there trou - ble an - y - where?
3. Are we weak and heav - y - la - den, Cum - bered with a load of care?
What a priv - i - lege to car - ry Ev - 'ry - thing to God in prayer!
We should nev - er be dis - cour - aged— Take it to the Lord in prayer.
Pre - cious Sav - ior, still our ref - uge— Take it to the Lord in prayer.
O what peace we oft - en for - feit, O what need - less pain we bear,
Can we find a friend so faith - ful Who will all our sor - rows share?
Do thy friends de - spise, for - sake thee? Take it to the Lord in prayer;
All be - cause we do not car - ry Ev - 'ry - thing to God in prayer!
Je - sus knows our ev - 'ry weak - ness— Take it to the Lord in prayer.
In His arms He'll take and shield thee— Thou wilt find a sol - ace there.

Tune: CONVERSE (Alternate, HOLY MANNA)

413 — Lord, Listen to Your Children Praying
KEN MEDEMA
KEN MEDEMA
Lord, lis - ten to Your chil-dren pray - ing— Lord, send Your Spir-it
in this place! Lord, lis - ten to Your chil-dren pray - ing—
1 (Optional)
D.C.
Final
Send us love, send us pow'r, send us grace! grace!
© Copyright 1973 and arr. © 1979 by Crescendo Publications, Inc. All rights reserved.
414 — Sweet Hour of Prayer
WILLIAM W. WALFORD
WILLIAM B. BRADBURY
1. Sweet hour of prayer, sweet hour of prayer, That calls me from a world of care,
2. Sweet hour of prayer, sweet hour of prayer, Thy wings shall my pe - ti - tion bear
And bids me at my Fa-ther's throne Make all my wants and wish - es known:
To Him whose truth and faith - ful - ness En - gage the wait-ing soul to bless:
Tune: SWEET HOUR
PRAYER

In sea-sons of dis-tress and grief My soul has oft-en found re-lief,
And since He bids me seek His face, Be-lieve His Word, and trust His grace,
And oft es-caped the tempt-er's snare By thy re-turn, sweet hour of prayer.
I'll cast on Him my ev-'ry care, And wait for thee, sweet hour of prayer.
Our Father in Heaven — 415
Based on Matthew 6:9-13
SARAH J. HALE
Welsh melody
Robert's Caniadau y Cyssegr
1. Our Fa-ther in heav-en, we hal-low Thy name, May Thy king-dom ho-ly on earth be the same; O give to us dai-ly our por-tion of bread: It is from Thy boun-ty that all must be fed.
2. For-give our trans-gres-sions and teach us to know That hum-ble com-pas-sion which par-dons each foe; Keep us from temp-ta-tion, from e-vil and sin, And Thine be the glo-ry for-ev-er! A-men.
Tune: ST. DENIO—higher key at 55
PRAYER

416 — Let Us Come Boldly
Hebrews 4:16
JON DREVITS
CHORAL CALL TO PRAYER
Let us come bold - ly un - to the throne of grace, that we
may ob - tain mer - cy and find grace to help in time of need.
© Singspiration 1979. All rights reserved.
417 — Pray for Me
NORMAN JOHNSON
NORMAN JOHNSON
*A. Pray for me when you kneel at the mer - cy seat— I'm so bur - dened
B. Pray for me when you bow at the throne of grace— I've a tri - al
C. Pray for me when you talk to the Lord a - bove— For, when two a -
with my heart-ache and care; I need help to lay it down at
just too heav - y to bear; I need some - one who will ear - nest -
gree to - geth - er to share, He will hear and He will an - swer
the Mas - ter's feet—When you pray, re-mem-ber me in your prayer.
ly plead my case—When you pray, re-peat my name in your prayer.
in ten - der love—When you pray, re-call my need in your prayer.

*Rather than a hymn, this is a prayer chorus in which one stanza is sufficient for any given service—preceding or following the voicing of prayer requests.

A
N. J.
NORMAN JOHNSON
We come un-to Your throne of grace, O Lord, in Je-sus' name. A-men.
© Singspiration 1967, arr. 1979.
B
Isaiah 26:3
Scottish Psalter
Thou wilt keep him in per-fect peace whose mind is stayed on Thee.*
C
J. D.
JON DREVITS
A. What our lips pro-fess may our lives ex-press: This we pray in Je-sus' name.*
B. As our hearts be-lieve we with joy re-ceive: For in Je-sus' name we pray.*
C. In the Sav-ior's name we the prom-ise claim: That You hear and answer prayer.*
D. What our mouths confess may our faith pos-sess: This we ask for Je-sus' sake.*
© Singspiration 1979.
D
N. J.
NORMAN JOHNSON
May our hearts a-gree with what we say, May our lives con-form to what we pray;
Our faith be strong, our mo-tives pure— Thy will be done in us to-day.*
© Singspiration 1970, arr. 1979.

419 — Tell It to Jesus

JEREMIAH E. RANKIN

EDMUND S. LORENZ

1. Are you wea - ry, are you heav - y - heart - ed? Tell it to Je - sus,
2. Do the tears flow down your cheeks un - bid - den? Tell it to Je - sus,
3. Do you fear the gath-'ring clouds of sor - row? Tell it to Je - sus,
4. Are you trou - bled at the thought of dy - ing? Tell it to Je - sus,
Tell it to Je - sus; Are you griev - ing o - ver joys de - part - ed?
Tell it to Je - sus; Have you sins that to men's eyes are hid - den?
Tell it to Je - sus; Are you anx - ious what shall be to - mor - row?
Tell it to Je - sus; For Christ's com - ing king - dom are you sigh - ing?
Tell it to Je - sus a - lone.
CHORUS
Tell it to Je - sus, tell it to
Je - sus, He is a friend that's well - known;
You've no oth - er
such a friend or broth - er—
Tell it to Je - sus a - lone.

CHALLENGE

In Times Like These — 420
RUTH CAYE JONES
RUTH CAYE JONES
1. In times like these you need a Sav-ior, In times like these you need an
2. In times like these you need the Bi - ble, In times like these O be not
3. In times like these I have a Sav-ior, In times like these I have an
an - chor; Be ver - y sure, be ver - y sure Your an-chor holds
i - dle; Be ver - y sure, be ver - y sure Your an-chor holds
an - chor; I'm ver - y sure, I'm ver-y sure My an-chor holds
REFRAIN
and grips the Sol-id Rock! This Rock is Je - sus, Yes, He's the
and grips the Sol-id Rock! This Rock is Je - sus, Yes, He's the
and grips the Sol-id Rock! This Rock is Je - sus, Yes, He's the
One; This Rock is Je - sus, The on - ly One! Be ver - y sure,
One; This Rock is Je - sus, The on - ly One! Be ver - y sure,
One; This Rock is Je - sus, The on - ly One! I'm ver - y sure,
be ver - y sure Your an-chor holds and grips the Sol - id Rock!
be ver - y sure Your an-chor holds and grips the Sol - id Rock!
I'm ver - y sure My an-chor holds and grips the Sol - id Rock!

421 — Who Is on the Lord's Side?
C. LUISE REICHARDT
Arr. by John Goss
FRANCES R. HAVERGAL
1. Who is on the Lord's side? Who will serve the King? Who will
2. Not for weight of glo - ry, Not for crown and palm, En - ter
3. Je - sus, Thou hast bought us, Not with gold or gem, But with
4. Fierce may be the con - flict, Strong may be the foe, But the
be His help - ers, Oth - er lives to bring? Who will leave the
we the ar - my, Raise the war - rior - psalm; But for Love that
Thine own life - blood, For Thy di - a - dem. With Thy bless - ing
King's own ar - my None can o - ver - throw. Round His stand - ard
world's side? Who will face the foe? Who is on the
claim - eth Lives for whom He died: He whom Je - sus
fill - ing Each who comes to Thee, Thou hast made us
rang - ing, Vic - t'ry is se - cure, For His truth un -
Lord's side? Who for Him will go? By Thy call of mer - cy,
nam - eth Must be on His side. By Thy love con - strain - ing,
will - ing, Thou hast made us free. By Thy grand re - demp - tion,
chang - ing Makes the tri - umph sure. Joy - ful - ly en - list - ing

Tune: ARMAGEDDON

CHALLENGE

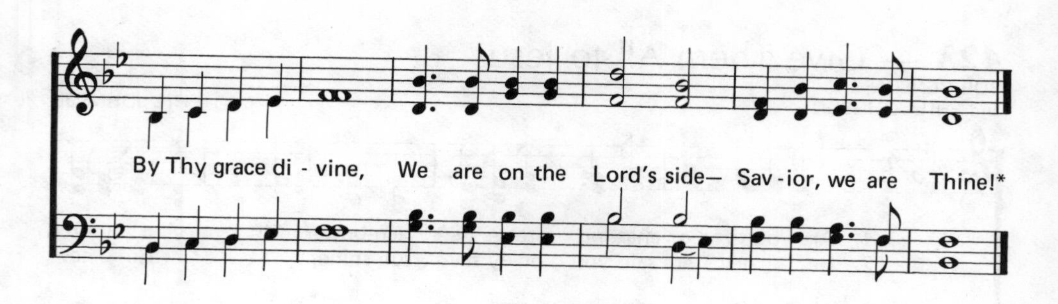
By Thy grace di - vine, We are on the Lord's side— Sav - ior, we are Thine!*

Take Time to Be Holy — 422

WILLIAM D. LONGSTAFF–alt.

GEORGE C. STEBBINS

1. Take time to be ho - ly, Speak oft with the Lord; A - bide in Him al - ways And feed on His Word. Make friends of God's chil-dren, Help those who are weak, For - get - ting in noth - ing His bless-ing to seek.
2. Take time to be ho - ly, The world rush-es on; Spend much time in se - cret With Je - sus a - lone. By look - ing to Je - sus, Like Him you will be— Your friends in your con - duct His like-ness will see.
3. Take time to be ho - ly, Let Him be your guide, And run not be - fore Him, What - ev - er be - tide. In joy or in sor - row Still fol - low the Lord, And, look - ing to Je - sus, Still trust in His Word.
4. Take time to be ho - ly, Be calm in your soul— Each tho't and each mo - tive Be - neath His con - trol. Thus led by His Spir - it To foun-tains of love, You soon will be fit - ted For serv - ice a - bove.

Tune: HOLINESS

423 — Give Them All to Jesus

BOB BENSON, Sr. and PHIL JOHNSON

PHIL JOHNSON

1. Are you tired of chas-ing pret - ty rain-bows? Are you tired of spin-ning round and round? Wrap up all the shat-tered dreams of your life And at the feet of Je - sus lay them down.
2. He nev - er said you'd on-ly see sun-shine, He nev-er said there'd be no rain; He on - ly prom-ised a heart full of sing-ing A - bout the ver - y things that once bro't pain.
CHORUS
Give them all, give them all, Give them all to Je - sus—
Shattered dreams, wounded hearts and broken toys;
Give them all, give them all,

Give them all to Je-sus, And He will turn your sor-row in-to joy!
Jesus Calls Us — 424
CECIL FRANCES ALEXANDER
Leavitt's The Christian Lyre
Arr. by Larry Leader
1. Je-sus calls us o'er the tu-mult Of our life's wild, rest-less sea;
2. In our joys and in our sor-rows, Days of toil and hours of ease,
Day by day His sweet voice sound-eth, Say-ing, "Chris-tian, fol-low Me."
Still He calls, in cares and pleas-ures, "Chris-tian, love Me more than these."
Je-sus calls us from the wor-ship Of the vain world's gold-en store,
Je-sus calls us– by Thy mer-cies, Sav-ior, may we hear Thy call,
From each i-dol that would keep us, Say-ing, "Chris-tian, love Me more."
Give our hearts to Thy o-be-dience, Serve and love Thee best of all.*
Tune: PLEADING SAVIOR (Alternate, GALILEE, doubled)
Arr. © Singspiration 1979. All rights reserved.
CHALLENGE

425 — Only Believe!

Based on Mark 9:23
PAUL RADER

PAUL RADER
1. Fear not, lit-tle flock, from the cross to the throne, From death in-to life He went for His own; All pow-er in earth, all pow-er a-bove, Is giv-en to Him for the flock of His love.
2. Fear not, lit-tle flock, what-ev-er your lot— He en-ters all rooms, "the doors be-ing shut;" He nev-er for-sakes, He nev-er is gone—So count on His pres-ence in dark-ness and dawn.
CHORUS
On-ly be-lieve, on-ly be-lieve: All things are pos-si-ble, on-ly be-lieve! On-ly be-lieve, on-ly be-lieve: All things are pos-si-ble, on-ly be-lieve!

CHALLENGE

Yield Not to Temptation — 426
HORATIO R. PALMER
HORATIO R. PALMER
1. Yield not to temp - ta - tion, For yield-ing is sin— Each vic - t'ry will help you Some oth-er to win; Fight man-ful - ly on - ward, Dark pas - sions sub - due, Look ev-er to Je - sus— He'll car-ry you through.
2. Shun e - vil com - pan - ions, Bad lan-guage dis - dain, God's name hold in rev - 'rence, Nor take it in vain; Be thought-ful and ear - nest, Kind-heart - ed and true, Look ev-er to Je - sus— He'll car-ry you through.
3. To him that o'er-com - eth God giv - eth a crown, Thru faith we will con - quer Tho oft - en cast down; He who is our Sav - ior Our strength will re - new, Look ev-er to Je - sus— He'll car-ry you through.
CHORUS
Ask the Sav - ior to help you, Com - fort, strength-en and keep you;
He is will - ing to aid you— He will car - ry you through.

CHALLENGE

427 — Reach Out to Jesus
RALPH CARMICHAEL
RALPH CARMICHAEL
1. Is your bur-den heav-y as you bear it all a-lone? Does the road you trav-el har-bor dan-ger yet un-known? Are you grow-ing wear-y in the strug-gle of it all? Je-sus will help you when on His name you call.
2. Is the life you're liv-ing filled with sor-row and de-spair? Does the fu-ture press you with its wor-ry and its care? Are you tired and friend-less, have you al-most lost your way? Je-sus will help you—just come to Him to-day.
REFRAIN
He is al-ways there hear-ing ev-'ry prayer, faith-ful and true, Walk-ing by our side— in His love we hide
© Lexicon Music, Inc. 1968, arr. 1976. All rights reserved.
CHALLENGE

all the day through; When you get dis - cour-aged just re - mem - ber
what to do— Reach out to Je - sus, He's reach - ing out to you.

We Are Climbing Jacob's Ladder — 428

Traditional
(Suggested by Genesis 28:10-15)

Traditional Spiritual
Arr. by Norman Johnson

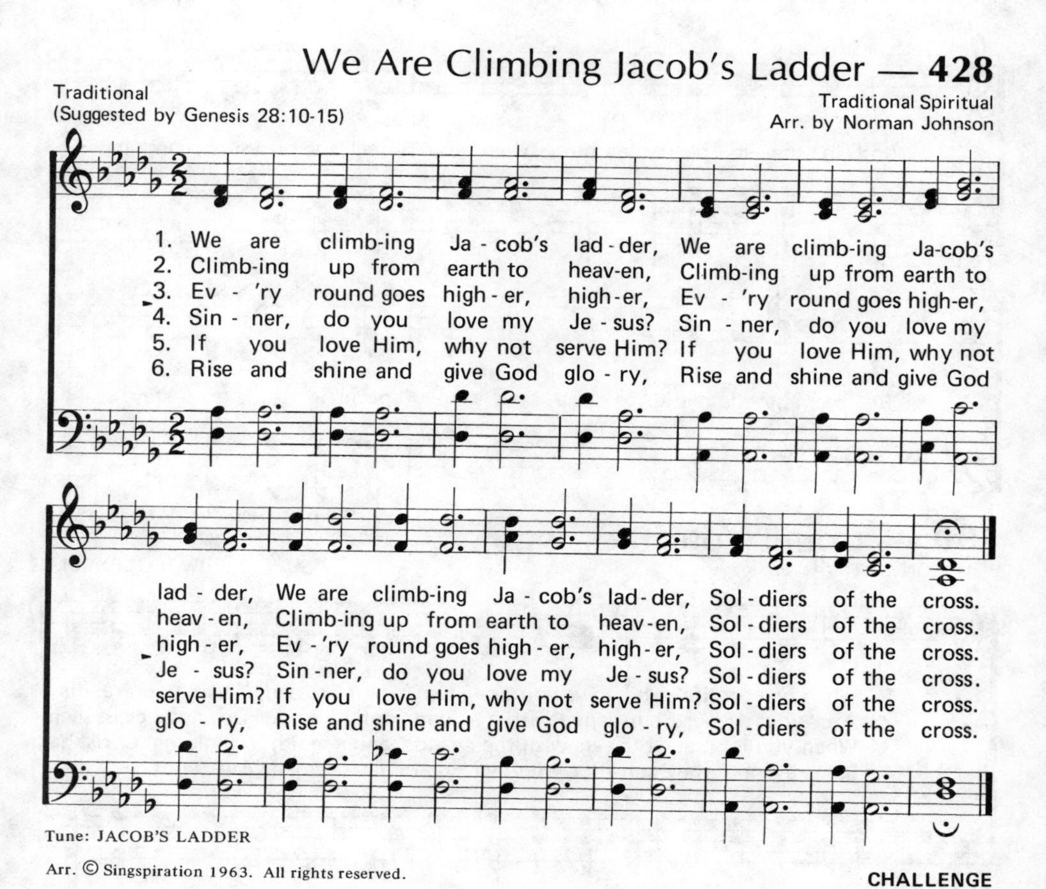
1. We are climb-ing Ja - cob's lad - der, We are climb-ing Ja-cob's lad - der, We are climb-ing Ja - cob's lad-der, Sol - diers of the cross.
2. Climb-ing up from earth to heav-en, Climb-ing up from earth to heav - en, Climb-ing up from earth to heav-en, Sol - diers of the cross.
3. Ev - 'ry round goes high - er, high-er, Ev - 'ry round goes high-er, high - er, Ev - 'ry round goes high - er, high - er, Sol - diers of the cross.
4. Sin - ner, do you love my Je - sus? Sin - ner, do you love my Je - sus? Sin - ner, do you love my Je - sus? Sol - diers of the cross.
5. If you love Him, why not serve Him? If you love Him, why not serve Him? If you love Him, why not serve Him? Sol - diers of the cross.
6. Rise and shine and give God glo - ry, Rise and shine and give God glo - ry, Rise and shine and give God glo - ry, Sol - diers of the cross.

Tune: JACOB'S LADDER

429 — All Day Song
JOHN FISCHER
JOHN FISCHER
Love Him in the morn - in' when you see the sun a - ris - in',
Love Him in the eve - nin' 'cause He took you thru the day.
And in the in - be - tween time when you feel the pres-sure com - in',
Re - mem-ber that He loves you, and He prom-is - es to stay.
© Lexicon Music, Inc. 1973, arr. 1976.
All rights reserved.
430 — Count Your Blessings
JOHNSON OATMAN, Jr.
EDWIN O. EXCELL
1. When up - on life's bil-lows you are tem - pest - tossed, When you are dis-
2. Are you ev - er bur-dened with a load of care? Does the cross seem
3. When you look at oth - ers with their lands and gold, Think that Christ has
4. So a - mid the con-flict, wheth-er great or small, Do not be dis-
CHALLENGE

cour-aged, think-ing all is lost, Count your man-y bless-ings—name them
heav - y you are called to bear? Count your man-y bless-ings— ev - 'ry
prom-ised you His wealth un - told; Count your man-y bless-ings—mon - ey
cour-aged—God is o - ver all; Count your man-y bless-ings—an - gels
one by one, And it will sur - prise you what the Lord hath done.
doubt will fly, And you will be sing - ing as the days go by.
can - not buy Your re-ward in heav - en nor your home on high.
will at - tend, Help and com-fort give you to your jour - ney's end.
CHORUS
Count your bless - ings—name them one by one; Count your bless-ings—
see what God hath done; Count your bless-ings— name them one by
one; Count your man- y bless-ings—see what God hath done.

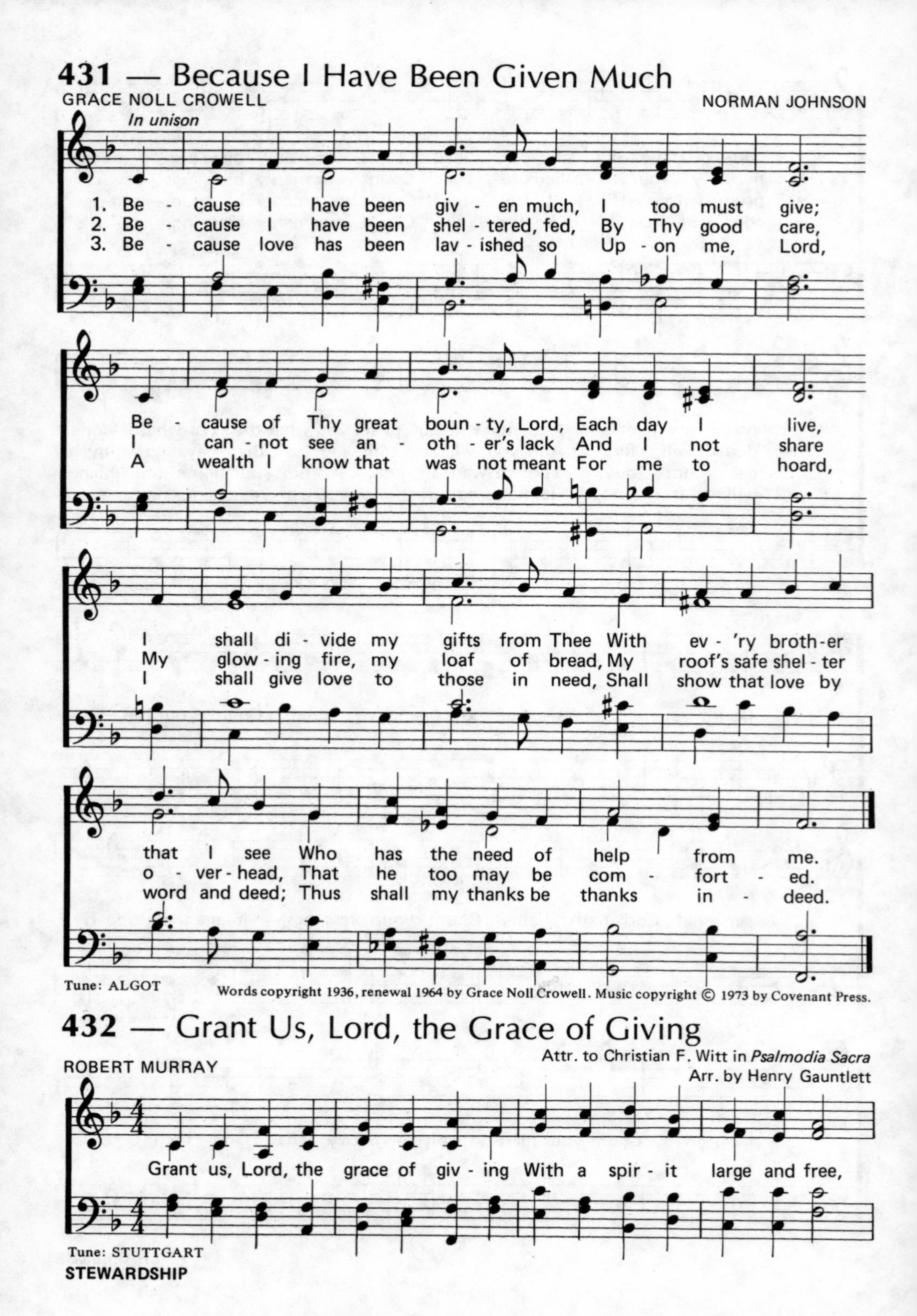
431 — Because I Have Been Given Much
GRACE NOLL CROWELL
NORMAN JOHNSON
In unison
1. Be - cause I have been giv - en much, I too must give;
2. Be - cause I have been shel - tered, fed, By Thy good care,
3. Be - cause love has been lav - ished so Up - on me, Lord,
Be - cause of Thy great boun - ty, Lord, Each day I live,
I can - not see an - oth - er's lack And I not share
A wealth I know that was not meant For me to hoard,
I shall di - vide my gifts from Thee With ev - 'ry broth - er
My glow - ing fire, my loaf of bread, My roof's safe shel - ter
I shall give love to those in need, Shall show that love by
that I see Who has the need of help from me.
o - ver - head, That he too may be com - fort - ed.
word and deed; Thus shall my thanks be thanks in - deed.
Tune: ALGOT
Words copyright 1936, renewal 1964 by Grace Noll Crowell. Music copyright © 1973 by Covenant Press.
432 — Grant Us, Lord, the Grace of Giving
Attr. to Christian F. Witt in Psalmodia Sacra
ROBERT MURRAY
Arr. by Henry Gauntlett
Grant us, Lord, the grace of giv - ing With a spir - it large and free,
Tune: STUTTGART
STEWARDSHIP

optional
That our-selves and all our liv-ing We may of-fer un-to Thee. A-men.
Little Is Much When God Is in It — 433
KITTIE J. SUFFIELD
KITTIE J. SUFFIELD
1. In the har-vest field now rip-ened There's a work for all to do;
2. Does the place you're called to la-bor Seem so small and lit-tle known?
3. Are you laid a-side from serv-ice, Bod-y worn from toil and care?
4. When the con-flict here is end-ed And our race on earth is run,
Hark! the voice of God is call-ing, To the har-vest call-ing you.
It is great if God is in it, And He'll not for-get His own.
You can still be in the bat-tle In the sa-cred place of pray'r.
He will say, if we are faith-ful, "Wel-come home, my child—well done."
CHORUS
Lit-tle is much, when God is in it! La-bor not for wealth or fame;
There's a crown—and you can win it, If you'll go in Je-sus' name.
STEWARDSHIP

434 — Something for Thee

SYLVANUS D. PHELPS ROBERT LOWRY

1. Sav - ior, Thy dy - ing love Thou gav - est me, Nor should I aught with-hold, Dear Lord, from Thee: In love my soul would bow, My heart ful - fill its vow, Some of-f'ring bring Thee now, Some-thing for Thee.
2. At the blest mer - cy seat, Plead - ing for me, My fee - ble faith looks up, Je - sus, to Thee: Help me the cross to bear, Thy won-drous love de-clare, Some song to raise, or prayer, Some-thing for Thee.
3. Give me a faith - ful heart, Like - ness to Thee, That each de - part - ing day Hence - forth may see Some work of love be - gun, Some deed of kind-ness done, Some wan-d'rer sought and won, Some-thing for Thee.
4. All that I am and have— Thy gifts so free— In joy, in grief, thru life, Dear Lord, for Thee! And when Thy face I see, My ran-somed soul shall be, Thru all e - ter - ni - ty, Some-thing for Thee.*

Tune: SOMETHING FOR JESUS

435 — We Give Thee But Thine Own

WILLIAM W. HOW Mason and Webb's *Cantica Laudis*

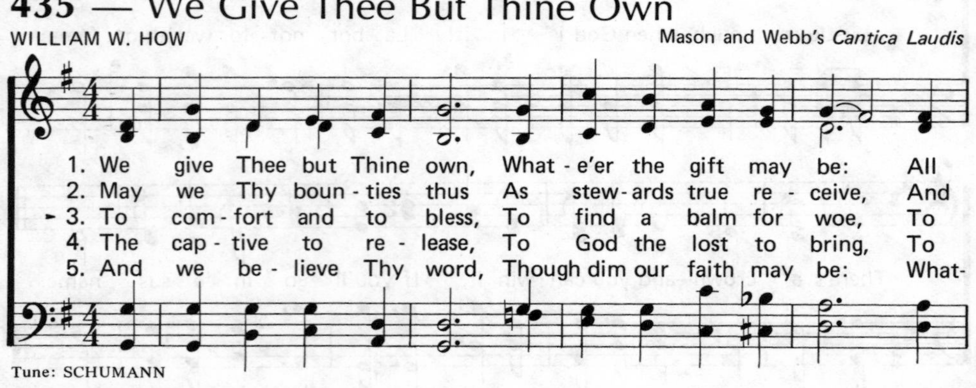
1. We give Thee but Thine own, What - e'er the gift may be: All
2. May we Thy boun - ties thus As stew - ards true re - ceive, And
3. To com - fort and to bless, To find a balm for woe, To
4. The cap - tive to re - lease, To God the lost to bring, To
5. And we be - lieve Thy word, Though dim our faith may be: What-

Tune: SCHUMANN

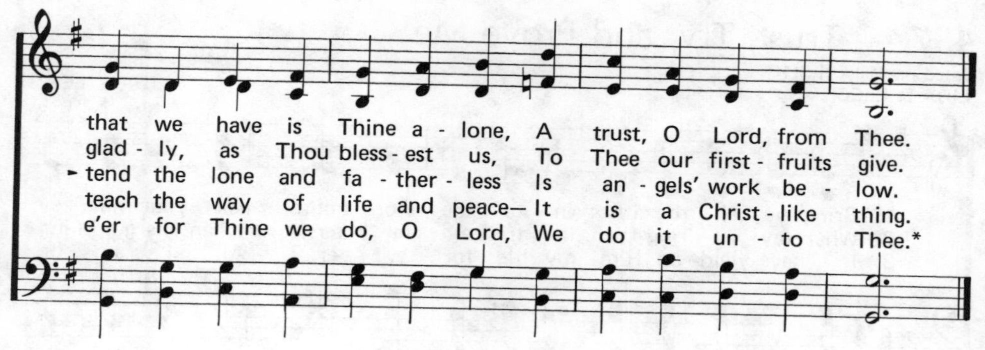
that we have is Thine a - lone, A trust, O Lord, from Thee.
glad - ly, as Thou bless - est us, To Thee our first - fruits give.
tend the lone and fa - ther - less Is an - gels' work be - low.
teach the way of life and peace— It is a Christ - like thing.
e'er for Thine we do, O Lord, We do it un - to Thee.*

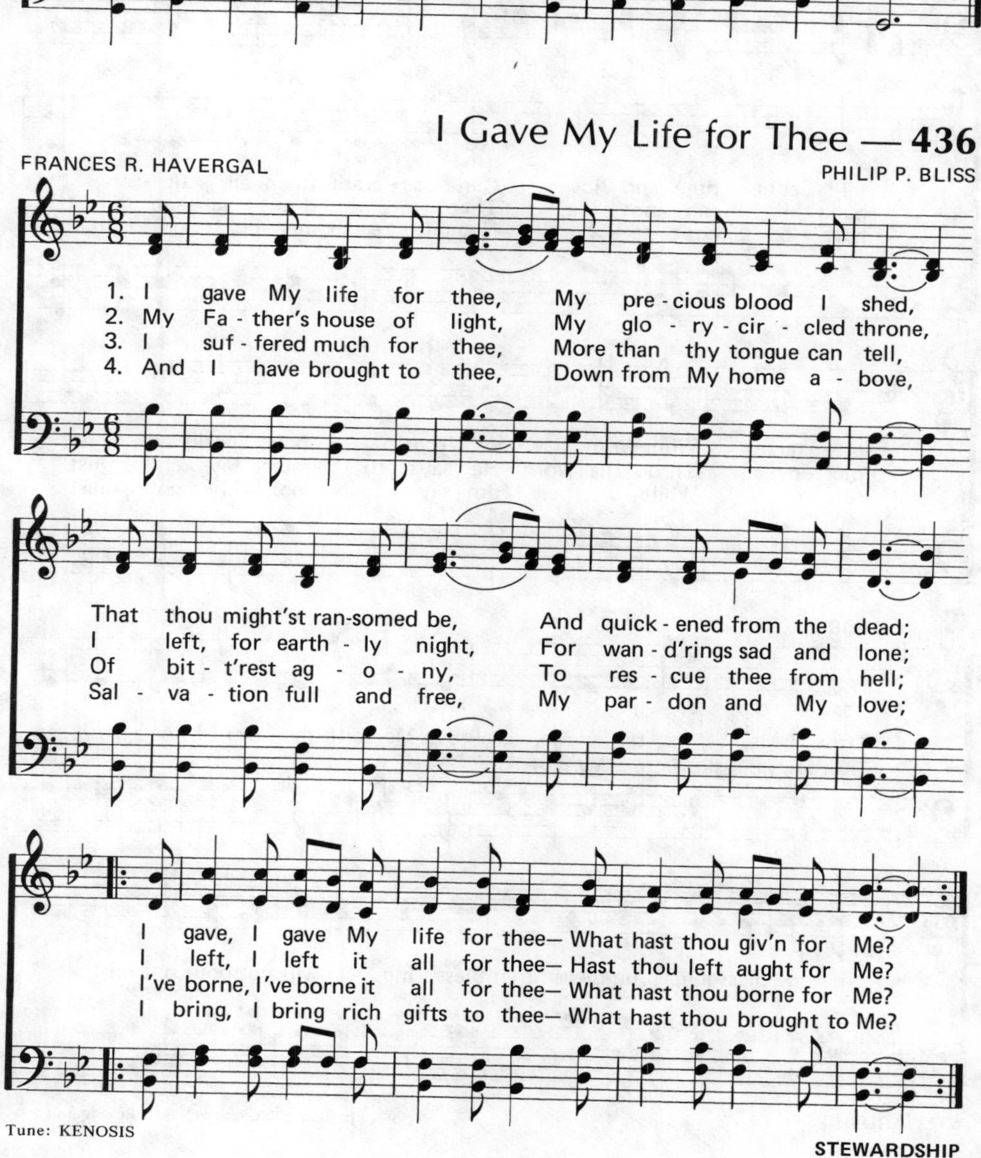
I Gave My Life for Thee — 436
FRANCES R. HAVERGAL
PHILIP P. BLISS
1. I gave My life for thee, My pre - cious blood I shed,
2. My Fa - ther's house of light, My glo - ry - cir - cled throne,
3. I suf - fered much for thee, More than thy tongue can tell,
4. And I have brought to thee, Down from My home a - bove,
That thou might'st ran-somed be, And quick - ened from the dead;
I left, for earth - ly night, For wan - d'rings sad and lone;
Of bit - t'rest ag - o - ny, To res - cue thee from hell;
Sal - va - tion full and free, My par - don and My love;
I gave, I gave My life for thee— What hast thou giv'n for Me?
I left, I left it all for thee— Hast thou left aught for Me?
I've borne, I've borne it all for thee— What hast thou borne for Me?
I bring, I bring rich gifts to thee— What hast thou brought to Me?

Tune: KENOSIS

437 — Trust, Try, and Prove Me

Based on Malachi 3:10
LIDA S. LEECH
LIDA S. LEECH
1. Bring ye all the tithes in - to the store - house, All your mon - ey tal - ents, time and love; Con - se - crate them all up - on the al - tar, While your Sav - ior from a - bove speaks sweet - ly:
2. When my wa-v'ring faith in tri - al fal - ters, When His guid - ing hand I can - not see, Then in won - drous love and ten - der mer - cy, Thru His Word He says to me: My child, just
3. I have yield - ed Him my life for - ev - er, All I am or have or hope to be; Naught on earth my hold on Him can sev - er, While I hear Him say to me: My child, just
CHORUS
Trust Me, try Me, Prove Me, saith the Lord of hosts, And see
Trust Me, yes, then try Me, prove Me,
if a bless-ing, un-meas - ured bless - ing, I will not pour out on thee.

STEWARDSHIP

Based on Matthew 6:33, 7:7
KAREN LAFFERTY
Seek Ye First — 438
KAREN LAFFERTY
Al - le - lu - ia, Al - le - lu - ia,
1. Seek ye first the king - dom of God And His righ - teous - ness,
2. Ask and it shall be giv - en un - to you, Seek and ye shall find,
Al - le - lu - ia, Al - le - lu - ia!
And all these things shall be add - ed un - to you— Al - le - lu, al - le - lu - ia!
Knock and it shall be o - pened un - to you— Al - le - lu, al - le - lu - ia!
St. 2 added by PRAISE! editor.
© 1972 Maranatha! Music. All rights reserved.
I'll Live for Him — 439
RALPH E. HUDSON
C. R. DUNBAR
1. My life, my love I give to Thee, Thou Lamb of God who died for me;
2. I now be - lieve Thou dost re - ceive, For Thou hast died that I might live;
3. O Thou who died on Cal - va - ry To save my soul and make me free,
Chorus—I'll live for Him who died for me, How hap - py then my life shall be!
D.C. for Chorus
O may I ev - er faith - ful be, My Sav - ior and my God!
And now hence - forth I trust in Thee, My Sav - ior and my God!
I'll con - se - crate my life to Thee, My Sav - ior and my God!
I'll live for Him who died for me, My Sav - ior and my God!
Tune: DUNBAR

440 — Follow On

WILLIAM O. CUSHING

ROBERT LOWRY

1. Down in the val - ley with my Sav - ior I would go, Where the flow'rs are bloom-ing and the sweet wa-ters flow; Ev - 'ry - where He leads me I would fol - low, fol - low on, Walk-ing in His foot-steps till the crown be won.
2. Down in the val - ley with my Sav - ior I would go, Where the storms are sweep-ing and the dark wa-ters flow; With His hand to lead me I will nev - er, nev - er fear, Dan - ger can - not fright me if my Lord is near.
3. Down in the val - ley or up - on the moun-tain steep, Close be - side my Sav - ior would my soul ev - er keep; He will lead me safe - ly in the path that He has trod, Up to where they gath - er on the hills of God.
CHORUS
Fol - low! fol - low! I would fol-low Je - sus! An - y - where, ev - 'ry-where, I would fol - low on! Fol - low! fol - low! I would

COMMITMENT

fol - low Je - sus! Ev - 'ry-where He leads me I would fol - low on!
Wherever He Leads I'll Go — 441
B. B. McKINNEY
B. B. McKINNEY
1. "Take up thy cross and fol - low Me," I heard my Mas - ter say;
2. He drew me clos - er to His side, I sought His will to know;
3. It may be thru the shad - ows dim Or o'er the storm - y sea:
4. My heart, my life, my all I bring To Christ who loves me so;
"I gave My life to ran - som thee— Sur - ren-der your all to - day."
And in that will I now a - bide— Wher - ev - er He leads I'll go.
I take my cross and fol - low Him— Wher - ev - er He lead - eth me.
He is my Mas - ter, Lord, and King— Wher - ev - er He leads I'll go.
CHORUS
Wher - ev - er He leads I'll go, Wher - ev - er He leads I'll go;
I'll fol-low my Christ who loves me so— Wher - ev - er He leads I'll go.
©Copyright 1936, renewal 1964 Broadman Press.
COMMITMENT

442 — A Flag to Follow
JOHN W. PETERSON
JOHN W. PETERSON
1. I sought a flag to fol - low, A cause for which to stand,
2. I sought a ring - ing an - swer For all my doubts in - side,
3. I sought for sat - is - fac - tion For yearn - ings deep with - in,
I sought a val - iant lead - er Who could my love com - mand;
A torch of truth up - lift - ed, My search - ing steps to guide;
I sought for full de - liv - 'rance From chains of guilt and sin;
I sought a stir - ring chal - lenge, Some no - ble work to try,
I sought a word of wis - dom, A true au - thor - i - ty,
I sought for peace and par - don, For free - dom from my fears,
To give my life ful - fill - ment, My dreams to sat - is - fy.
I sought to know life's pur - pose, To solve its mys - ter - y.
I sought a hope to cling to Be - yond these pass - ing years.
REFRAIN
I found them all in Je - sus, The Life, the Truth, the Way; Be - neath His
COMMITMENT
© 1959, 1961 by John W. Peterson Music Company.
All rights reserved. Used by permission.

CODA–optional
flag I'll take my stand And fol-low Him to-day. I'll fol-low Him to-day!
Only One Life — 443
AVIS B. CHRISTIANSEN
MERRILL DUNLOP
1. On-ly one life to of-fer— Je-sus, my Lord and King;
2. On-ly this hour is mine, Lord— May it be used for Thee;
3. On-ly one life to of-fer— Take it, dear Lord, I pray;
On-ly one tongue to praise Thee And of Thy mer-cy sing (for-ev-er);
May ev-'ry pass-ing mo-ment Count for e-ter-ni-ty (my Sav-ior);
Nothing from Thee with-hold-ing, Thy will I now o-bey (my Je-sus);
On-ly one heart's de-vo-tion— Sav-ior, O may it be Con-se-
Souls all a-bout are dy-ing, Dy-ing in sin and shame; Help me
Thou who hast free-ly giv-en Thine all in all for me, Claim this
crat-ed a-lone to Thy match-less glo-ry, Yield-ed ful-ly to Thee.
bring them the mes-sage of Cal-v'ry's re-demp-tion In Thy glo-ri-ous name.
life for Thine own to be used, my Sav-ior, Ev-'ry mo-ment for Thee.*
COMMITMENT

444 — The Master Has Come

SARAH DOUDNEY

Welsh melody

1. The Mas-ter has come, and He calls us to fol-low The track of the
2. The Mas-ter has called us— the road may be drear-y, And dan-gers and
3. The Mas-ter has called us in life's ear-ly morn-ing, With spir-its as
foot-prints He leaves on our way; Far o-ver the moun-tain and thru
sor-rows are strewn on the track; But God's Ho-ly Spir-it shall com-
fresh as the dew on the sod; We turn from the world with its smiles
the deep hol-low The path leads us on to the man-sions of day.
fort the wea-ry—We fol-low the Sav-ior and can-not turn back.
and its scorn-ing To cast in our lot with the peo-ple of God.
The Mas-ter has called us, the chil-dren who fear Him, Who march 'neath
The Mas-ter has called us— tho doubt and temp-ta-tion May com-pass
The Mas-ter has called us, His sons and His daugh-ters, We plead for
Christ's ban-ner, His own lit-tle band: We love Him and seek Him, we
our jour-ney, we cheer-ful-ly sing: "Press on-ward, look up-ward—thru
His bless-ing and trust in His love: And thru the green pas-tures, be-

Tune: ASH GROVE

COMMITMENT

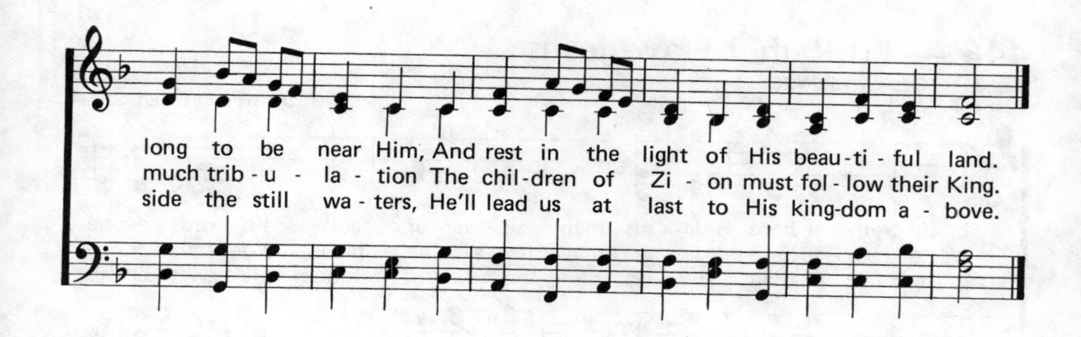
long to be near Him, And rest in the light of His beau-ti-ful land.
much trib-u-la-tion The chil-dren of Zi-on must fol-low their King.
side the still wa-ters, He'll lead us at last to His king-dom a-bove.

Have Thine Own Way, Lord! — 445

ADELAIDE A. POLLARD

GEORGE C. STEBBINS

1. Have Thine own way, Lord! Have Thine own way! Thou art the
2. Have Thine own way, Lord! Have Thine own way! Search me and
3. Have Thine own way, Lord! Have Thine own way! Wound-ed and
4. Have Thine own way, Lord! Have Thine own way! Hold o'er my
Pot-ter, I am the clay: Mold me and make me
try me, Mas-ter, to-day! Whit-er than snow, Lord,
wea-ry, Help me, I pray! Pow-er, all pow-er,
be-ing Ab-so-lute sway! Fill with Thy Spir-it
Aft-er Thy will, While I am wait-ing, Yield-ed and still.
Wash me just now, As in Thy pres-ence Hum-bly I bow.
Sure-ly is Thine! Touch me and heal me, Sav-ior di-vine!
Till all shall see Christ on-ly, al-ways, Liv-ing in me!*

Tune: ADELAIDE

COMMITMENT

446 — I'd Rather Have Jesus

Based on Matthew 16:24-26
RHEA F. MILLER
GEORGE BEVERLY SHEA
1. I'd rath - er have Je - sus than sil - ver or gold, I'd rath - er be
2. I'd rath - er have Je - sus than men's ap - plause, I'd rath - er be
3. He's fair - er than lil - ies of rar - est bloom, He's sweet - er than
His than have rich - es un - told; I'd rath - er have Je - sus than hous - es
faith - ful to His dear cause; I'd rath - er have Je - sus than world -
hon - ey from out the comb; He's all that my hun - ger - ing spir -
or land, I'd rath - er be led by His nail - pierced hand:
wide fame, I'd rath - er be true to His ho - ly name:
it needs—I'd rath - er have Je - sus and let Him lead:
REFRAIN
Than to be the
king of a vast do - main Or be held in sin's dread sway! I'd
rath - er have Je - sus than an - y - thing This world af - fords to - day.

COMMITMENT

Jesus, I My Cross Have Taken — 447

HENRY F. LYTE
Leavitt's *Christian Lyre*
Attr. to Wolfgang A. Mozart
1. Je - sus, I my cross have tak - en, All to leave and fol - low Thee;
2. Let the world de - spise and leave me— They have left my Sav - ior too;
3. Man may trou - ble and dis - tress me— 'Twill but drive me to Thy breast;
4. Has - ten on from grace to glo - ry, Armed by faith and winged by prayer;
Des - ti - tute, de - spised, for - sak - en— Thou from hence my all shalt be.
Hu - man hearts and looks de - ceive me— Thou art not, like man, un - true.
Life with tri - als hard may press me— Heav'n will bring me sweet - er rest.
Heav'ns e - ter - nal day's be - fore me— God's own hand shall guide me there.
Per - ish ev - 'ry fond am - bi - tion— All I've sought and hoped and known!
And while Thou shalt smile up - on me, God of wis - dom, love, and might,
O 'tis not in grief to harm me While Thy love is left to me;
Soon shall close my earth - ly mis - sion, Swift shall pass my pil - grim days;
Yet how rich is my con - di - tion— God and heav'n are still my own!
Foes may hate, and friends may shun me— Show Thy face, and all is bright!
O 'twere not in joy to charm me Were that joy un - mixed with Thee!
Hope shall change to glad fru - i - tion, Faith to sight, and prayer to praise!
Tune: ELLESDIE—lower key at 145

COMMITMENT

448 — Shepherd of Love
JOHN W. PETERSON
JOHN W. PETERSON
1. Shep-herd of love, You knew I had lost my way; Shep-herd of love, You cared that I'd gone a - stray. You sought and found me, placed a - round me Strong arms that car-ried me home; No foe can harm me or a - larm me— Nev - er a - gain will I roam!
2. Shep-herd of love, Con - tent-ment at last is mine; Deep in my heart There's peace and a joy di - vine. The fu - ture's bright-er, bur - den's light - er, My cup runs o - ver each day; Your grace sup - plied me now pro - vides me All that I need for the way.
Shep - herd of love, Sav - ior and Lord and Guide,
Shep - herd of love, Sav - ior and Lord and Guide,

COMMITMENT

Shep - herd of love, For - ev - er I'll stay by Your side.
Shep - herd of love, For - ev - er I'll stay by Your side.
Take My Life and Let It Be — 449
FRANCES R. HAVERGAL
H. A. CÉSAR MALAN
1. Take my life and let it be Con - se - cra - ted,
2. Take my hands and let them move At the im - pulse
3. Take my voice and let me sing Al - ways, on - ly,
4. Take my sil - ver and my gold— Not a mite would
5. Take my will and make it Thine— It shall be no
6. Take my love— my Lord, I pour At Thy feet its
Lord, to Thee; Take my mo - ments and my days— Let them
of Thy love; Take my feet and let them be Swift and
for my King; Take my lips and let them be Filled with
I with-hold; Take my in - tel - lect and use Ev - 'ry
long - er mine; Take my heart— it is Thine own, It shall
treas - ure store; Take my - self— and I will be Ev - er,
flow in cease - less praise, Let them flow in cease - less praise.
beau - ti - ful for Thee, Swift and beau - ti - ful for Thee.
mes - sag - es from Thee, Filled with mes - sag - es from Thee.
pow'r as Thou shalt choose, Ev - 'ry pow'r as Thou shalt choose.
be Thy roy - al throne, It shall be Thy roy - al throne.
on - ly, all for Thee, Ev - er, on - ly, all for Thee.*
Tune: HENDON (Alternate, TRYGGARE KAN INGEN VARA, adapted)

COMMITMENT

450 — Living for Jesus

THOMAS O. CHISHOLM

C. HAROLD LOWDEN

1. Liv-ing for Je-sus a life that is true, Striv-ing to please Him in all that I do, Yield-ing al - le - giance, glad-heart-ed and free— This is the path-way of bless-ing for me.
2. Liv-ing for Je-sus who died in my place, Bear-ing on Cal - v'ry my sin and dis - grace— Such love con-strains me to an - swer His call, Fol - low His lead - ing and give Him my all.
3. Liv-ing for Je-sus thru earth's lit - tle while, My dear - est treas - ure the light of His smile, Seek-ing the lost ones He died to re - deem, Bring-ing the wea - ry to find rest in Him.
CHORUS
O Je - sus, Lord and Sav - ior, I give my-self to Thee, For Thou in Thine a - tone-ment didst give Thy-self for me. I own no oth - er Mas-ter— my heart shall be Thy

COMMITMENT

throne: My life I give, hence-forth to live, O Christ, for Thee a - lone.
I Surrender All — 451
JUDSON W. VAN de VENTER
WINFIELD S. WEEDEN
1. All to Je - sus I sur-ren - der, All to Him I free - ly give;
2. All to Je - sus I sur-ren - der, Hum-bly at His feet I bow;
3. All to Je - sus I sur-ren - der, Make me, Sav - ior, whol - ly Thine;
4. All to Je - sus I sur-ren - der, Lord, I give my - self to Thee;
I will ev - er love and trust Him, In His pres - ence dai - ly live.
World - y pleas - ures all for - sak - en, Take me, Je - sus, take me now.
Let me feel the Ho - ly Spir - it— Tru - ly know that Thou art mine.
Fill me with Thy love and pow - er, Let Thy bless-ings fall on me.
CHORUS
I sur-ren - der all, I sur-ren - der all,
I sur - ren - der, I sur - ren-der all, I sur - ren - der, I sur-ren-der all,
All to Thee, my bless - ed Sav - ior, I sur-ren - der all.
COMMITMENT

452 — Where He Leads Me
E. W. BLANDY
JOHN S. NORRIS
1. I can hear my Sav - ior call - ing, I can hear my Sav - ior call - ing, I can hear my Sav - ior call - ing, "Take thy cross and fol - low, fol - low Me."
2. I'll go with Him thru the gar - den, I'll go with Him thru the gar - den, I'll go with Him thru the gar - den, I'll go with Him, with Him all the way.
3. I'll go with Him thru the judg - ment, I'll go with Him thru the judg - ment, I'll go with Him thru the judg - ment, I'll go with Him, with Him all the way.
4. He will give me grace and glo - ry, He will give me grace and glo - ry, He will give me grace and glo - ry, And go with me, with me all the way.
*Chorus—Where He leads me I will fol - low, Where He leads me I will fol - low, Where He leads me I will fol - low, I'll go with Him, with Him all the way.
D.C. for Chorus
*Optionally only after stanzas 1 and 4.
Tune: NORRIS
453 — All for Jesus
MARY D. JAMES
WILLIAM H. JUDE
1. All for Je - sus, all for Je - sus! All my be - ing's ransomed pow'rs:
2. Let my hands per - form His bid - ding, Let my feet run in His ways;
3. Since my eyes were fixed on Je - sus, I've lost sight of all be - side,
4. O what won - der! how a - maz - ing! Je - sus, glo - rious King of kings,
Tune: GALILEE
COMMITMENT

All my tho'ts and words and do - ings, All my days and all my hours.
Let my eyes see Je - sus on - ly, Let my lips speak forth His praise.
So en - chained my spir - it's vi - sion, Look-ing at the Cru - ci - fied.
Deigns to call me His be - lov - ed, Lets me rest be - neath His wings.

I Have Decided to Follow Jesus — 454

Attributed to an Indian prince
As sung in Garo, Assam

Folk melody from India
Arr. by Norman Johnson

1. I have de - cid - ed to fol - low Je - sus, I have de - cid - ed
2. Tho no one join me, still I will fol - low, Tho no one join me,
3. The world be-hind me, the cross be - fore me, The world be-hind me,
to fol - low Je - sus, I have de - cid - ed to fol - low Je - sus—
still I will fol - low, Tho no one join me, still I will fol - low—
the cross be - fore me, The world be-hind me, the cross be-fore me—
No turn - ing back, (No turn - ing back,) no turn - ing back!

455 — The Son of God Goes Forth to War

REGINALD HEBER
HENRY S. CUTLER
1. The Son of God goes forth to war, A kingly crown to gain; His blood-red banner streams afar: Who follows in His train? Who best can drink his cup of woe, Triumphant over pain, Who patient bears his cross below, He follows in His train.
2. The martyr first, whose eagle eye Could pierce beyond the grave, Who saw his Master in the sky And called on Him to save— Like Him, with pardon on his tongue In midst of mortal pain, He prayed for them that did the wrong: Who follows in his train?
3. A glorious band, the chosen few On whom the Spirit came, Twelve valiant saints, their hope they knew, And mocked the cross and flame— They met the tyrant's brandished steel, The lion's gory mane, They bowed their necks the death to feel: Who follows in their train?
4. A noble army, men and boys, The matron and the maid, Around the Savior's throne rejoice, In robes of light arrayed— They climbed the steep ascent of heav'n Thru peril, toil and pain: O God, to us may grace be giv'n To follow in their train!

Tune: ALL SAINTS NEW—lower key at 210

GEORGE DUFFIELD

GEORGE J. WEBB

1. Stand up, stand up for Je - sus, Ye sol - diers of the cross!
2. Stand up, stand up for Je - sus, The trum - pet call o - bey;
3. Stand up, stand up for Je - sus, Stand in His strength a - lone;
4. Stand up, stand up for Je - sus, The strife will not be long;

Lift high His roy - al ban - ner— It must not suf - fer loss.
Forth to the might - y con - flict In this His glo - rious day.
The arm of flesh will fail you— Ye dare not trust your own.
This day the noise of bat - tle— The next, the vic - tor's song.

From vic - t'ry un - to vic - t'ry His ar - my shall He lead,
Ye that are men now serve Him A - gainst un - num - bered foes;
Put on the gos - pel ar - mor, Each piece put on with prayer;
To Him that o - ver - com - eth A crown of life shall be:

Till ev - 'ry foe is van - quished And Christ is Lord in - deed.
Let cour - age rise with dan - ger, And strength to strength op - pose.
Where du - ty calls, or dan - ger, Be nev - er want - ing there.
He with the King of glo - ry Shall reign e - ter - nal - ly.

Tune: WEBB

457 — We Are More Than Conquerors

Based on Romans 8:37
RALPH CARMICHAEL

RALPH CARMICHAEL

We are more than con-quer-ors thru Him that loved us so— The Christ who
dwells with - in us is the great - est pow'r we know! He will fight be -
side us tho the en - e - my be great— Who can stand a - gainst us?
He's the Cap - tain of our fate. Then we will con-quer, nev - er fear—
Two parts
so let the bat-tle rage! He has prom-ised to be near
3

CHRISTIAN WARFARE

Four parts
un - til the end of the age. We are more than con-quer-ors thru
Him that loved us so— The Christ who dwells with - in us is the
Two parts
great - est pow'r we know! Then great - est pow'r we know!
Fight the Good Fight — 458
JOHN S. B. MONSELL
WILLIAM BOYD
1. Fight the good fight with all thy might! Christ is thy strength and Christ thy right;
2. Run the straight race thru God's good grace, Lift up thine eyes and seek His face;
3. Cast care a - side, lean on thy Guide, His bound-less mer - cy will pro - vide;
4. Faint not nor fear, for He is near, He chang-eth not and thou art dear;
Lay hold on life and it shall be Thy joy and crown e - ter - nal - ly.
Life with its way be - fore us lies, Christ is the path and Christ the prize.
Trust, and thy trust-ing soul shall prove Christ is its life and Christ its love.
On - ly be - lieve, and thou shalt see That Christ is all in all to thee.
Tune: PENTECOST
CHRISTIAN WARFARE

459 — Faith Is the Victory
JOHN H. YATES
IRA D. SANKEY
1. En - camped a-long the hills of light, Ye Chris-tian sol - diers, rise,
2. His ban - ner o - ver us is love, Our sword the Word of God;
3. To him that o - ver - comes the foe White rai - ment shall be giv'n;
And press the bat - tle ere the night Shall veil the glow - ing skies.
We tread the road the saints a - bove With shouts of tri - umph trod.
Be - fore the an - gels he shall know His name con-fessed in heav'n.
A - gainst the foe in vales be - low Let all our strength be hurled;
By faith they like a whirl-wind's breath Swept on o'er ev - 'ry field;
Then on - ward from the hills of light, Our hearts with love a - flame;
Faith is the vic - to - ry, we know, That o - ver-comes the world.
The faith by which they con-quered death Is still our shin - ing shield.
We'll van-quish all the hosts of night In Je - sus' con - q'ring name.
CHORUS
Faith is the vic - to - ry! Faith is the vic - to - ry!
Faith is the vic - to - ry! Faith is the vic - to - ry!
CHRISTIAN WARFARE

O glo-ri-ous vic-to-ry That o-ver-comes the world.
Lead On, O King Eternal — 460
ERNEST W. SHURTLEFF
HENRY SMART
1. Lead on, O King E-ter-nal, The day of march has come!
2. Lead on, O King E-ter-nal, Till sin's fierce war shall cease
3. Lead on, O King E-ter-nal, We fol-low—not with fears!
Hence-forth in fields of con-quest Thy tents shall be our home;
And ho-li-ness shall whis-per The sweet A-men of peace;
For glad-ness breaks like morn-ing Wher-e'er Thy face ap-pears;
Thru days of prep-a-ra-tion Thy grace has made us strong,
For not with swords loud clash-ing Nor roll of stir-ring drums—
Thy cross is lift-ed o'er us, We jour-ney in its light:
And now, O King E-ter-nal, We lift our bat-tle song.
With deeds of love and mer-cy The heav'n-ly king-dom comes.
The crown a-waits the con-quest—Lead on, O God of might.*
Tune: LANCASHIRE—lower key at 230
Arr. © Singspiration 1966. All rights reserved.
CHRISTIAN WARFARE

461 — The Banner of the Cross
DANIEL W. WHITTLE
JAMES McGRANAHAN
1. There's a roy - al ban - ner giv - en for dis - play To the sol - diers of the King;
As an en - sign fair we lift it up to - day, While as ran - somed ones we sing.
2. Tho the foe may rage and gath - er as a flood, Let the stan - dard be dis - played;
And be - neath its folds, as sol - diers of the Lord, For the truth be not dis - mayed.
3. O - ver land and sea, wher - ev - er men may dwell, Make the glo - rious ti - dings known;
Of the crim - son ban - ner now the sto - ry tell, While the Lord shall claim His own.
CHORUS
March - ing on, march - ing on, For Christ count ev - 'ry - thing but loss!
on, on, on, on, ev - 'ry - thing, ev - 'ry - thing but loss!
And to crown Him King, toil and sing 'Neath the ban - ner of the cross!
we'll Be - neath

I've a Home Beyond the River — 462

JOHN W. PETERSON JOHN W. PETERSON

1. O the bless - ed con-tem-pla-tion, When with trou - ble here I sigh:
2. Just a lit - tle more to la - bor, Tell the sto - ry, watch and pray;
3. O how sweet 'twill be to meet them—All the ran - somed host a - bove;
4. Tho the hills are rough and ston-y And the val - leys dark and cold,
I've a home be-yond the riv - er, That I'll en - ter by and by.
Just a few more earth-ly sor - rows, Then to heav'n we'll fly a - way.
Sweet-er still to see the Sav - ior, Praise Him for re-deem-ing love.
I must walk the path be - fore me— It will some day turn to gold.
CHORUS
I've a home be - yond the riv - er, I've a
I've a home be - yond the riv - er,
man - - sion bright and fair; I've a home
I've a man - sion bright and fair; (bright and fair;) home, a hap - py
be-yond the riv - er— I will dwell with Je - sus there.
home be - yond the riv - er—

ETERNAL DESTINY

463 — When the Roll Is Called Up Yonder

JAMES M. BLACK
JAMES M. BLACK
1. When the trum-pet of the Lord shall sound and time shall be no more
2. On that bright and cloudless morning when the dead in Christ shall rise
3. Let us la - bor for the Mas - ter from the dawn till set - ting sun,
And the morn-ing breaks e - ter - nal, bright and fair— When the saved of
And the glo - ry of His res - ur - rec - tion share— When His cho - sen
Let us talk of all His won-drous love and care; Then when all of
earth shall gath-er o - ver on the oth - er shore And the roll is called up
ones shall gath-er to their home be-yond the skies And the roll is called up
life is o - ver and our work on earth is done And the roll is called up
yon-der, I'll be there!
yon-der, I'll be there!
yon-der, I'll be there!
CHORUS
When the roll is called up yon - der,
When the roll
When the roll is called up yon - der, When the roll
When the roll
When the roll

is called up yon - der—When the roll is called up yon-der I'll be there!
He the Pearly Gates Will Open — 464
FREDRICK A. BLOM
Trans. by Nathaniel Carlson—alt.
ELSIE AHLWÉN
1. Love di - vine, so great and won - drous! Deep and might-y, pure, sub - lime!
2. Like a spar - row hunt-ed, fright-ened, Weak and help-less—so was I;
3. Love di - vine, so great and won - drous! All my sins He then for - gave!
4. In life's e - ven-tide, at twi - light, At His door I'll knock and wait;
Com - ing from the heart of Je - sus— Just the same thru tests of time.
Wound - ed, fall - en, yet He healed me— He will heed the sin - ner's cry.
I will sing His praise for - ev - er, For His blood, His pow'r to save.
By the pre - cious love of Je - sus I shall en - ter heav - en's gate.
CHORUS
He the pearl - y gates will o - pen, So that I may en - ter in;
For He pur-chased my re - demp - tion And for - gave me all my sin.
Arr. © Singspiration 1968, 1979. All rights reserved.
ETERNAL DESTINY

465 — My Savior First of All

FANNY J. CROSBY JOHN R. SWENEY

1. When my life-work is ended and I cross the swelling tide,
When the bright and glorious morning I shall see,
I shall know my Redeemer when I reach the other side,
And His smile will be the first to welcome me.

2. O the soul-thrilling rapture when I view His blessed face
And the luster of His kindly beaming eye;
How my full heart will praise Him for the mercy, love and grace
That prepare for me a mansion in the sky.

3. O the dear ones in glory, how they beckon me to come,
And our parting at the river I recall;
To the sweet vales of Eden they will sing my welcome home—
But I long to meet my Savior first of all.

4. Thru the gates to the city, in a robe of spotless white,
He will lead me where no tears will ever fall;
In the glad song of ages I shall mingle with delight—
But I long to meet my Savior first of all.

CHORUS

I shall know Him, I shall

know Him, And re - deemed by His side I shall stand, I shall know
Him, I shall know Him By the print of the nails in His hand.
When We See Christ — 466
ESTHER KERR RUSTHOI
ESTHER KERR RUSTHOI
It will be worth it all When we see Je - sus, Life's trials will
seem so small When we see Christ; One glimpse of His dear face
All sor-row will e-rase, So brave-ly run the race Till we see Christ.

ETERNAL DESTINY

467 — When We All Get to Heaven
ELIZA E. HEWITT
EMILY D. WILSON
1. Sing the won-drous love of Je - sus, Sing His mer - cy and His grace;
2. While we walk the pil - grim path-way Clouds will o - ver - spread the sky;
3. Let us then be true and faith-ful, Trust - ing, serv - ing ev - 'ry day;
4. On - ward to the prize be - fore us! Soon His beau - ty we'll be - hold;
In the man - sions bright and bless - ed He'll pre - pare for us a place.
But when trav - 'ling days are o - ver Not a shad - ow, not a sigh.
Just one glimpse of Him in glo - ry Will the toils of life re - pay.
Soon the pearl - y gates will o - pen—We shall tread the streets of gold.
CHORUS
When we all get to heav - en, What a day of re -
When we all
What a
joic - ing that will be! When we all see
day of re - joic - ing that will be!
When we all
Je - sus, We'll sing and shout the vic - to - ry.
shout, and shout the vic - to - ry.
ETERNAL DESTINY

SANFORD F. BENNETT
JOSEPH P. WEBSTER
1. There's a land that is fair - er than day, And by faith
2. We shall sing on that beau - ti - ful shore The me - lo -
3. To our boun - ti - ful Fa - ther a - bove We will of -
we can see it a - far, For the Fa - ther waits o -
di - ous songs of the blest; And our spir - its shall sor -
fer our trib - ute of praise, For the glo - ri - ous gift
ver the way To pre - pare us a dwell - ing place there.
row no more— Not a sigh for the bless - ing of rest.
of His love And the bless - ings that hal - low our days.
CHORUS
In the sweet by and by, We shall meet on that beau - ti - ful shore;
In the sweet by and by, We shall meet on that beau - ti - ful shore.

469 — Beyond the Sunset

VIRGIL P. BROCK BLANCHE KERR BROCK

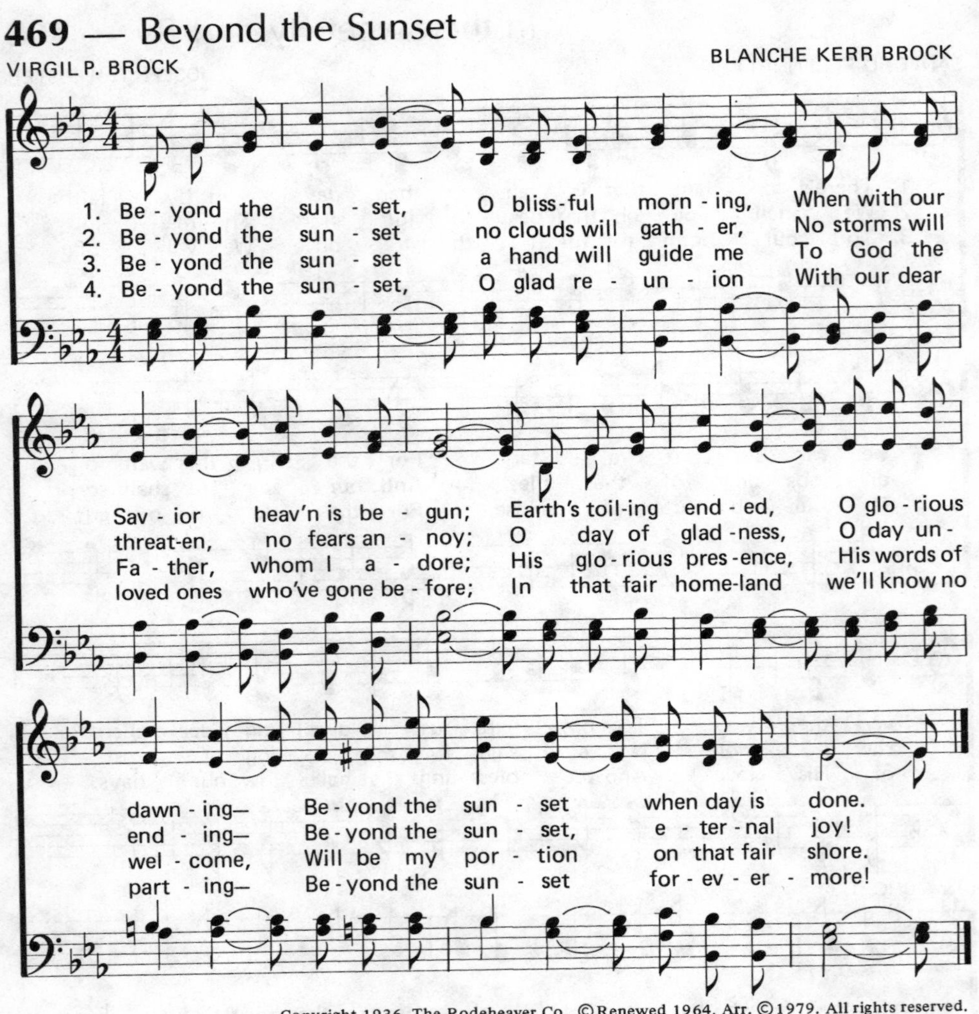
1. Be - yond the sun - set, O bliss-ful morn - ing, When with our
2. Be - yond the sun - set no clouds will gath - er, No storms will
3. Be - yond the sun - set a hand will guide me To God the
4. Be - yond the sun - set, O glad re - un - ion With our dear
Sav - ior heav'n is be - gun; Earth's toil-ing end - ed, O glo - rious
threat-en, no fears an - noy; O day of glad - ness, O day un -
Fa - ther, whom I a - dore; His glo - rious pres - ence, His words of
loved ones who've gone be - fore; In that fair home-land we'll know no
dawn - ing— Be - yond the sun - set when day is done.
end - ing— Be - yond the sun - set, e - ter - nal joy!
wel - come, Will be my por - tion on that fair shore.
part - ing— Be - yond the sun - set for - ev - er - more!

470 — What a Day That Will Be!

JIM HILL JIM HILL

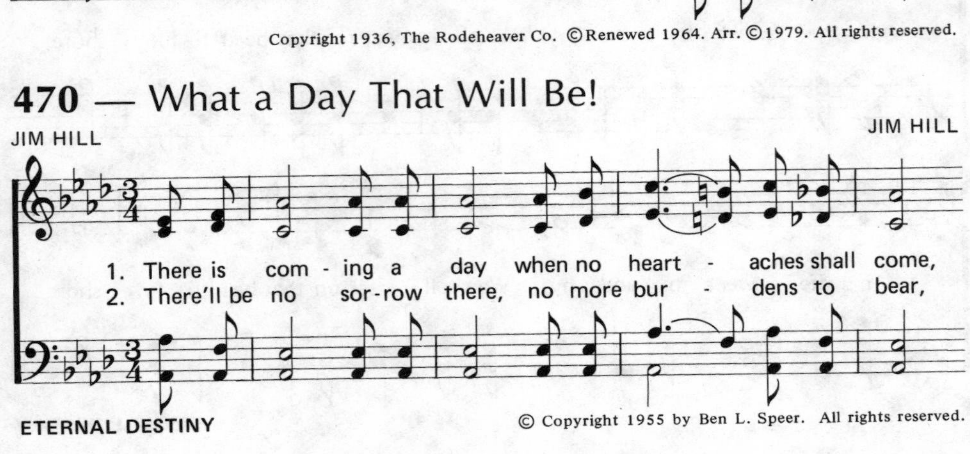
1. There is com - ing a day when no heart - aches shall come,
2. There'll be no sor - row there, no more bur - dens to bear,

No more clouds in the sky, no more tears to dim the eye;
No more sick - ness, no pain, no more part - ing o - ver there;
All is peace for - ev - er - more on that hap - py gold-en
And for - ev - er I will be with the One who died for
D.S. When He takes me by the hand and leads me thru the prom-ised
shore— What a day, glo - ri - ous day that will be!
me— What a day, glo - ri - ous day that will be!
land, What a day, glo - ri - ous day that will be!
Fine
CHORUS
What a day that will be when my Je - sus I shall see,
And I look up - on His face— the One who saved me by His grace;
D.S.

ETERNAL DESTINY

471 — Mansion over the Hilltop
IRA F. STANPHILL
IRA F. STANPHILL
1. I'm sat - is - fied with just a cot-tage be - low, A lit - tle
2. Tho oft - en tempt - ed, tor - ment-ed and test - ed And, like the
3. Don't think me poor or de - sert - ed or lone - ly— I'm not dis -
sil - ver and a lit - tle gold; But in that cit - y where the
proph-et, my pil-low a stone, And tho I find here no
cour-aged, I'm heav - en - bound; I'm just a pil - grim in
ran-somed will shine, I want a gold one that's sil - ver - lined.
per - ma - nent dwell-ing, I know He'll give me a man-sion my own.
search of a cit - y, I want a man-sion, a harp and a crown.
CHORUS
I've got a man - sion just o - ver the hill - top, In that bright
land where we'll nev-er grow old; And some-day yon - der we will

ETERNAL DESTINY

nev-er-more wan-der, But walk the streets that are pur-est gold.
Over the Sunset Mountains — 472
JOHN W. PETERSON
JOHN W. PETERSON
1. O-ver the sun-set moun-tains Some-day I'll soft-ly go,
2. Toil-ing will all be end-ed, Shad-ows will flee a-way;
In-to the arms of Je-sus— He who has loved me so.
Sor-row will be for-got-ten— O what a won-der-ful day!
REFRAIN
O-ver the sun-set moun-tains, Heav-en a-waits for me;
O-ver the sun-set moun-tains, Je-sus my Sav-ior I'll see.
© 1953, renewal 1981 by John W. Peterson Music Company.
All rights reserved. Used by permission.
ETERNAL DESTINY

473 — O That Will Be Glory
CHARLES H. GABRIEL
CHARLES H. GABRIEL
1. When all my la - bors and tri - als are o'er And I am safe on that
2. When, by the gift of His in - fi - nite grace, I am ac - cord - ed in
3. Friends will be there I have loved long a - go, Joy like a riv - er a -
beau - ti - ful shore, Just to be near the dear Lord I a - dore
heav - en a place, Just to be there and to look on His face
round me will flow; Yet, just a smile from my Sav - ior, I know,
CHORUS
Will thru the a - ges be glo - ry for me.
O that will be
O
that will
glo - ry for me, Glo - ry for me, glo - ry for me; When by His grace
be
glo - ry for
me,
Glo - ry for
me,
glo - ry for
me;
rit.
I shall look on His face, That will be glo - ry, be glo - ry for me!
ETERNAL DESTINY

Jesus Led Me All the Way — 474

JOHN W. PETERSON
JOHN W. PETERSON
1. Some day life's jour - ney will be o'er, And I shall reach that
2. If God should let me there re - view The wind - ing paths of
3. And hith - er - to my Lord hath led, To - day He guides each
dis - tant shore; I'll sing while en - t'ring heav - en's door,
earth I knew, It would be prov - en clear and true—
step I tread; And soon in heav'n it will be said,
"Je - sus led me all the way."
Je - sus led me all the way.
"Je - sus led me all the way."
CHORUS
Je - sus led me all the way,
Led me step by step each day; I will tell the saints and an - gels
as I lay my bur - dens down, "Je - sus led me all the way."

ETERNAL DESTINY

475 — We're Marching to Zion
ISAAC WATTS
Chorus—Robert Lowry
ROBERT LOWRY
1. Come, we that love the Lord, And let our joys be known;
2. Let those re - fuse to sing Who nev - er knew our God;
3. The hill of Zi - on yields A thou - sand sa - cred sweets
4. Then let our songs a - bound And ev - 'ry tear be dry;
Join in a song with sweet ac - cord, Join in a song with sweet ac -
But chil - dren of the heav'n-ly King, But chil - dren of the heav'n - ly
Be - fore we reach the heav'n-ly fields, Be - fore we reach the heav'n - ly
We're march - ing thru Im - man-uel's ground, We're march - ing thru Im - man - uel's
cord And thus sur - round the throne, And thus sur-round the throne.
King May speak their joys a - broad, May speak their joys a - broad.
fields Or walk the gold - en streets, Or walk the gold - en streets.
ground To fair - er worlds on high, To fair - er worlds on high.
CHORUS
We're march - ing to Zi - on, Beau - ti - ful, beau - ti - ful Zi - on; We're

marching upward to Zion, The beautiful city of God.
Shall We Gather at the River? — 476
Based on Revelation 22:21
ROBERT LOWRY
ROBERT LOWRY
1. Shall we gather at the river, Where bright angel feet have trod,
2. On the bosom of the river, Where the Savior-King we own,
3. Ere we reach the shining river, Lay we ev'ry burden down;
4. Soon we'll reach the shining river, Soon our pilgrimage will cease;
With its crystal tide forever Flowing by the throne of God?
We shall meet and sorrow never 'Neath the glory of the throne.
Grace our spirits will deliver And provide a robe and crown.
Soon our happy hearts will quiver With the melody of peace.
REFRAIN
Yes, we'll gather at the river, The beautiful, the beautiful river,
Gather with the saints at the river That flows by the throne of God.
ETERNAL DESTINY

477 — For All the Saints
WILLIAM W. HOW
RALPH VAUGHAN WILLIAMS
In unison
1. For all the saints who from their la - bors rest, Who
2. Thou wast their rock, their for - tress, and their might,
3. O may Thy sol - diers, faith - ful, true, and bold,
4. O blest com - mu - nion, fel - low - ship di - vine!
5. But lo! there breaks a yet more glo - rious day: The
6. From earth's wide bounds, from o - cean's far - thest coast, Thru
Thee by faith be - fore the world con - fessed, Thy
Thou, Lord, their cap - tain in the well - fought fight;
Fight as the saints who no - bly fought of old, And
We fee - bly strug - gle, they in glo - ry shine; Yet
saints tri - um - phant rise in bright ar - ray; The
gates of pearl streams in the count - less host,
name, O Je - sus, be for - ev - er blest:
Thou, in the dark - ness drear, their one true light:
win with them the vic - tor's crown of gold:
all are one in Thee, for all are Thine:
King of glo - ry pass - es on His way:
Sing - ing to Fa - ther, Son, and Ho - ly Ghost:
Tune: SINE NOMINE
ETERNAL DESTINY
From The English Hymnal.
By permission of Oxford University Press.

Al - le - lu - ia! Al - le - lu - ia!
Abide with Me — 478
HENRY F. LYTE
WILLIAM H. MONK
1. A - bide with me— fast falls the e - ven - tide! The dark-ness deep - ens— Lord, with me a - bide; When oth - er help - ers fail and com - forts flee, Help of the help - less, O a - bide with me!
2. Swift to its close ebbs out life's lit - tle day, Earth's joys grow dim, its glo - ries pass a - way; Change and de - cay in all a - round I see— O Thou who chang-est not, a - bide with me!
3. I need Thy pres - ence ev - 'ry pass-ing hour— What but Thy grace can foil the temp-ter's pow'r? Who like Thy - self my guide and stay can be? Thru cloud and sun-shine, O a - bide with me!
4. I fear no foe with Thee at hand to bless, Ills have no weight and tears no bit - ter - ness; Where is death's sting? where, grave, thy vic - to - ry? I tri - umph still if Thou a - bide with me!
5. Hold Thou Thy Word be - fore my clos - ing eyes, Shine thru the gloom and point me to the skies; Heav'n's morn-ing breaks and earth's vain shad - ows flee— In life, in death, O Lord, a - bide with me!*
Tune: EVENTIDE
ETERNAL DESTINY

479 — Face to Face

Based on I Corinthians 13:12
CARRIE E. BRECK

GRANT COLFAX TULLAR

1. Face to face with Christ, my Sav - ior, Face to face—what will it be?
When with rap-ture I be - hold Him, Je - sus Christ who died for me!

2. On - ly faint - ly now I see Him, With the dark-ling veil be - tween;
But a bless-ed day is com - ing, When His glo - ry shall be seen.

3. What re-joic - ing in His pres - ence, When are ban-ished grief and pain,
When the crook-ed ways are straightened And the dark things shall be plain.

4. Face to face—O bliss - ful mo - ment! Face to face—to see and know;
Face to face with my Re - deem - er, Je - sus Christ who loves me so!

CHORUS

Face to face I shall be - hold Him, Far be-yond the star - ry sky;
Face to face, in all His glo - ry, I shall see Him by and by!

Tune: FACE TO FACE

ETERNAL DESTINY

The Sands of Time Are Sinking — 480

ANNE ROSS COUSIN

CHRÉTIEN URHAN
Arr. by Edward F. Rimbault

1. The sands of time are sink - ing, The dawn of heav - en breaks;
2. O Christ, He is the foun - tain, The deep, sweet well of love;
3. O I am my Be - lov - ed's, And my Be - lov - ed's mine;
4. The Bride eyes not her gar - ment But her dear Bride-groom's face—
The sum - mer morn I've sighed for— The fair, sweet morn a - wakes.
The streams on earth I've tast - ed More deep I'll drink a - bove.
He brings a poor vile sin - ner In - to His "house of wine."
I will not gaze at glo - ry But on my King of grace,
Dark, dark hath been the mid - night, But day - spring is at hand,
There to an o - cean ful - ness His mer - cy doth ex - pand,
I stand up - on His mer - it— I know no oth - er stand,
Not at the crown He giv - eth But on His pierc - ed hand:
And glo - ry, glo - ry dwell - eth In Im - man - uel's land.
And glo - ry, glo - ry dwell - eth In Im - man - uel's land.
Not e'en where glo - ry dwell - eth In Im - man - uel's land.
The Lamb is all the glo - ry Of Im - man - uel's land.

Tune: RUTHERFORD

481 — Where the Roses Never Fade

JACK and ELSIE OSBORN
JAMES C. MILLER

JACK and ELSIE OSBORN
JAMES C. MILLER

1. I am go - ing to a cit - y Where the streets with gold are laid,
2. In this world we have our trou - bles— Sa - tan's snares we must e - vade;
3. Loved ones gone to be with Je - sus, In their robes of white ar - rayed,
Fine
Where the tree of life is bloom - ing And the ros - es nev - er fade.
We'll be free from all temp - ta - tions Where the ros - es nev - er fade.
Now are wait - ing for my com - ing Where the ros - es nev - er fade.
D.S. I am go - ing to a cit - y Where the ros - es nev - er fade.
REFRAIN
D.S.
Here they bloom but for a sea - son, Soon their beau - ty is de - cayed;

482 — We Shall Walk Through the Valley

Traditional American melody
Arr. by Fred Bock

Traditional

1. We shall walk thru the val - ley in peace, We shall walk thru the
2. There will be no sor - row there, There will be no
3. We shall meet our loved ones there, We shall meet our
4. We shall meet our Sav - ior there, We shall meet our

val - ley in peace; If Je - sus Him - self will be our
sor - row there; If Je - sus Him - self will be our
loved ones there; If Je - sus Him - self will be our
Sav - ior there; If Je - sus Him - self will be our
lead - er, We shall walk thru the val - ley in peace.
lead - er, There will be no sor - row there.
lead - er, We shall meet our loved ones there.
lead - er, We shall meet our Sav - ior there.
I've a Longing in My Heart — 483
DOROTHY MASTER GREEN
DOROTHY MASTER GREEN
I've a long-ing in my heart for Je - sus, I've a long-ing in my
heart to see His face; I am wea - ry, O so wea - ry of
trav - 'ling here be - low— I've a long - ing in my heart for Him.
ETERNAL DESTINY

484 — On Jordan's Stormy Banks

SAMUEL STENNETT

Traditional American melody
Adapted by Rigdon M. McIntosh

1. On Jor-dan's storm-y banks I stand And cast a wish-ful eye
To Ca-naan's fair and hap-py land, Where my pos-ses-sions lie.

2. All o'er those wide-ex-tend-ed plains Shines one e-ter-nal day;
There God the Son for-ev-er reigns And scat-ters night a-way.

3. No chill-ing winds nor poi-s'nous breath Can reach that health-ful shore;
Sick-ness and sor-row, pain and death Are felt and feared no more.

4. When shall I reach that hap-py place And be for-ev-er blest?
When shall I see my Fa-ther's face And in His bos-om rest?

CHORUS

I am bound for the prom-ised land, I am bound for the prom-ised land;
O who will come and go with me? I am bound for the promised land.

PART 3

THE OUTWARD LOOK

OUR SONGS AND HYMNS OF TESTIMONY AND CHRISTIAN RESPONSIBILITY

"Sing unto the Lord,
bless His name;
show forth His salvation
from day to day.
Declare His glory among the heathen,
His wonders among all people."

Psalm 96:1,2

485 — America the Beautiful

KATHARINE LEE BATES

SAMUEL A. WARD

1. O beau - ti - ful for spa-cious skies, For am - ber waves of grain,
2. O beau - ti - ful for pil - grim feet, Whose stern, im - pas-sioned stress
3. O beau - ti - ful for he - roes proved In lib - er - at - ing strife,
4. O beau - ti - ful for pa - triot dream That sees, be - yond the years,

For pur - ple moun-tain maj - es- ties A - bove the fruit - ed plain!
A thor - ough-fare for free-dom beat A - cross the wil - der - ness!
Who more than self their coun-try loved And mer - cy more than life!
Thine al - a - bas - ter cit - ies gleam—Un-dimmed by hu - man tears!

A - mer - i - ca! A - mer - i - ca! God shed His grace on thee,
A - mer - i - ca! A - mer - i - ca! God mend thine ev - 'ry flaw,
A - mer - i - ca! A - mer - i - ca! May God thy gold re - fine,
A - mer - i - ca! A - mer - i - ca! God shed His grace on thee,

And crown thy good with broth - er - hood From sea to shin - ing sea.
Con - firm thy soul in self - con - trol, Thy lib - er - ty in law.
Till all suc - cess be no - ble - ness, And ev - 'ry gain di - vine.
And crown thy good with broth - er - hood From sea to shin - ing sea.

Tune: MATERNA

CHRISTIAN CITIZENSHIP

My Country, 'Tis of Thee — 486

SAMUEL F. SMITH

Thesaurus Musicus

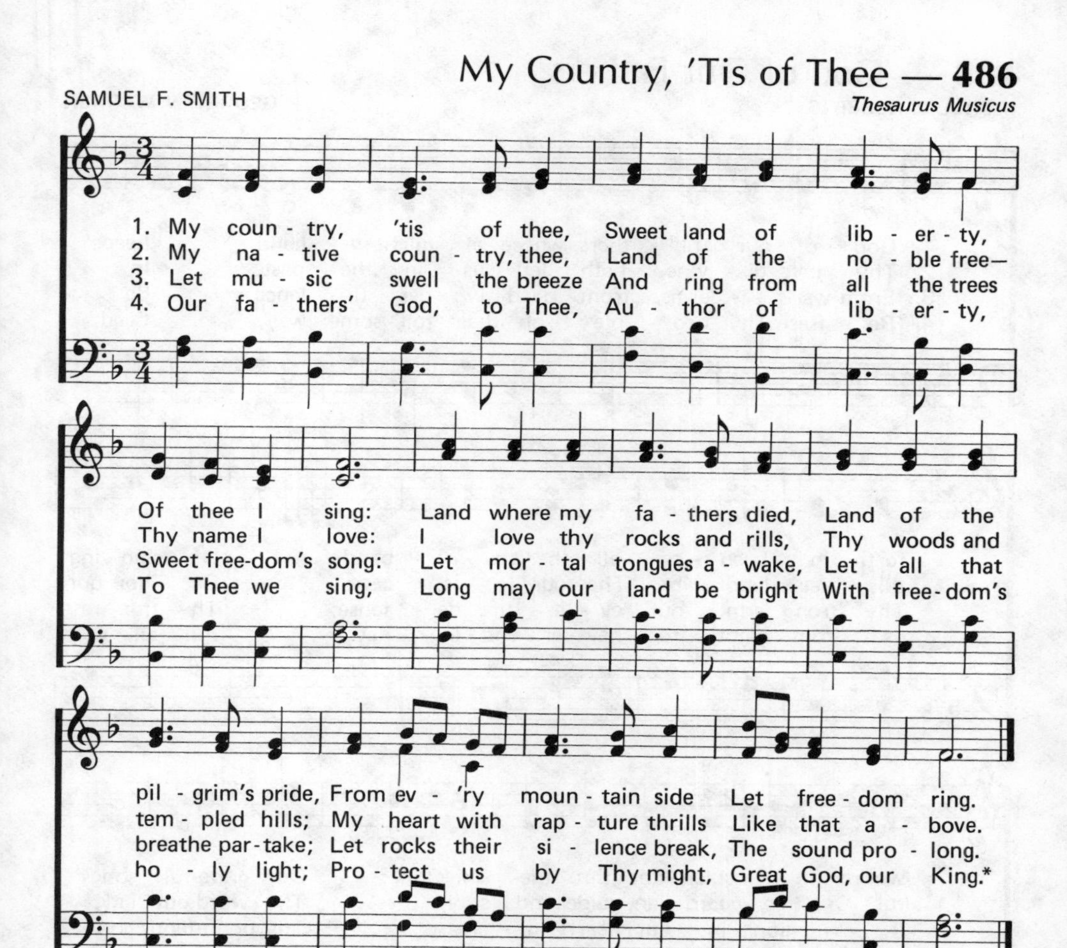
1. My coun - try, 'tis of thee, Sweet land of lib - er - ty,
2. My na - tive coun - try, thee, Land of the no - ble free—
3. Let mu - sic swell the breeze And ring from all the trees
4. Our fa - thers' God, to Thee, Au - thor of lib - er - ty,
Of thee I sing: Land where my fa - thers died, Land of the
Thy name I love: I love thy rocks and rills, Thy woods and
Sweet free-dom's song: Let mor - tal tongues a - wake, Let all that
To Thee we sing; Long may our land be bright With free-dom's
pil - grim's pride, From ev - 'ry moun - tain side Let free - dom ring.
tem - pled hills; My heart with rap - ture thrills Like that a - bove.
breathe par-take; Let rocks their si - lence break, The sound pro - long.
ho - ly light; Pro - tect us by Thy might, Great God, our King.*

Tune: AMERICA

God Bless Our Native Land — 487

1, 2 - SIEGFRIED A. MAHLMANN
Trans. by Charles T. Brooks, John S. Dwight
3 - WILLIAM E. HICKSON

Thesaurus Musicus

1. God bless our native land—
Firm may she ever stand
Through storm and night:
When the wild tempests rave,
Ruler of wind and wave,
Do Thou our country save
By Thy great might.

2. For her our prayers shall rise
To God above the skies—
On Him we wait:
Thou who art ever nigh,
Guarding with watchful eye,
To Thee aloud we cry,
God save the state!

3. And not to us alone,
But be Thy mercies known
From shore to shore:
Lord, make the nations see
That men should brothers be,
And form one family
The wide world o'er.*

Tune: AMERICA–(at 486)

488 — God of Our Fathers
DANIEL C. ROBERTS
GEORGE W. WARREN
1. God of our fa - thers, whose al - might - y hand Leads
2. Thy love di - vine hath led us in the past, In
3. From war's a - larms, from dead - ly pes - ti - lence, Be
4. Re - fresh Thy peo - ple on their toil - some way, Lead
forth in beau - ty all the star - ry band Of shin - ing
this free land by Thee our lot is cast; Be Thou our
Thy strong arm our ev - er - sure de - fense; Thy true re -
us from night to nev - er - end - ing day; Fill all our
worlds in splen - dor thru the skies, Our grate-ful songs
rul - er, guard - ian, guide and stay, Thy word our law,
li - gion in our hearts in - crease, Thy boun-teous good -
lives with love and grace di - vine, And glo - ry, laud
be - fore Thy throne a - rise.
Thy paths our cho - sen way.
ness nour - ish us in peace.
and praise be ev - er Thine!*
1-3
D.C.
4

Tune: NATIONAL HYMN

CHRISTIAN CITIZENSHIP

Thou, by Heavenly Hosts Adored — 489

HENRY HARBAUGH–alt.

SIMEON B. MARSH
Arr. by Larry Leader

1. Thou, by heav'n-ly hosts a-dored, Gra-cious, might-y, sov-'reign Lord,
2. From all pub-lic sin and shame, From am-bi-tion's grasp-ing aim,
3. Let our rul-ers ev-er be Men that love and hon-or Thee,
God of na-tions, King of kings, Head of all cre-a-ted things,
From re-bel-lion, death and war, From de-stroy-ing na-ture's store,
Let the pow'rs by Thee or-dained Be in right-eous-ness main-tained;
By the Church with joy con-fessed, God o'er all, for-ev-er blest,
From dread fam-ine's aw-ful stroke, From op-pres-sion's gall-ing yoke,
In the peo-ple's hearts in-crease Love of pi-e-ty and peace:
Plead-ing at Thy throne we stand: Save this peo-ple, bless our land.
From the judg-ments of Thy hand: Spare this peo-ple, spare our land.
Thus u-nit-ed, may we stand One wide, free and hap-py land.*

Tune: MARTYN (Alternate, ST. GEORGE'S, WINDSOR)

490 — Where Cross the Crowded Ways of Life
FRANKLIN MASON NORTH
Gardiner's Sacred Melodies
1. Where cross the crowd - ed ways of life, Where sound the
2. In haunts of wretch - ed - ness and need, On shad - owed
3. The cup of wa - ter giv'n for Thee Still holds the
4. O Mas - ter, from the moun - tain side, Make haste to
5. Till sons of men shall learn Thy love And fol - low
cries of race and clan, A - bove the noise of
thresh - olds dark with fears, From paths where hide the
fresh - ness of Thy grace; Yet long these mul - ti -
heal these hearts of pain; A - mong these rest - less
where Thy feet have trod; Till glo - rious, from Thy
self - ish strife We hear Thy voice, O Son of man!
lures of greed, We catch the vi - sion of Thy tears.
tudes to see The sweet com - pas - sion of Thy face.
throngs a - bide, O tread the cit - y streets a - gain:
heav'n a - bove, Shall come the cit - y of our God.*
Tune: GERMANY—lower keys at 112 and 287
491 — When Your Heart, with Joy O'erflowing
THEODORE C. WILLIAMS—alt. N. J.
ETHELBERT W. BULLINGER
1. When your heart, with joy o'er - flow - ing, Sings a thank - ful prayer,
2. When a har - vest God has giv - en Fills your barn with store,
3. E - ven if your gift be mea - ger, Plant it as a seed;
4. Share with him your bread of bless - ing, Thus to show you care;

Tune: BULLINGER

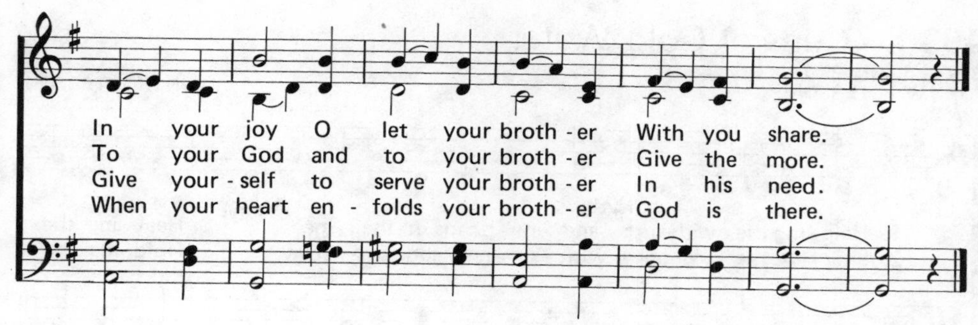

In your joy O let your broth - er With you share.
To your God and to your broth - er Give the more.
Give your - self to serve your broth - er In his need.
When your heart en - folds your broth - er God is there.

Let Your Heart Be Broken — 492

BRYAN JEFFERY LEECH

JAMES MOUNTAIN

1. Let your heart be bro - ken For a world in need— Feed the mouths that
2. Here on earth ap - ply - ing Prin - ci - ples of love— Vis - i - ble ex -
3. Blest to be a bless - ing, Priv - i - leged to care, Chal - lenged by the
4. Add to your be - liev - ing Deeds that prove it true— Know - ing Christ as
5. Let your heart be ten - der And your vi - sion clear— See man - kind as
hun - ger, Soothe the wounds that bleed, Give the cup of wa - ter And the
pres - sion God still rules a - bove, Liv - ing il - lus - tra - tion Of the
need Ap - par - ent ev - 'ry - where, Where mankind is want - ing Fill the
Sav - ior, Make Him Mas - ter too: Fol - low in His foot - steps, Go where
God sees, Serve Him far and near; Let your heart be bro - ken By a
loaf of bread— Be the hands of Je - sus, Serv - ing in His stead:
Liv - ing Word To the minds of all who've Nev - er seen and heard.
va - cant place, Be the means thru which the Lord re - veals His grace.
He has trod, In the world's great trou - ble Risk your-self for God.
broth - er's pain, Share your rich re - sourc - es— Give and give a - gain.

Tune: WYE VALLEY (abridged)

493 — Cups of Cold Water

Based on Mark 9:41
JOHN W. PETERSON
JOHN W. PETERSON
1. Help-ing the wid-ows and or-phans in their need, Heal-ing the sick ones and bind-ing hearts that bleed, Feed-ing the hun-gry con-cerns the Lord a-bove— By this we serve Him and dem-on-strate His love.
2. Shar-ing the gos-pel with sin-ners gone a-stray, Hold-ing the light up so they can find the way, Lift-ing the fall-en—this we must sure-ly do, If to our call-ing as Chris-tians we are true.
CHORUS
Cups of cold wa-ter giv'n in Je-sus' name— Cups of cold wa-ter are nev-er giv'n in vain; Some day in heav-en, when we

meet the Lord, Each deed of kind - ness will bring a rich re - ward.
Share Jesus with Others — 494
JOHN W. PETERSON
JOHN W. PETERSON
1. Sin - ful and lone-ly and dy - ing, Wan-d'ring far in the night,
2. This is the ul - ti - mate kind-ness, This is love at its best:
Wait - ing, long-ing for some - one To lead them to Christ and the light. . .
Shar - ing Je - sus with oth - ers, The lone- ly, the lost and op - pressed.
CHORUS
Share Je-sus with oth-ers— He loves and will save them too;
Share Je-sus with oth-ers— That's what a Chris - tian should do.

495 — Jesus Saves!

PRISCILLA J. OWENS WILLIAM J. KIRKPATRICK

1. We have heard the joy - ful sound— Je - sus saves! Je - sus saves!
2. Waft it on the roll - ing tide— Je - sus saves! Je - sus saves!
3. Sing a - bove the bat - tle strife— Je - sus saves! Je - sus saves!
4. Give the winds a might - y voice— Je - sus saves! Je - sus saves!
Spread the ti - dings all a - round— Je - sus saves! Je - sus saves!
Tell to sin - ners far and wide— Je - sus saves! Je - sus saves!
By His death and end - less life— Je - sus saves! Je - sus saves!
Let the na - tions now re - joice— Je - sus saves! Je - sus saves!
Bear the news to ev - 'ry land, Climb the steeps and cross the waves;
Sing, ye is - lands of the sea! Ech - o back, ye o - cean caves!
Sing it soft - ly thru the gloom, When the heart for mer - cy craves;
Shout sal - va - tion full and free, High - est hills and deep - est caves;
On - ward! 'tis our Lord's com - mand— Je - sus saves! Je - sus saves!
Earth shall keep her ju - bi - lee— Je - sus saves! Je - sus saves!
Sing in tri - umph o'er the tomb— Je - sus saves! Je - sus saves!
This our song of vic - to - ry— Je - sus saves! Je - sus saves!

Hear the Voice of Jesus Calling — 496

From a Gregorian Chant
Adapted by Lowell Mason

DANIEL MARCH—alt.

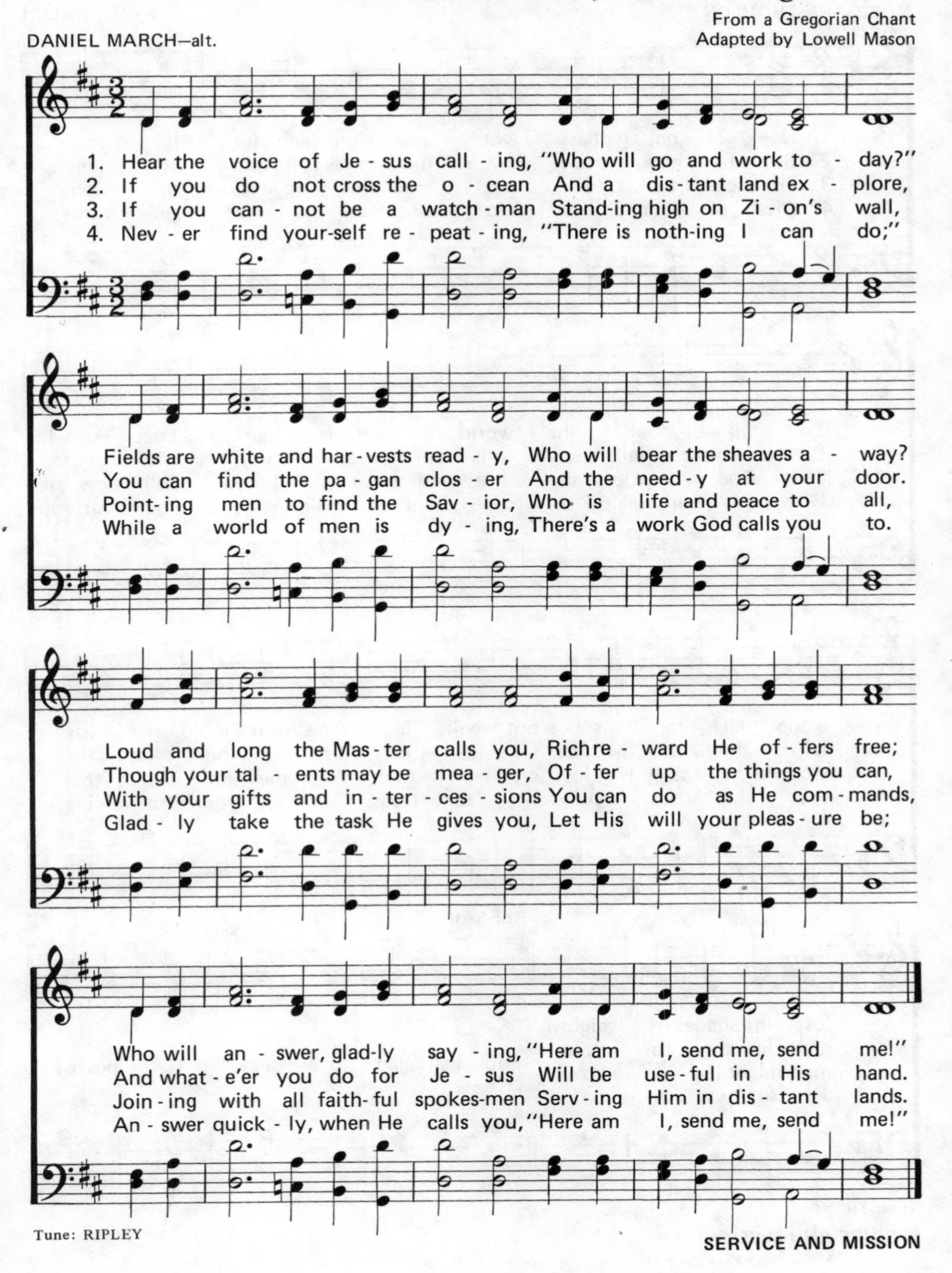
1. Hear the voice of Je - sus call - ing, "Who will go and work to - day?"
2. If you do not cross the o - cean And a dis - tant land ex - plore,
3. If you can - not be a watch - man Stand-ing high on Zi - on's wall,
4. Nev - er find your-self re - peat - ing, "There is noth-ing I can do;"
Fields are white and har - vests read - y, Who will bear the sheaves a - way?
You can find the pa - gan clos - er And the need - y at your door.
Point-ing men to find the Sav - ior, Who is life and peace to all,
While a world of men is dy - ing, There's a work God calls you to.
Loud and long the Mas - ter calls you, Rich re - ward He of - fers free;
Though your tal - ents may be mea - ger, Of - fer up the things you can,
With your gifts and in - ter - ces - sions You can do as He com - mands,
Glad - ly take the task He gives you, Let His will your pleas - ure be;
Who will an - swer, glad-ly say - ing, "Here am I, send me, send me!"
And what - e'er you do for Je - sus Will be use - ful in His hand.
Join - ing with all faith - ful spokes-men Serv - ing Him in dis - tant lands.
An - swer quick - ly, when He calls you, "Here am I, send me, send me!"

Tune: RIPLEY

497 — O Zion, Haste
MARY ANN THOMSON
JAMES WALCH
1. O Zi - on, haste, your mis - sion high ful - fill - ing,
2. Be - hold how man - y thou - sands still are ly - ing
3. Pro - claim to ev - 'ry peo - ple, tongue and na - tion
4. Give of your sons to bear the mes - sage glo - rious,
To tell to all the world that God is Light, That He who
Bound in the dark - some pris - on - house of sin, With none to
That God in whom they live and move is Love: Tell how He
Give of your wealth to speed them on their way; Pour out your
made all na - tions is not will - ing One soul should per - ish,
tell them of the Sav - ior's dy - ing Or of the life He
stooped to save His lost cre - a - tion And died on earth that
soul for them in prayer vic - to - rious, And all your spend - ing
REFRAIN
lost in shades of night.
died for them to win.
man might live a - bove.
Je - sus will re - pay.
Pub - lish glad ti - dings, Ti - dings of

Tune: TIDINGS

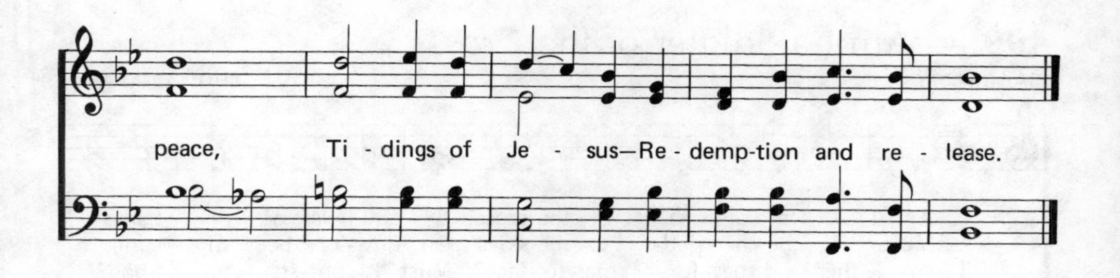
peace, Ti - dings of Je - sus—Re - demp-tion and re - lease.

Christ for the World We Sing! — 498

SAMUEL WOLCOTT

FELICE de GIARDINI

1. Christ for the world we sing! The world to Christ we bring
2. Christ for the world we sing! The world to Christ we bring
3. Christ for the world we sing! The world to Christ we bring
4. Christ for the world we sing! The world to Christ we bring
With lov - ing zeal: The poor and them that mourn, The faint and
With fer - vent prayer: The way - ward and the lost, By rest - less
With one ac - cord: With us the work to share, With us re -
With joy - ful song: The new - born souls, whose days, Re-claimed from
o - ver-borne, Sin - sick and sor - row worn, Whom Christ doth heal.
pas - sions tossed, Re - deemed at count - less cost From dark de - spair.
proach to dare, With us the cross to bear For Christ our Lord.
er - ror's ways, In - spired with hope and praise, To Christ be - long.

Tune: ITALIAN HYMN—higher key at 48

499 — Am I a Soldier of the Cross?

ISAAC WATTS THOMAS A. ARNE

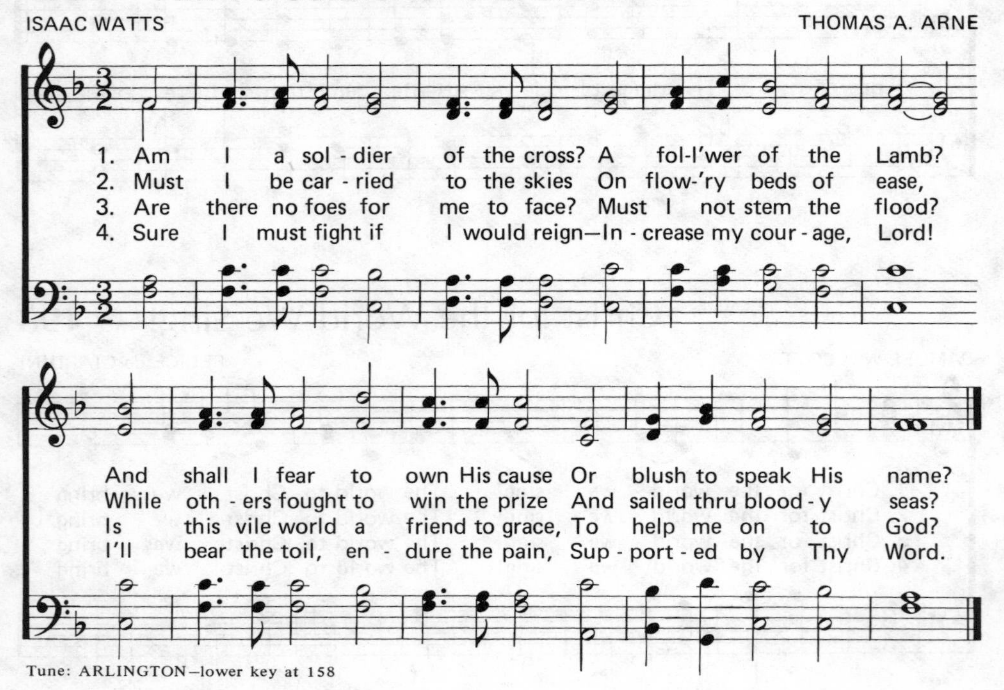

1. Am I a sol - dier of the cross? A fol-l'wer of the Lamb?
2. Must I be car - ried to the skies On flow-'ry beds of ease,
3. Are there no foes for me to face? Must I not stem the flood?
4. Sure I must fight if I would reign—In - crease my cour - age, Lord!
And shall I fear to own His cause Or blush to speak His name?
While oth - ers fought to win the prize And sailed thru blood - y seas?
Is this vile world a friend to grace, To help me on to God?
I'll bear the toil, en - dure the pain, Sup - port - ed by Thy Word.

Tune: ARLINGTON—lower key at 158

500 — So Send I You—by Grace Made Strong

Based on John 20:21
E. MARGARET CLARKSON

1. So send I you—
   by grace made strong to triumph
   O'er hosts of hell,
   o'er darkness, death and sin,
   My name to bear,
   and in that name to conquer—
   So send I you,
   My victory to win.

2. So send I you—
   to take to souls in bondage
   The word of truth
   that sets the captive free,
   To break the bonds
   of sin, to loose death's fetters—
   So send I you,
   to bring the lost to Me.

3. So send I you—
   My strength to know in weakness,
   My joy in grief,
   My perfect peace in pain,
   To prove My pow'r,
   My grace, My promised presence—
   So send I you,
   eternal fruit to gain.

4. So send I you—
   to bear My cross with patience,
   And then one day
   with joy to lay it down,
   To hear my voice,
   "Well done, My faithful servant—
   Come, share My throne,
   My kingdom and My crown!"

CODA: "As the Father hath sent Me, So send I you."

Tune: SO SEND I YOU—(at 501); adaptable, without Coda, to FINLANDIA—(at 147, 334)

Based on John 20:21
E. MARGARET CLARKSON
JOHN W. PETERSON
1. So send I you— to la - bor un - re - ward - ed, To serve un -
2. So send I you— to bind the bruised and bro - ken, O'er wan-d'ring
3. So send I you— to lone - li - ness and long - ing, With heart a -
4. So send I you— to leave your life's am - bi - tion, To die to
5. So send I you— to hearts made hard by ha - tred, To eyes made
paid, un - loved, un-sought, un - known, To bear re - buke, to suf - fer
souls to work, to weep, to wake, To bear the bur - dens of a
hun - g'ring for the loved and known, For-sak - ing home and kin-dred,
dear de - sire, self - will re - sign, To la - bor long, and love where
blind be - cause they will not see, To spend, tho it be blood, to
scorn and scoff - ing— So send I you, to toil for Me a - lone.
world a - wea - ry— So send I you, to suf - fer for My sake.
friend and dear one— So send I you, to know My love a - lone.
men re - vile you— So send I you, to lose your life in Mine.
spend and spare not— So send I you, to taste of Cal - va -
1-4
D.C.
5
ry. "As the Fa - ther hath sent Me, So send I you."

502 — We've a Story to Tell

H. ERNEST NICHOL

H. ERNEST NICHOL

1. We've a sto - ry to tell to the na - tions That shall turn their hearts
2. We've a song to be sung to the na - tions That shall lift their hearts
3. We've a mes - sage to give to the na - tions—That the Lord who reigns
4. We've a Sav - ior to show to the na - tions Who the path of sor -

to the right, A sto - ry of truth and mer - cy, A sto - ry of
to the Lord, A song that shall con - quer e - vil And shat - ter the
from a - bove Has sent us His Son to save us And show us that
row has trod, That all of the world's great peo - ples Might come to the

peace and light, A sto - ry of peace and light.
spear and sword, And shat - ter the spear and sword.
God is love, And show us that God is love.
truth of God, Might come to the truth of God.

REFRAIN

For the dark-ness shall turn to dawn - ing, And the dawn-ing to noon-day bright, And Christ's

great king-dom shall come to earth, The king - dom of love and light.
The Church of God Is Debtor — 503
E. MARGARET CLARKSON
NORMAN JOHNSON
1. The Church of God is debt - or To Him who shed His blood
2. The Church of God is debt - or To all men far and near,
3. The Church of God is debt - or— O may we not for - get
That all earth's teem-ing mil - lions Might be re - deemed to God;
To tell the name of Je - sus Till all the world shall hear;
Our all to Christ is for - feit If we would pay that debt!
Is debt - or to His mer - cy, Is debt - or to His grace,
Is debt - or to the stran - ger, To a - lien, foe and kin,
We lay our lives be - fore Him To pray, to give, to go:
Is debt - or till all crea - tures Shall know His love's em - brace.
Is debt - or till for - give - ness Shall tri - umph o - ver sin.
The Church of God is debt - or Till all the world shall know!
Tune: SALINA (Alternates, AURELIA, LANCASHIRE)
Words © Singspiration 1967, music © Singspiration 1976. All rights reserved.
SERVICE AND MISSION

504 — Go Ye into All the World

JAMES McGRANAHAN
Chorus—Mark 16:15

JAMES McGRANAHAN

1. Far, far a-way, in hea-then darkness dwell-ing, Mil-lions of souls for-ev-er may be lost; Who, who will go, sal-va-tion's sto-ry tell-ing, Look-ing to Je-sus, mind-ing not the cost?

2. See o'er the world wide o-pen doors in-vit-ing— Sol-diers of Christ, a-rise and en-ter in! Chris-tians, a-wake! your forc-es all u-nit-ing, Send forth the gos-pel, break the chains of sin.

3. God speed the day when those of ev-'ry na-tion "Glo-ry to God!" tri-um-phant-ly shall sing; Ran-somed, re-deemed, re-joic-ing in sal-va-tion, Shout "Hal-le-lu-jah, for the Lord is King!"

CHORUS

"All pow'r is giv-en un-to Me, All pow'r is giv-en un-to Me, Go ye in-to all the world and preach the gos-pel, And lo, I am with you al-way."

CHARLES H. GABRIEL

CHARLES H. GABRIEL
Arr. by Larry Leader

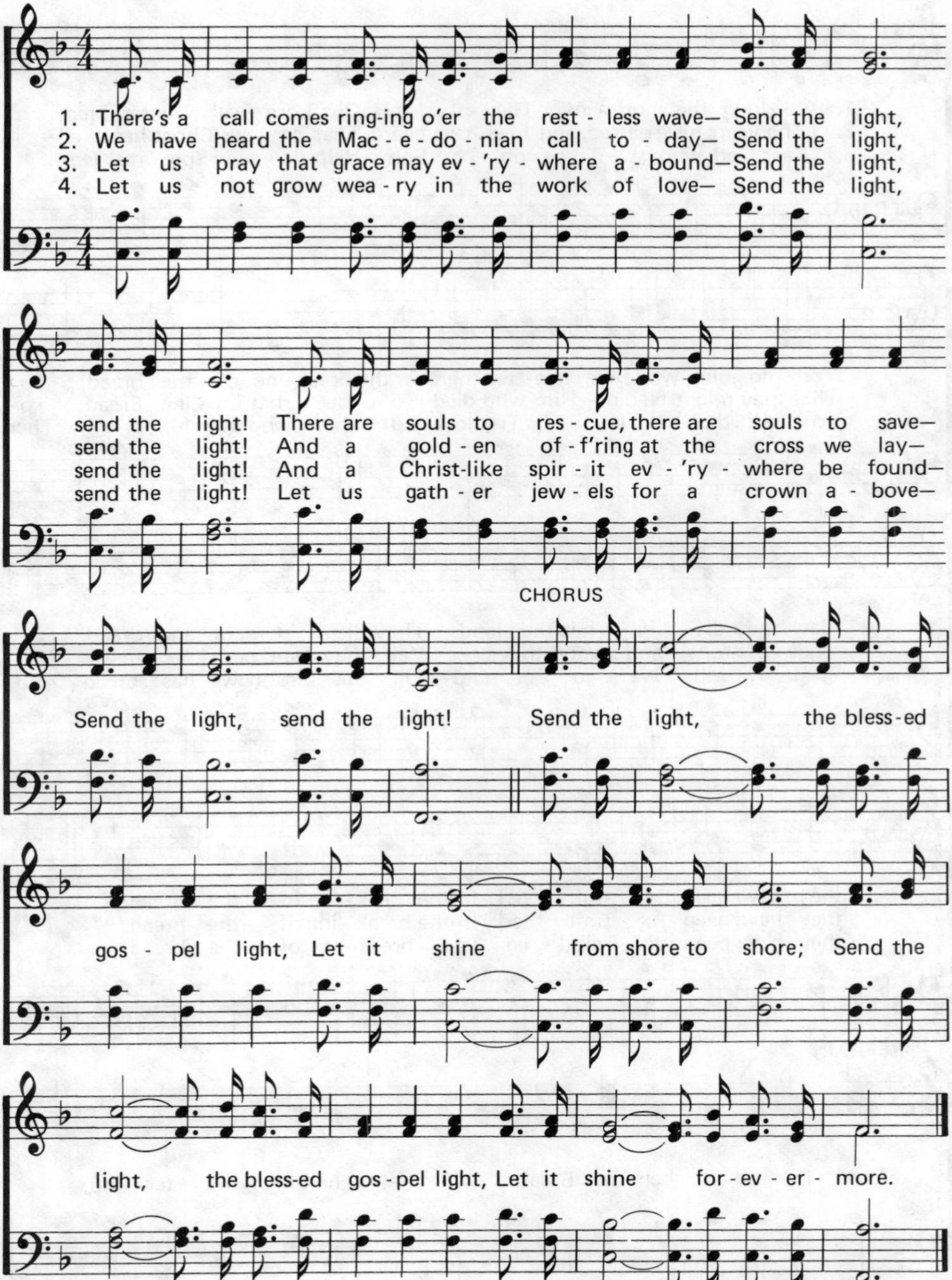

1. There's a call comes ring-ing o'er the rest - less wave— Send the light,
2. We have heard the Mac - e - do - nian call to - day— Send the light,
3. Let us pray that grace may ev - 'ry - where a - bound—Send the light,
4. Let us not grow wea - ry in the work of love— Send the light,

send the light! There are souls to res - cue, there are souls to save—
send the light! And a gold - en of - f'ring at the cross we lay—
send the light! And a Christ-like spir - it ev - 'ry - where be found—
send the light! Let us gath - er jew - els for a crown a - bove—

Send the light, send the light!

CHORUS

Send the light, the bless-ed gos - pel light, Let it shine from shore to shore; Send the light, the bless-ed gos - pel light, Let it shine for - ev - er - more.

506 — The Breaking of the Bread

Based on Mark 6:34-44
BEATRICE BUSH BIXLER

BEATRICE BUSH BIXLER

1. A - long the shores of Gal - i - lee Our Lord five thou - sand fed,
2. Long years have passed, and few have heard That Je - sus Christ has bled—
3. Great God, who gave Thine on - ly Son, Help us— now Spir - it - led—
Yet no one was o - mit - ted there In the break - ing of the bread; To -
That they might feed on Him who died To be that Liv - ing Bread; To -
To tell the sto - ry of Thy love To those who ask for bread; Then
day they die in hea-then lands, They die in want and dread, For
gods of stone and wood they cry, Yet they are nev - er fed, For
glad - ly will we go or send— Till this blest news has spread And
they have been o - mit - ted In the break - ing of the bread.
they have been o - mit - ted In the break - ing of the bread.
they have been in - clud - ed In the break - ing of the bread.
REFRAIN
Lord, I would give them the Bread of Life, The Liv-ing Wa - ter too;

My heart cries out, "O here am I— Read-y Thy will to do!"
Pass It On — 507
KURT KAISER
KURT KAISER
1. It only takes a spark to get a fire going,
2. What a wondrous time is spring—when all the trees are budding,
3. I wish for you, my friend, this happiness that I've found—
pass it on!
And soon all those around can warm up in its glowing;
The birds begin to sing, the flowers start their blooming;
You can depend on Him, it matters not where you're bound;
pass it on!
That's how it is with God's love, once you've experienced it: You
That's how it is with God's love, once you've experienced it: You
I'll shout it from the mountain top, I want my world to know: The
spread His love to ev'ryone, you want to pass it on.
want to sing, it's fresh like spring, you want to pass it on.
Lord of love has come to me, I want to pass it on.

508 — O Master, Let Me Walk with Thee
WASHINGTON GLADDEN
H. PERCY SMITH
1. O Mas - ter, let me walk with Thee In low - ly paths of serv - ice free; Tell me Thy se - cret— help me bear The strain of toil, the fret of care.
2. Help me the slow of heart to move By some clear, win - ning word of love; Teach me the way - ward feet to stay And guide them in the home - ward way.
3. Teach me Thy pa - tience! still with Thee In clos - er, dear - er com - pa - ny, In work that keeps faith sweet and strong, In trust that tri - umphs o - ver wrong.
4. In hope that sends a shin - ing ray Far down the fu - ture's broad - 'ning way, In peace that on - ly Thou canst give, With Thee, O Mas - ter, let me live.*
Tune: MARYTON
509 — In Christ There Is No East or West
JOHN OXENHAM
Traditional Spiritual
1. In Christ there is no East or West, In Him no South or North,
2. In Him shall true hearts ev - 'ry-where Their high com-mun - ion find;
3. Join hands then, broth-ers of the faith, What - e'er your race may be;
4. In Christ now meet both East and West, In Him meet South and North:
Tune: McKEE (Alternate, ST. PETER)
Words by permission of Miss Theo Oxenham.
Arr. © Singspiration 1979. All rights reserved.
SERVICE AND MISSION

But one great fel - low - ship of love Thru - out the whole wide earth.
His serv - ice is the gold - en cord Close - bind - ing all man - kind.
Who serves my Fa - ther as a son Is sure - ly kin to me.
All Christ - ly souls are one in Him Thru - out the whole wide earth.
Lord, Speak to Me — 510
FRANCES R. HAVERGAL
ROBERT SCHUMANN
1. Lord, speak to me, that I may speak In liv - ing ech - oes of Thy tone; As Thou hast sought, so let me seek Thy err - ing chil - dren lost and lone.
2. O teach me, Lord, that I may teach The pre - cious things Thou dost im - part; And wing my words that they may reach The hid - den depths of man - y a heart.
3. O fill me with Thy full - ness, Lord, Un - til my ver - y heart o'er - flow In kin - dling tho't and glow - ing word, Thy love to tell, Thy praise to show.
4. O use me, Lord, use e - ven me, Just as Thou wilt, and when, and where, Un - til Thy bless - ed face I see— Thy rest, Thy joy, Thy glo - ry share.*
Tune: CANONBURY

511 — Show a Little Bit of Love and Kindness

JOHN W. PETERSON JOHN W. PETERSON

1. Sing a song, (Sing a song,) spread some cheer, (spread some cheer,) There are
2. Of - fer help, (Of - fer help,) bring some hope, (bring some hope,) To the
3. Be a light, (Be a light,) show the way, (show the way,) Be a
sad and lone-ly peo-ple ev - 'ry - where; Be a friend, (Be a friend,) show some
faint-ing and dis-cour-aged on life's road; See a need, (See a need,) lend a
light with-in the night for those a - stray; Speak a word, (Speak a word,) lov - ing
love, (show some love,) It will lift them from the dungeons of de - spair.
hand, (lend a hand,) There are man - y who are crushed beneath their load.
word, (lov - ing word,) That will bring them back to walk the nar - row way.
CHORUS
Show a lit - tle bit of love and kind - ness, Nev-er go a-long with ha-tred's
blind - ness, Take a lit - tle time to reach for joy, and wear a hap-py face;

Sing a lit - tle bit when the days are drear-y, Give a lit - tle help to a friend who's
wea-ry— That's the way to make the world a hap - py place!
1,2 (3)
(a hap-py place!)
CODA ending (optional)
place, That's the way to make the world a hap-py place, a hap - py place!

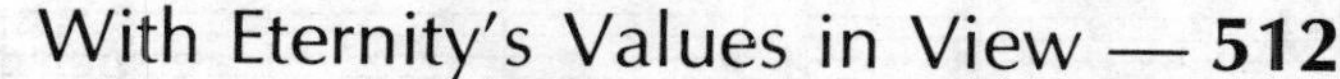

With Eternity's Values in View — 512

ALFRED B. SMITH

ALFRED B. SMITH

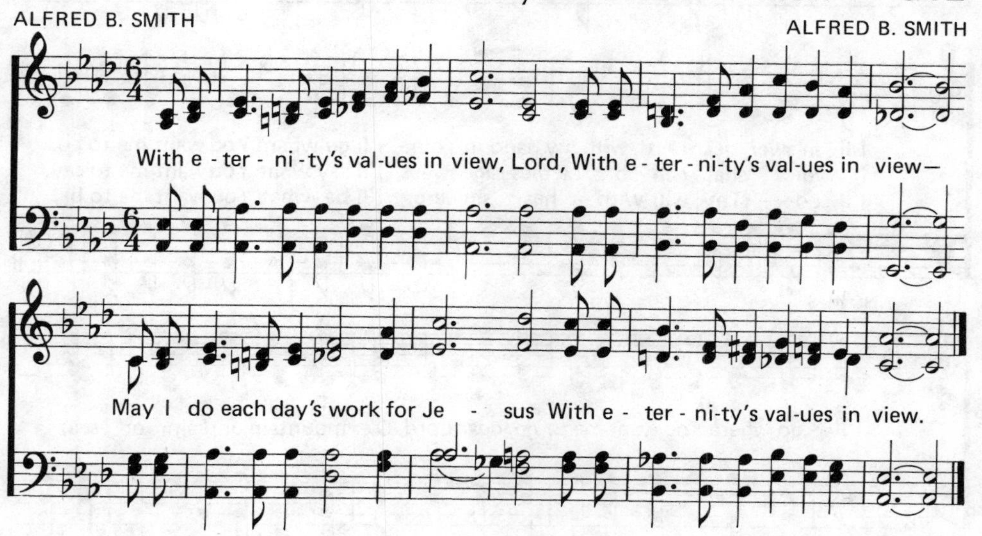
With e - ter - ni - ty's val-ues in view, Lord, With e - ter - ni - ty's val-ues in view—
May I do each day's work for Je - sus With e - ter - ni - ty's val-ues in view.

513 — I'll Go Where You Want Me to Go

1 - MARY BROWN
2,3 - CHARLES E. PRIOR

CARRIE E. ROUNSEFELL

1. It may not be on the mountain's height Or o - ver the storm-y sea,
2. Per - haps to - day there are lov - ing words Which Je - sus would have me speak,
3. There's sure-ly somewhere a low - ly place In earth's har-vest fields so wide,

It may not be at the bat - tle's front My Lord will have need of me;
There may be now, in the paths of sin, Some wand'rer whom I should seek;
Where I may la - bor thru life's short day For Je - sus the Cru - ci - fied;

But if by a still, small voice He calls To paths I do not know,
O Sav - ior, if Thou wilt be my Guide, Tho dark and rug-ged the way,
So, trust-ing my all un - to Thy care— I know Thou lov - est me—

I'll an-swer, dear Lord, with my hand in Thine, I'll go where You want me to go.
My voice shall ech - o the mes-sage sweet, I'll say what You want me to say.
I'll do Thy will with a heart sin-cere, I'll be what You want me to be.

CHORUS

I'll go where You want me to go, dear Lord, O'er mountain or plain or sea;

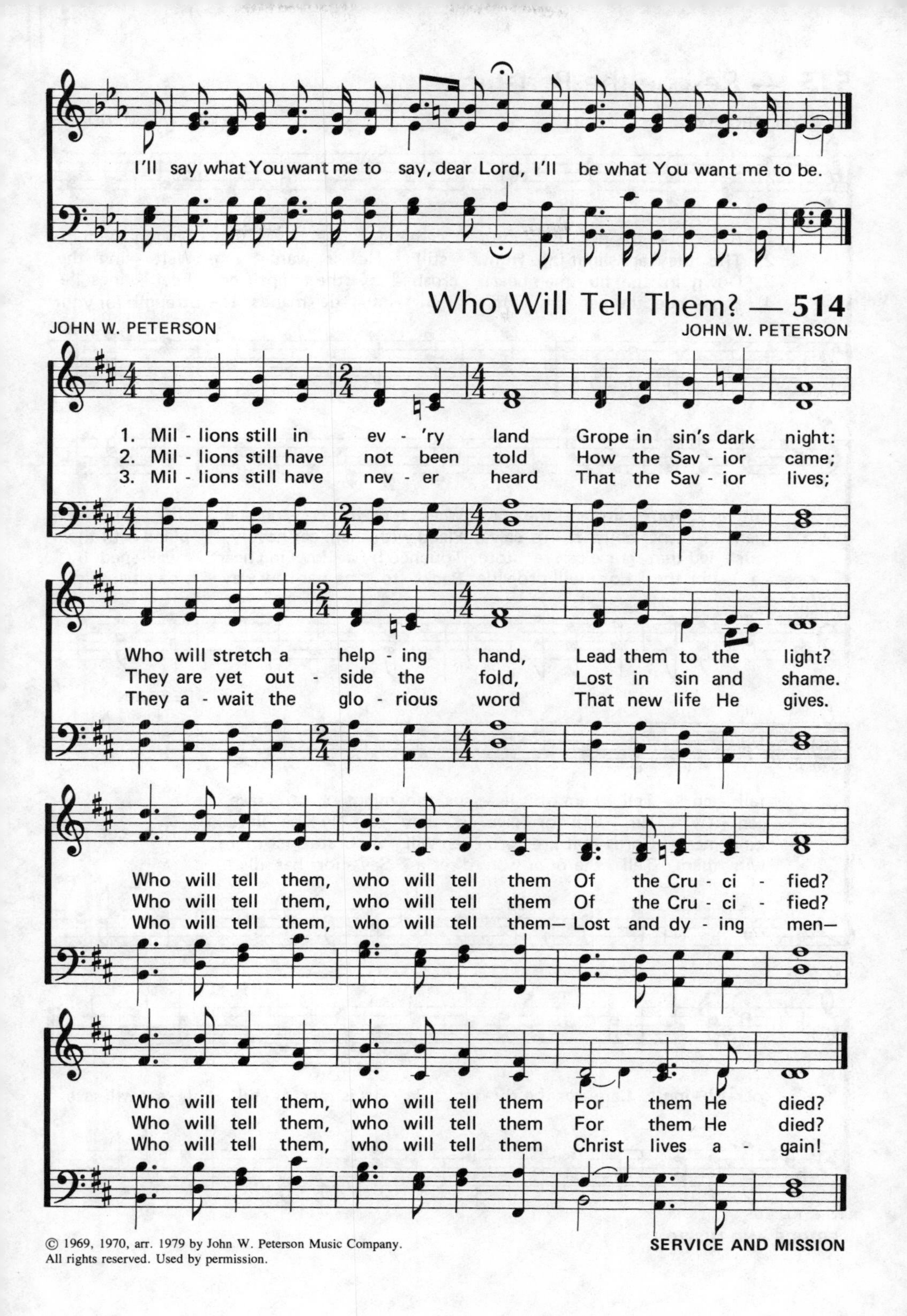
I'll say what You want me to say, dear Lord, I'll be what You want me to be.
Who Will Tell Them? — 514
JOHN W. PETERSON
JOHN W. PETERSON
1. Mil - lions still in ev - 'ry land Grope in sin's dark night:
2. Mil - lions still have not been told How the Sav - ior came;
3. Mil - lions still have nev - er heard That the Sav - ior lives;
Who will stretch a help - ing hand, Lead them to the light?
They are yet out - side the fold, Lost in sin and shame.
They a - wait the glo - rious word That new life He gives.
Who will tell them, who will tell them Of the Cru - ci - fied?
Who will tell them, who will tell them Of the Cru - ci - fied?
Who will tell them, who will tell them— Lost and dy - ing men—
Who will tell them, who will tell them For them He died?
Who will tell them, who will tell them For them He died?
Who will tell them, who will tell them Christ lives a - gain!

515 — Rescue the Perishing

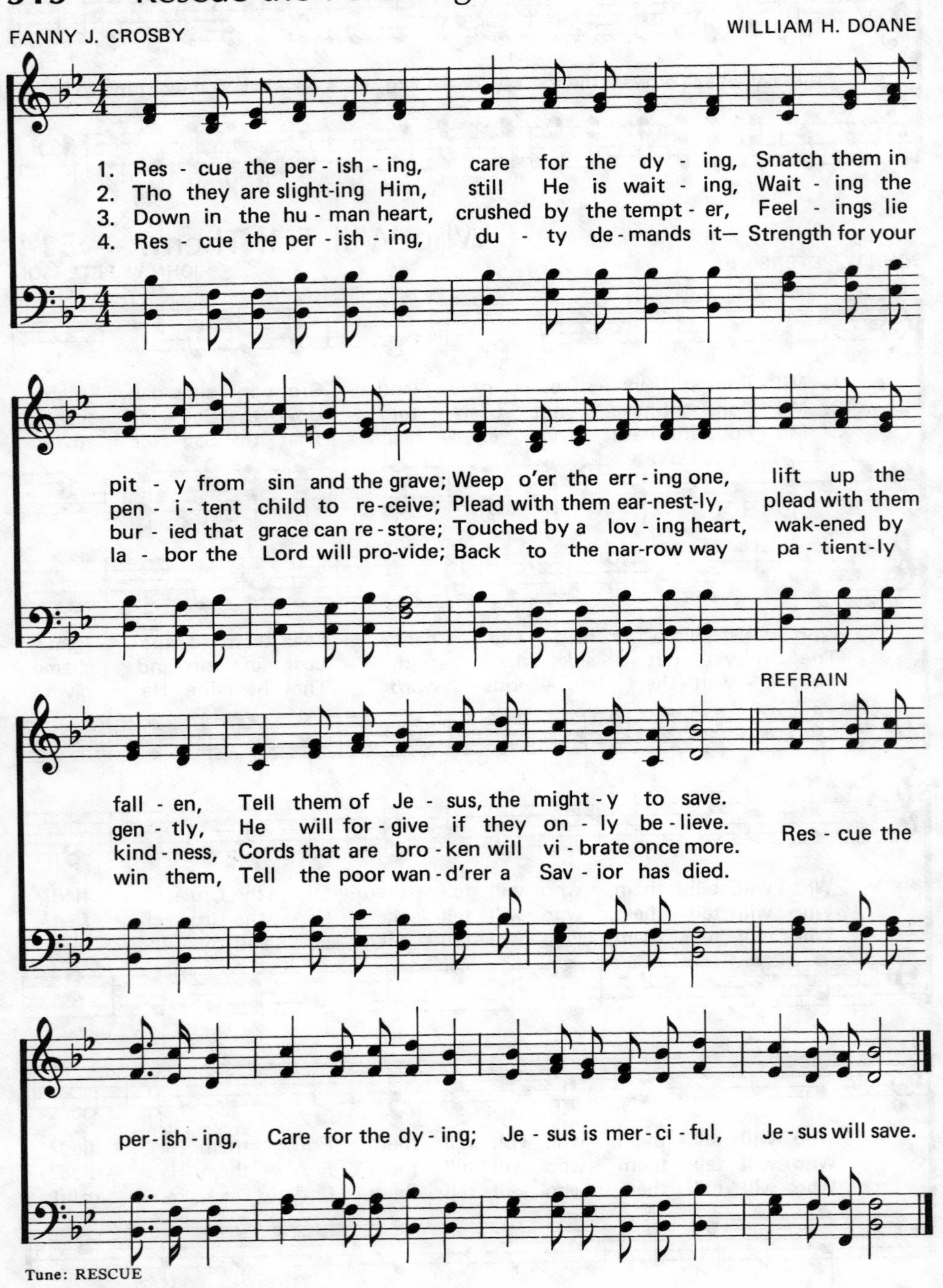

FANNY J. CROSBY
WILLIAM H. DOANE
1. Res - cue the per - ish - ing, care for the dy - ing, Snatch them in pit - y from sin and the grave; Weep o'er the err - ing one, lift up the fall - en, Tell them of Je - sus, the might - y to save.
2. Tho they are slight-ing Him, still He is wait - ing, Wait - ing the pen - i - tent child to re-ceive; Plead with them ear-nest-ly, plead with them gen - tly, He will for - give if they on - ly be - lieve.
3. Down in the hu - man heart, crushed by the tempt - er, Feel - ings lie bur - ied that grace can re - store; Touched by a lov - ing heart, wak-ened by kind - ness, Cords that are bro - ken will vi - brate once more.
4. Res - cue the per - ish - ing, du - ty de - mands it— Strength for your la - bor the Lord will pro-vide; Back to the nar-row way pa - tient-ly win them, Tell the poor wan - d'rer a Sav - ior has died.
REFRAIN
Res - cue the per-ish - ing, Care for the dy - ing; Je - sus is mer - ci - ful, Je - sus will save.

Tune: RESCUE

I Love to Tell the Story — 516
A. CATHERINE HANKEY
WILLIAM G. FISCHER
1. I love to tell the sto - ry of un - seen things a - bove, Of Je - sus
2. I love to tell the sto - ry—'tis pleas - ant to re - peat What seems, each
3. I love to tell the sto - ry, for those who know it best Seem hun-ger-
and His glo - ry, of Je - sus and His love; I love to tell the
time I tell it, more won-der-ful - ly sweet; I love to tell the
ing and thirst-ing to hear it like the rest; And when in scenes of
sto - ry be - cause I know 'tis true, It sat - is-fies my long-ings
sto - ry, for some have nev - er heard The mes-sage of sal - va - tion
glo - ry I sing the new, new song, 'Twill be the old, old sto - ry
REFRAIN
as noth - ing else can do.
from God's own ho - ly Word.
that I have loved so long.
I love to tell the sto - ry! 'Twill be my
theme in glo - ry— To tell the old, old sto - ry Of Je - sus and His love.

517 — Freely, Freely

CAROL OWENS
Based on Matthew 10:8; 28:18

CAROL OWENS

1. God for - gave my sin in Je - sus' name, I've been born a - gain in
2. All pow'r is giv'n in Je - sus' name, In earth and heav'n in
Je - sus' name; And in Je - sus' name I come to you To share
Je - sus' name; And in Je - sus' name I come to you To share
His love as He told me to:
His pow'r as He told me to:
REFRAIN
He said, "Free - ly, free - ly
you have re - ceived—Free - ly, free - ly give; Go in my
name and, be - cause you be - lieve, Oth - ers will know that I live."

SERVICE AND MISSION

It Took a Miracle — 518

JOHN W. PETERSON JOHN W. PETERSON

1. My Fa - ther is om - ni - po - tent, And that you can't de - ny;
2. Tho here His glo - ry has been shown, We still can't ful - ly see
3. The Bi - ble tells us of His pow'r And wis - dom all way thru,
A God of might and mir - a - cles— 'Tis writ - ten in the sky.
The won - ders of His might, His throne—'Twill take e - ter - ni - ty.
And ev - 'ry lit - tle bird and flow'r Are tes - ti - mo - nies too.
CHORUS
It took a mir - a - cle to put the stars in place, It took a
mir - a - cle to hang the world in space; But when He saved my soul,
Cleansed and made me whole, It took a mir - a - cle of love and grace.

519 — Love Lifted Me

JAMES ROWE HOWARD E. SMITH

1. I was sink-ing deep in sin, Far from the peace-ful shore, Ver-y deep-ly
2. All my heart to Him I give, Ev-er to Him I'll cling, In His bless-ed
3. Souls in dan-ger, look a-bove, Je-sus com-plete-ly saves; He will lift you
stained with-in, Sink-ing to rise no more; But the Mas-ter of the sea
pres-ence live, Ev-er His prais-es sing. Love so might-y and so true
by His love Out of the an-gry waves. He's the Mas-ter of the sea,
Heard my de-spair-ing cry, From the wa-ters lift-ed me—Now safe am I.
Mer-its my soul's best songs; Faith-ful, lov-ing serv-ice too To Him be-longs.
Bil-lows His will o-bey; He your Sav-ior wants to be— Be saved to-day.
CHORUS
Love lift-ed me, Love lift-ed me; When noth-ing
e-ven me, e-ven me;
else could help, Love lift-ed me. Love lift-ed me,
e-ven me,

Love lift - ed me; When noth-ing else could help, Love lift-ed me.
e - ven me;
O How I Love Jesus — 520
FREDERICK WHITFIELD
American melody
Arr. by John W. Peterson
1. There is a name I love to hear, I love to sing its worth;
2. It tells me of a Sav - ior's love, Who died to set me free;
3. It tells me what my Fa - ther hath In store for ev - 'ry day,
4. It tells of One whose lov - ing heart Can feel my deep - est woe,
It sounds like mu - sic in mine ear, The sweet - est name on earth.
It tells me of His pre-cious blood, The sin - ner's per-fect plea.
And, tho I tread a dark - some path, Yields sun-shine all the way.
Who in each sor - row bears a part That none can bear be - low.
CHORUS
O how I love Je - sus, O how I love Je - sus,
O how I love Je - sus— Be - cause He first loved me!
Arr. © Singspiration 1966. All rights reserved.
WITNESS AND TESTIMONY

521 — I've Found a Friend

JAMES G. SMALL GEORGE C. STEBBINS

1. I've found a friend, O such a friend! He loved me ere I knew Him;
2. I've found a friend, O such a friend! He bled, He died to save me;
3. I've found a friend, O such a friend! All pow'r to Him is giv - en
4. I've found a friend, O such a friend! So kind and true and ten - der,
He drew me with the cords of love, And thus He bound me to Him.
And not a - lone the gift of life, But His own self He gave me.
To guard me on my on-ward course And bring me safe to heav-en.
So wise a coun-sel - lor and guide, So might - y a de - fend-er!
And round my heart still close - ly twine Those ties which naught can sev-er,
Naught that I have my own I call, I hold it for the giv - er:
Th'e - ter - nal glo - ries gleam a - far To nerve my faint en - deav-or:
From Him who loves me now so well, What pow'r my soul can sev - er?
For I am His and He is mine, For - ev - er and for - ev - er.
My heart, my strength, my life, my all Are His, and His for - ev - er.
So now to watch, to work, to war, And then to rest for - ev - er.
Shall life or death or earth or hell? No— I am His for - ev - er.

Tune: FRIEND

WITNESS AND TESTIMONY

CHARLES H. GABRIEL

CHARLES H. GABRIEL

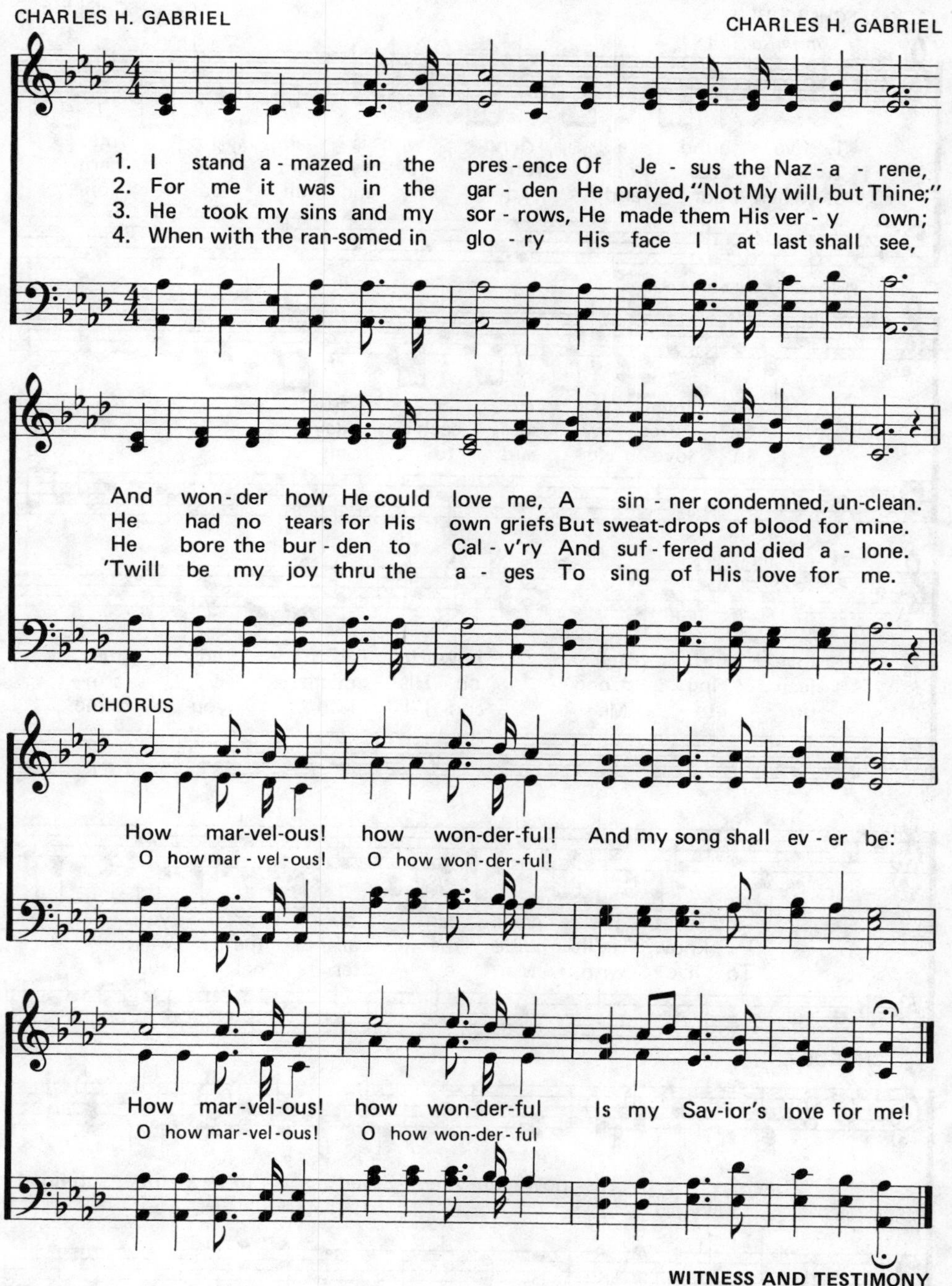
1. I stand a-mazed in the pres-ence Of Je-sus the Naz-a-rene,
2. For me it was in the gar-den He prayed, "Not My will, but Thine;"
3. He took my sins and my sor-rows, He made them His ver-y own;
4. When with the ran-somed in glo-ry His face I at last shall see,
And won-der how He could love me, A sin-ner condemned, un-clean.
He had no tears for His own griefs But sweat-drops of blood for mine.
He bore the bur-den to Cal-v'ry And suf-fered and died a-lone.
'Twill be my joy thru the a-ges To sing of His love for me.
CHORUS
How mar-vel-ous! how won-der-ful! And my song shall ev-er be:
O how mar-vel-ous! O how won-der-ful!
How mar-vel-ous! how won-der-ful Is my Sav-ior's love for me!
O how mar-vel-ous! O how won-der-ful

523 — Saved, Saved!

JACK P. SCHOLFIELD JACK P. SCHOLFIELD

In unison

1. I've found a friend who is all to me,
2. He saves me from ev - 'ry sin and harm,
3. When poor and need - y and all a - lone,

Play melody and bass in octaves

His love is ev - er true; I
Se - cures my soul each day; I'm
In love He said to me, "Come

love to tell how He lift - ed me
lean - ing strong on His might - y arm—
un - to Me and I'll lead you home

And what His grace can do for you.
I know He'll guide me all the way.
To live with Me e - ter - nal - ly."

CHORUS *Parts*

Saved by His pow'r di - vine, Saved to new life sub - lime!
I'm saved I'm saved

Life now is sweet and my joy is com-plete, For I'm saved, saved, saved!
At Calvary — 524
WILLIAM R. NEWELL
DANIEL B. TOWNER
1. Years I spent in van - i - ty and pride, Car - ing not my Lord was cru - ci - fied, Know-ing not it was for me He died On Cal - va - ry.
2. By God's Word at last my sin I learned— Then I trem-bled at the law I'd spurned, Till my guilt - y soul im - plor-ing turned To Cal - va - ry.
3. Now I've giv'n to Je - sus ev - 'ry - thing, Now I glad - ly own Him as my King, Now my rap-tured soul can on - ly sing Of Cal - va - ry
4. O the love that drew sal - va - tion's plan! O the grace that bro't it down to man! O the might - y gulf that God did span At Cal - va - ry.
CHORUS
Mer - cy there was great and grace was free, Par - don there was mul - ti - plied to me, There my bur-dened soul found lib-er-ty—At Cal - va - ry.
WITNESS AND TESTIMONY

525 — Heaven Came Down

JOHN W. PETERSON JOHN W. PETERSON

1. O what a won-der-ful, won-der-ful day— Day I will nev-er for - get;
2. Born of the Spir-it with life from a-bove In - to God's fam-'ly di - vine,
3. Now I've a hope that will sure-ly en-dure Aft - er the pass-ing of time;
Aft - er I'd wandered in dark-ness a - way, Je - sus my Sav-ior I met.
Jus - ti-fied ful-ly thru Cal - va-ry's love, O what a stand-ing is mine!
I have a fu-ture in heav - en for sure, There in those mansions sub - lime.
O what a ten - der, com-pas - sion-ate friend—He met the need of my heart;
And the trans-ac-tion so quick-ly was made When as a sin - ner I came,
And it's be-cause of that won-der-ful day When at the cross I be - lieved;
Shadows dispelling, With joy I am tell-ing, He made all the dark-ness de-part!
Took of the of-fer Of grace He did proffer—He saved me, O praise His dear name!
Rich-es e - ter-nal And blessings su-per-nal From His precious hand I re - ceived.

WITNESS AND TESTIMONY

CHORUS
Heav-en came down and glo-ry filled my soul,
filled my soul,
When at the cross the Sav-ior made me whole;
made me whole;
My
sins were washed a - way And my night was turned to day—
D.C.
Heav-en came down and glo-ry filled my soul!
filled my soul!
CODA (after last chorus only)
Heav - en came down and glo - ry filled my soul!

WITNESS AND TESTIMONY

526 — Victory in Jesus

EUGENE M. BARTLETT EUGENE M. BARTLETT

1. I heard an old, old sto - ry, how a Sav - ior came from glo - ry,
2. I heard a - bout His heal - ing, of His cleans-ing pow'r re - veal - ing,
3. I heard a - bout a man - sion He has built for me in glo - ry,

How He gave His life on Cal - va - ry to save a wretch like me;
How He made the lame to walk a - gain and caused the blind to see;
And I heard a - bout the streets of gold be - yond the crys - tal sea,

I heard a - bout His groan - ing, of His pre-cious blood's a - ton - ing,
And then I cried, "Dear Je - sus, come and heal my bro - ken spir - it,"
A - bout the an - gels sing - ing and the old re - demp - tion sto - ry—

Then I re - pent - ed of my sins and won the vic - to - ry.
And some - how Je - sus came and brought to me the vic - to - ry.
And some sweet day I'll sing up there the song of vic - to - ry.

CHORUS

O vic - to - ry in Je - sus, my Sav - ior, for - ev - er! He sought me and

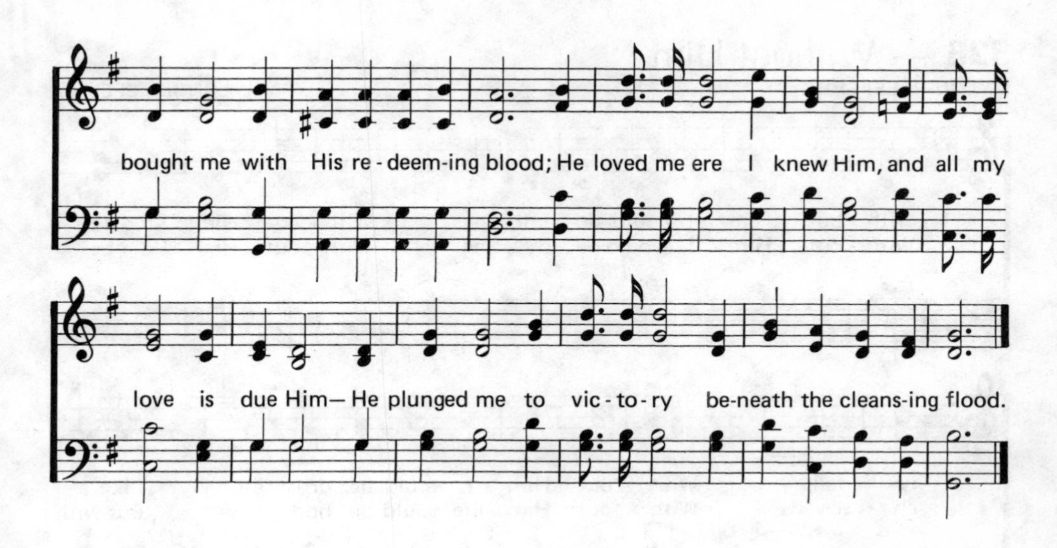
bought me with His re-deem-ing blood; He loved me ere I knew Him, and all my
love is due Him— He plunged me to vic-to-ry be-neath the cleans-ing flood.

Got Any Rivers? — 527

OSCAR ELIASON

OSCAR ELIASON

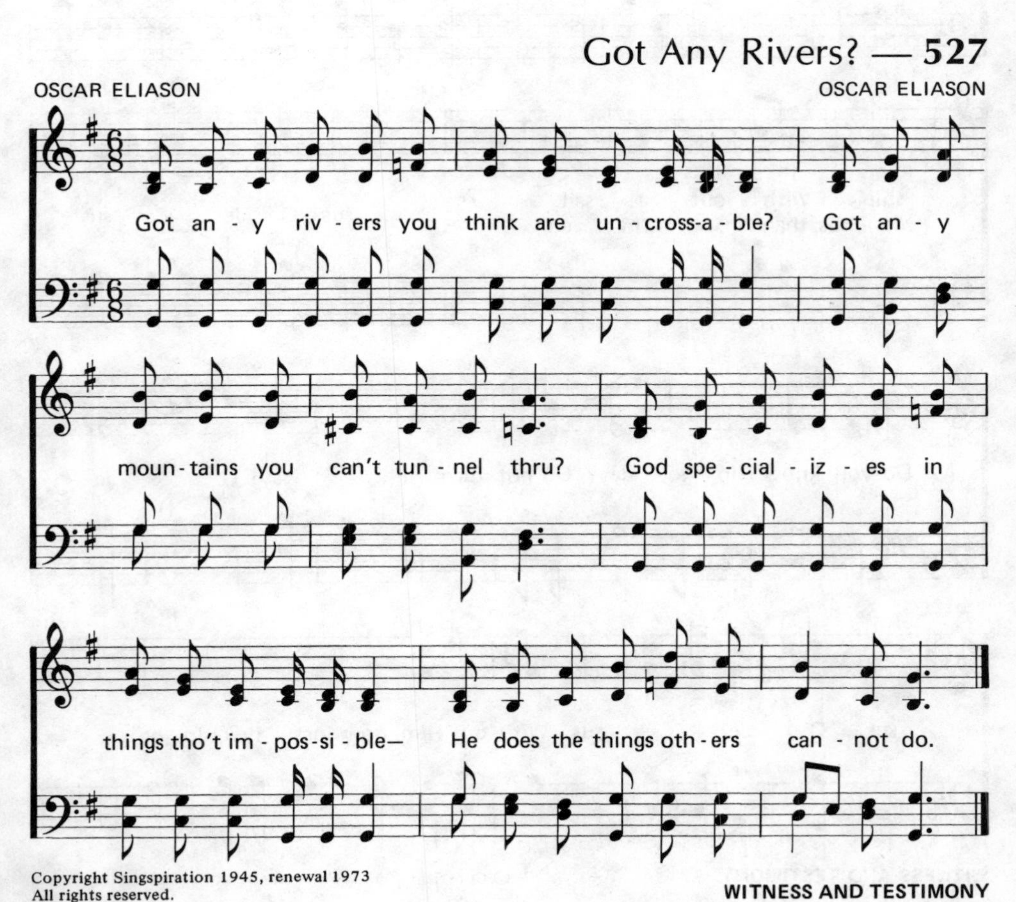
Got an-y riv-ers you think are un-cross-a-ble? Got an-y
moun-tains you can't tun-nel thru? God spe-cial-iz-es in
things tho't im-pos-si-ble— He does the things oth-ers can-not do.

528 — Without Him

MYLON R. LEFEVRE — MYLON R. LEFEVRE

1. With - out Him I could do noth - ing, With - out Him I'd sure - ly fail; With - out Him I would be drift - ing Like a ship with - out a sail.

2. With - out Him I would be dy - ing, With - out Him I'd be en - slaved; With - out Him life would be hope - less— But with Je - sus, thank God, I'm saved.

CHORUS

Je - sus, O Je - sus! Do you know Him to - day? Do not turn Him a - way! O Je - sus, O Je - sus, With - out Him, how lost I would be.

JOHNSON OATMAN, Jr.

GEORGE C. HUGG

1. There's not a friend like the low-ly Je-sus— No, not one! no, not one!
2. No friend like Him is so high and ho-ly— No, not one! no, not one!
3. There's not an hour that He is not near us— No, not one! no, not one!
4. Did ev-er saint find this friend for-sake Him? No, not one! no, not one!
5. Was e'er a gift like the Sav-ior giv-en? No, not one! no, not one!
None else could heal all our soul's dis-eas-es— No, not one! no, not one!
And yet no friend is so meek and low-ly— No, not one! no, not one!
No night so dark but His love can cheer us— No, not one! no, not one!
Or sin-ner find that He would not take Him? No, not one! no, not one!
Will He re-fuse us a home in heav-en? No, not one! no, not one!
REFRAIN
Je-sus knows all a-bout our strug-gles, He will guide till the day is done;
There's not a friend like the low-ly Je-sus— No, not one! no, not one!

530 — He Was There All the Time
GARY S. PAXTON
GARY S. PAXTON
1. Time aft - er time I went search-ing for peace in some void— I was
2. Nev - er a - gain will I look for a fake rain-bow's end— Now that
try - ing to blame all my ills on this world I was in;
I have the an - swer my life is just start - ing to rhyme;
Sur - face re - la - tion - ships used me till I was done in—
Shar - ing each new day with Him is a cup of fresh life—
And all the while Some-one was beg - ging to free me from sin!
But O what I missed! He'd been wait - ing right there all the time!
CHORUS
He was there all the time, He was there all the time;
WITNESS AND TESTIMONY
© Copyright 1975 by New Pax Music Press. All rights reserved.

Wait-ing pa-tient-ly in line, He was there all the time!
What a Wonderful Savior! — 531
ELISHA A. HOFFMAN
ELISHA A. HOFFMAN
1. Christ has for sin a-tone-ment made—What a won-der-ful Sav-ior!
2. I praise Him for the cleans-ing blood—What a won-der-ful Sav-ior!
3. He cleansed my heart from all its sin— What a won-der-ful Sav-ior!
4. He gives me o-ver-com-ing pow'r—What a won-der-ful Sav-ior!
We are re-deemed, the price is paid—What a won-der-ful Sav-ior!
That rec-on-ciled my soul to God—What a won-der-ful Sav-ior!
And now He reigns and rules there-in— What a won-der-ful Sav-ior!
And tri-umph in each try-ing hour—What a won-der-ful Sav-ior!
REFRAIN
What a won-der-ful Sav-ior is Je-sus, my Je-sus!
What a won-der-ful Sav-ior is Je-sus, my Lord!

532 — He Touched Me
WILLIAM J. GAITHER
WILLIAM J. GAITHER
1. Shack-led by a heav - y bur-den, 'Neath a load of guilt and shame— Then the hand of Je - sus touched me, And now I am no long - er the same.
2. Since I met this bless - ed Sav - ior, Since He cleansed and made me whole, I will nev-er cease to praise Him— I'll shout it while e - ter - ni - ty rolls.
CHORUS
He touched me, O He touched me, And O the joy that floods my soul! Some-thing happened, and now I know He touched me and made me whole.
WITNESS AND TESTIMONY
©Copyright 1963 by William J. Gaither. All rights reserved.

I Believe in Miracles — 533
CARLTON C. BUCK
JOHN W. PETERSON
1. Cre - a - tion shows the power of God—There's glo-ry all a - round, And
2. I can-not doubt the work of God—It's plain for all to see; The
3. The love of God! O pow'r di - vine! 'Tis won-der-ful to see The
those who see must stand in awe, For mir - a - cles a - bound.
mir - a - cles that He has wrought Should lead to Cal - va - ry.
mir - a - cle of grace per-formed With - in the heart of me.
CHORUS
I be-lieve in mir-a-cles—I've seen a soul set free, Mi - rac - u-lous the
change in one Re-deemed thru Cal-va - ry; I've seen the lil - y push its way Up
thru the stub-born sod— I be-lieve in mir-a-cles, For I be-lieve in God!

534 — Love Found a Way

AVIS B. CHRISTIANSEN | HARRY DIXON LOES

1. Won-der-ful love that res-cued me, Sunk deep in sin, Guilt-y and
2. Love bro't my Sav-ior here to die On Cal-va-ry, For such a
3. Love o-pened wide the gates of light To heav'n's do-main, Where in e-

vile as I could be— No hope with-in; When ev-'ry ray of
sin-ful wretch as I— How can it be? Love bridged the gulf 'twixt
ter-nal pow'r and might Je-sus shall reign; Love lift-ed me from

light had fled, O glo-rious day! Rais-ing my soul from out the dead,
me and heav'n, Taught me to pray; I am re-deemed, set free, for-giv'n—
depths of woe To end-less day; There was no help in earth be-low—

CHORUS
Love found a way. Love found a way to re-deem my soul,
Love found a way that could make me whole; Love sent my Lord

to the cross of shame, Love found a way—O praise His ho-ly name!
Satisfied — 535
CLARA TEAR WILLIAMS
RALPH E. HUDSON
1. All my life long I had pant-ed For a drink, from some clear spring,
2. Feed-ing on the husks a-round me, Till my strength was al-most gone,
3. Well of wa-ter ev-er spring-ing, Bread of life so rich and free,
That I hoped would quench the burn-ing Of the thirst I felt with-in.
Longed my soul for some-thing bet-ter, On-ly still to hun-ger on.
Un-told wealth that nev-er fail-eth, My Re-deem-er is to me.
CHORUS
Hal-le-lu-jah! I have found Him Whom my soul so long has craved!
Je-sus sat-is-fies my long-ings—Thru His blood I now am saved.
WITNESS AND TESTIMONY

536 — My Tribute

ANDRAÉ CROUCH

ANDRAÉ CROUCH

How can I say thanks for the things You have done for me— Things
so un - de - served, yet You give to prove Your love for me? The voic - es
of a mil - lion an - gels could not ex - press my grat - i - tude— All
that I am and ev - er hope to be, I owe it all to Thee.
To God be the glo - ry, To God be the glo - ry, To

God be the glo - ry For the things He has done! With His
blood He has saved me, With His pow'r He has raised me— To
blood He has saved me, With His pow'r He has raised me— To
1
To next strain
2
Fine
God be the glo - ry For the things He has done!
God be the glo - ry For the things He has done!
Just let me live my life— Let it be pleas-ing, Lord, to Thee; And
D.S.
should I gain an - y praise, Let it go to Cal - va - ry. With His

537 — New Life!
JOHN W. PETERSON
JOHN W. PETERSON
1. Gone is the guilt of my sin, (my sin,) Peace is now reign-ing with - in; (with-in;) Since I be-lieved—par-don re-ceived— Hap-py, so hap-py I've been. (I've been.)
2. Bright-er the jour-ney each day, (each day,) Tho there is much to dis - may; (dis-may;) Heav-en a - waits—bright pearl-y gates— There at the end of the way. (the way.)
3. Come with your sin - bur-dened heart, (your heart,) Christ will His cleans-ing im - part; (im-part;) He will for-give— in Him you'll live— O how the joy-bells will start. (will start.)
CHORUS
New life in Christ, a - bun - dant and free! What glo-ries shine, what joys are mine, What wondrous blessings I see! My past with its sin, the search-ing and strife, For-

ev-er gone—there's a bright new dawn! For in Christ I have found new life!
Now I Belong to Jesus — 538
NORMAN J. CLAYTON
NORMAN J. CLAYTON
1. Je - sus my Lord will love me for-ev - er, From Him no pow'r of
2. Once I was lost in sin's deg-ra-da - tion, Je - sus came down to
3. Joy floods my soul, for Je - sus has saved me, Freed me from sin that
e - vil can sev - er; He gave His life to ran - som my soul—
bring me sal - va - tion, Lift - ed me up from sor - row and shame—
long had en-slaved me; His pre-cious blood He gave to re - deem—
CHORUS
Now I be-long to Him! Now I be-long to Je - sus, Je - sus belongs to me— Not for the years of time a - lone, But for e - ter - ni - ty.
WITNESS AND TESTIMONY

539 — I Will Sing of My Redeemer
PHILIP P. BLISS
JAMES McGRANAHAN
1. I will sing of my Re-deem-er And His won-drous love to me;
2. I will tell the won-drous sto-ry, How, my lost es-tate to save,
3. I will praise my dear Re-deem-er, His tri-um-phant pow'r I'll tell,
4. I will sing of my Re-deem-er And His heav'n-ly love to me;
On the cru-el cross He suf-fered, From the curse to set me free.
In His bound-less love and mer-cy, He the ran-som free-ly gave.
How the vic-to-ry He giv-eth O-ver sin and death and hell.
He from death to life hath bro't me, Son of God with Him to be.
CHORUS
Sing, O sing of my Re-deem-er,
of my Re-deem-er, Sing, O sing of my Re-deem-er,
With His blood He pur-chased me;
He pur-chased me, With His blood He pur-chased me;

Alternative tune, HYFRYDOL (57, 172)

On the cross He sealed my par - don,
He sealed my par - don, On the cross He sealed my par - don,
Paid the debt and made me free.
and made me free, and made me free.
I Can Do All Things — 540
Based on Philippians 4:13
HOMER W. GRIMES
HOMER W. GRIMES
Arr. by Jon Drevits
I can do all things thru Christ who strength-ens me! I can do all
things thru Christ who strength-ens me! Day by day, hour by hour, I am
kept by His pow'r: I can do all things thru Christ who strength-ens me!

541 — In the Garden

C. AUSTIN MILES
C. AUSTIN MILES
1. I come to the gar - den a - lone, While the dew is still on the ros - es; And the voice I hear, fall - ing on my ear, The Son of God dis - clos - es.
2. He speaks, and the sound of His voice Is so sweet the birds hush their sing - ing; And the mel - o - dy that He gave to me With - in my heart is ring - ing.
3. I'd stay in the gar - den with Him Tho the night a - round me be fall - ing; But He bids me go— thru the voice of woe, His voice to me is call - ing.
REFRAIN
And He walks with me, and He talks with me, And He tells me I am His own; And the joy we share as we tar - ry there None oth - er has ev - er known.

WITNESS AND TESTIMONY

Jesus Loves Even Me — 542
PHILIP P. BLISS
PHILIP P. BLISS
1. I am so glad that our Fa - ther in heav'n Tells of His love in the Book He has giv'n; Won - der - ful things in the Bi - ble I see— This is the dear - est, that Je - sus loves me.
2. Tho I for - get Him and wan - der a - way, Still He doth love me wher - ev - er I stray; Back to His dear lov - ing arms would I flee When I re - mem - ber that Je - sus loves me.
3. O if there's on - ly one song I can sing When in His beau - ty I see the great King, This shall my song in e - ter - ni - ty be: "O what a won - der that Je - sus loves me!"
CHORUS
I am so glad that Je - sus loves me, Je - sus loves me, Je - sus loves me;
I am so glad that Je - sus loves me, Je - sus loves e - ven me.

543 — Through It All
ANDRAÉ CROUCH
ANDRAÉ CROUCH
1. I've had man - y tears and sor-rows, I've had ques-tions for to - mor-row, There've been times I did-n't know right from wrong; But in ev - 'ry sit - u - a - tion God gave bless - ed con - so - la - tion That my tri - als come to on - ly make me strong.
2. I've been to lots of plac-es, And I've seen a lot of fac - es, There've been times I felt so all a - lone; But in my lone - ly hours, Yes, those pre - cious lone - ly hours, Je - sus let me know that I was His own.
3. I thank God for the moun-tains, And I thank Him for the val - leys, I thank Him for the storms He bro't me through; For if I'd nev - er had a prob - lem I would - n't know that He could solve them, I'd nev - er know what faith in God could do.
CHORUS
Through it all, Through it all, I've learned to trust in
WITNESS AND TESTIMONY
©Copyright 1971, arr. 1974 by Manna Music, Inc. All rights reserved.

Je - sus, I've learned to trust in God; Through it all,
Through it all, I've learned to de - pend up - on His Word.
Something Beautiful — 544
GLORIA GAITHER
WILLIAM J. GAITHER
Some-thing beau-ti - ful, some-thing good— All my con-
fu - sion He un-der - stood; All I had to of-fer Him was
bro-ken-ness and strife, But He made some - thing beau-ti-ful of my life.
© Copyright 1971 by William J. Gaither. All rights reserved.
WITNESS AND TESTIMONY

545 — He Lifted Me

CHARLES H. GABRIEL CHARLES H. GABRIEL

1. In lov-ing-kind-ness Je-sus came My soul in mer-cy to re-claim,
2. He called me long be-fore I heard, Be-fore my sin-ful heart was stirred,
3. His brow was pierced with man-y a thorn, His hands by cru-el nails were torn,
4. Now on a high-er plane I dwell, And with my soul I know 'tis well;
And from the depths of sin and shame Thru grace He lift-ed me.
But when I took Him at His word, For-giv'n He lift-ed me.
When from my guilt and grief, for-lorn, In love He lift-ed me.
Yet how or why, I can-not tell, He should have lift-ed me.
He lift-ed me.
CHORUS
From sink-ing sand He lift-ed me, With ten-der hand He lift-ed me;
From shades of night to plains of light, O praise His name, He lift-ed me!

I Will Sing the Wondrous Story — 546

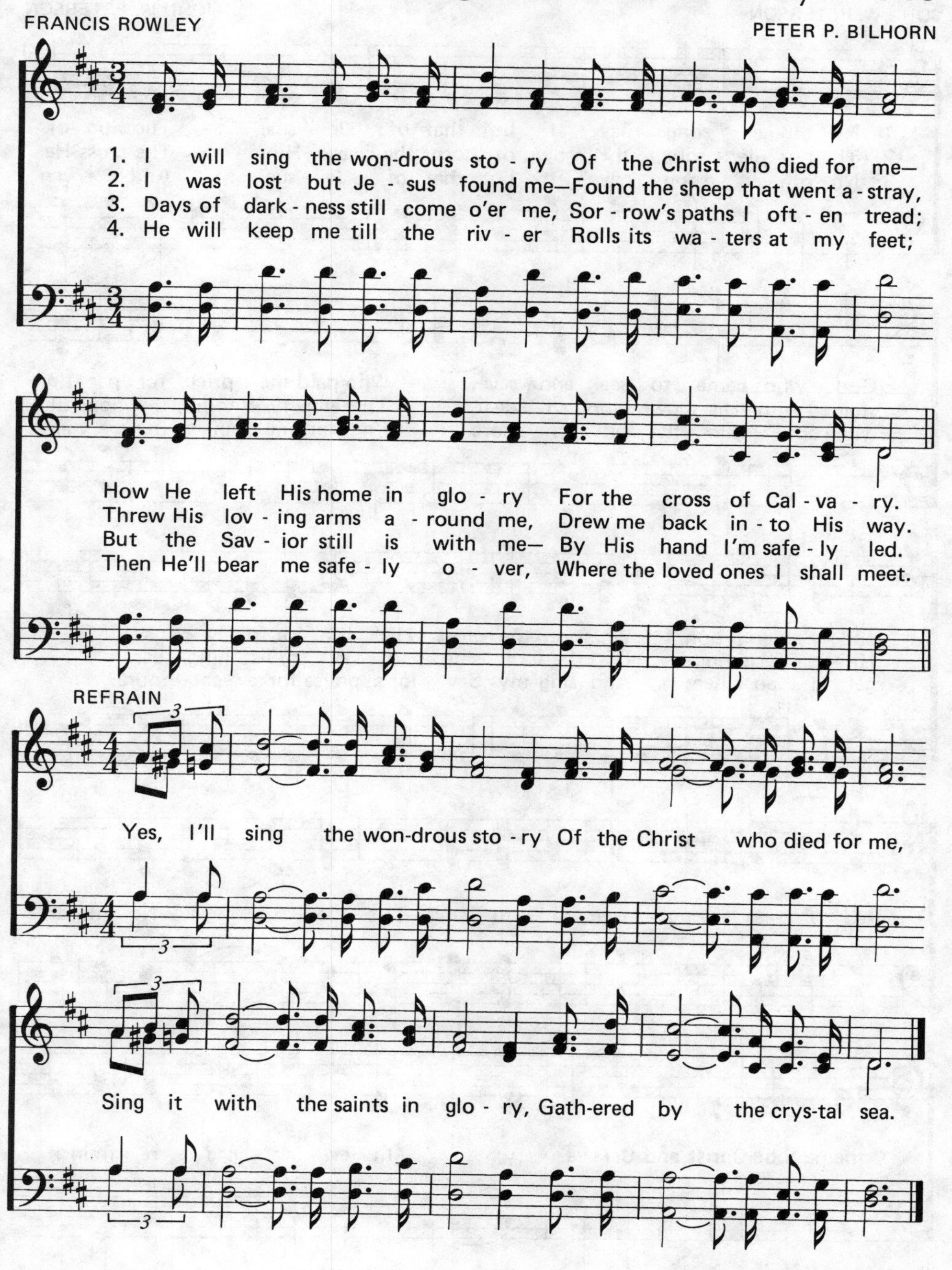
FRANCIS ROWLEY
PETER P. BILHORN
1. I will sing the won-drous sto - ry Of the Christ who died for me—
2. I was lost but Je - sus found me—Found the sheep that went a - stray,
3. Days of dark - ness still come o'er me, Sor - row's paths I oft - en tread;
4. He will keep me till the riv - er Rolls its wa - ters at my feet;
How He left His home in glo - ry For the cross of Cal - va - ry.
Threw His lov - ing arms a - round me, Drew me back in - to His way.
But the Sav - ior still is with me— By His hand I'm safe - ly led.
Then He'll bear me safe - ly o - ver, Where the loved ones I shall meet.
REFRAIN
Yes, I'll sing the won-drous sto - ry Of the Christ who died for me,
Sing it with the saints in glo - ry, Gath-ered by the crys-tal sea.

547 — No Other Song
JOHN W. PETERSON
JOHN W. PETERSON
1. No oth - er song have I but that of Je - sus, The Son of God who came to seek and save, Who paid the price for par - don and re - demp-tion When on the cross His life He free-ly gave.
2. The pur - ple robe, the crown of thorns they gave Him, The cross He stained with His own blood so dear, The emp - ty tomb, the hope of His re - turn - ing— Of these I'll sing to ev - 'ry list-'ning ear.
3. No oth - er song have I but that of Je - sus, And e - ven when I gain the oth - er shore I'll join me in the great an - gel - ic an - them And sing my Sav - ior's praise for - ev - er - more.
CHORUS
No oth - er song have I to sing but Je - sus, No oth - er theme but Christ and Cal - va - ry; In ev - 'ry glad re - frain I

would be tell - ing The won-ders of His might-y love for me.
Glory to His Name — 548
ELISHA A. HOFFMAN
JOHN H. STOCKTON
1. Down at the cross where my Sav - ior died, Down where for cleans - ing from sin I cried, There to my heart was the blood ap - plied—
2. I am so won-drous-ly saved from sin, Je - sus so sweet - ly a - bides with-in; There at the cross where He took me in—
3. O pre - cious foun-tain that saves from sin, I am so glad I have en - tered in; There Je - sus saves me and keeps me clean—
4. Come to this foun-tain so rich and sweet, Cast thy poor soul at the Sav - ior's feet; Plunge in to-day and be made com-plete—
Glo - ry to His name.
REFRAIN
Glo-ry to His name, Glo - ry to His name; There to my heart was the blood ap - plied— Glo - ry to His name.
WITNESS AND TESTIMONY

549 — He's Everything to Me

RALPH CARMICHAEL RALPH CARMICHAEL

In the stars His hand-i - work I see, On the wind He speaks with maj - es - ty, Tho He rul - eth o - ver land and sea, *in unison* What is that to me? *in parts* I will cel - e-brate Na - tiv - i - ty, for it has a place in his - to - ry; Sure, He came to set His peo - ple free— *in unison* What is that to me? *in parts* Till by faith I met Him face to face

And I felt the won-der of His grace— Then I knew that
He was more than just a God who did-n't care That lived a-way out
there And now He walks be-side me day by day, Ev-er
watch-ing o'er me lest I stray, Help-ing me to find that nar-row way—
1
2
He's ev-'ry-thing to me. He's ev-'ry-thing to me.
WITNESS AND TESTIMONY

550 — He Lives
ALFRED H. ACKLEY
ALFRED H. ACKLEY
1. I serve a ris - en Sav - ior— He's in the world to - day,
2. In all the world a - round me I see His lov - ing care,
3. Re - joice, re - joice, O Chris - tian, lift up your voice and sing
I know that He is liv - ing, what - ev - er men may say;
And tho my heart grows wea - ry I nev - er will de - spair;
E - ter - nal hal - le - lu - jahs to Je - sus Christ the King!
I see His hand of mer - cy, I hear His voice of cheer,
I know that He is lead - ing thru all the storm-y blast,
The hope of all who seek Him, the help of all who find,
And just the time I need Him He's al - ways near.
The day of His ap - pear-ing will come at last.
None oth - er is so lov - ing, so good and kind.
CHORUS
He lives, He lives, Christ Je - sus lives to - day!
He lives, He lives,
WITNESS AND TESTIMONY
Copyright 1933 The Rodeheaver Co.
©Renewed 1961. All rights reserved.

He walks with me and talks with me a - long life's nar - row way.
He lives, He lives, sal - va - tion to im - part!
He lives, He lives,
You ask me how I know He lives? He lives with - in my heart.

Jesus Christ Is the Way — 551

Based on John 14:6
LETITIA SCHULER

ELEANOR S. MURRAY

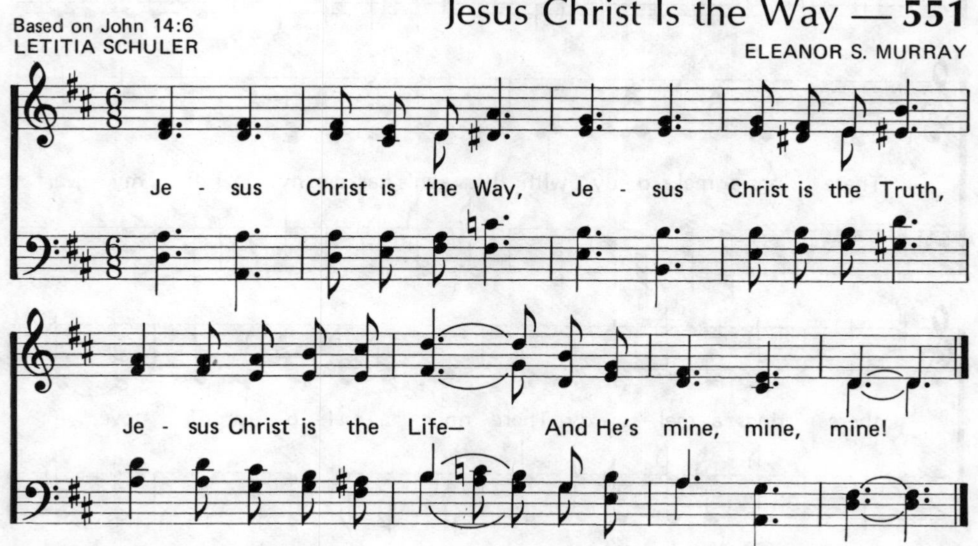
Je - sus Christ is the Way, Je - sus Christ is the Truth,
Je - sus Christ is the Life— And He's mine, mine, mine!

552 — In My Heart There Rings a Melody

ELTON M. ROTH ELTON M. ROTH

1. I have a song that Je - sus gave me, It was sent from
2. I love the Christ who died on Cal - v'ry, For He washed my
3. 'Twill be my end - less theme in glo - ry, With the an - gels
heav'n a - bove; There nev - er was a sweet - er mel - o - dy,
sins a - way; He put with - in my heart a mel - o - dy,
I will sing; 'Twill be a song with glo - rious har - mo - ny,
'Tis a mel - o - dy of love.
And I know it's there to stay.
When the courts of heav - en ring.
CHORUS
In my heart there rings a mel - o - dy,
There rings a mel - o - dy with heav - en's har - mo - ny; In my heart
there rings a mel - o - dy, There rings a mel - o - dy of love.

WITNESS AND TESTIMONY

Isn't the Love of Jesus Something Wonderful! — 553

JOHN W. PETERSON JOHN W. PETERSON

1. There will nev - er be a sweet - er sto - ry— Sto - ry of the
2. Bound-less as the u - ni - verse a - round me, Reach-ing to the
3. Love be-yond our hu - man com - pre - hend - ing, Love of God in
Sav - ior's love di - vine, Love that bro't Him from the realms of
far - thest soul a - way— Sav - ing, keep - ing love it was that
Christ—how can it be! This will be my theme and nev - er
CHORUS
glo - ry Just to save a sin - ful soul like mine.
found me, That is why my heart can tru - ly say: Is-n't the love of
end - ing, Great re-deem-ing love of Cal - va - ry.
Je - sus some-thing won-der-ful, Won-der-ful, won-der-ful; O is - n't the
it is
love of Je - sus some-thing won-der-ful! Won-der-ful it is to me.

554 — The Old Rugged Cross

GEORGE BENNARD GEORGE BENNARD

1. On a hill far a - way stood an old rug - ged cross, The
2. O that old rug - ged cross, so de - spised by the world, Has a
3. In the old rug - ged cross, stained with blood so di - vine, A
4. To the old rug - ged cross I will ev - er be true, Its
em - blem of suf - f'ring and shame; And I love that old cross where the
won-drous at - trac - tion for me; For the dear Lamb of God left His
won - drous beau - ty I see; For 'twas on that old cross Je - sus
shame and re-proach glad - ly bear; Then He'll call me some day to my
dear - est and best For a world of lost sin - ners was slain.
glo - ry a - bove To bear it to dark Cal - va - ry.
suf - fered and died To par - don and sanc - ti - fy me.
home far a - way, Where His glo - ry for - ev - er I'll share.
CHORUS
So I'll cher - ish the old rug - ged cross, Till my
cross, the old rug - ged cross,

tro - phies at last I lay down; I will cling to the old rug - ged
cross, the
cross, And ex - change it some day for a crown.
old rug - ged cross,
Jesus Loves Me — 555
ANNA B. WARNER–alt.
WILLIAM B. BRADBURY
1. Je - sus loves me! this I know, For the Bi - ble tells me so; Lit - tle
2. Je - sus loves me! He who died Heav-en's gate to o - pen wide; He will
3. Je - sus loves me! He will stay Close be-side me all the way; He's pre-
CHORUS
ones to Him be - long, They are weak but He is strong.
wash a - way my sin, Let His lit - tle child come in. Yes, Je - sus loves me!
pared a home for me, And some day His face I'll see.
Yes, Je - sus loves me! Yes, Je - sus loves me! The Bi - ble tells me so.

556 — Jesus Is All the World to Me
WILL L. THOMPSON
WILL L. THOMPSON
1. Je - sus is all the world to me, My life, my joy, my all;
2. Je - sus is all the world to me, My friend in tri - als sore;
3. Je - sus is all the world to me, And true to Him I'll be;
4. Je - sus is all the world to me, I want no bet - ter friend;
He is my strength from day to day, With - out Him I would fall.
I go to Him for bless-ings, and He gives them o'er and o'er.
O how could I this friend de - ny, When He's so true to me?
I trust Him now, I'll trust Him when Life's fleet - ing days shall end.
When I am sad to Him I go, No oth - er one can cheer me
He sends the sun - shine and the rain, He sends the har - vest's gold - en
Fol - low-ing Him I know I'm right, He watch-es o'er me day and
Beau - ti - ful life with such a friend, Beau - ti - ful life that has no
so; When I am sad He makes me glad— He's my friend.
grain; Sun - shine and rain, har - vest of grain— He's my friend.
night; Fol - low - ing Him by day and night— He's my friend.
end; E - ter - nal life, e - ter - nal joy— He's my friend.

Redeemed — 557
FANNY J. CROSBY —alt.
WILLIAM J. KIRKPATRICK
1. Re - deemed—how I love to pro - claim it! Re - deemed by the
2. Re - deemed—and so hap - py in Je - sus, No lan - guage my
3. I think of my bless - ed Re - deem - er, I wor - ship Him
4. I know I shall see in His beau - ty The King in whose
blood of the Lamb! Re - deemed thru His in - fin - ite mer - cy,
rap - ture can tell; I know that the light of His pres - ence
all the day long; I sing, for I can - not be si - lent!
law I de - light, Who lov - ing - ly guards all my foot - steps
His child, and for - ev - er, I am.
With me does con - tin - ual - ly dwell.
His love is the theme of my song.
And gives to me songs in the night.
CHORUS
Re - deemed, re - deemed, Re - deemed by the blood of the Lamb; Re - deemed, re - deemed, His child, and for - ev - er, I am.
WITNESS AND TESTIMONY

558 — Springs of Living Water

JOHN W. PETERSON JOHN W. PETERSON

1. I thirst-ed in the bar-ren land of sin and shame, And noth-ing sat - is - fy - ing there I found; But to the bless - ed cross of Christ one day I came, Where springs of liv - ing wa - ter did a - bound.
2. How sweet the liv - ing wa-ter from the hills of God, It makes me glad and hap - py all the way; Now glo - ry, grace and bless - ing mark the path I've trod, I'm shout - ing "Hal - le - lu - jah" ev - 'ry day.
3. O sin - ner, won't you come today to Cal - va - ry? A foun-tain there is flow-ing deep and wide; The Sav - ior now in - vites you to the wa - ter free, Where thirst - ing spir - its can be sat - is - fied.
CHORUS
Drink-ing at the springs of liv - ing wa - ter, Hap - py now am I, My soul they sat - is - fy;
Hap - py now am I, My soul they sat - is - fy; I'm
Drink-ing at the

springs of liv - ing wa - ter, O won-der-ful and boun-ti-ful sup - ply!
Sunshine in My Soul — 559
ELIZA E. HEWITT
JOHN R. SWENEY
1. There is sun-shine in my soul to - day, More glo - ri - ous and bright
2. There is mu - sic in my soul to - day, A car - ol to my King,
3. There is spring-time in my soul to - day, For when the Lord is near
4. There is glad - ness in my soul to - day, And hope and praise and love,
Than glows in an - y earth - ly sky, For Je - sus is my light.
And Je - sus, lis - ten - ing, can hear The songs I can - not sing.
The dove of peace sings in my heart, The flow'rs of grace ap - pear.
For bless-ings which He gives me now, For joys laid up a - bove.
CHORUS
O there's sun - shine, bless - ed sun - shine, When the peace - ful, happy moments
roll; When Je-sus shows His smil - ing face, There is sun-shine in my soul.

560 — Yes, He Did!

Traditional Spiritual
Arr. by Frank Anderson

Traditional

1. He took my feet from the mir - y clay— Yes, He did!
2. O my Lord did just what He said— Yes, He did!
3. He died on the cross to save my soul— Yes, He did!
4. O Je - sus washed my sins a - way— Yes, He did!
Yes, He did! And placed them on the Rock to stay—
Yes, He did! He healed the sick and He raised the dead—
Yes, He did! He ran - somed me and He made me whole—
Yes, He did! And made me hap - py all the day—
CHORUS
Yes, He did! Yes, He did! I can tell the world a - bout this,
I can tell the na - tions I'm blest, Tell them that Je - sus
made me whole, And He brought joy, joy to my soul!

Since Jesus Came into My Heart — 561

RUFUS H. McDANIEL

CHARLES H. GABRIEL

1. What a won-der-ful change in my life has been wrought Since Je-sus came
2. I have ceased from my wan-d'ring and go-ing a-stray, Since Je-sus came
3. I shall go there to dwell in that Cit-y, I know, Since Je-sus came
in-to my heart! I have light in my soul for which long I have sought,
in-to my heart! And my sins, which were man-y, are all washed a-way,
in-to my heart! And I'm hap-py, so hap-py, as on-ward I go,
Since Je-sus came in-to my heart!
CHORUS
Since Je-sus came in-to my heart, Since Je-sus came in-to my heart, Floods of joy o'er my soul like the sea bil-lows roll, Since Je-sus came in-to my heart.

562 — You Can Have a Song in Your Heart

IRA F. STANPHILL
and EDWARD L. SLAVENS

IRA F. STANPHILL

1. You can have a mel-o-dy down in your heart When it's ach-ing, al-most break-ing; E-ven tho the sor-row makes the tear-drops start, You can have a mel-o-dy down in your heart.
2. Do not let your wor-ries drive your song a-way! Tho to-mor-row bring its sor-row, Just re-mem-ber aft-er night-time comes the day— Do not let your wor-ries drive your song a-way!
3. Soon the night will pass and morn-ing bring the day— I am long-ing for its dawn-ing; Un-til then let's la-bor here and watch and pray— Soon the night will pass and morn-ing bring the day.
CHORUS
You can have a song in your heart in the night, Aft-er ev-'ry trial, Aft-er ev-'ry mile; An-y-one can sing when the

sun's shin - ing bright, But you need a song in your heart at night.
All That Thrills My Soul — 563
THORO HARRIS
THORO HARRIS
1. Who can cheer the heart like Je - sus, By His pres - ence all di - vine?
2. Love of Christ so free - ly giv - en, Grace of God be - yond de - gree,
3. Ev - 'ry need His hand sup - ply - ing— Ev - 'ry good in Him I see;
4. By the crys - tal flow - ing riv - er With the ran - somed I will sing,
True and ten - der, pure and pre - cious, O how blest to call Him mine!
Mer - cy high - er than the heav - en, Deep - er than the deep - est sea!
On His strength di - vine re - ly - ing— He is all in all to me.
And for - ev - er and for - ev - er Praise and glo - ri - fy the King.
REFRAIN
All that thrills my soul is Je - sus, He is more than life to me;
to me;
And the fair - est of ten thou - sand In my bless - ed Lord I see.

564 — His Banner over Me Is Love
Traditional
Song of Solomon 2:4,16; 5:10
Attr. to B. C. Laurelton
Arr. by Larry Leader
1. I am my Be - lov - ed's and He is mine—
2. He brought me to His ban-quet-ing ta - ble— His
3. He's fair - est of ten thou - sand to my soul—
ban-ner o - ver me is love, He brought me to His
I am my Be - lov - ed's and
He's fair - est of ten thou - sand
He is mine—
ban-quet-ing ta - ble— His ban-ner o - ver me is love; He
to my soul— He's
I am my Be - lov - ed's and He is mine—
brought me to His ban-quet-ing ta - ble— His ban-ner o - ver
fair-est of ten thou - sand to my soul—
me is love, His ban - ner o - ver me is love.
WITNESS AND TESTIMONY
Arr. © Singspiration 1979. All rights reserved.

ADDITIONAL STANZAS FOR OPTIONAL SELECTION:

4. He is the Rock of my salvation—(Ps. 95:1)
5. He placed my feet on the firm foundation—(Ps. 40:2b; II Tim. 2:19)
6. He gave me peace thru the power of the cross—(Eph. 2:13,14)
7. And now I am a new creation—(IICor. 5:17)
8. There's therefore now no condemnation—(Rom.8:10)
9. He calls me by my name and I follow where He leads me—(John 10:3,4)
10. I'm seated with Him in heavenly places—(Eph. 2:6)
11. He fills my cup to overflowing—(Ps. 23:5c)
12. He's working in me by His Holy Spirit—(Eph. 3:20b)
13. He's gone to prepare a place for me—(John 14:2c)
14. He'll come again that we may be together—(John 14:3)

Wonderful, Wonderful Jesus — 565

BENJAMIN A. BAUR

BENJAMIN A. BAUR

Won-der-ful, won-der-ful Je - sus, Who can com - pare with Thee!
Won-der-ful, won-der-ful Je - sus, Fair - er than all art Thou to me!
Won-der-ful, won-der-ful Je - sus, O how my soul loves Thee!
Fair - er than all the fair - est, Je - sus, art Thou to me!

566 — Happiness Is the Lord
IRA F. STANPHILL
IRA F. STANPHILL
1. Hap-pi-ness is to know the Sav-ior, Liv-ing a life with-in His fa-vor, Hav-ing a change in my be-hav-ior— Hap-pi-ness is the Lord;
2. Hap-pi-ness is a new cre-a-tion, "Je-sus and me" in close re-la-tion, Hav-ing a part in His sal-va-tion— Hap-pi-ness is the Lord. Real joy is mine, no mat-ter if tear-drops start; I've found the se-cret—it's Je-sus in my heart!
3. Hap-pi-ness is to be for-giv-en, Liv-ing a life that's worth the liv-in', Tak-ing a trip that leads to heav-en— Hap-pi-ness is the Lord, Hap-pi-ness is the Lord, Hap-pi-ness is the Lord!
to vs. 2
D.C. to vs. 3
1
2
3

Learning to Lean — 567
JOHN STALLINGS
JOHN STALLINGS
Learn-ing to lean, learn-ing to lean, I'm learn-ing to lean on Je - sus;
Fine
Find-ing more pow-er than I'd ev - er dreamed, I'm learn-ing to lean on Je - sus.
1. A joy I can't ex - plain is fill - ing my soul Since the day
2. There's glo - ri - ous vic - t'ry each day now for me As I dwell
I met Je - sus my King; His bless - ed Ho - ly Spir - it is
in His peace so se - rene; He helps me with each task if
D.C.
lead - ing my way— He is teach - ing, and I'm learn - ing to lean.
on - ly I ask— Ev - 'ry day now I am learn - ing to lean.
© 1976 by Heart Warming Music. All rights reserved.
WITNESS AND TESTIMONY

568 — He's the One!
JOHN W. PETERSON
JOHN W. PETERSON
1. Who can move the mountains that are hin-d'ring you to - day?
2. Who can heal the heart-ache that is crush-ing you with - in?
3. Who can keep you from all harm and guide you by His hand?
Who can pick them up like peb - bles, clear them from the way?
Who can pour the balm of heav - en where the hurt has been?
Who can give you pow'r for serv - ice and the strength to stand?
Who can prove His pow - er when a Chris - tian kneels to pray?
Who can chase the shad - ows, make the song of joy be - gin?
Who can give you grace for all that liv - ing may de - mand?
CHORUS
It is Je - sus— He's the One!
It is Je - sus— He's the One!
It is Je - sus— He's the One!
Je - sus holds all
pow - er in His might-y hands di - vine, He's the One who healed the

sick, turned wa - ter in - to wine; He makes all things pos - si - ble and
He's a friend of mine: Bless-ed Je - sus— He's the One!
He's the Savior of My Soul — 569
Traditional
Latin-American melody
He's the Sav-ior of my soul, My Je - sus, my Je - sus;
He's the Sav - ior of my soul, He's the Sav - ior of my soul.
D.S.– Sav - ior of my soul, He's the Sav - ior of my soul.
Fine
D.S.
Je - sus, Je - sus, Je - sus, Je - sus! He's the

Optional: 2. He is light and life and love... 3. He is all the world to me...
4. He is coming back again... (Further stanzas may be added.)

570 — No One Ever Cared for Me Like Jesus

CHARLES F. WEIGLE — CHARLES F. WEIGLE

1. I would love to tell you what I think of Je - sus Since I found in Him a friend so strong and true; I would tell you how He chang'd my life com - plete - ly— He did some - thing that no oth - er friend could do.

2. All my life was full of sin when Je - sus found me, All my heart was full of mis - er - y and woe; Je - sus placed His strong and lov - ing arms a - round me, And He led me in the way I ought to go.

3. Ev - 'ry day He comes to me with new as - sur - ance, More and more I un - der - stand His words of love; But I'll nev - er know just why He came to save me, Till some day I see His bless - ed face a - bove.

CHORUS

No one ev - er cared for me like Je - sus, There's no oth - er friend so kind as He; No one else could

WITNESS AND TESTIMONY

take the sin and dark-ness from me— O how much He cared for me!
Happy Am I! — 571
MICKEY HOLIDAY
MICKEY HOLIDAY
1. Hap - py am I! Je - sus is mine for - ev - er,
2. Hap - py am I! All of my sins for - giv - en,
3. Hap - py am I! How can I help but shout it?
(am I!)
Nev - er to leave! Al - ways in each en - deav - or
What a great day! Life is now worth the liv - in';
Ev - er - y day Tell - ing the world a - bout it;
Lead - ing me on In a life end - ing nev - er:
One of these days I'll be en - joy - ing heav - en:
Je - sus is real On - ly be - lieve, don't doubt it:
(O yes!)
Giv - ing a smile Ev - er - y mile, Hap - py am I!
Now that I know Up - ward I'll go, Hap - py am I!
Then you will be Hap - py like me— Hap - py am I!
© Singspiration 1971, arr. 1979. All rights reserved.
WITNESS AND TESTIMONY

572 — He Keeps Me Singing

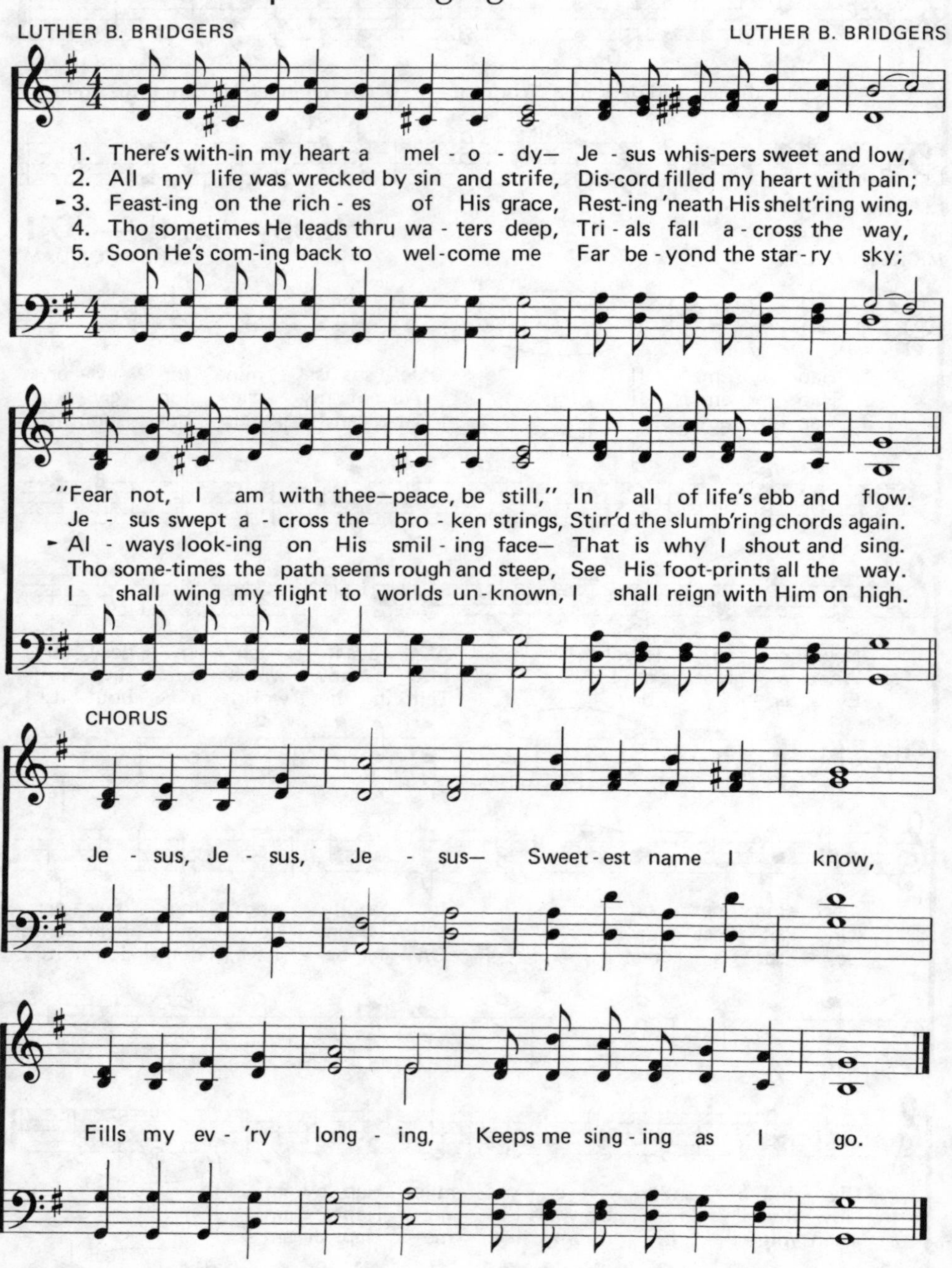
LUTHER B. BRIDGERS
LUTHER B. BRIDGERS
1. There's with-in my heart a mel - o - dy— Je - sus whis-pers sweet and low,
2. All my life was wrecked by sin and strife, Dis-cord filled my heart with pain;
3. Feast-ing on the rich - es of His grace, Rest-ing 'neath His shelt'ring wing,
4. Tho sometimes He leads thru wa - ters deep, Tri - als fall a - cross the way,
5. Soon He's com-ing back to wel - come me Far be - yond the star - ry sky;
"Fear not, I am with thee—peace, be still," In all of life's ebb and flow.
Je - sus swept a - cross the bro - ken strings, Stirr'd the slumb'ring chords again.
Al - ways look-ing on His smil - ing face— That is why I shout and sing.
Tho some-times the path seems rough and steep, See His foot-prints all the way.
I shall wing my flight to worlds un-known, I shall reign with Him on high.
CHORUS
Je - sus, Je - sus, Je - sus— Sweet - est name I know,
Fills my ev - 'ry long - ing, Keeps me sing - ing as I go.

PART 4

WORSHIP RESOURCES

THE SCRIPTURES

PSALMS
•
OLD TESTAMENT
•
NEW TESTAMENT
•
ANTIPHONAL READINGS

Scripture Readings from the **New International Version** of the Bible

573—The Blessed Man
Psalm 1

Blessed is the man
who does not walk in the counsel of the wicked
or stand in the way of sinners
or sit in the seat of mockers.

But his delight is in the law of the LORD,
and on his law he meditates day and night.

He is like a tree planted by streams of water,
which yields its fruit in season
and whose leaf does not wither.
Whatever he does prospers.

Not so the wicked!
They are like chaff
that the wind blows away.

Therefore the wicked will not stand in the judgment,
nor sinners in the assembly of the righteous.

For the LORD watches over the way of the righteous,
but the way of the wicked will perish.

574—God and Man
Psalm 8

O LORD, our Lord,
how majestic is your name in all the earth!
You have set your glory
above the heavens.

From the lips of children and infants
you have ordained praise
because of your enemies,
to silence the foe and the avenger.

When I consider your heavens,
the work of your fingers,
the moon and the stars,
which you have set in place,

what is man that you are mindful of him,
the son of man that you care for him?

You made him a little lower than the heavenly beings
and crowned him with glory and honor.

You made him ruler over the works of your hands;
you put everything under his feet:

all flocks and herds,
and the beasts of the field,
the birds of the air,
and the fish of the sea,
all that swim the paths of the seas.

O LORD, our Lord,
how majestic is your name in all the earth!

575—The Shepherd
Psalm 23

The LORD is my shepherd, I shall lack nothing.
He makes me lie down in green pastures,
he leads me beside quiet waters,
he restores my soul.
He guides me in paths of righteousness
for his name's sake.
Even though I walk
through the valley of the shadow of death,
I will fear no evil,
for you are with me;
your rod and your staff,
they comfort me.
You prepare a table before me
in the presence of my enemies.
You anoint my head with oil;
my cup overflows.
Surely goodness and love will follow me
all the days of my life,
and I will dwell in the house of the LORD
forever.

576—Protection
Psalm 27:1-5, 10, 13, 14

The LORD is my light and my salvation—
whom shall I fear?
The LORD is the stronghold of my life—
of whom shall I be afraid?

When evil men advance against me
to devour my flesh,
when my enemies and my foes attack me,
they will stumble and fall.

Though an army besiege me,
my heart will not fear;
though war break out against me,
even then will I be confident.

One thing I ask of the LORD,
this is what I seek:
that I may dwell in the house of the LORD
all the days of my life,
to gaze upon the beauty of the LORD
and to seek him in his temple.

For in the day of trouble
he will keep me safe in his dwelling;
he will hide me in the shelter of his tabernacle
and set me high upon a rock.

Though my father and mother forsake me,
the LORD will receive me.

I am confident of this:
I will see the goodness of the LORD
in the land of the living.

Wait for the LORD;
be strong and take heart
and wait for the LORD.

577—Facing Fear
Psalm 34:1-4, 6-10, 17-20, 22

I will extol the LORD at all times;
his praise will always be on my lips.
My soul will boast in the LORD;
let the afflicted hear and rejoice.
Glorify the LORD with me;
let us exalt his name together.

I sought the LORD, and he answered me;
he delivered me from all my fears.
This poor man called, and the LORD heard him;
he saved him out of all his troubles.
The angel of the LORD encamps around those who fear him,
and he delivers them.

Taste and see that the LORD is good;
blessed is the man who takes refuge in him.
Fear the LORD, you his saints,
for those who fear him lack nothing.
The lions may grow weak and hungry,
but those who seek the LORD lack no good thing.

The righteous cry out, and the LORD hears them;
he delivers them from all their troubles.
The LORD is close to the brokenhearted
and saves those who are crushed in spirit.

A righteous man may have many troubles,
but the LORD delivers him from them all;
he protects all his bones,
not one of them will be broken.

The LORD redeems his servants;
no one who takes refuge in him will be condemned.

578—Confession
Psalm 51:1-13; 16, 17

Have mercy on me, O God,
according to your unfailing love;
according to your great compassion
blot out my transgressions.
Wash away all my iniquity
and cleanse me from my sin.

For I know my transgressions,
and my sin is always before me.
Against you, you only, have I sinned
and done what is evil in your sight,
so that you are proved right when you speak
and justified when you judge.

Surely I have been a sinner from birth,
sinful from the time my mother conceived me.
Surely you desire truth in the inner parts;
you teach me wisdom in the inmost place.

Cleanse me with hyssop, and I will be clean;
wash me, and I will be whiter than snow.
Let me hear joy and gladness;
let the bones you have crushed rejoice.

Hide your face from my sins
and blot out all my iniquity.
Create in me a pure heart, O God,
and renew a steadfast spirit within me.

Do not cast me from your presence
or take your Holy Spirit from me.
Restore to me the joy of your salvation
and grant me a willing spirit, to sustain me.

Then I will teach transgressors your ways,
and sinners will turn back to you.

You do not delight in sacrifice, or I would bring it;
you do not take pleasure in burnt offerings.
The sacrifices of God are a broken spirit;
a broken and contrite heart,
O God, you will not despise.

579—Thirst for God
Psalm 63

O God, you are my God,
earnestly I seek you;
my soul thirsts for you,
my body longs for you,
in a dry and weary land
where there is no water.

I have seen you in the sanctuary
and beheld your power and your glory.

Because your love is better than life,
my lips will glorify you.
I will praise you as long as I live,
and in your name I will lift up my hands.

My soul will be satisfied as with the richest of foods;
with singing lips my mouth will praise you.

On my bed I remember you;
I think of you through the watches of the night.

Because you are my help,
I sing in the shadow of your wings.
I stay close to you;
your right hand upholds me.

They who seek my life will be destroyed;
they will go down to the depths of the earth.
They will be given over to the sword
and become food for jackals.

But the king will rejoice in God;
all who swear by God's name will praise him,
while the mouths of liars will be silenced.

580—God is Good

Psalm 73:1-5, 12, 16-18, 21, 22, 25-28

Surely God is good to Israel,
to those who are pure in heart.
But as for me, my feet had almost slipped;
I had nearly lost my foothold.
For I envied the arrogant
when I saw the prosperity of the wicked.

They have no struggles;
their bodies are healthy and strong.
They are free from the burdens common to man;
they are not plagued by human ills.
This is what the wicked are like—
always carefree, they increase in wealth.

When I tried to understand all this,
it was oppressive to me
till I entered the sanctuary of God;
then I understood their final destiny.
Surely you place them on slippery ground;
you cast them down to ruin.

When my heart was grieved
and my spirit embittered,
I was senseless and ignorant;
I was a brute beast before you.

Whom have I in heaven but you?
And being with you, I desire nothing on earth.
My flesh and my heart may fail,
but God is the strength of my heart
and my portion forever.

Those who are far from you will perish;
you destroy all who are unfaithful to you.
But as for me, it is good to be near God.
I have made the Sovereign LORD my refuge;
I will tell of all your deeds.

581—God's House

Psalm 84:1-5a, 8-12

How lovely is your dwelling place,
O LORD Almighty!

My soul yearns, even faints
for the courts of the LORD;
my heart and my flesh cry out
for the living God.

Even the sparrow has found a home,
and the swallow a nest for herself,
where she may have her young—
a place near your altar,
O LORD Almighty, my King and my God.

Blessed are those who dwell in your house;
they are ever praising you.
Blessed are those whose strength is in you,

Hear my prayer, O LORD God Almighty;
listen to me, O God of Jacob.
Look upon our shield, O God;
look with favor on your anointed one.

Better is one day in your courts
than a thousand elsewhere;
I would rather be a doorkeeper in the house of my God
than dwell in the tents of the wicked.
For the LORD God is a sun and shield;
the LORD bestows favor and honor;
no good thing does he withhold
from those whose walk is blameless.

O LORD Almighty,
blessed is the man who trusts in you.

582—Worship

Psalm 89:1, 6-9, 11, 13, 15-18

I will sing of the love of the LORD forever;
with my mouth I will make your faithfulness known through all generations.

For who in the skies above can compare with the LORD?
Who is like the LORD among the heavenly beings?

In the council of the holy ones God is greatly feared;
he is more awesome than all who surround him.

O LORD God Almighty, who is like you?
You are mighty, O LORD, and your faithfulness surrounds you.

You rule over the surging sea;
when its waves mount up, you still them.

The heavens are yours, and yours also the earth;
you founded the world and all that is in it.

Your arm is endued with power;
your hand is strong, your right hand exalted.

Blessed are those who have learned to acclaim you,
who walk in the light of your presence, O LORD.

They rejoice in your name all day long;
they exult in your righteousness.

For you are their glory and strength,
and by your favor you exalt our horn.
Indeed, our shield belongs to the LORD,
our king to the Holy One of Israel.

583—Refuge

Psalm 91

He who dwells in the shelter of the Most High
will rest in the shadow of the Almighty.

I will say of the LORD, "He is my refuge and my fortress,
my God, in whom I trust."
Surely he will save you from the fowler's snare
and from the deadly pestilence.
He will cover you with his feathers,
and under his wings you will find refuge;
his faithfulness will be your shield and rampart.

You will not fear the terror of night,
nor the arrow that flies by day,
nor the pestilence that stalks in the darkness,
nor the plague that destroys at midday.

A thousand may fall at your side,
ten thousand at your right hand,
but it will not come near you.
You will only observe with your eyes
and see the punishment of the wicked.

If you make the Most High your dwelling—
even the LORD, who is my refuge—
then no harm will befall you,
no disaster will come near your tent.

For he will command his angels concerning you
to guard you in all your ways;
they will lift you up in their hands,
so that you will not strike your foot against a stone.

You will tread upon the lion and the cobra;
you will trample the great lion and the serpent.
"Because he loves me," says the LORD, "I will rescue him;
I will protect him, for he acknowledges my name.

He will call upon me, and I will answer him;
I will be with him in trouble,
I will deliver him and honor him.
With long life will I satisfy him
and show him my salvation."

584—Give Thanks

Psalm 105:1-8; 106:1-3, 47, 48

Give thanks to the LORD, call on his name;
make known among the nations what he has done,

Sing to him, sing praise to him;
tell of all his wonderful acts.

Glory in his holy name;
let the hearts of those who seek the LORD rejoice.

Look to the LORD and his strength;
seek his face always.

Remember the wonders he has done,
his miracles, and the judgments he pronounced,

O descendants of Abraham his servant,
O sons of Jacob, his chosen ones.

He is the LORD our God;
his judgments are in all the earth.

He remembers his covenant forever,
the word he commanded, for a thousand generations,

Praise the LORD.
Give thanks to the LORD, for he is good;
his love endures forever.

Who can proclaim the mighty acts of the LORD
or fully declare his praise?

Blessed are they who maintain justice,
who constantly do what is right.

Save us, O LORD our God,
and gather us from the nations,
that we may give thanks to your holy name.
and glory in your praise.

Praise be to the LORD, the God of Israel,
from everlasting to everlasting.
Let all the people say, "Amen!"
Praise the LORD.

585—Love to God

Psalm 116:1-6, 12-14, 17-19

I love the LORD, for he heard my voice;
he heard my cry for mercy.
Because he turned his ear to me,
I will call on him as long as I live.

The cords of death entangled me,
the anguish of the grave came upon me;
I was overcome by trouble and sorrow.
Then I called on the name of the LORD:
"O LORD, save me!"

The LORD is gracious and righteous;
our God is full of compassion.
The LORD protects the simplehearted;
when I was in great need, he saved me.

How can I repay the LORD
for all his goodness to me?

I will lift up the cup of salvation
and call on the name of the LORD.
I will fulfill my vows to the LORD
in the presence of all his people.

I will sacrifice a thank offering to you
and call on the name of the LORD.
I will fulfill my vows to the LORD
in the presence of all his people,

in the courts of the house of the LORD—
in your midst, O Jerusalem.
Praise the LORD.

586—Praise

Psalm 149:1-9

Praise the LORD.
Sing to the LORD a new song,
his praise in the assembly of the saints.

Let Israel rejoice in their Maker;
let the people of Zion be glad in their King.

Let them praise his name with dancing
and make music to him with tambourine and har

For the LORD takes delight in his people;
he crowns the humble with salvation.

Let the saints rejoice in this honor
and sing for joy on their beds.

May the praise of God be in their mouths
and a double-edged sword in their hands,

to inflict vengeance on the nations
and punishment on the peoples,

to bind their kings with fetters,
their nobles with shackles of iron,

to carry out the sentence written against them.
This is the glory of all his saints.
Praise the LORD.

587—The Commandments

—from Exodus 20, Matthew 22

And God spoke all these words:

You shall have no other gods before me.
You shall not make for yourself an idol in the form of anything... You shall not bow down to them or worship them;
You shall not misuse the name of the LORD your God,
Remember the Sabbath day by keeping it holy.
Honor your father and your mother, so that you may live long in the land the LORD your God is giving you.

You shall not murder.
You shall not commit adultery.
You shall not steal.
You shall not give false testimony against your neighbor.
You shall not covet anything that belongs to your neighbor.

Jesus replied:

Love the LORD your God with all your heart and with all your soul and with all your mind.
Love your neighbor as yourself.
All the Law and the Prophets hang on these two commandments.

588—Family Instruction

Deuteronomy 6:1-7, 20-25

These are the commands, decrees and laws the LORD your God directed me to teach you to observe in the land that you are crossing the Jordan to possess, so that you, your children and their children after them may fear the LORD your God as long as you live by keeping all his decrees and commands that I give you, and so that you may enjoy long life.

Hear, O Israel, and be careful to obey so that it may go well with you and that you may increase greatly in a land flowing with milk and honey, just as the LORD, the God of your fathers, promised you. Hear, O Israel: The LORD our God, the LORD is one. Love the LORD your God with all your heart and with all your soul and with all your strength. These commandments that I give you today are to be upon your hearts. Impress them on your children. Talk about them when you sit at home and when you walk along the road, when you lie down and when you get up.

In the future, when your son asks you, "What is the meaning of the stipulations, decrees and laws the LORD our God has commanded you?" tell him: "We were slaves of Pharaoh in Egypt, but the LORD brought us out of Egypt with a mighty hand. Before our eyes the LORD sent miraculous signs and wonders—great and terrible—upon Egypt and Pharaoh and his whole household. But he brought us out from there to bring us in and give us the land that he promised on oath to our forefathers. The LORD commanded us to obey all these decrees and to fear the LORD our God, so that we might always prosper and be kept alive, as is the case today. And if we are careful to obey all this law before the LORD our God, as he has commanded us, that will be our righteousness."

589—Wisdom

Proverbs 3:13-26

Blessed is the man who finds wisdom,
the man who gains understanding,
for she is more profitable than silver
and yields better returns than gold.
She is more precious than rubies;
nothing you desire can compare with her.
Long life is in her right hand;
in her left hand are riches and honor.
Her ways are pleasant ways,
and all her paths are peace.
She is a tree of life to those who embrace her;
those who lay hold of her will be blessed.
By wisdom the LORD laid the earth's
foundations,
by understanding he set the heavens in
place;
by his knowledge the deeps were divided,
and the clouds let drop the dew.

My son, preserve sound judgment and
discernment.
do not let them out of your sight;
they will be life for you,
an ornament to grace your neck.
Then you will go on your way in safety,
and your foot will not stumble;
when you lie down, you will not be afraid;
when you lie down, your sleep will be sweet.
Have no fear of sudden disaster
or of the ruin that overtakes the wicked,
for the LORD will be your confidence
and will keep your foot from being snared.

590—God Exalted

Isaiah 6:1-8

In the year that King Uzziah died, I saw the Lord seated on a throne, high and exalted, and the train of his robe filled the temple. Above him were seraphs, each with six wings: With two wings they covered their faces, with two they covered their feet, and with two they were flying. And they were calling to one another:

"Holy, holy, holy is the LORD Almighty;
the whole earth is full of his glory."

At the sound of their voices the doorposts and thresholds shook and the temple was filled with smoke.

"Woe to me!" I cried. "I am ruined! For I am a man of unclean lips, and I live among a people of unclean lips, and my eyes have seen the King, the LORD Almighty."

Then one of the seraphs flew to me with a live coal in his hand, which he had taken with tongs from the altar. With it he touched my mouth and said, "See, this has touched your lips; your guilt is taken away and your sin atoned for."
Then I heard the voice of the Lord saying,

"Whom shall I send? And who will go for us?" And I said, "Here am I. Send me!"

591—Prophecy and Reality

Isaiah 53; Matthew 27:27-31; 2 Corinthians 5:21; 1 Peter 2; Matthew 26:59-63; Philippians 2

Who has believed our message
and to whom has the arm of the LORD been revealed?
He grew up before him like a tender shoot,
and like a root out of dry ground.
He had no beauty or majesty to attract us to him,
nothing in his appearance that we should desire him.
He was despised and rejected by men,
a man of sorrows, and familiar with suffering.
Like one from whom men hide their faces
he was despised, and we esteemed him not.

Then the governor's soldiers took Jesus into the Praetorium and gathered the whole company of soldiers around him. They stripped him and put a scarlet robe on him, and then wove a crown of thorns and set it on his head. They put a staff in his right hand and knelt in front of him and mocked him. "Hail, King of the Jews!" they said. They spit on him, and took the staff and struck him on the head again and again. After they had mocked him, they took off the robe and put his own clothes on him. Then they led him away to crucify him.

Surely he took up our infirmities
and carried our sorrows,
yet we considered him stricken by God,
smitten by him, and afflicted.
But he was pierced for our transgressions,
he was crushed for our iniquities;
the punishment that brought us peace was upon him,
and by his wounds we are healed.

We all, like sheep, have gone astray,
each of us has turned to his own way;
and the LORD has laid on him
the iniquity of us all.

God made him who had no sin to be sin for us, so that in him we might become the righteousness of God. He himself bore our sins in his body on the tree, so that we might die to sins and live for righteousness; by his wounds you have been healed.

He was oppressed and afflicted,
yet he did not open his mouth;
he was led like a lamb to the slaughter,
and as a sheep before her shearers is silent,
so he did not open his mouth.
By oppression and judgment, he was taken away.
And who can speak of his descendants?
For he was cut off from the land of the living;
for the transgression of my people he was stricken.
He was assigned a grave with the wicked,
and with the rich in his death,
though he had done no violence,
nor was any deceit in his mouth.

The chief priest and the whole Sanhedrin were looking for false evidence against Jesus so that they could put him to death. But they did not find any, though many false witnesses came forward.
Finally two came forward and declared, "This fellow said, 'I am able to destroy the temple of God and rebuild it in three days.'"
Then the high priest stood up and said to Jesus, "Are you not going to answer? What is this testimony that these men are bringing against you?" But Jesus remained silent.

Yet it was the LORD'S will to crush him and cause him to suffer,
and though the LORD makes his life a guilt offering,
he will see his offspring and prolong his days,
and the will of the LORD will prosper in his hand.
After the suffering of his soul,
he will see the light of life and be satisfied;
by his knowledge my righteous servant will justify many,
and he will bear their iniquities.
Therefore I will give him a portion among the great,
and he will divide the spoils with the strong,
because he poured out his life unto death,
and was numbered with the transgressors.
For he bore the sin of many,
and made intercession for the transgressors.

And being found in appearance as a man,
he humbled himself
and became obedient to death—even death on a cross!
Therefore God exalted him to the highest place
and gave him the name that is above every name,
that at the name of Jesus every knee should bow,
in heaven and on earth and under the earth,
and every tongue confess that Jesus Christ is Lord,
to the glory of God the Father.

592—Pardon

Isaiah 55:1-3, 6-11

"Come, all you who are thirsty,
come to the waters;
and you who have no money,
come, buy and eat!
Come, buy wine and milk
without money and without cost.
Why spend money on what is not bread,
and your labor on what does not satisfy?
Listen, listen to me, and eat what is good,
and your soul will delight in the richest of fare.
Give ear and come to me;
hear me, that your soul may live.
I will make an everlasting covenant with you,
my unfailing kindnesses promised to David.

Seek the LORD while he may be found;
call on him while he is near.
Let the wicked forsake his way
and the evil man his thoughts.
Let him turn to the LORD, and he will have mercy on him,
and to our God, for he will freely pardon.

"For my thoughts are not your thoughts,
neither are your ways my ways,"
declares the LORD.
"As the heavens are higher than the earth,
so are my ways higher than your ways
and my thoughts than your thoughts.
As the rain and the snow
come down from heaven,
and do not return to it
without watering the earth
and making it bud and flourish,
so that it yields seed for the sower and bread for the eater,
so is my word that goes out from my mouth:
It will not return to me empty,
but will accomplish what I desire
and achieve the purpose for which I sent it.

593—Tithes/Offerings

Malachi 3:8-12;
2 Corinthians 9:6-8;
1 Peter 4:10

"Will a man rob God? Yet you rob me.
"But you ask, 'How do we rob you?"
"In tithes and offerings. You are under a curse—the whole nation of you—because you are robbing me. Bring the whole tithe into the storehouse, that there may be food in my house. Test me in this," says the LORD Almighty, "and see if I will not throw open the floodgates of heaven and pour out so much blessing that you will not have room enough for it. I will prevent pests from devouring your crops, and the vines in your fields will not cast their fruit," says the LORD Almighty. "Then all the nations will call you blessed, for yours will be a delightful land," says the LORD Almighty.

Remember this: Whoever sows sparingly will also reap sparingly, and whoever sows generously will also reap generously. Each man should give what he has decided in his heart to give, not reluctantly or under compulsion, for God loves a cheerful giver. And God is able to make all grace abound to you, so that in all things at all times, having all that you need, you will abound in every good work.

Each one should use whatever gift he has received to serve others, faithfully administering God's grace in its various forms.

594—The Beatitudes

Matthew 5:3-12

Blessed are the poor in spirit,

for theirs is the kingdom of heaven.

Blessed are those who mourn,

for they will be comforted.

Blessed are the meek,

for they will inherit the earth.

Blessed are those who hunger and thirst for righteousness,

for they will be filled.

Blessed are the merciful,

for they will be shown mercy.

Blessed are the pure in heart,

for they will see God.

Blessed are the peacemakers,

for they will be called sons of God.

Blessed are those who are persecuted because of righteousness,

for theirs is the kingdom of heaven.

Blessed are you when people insult you, persecute you and falsely say all kinds of evil against you because of me.

Rejoice and be glad, because great is your reward in heaven, for in the same way they persecuted the prophets who were before you.

595—Prayer
Matthew 6:5-13

But when you pray, do not be like the hypocrites, for they love to pray standing in the synagogues and on the street corners to be seen by men. I tell you the truth, they have received their reward in full.

When you pray, go into your room, close the door and pray to your Father, who is unseen. Then your Father, who sees what is done in secret, will reward you.

And when you pray, do not keep on babbling like pagans, for they think they will be heard because of their many words.

Do not be like them, for your Father knows what you need before you ask him.

This is how you should pray:
Our Father in heaven,
hallowed be your name,
your kingdom come,
your will be done
on earth as it is in heaven.
Give us today our daily bread.
Forgive us our debts,
as we also have forgiven our debtors.
And lead us not into temptation,
but deliver us from the evil one.

596—Anxiety
Matthew 6:19-21, 24-34

Do not store up for yourselves treasures on earth, where moth and rust destroy, and where thieves break in and steal. But store up for yourselves treasures in heaven, where moth and rust do not destroy, and where thieves do not break in and steal. For where your treasure is, there your heart will be also.

No one can serve two masters. Either he will hate the one and love the other, or he will be devoted to the one and despise the other. You cannot serve both God and Money. Therefore I tell you, do not worry about your life, what you will eat or drink; or about your body, what you will wear. Is not life more important than food, and the body more important than clothes?

Look at the birds of the air; they do not sow or reap or store away in barns, and yet your heavenly Father feeds them. Are you not much more valuable than they?

Who of you by worrying can add a single hour to his life?

And why do you worry about clothes? See how the lilies of the field grow. They do not labor or spin. Yet I tell you that not even Solomon in all his splendor was dressed like one of these. If that is how God clothes the grass of the field, which is here today and tomorrow is thrown into the fire, will he not much more clothe you, O you of little faith?

So do not worry saying, "What shall we eat?" or "What shall we drink?" or "What shall we wear?" For the pagans run after all these things, and your heavenly Father knows that you need them.

But seek first his kingdom and his righteousness, and all these things will be given to you as well.

Therefore do not worry about tomorrow, for tomorrow will worry about itself. Each day has enough trouble of its own.

597—Incarnation

Luke 1:26-33; 2:1-14

In the sixth month, God sent the angel Gabriel to Nazareth, a town in Galilee, to a virgin pledged to be married to a man named Joseph, a descendant of David. The virgin's name was Mary. The angel went to her and said,

"Greetings, you who are highly favored! The Lord is with you... You have found favor with God. You will be with child and give birth to a son, and you are to give him the name Jesus. He will be great and will be called the Son of the Most High. The Lord God will give him the throne of his father David, and he will reign over the house of Jacob forever; his kingdom will never end."

In those days Caesar Augustus issued a decree that a census should be taken of the entire Roman world. (This was the first census that took place while Quirinius was governor of Syria.) And everyone went to his own town to register. So Joseph also went up from the town of Nazareth in Galilee to Judea, to Bethlehem the town of David, because he belonged to the house and line of David. He went there to register with Mary, who was pledged to be married to him and was expecting a child. While they were there, the time came for the baby to be born, and she gave birth to her firstborn, a son. She wrapped him in strips of cloth and placed him in a manger, because there was no room for them in the inn. And there were shepherds living out in the fields nearby, keeping watch over their flocks at night. An angel of the Lord appeared to them, and the glory of the Lord shone around them, and they were terrified. But the angel said to them,

"Do not be afraid. I bring you good news of great joy that will be for all the people. Today in the town of David a Savior has been born to you; he is Christ the Lord. This will be a sign to you: You will find a baby wrapped in strips of cloth and lying in a manger."

Suddenly a great company of the heavenly host appeared with the angel, praising God and saying,

"Glory to God in the highest,
and on earth peace to men on whom his favor rests."

598—Heaven

John 14:1-6; 2 Corinthians 5:1-4, 6-8

Do not let your hearts be troubled. Trust in God; trust also in me. In my Father's house are many rooms; if it were not so, I would have told you. I am going there to prepare a place for you. And if I go and prepare a place for you, I will come back and take you to be with me that you also may be where I am. You know the way to the place where I am going.

Thomas said to him, "Lord, we don't know where you are going, so how can we know the way?" Jesus answered, "I am the way and the truth and the life. No one comes to the Father except through me."

Now we know that if the earthly tent we live in is destroyed, we have a building from God, an eternal house in heaven, not built by human hands. Meanwhile we groan, longing to be clothed with our heavenly dwelling, because when we are clothed, we will not be found naked. For while we are in this tent, we groan and are burdened, because we do not wish to be unclothed but to be clothed with our heavenly dwelling, so that what is mortal may be swallowed up by life.

Therefore we are always confident and know that as long as we are at home in the body we are away from the Lord. We live by faith, not by sight. We are confident, I say, and would prefer to be away from the body and at home with the Lord.

599—Justification by Faith

Romans 5:1, 2, 6-12, 18-21

Therefore, since we have been justified through faith, we have peace with God through our Lord Jesus Christ, through whom we have gained access by faith into this grace in which we now stand. And we rejoice in the hope of the glory of God.

You see, at just the right time, when we were still powerless, Christ died for the ungodly. Very rarely will anyone die for a righteous man, though for a good man someone might possibly dare to die. But God demonstrates his own love for us in this: While we were still sinners, Christ died for us.

Since we have now been justified by his blood, how much more shall we be saved from God's wrath through him! For if, when we were God's enemies, we were reconciled to him through the death of his Son, how much more, having been reconciled, shall we be saved through his life! Not only is this so, but we also rejoice in God through our Lord Jesus Christ, through whom we have now received reconciliation.

Consequently, just as the result of one trespass was condemnation for all men, so also the result of one act of righteousness was justification that brings life for all men. For just as through the disobedience of the one man the many were made sinners, so also through the obedience of the one man the many will be made righteous.

The law was added so that the trespass might increase. But where sin increased, grace increased all the more, so that, just as sin reigned in death, so also grace might reign through righteousness to bring eternal life through Jesus Christ our Lord.

600—Spiritual Gifts

Romans 12:3-8; 1 Corinthians 12:4-6, 18-25, 31a

For by the grace given me I say to every one of you: Do not think of yourself more highly than you ought, but rather think of yourself with sober judgment, in accordance with the measure of faith God has given you. Just as each of us has one body with many members, and these members do not all have the same function, so in Christ we who are many form one body, and each member belongs to all the others.

We have different gifts, according to the grace given us. If a man's gift is prophesying, let him use it in proportion to his faith. If it is serving, let him serve; if it is teaching, let him teach; if it is encouraging, let him encourage; if it is contributing to the needs of others, let him give generously; if it is leadership, let him govern diligently; if it is showing mercy, let him do it cheerfully.

There are different kinds of gifts, but the same Spirit. There are different kinds of service, but the same Lord. There are different kinds of working, but the same God works all of them in all men.

But in fact God has arranged the parts in the body, every one of them, just as he wanted them to be. If they were all one part, where would the body be? As it is, there are many parts, but one body.

The eye cannot say to the hand, "I don't need you!" And the head cannot say to the feet, "I don't need you!" On the contrary, those parts of the body that seem to be weaker are indispensable, and the parts that we think are less honorable we treat with special honor. And the parts that are unpresentable are treated with special modesty, while our presentable parts need no special treatment. But God has combined the members of the body and has given greater honor to the parts that lacked it, so that there should be no division in the body, but that its parts should have equal concern for each other.

But eagerly desire the greater gifts.

601—Love Preeminent

1 Corinthians 13

If I speak in the tongues of men and of angels, but have not love, I am only a resounding gong or a clanging cymbal. If I have the gift of prophecy and can fathom all mysteries and all knowledge, and if I have a faith that can move mountains, but have not love, I am nothing. If I give all I possess to the poor and surrender my body to the flames, but have not love, I gain nothing.

Love is patient, love is kind. It does not envy, it does not boast, it is not proud. It is not rude, it is not self-seeking, it is not easily angered, it keeps no record of wrongs. Love does not delight in evil but rejoices with the truth. It always protects, always trusts, always hopes, always perseveres.

Love never fails. But where there are prophecies, they will cease; where there are tongues, they will be stilled; where there is knowledge, it will pass away. For we know in part and we prophesy in part, but when perfection comes, the imperfect disappears. When I was a child, I talked like a child, I thought like a child, I reasoned like a child. When I became a man, I put childish ways behind me. Now we see but a poor reflection; then we shall see face to face. Now I know in part; then I shall know fully, even as I am fully known.

And now these three remain: faith, hope and love. But the greatest of these is love.

602—Resurrection
1 Corinthians 15:19-23, 51-58

If only for this life we have hope in Christ, we are to be pitied more than all men. But Christ has indeed been raised from the dead, the firstfruits of those who have fallen asleep. For since death came through a man, the resurrection of the dead comes also through a man. For as in Adam all die, so in Christ all will be made alive. But each in his own turn: Christ, the firstfruits; then, when he comes, those who belong to him.

Listen, I tell you a mystery: We will not all sleep, but we will all be changed—in a flash, in the twinkling of an eye, at the last trumpet. For the trumpet will sound, the dead will be raised imperishable, and we will be changed. For the perishable must clothe itself with the imperishable, and the mortal with immortality. When the perishable has been clothed with the imperishable, and the mortal with immortality, then the saying that is written will come true: "Death has been swallowed up in victory."

"Where, O death, is your victory?
"Where, O death, is your sting?"

The sting of death is sin, and the power of sin is the law. But thanks be to God! He gives us the victory through our Lord Jesus Christ.

Therefore, my dear brothers, stand firm. Let nothing move you. Always give yourselves fully to the work of the Lord, because you know that your labor in the Lord is not in vain.

603—Christ Has Set Us Free
Galatians 3:13, 14, 23-26; 5:1, 13, 14, 16-18

Christ redeemed us from the curse of the law by becoming a curse for us, for it is written: "Cursed is everyone who is hung on a tree." He redeemed us in order that the blessing given to Abraham might come to the Gentiles through Christ Jesus, so that by faith we might receive the promise of the Spirit.

Before this faith came, we were held prisoners by the law, locked up until faith should be revealed. So the law was put in charge to lead us to Christ that we might be justified by faith. Now that faith has come, we are no longer under the supervision of the law. You are all sons of God through faith in Christ Jesus.

It is for freedom that Christ has set us free. Stand firm, then, and do not let yourselves be burdened again by a yoke of slavery. You, my brothers, were called to be free. But do not use your freedom to indulge the sinful nature; rather, serve one another in love. The entire law is summed up in a single command: "Love your neighbor as yourself."

So I say, live by the Spirit, and you will not gratify the desires of the sinful nature. For the sinful nature desires what is contrary to the Spirit, and the Spirit what is contrary to the sinful nature. They are in conflict with each other, so that you do not do what you want. But if you are led by the Spirit, you are not under law.

604—Christian Marriage
Ephesians 5:1, 2, 21-33

Be imitators of God, therefore, as dearly loved children and live a life of love, just as Christ loved us and gave himself up for us as a fragrant offering and sacrifice to God. Submit to one another out of reverence for Christ.

Wives, submit to your husbands as to the Lord. For the husband is the head of the wife as Christ is the head of the church, his body, of which he is the Savior. Now as the church submits to Christ, so also wives should submit to their husbands in everything.

Husbands, love your wives, just as Christ loved the church and gave himself up for her to make her holy, cleansing her by the washing with water through the word, and to present her to himself as a radiant church, without stain or wrinkle or any other blemish, but holy and blameless. In this same way, husbands ought to love their wives as their own bodies. He who loves his wife loves himself. After all, no one ever hated his own body, but he feeds and cares for it, just as Christ does the church—for we are members of his body. For this reason a man will leave his father and mother and be united to his wife, and the two will become one flesh.

This is a profound mystery—but I am talking about Christ and the church. However, each one of you also must love his wife as he loves himself, and the wife must respect her husband.

605—Rules for Living
Philippians 4:4-9, 13

Rejoice in the Lord always. I will say it again: Rejoice!

Let your gentleness be evident to all. The Lord is near.

Do not be anxious about anything, but in everything, by prayer and petition, with thanksgiving, present your requests to God. And the peace of God, which transcends all understanding, will guard your hearts and your minds in Christ Jesus.

Finally, brothers, whatever is true, whatever is noble, whatever is right, whatever is pure, whatever is lovely, whatever is admirable—if anything is excellent or praiseworthy—think about such things.

Whatever you have learned or received or heard from me, or seen in me—put it into practice. And the God of peace will be with you.

I can do everything through him who gives me strength.

606—Christ's Coming

1 Thessalonians 4:13—5:6, 8-10, 23

Brothers, we do not want you to be ignorant about those who fall asleep, or to grieve like the rest of men, who have no hope. We believe that Jesus died and rose again and so we believe that God will bring with Jesus those who have fallen asleep in him. According to the Lord's own word, we tell you that we who are still alive, who are left till the coming of the Lord, will certainly not precede those who have fallen asleep. For the Lord himself will come down from heaven, with a loud command, with the voice of the archangel and with the trumpet call of God, and the dead in Christ will rise first. After that, we who are still alive and are left will be caught up with them in the clouds to meet the Lord in the air. And so we will be with the Lord forever. Therefore encourage each other with these words.

Now, brothers, about times and dates we do not need to write to you, for you know very well that the day of the Lord will come like a thief in the night. While people are saying, "Peace and safety," destruction will come on them suddenly, as labor pains on a pregnant woman, and they will not escape.

But you, brothers, are not in darkness so that this day should surprise you like a thief. You are all sons of the light and sons of the day. We do not belong to the night or to the darkness. So then, let us not be like others, who are asleep, but let us be alert and self-controlled. But since we belong to the day, let us be self-controlled, putting on faith and love as a breastplate, and the hope of salvation as a helmet. For God did not appoint us to suffer wrath but to receive salvation through our Lord Jesus Christ. He died for us so that, whether we are awake or asleep, we may live together with him.

May God himself, the God of peace, sanctify you through and through. May your whole spirit, soul and body be kept blameless at the coming of our Lord Jesus Christ.

607—Faith in Action

Hebrews 11:1-3, 6, 32-40; 12:1, 2

Now faith is being sure of what we hope for and certain of what we do not see. This is what the ancients were commended for.

By faith we understand that the universe was formed at God's command, so that what is seen was not made out of what was visible.

And without faith it is impossible to please God, because anyone who comes to him must believe that he exists and that he rewards those who earnestly seek him.

And what more shall I say? I do not have time to tell about Gideon, Barak, Samson, Jephthah, David, Samuel and the prophets, who through faith conquered kingdoms, administered justice, and gained what was promised; who shut the mouths of lions, quenched the fury of the flames, and escaped the edge of the sword; whose weakness was turned to strength; and who became powerful in battle and routed foreign armies. Women received back their dead, raised to life again. Others were tortured and refused to be released, so that they might gain a better resurrection. Some faced jeers and flogging, while still others were chained and put in prison. They were stoned; they were sawed in two; they were put to death by the sword. They went about in sheepskins and goatskins, destitute, persecuted and mistreated—the world was not worthy of them. They wandered in deserts and mountains, and in caves and holes in the ground.

These were all commended for their faith, yet none of them received what had been promised. God had planned something better for us so that only together with us would they be made perfect.

Therefore, since we are surrounded by such a great cloud of witnesses, let us throw off everything that hinders and the sin that so easily entangles, and let us run with perseverance the race marked out for us. Let us fix our eyes on Jesus, the author and perfecter of our faith, who for the joy set before him endured the cross, scorning its shame, and sat down at the right hand of the throne of God.

608—If…
—from 1 John 1, 2, 4 and 5

If we claim to have fellowship with him yet walk in the darkness, we lie and do not live by the truth. But if we walk in the light, as he is in the light, we have fellowship with one another, and the blood of Jesus, his Son, purifies us from every sin.

If we claim to be without sin, we deceive ourselves and the truth is not in us. If we confess our sins, he is faithful and just and will forgive us our sins and purify us from all unrighteousness. If we claim we have not sinned, we make him out to be a liar and his word has no place in our lives.

If anybody does sin, we have one who speaks to the Father in our defense—Jesus Christ, the Righteous One. He is the atoning sacrifice for our sins, and not only for ours but also for the sins of the whole world.

If anyone loves the world, the love of the Father is not in him. For everything in the world—the cravings of sinful man, the lust of his eyes and the boasting of what he has and does—comes not from the Father but from the world.

If anyone says, "I love God," yet hates his brother, he is a liar. For anyone who does not love his brother, whom he has seen, cannot love God, whom he has not seen. And he has given us this command: Whoever loves God must also love his brother.

If we ask anything according to his will, he hears us. And if we know that he hears us—whatever we ask—we know that we have what we asked of him.

609—The Exalted Christ
—from Revelation 5 and 7

Then I saw a Lamb, looking as if it had been slain, standing in the center of the throne, encircled by the four living creatures and the elders. He had seven horns and seven eyes, which are the seven spirits of God sent out into all the earth. He came and took the scroll from the right hand of him who sat on the throne. And when he had taken it, the four living creatures and the twenty-four elders fell down before the Lamb. Each one had a harp and they were holding golden bowls full of incense, which are the prayers of the saints. And they sang a new song:

"You are worthy to take the scroll
and to open its seals,
because you were slain,
and with your blood you purchased men for God
from every tribe and language and people and nation.
You have made them to be a kingdom and priests
to serve our God,
and they will reign on the earth."

Then I looked and heard the voice of many angels, numbering thousands upon thousands, and ten thousand times ten thousand. They encircled the throne and the living creatures and the elders. In a loud voice they sang:

"Worthy is the Lamb, who was slain,
to receive power and wealth and wisdom and strength
and honor and glory and praise!"

Then I heard every creature in heaven and on earth and under the earth and on the sea, and all that is in them, singing:

"To him who sits on the throne and to the Lamb
be praise and honor and glory and power,
for ever and ever!"

After this I looked and there before me was a great multitude that no one could count, from every nation, tribe, people and language, standing before the throne and in front of the Lamb. They were wearing white robes and were holding palm branches in their hands. And they cried out in a loud voice:

"Salvation belongs to our God,
who sits on the throne,
and to the Lamb."

All the angels were standing around the throne and around the elders and the four living creatures. They fell down on their faces before the throne and worshiped God, saying:

"Amen!
Praise and glory
and wisdom and thanks and honor
and power and strength
be to our God for ever and ever.
Amen!"

610—New Heaven and Earth
Revelation 21:1-4, 22-27; 22:1-7

Then I saw a new heaven and a new earth, for the first heaven and the first earth had passed away, and there was no longer any sea. I saw the Holy City, the new Jerusalem, coming down out of heaven from God, prepared as a bride beautifully dressed for her husband. And I heard a loud voice from the throne saying, "Now the dwelling of God is with men, and he will live with them. They will be his people, and God himself will be with them and be their God. He will wipe every tear from their eyes. There will be no more death or mourning or crying or pain, for the old order of things has passed away."

I did not see a temple in the city, because the Lord God Almighty and the Lamb are its temple. The city does not need the sun or the moon to shine on it, for the glory of God gives it light, and the Lamb is its lamp. The nations will walk by its light, and the kings of the earth will bring their splendor into it. On no day will its gates ever be shut, for there will be no night there. The glory and honor of the nations will be brought into it. Nothing impure will ever enter it, nor will anyone who does what is shameful or deceitful, but only those whose names are written in the Lamb's book of life.

Then the angel showed me the river of the water of life, as clear as crystal, flowing from the throne of God and of the Lamb down the middle of the great street of the city. On each side of the river stood the tree of life, bearing twelve crops of fruit, yielding its fruit every month. And the leaves of the tree are for the healing of the nations. No longer will there be any curse. The throne of God and of the Lamb will be in the city, and his servants will serve him. They will see his face, and his name will be on their foreheads. There will be no more night. They will not need the light of a lamp or the light of the sun, for the Lord God will give them light. And they will reign for ever and ever.

The angel said to me, "These words are trustworthy and true. The Lord, the God of the spirits of the prophets, sent his angel to show his servants the things that must soon take place. Behold, I am coming soon! Blessed is he who keeps the words of the prophecy in this book."

611—Christmas
—from Matthew 1 and 2

This is how the birth of Jesus Christ came about. His mother Mary was pledged to be married to Joseph, but before they came together, she was found to be with child through the Holy Spirit. Because Joseph her husband was a righteous man and did not want to expose her to public disgrace, he had in mind to divorce her quietly. But after he had considered this, an angel of the Lord appeared to him in a dream and said, "Joseph son of David, do not be afraid to take Mary home as your wife, because what is conceived in her is from the Holy Spirit. She will give birth to a son, and you are to give him the name Jesus, because he will save his people from their sins." All this took place to fulfill what the Lord had said through the prophet:

"The virgin will be with child and will give birth to a son, and they will call him Immanuel"—which means, "God with us."

After Jesus was born in Bethlehem in Judea, during the time of King Herod, Magi from the east came to Jerusalem and asked, "Where is the one who has been born king of the Jews? We saw his star in the east and have come to worship him." When King Herod heard this he was disturbed, and all Jerusalem with him. When he had called together all the people's chief priests and teachers of the law, he asked them where the Christ was to be born. "In Bethlehem in Judea," they replied, "for this is what the prophet has written:

"But you, Bethlehem, in the land of Judah,
are by no means least among the rulers of Judah;
for out of you will come a ruler
who will be the shepherd of my people Israel."

On coming to the house, they saw the child with his mother Mary, and they bowed down and worshiped him. Then they opened their treasures and presented him with gifts of gold and of incense and of myrrh. And having been warned in a dream not to go back to Herod, they returned to their country by another route.

When they had gone, an angel of the Lord appeared to Joseph in a dream. "Get up," he said, "take the child and his mother and escape to

Egypt. Stay there until I tell you, for Herod is going to search for the child to kill him." So he got up, took the child and his mother during the night and left for Egypt, where he stayed until the death of Herod. And so was fulfilled what the Lord had said through the prophet:

"Out of Egypt I called my son."

When Herod realized that he had been outwitted by the Magi, he was furious, and he gave orders to kill all the boys in Bethlehem and its vicinity who were two years old and under, in accordance with the time he had learned from the Magi. Then what was said through the prophet Jeremiah was fulfilled:

"A voice is heard in Ramah,
weeping and great mourning,
Rachel weeping for her children
and refusing to be comforted,
because they are no more."

After Herod died, an angel of the Lord appeared in a dream to Joseph in Egypt and said, "Get up, take the child and his mother and go to the land of Israel." And he went and lived in a town called Nazareth. So was fulfilled what was said through the prophets:

"He will be called a Nazarene."

612—Easter—As He Said

—from Luke 24, John 2, Matthew 16, 17, 20 and 26

He is not here; he has risen! Remember how he told you, while he was still with you in Galilee:

Jesus answered them, "Destroy this temple, and I will raise it again in three days."

He is not here; he has risen! Remember how he told you, while he was still with you in Galilee.

From that time on Jesus began to explain to his disciples that he must go to Jerusalem and suffer many things at the hands of the elders, chief priests and teachers of the law, and that he must be killed and on the third day be raised to life.

He is not here; he has risen! Remember how he told you, while he was still with you in Galilee:

When they came together in Galilee, he said to them, "The Son of Man is going to be betrayed into the hands of men. They will kill him, and on the third day he will be raised to life."

He is not here; he has risen! Remember how he told you, while he was still with you in Galilee:

"We are going up to Jerusalem, and the Son of Man will be betrayed to the chief priests and the teachers of the law. They will condemn him to death and will turn him over to the Gentiles to be mocked and flogged and crucified. On the third day he will be raised to life!"

He is not here, but is risen: remember how he spoke unto you when he was yet in Galilee.

Then Jesus told them, "This very night you will all fall away on account of me, for it is written:
'I will strike the shepherd,
and the sheep of the flock will be scattered.'
But after I have risen, I will go ahead of you into Galilee."

Then they remembered his words.

613—Pentecost

—from Acts 1 and 2

On one occasion, while he was eating with them, he gave them this command: "Do not leave Jerusalem, but wait for the gift my Father promised, which you have heard me speak about. For John baptized with water, but in a few days you will be baptized with the Holy Spirit."

When the day of Pentecost came, they were all together in one place. Suddenly a sound like the blowing of a violent wind came from heaven and filled the whole house where they were sitting. They saw what seemed to be tongues of fire that separated and came to rest on each of them. All of them were filled with the Holy Spirit and began to speak in other tongues as the Spirit enabled them.

He said to them: It is not for you to know the times or dates the Father has set by his own authority. But you will receive power when the Holy Spirit comes on you; and you will be my witnesses in Jerusalem, and in all Judea and Samaria, and to the ends of the earth."

Now there were staying in Jerusalem God-fearing Jews from every nation under heaven. When they heard this sound, a crowd came together in bewilderment, because each one heard them speaking in his own language.

This is what was spoken by the prophet Joel:
"In the last days, God says,
I will pour out my Spirit on all people.
Your sons and daughters will prophesy,
your young men will see visions,
your old men will dream dreams.
Even on my servants, both men and women,
I will pour out my Spirit in those days,
and they will prophesy."

They devoted themselves to the apostles' teaching and to the fellowship, to the breaking of bread and to prayer. Everyone was filled with awe, and many wonders and miraculous signs were done by the apostles.

Every day they continued to meet together in the temple courts. They broke bread in their homes and ate together with glad and sincere hearts, praising God and enjoying the favor of all the people. And the Lord added to their number daily those who were being saved.

614—Jesus!

Luke 2, 19, 23; Matthew 9; Mark 1; Acts 10; 1 Peter 1; Revelation 1

Leader:
A Savior has been born to you...

People:
Today in the town of David a Savior has been born to you; he is Christ the Lord.

Choir:
Glory to God in the highest,
and on earth peace to men on whom his favor rests.

Leader:
He was named Jesus...

People:
On the eighth day, when it was time to circumcise him, he was named Jesus, the name the angel had given him before he had been conceived.

Choir:
For my eyes have seen your salvation,
which you have prepared in the sight of all people,
a light for revelation to the Gentiles
and for glory to your people Israel."

Leader:
Jesus...was baptized...

People:
At that time Jesus came from Nazareth in Galilee and was baptized by John in the Jordan.

Choir:
As Jesus was coming up out of the water, he saw heaven being torn open and the Spirit descending on him like a dove. And a voice came from heaven: "You are my Son, whom I love; with you I am well pleased."

Leader:
He went around doing good...

People:
God anointed Jesus of Nazareth with the Holy Spirit and power, and he went around doing good and healing all who were under the power of the devil, because God was with him.

Choir:
When the crowd saw this, they were filled with awe; and they praised God, who had given such authority to men.

Leader:
He came near the place where the road goes down the Mount of Olives...

People:
When he came near the place where the road goes down the Mount of Olives, the whole crowd of disciples began joyfully to praise God in loud voices for all the miracles they had seen:

Choir:
"Blessed is the king who comes in the name of the Lord!
Peace in Heaven and glory in the highest!"

Leader:
When they came to the place called The Skull...

People:
When they came to the place called The Skull, there they crucified him, along with the criminals—one on his right, the other on his left.

Choir:
The centurion, seeing what had happened, praised God and said, "Surely this was a righteous man."

Leader:
God raised him from the dead...

People:
We are witnesses of everything he did in the country of the Jews and in Jerusalem. They killed him by hanging him on a tree, but God raised him from the dead on the third day and caused him to be seen.

Choir:
Praise be to the God and Father of our Lord Jesus Christ! In his great mercy he has given us new birth into a living hope through the resurrection of Jesus Christ from the dead.

Leader:
Look, he is coming with the clouds...

People:
Look, he is coming with the clouds,
and every eye will see him,
even those who pierced him;
and all the people of the earth will
mourn because of him.

All:
So shall it be! Amen.

615—The Communion Service

—from 1 Corinthians 11; Psalm 139, 19, 51; John 6; Matthew 26; Revelation 22

Therefore, whoever eats the bread or drinks the cup of the Lord in an unworthy manner will be guilty of sinning against the body and blood of the Lord. A man ought to examine himself before he eats of the bread and drinks of the cup.

Search me, O God and know my heart;
test me and know my anxious thoughts.
See if there is any offensive way in me,
and lead me in the way everlasting.

For anyone who eats and drinks without recognizing the body of the Lord eats and drinks judgment on himself. That is why many among you are weak and sick, and a number of you have fallen asleep.

Who can discern his errors?
Forgive my hidden faults.
Keep your servant also from willful sins;
may they not rule over me.
Then will I be blameless,
innocent of great transgression.
May the words of my mouth and the meditation of my heart
be pleasing in your sight,
O Lord, my Rock and my Redeemer.

But if we judged ourselves, we would not come under judgment. When we are judged by the Lord, we are being disciplined so that we will not be condemned with the world.

For I know my transgressions,
and my sin is always before me.
Cleanse me with hyssop, and I will be clean;
wash me, and I will be whiter than snow.
Create in me a pure heart, O God,
and renew a steadfast spirit within me.

For I received from the Lord what I also passed on to you: The Lord Jesus, on the night he was betrayed, took bread, and when he had given thanks, he broke it and said, "This is my body, which is for you; do this in remembrance of me."

Here is the bread that comes down from heaven, which a man may eat and not die. I am the living bread that came down from heaven. If a man eats of this bread, he will live forever. This bread is my flesh, which I will give for the life of the world.

In the same way, after supper he took the cup, saying, "This cup is the new covenant in my blood; do this, whenever you drink it, in remembrance of me."

This is my blood of the covenant, which is poured out for many for the forgiveness of sins.

For whenever you eat this bread and drink this cup, you proclaim the Lord's death until he comes.

Come, Lord Jesus.

616—Believer's Baptism

—from Matthew 3, 28; Ephesians 4; Romans 6; Colossians 2, 3

Minister:
Then Jesus came from Galilee to the Jordan to be baptized by John. But John tried to deter him, saying, "I need to be baptized by you, and do you come to me?" Jesus replied, "Let it be so now; it is proper for us to do this to fulfill all righteousness." Then John consented. As soon as Jesus was baptized, he went up out of the water. At that moment heaven was opened, and he saw the Spirit of God descending like a dove and

lighting on him. And a voice from heaven said, "This is my Son, whom I love; with him I am well pleased."

Congregation:
Then the eleven disciples went to Galilee, to the mountain where Jesus had told them to go. When they saw him, they worshiped him; but some doubted. Then Jesus came to them and said, "All authority in heaven and on earth has been given to me. Therefore go and make disciples of all nations, baptizing them in the name of the Father and of the Son and of the Holy Spirit, and teaching them to obey everything I have commanded you. And surely I will be with you always, to the very end of the age."

Candidates:
There is one body and one Spirit—just as you were called to one hope when you were called—one Lord, one faith, one baptism; one God and Father of all, who is over all and through all and in all.

Or don't you know that all of us who were baptized into Christ Jesus were baptized into his death? We were therefore buried with him through baptism into death in order that, just as Christ was raised from the dead through the glory of the Father, we too may live a new life.

Minister:
Having been buried with him in baptism and raised with him through your faith in the power of God, who raised him from the dead. When you were dead in your sins and in the uncircumcision of your sinful nature, God made you alive with Christ. He forgave us all our sins.

Since, then, you have been raised with Christ, set your hearts on things above, where Christ is seated at the right hand of God.

617—The Blessing of Children

Matthew 18:2-6, 19:15; Luke 18:15-17

He called a little child and had him stand among them. And he said:

I tell you the truth, unless you change and become like little children, you will never enter the kingdom of heaven.

Therefore, whoever humbles himself like this child is the greatest in the kingdom of heaven. And whoever welcomes a little child like this in my name welcomes me.

But if anyone causes one of these little ones who believe in me to sin, it would be better for him to have a large millstone hung around his neck and to be drowned in the depths of the sea.

See that you do not look down on one of these little ones. For I tell you that their angels in heaven always see the face of my Father in heaven.

People were also bringing babies to Jesus to have him touch them. When the disciples saw this, they rebuked them.

But Jesus called the children to him and said, Let the little children come to me, and do not hinder them, for the kingdom of God belongs to such as these.

I tell you the truth, anyone who will not receive the kingdom of God like a little child will never enter it.

When he had placed his hands on them, he went on from there.

618—A Family Celebration

—from Proverbs 18, 31; Ephesians 5; 1 Peter 3; Psalm 127; Isaiah 54; Deuteronomy 5; Proverbs 6; Ephesians 6; Joshua 24.

Husband to Wife:

He who finds a wife finds what is good
and receives favor from the Lord.

A wife of noble character who can find?
She is worth far more than rubies.
Her husband has full confidence in her
and lacks nothing of value.
Her children arise and call her blessed;
her husband also, and he praises her:
"Many women do noble things,
but you surpass them all."
Charm is deceptive, and beauty is fleeting;
but a woman who fears the LORD is
to be praised.

Wife to Husband:

Husbands, love your wives, just as Christ loved the church and gave himself up for her to make her holy, cleansing her by the washing with water through the word, and to present her to himself as a radiant church, without stain or wrinkle or any other blemish, but holy and blameless. In this same way, husbands ought to love their wives as their own bodies. He who loves his wife loves himself.

Husbands, in the same way be considerate as you live with your wives, and treat them with respect as the weaker partner and as heirs with you of the gracious gift of life, so that nothing will hinder your prayers.

Children to Parents:

Sons are a heritage from the LORD,
children a reward from him.
Like arrows in the hands of a warrior
are sons born in one's youth.
Blessed is the man
whose quiver is full of them.
They will not be put to shame
when they contend with their enemies in the gate.

All your sons will be taught by the LORD,
and great will be your children's peace.

Parents to Children:

"Honor your father and your mother, as the LORD your God has commanded you, so that you may live long and that it may go well with you in the land the LORD your God is giving you.

My son, keep your father's commands
and do not forsake your mother's teaching.
Bind them upon your heart forever;
fasten them around your neck.
When you walk, they will guide you;
when you sleep, they will watch over you;
when you awake, they will speak to you.
For these commands are a lamp,
this teaching is a light,
and the corrections of discipline
are the way to life.

"Honor your father and mother"—which is the first commandment with a promise.

Entire Family:

Now fear the Lord and serve him with all faithfulness. Throw away the gods your forefathers worshiped beyond the River and in Egypt, and serve the Lord. But if serving the Lord seems undesirable to you, then choose for yourselves this day whom you will serve...But as for me and my household, we will serve the Lord.

619—The Fruit of the Spirit

Galatians 5:22, 23, and other texts

The fruit of the Spirit is love...

Dear friends, let us love one another, for love comes from God. Everyone who loves has been born of God and knows God.

The fruit of the Spirit is...joy...

Be filled with the Spirit. Speak to one another with psalms, hymns, and spiritual songs. Sing and make music in your heart to the Lord.

The fruit of the Spirit is...peace...

Peace I leave with you; my peace I give you. I do not give to you as the world gives. Do not let your hearts be troubled and do not be afraid.

The fruit of the Spirit is...patience...

Being strengthened with all power according to his glorious might so that you may have great endurance and patience.

The fruit of the Spirit is...kindness...

And the Lord's servant must not quarrel; instead, he must be kind to everyone, able to teach, not resentful.

The fruit of the Spirit is...goodness...

For the fruit of the light consists in all goodness, righteousness and truth.

The fruit of the Spirit is...faithfulness...

Now it is required that those who have been given a trust must prove faithful.

The fruit of the Spirit is...gentleness...

As a prisoner for the Lord, then, I urge you to live a life worthy of the calling you have received. Be completely humble and gentle; be patient, bearing with one another in love.

The fruit of the Spirit is...self-control...

Everyone who competes in the games goes into strict training. They do it to get a crown that will not last; but we do it to get a crown that will last forever.

Against such things there is no law.

620—More Than Conquerors
Romans 8:31-35, 37-39

What, then, shall we say in response to this? If God is for us, who can be against us?

He who did not spare his own Son, but gave him up for us all—how will he not also, along with him, graciously give us all things?

Who will bring any charge against those whom God has chosen?

It is God who justifies.

Who is he that condemns?

Christ Jesus, who died—more than that, who was raised to life—is at the right hand of God and is also interceding for us.

Who shall separate us from the love of Christ? Shall trouble or hardship or persecution or famine or nakedness or danger or sword?

No, in all these things we are more than conquerors through him who loved us. For I am convinced that neither death nor life, neither angels nor demons, neither the present nor the future, nor any powers, neither height nor depth, nor anything else in all creation, will be able to separate us from the love of God that is in Christ Jesus our Lord.

REFERENCE INDEX OF SCRIPTURE READINGS

In some instances where entire chapters are listed below, the Reading may actually contain only certain passages or a number of scattered and selected verses.

OTHER WORSHIP RESOURCES

AFFIRMATIONS OF FAITH
PRAYERS
DEVOTIONAL READINGS

621—An Affirmation of Faith

We believe in Jesus Christ the Lord,
Who was promised to the people of Israel,
Who came in the flesh to dwell among us,
Who announced the coming of the rule of God,
Who gathered disciples and taught them,
Who died on the cross to free us from sin,
Who rose from the dead to give us life and hope,
Who reigns in heaven at the right hand of God,
Who comes to judge and bring justice to victory.

We believe in God His Father,
Who raised Him from the dead,
Who created and sustains the universe,
Who acts to deliver His people in times of need,
Who desires all men everywhere to be saved,
Who rules over the destinies of men and nations,
Who continues to love men even when they reject Him.

We believe in the Holy Spirit,
Who is the form of God present in the church,
Who moves men to faith and obedience,
Who is the guarantee of our deliverance,
Who leads us to find God's will in the Word,
Who assists those whom He renews in prayer,
Who guides us in discernment,
Who impels us to act together.

We believe God has made us His people,
To invite others to follow Christ,
To encourage one another to deeper commitment,
To proclaim forgiveness of sins and hope,
To reconcile men to God through word and deed,
To bear witness to the power of love over hate,
To proclaim Jesus the Lord over all,
To meet the daily tasks of life with purpose,
To suffer joyfully for the cause of right,
To the ends of the earth,
To the end of the age,
To the praise of His glory. Amen.

622—The Apostles' Creed

I believe in God the Father Almighty, maker of heaven and earth.

And in Jesus Christ, His only begotten Son, our Lord, who was conceived by the Holy Spirit, born of the virgin Mary, suffered under Pontius Pilate, was crucified, dead and buried; He descended into hell; the third day He rose again from the dead; He ascended into heaven, and sitteth at the right hand of God the Father Almighty; from thence He shall come to judge the quick and the dead.

I believe in the Holy Spirit, the holy Christian church, the communion of saints, the forgiveness of sins, the resurrection of the body, and the life everlasting. Amen.

623—Confession of Faith

I believe, O Lord, in You,
Father, Word, Spirit, One God;
that by Your fatherly love and power all things were created;
that by Your goodness and love to man
all things have been gathered into one
in Your Word,
Who, for us men and for our salvation,
became flesh,
was conceived, was born,
suffered, was crucified,
died, was buried,
descended, rose again,
ascended, sat down,
will return, will repay;
that by the forth-shining and operation of Your Holy Spirit
has been called out of the whole world a peculiar people,
into a commonwealth of faith in the truth
and holiness of life,
in which we are partakers of the communion of saints
and forgiveness of sins in this world,
and in which we look for the resurrection of the flesh
and the life everlasting
in the world to come.
This most holy faith once delivered to the saints
I believe, O Lord;
help my unbelief,
increase my little faith.

624—An Affirmation of Faith

Leader:
We affirm our faith in the Bible.

People:
We believe the Bible to be the inspired, the only infallible authoritative Word of God.

Leader:
We affirm our faith in God.

People:
We believe that there is one God, eternally existent in three persons, Father, Son and Holy Ghost.

Leader:
We affirm our faith in Jesus Christ.

People:
We believe in the deity of our Lord Jesus Christ, in His virgin birth, in His sinless life, in His miracles, in His vicarious and atoning death through His shed blood, in His bodily resurrection, in His ascension to the right hand of the Father, and in His personal return in power and glory.

Leader:
We affirm our faith in salvation.

People:
We believe that, for the salvation of lost and sinful man, regeneration by the Holy Spirit is absolutely essential.

Leader:
We affirm our faith in the Holy Spirit.

People:
We believe in the present ministry of the Holy Spirit by whose indwelling the Christian is enabled to live a godly life.

Leader:
We affirm our faith in the Resurrection.

People:
We believe in the resurrection of both the saved and the lost; they that are saved unto the resurrection of life and they that are lost unto the resurrection of damnation.

Leader:
We affirm our faith in spiritual unity.

People:
We believe in the spiritual unity of believers in our Lord Jesus Christ.

625—The Purpose of God

We affirm our belief in the one eternal God,
Creator and Lord of the World,
Father,
Son, and
Holy Spirit,
who governs all things
according to the purpose of his will.
He has been calling out from the world a people for Himself,
and sending his people back into the world
to be his servants and his witness,
for the extension of his kingdom,
the building up of Christ's body,
and the glory of his name.
We confess with shame that we have often denied
our calling
and failed in our mission,
by becoming conformed to the world
or by withdrawing from it.
Yet we rejoice that even when borne by earthen vessels
the gospel is still a precious treasure.
To the task of making that treasure known
in the power of the Holy Spirit
we desire to dedicate ourselves anew.

626—Te Deum

We praise Thee, O God:
We acknowledge Thee to be the Lord.
All the earth doth worship Thee, the Father everlasting.
To Thee all angels cry aloud;
The heavens and all the powers therein.
To Thee cherubim and seraphim continually do cry:
Holy, Holy, Holy, Lord God of Sabaoth.
Heaven and earth are full of the majesty of Thy glory.
The glorious company of the apostles praise Thee.
The goodly fellowship of the prophets praise Thee.
The noble army of martyrs praise Thee.
The holy Church, throughout all the world, doth acknowledge Thee,
The Father of an infinite majesty;
Thine adorable, true, and only Son,
Also the Holy Spirit, the comforter.
Thou art the King of glory, O Christ.
Thou art the everlasting Son of the Father.
When Thou tookest upon Thee to deliver man,
Thou didst humble Thyself to be born of a virgin.
When Thou hadst overcome the sharpness of death,
Thou didst open the kingdom of heaven to all believers.
Thou sittest at the right hand of God, in the glory of the Father.
We believe that Thou shalt come to be our Judge.
We therefore pray Thee, help Thy servants,
Whom Thou hast redeemed with Thy precious blood.
Make them to be numbered with Thy saints in glory everlasting.
O Lord, save Thy people, and bless Thy heritage.
Govern them, and lift them up forever.
Day by day we magnify Thee;
And we worship Thy name ever, world without end.
Vouchsafe, O Lord, to keep us this day without sin.
O Lord, have mercy upon us, have mercy upon us.
O Lord, let Thy mercy be upon us, as our trust is in Thee.
O Lord, in Thee have I trusted;
Let me never be confounded.

627—Father, We Seek Thee

Father:

We seek Thy truth lest we be deceived and misled.
We seek Thy love lest we go unloving and
uncaring through the day.
We seek Thy peace lest we waste our time in
anxieties that eat up our energies and profit
neither ourselves nor others.
We seek Thyself lest, living to ourselves,
we remain lonely and alien and frustrated.
May we know today what it means to live in
Christ's life, to be open to His mind, to be
governed by His love, to be ruled by His purpose.
For Jesus Christ's sake. Amen.

628—The Intent of My Heart

Lord,
I would trust Thee completely;
I would be altogether Thine;
I would exalt Thee above all.

I desire that I may feel no sense of possessing anything
outside of Thee.
I want constantly to be aware of Thy overshadowing Presence
and to hear Thy Voice.
I long to live in restful sincerity of heart.
I want to live so fully in the Spirit
that all my thoughts may be as sweet incense
ascending to Thee
and every act of my life may be an act of worship.

Therefore I pray in the words of Thy great servant of old,
"I beseech Thee so for to cleanse
the intent of mine heart with the
unspeakable gift of Thy grace,
that I may perfectly love Thee
and worthily praise Thee."

And all this I confidently believe Thou wilt grant me through
the merits of Jesus Christ Thy Son. Amen.

629—Be, Lord, Within Me

Be, Lord,
within me to strengthen me,
without me to guard me,
over me to shelter me,
beneath me to stablish me,
before me to guide me,
after me to forward me,
round about me to secure me.

630—Submission

O Lord,
let me not henceforth desire health or life,
except to spend them for You,
with You,
and in You.
You alone know what is good for me:
Do, therefore, what seems best to You.
Give to me, or take from me;
Conform my will to Yours;
And grant that, with humble and perfect
submission, and in holy confidence, I
may receive the orders of Your eternal
Providence;
And may equally adore all that
comes to me from You;

through Jesus Christ our Lord. Amen.

631—In Life's Seasons

God for all seasons,
Who gives summer's warm breezes the crispness of autumn,
Who lays upon earth's breast the snows of winter,
Who makes streams flow in springtime,
Who in summer calls forth to fruit the sleeping folds of nature,
be the God for all seasons of my life:
days of joy and nights of sorrow,
weeks of anxiety and years of patience,
lifetime of work and play,
the eternity of Thy grace.

Some of my days fly by with creative work or relaxation;
others linger with their tiring requirements.

Some days I would cling to with joy;
others I would cast away with vengeance.

Some days escape me through the work to be done;
others never seem to end.

Strengthen me to live all my days not only in the time it takes to live them
but with the peace and patience necessary.

Save me from the waste of today caused by wanting tomorrow.

Help me to stop fighting against time and tide.
Cleanse me of anxiety so I may take my days in stride.

Shed Thy Spirit upon me so I may cease worrying about the mysteries of life
and wholly enjoy the blessings I can count.

Lead me in my waking moments so I may conquer life rather than complain about it.

Comfort me in my resting moments so I may be strengthened in soul and body for
the living of the next day given to me by Thy providence.

632—Quietness of Heart

Give me, O Lord
that quietness of heart that makes the most of labor and of rest. Save me from passionate excitement, petulant fretfulness, and idle fear, keeping me ever in the restful presence of Thy love.

Teach me to be alert and wise in all responsibilities, without hurry and without neglect. Tame Thou and rule my tongue, that I may not transgress Thy law of love. When others censure, may I seek Thine image in each fellow man, judging with charity, as one who shall be judged.

Banish envy and hatred from my thoughts.

Help me to be content amid the strife of tongues, with my unspoken thought. When anxious cares threaten my peace, help me to run to Thee, that I may find my rest and be made strong for calm endurance and valiant service.

633—As If at Sea...

O God, my sea is so great
And my boat is so small.
Fill my sails with the winds of the Spirit.

May I trust your steady hand on the helm of my life.
Keep my eyes each alternating between the compass of your Word
And the distant horizons.
And at the end of my journey
May I cast my anchor in the quiet harbor of your love.
In the name of Christ my Savior I pray. Amen.

634—An Act of Pleading

Two things I recognize in myself, O Lord;
the nature which You have made,
the sin which I have added.
I confess that by my fault I have disfigured nature:
but You remember that I am a wind,
that passes away and comes not again.
For of myself I cannot come again from sin.
Alas! take away from me what I have done;
let that abide in me which You have made;
that so, that perish not which You have redeemed with Your
precious blood.
Alas! Let not my wickedness destroy
what Your goodness has redeemed.
O Lord my God, if I have so done as to be Your criminal,
yet could I so do as not to be Your servant?
If thereby I have done away my innocence,
yet have I thereby withal destroyed Your mercy?
If I have wrought that for which You might condemn me,
yet have You also lost that whereby You are used to save?
'Tis true, O Lord, my conscience deserves condemnation;
but Your mercy overtops all offence.
Spare therefore,
forasmuch as it is not difficult to Your power
illsorting with Your justice
unwonted with Your loving kindness
to spare the wrongdoer.
You that have created me, redeemed me,
do not destroy me, condemn me.
You that have created me by Your goodness,
let not Your work perish by my iniquity.
Acknowledge in me that is Yours,
and take away from me that is mine.

635—Confession

O Father of heaven,
O Son of God, Redeemer of the world,
O Holy Spirit,
Three Persons and one God:

Have mercy upon me, the most wretched and miserable of sinners. I have offended both against heaven and earth more than tongue can express. Whither then may I go, or whither should I fly? To heaven, I may be ashamed to lift up my eyes, and in earth I find no place of refuge or succor. To Thee, therefore, O Lord, do I run; to Thee do I humble myself, saying: O Lord, my God, my sins are great but yet have mercy upon me for Thy great mercy. The great mystery that God became man was not wrought for little or few offenses. Thou didn't give Thy Son, O heavenly Father, unto death for small sins only, but for all the greatest sins of the world, so that the sinner might return unto Thee with his whole heart, as I do now. Wherefore, have mercy on me, O God, whose propiety is always to have mercy; have mercy on me, O Lord, for Thy great mercy. I crave nothing, O Lord, for my own merits, but for Thy Name's sake, that it may be hallowed thereby, and for Thy dear Son, Jesus Christ's sake;

And now therefore, my Father in heaven, hallowed be Thy name...

636—When We Have Failed

O God, you know how badly I have failed in the task which I attempted, and which was given me to do, and in which I so much wanted to do well.

> Don't let me become too depressed and discouraged; help me to have the determination to try again and to work still harder.
>
> Don't let me try to put the blame on everyone and on everything except myself.
>
> Don't let me be resentful and bitter about this failure; but help me to accept both success and failure with a good grace.
>
> Don't let me be envious and jealous of those who have succeeded where I have failed.
>
> Don't ever let me talk about giving up and giving in; but help me to refuse to be beaten.

Help me to learn the lesson which you want me to learn even from this failure; help me to begin again, and not to make the same mistakes again.

Maybe it is hardest of all to meet the eyes of those who are disappointed in me. Help me even yet to show them that I deserve their trust and to let them see what I can do.

This I ask for your love's sake. Amen.

637—Listening

Lord, teach me to listen.
The times are noisy
and my ears are weary with the thousand
raucous sounds which continuously assault them.
Give me the spirit of the boy Samuel
when he said to Thee,
"Speak, for Thy servant heareth."
Let me hear Thee speaking in my heart.
Let me get used to the sound of Thy Voice,
that its tones may be familiar
when the sounds of faith die away
and the only sound will be the
music of Thy speaking Voice.
Amen.

638—A Prayer for the Church

Grant, O Almighty God,
that we may learn to cast our eyes
upon the state of thine ancient Church,
since at the present day the sorrowful and
manifest dispersion of thy Church
seems to threaten its complete destruction:

Grant also,
that we may look upon those promises
which are common to us also,
that we may wait till thy Church
emerges again from the darkness of death.
Meanwhile,
may we be content with thy help,
however weak as to outward appearance,
till at length it shall appear
that our patience was not delusive,
when we enjoy the reward of our faith
and patience
in thy heavenly kingdom,
through Jesus Christ our Lord. Amen.

639—A Prayer for Missionaries

O God, bless all those who have gone out to bring the message of the Gospel to other lands.

I remember before You
Those who have to endure hardship and discomfort;
Those who have to face peril and danger;
Those who have had to leave their families and their children behind while they went out to other lands;
Those who have had to struggle with a new language and with new ways of thought;
Those whose health has broken down under the strain, and who have had to come home, not knowing whether they will ever be fit for their task again;
Those who have to face constant discouragement in a situation in which no progress ever seems to be made.

Especially bless those who work in countries where new nations are being born, and where there is strife and trouble and bitterness in the birth-pangs of the new age.

Bless those who preach in the villages and the towns and the cities; those who teach in the schools and the colleges; those who work in the hospitals and among the sick; those who have laid their gifts of craftsmanship or administration on the altar of missionary service.

Help us at home never to forget them and always to pray for them. And help us to give generously of our money to their work so that it may go where we ourselves cannot go.

And bring quickly the day when the knowledge of You will cover the earth as the waters cover the sea: through Jesus Christ my Lord. Amen.

640—A Prayer, When You Cannot Pray

O my Father, I have moments of deep unrest—
Moments when I know not what to ask
for reason of the very excess
of my wants.
I have in these hours no words for You;
no conscious prayers for You.
My prayer seems purely worldly;
I want only the wings of a dove that
I may flee away.

Yet all the time
You have accepted my unrest as a prayer,
You have interpreted its cry for a dove's wings as a cry for You,
You have received the nameless longing of my heart as the intercessions of Your Spirit.

They are not yet the intercessions of my spirit.

I know not what I ask.
But You know what I ask, O my God.
You know the name of that need which lies beneath my speechless groan.
You know that, because I am made in Your image, I can find rest only in what gives rest to You;

Therefore You have counted my unrest
unto me for righteousness and have
called my groaning Your Spirit's prayer.
Amen.

641—A Benediction

"May the roads rise up to meet you;
May the winds be always at your back;
May the sun shine warmly upon your face,
And the rains fall softly on your fields.
Until we meet again
May the good Lord hold you in the hollow of His hand.
And may He keep your hand steady...steady now...
Till the setting of the golden sun. Amen."

642—Incarnation

God is love in action—love rushing on a rescue mission.
He never intended His beloved man to be lonely and miserable,
wandering in a dark forest.
That is against His Own nature of light.

God took the initiative in Bethlehem when He became
a human being in the Person of Jesus Christ.
He joined us in the darkness of life and said,
"I am the Light of the world."
The dark forest of human existence was lit up.

When Christ lived among men, He knew what poverty was.
He was hungry,
thirsty,
sorrowful,
lonely and tired.
He relieved pain in others,
but He experienced the full force of it Himself.

When Christ died on the cross, He bore the shattering responsibility of guilt.
He lifted the heaviest burden from man's most sensitive part—his conscience.
He brought peace to his mind by forgiving the sins which caused the guilt.
Receiving Him is the greatest miracle in life.
Christ called it
"to be born anew."
Paul called it
"to become a new person altogether."

The broken relationship with God is restored.
We are at home with God, and therefore
at home with ourselves,
at home with our fellow men,
and at home in our world.

643—I Love You, Lord

I love you, Lord,
not doubtingly,
but with absolute certainty.
Your Word beat upon my heart until I fell in love with You,
and now the universe and everything in it tells me to love You,
and tells the same thing to us all,
so that we are without excuse.

And what do I love when I love you?
Not physical beauty,
or the grandeur of our existence in time,
or the radiance of light that pleases the eye,
or the sweet melody of old familiar songs,
or the fragrance of flowers
and ointments
and spices,
or the taste of manna or honey,
or the arms we use to clasp each other.
None of these do I love when I love my God.

Yet there is a kind of light,
and a kind of melody,
and a kind of fragrance,
and a kind of food,
and a kind of embracing,
when I love my God.
They are the kind of light and sound and odor and food and love that affect the senses of my inner man.
There is another dimension of life in which my soul reflects a light that space itself cannot contain.
It hears melodies that never fade with time.
It inhales lovely scents that are not blown away by the wind.

It eats without diminishing or consuming the supply.
It never gets separated from the embrace of God and
never gets tired of it.

That is what I love when I love my God.

644—Jesus! Jesus! Jesus!

To many, Jesus Christ is only a grand subject for a painting,
a heroic theme for a pen,
a beautiful form for a statute,
or a thought for a song.
But to those who have heard His voice,
who have felt His pardon,
who have received His benediction,
He is music—light—joy—hope and salvation—
a Friend who never forsakes, lifting you up
when others try to put you down,
There is no name like His.
It is more inspiring than Caesar's,
more musical than Beethoven's,
more eloquent than Demosthenes',
more patient than Lincoln's.
The name of Jesus throbs with all life,
weeps with all pathos,
groans with all pains,
stoops with all love.
Who like Jesus can pity a homeless orphan?
Who like Jesus can welcome a wayward prodigal back home?
Who like Jesus can make a drunkard sober?
Who like Jesus can illuminate a cemetery plowed with graves?
Who like Jesus can make a queen unto God out of a lost woman of the street?
Who like Jesus can catch the tears of human sorrow in His bowl?
Who like Jesus can kiss away our sorrow?

I struggle for a metaphor with which to express Jesus.
He is not like the bursting forth of an orchestra.
That is too loud and it might be out of tune.
He is not like the sea when lashed by a storm,
That is too boisterous.
He is not like a mountain canopied with snow,
That is too solitary and remote.
He is the Lily of the Valley;
the Rose of Sharon;
a gale of sweet spices from Heaven.
He is our home.

645—Loyalty to Jesus

In a remote province of Galilee
at the high point of Roman power,
there appeared a man dressed in peasant garb,
with the calloused hands of a laborer,
who awakened unprecedented interest
by His astonishing words and works.

He was a young man of about 30 years of age.
He had only the elementary schooling of the village synagogue.
He had no political or financial backing.

His itinerate ministry of teaching and healing was of short duration—
about three years—
and then He was crucified at the hands
of the religious and political authorities
who feared His growing popularity.

Rather than scatter His followers, His death was followed
by a movement of revolutionary impact and power.

The effects of that spiritual explosion
remain a major factor in our world today—
the strongest influence for good
and for God
our world knows.

What do we do with this man Jesus?
If He is not the Son of God and Savior of mankind,
then let us get down to the
bitter business of adjusting
to a grim and hopeless world.
If He is, then let us give Him the full measure of our loyalty and love.

646—Thine Is the Power

I am startled by an atomic explosion 250 times the power of the Hiroshima bomb.
I am impressed when scientists develop instruments so powerful
they can pick up the sound of galaxies in collision
270 million light years away.
I am amazed to see a laser beam cut through a diamond
as if it were paper.
I marvel at the quiet power of a few drops of water which,
when frozen, can tear apart a brass valve
a half-dozen men cannot turn.

But I am completely lost attempting to search out the power of God.
I try to say it all by simply saying 'God,'
but to expect one word to explain His power is like
looking out on the setting sun,
exhausting in its beauty,
its hundred hues glowing indescribably,
cloud formations around it like the skill of a thousand masters
expressed in one piece of art,
silhouettes before it cut with
exactness and painted with ebony
against the sun,
and calling all this simply 'Sunset.'

Who can express in a word or even a thousand words
the magnitude and grandeur of the power of God?
It is like putting a wet finger to a penlight battery and,
by the sensation you feel,
defining all the properties,
potentiality, and powers of
electricity.

God has been known to bring giants to their knees, weeping like babies,
God has been known to take corrupt minds and give them thoughts
as pure as fresh-fallen snowflakes.
God has been known to take a home, torn by strife,
and make it the sweetest place this side of heaven.
God has been known to take crippled men,
who scrape the earth as they pull along
their weakened torsos,
and stand them, whole and healthy,
upon their feet.
God has been known to take men rotten and ripe for hell,
and make them jewels in the kingdom of heaven.
God has been known to displace hate with love,
sorrow with joy
war with peace
ashes with fire.

God can do all things possible, and—
"Father! All things are possible with thee."

647—To Sinners with Tears

Go to sinners with tears in your eyes.
Let them see that you yearn over them and that
it is the earnest desire of your heart
to do them good.
Let them perceive that you have no other end
but their eternal happiness,
and that it is your love that forces you
to speak.
I know it must be God that changes men's hearts,
but I know also that God works by means,
and when he means to prevail with men
he usually suits the means to the end,
and stirs up men to plead with them
in a kindly way,
and so makes it successful.

Do it from compassion and love.
We have many reprovers,
but their manner shows
too plainly
that they are not influenced by love.
Villifying or reproaching a man for his faults
is not likely to work his reformation
or convert him to God.
Men will consider people who so deal with them
to be enemies,
and the words of an enemy
are not very persuasive.

648—If I Were the Devil

If I were the Prince of Darkness I would want to engulf the whole earth in darkness.

I would begin with a campaign of whispers. With the wisdom of a serpent, I would whisper to you as I whispered to Eve, "Do as you please."

To the young I would whisper, "The Bible is a myth." I would convince them that "man created God," instead of the other way around. I would confide that "what is bad is good and what is good is square."

In the ears of the young married I would whisper that work is debasing, that cocktail parties are good for you. I would caution them not to be "extreme" in religion, in patriotism, in moral conduct.

I would encourage schools to confine young intellects, but neglect to discipline emotions; let those run wild.

I'd designate an atheist to front for me before the highest courts and I'd get preachers to say, "She's right."

With flattery and promises of power I would get the courts to do what I construe as against God and in favor of pornography. Thus I would evict God from the courthouse, then the schoolhouse, then from the houses of Congress.

Then in his own churches I'd substitue psychology for religion and deify science.

If I were Satan I'd make the symbol of Easter an egg...and the symbol of Christmas a bottle.

Then I would separate families, putting children in uniform, women in coal mines and objectors in slave-labor camps.

If I were Satan I'd just keep doing what he's doing.

649—My Prayer Was Answered

I asked for strength that I might achieve;
He made me weak that I might obey.
I asked for health that I might do greater things;
I was given grace that I might do better things.
I asked for riches that I might be happy;
I was given poverty that I might be wise.
I asked for power that I might have the praise of men;
I was given weakness that I might feel the need of God.
I asked for all things that I might enjoy life;
I was given life that I might enjoy all things.
I received nothing that I asked for, all that I hoped for,
My prayer was answered.

650—The Only True Values

I have concluded that the accumulation of wealth, even if I could achieve it, is an insufficient reason for living. When I reach the end of my days, a moment or two from now, I must look backward on something more meaningful than the pursuit of houses and land and machines and stocks and bonds. Nor is fame of any lasting benefit. I will consider my earthly existence to have been wasted unless I can recall a loving family, a consistent investment in the lives of people,. and an earnest attempt to serve the God who made me. Nothing else makes much sense.

651—Not I, But Christ

"Not I, but Christ," is a fact meant to shine out. It is designed, calculated, to light up the common daily path of the person whose will has really let it in. Have you said that Self, and all Self's interests and aims, are now laid at, laid under, the Master's feet? That you are literally, and wholly, not your own, but His? Then the spring and center of your life being transferred to Another, there will be a quiet but real revolution in the working.

652—Suffering—Hurting

Am I wounded? He is balm.
    Am I sick? He is medicine.
Am I poor? He is wealth.
    Am I hungry? He is bread.
Am I thirsty? He is water.
    Am I in debt? He is my surety.
Am I in darkness? He is my sun and shield.
    Must I face black clouds and a gathering storm?
He is an anchor both sure and steadfast.
    Am I being tried?
He pleads for me as my perfect Advocate.
    Yes, in every human need Christ is my all!

653—Redemption

A famous American scientist once said, "If you want to send an idea, wrap it up in a person." This is exactly what God did at Bethlehem. He sent unto our lost world the saving truth of His grace, wrapped up in a virgin-born baby...a baby who, in manhood, said "I AM the Truth."

An anonymous author, in commenting on this One has written, "Longfellow could take a worthless sheet of paper, write a poem on it and make it worth $6,000.00...that is genius! Rockefeller can sign his name to a piece of paper and make it worth millions...that is capital! A mechanic can take a piece of metal worth $5.00 and make an article worth $20.00...that is skill! An artist can take a cheap piece of canvas, paint a picture on it and make it worth $1,000,000.00...that is art! The Lord Jesus Christ can take a worthless life, put His Spirit into it and make it both a blessing to humanity and fit for citizenship in Heaven...that is salvation!

The apostle Paul, realizing the truth of this, was inspired to write in II Corinthians 5:17, "If any man be in Christ, he is a new creation; old things pass away; behold, all things become new."

And this is what redemption is all about!

654—What Is a Christian?

What is a Christian? The question can be answered in many ways, but the richest answer I know is that a Christian is one who has God for his Father.

But cannot this be said of every man, Christian or not? Emphatically no! The idea that all men are children of God is not found in the Bible anywhere. The Old Testament shows God as the Father, not of all men, but of His own people, the seed of Abraham. 'Israel is my son, even my firstborn: and I say unto thee, Let my son go...' (Exodus 4:22f). The New Testament has a world vision, but it too shows God as the Father, not of all men, but of those who, knowing themselves to be sinners, put their trust in the Lord Jesus Christ as their divine sin-bearer and master, and so become Abraham's spiritual seed. 'Ye are all sons of God, through faith, in Christ Jesus...ye all are one man in Christ Jesus. And if ye are Christ's, then are ye Abraham's seed' (Galatians 3:26ff.). Sonship to God is not, therefore, a universal status upon which everyone enters by natural birth, but a supernatural gift which one receives through receiving Jesus. 'No man cometh unto the Father'—in other words, is acknowledged by God as a son—'but by me' (John 14:6). The gift of sonship to God becomes ours, not through being born, but through being born again. '***As many as received Him, to them*** gave He power to become the sons of God, even to them that believe on His name: which were born, not of blood, nor of the will of the flesh, nor of the will of man, but of God' (John 1:12f.).

655—To See As Jesus Sees

Lord Jesus,
by the indwelling of Thy Holy Spirit,
purge our eyes to discern and
contemplate Thee
until we attain to see as Thou seest,
judge as Thou judgest,
choose as Thou choosest;
and, having sought and found Thee,
to behold Thee for ever and ever.
We ask this for Thy name's sake. Amen.

AUTHOR AND CONTRIBUTOR INDEX

OUR THANKS to those who submitted material selected for the supplementary readings: F. Carlton Booth—632, 644; Harold L. Fickett, Jr.—653; Dick Hillis—645, 649, 652; David Howard—634; Billy Melvin—624; Jess C. Moody—633, 641; Raymond C. Ortlund—629; Paul S. Rees—627, 651; Russell A. Shive—628; Charles A. Wickman—630, 635, 640; Sherwood E. Wirt—647.

SUBJECT INDEX OF SCRIPTURE AND OTHER READINGS

TITLE INDEX OF SCRIPTURE AND OTHER READINGS

PART 5

INDEXES

for the hymns

ACKNOWLEDGMENTS of Hymn Copyrights:

The use of the valid copyrights of the following publishers and individuals is gratefully acknowledged. In each case, rearranging, photocopying, or reproduction by any other means, as well as the use of the song in performance for profit, is specifically prohibited by law without the written permission of the copyright owner. Recordings must be licensed by the agency shown in parentheses.

Songs showing a copyright as © are protected by the Berne Convention throughout Europe and Canada. Songs showing "all rights reserved" are protected throughout Latin and South America. Those who abuse the rights of copyright are subject to severe penalty according to federal law, and must also face the moral implications of the Christian ethic.

USED BY PERMISSION:

ABINGDON 201 Eighth Avenue South, Nashville, TN 37202—(615) 749-6421: Song 173w.

ALBERT E. BRUMLEY AND SONS Powell, MO 65730—(417) 435-2225: (SESAC) Songs 256, 526.

AUGSBURG PUBLISHING HOUSE 426 South Fifth Street, Minneapolis, MN 55415—(612) 332-4561:(SESAC) Song 210w.

BARHAM-GOULD, A. CYRIL—contact D.R. Gould: Song 388m.

BELINDA MUSIC—contact Unichappell Music, Inc.: Song 374.

BEN SPEER MUSIC PO box 9201, Nashville, TN 37204—(615) 329-9999: (BMI) Song 470.

BENSON COMPANY, THE 365 Great Circle Road, Nashville, TN 37228—(615) 259-9111: Songs listed under names shown in copyright notices.

BENSON, JOHN T., Jr. —contact Singspiration: (ASCAP) Songs 218, 519, 570.

BREITKOPF & HARTEL Postfach 1707, D-6200 Weisbaden 1, Germany—(06121) 40 20 31: Songs 147 melody, 334 melody.

BROADMAN PRESS 127 Ninth Avenue North, Nashville, TN 37234—(615) 251-2000: (SESAC) Songs 120, 409, 437, 449, 572. (Affiliate of The Sunday School Board of the Southern Baptist Convention.)

CHANCEL MUSIC, INC. 4068 Garden Ave., Western Springs, IL 60558—Song 446.

CHATTO AND WINDUS LTD. 40-42 William IV Street, London WC2N 4DF, England—01-836-0127: Song 378w.

COBER, KENNETH L.—contact Judson Press: Song 141w.

COVENANT PRESS 5101 Francisco Avenue North, Chicago, IL 60625—(312) 784-3000: Songs 40m, 122m, 195w, 209, 270, 431m.

CRESCENDO PUBLICATIONS, INC. PO box 28218, Dallas, TX 75228—(214) 324-2451: (BMI) Song 413.

CROWELL, REID 719 Lowell Street, Dallas, TX 75214: Song 431w.

CROWN ROYAL MUSIC COMPANY—contact The Benson Company: (BMI) Song 309.

DIMENSION MUSIC—contact The Benson Company: (SESAC) Songs 98, 229, 272, 423.

DUNAMIS MUSIC 8319 Lankershim Boulevard, North Hollywood, CA 91605—(213) 767-4522: Song 10.

EDEN PUBLISHING HOUSE—contact Abingdon: Song 173w.

EVANGELICAL COVENANT CHURCH OF AMERICA 5101 Francisco Avenue North, Chicago, IL 60625—(312) 784-3000: Song 492w.

EVANS, DILYS Tan-y-Coed, Uxbridge Square, Caernarfon, Gwynedd, North Wales: Song 81m.

FRED BOCK MUSIC COMPANY PO box 333, Tarzana, CA 91356—(213) 996-6181: (ASCAP) **Songs 72, 391.**

GAITHER, WILLIAM J.— contact Gaither Music Company, P.O. Box 300, Alexandria, IN 46001: Songs 66, 69, 79, 138, 238, 532, 544.

GEOFFREY CHAPMAN LTD. 35 Red Lion Square, London WC1R 4SG, England—01-831-6100: Song 390w.

GOOD NEWS BROADCASTING ASSOCIATION, INC., THE Box 82808 (301 South Twelfth Street), Lincoln, NB 68501—(402) 474-4567: Song 337.

GOULD, D. R. 34 Pollards Drive, Horsham, Sussex RH13 5HH, England: Song 388m.

G. SCHIRMER, INC. 866 Third Avenue, New York, NY 10022—(212) 935-5100: Song 37w.

HAMBLEN MUSIC COMPANY— 26101 Ravenhill Road, Canyon Country, CA 91351: Song 331.

HEART WARMING MUSIC—contact The Benson Company: (BMI) Song 567.

HILL & RANGE SONGS, INC.—contact Unichappell Music, Inc.: Song 374.

HOPE PUBLISHING COMPANY 380 South Main Place, Carol Stream, IL 60187—(312) 665-3200: (ASCAP) Songs 54, 57, 107, 140, 221, 248, 291, 297, 311, 339, 445, 552.

J. CURWEN & SONS—contact G. Schirmer, Inc.: Song 37w.

JOHN T. BENSON PUBLISHING COMPANY—contact The Benson Company: (ASCAP) Song 236.

JONES, TOM—contact Ronald M. Jones, 22 Wentworth Road, Chilwell, Nottingham, England: Song 383.

JUDSON PRESS Educational Ministries–ABC (Division of Publishing and Business), Valley Forge, PA 19481—(215) 768-2000: Song 141.

LANNY WOLFE MUSIC COMPANY—contact The Benson Company: (SESAC) Song 97.

LE FEVRE/SING PUBLISHING COMPANY PO box 43703, Atlanta, GA 30336—(404) 696-6302: (BMI) Song 52.

LEXICON MUSIC, INC. PO box 926, Woodland Hills, CA 91365—(213) 884-0333: (ASCAP) Songs 34, 51, 263, 427, 429, 457, 507, 517, 536, 549.

LILLENAS PUBLISHING COMPANY Box 527, Kansas City, MO 64141—(816) 931-1900: (SESAC) Songs 11, 137, 360.

MANNA MUSIC, INC. PO box 3257 (2111 Kenmere Avenue), Burbank, CA 91504—(213) 843-8100: (ASCAP) Songs 16, 30, 65, 89, 276, 543.

MARANATHA! MUSIC PO box 1396, Costa Mesa, CA 92626—(714) 546-9206: Songs 45, 438.

MARSHALL, MORGAN & SCOTT PUBLICATIONS LTD. 1 Bath Street, London EC1V 9QA, England—01-251-2925: Songs 70m, 325m, 343m, 492m.

MECHANICAL-COPYRIGHT PROTECTION SOCIETY LIMITED Elgar House, 380 Streatham High Road, London SW16 6HR, England—01-769-3181: Song 359m. Reproduced by permission of the legal representatives of the composer who reserve all rights therein.

MOODY BIBLE INSTITUTE 820 North LaSalle Street, Chicago, IL 62610—(312) 329-4332: Song 90.

MOTHERS' UNION, THE The Mary Sumner House, 24 Tufton Street, London SW1P 3RB, England—01-222-5533: Song 150w.

NAZARENE PUBLISHING HOUSE—contact Lillenas Publishing Company: (SESAC) Songs 290, 563.

NEW PAX MUSIC PRESS—contact Paragon Associates, Inc.: (BMI) Song 530.

NORMAN CLAYTON PUBLISHING COMPANY—contact The Rodeheaver Company: (SESAC) Songs 266, 351, 538.

NOVELLO & COMPANY LTD. 145 Palisade Street, Dobbs Ferry, New York 10522—(914) 693-5445: Song 215w.

OXENHAM, THEO — contact Mr. Desmond Dunkerly, 23 Haslemere Road, South Sea, Portsmouth, Hampshire, P.O. 4 8BB England: Song 509w.

OXFORD UNIVERSITY PRESS 44 Conduit Street, London WIR ODE, England—01-629-8494: Song 477m.

PARAGON MUSIC CORPORATION—contact The Benson Company: (ASCAP) Song 6.

PEARCE, MRS. ROWAN (ALMEDA J.) 510 Elizabeth Drive, Lancaster, PA 17601: Song 249.

QUINN, JAMES, SJ—contact Geoffrey Chapman Ltd.: Song 390w.

RODEHEAVER COMPANY, THE Winona Lake, IN 46590—(219) 267-5116: (ASCAP) Songs 95, 96, 167, 260, 278, 384, 389, 425, 450, 469, 541, 550, 554, 561. (Rodeheaver is affiliated with Word Music, Inc.)

SACRED SONGS (a division of Word, Inc.)—contact Word Music, Inc.: (ASCAP) Song 300.

SALVATION ARMY—contact Salvationist Publishing and Supplies Ltd., 117-121 Judd Street, King's Cross, London WC1H 9NN, England—01-387-1656: Songs 273, 344.

SINGSPIRATION, Division of The Zondervan Corporation 1415 Lake Drive SE, Grand Rapids, MI 49506—(616) 459-6900. Listed for your convenience. (ASCAP)

SPEER, BEN L.—contact Ben Speer Music: (SESAC) Song 470.

STAMPS-BAXTER MUSIC of The Zondervan Corporation PO Box 4007 (201-211 South Tyler), Dallas, TX 75208—(214) 943-1155: (AME/Harry Fox) Songs 354, 470.

UNICHAPPELL MUSIC, INC. 729 Seventh Avenue, New York, NY 10019—(212) 575-4971: Song 374.

WEBB, DILYS—contact Mechanical-Copyright Protection Society Ltd.: Song 359m.

WORD MUSIC, INC. 4800 West Waco Drive, Waco, TX 76703—(817) 772-7650: (ASCAP) Songs 91, 214, 271.

ZONDERVAN FIESTA MUSIC—contact Singspiration. (BMI).

ZONDERVAN HERMAN CORPORATION—contact Singspiration. (ASCAP).

ZONDERVAN MUSIC PUBLISHERS—contact Singspiration. (SESAC)

We have been unable to determine the current copyright status of song 540, "I Can Do All Things" but have added our own protective copyright.
Any omission or inaccuracy of copyright notices on individual hymns will be corrected in subsequent printings wherever valid information is offered by the claimants.

ACKNOWLEDGMENTS of Copyrights for "Other Worship Resources:"

621 From *The Mennonite Hymnal,* copyrighted 1969 by Herald Press, Scottdale, PA 15683 and Faith and Life Press, Newton, KS 67114. Used by permission.
623 From *The Private Devotions of Lancelot Andrewes,* Meridian Books, Inc., New York. 1961.
624 From *Statement of Faith,* National Association of Evangelicals, Wheaton, IL 60187. Used by permission.
625 Excerpt from *Lausanne Covenant — 1974,* by the Editorial Staff of "Christianity Today," August 16, 1974. Used by permission.
627 By Paul S. Rees. All rights reserved. Used by permission.
628 From *The Pursuit of God,* by A.W. Tozer. Used by permission of Christian Publications, Inc., Harrisburg, PA 17101. 1948.
629 From *Lancelot Andrewes and His Private Devotions,* by Alexander Whyte, Oliphant Anderson and Ferrier, London. (1896 — now in public domain.)
630 From *Prayers, Ancient & Modern,* by Mary Wilder Tileston. Little, Brown & Company, Boston (1906 — now in public domain.)
631 From *Dialogues with God,* by O. Thomas Miles. Wm. B. Eerdmans Publishing Company, Grand Rapids, MI 49503 (LC #66-22947). Used by permission.
632 By W. Lewis of Milan. Source of quotation unknown.
633 By Jess C. Moody. All rights reserved. Used by permission.
634 From *The Private Devotions of Lancelot Andrewes,* Meridian Books, Inc., New York. 1961.
635 From *Miscellaneous Writings and Letters* of Thomas Cranmer. Parker Society, Cambridge. (1846 — now in public domain.)
636 From *A Guide to Daily Prayer,* by William Barclay. Copyright © 1962 by William Barclay. Reprinted by permission of Harper & Row, Publishers, Inc.
637 From *The Pursuit of God,* by A.W. Tozer. Used by permission of Christian Publications, Inc., Harrisburg, PA 17101. 1948
638 From *Commentaries on the First 20 Chapters of Ezekiel, Volume I,* by John Calvin, translated by Thomas Myers. Wm. B. Eerdmans Publishing Company, Grand Rapids, MI 49503. 1948. Used by permission.
639 From *A Guide to Daily Prayer,* by William Barclay. Copyright © 1962 by William Barclay. Reprinted by permission of Harper & Row, Publishers, Inc.
640 From *Prayers, Ancient & Modern,* by Mary Wilder Tileston. Little, Brown & Company, Boston. (1906 — now in public domain.)
641 The "Gaelic Prayer," with adaptations by Jess C. Moody. All rights reserved. Used by permission.
642 By Bishop Festo Kivengere. Used by permission.
643 From *The Confessions of Augustine in Modern English, Book Ten,* by Sherwood E. Wirt. © 1971 by Sherwood Eliot Wirt under the title, *Love Song.* Used by permission of Zondervan Publishing House.
644 By Billy Sunday. Source of quotation unknown.
645 *What Jesus Says* by Robert Boyd Munger. Copyright © 1955 by Fleming H. Revell Company. Used by permission.
646 By Charles A. Wickman. All rights reserved. Used by permission.
647 From *The Saint's Everlasting Rest,* by Richard Baxter.
648 Excerpts from Paul Harvey News, American Broadcasting Company, January 15, 1966. Used by permission.
650 From *What Wives Wish Their Husbands Knew About Women,* by James C. Dobson. Used by permission of Tyndale House Publishers, Wheaton, IL 60187.
651 From *Thoughts on Christian Sanctity,* by Bishop Handley Moule. Seeley & Company, London. (1906 — now in public domain.)
653 By Harold L. Fickett, Jr. All rights reserved. Used by permission.
654 From *Knowing God,* by J.I. Packer. © 1973 by J.I. Packer. Used by permission of InterVarsity Press, Downers Grove, IL 60515.
655 By Christina G. Rossetti. Source of quotation unknown.

INDEX OF AUTHORS, COMPOSERS AND SOURCES including translators and arrangers

METRICAL INDEX

Tune names in *parentheses* are of a different basic meter but are readily adaptable to the meter indicated.
Tune names with an *asterisk* require an extension by *repetition* of text.

TUNE INDEX

(**R** indicates "with Refrain;" **A** indicates "with Alleluias.")

SCRIPTURAL TEXTS AND ADAPTATIONS IN THE HYMNS

TOPICAL INDEX

GENERAL INDEX

A WORD FROM THE EDITOR

A small **arrowhead** appears at the left side of hymns having five or more stanzas. This is designed as an aid for locating the middle stanza or stanzas more easily as the eye travels from one staff to the next.

An **asterisk** following the last word of the final stanza of a hymn denotes the appropriateness of a concluding **Amen,** if that should be the custom or preference of the local church. A congregational **Amen** must always employ a plagal cadence (IV — I, subdominant to tonic), sung and played with affirmative vigor in the same tempo as the hymn without obvious slowing or relaxation of intensity.

All **Service Music** (calls-to-worship, doxologies, prayer responses, and the like) has been placed within the general body of hymns rather than in an isolated choral section. By this we wish to encourage the worshipers to consider these materials their own — and indeed to sing them together congregationally at least part of the time. Refer to the Topical Index for suggestions.

And, lastly, you are encouraged to familiarize yourself with the function and value of each of the various Indexes (pp. 553-576). Their use can enhance your understanding and appreciation of the hymns and make possible new spiritual insights.

Hymn 136—In all 1979–1980 printings of the hymnal, the song "They'll Know We Are Christians by Our Love" appears at this location. Due to circumstances beyond our control, we have found it necessary to substitute another song ("Praise God for the Body!") in all 1981 and subsequent printings of the hymnal.

Hymn 349—Because of a challenge regarding the copyright status of "There Is a Balm in Gilead," all 1981 and subsequent printings of the hymnal contain a slightly different version from that found in the 1979–1980 editions.